JOHN + SIENA

THE COMPLETE DUET

BETHANY-KRIS

Published by Bethany-Kris
www.bethanykris.com

eISBN 13: 978-1-988197-87-6

Editor: Eli Peters
.

Proofreaders: Eli, Tracy, Felicia, Mia.

Cover Design © London Miller

This is a work of fiction. Names, characters, places, organizations, corporations, locales and so forth are a product of the author's imagination, or if real, used fictitiously. Any resemblance to a person, living or dead, is entirely coincidental.

CONTENTS

LOYALTY

JOHN + SIENA, BOOK 1

ONE

The black car pulled up and parked alongside of Johnathan. The sight of a dark vehicle with tinted windows was so familiar to him he almost smiled. *Almost.*

A good portion of his life was filled with memories of cars just like this one picking him up for one thing or another. Likely some situation he'd gotten himself in to and needed out of.

The passenger window rolled down and revealed the person who had come to pick John up this time. He *did* smile at the sight of Giovanni behind the wheel.

"*Zio,*" John greeted.

Uncle.

Truth be told, Giovanni had always been more like a friend and brother to John than just an uncle. Especially now that John was thirty and not just a kid under his uncle's feet anymore.

Still, Giovanni was the one person in John's family that he connected with on a level of trust that he didn't have with anyone else. Despite the salt peppering the fifty-seven-year-old's hair, and the lines on his face that said Giovanni was not a young man, he somehow still gave off the air of youth. Antony, John's grandfather, always said that Giovanni had a young soul.

Whatever that meant.

"John," his uncle replied. "Get in. We're going to be late as it is with the drive. They told me you would be getting out at twelve, and it's already one."

"They had some kind of delay on the paperwork."

Giovanni pointed at the passenger door. "Don't care. Get in."

Johnathan knew better than to disobey Giovanni. Pulling open the passenger door, he tossed the large brown paper bag to the floor of the car and climbed in. He hadn't even shut the door completely before the Gio hit the gas, and the car lurched forward.

"Shit," John said, grabbing for something to steady himself and laughing. "Slow down. I'd like to see Ma at least once more before I die, all right."

Gio smirked. "Not your father?"

"You know how it is."

"I don't, actually. Lucian, like Dante, is my best friend. We've always been close, John. When I was younger, had no self-control and too many issues to name, I always had my brothers. When my father felt a million miles away, my brothers were still there. So, no, I don't understand."

"It's like this, he's not my brother."

Gio hummed under his breath. "He's your father, I know."

John had never seen eye to eye with his father on a lot of things. Lucian was a good father, as far as that went. He'd always been good to John and his sisters. He loved his children totally. But John had always felt misplaced somehow in his life. Or even out of touch with the people around him, his father included. It made it difficult to have a connection like his younger sisters had to their mother and

2

father.

"What is in the bag?" Gio asked, passing the brown sack John had tossed to the car floor a look.

John shrugged. "Shit I went in with. Clothes, a watch, stuff like that. Nothing important."

"Let me see your band, John."

"Why?"

"Let me see it."

Sighing, John lifted his hand up to show off the leather wrist band he wore with his family's crest embossed across the middle. "Happy?"

"Just making sure you got that back, too."

"Everything that I took in came back out with me, *Zio*."

"I don't trust the system, John."

Neither did John, really.

"Thanks for sending a package to the prison for me to have clean, decent clothes to come out with today," John said.

Gio shot his nephew a look. "I didn't send anything, John."

"Who did?"

"Your father. He sent it up a couple of weeks ago, so you would have a suit to wear today. He thinks about you even when you're not thinking about him."

John wished that made him feel something, but all he got was a twinge in his chest that reminded him of how detached he truly was. It had always been this way for him. He never felt at home; he always looked at the people around him like he was on the outside looking in.

"So, what is your next week looking like?" Gio asked.

"Nothing unusual. I have to check in with the probation officer. Three years of that nonsense should be fun."

Gio laughed. "Or we could just pay the fucker off."

John scowled. "Bribing people was one of the reasons I spent three years behind bars instead of the one year it would have been, *Zio*."

"Yeah," Gio said, wincing. "You're right. Better to let it lie."

Attempted bribery of officials to drop the charges he faced. Possession of an unregistered weapon. Discharging an unregistered weapon. Assault on a police officer. Actually, *several* police officers.

The charges had racked up one after the other on John. Before he knew it, a five-year term slammed down on him with the bang of a judge's gavel. Not even his family's money, status, or connections had been able to get him out of that one.

John was pretty sure his father and uncle, Dante, had a bit of a hand in it all. To Lucian, John was out of control. Or rather, out of his father's control. He didn't always follow the rules. He liked to do things his way, which wasn't always the Marcello way.

Wherever John went, trouble usually followed.

Lucian had said more than once that it was time for John to grow the fuck up. John supposed he finally had, in a way.

He just wished his father hadn't let him take a five-year rap to get his head straightened out. Thankfully, John served his time in three years with good behavior and probation for the foreseeable future, but it still stunk like shit no matter which way he looked at it.

"Hey," Gio said.

John fell out of his troubled thoughts and gave his uncle the attention and respect the man deserved.

That was the Marcello way.

It was a rule John didn't mind following.

Respect and honor.

Always.

"What?" John asked.

"What do you want to do right now?"

"We've got a party to make it to, don't we?"

"Fashionably late is the thing or so I hear," Gio replied. "Just tell me something you'd like to do, John."

"A beer. I'd like to have a beer."

Gio chuckled. "Are you supposed to with—"

"It's fine. One won't kill me."

"I think we can manage that without Dante sending people out looking for us."

John frowned at the mention of his uncle ... and boss. "It's my first day out. Are you seriously urging me to irk Dante? Dante, who has a shorter fuse than even I do?"

The older Dante Marcello got the less tolerable to bullshit he seemed to be. John was smart enough to know that his uncle, the Don of the Marcello Cosa Nostra, would kick his ass first and then ask questions later if need be.

Gio smiled. "It's not him you should be worried about."

"Oh?"

"No. Worry about when your mother gets her hands on you for not calling her for three months."

Shit.

Family first, John. Always.

His father's words were a mantra John couldn't forget.

John's mother, Jordyn, had gotten progressively more concerned the closer his release date loomed. She voiced her worries about his release, and a possible relapse into another one of his episodes enough that it started to grate on John's nerves. His focus was simply getting out of prison and what he was going to do after he was out. To do that, he had put a block of sorts between him and his mother.

It probably wasn't the right thing to do.

"Maybe we should stop at a flower shop on the way to Tuxedo Park," John murmured.

Gio nodded. "Maybe we should."

"And the jewelry store."

"Now you're getting it, man. Lucian taught you well, regardless of what you think."

John laughed. "I know my mother worries because she loves me."

"But?"

"She suffocates me," John admitted. "I'm an adult, not a child. She acts like

I'm seventeen and not thirty. She still thinks I'm a boy."

"For the record, all mothers see their children as their babies. Jordyn isn't a special case. Cecelia still thinks she has to fix my damned tie if it's crooked."

"You know it's not the same."

Gio sighed heavily. "Or maybe you just don't understand your mother and father, John."

"I think I do."

"Do you? They almost lost you twice. Have you ever thought that letting you go too far ahead where they can't reach makes them feel suffocated? That being unable to keep you close takes away the security they have?"

John didn't answer his uncle, but he knew Giovanni had a good point. When he was just a baby, his aunt, Catrina, had been involved with a cartel that had taken John as a way to draw Catrina out. He'd nearly lost his life, as had his father, uncles, and aunt when they'd made the attempt to save him.

Clearly, his family won that battle.

The Marcellos always won.

And then John's first episode had happened when he was seventeen. In the process of losing himself in the manic chaos of his brain, and the torrent of his uncontrollable, rash decisions that led him to a bad place, he nearly died again. Self-medicating, living fast, and almost dying young.

He might as well have been a walking cliché.

Except he wasn't.

His life was real, and so was the manic bipolar disorder he had been diagnosed with at seventeen, and then severely failed to manage as an adult.

"John," Giovanni said quietly. "I'd like an answer."

"How close did my father keep me when he let me be carted off to prison for three years?"

"You didn't give Lucian a choice. You were running crazy, John, doing stupid shit. The faster you ran, the more frenzied you became. You were refusing to work with your father or the people set up for you. On more than one occasion, you put everyone in terrible situations that could have cost us all a lot. You were self-medicating between chemicals and prescriptions. *Cristo*, John, you went missing for two weeks!"

He had.

He had done all of that.

"I thought I had it under control," John said.

"That was your first mistake because clearly you were lost. Everybody was trying to help you, but you just kept pushing us away until we couldn't even see you anymore."

Not one word was a lie.

John wouldn't deny it.

His last manic episode had begun shortly after his twenty-sixth birthday, and the cycles of the disorder went on for weeks at a time, and lasted for over a year. It almost mirrored his first episode from his teenaged years when his family had finally gotten a diagnosis for what was wrong inside his head.

Chemical imbalances.

Bipolar.

John's biggest mistake back then was thinking he could manage his mental health without medications. Those pills labeled him crazy. He didn't need them. He was wrong, and the longer he was without them the more manic he became in his daily life. He'd go from stealing because of the rush, fighting because of the high, using substances to manage the highs and the lows, to fucking any female within arm's reach just to feel.

When he was in a high cycle of the mania, he'd be up for days, running non-stop, and obsessive to an extreme. When the lows of the cycle hit, he would do anything just to get out of it, if he could even manage to function.

Yeah, he'd lost that battle with a bang.

Literally.

His parents hadn't been able to step in like they had when he was a teen because he was an adult the second time around. When his episode came to a head and John finally hit bottom, he nearly killed his cousin, Andino, during an argument over territory and men on the streets. It should have been a simple discussion between Capos. John was far too lost in his own nonsense to fully understand what he was doing when he pulled that gun on his cousin in a busy restaurant.

How Gio was even sitting in a car with John after what he'd almost done to the man's son, John didn't understand.

Well, truthfully, he did know how.

Family first.

"I'm good," John said firmly.

"Now," Gio agreed.

John decided right then and there to end the conversation. He didn't want to talk about his mental health with his uncle, or anyone for that matter. He had a fucking doctor for that shit. Or he'd had before.

"Drop it, *Zio*," John said.

"You brought it up first."

"And now I'm done."

Gio glared at the highway they were driving down. "Your crew has been divided between a few of the family Capos."

"Better than Dante handing my position and men off to someone else entirely."

"You could say that."

Oh, for fuck's sake.

John could hear the hesitance in his uncle's tone, which wouldn't lead to anything good.

"What now?" he demanded.

Gio rapped his fingers to the leather-bound steering wheel. "Just to be sure that you're not going to have a relapse the moment you're out and free to do your own thing, Dante and Lucian decided that it would be better if you worked alongside Andino and Timothy with their crews for a while."

Anger surged through John like he hadn't felt in a long time. It was good. So fucking good. Like a shot of adrenaline straight to his bloodstream.

But that feeling was also addictive and bad for him. Bad for his mania and bad for the bipolar currents of his emotions that he fought with daily. He wasn't that crazy, out of control, unmanageable person. He got that his behavior and issues had put his family and *la famiglia* through hell, but he was good.

Wasn't he?

Now?

Did his family not trust him?

Christ.

It pissed him off even more.

"Just to be clear, I don't get a say here, right?" John asked.

Gio shrugged. "No, you don't."

Because that's how Cosa Nostra worked, and his family was knee-deep in that life and culture. Nobody could possibly begin to understand their life. With his uncle being the head boss of the family, his other uncle acting as Dante's consigliere, and John's own father being the family underboss, there was no escaping who he was.

Mafia.

Made.

Cosa Nostra.

When it came to family decisions, especially ones made about him, John didn't get a bone in the fight. His uncles pulled rank, as did his father.

Rules.

His life was dictated, surrounded, and determined by rules.

John stifled the familiar urge to push back against the walls closing in on him again. They were only in his own mind, after all.

"There's something else I have to do this week," John said, dropping the conversation. He didn't want to fight with his uncle about something that neither of them could do anything about at the moment. "I should do it tomorrow, but I need some contacts."

Gio cocked a brow and passed John a look. "What is that?"

"I need a new therapist. One that my father doesn't have on his payroll."

"John—"

"I'll follow his fucking rules and give him what he wants, but he's not having control over that. Not now. It's been three years since my last episode. Give me a fucking break here. I've earned that, Gio."

"You were wrong," Gio said quietly.

"About what?"

"Your father. He did give you a choice, John. You know he did."

John forced back his irritation. "Leave it alone."

"He gave you a choice. An institution to get yourself checked out and settled, or time behind bars. You made the choice, John, not Lucian."

"I'm not crazy," John said.

"No one ever said that."

But they might as well have.

"Putting me in an institution would have labeled me exactly that."

"We just wanted you healthy."

"I am."

Gio passed him another look. "Let's hope you stay that way."

"Thanks for that, asshole."

"I'm just being real, John. We both know if you don't keep managing this like you've been forced to for the last three years, you can easily relapse into another episode."

John knew that, but it still made his anger rear its ugly head. His saving grace was being able to control it now, whereas he couldn't before.

"By the way," Gio said as he pushed the gas pedal harder.

"What?"

"Happy birthday, John."

A drop of tension crawled down John's spine as his uncle pulled up to the iron-wrought gate. A long, twisty driveway led up to a mansion with two wings, three floors, a pool, and a guest house out back. The estate rested on six acres of property in Tuxedo Park.

The Marcello family home was massive.

"Passcode, please," a robotic voice commanded from the speaker Gio was talking in to.

"Seven, two, six, nine, five, five," his uncle replied.

"Please speak your name clearly for voice recognition."

"Giovanni David Marcello."

The speaker buzzed for a split second before the gate shuddered and began to open automatically. Gio pulled the car through the opening the moment the vehicle could fit through. It never failed to amaze John how careful and protective their family was about keeping their private lives hidden from public view. He understood, of course, but it was still amusing.

"Voice recognition?" John asked. "When did Antony have that put in?"

"A year ago."

"Why?"

Gio stilled in his seat. "Just because, I suppose."

"Are you being purposely difficult, or what?"

Quickly, Gio put the car in park at the mid-way point on the driveway between the gate and the house.

"He put it in because he's not young, John. He's eighty-seven, and he doesn't like to be reminded of the things he's not capable of doing at his age. He's not quick on his feet, his eyesight is terrible, and he wants his wife to feel safe."

"What happened to the guard he had?"

"You'll see," Gio muttered as he put the car in drive again. "Just don't say anything to him about his age or the changes. It bothers him and then Cecelia gets pissy."

"I got it."

"Good."

John found the guard in question the moment the front entrance to the Marcello home was in full view. Dressed in all black, the man rested beside a dark sedan with a cigarette in one hand and a gun at his waist. John knew the man had to be the guard because no one else was permitted to smoke in front of the Marcello home. They had areas designated for that sort of thing.

"He's keeping him closer," John noted.

"Yeah."

"Any particular reason why?"

Gio shrugged. "You can never be too safe."

Why didn't John believe that?

"Hey," Gio said quietly.

John gave his uncle a look. "Hmm?"

"You good?"

"Yeah."

His tension was still there, dancing hand in hand with his anxiety. Three years in lock-up was a long time to be gone. How many things had changed since he'd went to prison? How much more distance had he forced between him and his family in that time?

Gio turned the car off and put his hand on the door handle. "For the record, John …"

"What about it?"

"I thought you made the right choice three years ago."

John's brow furrowed. "I don't know what you mean."

"When your father bribed the judge with the option of an institution or jail time. I thought you made the right choice."

Well, that was not what John expected to hear.

"Why is that?"

"Because despite how irrational everything you were doing seemed to be, I don't believe for a second that any hospital in the country would have sorted you out like prison did. Thirty days in an institution with a couple of therapists, new meds, and little else wasn't what you needed. Time was what you needed, John. You still got the doctors, you got the meds, but you also got the break. You made the right choice."

John let out a slow breath. "Who else feels that way?"

Gio laughed. "I know what you're asking without outright asking it."

"So?"

"Your mother is probably at the front door about ready to blow it down and come out here."

John nodded, knowing his uncle wasn't going to answer his question. "I better get my ass in the house before she comes out."

"Yeah, probably. I bet your father is waiting, too."

"We haven't talked a lot since I went in."

"All you had to do was pick up the phone, John."

John glanced at the mansion. "I know."

"Lucian thinks you made the right choice for you. In case you were wondering."

"I wasn't."

"Lying is a terrible habit, Johnathan."

It was.

9

But John was too damned good at it.

"Oh, *il mio ragazzo!*"

John barely heard the words come out of his mother's mouth before he was engulfed in tiny arms that squeezed him nearly to death. For such a tiny thing, his mother was strong as hell. She literally knocked him off balance forcing them both to spin in a half circle, so they were facing the front door and not the large entryway like before.

"Hey, Ma," John said, letting her crush him for all she was worth.

Gio grinned as he strolled on by.

Asshole.

He could have helped John a little. Physical expressions of emotions and John had never mixed well together. Not unless he was the one doing the expressing. And when he physically expressed emotions, it usually never ended well for anyone involved. Mushy, lovey nonsense didn't do very damned much for him, either.

Jordyn squeezed her son harder. "I missed you."

"You saw me a few months ago, Ma."

"So?"

John bent down when Jordyn finally loosened her grip around his chest and gave his mother a quick kiss to the cheek. "So nothing, Ma. I missed you, too."

Jordyn's face lit up with happiness.

Guilt stabbed at John's insides.

He didn't verbally express his feelings very well, either. He felt a lot of shit, and that was just the by-product of his disorder. Processing, understanding, and communicating his inner thoughts and emotions was difficult. It had clearly been too long since he'd given any affection to his mother if her joy over a simple admission was any indication.

"Liliana couldn't make it down from Chicago with Joseph," Jordyn said as she fiddled with John's crooked tie. "She tried, but she couldn't get out of the shifts at the hospital."

Liliana, John's younger sister, had married a man involved with the Chicago Outfit. John barely remembered the wedding, as he'd been right in the thick of his manic episode.

"But she's coming down next month," Jordyn added.

"Lucia?" John asked.

"She's here," his mother said about his youngest sister.

"And Cella?"

John's other sister, also married but to a man who was unaffiliated to the mob, had never been very close to him. He wouldn't be surprised if she hadn't shown up for his welcome-home-slash-birthday party.

"She's here, sneaking food while everyone else waits to eat," came a darker, familiar voice from behind John.

Jordyn took a step back from her son. John spun on his heel only to come face to face with his father.

For John, it was like looking in an aging mirror. As he grew up, almost everyone he knew felt the need to point out how much he resembled his father. A twin, they said. Hazel eyes that matched John's looked him up and down. His father smiled a little, making the sharp lines of his features soften briefly. Even at sixty, Lucian Marcello stood tall and straight, matching John's height at six feet, three inches tall. Lucian commanded a room with his no-nonsense demeanor and his blunt attitude. He could also be intimidating with his quietness and watchful eye.

"Son," Lucian greeted.

"Hey," John replied.

"You look good."

"I hope so."

"Seems prison has its benefits, hmm?"

John let the comment roll off his shoulders, knowing his father hadn't meant it as an insult. "I think it did for me."

"How was the drive?"

"Long," John answered.

Lucian chuckled. "With Gio, any drive is long."

"He talks a lot."

"That he does." Lucian jerked a thumb over his shoulder. "As I said, Cella is here and sneaking food. We're letting it go what with the pregnancy and all. She has to feed the baby."

John cleared his throat. "I didn't know she was pregnant."

"Phones work, John, even in prison."

Ouch. That comment didn't roll off like the first one did.

"Lucian," Jordyn said, coming to stand beside her son. "Don't."

Lucian's jaw tightened before he frowned. "*Mi scusi*, I'm sorry. That was out of line, son. I'm happy you're home. We all are."

John wished he could say the same, but for a split second he was back to feeling like the outsider in his family again. No one in particular made him feel that way directly, but the disconnect he experienced with his own father made everyone else seem distant, too.

"John!"

The shout of his name drew John's attention away from Lucian.

John stiffened when his cousin, Andino, moved past his uncle with a wide grin. Andino stood toe-to-toe with John. Before the incident that landed John in prison and nearly took Andino's life, the two cousins had been inseparable.

Ride or die, their family said. Because the two cousins always found trouble together. They had always been close, best friends even, and one mistake ruined it all.

At twenty-eight, Andino was the closest cousin in relation to his own age that John had.

"Jordyn," Lucian said with a pointed look in his wife's direction, "… why don't we go let everyone know that the man of the hour has arrived."

"Sure," Jordyn replied.

With a squeeze of her hand on John's arm, his parents disappeared.

"It's good to see you, man," Andino said.

John smirked. "And you, *cugino*."

Andino grinned at the Italian word for cousin. "I would have made the trip up to see you, but I wasn't sure if that was good for you."

"I wouldn't have turned you away, Andi."

Andino held out a hand.

John passed it a wary glance.

"John?" Andino asked.

"Yeah?"

"We're good, man."

Just like that, three words ripped away the concern John had about his friendship with Andino.

"Are we?" John asked.

Andino didn't drop his hand. "Family first, John."

John shook his cousin's hand. Home started to feel a little more real. The distance keeping John and his emotional attachments to his family at bay began to close.

"I hope you don't mind a crowd," Andino said.

John cocked a brow. "I never do."

"Good, because the whole damn city might as well be here to welcome you home."

"Seriously?"

"Open invitation to anyone in *la famiglia*, man," Andino said, chuckling. "I don't think anyone refused it."

Huh.

"I have to start looking for a place," John said.

Andino took a drag off his cigarette, and eyed his companion in the Lexus. "I told you that it was all right if you stayed with me for a bit."

"I like being alone, Andi. It's not about you."

"Fine. You've only been home a couple of days, John. Give it a bit of time. You've got a lot of adjustment to do. Work in to it all slowly. You don't have to do it all at once."

John disagreed. He wanted to get back to his old routine of things as quickly as he possibly could. Part of that was not being under his cousin's watch all of the damned time. It wasn't Andino's fault because the man was just following orders. But John felt suffocated all the same.

"I still need to find my own place."

Andino tossed his nearly finished cigarette out of the window. "We can do that."

"Good."

"So hey, I've got to handle some business over at one of my restaurants. Are you interested in coming or do you have things to do?"

John shrugged. "I've got shit to do."

"I'm not giving you my car."

Laughing, John said, "I don't need it, asshole."

But he did need to get his own and soon. It was in the works.

"I'll take the bus," John added. "The warehouse is only a couple of blocks from here."

"Careful and clean, right?"

John glowered. "Back off."

"I'm just making sure."

"It's on the up. It's your goddamn guys I'm working with."

"I know," Andino said. "But not all of those fools are good, either. I'll see you later."

John climbed out of the Lexus without another word to his cousin. As Andino pulled away from the side of the road, John strolled down the sidewalk to where the bus stop was and waited. Less than ten minutes later, a bus heading straight into the heart of Hell's Kitchen pulled over, and John stepped in the vehicle.

Pulling out a phone from his pocket, John dialed his father's cell phone number as he walked toward the back of the bus with his eyes on the ground.

"*Ciao,*" Lucian said when he picked up John's call.

"Hey, Dad."

"John."

"I'm not going to make it for dinner. Give Ma my apologies."

Lucian sighed heavily. "Why not?"

"Business in the Kitchen."

Technically, it was a lie. He didn't have to work today if he didn't want to, but he needed something to do other than be under his cousin's watch. John simply didn't want to go through another round with his parents and their concerns. He needed space and time to breathe. He needed to be his own person without everyone else's worries and influence.

His parents didn't understand.

"Breakfast tomorrow then," Lucian said.

"I—"

"It's not a request, John," his father cut in harshly. "When you flake on your mother, I expect you to make it up to her."

"Fine, tomorrow."

"Good."

Lucian hung up the call before John could.

Shoving his phone in his pocket, John took the first seat he could. Glancing up from his clenched hands that rested in his lap, he came face-to-face with sapphire eyes.

John blinked. The woman smiled.

She had a tablet in her hands and one earbud in her ear. A messenger bag rested at her feet, drawing John's gaze down to the leather boots she wore. Skinny jeans showcased the length of her legs and the curve of her hips. He didn't recognize her, but something about her was familiar.

Tucking a strand of her caramel-toned curls behind her ear, the woman met his gaze again. His mouth went dry and he didn't have the first clue of why. Maybe it was because he'd spent three years in prison, and the only females he'd had contact with since he got out were family.

Or maybe it was because the girl was fucking beautiful.

Every part of him knew it.

"Hi," she said, still smiling.

"Hi." John grinned back. "Johnathan Marcello."

"*The* Johnathan Marcello?"

John chuckled. "There's only one alive in this city, as far as I know."

The woman's smile turned wider. "Siena."

"Like the city in Italy?"

"Just like that," she replied.

"A last name?" John asked.

"Calabrese. It's very nice to meet you, John."

Shit.

TWO

Johnathan's eyes widened, and Siena grinned at the sight. Surprise looked good on the man. His confident smile earlier had sharpened his strong jaw and chiseled cheekbones, and made her think, *I bet he could kill a woman with that smile. Stop her heart with a look, and restart it with a wink.*

The surprise, though?

That took his sexiness, and turned it almost boyish in a blink.

"You didn't know who I was?" Siena asked.

"Marcellos don't tend to … mix a lot of business with the Calabrese family." Johnathan's confident grin took over once more, and his gaze traveled over her form. "You must be Matteo's daughter."

"One of a few," she replied.

Johnathan cocked a brow. "I only know the Calabrese boss to have one."

"The three illegitimate ones don't get much recognition in the family."

Across from her on the bus, Johnathan cleared his throat.

"Ah, I see," he said.

So was the way of their life.

Nobody ever said being a *principessa della mafia* was an easy thing. In fact, it was one of the most suffocating things to be. All the rules and expectations that never ended. Having a Cosa Nostra boss for a father—and high-ranking brothers—left a young woman like Siena under their control and demands.

She was used to it, now.

Twenty-five years dealing with it all had done that to her.

"Kind of strange to see a Capo riding on a city bus," Siena said.

"And what do you know about Capos, *donna?*"

The way he called her woman, and his hazel gaze drifted down over her jean-clad legs left a heavy feeling thumping in her throat. Siena was used to men staring—a byproduct of having taken after her exceptionally beautiful, but cold, mother. She wasn't, however, used to a man like Johnathan doing it.

A man connected to the mafia. One that might face punishment from her father or brothers for disrespecting their family name by treating one of their women in any way that wasn't honest and pure.

Like she was some angel.

Or a saint.

Siena was *none* of those things.

She quite liked the way Johnathan was looking at her.

"Well?" Johnathan asked. "What do you know about the business, huh?"

A lot.

More than he probably thought she did.

Siena simply said, "Do you think I shouldn't know who is who when it comes to the Three Families in New York? Wouldn't that be a little dumb of me, considering who my father is and all?"

"Fair enough."

She mentally patted herself on the back for dodging that bullet. After all, one who dealt in the business did not discuss the business.

It was a rule.

Siena's father repeated it to her a little more often than he did to everyone else. She figured that was because she was a woman, and no made man in the mafia wanted other *Mafiosi* to know a woman was handling business.

Especially … numbers.

"Isn't it always black cars, and ten under the speed limit for Capos?" Siena asked.

"For some, maybe." Johnathan chuckled. "My car is still in shipping somewhere between the Rust Belt and here."

"But is it black?" she asked.

Johnathan smirked. "Possibly."

"And do you drive ten under the limit?"

"Possibly."

"I knew it," Siena said, winking. "So, for now you're slumming it on a bus, then?"

"I don't mind the bus. I get to be around people without actually engaging with people."

Siena lifted a single eyebrow. "Is that a shot at me—I shouldn't be engaging you, or something?"

Johnathan's grin deepened, and he looked her over once more. "Nah, I don't mind engaging you, Siena."

"It's just a shame my last name is Calabrese, huh?"

He waved a hand, and said, "It is what it is."

Johnathan looked out the bus window, and stayed silent for a few moments. As the bus stopped to let more people on, and a few off, Siena took the chance to take Johnathan's profile in. A lax, easy smile. Strong lines shaped his jaw and cheekbones. A single dimple in his right cheek peeked out whenever his grin deepened. His bottom lip was slightly fuller than his top, and his olive complexion spoke of his Italian bloodline.

He had to be at least six-foot-three, or taller when standing up. The black suit he wore looked cut perfectly to his form—a lean, yet fit, form. The diamond incrusted Rolex on one wrist, a leather band embossed with something on the other, and black leather shoes gave credence to the wealth the Marcello family had.

Everything about Johnathan screamed handsome, bad news, and entirely interesting to Siena. His good looks certainly couldn't be denied, and his last name—without needing him to confirm or deny—was enough to tell her he was probably mixed up in *la famiglia*.

The interesting bit, though, was a little harder to explain.

Other than how he looked at her?

Something different from how his dark grin made her pulse quicken?

Maybe it was because the Marcello family kind of felt like an enigma to her. She knew they were real, and heard enough about them to respect how they controlled New York. Yet, at the same time, the Marcellos were also illusive. A crime organization just like her father's, but one her family only whispered about over the years.

Johnathan was, essentially, one big mystery.

Just like his family.

Straight, thick brows gave him a disinterested expression, except when he turned his hazel gaze on her. The cool, calm demeanor of Johnathan Marcello was shattered when someone got a good look at his eyes—a wild, lost man stared back.

Johnathan glanced away from the window. He caught Siena staring at him like a foolish girl, but she didn't look away.

"Yes?" he asked.

Lying really wasn't her forte.

She wasn't very good at it.

"You're very handsome, Johnathan," she said.

Those dark eyes of his flashed with something unknown before he said, "I prefer John."

"John."

"Yeah."

"What I said remains the same, John."

Siena was not usually so bold. Daring statements like those to a man like Johnathan could possibly get her in trouble, all things considered.

Still, she said it.

It had to be said.

He arched a brow. "Why did you call me *the* Johnathan Marcello earlier?"

Siena cleared her throat. "You're a little infamous, aren't you?"

"Me?"

"All the Marcellos, really."

Johnathan nodded. "I suppose."

Then, the bus came to another slow stop. Johnathan glanced out the window, and cussed before he stood up. His back was already turned to her, and he was heading for the door when he looked back over his shoulder.

All over again, with one single look, Siena's heart thumped hard in her throat. A rhythm that intrigued and frightened her.

How did he do that by only staring?

Why couldn't she control her own body?

"Maybe I'll see you around, *bella*."

Siena stilled.

He'd called her beautiful.

"Maybe," she agreed.

Johnathan didn't hear her.

He had already exited the bus.

"You're late."

Matteo's voice boomed over the bustling Brooklyn restaurant. Siena's father was a lot of things, but overwhelming was highest on the list. He towered over her

17

mother who stood next to him at the table, and was wide enough that Siena's arms couldn't reach all the way around him when she hugged him.

"Traffic was bad," Siena told him. "Hi, Dad."

Matteo scowled at her when she stepped back. "Taking the bus again?"

"I like the bus. It's ... responsible."

And it gives me a little less time with you.

She didn't add that last part out loud.

Siena knew better.

"You have a brand new Lexus sitting in your apartment's lot," her father said, shaking his head full of dark brown hair, although it had started to thin a bit at the top. He didn't like for anyone to point it out. "I bought you that car for you to do your business, and get to places *on time*, Siena."

"Oh, leave her alone, Matteo. So, she likes the bus, who cares?"

Siena's mother—Coraline—smiled sweetly at her daughter. She returned the smile, but hers wasn't as honest or wide.

Sure, she loved her parents.

They had given her life, after all.

The two were still ... difficult. Siena had grown up as the afterthought in her parents' lives. Her brothers, Kev and Darren, had always taken center stage with Matteo and Coraline. Siena, on the other hand, had simply been given direction and restrictions. Rules she was meant to follow with no questions asked, and a set path in life chosen by these two people in front of her.

It certainly left her with a bitter taste.

"Because riding a bus with the money she makes is undignified," Matteo said.

"Or economically and fiscally smart," Siena put in.

Matteo passed her a look, and narrowed his gaze. "No, I told you what it is."

Yes, undignified.

Heaven forbid she ride the bus with the rest of the lowly people. She might catch their poor people cooties, or something.

Siena had all she could do not to roll her damn eyes. Matteo wouldn't like that, either. Respect needed to be shown at all times when it came to her father. He expected nothing less from his children.

At least that was one thing she had in common with her brothers where their father was concerned. Matteo treated them all equally in that respect. One of the only fucking things.

"Sit, sit," her father demanded with a wave at the table.

Matteo didn't bother holding out a chair for Siena, but he did for his wife. Siena pulled her own chair out, and sat down. She was hoping this lunch with her parents would be over quickly enough because she had a million other things she'd rather be doing.

Coraline reached across the table to tap the napkin in front of Siena. "You'll be staying a while—act like it, sweetheart."

Damn.

Siena picked up the napkin, flicked it open, and set it on her lap. At least the place had decent food, and that would make this lunch slightly more bearable. For now, anyway.

Matteo waved at a waiter who was handling another table. At the sight of her father gesturing for him, the man instantly left the couple whose coffees were not yet poured, and came their way.

So was the way of Matteo Calabrese.

He did not like to wait, or be left waiting.

He did not like to be ignored.

He was king of the room, always.

Luckily for her father, Matteo owned this particular restaurant. Actually, he owned quite a few businesses, and so did Siena's older brothers. Between restaurants, clubs, used car dealerships, a couple of barber shops, pizza joints, a laundry mat, and a pub in Manhattan, they had more businesses than they knew what to do with.

None of the men in her family seemed particularly good with numbers unless it included counting up their profits for the month. Taxes were a thing to be avoided at all costs. Every single nickel and dime needed accounted for at the end of the day.

Given how they used their legal businesses to hide their illegal profits from the criminal side of their lives, her father and brothers needed someone good with numbers. Someone who could scrub books clean, and hide dirty cash.

They needed her.

Siena was ... exceptional with numbers. She could take a business's books, hide a couple of hundred grand in dirty money through different receivables accounts, and push the cleaned money straight out the other end.

It was the one thing she could do that her brothers could not. It was the only reason why Siena suspected her father hadn't tried to force her into some arranged marriage to get the responsibility of her off his hands.

After all, a girl was only useful if she wasn't useless.

Without numbers ... without her talent of scrubbing books for her father's Cosa Nostra, that's all Siena would be. Entirely useless to the men in her family.

It gave her a little bit of control. She had no problems running with it every chance she could. It wasn't her fault if Matteo and her brothers couldn't see that she was manipulating them sometimes to get what she wanted.

"Mr. Calabrese," the waiter said with a smile. "Good afternoon, sir."

"Yes, yes, I'm ready to order now."

"Pen's ready, sir."

Like always, Matteo ordered for himself, his wife, and Siena. Had her brothers been there, he would have ordered for them, too.

Anything her father could control, he did. Even if it was something as simple as what they wanted to eat for lunch.

"Shoo," Matteo told the waiter with a flick of his wrist. "I'm hungry."

"Yes, sir."

The young man—who didn't look old enough to be serving liquor, likely— darted off, and headed right for the kitchen. He didn't even go back to the table where the couple was still waiting with their still-empty coffee cups.

"New boy," Matteo told Coraline. "I like him so far."

"He seems quiet," her mother agreed.

"For now."

Then, Matteo turned his dark eyes on the phone he had pulled from his inner jacket pocket. Just like that, Coraline and Siena were dismissed from the man's attention. Coraline didn't really seem all that bothered, as she simply stared out the window at the passersby on the street.

Siena was never more aware of how much she took after her mother in appearance and behavior than in that moment. Sure, her slyness and attitude came from her father, not to mention her determination to get shit done.

The rest?

All her mom.

From the blues of her wide eyes, to the caramel of her long, wavy hair. Standing side by side, the two only reached five-foot-seven in four-inch heels. Their full lips curved the same way when they smiled, or smirked, and even the button nose was compliments of her mother's delicate features.

The physical appearance was about as far as it went, though.

Coraline was quiet, and quick to bend to the whims of the men around her. Siena was far more likely to find a way out of it, or speak loudly enough for someone to listen.

Her mother was happy in her place, spoiled and content. She never batted an eye at the three daughters her husband fathered with a mistress over the period of twenty years, or the fact that mistress lived in a bigger house than she did.

Siena was not the kind of woman to stick her head in the sand.

She just couldn't.

She certainly wasn't going to turn her cheek, and pretend like the men in her life were some kind of good, godly creatures who gave back to society, and attended church every Sunday. Sure, they did those things—they also sold drugs, laundered money, blackmailed anyone they could, and murder was always at the top of someone's to-do list.

Coraline could pretend all she wanted about her family, and live in her gilded cage of clouds where the bad stuff didn't touch her.

Siena's feet were still firmly planted on the ground. She liked it here better.

"Don't pull this tardiness nonsense on your brother later," Matteo said.

Siena's attention was back on her father in a blink. "Pardon?"

"Later—you're heading over to Kev's club, aren't you? You've got books to scrub for him."

"Of course."

"Don't be late again. It's rude, Siena."

"I know, Dad. I won't be late."

Lies. She would make sure to be late.

Besides, she did need a couple of new books to put on her nightstand. The old bookshop a couple of blocks away from her brother's club sounded like a good place to get lost in for an hour or so.

If she could do it, and get away with it, then what was stopping her?

It was the Calabrese way.

20

Siena thumbed through the brand new paperback of a romance she had asked the old shopkeeper to order in for her well over a month ago. Sure, she had an e-reader and could have purchased a digital copy instantly, but she still liked a good old paperback once in a while.

"How long are you gonna caress that book, girly?"

Siena gave Eugene a smile.

Well in to his seventies, Eugene had been supplying Siena's addiction to romance and thrillers since she was seventeen or so. Sometimes, she came in the shop just to help him rearrange shelves, or unload the new releases for the month. He didn't need to be lifting things, anyway. His aged face showed more wrinkles when he smiled, and told the story of his life.

"I'm going to touch it and love it for as long as I want to, thank you," she said, smiling sweetly.

Eugene sighed. "You and those damn romances. You're going to give yourself an unhealthy outlook on men. No real life man will stand up to the kinds of heroes in those books."

Siena shrugged. "My standards are already pretty sky-high."

The man chuckled hoarsely. "As they should be, Siena. You take the book, and have a good day, sweetheart."

"You didn't ring me up yet."

From the other side of the counter, the man winked. "Call it even for you doing my books last month for the quarter."

Siena gave him a look. "Yeah, and I saw how much you're making, too. So, let me pay for the damn book."

"No way. It's all yours. I already paid for it. You thought I would forget, I bet."

"Eugene."

"I remembered your birthday was today. Twenty-five."

"*Eugene.*"

The old man smiled. "You didn't ask for a thing to do my books, girly. Plus, you filed my taxes last year and wouldn't let me pay you for that, either. Consider it payback, and a birthday gift. It's just a book."

"I didn't want anything," she replied, giving him a look.

It literally took her all of an hour to do his books, and twenty minutes to file his taxes.

Eugene shrugged. "The least you could do is allow me to buy you a book—one you've been waiting a long time for me to get. I know you have one of those fancy e-reader thingys. You could have just as easily gotten yourself a copy on that reading thing, and not from me. It's one book. Don't worry about it. Your reading addiction keeps me in business."

Siena knew that was only partly true. She still adored Eugene for saying it. Both sets of her grandparents had died—one after the other over the span of a decade. Before she ever even reached sixteen years old.

Now, at twenty-five, she kind of felt like she had found a stand-in for a grandparent with Eugene. Seeing him once or twice a week made her whole day.

Leaning across the counter, Siena pulled Eugene in for a tight one-armed hug.

"Thank you, Eugene."

"Ah, no need for that. You let me know if the book is as good as you wanted it to be, okay?"

Siena tapped the paperback against her palm, and cocked a brow. "Even though you think romance novels are just trashy sex scenes now?"

The old man laughed. "Now, I read some … mostly because you made me, but they're okay."

"Just okay?"

"How about you don't go getting unrealistic ideas in your head about what a real man is, huh?"

Siena nodded. "I won't."

"But make sure he treats you like a queen."

Exactly.

"Got it."

Eugene waved at the door. "Have a good day, Siena. By the way, I know that's a series, and I have already ordered the following two for you. This time, *you* can pay. They should get here in a couple of weeks."

"*Grazie.*"

"*Ciao,*" Eugene replied in kind, butchering the Italian greeting.

It still made Siena smile as she headed out of the bookshop. Eugene didn't need to make her feel special by saving or buying her books, or greeting her the way she greeted him every time she entered or exited his shop. Yet, he still did all of those things.

She suspected he was the one and only reason why people like her kept going back to him, and his bookshop. Because he was so sweet, he cared, and he never forgot to make someone who came into his business feel important while they were there.

The man should have retired years ago—he wasn't willing to give up his shop, though. Never was married, apparently, so he didn't have a wife or kids to pull him away from work and show him the world.

Siena thumbed through the first few pages of the paperback as she headed out of the bookshop. Her attention was fully engrossed in the opening paragraph introducing a CEO heroine getting ready for what was intended to be the biggest meeting of the woman's life.

She was so engaged in the book she had waited forever for, that she wasn't even paying attention to the people blowing by her on the street. It was only a couple of blocks to her brother's club. Kev had texted her four times and left one voicemail asking where the hell she was and why she was late.

Siena didn't bother to respond.

Who else was going to cook and scrub their books?

Nobody but her.

He could wait.

Siena flipped to the second page in the book, and not a breath later rammed straight into something hard. Her book went sprawling to the—thankfully dry—pavement, and landed with the cover up. She stumbled backwards, and almost fell herself.

A dark chuckle and a hand wrapping around her back kept her from hitting the ground as well.

The spicy cologne of the man helping her up was the first thing Siena noticed about the guy. His familiar black suit was the second thing.

She stared Johnathan Marcello right in the face as he helped her to stand straight. He flashed her a smile, showing off straight, white teeth and his charm in a blink.

"Two meetings in one day, huh?" he asked

Siena wondered why her throat had gone tight again. Still, she managed to speak. "Sorry about that. I was—"

Johnathan bent down and picked up her book. He eyed the title and the cover, and handed it over with another brilliant smile. "Distracted, I think. I can see why—the guy on that cover looks like he bathed himself in body oil, or something."

"They do say sex sells."

That smile of Johnathan's turned suggestive in a blink. "That it does."

"It's actually a book I've been waiting forever for," she admitted. "My birthday is today, and the shopkeeper remembered. It's my gift from him."

Johnathan chuckled. "A *gift*, huh?"

"He's old enough to be my grandfather."

"Well, happy birthday."

"Big, old twenty-five," she half-grumbled.

Johnathan scoffed. "*Old*, right. You're five years away from my thirty, and only when you get to there can you come talk to me about old."

"Thirty isn't old."

And he didn't look anything beyond twenty-six, *maybe*.

Johnathan shrugged. "It's all in how you feel, I guess."

Siena didn't believe in shit like fate or any of that kind of nonsense. Not being a numbers girl like she was. She much preferred to see things in black and white. Reality. Written in stone, not a what-could-be kind of thing.

She wondered, however, what the odds were that she would randomly run in to Johnathan like this again. Twice. In one day.

Should she consider that a sign, or something?

Maybe she could try for a third time to see him, except without it being entirely random. More ... planned.

The outspoken part of Siena's personality came forward before she could stop it with trivial things like nerves or anxiety.

"Hey, do you have somewhere—"

Johnathan's phone ringing loudly inside his pocket stopped Siena from asking him to dinner like she wanted. He pulled out the phone, and put it to his ear while he held up a finger for her to ask for a minute.

"Yeah, John here." A beat of silence passed, and then Johnathan said, "All right, man. I'm on my way."

Johnathan hung up the phone, gave Siena a wink, and shoved the device in his jacket.

"Business calls," he told her. "Try looking up when you walk, huh? Gotta be safe, *bella donna*. You don't know the kind of crazy you might run in to around here."

With a wave, John darted out into the street, and didn't give Siena another look.

She hadn't gotten to ask him out.

Maybe *that* was the sign.

Who knew?

Darren chewed loudly on an apple in the corner chair as Siena strolled into the club's office. You would think, given the kind of private work she did for her family, that they would allow her the privacy of her own office.

No way.

She almost always worked out of one of their offices.

"Late, aren't you?" Darren asked.

Siena shrugged as she dropped in the office chair, and turned the PC monitor the way she liked. "I'm here, aren't I?"

"Kev isn't happy."

Their oldest brother was never happy.

"Kev can chill," Siena said.

A couple of passwords, and one encrypted file later, and Siena had brought up the dirty books for the club. Next week, she would be at another office owned by her family to scrub out and cook those books, too.

It changed a lot.

Her bachelor's degree in accounting afforded her the knowledge of cooking and scrubbing books, but her respect for numbers kept her attention focused and interested. That was what mattered most.

She actually liked doing it.

The numbers in the excel charts were a comforting place for Siena. It was all about balances and checks. Numbers were straightforward, and didn't leave questions behind. Something either added up, or it didn't.

She liked that.

"Oh, so you finally fucking showed up, did you?"

Kev's voice—much like their father's—boomed. It could travel down hallways, and through walls. The men in her family didn't know how to have a quiet conversation if their lives depended on it.

Siena didn't look away from the computer screen as she brought up the accounts receivable and payable for the club. The proper books this time—not the ones she was about to make look proper.

"Got caught up in something," Siena said.

"Something like what?"

Shit.

She didn't want to mention the bookstore to her brothers. The two didn't have any respect or appreciation for things like books and escapism. They only respected and understood the life, Cosa Nostra, and their father.

She decided to deflect Kev's question with one of her own.

"So, I guess Johnathan Marcello is out of prison now, huh?" she asked.

Johnathan's prison sentence had been widely known across New York. It had been in the news, and even his sentencing had been publicized. It was one of the reasons she had called him infamous, though she thought it might be rude to point it out.

Siena peered over the PC screen.

Sure enough, Kev's brow had raised as he shot Darren a look. She mentally patted herself on the back.

"Did you know that?" Kev asked Darren.

"I didn't. How does she know it?"

Both Siena's brothers looked to her.

"I ran in to him on the bus," she said, shrugging.

She didn't mention the street, too.

"I guess we should let Dad know," Kev said.

Siena almost asked why.

She knew better.

They wouldn't answer.

THREE

Two weeks after beginning to look for a place of his own, and John finally had one. Well, he'd actually had it for a couple of days, but today was his move in day.

"All the money you have, and you rented a two-bedroom house in Queens," Andino said.

"Listen, not every fucker is like you, Andi. We don't all want to have the big mansion in Tuxedo Park."

"I don't have a mansion in Tuxedo Park."

"Yet," John shot back.

Andino chuckled. "Truth. You do have too much money to be living in a tiny house in Queens, though. Deny it."

"Money?" John scoffed. "I *had* money. Now I have investments, and a money manager who doesn't allow me very much control, man."

Andino shot John and look, but said nothing. He could still tell his cousin—and best friend—wanted to ask more questions.

"Go ahead," John muttered.

He unlocked the front door of the rental home while his cousin shoved his hands in his pockets. Andino shifted from foot to foot—maybe he was trying to figure out a way to phrase his question. John didn't know.

"Was that by choice, or …?"

John shrugged, and pushed the door open. "I mean, mostly. Do you know how much money I blew through during my last manic episode?"

"No."

"A little under three million."

Andino coughed hard, and looked like he couldn't breathe. "In a few months?"

"Yeah."

"That poor money."

John laughed loudly as they stepped into the house together. "It's one of my behaviors, that's all. Spending money. Hyper-sexuality. Bad decision after bad decision."

"The second one might not be such a bad thing."

"It is when you'll fuck anything that moves just to feel something, Andi. It's just another reckless behavior to add on top of the already reckless behaviors I seek out in an episode."

Andino blew out a breath, and then tossed his jacket to a bare corner. "Yeah, I know. I was just … kidding with you."

His cousin was just about the only person John allowed to kid with him about his bipolar disorder. Anyone else, and he was quick to point out he wasn't the fucking butt of anybody's jokes.

Andino meant no harm, though, and he was always down to help John. Or, keep him out of trouble, even. The two had been that way—ride or die—since they were kids.

"Anyway," John said, waving the moving guys in from the doorway, "now the money manager keeps me on track with everything regarding my trust fund from my biological grandfather. He earns me money, and gives me some to spend. I'm still working with a ten-thousand-dollar stipend every month, plus whatever I make working. He doesn't get that, you know."

"Yeah, it's not clean money, right? Wouldn't want somebody looking too deep in to how you made it, never mind the government getting easy access to documents that showed no taxes paid on it."

"Exactly."

John turned his back to the guys bringing the furniture and boxes in. Some had been in storage while he was in prison, and other things were brand new. Shit he had purchased over the last couple of weeks while he looked for a place.

"You said mostly, though," Andino pointed out.

"Huh?"

Adriano tipped his head to the side. "When I asked if it was by choice about the money manager, you said mostly."

"I recognized I had an issue that needed handling."

"But?"

"Dad threatened to file legal action against me if I didn't do it willingly," John admitted.

Andino flinched. "Ouch."

"Is what it is. So far, my disorder has never been brought into the public record. I don't want people in this life to know that I am bipolar."

"Like a target someone might see and use against you, huh?"

"Essentially. We're all fine and good pretending *mafiosi* are honorable made men, but the truth is a hell of a lot simpler, Andi."

Andino nodded. "We see a perceived weakness, and we exploit it."

"Yeah. Dad knows that, and if it gets him what he wants, he doesn't mind using the idea that my disorder will somehow get into a public record on me to make me do what he needs me to do. Filing legal action against me to take control of my assets or whatever else due to my failing to take care of it myself would absolutely do that."

"John, you know Lucian is only looking out for—"

"I know *why*," John interjected sharply. "That doesn't make it right."

Andino shoved his hands deep in his pockets again. "Point taken."

It was another reason why John held bitterness toward his father, sure, even if a part of him understood it had been for the best. The thing about Lucian Marcello and his only son was that a lot of the time, John was left feeling like his father was stripping the control of his life away from him.

Slowly.

One by one.

A thing at a time.

Or maybe his father didn't want to do that at all, and that was just John's misfiring emotions and brain working against each other again. Who fucking knew?

It didn't take long for the movers to get all the furniture and boxes inside the house. John simply directed them to drop everything in the middle of the large living room. He was so particular about his things and how it all needed to be placed that someone else doing it could send him into some kind of fit.

Anxiety.

Anger.

Sometimes both.

Sure, his meds helped a lot to keep him settled and allowed him a bit more breathing room to think before he spoke or reacted, but it wasn't a whole lot of space. Mostly just enough for him to recognize he might be making a bigger deal out of something than it actually was.

That didn't mean his brain accepted the conclusion, or that the problem still didn't feel *very* real to John.

It was hard to explain that to others. How could he explain something when sometimes, he didn't even know what he was feeling himself?

Andino knew, though. A byproduct of once trying to help John clean up his room as a teenager after his mother, Jordyn, had a fit about the mess.

His cousin looked over the boxes in the Queens house, but didn't touch a thing. He *did* ask.

"Anything you want me to help you with?"

John made a noise in the back of his throat, and scrubbed his hands together. A nervous tic that helped to give him an outlet for his simmering anxieties. "Maybe move some furniture once I know where I want to put it."

"I could unpack some stuff, and just not *put* it anywhere, too."

"No, don't do that."

Andino put a hand up. "All right."

There was something Andino was especially good at that John didn't mind letting his cousin do without looking over his shoulder the entire time.

"I filled the fridge and cupboards yesterday."

Andino smirked. "Still can't cook worth shit, can you?"

"I'm learning."

John tried not to sound defensive, and failed like a fucker. With a laugh and a clap to John's shoulder, Andino headed for the open concept kitchen. He still talked as he began pulling dishes from the cupboard, and then moved to another one where the food was.

"Right, right." Andino sighed loudly. "What is with all this organic shit, John? Haven't you heard of proper butter or sugar?"

"Every little thing helps to keep me at stable levels—diet, exercise, the money manager … all of it."

"Ah."

John opted to change the topic. "How was Atlantic City?"

Andino kept his back turned to John. "Interesting. A nice break, anyway."

"Kind of surprised the boss let you head out for a couple of weeks when you had business here."

Andino stayed silent.

John didn't miss it.

"Something up?" John asked.

Slowly, Andino turned around at the island so that John could see his face. Like with so many other things that were affected by his disorder, eye contact was a big thing. For those he trusted, he preferred to see their face and look in their eyes when they delivered him any kind of news that he might perceive as bad.

It just *helped*.

John braced for the impact.

"Dante didn't have a choice but to let me take a break," Andino said.

"Shit, rub some of that magic on me because that man keeps riding my ass about everything."

"Don't you want to know why he didn't have a choice?"

"There's a reason?" John asked back, joking.

Andino laughed quietly. "Yeah, uh … they want to move me up in *la famiglia*, John. The end goal is for me to take control after Dante is done."

Like a boss.

The boss.

A Cosa Nostra Don.

John took in the news, and let it process before he spoke. Not because he felt bad about it, or wondered why. He knew that was the best choice for the Marcello organization. *Andino* was the best choice, for more reasons than John could name.

Seems John would now have something to discuss with his father when he went to have dinner with his parents tomorrow. Their dinners were already stilted because John didn't have a lot to say.

"Okay," John said. "I don't understand what the problem is."

Andino blinked. "No?"

"No."

"A lot of us figured it would be you to do that, John."

Oh.

"Me, too," John said, chuckling, "a long time ago."

"I'm sorry, man."

John shook his head. "They're making the right choice, Andi."

Andino glanced down. "I didn't ask for this, John. I woke up being a very content Capo, and good at what I do. It's what I wanted to do, and they just shoved this at me. Like here you fucking go, so be thankful."

"You're the right choice. You already look out for this family like it's your first job, anyway."

"Family first," Andino said, nodding.

"God is a very close second."

So was the Marcello way.

"Johnathan."

At the sound of his mother's sweet voice, John's anxiety slipped away. It wouldn't last for long, he knew, but he enjoyed it while he could.

Bending down, he kissed Jordyn's smiling cheek. "Hey, Ma."

Jordyn's blue gaze took a silent inventory of her son. "You look well."

"I looked well when I was here a couple of weeks ago, too."

"Mmhmm, but you don't come over often enough for me to make sure you are always well, John."

"Ma," he said quietly.

Jordyn waved a hand as if to dismiss what she had said. "Never mind. It's just me thinking out loud."

John offered his mother a hand to help her up from the couch. He followed behind her as she headed for the kitchen. His mother's favorite room in the entire house. Despite all her efforts to teach him how to cook, John still sucked.

Jordyn checked the casserole in the oven as she said, "I didn't know if you were coming today or not, but I made you chicken and salad—all organic, John."

He smiled, and moved closer to wrap one arm around his mother's shoulders. He pulled her in for a quick hug because his mother always took care of him even when it was no longer her job to do so.

"Thanks, Ma."

Jordyn patted his cheek. "I know you have problems to work out with Lucian, but won't you come visit me more often? I've gone three years only seeing you occasionally, and it was always behind a Plexiglas window. The least you could do—"

"I will come visit you more often."

Her smile bloomed in to a brilliant sight. "That's my boy."

Thirty years old, and he was still a boy to his mother. He would blame it on the fact they were an Italian family, and the old saying about Italian mothers and their sons, but he couldn't. His mother's heritage sported maybe a twenty percent Italian bloodline—unlike his father's three quarter bloodline.

Still, Jordyn fit the bill perfectly.

"What are we talking about visits, now?" Lucian asked from the kitchen entryway.

Lucian Marcello was not a loud man, but he was a domineering man. He could easily silence people with a look, or make them uncomfortable with a single, soft spoken word. He rarely needed to use threats or violence to scare people, as a promise and a cold smile worked just as well.

Intimidating best described John's father.

Lucian didn't even have to try—he just was.

John nodded at his father, and then headed for the table. "Papa."

"I missed you when you came in," Lucian said.

"I was told not to flake on my mother, remember?"

One of those cool, calm smiles curved his father's mouth. "That you were."

Lucian crossed the kitchen, and dropped a kiss to his wife's forehead. He overlooked the food Jordyn was putting together, and then finally turned back to John.

"I heard Andino was helping to get your new place set up."

"He did."

"Do you think Queens is the best place when you do most of your work in the heart of Brooklyn, or over in Manhattan?"

Instantly, John's defenses started to raise. It wasn't even his father's fault, but their long history of John's choices being constantly overturned or undermined by his father made even the simplest of conversations difficult.

Mostly because John refused to open up another avenue where his father might step in and try to change or control something. Lucian hadn't even implied he thought one way or the other about where John chose to live—he only asked *a question.*

It didn't matter.

John's defenses worked their way up all the same. "I think I have a lot of people and connections in Queens, and some business there, too. It's close enough to Manhattan and Brooklyn. I'm not concerned, and you shouldn't be, either."

Lucian stilled, and eyed John like he didn't quite know how to reply to that. "I only wanted to know how you felt about it, son."

"I feel fine about it, Papa."

"Good. You're liking the house, then?"

John's defensive posture and tone lessened when he said, "It's all right. I grew up in bigger, but I just spent three years in an eight by eight cell, too."

Lucian chuckled. "Anything is better than a cell, right?"

"You could say that."

Jordyn gestured for Lucian to come taste what she held out on the spoon. Thankfully, it took Lucian's attention away from his son for the moment. John was grateful, as it allowed him to take a breath, and settle the rising irritation.

It wasn't his father's fault. Lucian hadn't pushed for information beyond what John had been willing to give. John was simply reactive to these kinds of things with his dad.

Taking his focus away from his father and mother, John realized then that someone else was missing from the table.

His littlest sister.

"Where's Lucia?"

Lucian passed Jordyn a look, but said nothing. John's mother quickly went back to putting together the dishes for supper.

John's youngest sister—the one sibling he was closest to for reasons stemming back to his childhood—still lived with their parents at her age. He tried to make time for her since getting out of prison, but shit kept coming up.

"The last time I saw her was last week after my car finally got shipped in," John said. "I took her out for a drive. She hasn't tried to get ahold of me since."

Which was entirely unusual for his little sister.

Lucian cleared his throat, and came to sit at the head of the table. A seat only reserved for him that no one else was ever allowed to sit in. John wasn't sure if that was something his father demanded, or a rule his mother made up.

It could have been both, knowing his parents.

"Lucia had to work late at the shelter today," Lucian said.

John raised a brow. "You don't sound sure."

"She's been ... different lately."

All over again, John's instincts went into overdrive. If it wasn't anger, then it was anxiety. If not those, then concern or defensiveness. Sometimes he cycled so fast between them, or ran through the entire gamut of them all at once that it was hard to keep up.

"Different how?" he asked.

Lucian shrugged. "Don't worry about it, John. I think she's just made a friend, and while I don't approve of him, it will run its course soon enough."

Him.

"Who?"

Lucian sighed. "It doesn't—"

"It does to me. I look out for Lucia. She's the only one of my sisters that lets me look out for her. So, who is it?"

"Well, you would probably know him better than I do, but I've looked in to him. Renzo is his name."

John stilled in the chair. "Renzo Zulla?"

Lucian nodded. "That would be him."

Shit.

A foot solider for a crew John controlled as the Capo. Ren, the guy liked to be called. He grew up poor, and followed the footsteps of his father when it came to running the streets. The guy was nineteen, or maybe twenty.

"I don't know where she would have met him," Lucian said, sounding both irritated and confused at the same time.

"I do," John replied.

His mother looked to him, and so did his father.

"How?" Jordyn asked.

"Me," John said before scrubbing a hand over his face. "We took a drive, and I had some work to do. Ren was one of those things I had to handle. They didn't even talk, though. She never even got out of the car."

"That boy is trouble, John," Lucian said. "I already had one daughter get mixed up with a man that almost killed her, and I do not want another one falling into the same trap. I don't know this young man, but I know he did not grow up in a very good situation. That typically means he wasn't brought up to be a decent man. Hell, maybe he doesn't even know how to be one. I don't know, and I don't care. I just don't want my daughter involved with him."

John didn't need to be told.

Renzo was a street kid that would soon be looking at a prison sentence, or he'd simply serve more time on the streets. So was the way of their life—or rather, Ren's life.

Lucia was not a part of that world.

"I'll have a chat with him," John said.

Lucian cocked a brow. "Do you think you should?"

John didn't even let his defensiveness come out to play this time. "I think if you approach Renzo, he'll laugh in your face. He knows me, though. It's not the same."

"All right."

That was that.

John thought this part of Brooklyn was a little upper crust for Renzo's taste, but this was apparently where the kid was supposed to be today. Well, calling Ren a kid was a little disrespectful considering the guy's age, but whatever.

Pulling his new Mercedes over into one of the only parking spots available on the block, John turned off the engine. He excited the car, and strolled into the people walking on the sidewalk.

John checked over his phone again—details he had gotten from a friend of a friend about what Renzo's usual schedule was like through the week. It had taken him a couple of days, but John now had sufficient enough information to believe Renzo was in this area of Brooklyn because of his seventeen-year-old sister.

Apparently, the girl attended a private school for the arts in these parts, and Renzo came to visit her every few days. Today was supposed to be one of those days.

John had no idea how Renzo, or his delinquent parents, were apparently paying for a private school for the girl. He also didn't care, as that wasn't any of his business. He simply wanted to let the guy know to stay the hell away from his sister, and nothing else.

Across the street, a familiar sight caught John's eye. His walk slowed for a split second as he did a double take of the woman coming out of an old bookstore.

John didn't think he would see her again after the bus incident, not to mention running in to her right here almost two weeks ago.

Their families just didn't mingle.

Siena.

The woman had lost the jeans, blouse, and messenger bag from the first time they met. Today, she wore a knee-length black dress, suede ankle books, and carried a leather Gucci bag. She seemed caught up in the paperback she held—that was the same as before.

John had shit to do.

A guy to threaten.

A million other things he needed to take care of except Siena Calabrese. The bad blood between their respective mafia organizations should have been enough to keep him on that side of the street. Hell, her grandfather had been the man who killed his biological great-grandfather and the man's family decades and decades ago. That *should* have been enough to keep John away.

He was crossing the busy street before he even knew what he was doing. He flipped the middle finger to a car that was forced to stop to let him jaywalk.

Siena still had her head stuck down in the book when John came up in front of her.

"I thought I told you to watch where you were walking around these parts, *donna.*"

Her head popped up, and those cerulean eyes of hers widened. She didn't even try to hide the shock of seeing him again.

"John," Siena murmured.

Now that he was right in front of her, he was able to get an even better look at the body-hugging dress she wore, and the heels that made her legs look fucking fantastic. His gaze traveled over her curves before settling back on her face once more.

"That's me," he said, grinning.

A pretty pink colored her cheeks when she returned his smile. "Any reason you're hanging around this part of Brooklyn again?"

"Business."

Siena raised a brow. "That so?"

John stuffed his hands in his pockets. "That's my story."

"Well, I'm heading to my brother's club for work. I'm late, so I have to go."

No, he couldn't just let her go this time. He was pretty sure the last time they had run in to each other like this, she had meant to ask him out. A phone call hadn't let her finish the sentence. John had to go right after, and he figured it was what it was.

Fate had different plans, it seemed.

"Can I walk you?" he asked.

"I don't know, *can* you?"

Just like that, his job to talk with Renzo was forgotten.

Someone far more beautiful and interesting had all of his attention now.

John chuckled. "May I walk you?"

Siena's smile softened. "You know what, yeah. Sure, John."

He moved into step with her as she headed down the road. Before she could shove the book she had been reading in her bag, he grabbed it out of her hand.

All over again, her cheeks lit up with that pretty pink.

John kind of liked it.

Another bare-chested man looked up at him from the cover, although this time, the guy did have a dress shirt opened, and he was working on tying a tie.

John cocked a brow. "Who knots their tie while their shirt is still open, anyway?"

"Oh, my God. Give me that back." Siena snatched the book out of his hand, and gave him a little glare. "Don't make fun of my books."

"I definitely wasn't. I was just saying that makes no sense."

"Mmhmm. Sure."

"The first full-length paperback I ever read was one of my mother's romances, actually. She was a huge fan."

Siena grinned. "Really?"

"Yeah, I mean, I was grounded, and couldn't do anything. She left it sitting around, so I picked it up and started reading. Took me a week or so to get through it—I was nine or something."

"She never noticed?"

John shrugged. "Yeah, I think she did, but it kept me quiet and out of her hair. You know?"

Siena's laughter sounded like wind chimes. John couldn't help but stare at her while she did it. Her delicate features lit up and natural pouty lips curved with happiness. She was quite a sight like that, he thought. Carefree and beautiful.

The heat that shot through his gut was such a foreign feeling that he didn't recognize it at first. It had been so long since he actually felt attraction and lust together. The past three years had been spent dealing with far too many other things that had very little to do with women, dating, or sex.

It took him by surprise.

"I know you're heading to your brother's place for work," John said, "but do you want to grab coffee or something later?"

Siena's steps hesitated, and the two stopped altogether on the sidewalk. "I—"

John's phone rang.

Just like the last time.

Again.

Fuck.

"Sorry," he told her.

Siena shrugged, and looked away. He didn't miss the flash of disappointment in her gaze, though.

John answered the phone with a sharp, "What?"

"Mr. Marcello, Dr. Goodane would like to confirm your appointment in two hours."

Shit.

John checked his watch, and realized he had forgotten one very important thing today. His therapist. It was one of the many requirements of his parole, not that he minded. A good therapist kept him on track with his bipolar disorder, anyway.

He couldn't refuse. The doctor would have to report a missed appointment to his parole officer. Then, that asshole would get on his ass, too.

"Yeah, I'll be there."

He would just have to leave *right now*.

John hung up the phone, and turned to Siena. Even though he had to go, he was still determined to get her number, and meet up sometime. Three random run-ins had to be a sign of something, right?

"So—"

Siena held up a hand, and stopped John from saying more. "Hey, it's okay. Maybe we'll have another one of these meetings, John."

She didn't give him a chance to say anything before she headed down the street. John was stuck staring after her.

Fuck his whole life.

John tried to brush off the pissy mood as he headed into the therapist's office. Amelia—a forty-year-old married mother with two teenaged sons whose pictures littered the walls—already sat waiting for him in the chair.

He took the couch across from her.

Twice a week, he had these appointments.

Mostly, he didn't mind.

Today, he did mind.

"John," she greeted.

"Amelia."

Down to business first, he knew.

It was just how she worked.

Amelia looked over the papers in the file. "How's the change in the dose of the Lithium working?"

"The first few days were a bad fog."

"We figured that, though, right?"

John shrugged. "It's still pretty thick most days. The medication fog, I mean."

"It's only been a couple of weeks since we changed the dose, right?"

"Something like that."

Amelia scratched something down to the paper. "I need you to give it some time to readjust, John. Lowering the dose could have bad consequences."

Sometimes, the meds were just … too much. A hazy fog descended over his brain, and took over everything. A single missed pill, or the wrong dose, could send him into a manic spiral within days.

"Yeah, I know," John finally said.

Not that he liked it.

"Every person managing their bipolar disorder is different," Amelia said. "You have to allow the medication time to settle with you, and your disorder."

"I'm aware. Except I was just fine for three years in prison taking only the Lithium. On your suggestion, I've added more medications to that, and all it's done is put me in a fog. I can't exactly be productive when my mind is like looking through frosted glass."

He'd been dealing with this and medications and everything else related to this disorder since he had been diagnosed as an older teen.

It never ended.

"You also deal with depression and anxiety, and the new med change should help with that. We discussed this. It's why we chose the med change."

She said *we*.

Truth was, she decided that.

John went along with it for now. Based on the way the new med regime left him feeling on a daily basis, he couldn't say how long it would last. Sure, some bipolar people needed more than just one med to manage their disorder—he wasn't sure he was one of those people based on his past experience. His therapist had a different opinion, but then again, she had only been treating him since his release, and not since his diagnosis.

Some therapists worked that way—they made decisions on medications, and the patients went along with it until they found the combination that worked. He preferred telling Amelia what worked best for him, and having her work that way.

So far, that's not how this whole thing had gone down.

Amelia rested back in her chair, and said, "For some people, bipolar is just one part of their life. A background thought that they manage with medication and whatever else. So today, I would like to talk about what being bipolar is—and means—to you, John."

Great.

He chuckled dryly, and toyed with the Rolex on his wrist. "For me, bipolar makes up a great portion of who I am. A lot of my relationships had been forged or broken because of this disorder. How I eat is determined by which foods might hinder or help my mood swings. It controls the fact that the first thing I do in the morning is take several pills because I won't remember if they're not the first thing

I go to. What else do you want to know?"

"What's it like for you day to day?"

"Depends on where I am in a cycle," he replied.

"And where are you right now?"

"Low."

She raised a brow. "Low as in a depression, or …?"

"No, just fine. There's low, and then there's low. I only get really low after the mania breaks. I mean, the depression is always there warring back and forth, but it never gets dangerous for me until after a manic episode."

"And how does that usually feel for you—depression *after* mania, I mean?"

"The way depression usually feels. Add in suicidal thoughts manifesting, and you've got depression after a manic break for me."

Amelia didn't seem to miss the bite in John's tone if her narrowed eyes were any indication. "You're not typically this snappy, Johnathan. Is something different? How are you feeling today?"

"At the moment, kind of pissed off."

"Why is that?"

"Your secretary interrupted me when I was trying to set up a date with somebody."

Amelia coughed, and hid her small smile by looking away. "Like a woman, or a business thing?"

"What do you think?"

The therapist sighed.

John knew what she was going to say before she even spoke.

"As good as it may be on the surface that you're trying to get back to a normal routine, you have to remember that you're still getting assimilated outside of confinement, John. I have to remind you that dating or sex or anything emotionally intense like those things could be detrimental to your success outside of prison while you're still attempting to adapt to these sudden changes. You have a history of hyper-sexuality, for one. Given how delicate the balance is while we work on med changes right now, I wouldn't toy too much with that behavior."

He knew she was right.

His disorder could be fickle—and predictable—in that way. Changes in his life, especially big ones, could easily tip the scales and lead him toward another manic cycle.

"I'll keep it in mind," he told her.

"Please do."

It was the best he could do.

Siena was still in the back of his mind, and she didn't seem to be going away anytime soon.

FOUR

Siena checked the calendar on her phone again—something she did upwards of twenty times a day. Like all the things she had put in to-do slots would suddenly change or disappear. Everything was still there, including the fact she was supposed to be at Kev's restaurant over an hour ago to look over some changes he wanted made to his books.

Also, it was the end of August.

How in the hell did two weeks slip by without her noticing?

She was losing it.

That, or she was too busy to have a freaking life.

Siena headed inside Kev's restaurant, and went to the back offices. She didn't even stop to say hello to her friend that was waiting tables. She didn't have the time.

The restaurant was full, though. The scrape of utensils against plates, and the conversations echoed behind her as she slipped into the back hallway.

Funny.

She worked here at least once or twice a month, but she had never actually eaten at the place. No, her whole life just revolved around which business she needed to be at from one day to the next in order to keep her brothers and father happy.

Siena tried to shrug off the irritation as she stepped up to the closed office door. Normally, she would have knocked if a door was closed. Her brothers demanded that she did for privacy. Not today, however.

She was too busy, and lost in her thoughts.

Siena opened the office door, and headed inside. She was still looking down at the calendar on her phone when someone cleared their throat.

Her head popped up.

Kev and Darren were both staring at her.

So was another guy.

She recognized Andino Marcello instantly. Of course, she only knew *of* the man, and very little else. He usually came to have meetings with one or both of her brothers every couple of months for Cosa Nostra business.

Something about crews, or streets.

Siena didn't really know.

She wasn't supposed to.

"Oh," she said, taking a small step back. "Sorry about that."

Kev cocked a brow at her. "You don't know how to knock today, or what?"

"I'm late."

Darren scowled. "Again."

"How about you two do even half of the stuff I have to do, and then tell me how well you're able to manage your fucking time."

That quieted her brothers.

Siena mentally patted herself on the back.

"I'll just wait outside until you're done," she said.

Kev sighed, and stood from the chair. "No, it's fine. We were going to continue our discussion over a meal, anyway. Better for you to get to work while you're actually here. And don't even think about taking off before the changes are made to the books, Siena."

She resisted the urge to roll her eyes, or tell her brother off. She only opted not to because Andino was there, and it wouldn't lead to anything good for her in the end. One of her brothers would tell their father that she had disrespected them in front of a man from another organization, and she would never hear the goddamn end of it.

All of these rules suffocated her.

It never ended.

Siena moved to the side of the doorway as her brothers moved past her to leave the office. Andino followed behind them. He gave her a tight smile, but nothing else.

She wasn't sure why, but her mouth decided to open up and ask something she had no business knowing. Andino was a Marcello, after all. He would have to know Johnathan. Cousins, or something.

It had been two weeks since she last saw Johnathan on the busy Brooklyn street. She had been so busy that when he got another phone call, she didn't mind letting him rush off even it was the second time he left her hanging.

Sort of …

"How's John, Andino?" Siena asked.

The man's steps halted instantly.

So did her brothers' in the hallway.

"Pardon?" Andino asked.

"Johnathan. He's like a cousin of yours, right?"

Andino nodded. "He is, yeah."

"How is he?"

"Busy," Andino said, chuckling. "I didn't know you knew him."

She could plainly see the way he probed for information without outright asking her, but she didn't mind indulging him. If only because she was hoping to get a little bit of her own information, too.

"We've run in to each other a couple of times, I guess. Talked a bit."

Andino stuffed his hands in his pockets, and glanced at her brothers who had come closer to them again. Despite how the Marcello man was built, like a linebacker ready to tackle someone, he seemed uncomfortable discussing his family.

Or maybe it was just because *her* family was there. The Marcello and the Calabrese families never did mingle beyond business.

Bad blood.

That shit didn't wash out.

"The last time we talked, he had to run off," Siena said, shrugging. "I just wanted to make sure he was okay."

Andino cleared his throat, and smiled again. "He's good, Siena. Thanks for asking."

"Siena, get to work, huh?" Kev clapped Andino on the shoulder, and directed him past Siena. "And mind your damn business, *donna*."

She heard her brother's warning loud and clear, and chose for now, to heed it. What else could she do?

Once all the men had disappeared down the hallway, Siena headed into the office. She closed the door behind her, and locked it seeing as how she didn't need or want her brothers interrupting her.

She was a good thirty minutes in to reworking accounts for the restaurant's books, and the numbers were already starting to bleed together. A knock on the office door made her pop her head up from the PC screen for the first time.

Thankful for the break it would take to get up and unlock the door, Siena shook her wrists and cracked her neck as she stood. She figured it would be one of her brothers on the other side of the door, but it wasn't.

Andino Marcello stood there.

Hands shoved in his pockets.

A cocked eyebrow.

Smile gone.

The politeness he had shown her earlier seemed to be entirely gone. His warm gaze now felt cold as he looked her over.

Siena's gaze darted over his shoulder to check for her brothers. Neither Kev, nor Darren stood there with Andino.

"They're busy—having a smoke in the back," Andino said, flashing a smirk. "I don't smoke. At least, not with them."

Siena wasn't sure why exactly, but the way he sought her out like this did not feel friendly at all.

"What can I do for you, Andino?" she asked.

"Step inside," he said.

When she didn't move as quickly as he wanted her to, Andino simply put a hand to Siena's shoulder, and moved her inside the office. He kicked the door closed behind him, and completely ignored her indignant shout.

Siena hit his hand from her shoulder, and glared at him. "Who in the hell do you think you are?"

"What do you want with my cousin?"

She blinked. "What?"

"Is it your brothers—your father, maybe? Did they put you up to engaging with John, or what?"

Siena shook her head, so confused that it wasn't even funny. "We sat across from each other on the bus, and then randomly ran in to each other on the street a couple of times outside the bookstore where I get my books."

Andino sucked air through his teeth. "That all?"

"What the fuck is it any of your business?"

He moved closer—just an inch.

It was enough to make Siena take a step back.

"It's my business because I look out for John. I've had his back since we were kids. He doesn't have very many people thinking about his interests, so I make sure to be one of them. Got it?"

Siena swallowed the lump that had formed in her throat. "Okay, I got it."

"What else was there?"

"Nothing. We had a walk, chatted a bit, and he asked me to go for coffee once, but we didn't. Seems like he's always running off and leaving me hanging, you know?"

Andino simply stared at her for a long while before he finally said, "And no one has said anything to you about John, or the Marcellos?"

"No." Siena's gaze narrowed as she added, "You heard my brothers—I ask anything, and I get told to mind my fucking business. I just wanted to make sure John was doing okay. Friends *can* ask after friends."

"You don't know my cousin from a fucking hole in the ground, girl. How can you be his friend?"

"Maybe I would like to be," she shot back.

Andino tipped his chin up, and continued eyeing her in that intense way of his. It made her want to move back again, or fidget. Something.

"He keeps running off, you said?" Andino asked.

Siena shrugged. "Kind of. I don't think he means to. I've never even gotten his number, or whatever."

"Maybe he didn't want to give it to you, then. Ever consider that?"

Ouch.

She ignored that jibe.

"I did *only* want to check up on him," she said. "I didn't mean any harm."

Andino cleared his throat, and took a step back. It was enough to let the office feel like the large space it was when his imposing presence wasn't taking up a lot of her fucking air. Christ, the man was something else.

And for Siena?

That was not a good thing.

"How about I help you out?" Andino asked.

"How?"

The man grinned. "John works out of a club every other weekend. For specific people, it's just easier to find him there than to make him run for them. Not a lot of people know that he's been using that spot to do his business occasionally. His next weekend working at the club should be in a couple of weeks, if you're curious."

"And what does that mean for me?"

"You show up—only you, girl—and maybe you'll get more than five minutes with him."

"Just me."

"I don't trust your family. No Marcello does."

Siena pursed her lips in an effort to hide her frown. "Not even me?"

"Not while you still have that last name, anyway."

It was not as easy to let that insult roll off her shoulders, but she tried.

"Which club?" she asked.

Andino smiled, and this time, it was warm.

Siena was fifty pages into her new novel about a mercenary hero and heroine thrown together by circumstance when a knock on her apartment door interrupted her. She had all she could do not to glare at the door from across the living room.

The few minutes she was allowed to sit down and relax, and someone had to come over. It wasn't like she had a lot of friends or anything, and her brothers barely wanted anything to do with her unless it related to work somehow.

"The door is unlocked," she called out.

Siena went back to her book.

However, she eyed her father as he slipped in her apartment. Matteo practically swallowed the space with his large stature. His dark gaze looked over the place, and then skipped to where his daughter sat with a book in her hands.

"Don't you lock your door?" he asked.

"Why would I?"

"Because it's safer, Siena."

"Safer for whom?" She smiled sweetly. "Pretty sure if someone wanted me out of here for whatever reason, they would just break it down, Dad."

Matteo clicked his tongue at her. One of his many signs of annoyance or disappointment. "This is what you do with your free time—read?"

"Reading is good for the brain."

She didn't bother to add how reading also helped to shut off her brain when she spent eight or more hours a day looking at numbers, and falsifying them. Being a bookkeeper and accountant was only made harder by the fact that every book she opened, she had to scrub it clean, and cook it up.

It added more work and time.

Matteo came closer, and seemed to be peering at the cover. "There's a half-naked man on the cover. What is that garbage?"

"It's not garbage. It's a romance."

"Mmhmm."

"He's a mercenary."

"That so?"

"Apparently. What do you want, Dad?"

Might as well get right to it, she thought. For the three years she had lived in this apartment, she could count on one hand the amount of times her father had come to visit her. Typically, her mother came over a couple of times a month, but Matteo never joined her.

Besides, Siena spent enough time with her father through the week when she worked. Him and her brothers.

She didn't need more time with him.

"I can't visit my daughter?" he asked, taking a seat on the couch beside her.

"You don't typically make an effort to, no."

Matteo chuckled, and the force rocked them both on the couch. "Perhaps I'm making an effort to do just that, Siena. Your mother is always telling me how there's more to you than the numbers in your head."

She side-eyed her father, and doubted every single word he spoke.

She still kept quiet.

Matteo continued talking, anyway. "Besides, you *are* my daughter. My only—"

Siena couldn't keep quiet at that statement. "You have three daughters with Joy Kennedy."

The reddening of her father's cheeks almost made her grin. She held it back, but still took great satisfaction at the sight.

"Yes, well, I meant my only legitimate daughter," Matteo grumbled.

"I'm sure Ma appreciated that when she found out about the other ones."

"We're not talking about that right now, Siena."

No, they never did.

Another rule to add to the pile.

Nothing was discussed that her father didn't approve. That absolutely included his mistress, and the children she birthed him.

"As I was saying," Matteo muttered heavily, giving her a pointed look, "you are my daughter. I don't think I need a reason to check in with you every once in a while. Do I?"

Siena was desperately trying to focus on the words in her book, and not whatever information her father had come here to pry out of her. That's the only reason she figured he was there. Her lack of focus on the book made it difficult to ignore Matteo.

Besides, if she pissed him off, he would just make the next couple of weeks a living hell for her when it came to work.

He was not very sly in that way.

"I guess so," she finally said.

Matteo smiled, and patted a beefy hand to her knee. "Good. How about you go make me a coffee?"

Great.

Bookkeeper, and a server.

Perfect.

Siena tossed her book aside with a soft sigh, and stood from the couch. Her father followed behind as she headed for the kitchen. With the electric kettle turned on, she kept her back turned to her father as she pulled out instant coffee, sugar, and a mug from the cupboard. At least this way, she figured her father might get the hint that she was not up for conversation.

Apparently not …

"I wondered if maybe you would be out tonight," he said behind her.

Siena stiffened. "Why would I be out?"

"You're twenty-five. Surely you have friends, and you like to do things. Don't most girls your age?"

"Haven't you told me for basically my whole life that idle hands and bad behavior would only shame you and the family?"

Matteo chuckled darkly. "That I did."

"I don't go out very much, Dad."

Mostly true.

"No friends, either?"

"A couple."

"What about men?"

A knot of tension tightened around Siena's spine. She tried not to show how uncomfortable the question made her as she turned around to face her father.

"Like dating?" she asked.

Matteo nodded. "Exactly that. Are you seeing someone?"

"Would it matter if I was?"

"I should think it would be my business if you were," he replied.

"Yet, I'm not."

"At all?" he pressed.

Siena's gaze narrowed. "Where is this coming from, Dad?"

Because it all screamed strange and odd to her. It wasn't like her father to care much about her personal life as long as she kept it quiet, and private. As long as nothing she did brought shame to her family, then he never spoke a word about it.

After all, he wanted a compliant, easily controlled daughter. Much like how he preferred his wife, too.

Matteo waved a large hand. "Your brothers mentioned maybe you were dating, and I thought I should ask."

What?

When would her brothers—

Siena's thoughts slammed together with a heavy realization. All she did was ask about one single man in front of her brothers, and the first thing they did was run to her father with the information.

Like a bunch of assholes.

She was, however, planning on seeking Johnathan Marcello out in a week at the club he apparently worked out of every other weekend. She even made sure to clear things off her schedule so that nothing would be taking her away.

Siena was not telling her father that, though.

Andino had been clear.

Her family was not welcome.

"I'm not seeing anyone," she told her father. "At all."

"Do let me know if that changes," Matteo said, grinning.

With that, her father moved away from the small island, and headed for the door. As though he were completely finished with their conversation, and now had better things to do that did not include being there with her.

"What about your coffee?" Siena asked.

Matteo looked over his shoulder as he pulled open the door. "I'm not really in the mood to stay and chat longer."

Yeah, she hadn't thought so.

He had only come to pry information out of her.

But why?

Why?

Siena filed the strange encounter away in the back of her mind, and decided it was probably nothing.

For now, anyway.

Despite the name of the club, Heavy Metal had very little to do with scream-o music or hard rock. Siena figured that out the second she stepped inside the joint. The reflective lights and metallic accents left shimmering colors cascading over her body-con red dress, and the matching four-inch stilettos on her feet.

The bouncer at the front of the club had only nodded at her when she mentioned being there to see a Marcello, even though she hadn't technically been told to do that by Andino.

Whatever.

It got her through the door.

Siena kept a firm grip on the red clutch in her hand as she weaved in and out of the moving people. The flickering lights and bass pounding through the hardwood floors made for quite an experience.

She wasn't really a partier.

Clubs weren't her thing.

She did kind of like this, though.

Siena found herself moving toward the bar while her gaze scanned the crowd for a familiar face …

For John.

The bartender came down her way, and tossed a rag over his shoulder. With a warm smile, he asked, "What can I get for you, pretty girl?"

Siena smiled. "Something light."

"I can mix you up something virgin, but it'll look like the real thing if you want really light."

"Sure, do that."

It was a couple of minutes before the guy came back with her drink. As she paid for it, Siena thought to ask, "Do you know where Johnathan is by chance?"

The bartender cocked a brow. "Marcello?"

"There's only one, right?"

"That there is. He's usually upstairs in the VIP, or working out of an office. Either way, you won't find him on the floor."

"Thanks."

"Just tell the guys guarding the entrance that John asked for you, and they'll let you through."

Siena laughed. "Even if he doesn't know I'm here?"

"Only one way to find out." The bartender winked, adding, "And I bet he won't say no to your pretty face."

Well, then …

FIVE

Andino passed John a subtle nod as he handed his cousin a glass of what would look like vodka to anyone else watching. Around the table tucked in the back section of the VIP area of the club, the two were working out a deal with a local gang leader who had been encroaching on their territories.

Capos had to talk a lot to make shit work, especially on the streets. Business could not always be done through bloodshed. It drew too much attention, and left them wide open for retribution. A good Capo could get anything done that needed handling with a few words, and a drink.

Or, that's how John had learned the business.

The gang leader—Maverick—took the second glass Andino had been holding with a nod, and thanks. Maverick held the glass up to John, and he did the same with his own, clinking the two together.

A peace offering.

After three years of lockup, it felt damn good to get back into business. Being a Capo—even if he did have other Capos looking over his fucking shoulder—was what he did best.

"Pleasure doing business with you, Johnathan," Maverick said.

John tipped his glass up for a drink, and smirked. "And you."

The two men sipped their drinks, although John's was nothing more than water. He didn't drink—or usually—as it wasn't good to mix alcohol with his meds.

Only a select few people knew that, though.

Andino was one of them.

John quickly finished his water, and set the glass to the table. Maverick followed along, and finished his own drink as well.

"So that's settled then," Johnathan said.

Maverick stood from the table. "Seems so. You'll supply, and I'll buy from only you."

"Keep that agreement, and you won't need to see us again."

"We wouldn't be as nice the second time," Andino added.

The gang leader gave a single nod in response, held up two fingers, and gestured at his men waiting a few tables over. With a quick goodbye between the three men, Maverick headed for the exit with his three men flanking him from the sides and behind.

John and Andino's two enforcers came closer damn near instantly. Their empty glasses on the table, and the one Maverick left behind, were picked up by the enforcers, and removed.

"Thanks," John said to Andino.

His cousin grinned. "For what, man? You handled that on your own. I don't know what the hell Dante is worried about with you. I wasn't even needed here tonight."

John chuckled. "Tell him that."

"I will."

He didn't doubt his cousin.

"I meant, thanks for the water," John said.

Andino shrugged a single shoulder, and shoved his hands in his pockets. "I've always got your back, John. Even when you don't know it."

John gave Andino a look. "Not really your job, though."

"Still going to do it."

"What about when you don't have the time anymore, huh?"

Andino's gaze narrowed. "Like fucking when?"

"How about when you're the boss, and have a whole organization to manage? You don't need to be worrying about me when that happens, Andi."

"Yeah, sure, but—"

"No buts. You work on you—make sure you are where you need to be in this organization, Andino. I'll handle me."

Andino scoffed, but clapped John hard on the shoulder at the same time. The two stood at the same six-foot-three height, yet Andino had a good thirty pounds of muscle on John's lean form. Still, he had never felt like the lesser when it came to his cousin. He appreciated Andino for that more than anything else.

"Man, even when I am looking out for me, I am still going to be looking out for you," Andino said, shrugging. "I don't know how to do anything different. Not after everything."

John knew Andino was telling the truth.

He wished he knew how to tell his cousin that it would be okay, one way or the other. It wouldn't matter. Not to his cousin.

Andino was going to do him, and that meant looking out for anybody he gave a shit about.

John included.

"Speaking of looking out for you," Andino said quieter.

John glanced at his cousin. "Pardon?"

"I ran in to somebody—looks like she listened to me."

"What are you talking about?"

Andino pointed over Johnathan's shoulder. He turned to see the sight of Siena Calabrese being escorted across the VIP floor by one of Johnathan's enforcers. The man stayed close to her side, like if she moved out of step, he was ready to grab her.

John hadn't expected to see her.

Especially not *here*.

"I figured that was fucked—finished," John said, more to himself than anyone else.

Andino cocked a brow. "What—her? I ran in to her when I had to handle some business with the Calabrese brothers. I hate them fuckers."

"Yeah, but no. I meant, I kind of ducked out on her. What did you do?"

A sly smile and another clap on John's shoulder accompanied Andino's next words. "She asked about you when I ran in to her. Kind of figured you must have made … an impression."

John cleared his throat. "Not really supposed to be dating."

Or fucking.

Or *anything*.

His therapist made that clear at every appointment. He was supposed to give it time, and work on getting himself straightened out and on the up before he worried about anything else. For good reason …

Relationships, women, and sex were intense things for John. When he mixed all three together, it could be one hell of a hurricane for him.

A good hurricane.

Damn, so good.

It could be a bad one, too.

"Who said anything about *dating*?" Andino asked like the word tasted bad in his mouth. "Have some fun, John. That's all."

It wasn't that simple.

John actually had an interest in Siena Calabrese. Her and those sweet smiles, the romance novels she always seemed to have, and her soft-spoken demeanor. It was only a little bit about her, but he liked it.

There was a lot about her he didn't know but wanted to, as well.

The two quieted as the enforcer finally approached with Siena at his side. She flashed John a blinding smile. He was so caught up in the way she looked at him, that he barely noticed the fact she was wearing a dress that showed off all her curves, and heels that made her legs look … fan-fucking-tastic.

Painted red lips.

Hair in curls.

Blue eyes lined in kohl.

All club and ready to dance.

She was not the same woman he had met on the street, and yet she was exactly that person, too.

"Siena," the enforcer said, jerking a thumb in her direction, "said she was told to come see you here tonight, Skip."

Siena glanced at Andino, and then back to John.

John waved a hand at the enforcer to make him scatter. The man went back to his post without a word.

Andino cleared his throat, and picked his jacket off the back of the chair. "John, I will see you … tomorrow, or something. I have business to do."

Sure you do.

John didn't really mind.

"Nice to see you again, Siena," Andino added as he passed her by. "Thanks for following directions."

"And you," she said quietly.

Then, they were alone.

Not entirely alone, as the VIP area still had a few other people partying, but no one was paying them any mind. For a long time, Siena and John simply stared at one another. He broke the silence first.

"I can't decide if you are out of your element, or not," he said.

She flashed him a smile.

Sexy and pretty in a blink.

How in the hell did she manage that?

"This is a little new for me—a club, I mean," she said.

John grinned. "That so?"

"Yep."

His gaze traveled up from her heels to her delicate features. He didn't hide his staring, and she didn't act like it bothered her.

John liked that *a lot*.

"That dress says differently—like you might know a bit more about this kind of place than you let on," he said.

Siena winked. "Guess you'll have to find out."

He laughed, loud and hard.

It had been too long since he laughed like that.

Way too long.

"I do owe you a coffee," he said.

"Coffee in a club?"

"I don't drink."

A beer once in a blue moon, but even that wasn't usual.

She didn't even blink.

She didn't ask a thing.

Instead, Siena said, "I know a place down the block, if you want to go?"

John's hand on her lower back led them both out. He left his anxiety about the rest at the door.

"Here," John said.

His fingers circled around Siena's small wrist to stop her from walking further. The cool September air had mixed in with the nighttime breeze, and made him think the thin sleeves of her tight dress were not enough to keep her warm.

"What—"

He already slipped his suit jacket off, and tossed it around her shoulders before she could protest, or say anything. He fixed the collar a bit, and the tips of his fingers grazed her collarbones peeking out.

John didn't miss the shiver that raced through Siena at the touch. He didn't think it was the cool breeze that time.

Her blue gaze stayed locked on him, even after he let her go. She didn't move to start walking down the sidewalk again, either.

"You didn't have to do that," she whispered.

John chuckled. "Sure I did, *bella*." He glanced down at the heels on her feet. "Let me know if your feet get tired because I don't mind helping you out there, either."

"And just how would you do that?"

"Carry you."

Siena stilled on the spot, and peeked up at him through long, dark lashes. "You're kidding, aren't you?"

"No."

Not in the least.

"Oh," she said softly.

"I don't mind."

She sighed. "You know, your cousin is kind of scary."

"Who, Andino?" John let out a laugh. "He's a fucking teddy bear."

"If by teddy bear, you mean a teddy bear built like a linebacker with the attitude of somebody ready to take you out, then sure."

John barely held back his smirk. "Really, he's harmless."

"Not if he thinks someone is trying to mess with you."

John sobered instantly. "Yeah, he doesn't play there. What did he say to you?"

Siena shrugged under his jacket. "Basically demanded to know what I wanted with you."

"Because …?"

"I asked about you?"

He liked how she posed that as a question.

"You don't seem sure," he said, giving her a look.

"That's all I did. Like I said, kind of scary."

John shifted from foot to foot, and glanced down the quiet sidewalk. "And what do you want with me, huh?"

"Not really sure."

When he looked back at her, she was still staring at him. Not like she was looking for something in his eyes, or anything. No, she was just there … with him.

Present.

Curious.

It was a strange feeling for John.

And definitely not something he was used to.

"Are you really interested in coffee?" John asked.

Siena shook her head. "Not really, no."

"So, I can assume you came looking for me tonight because you're interested in something else."

"You can definitely assume that, John."

Well, then …

He didn't get the chance to reply because Siena pushed up on her tiptoes, and kissed him. It took him all of three seconds to snap out of the shock, and act. He did just that by wrapping an arm around her back, and grabbing her jaw. He pulled her closer, felt her soft lips grin against his, and just like that …

John felt alive again.

Kind of like when he met her gaze that first time on the bus.

When she blushed …

Siena's lips parted at his tongue teasing against the seam, and he got his first taste of her. A heady sweetness that reminded him of cherries and vanilla. Wicked and pure.

John would have happily stayed like that with her on the sidewalk, until he remembered where exactly they were. Siena's tongue peeked out to touch her bottom lip as he pulled away.

Her lips curved sweetly, while her blue eyes flashed with something that spoke of sex and sin. It was such a juxtaposition. A contrast that took him by surprise each time she did it.

John's thumb stroked her cheek. "So what did make you come find me, then?"

"I thought … why not do something different?" Siena asked. "Besides, how many more times do we have to run in to each other before we get a chance to actually finish a conversation? Kind of leaves a person wanting more, doesn't it?"

"It can."

"Like I said, I'm just doing something different. Giving us another option, if you want to put it that way. If you don't run off tonight, maybe we'll actually be able to have one of those conversations, John."

He didn't think she meant *just* talking. That wasn't a bad thing. Not at all. "Oh?"

"Mmhmm." She gave him a look. "You seem unsure, John."

"It's been a long time for me—for something like this, I mean. Maybe I'm a bit rusty."

"About three years or so, huh?"

"How did you know that?"

"Infamous, remember?"

John nodded, and let out a dry laugh. "Yeah, that."

"I don't do this often, either," she admitted.

"No?"

"Nope."

John wet his lips. "I live in Queens."

Siena smiled. "I live five blocks away."

"Do you feel better with your place?"

"I would, actually."

John's hand rested just above the curve of Siena's ass as they began walking back in the direction they had come. He would be needing his Mercedes, now. Siena tucked tightly into his side the whole way.

"You're not second-guessing being here, are you?"

Siena's soft question drew his attention away from the window overlooking the street below. Her Brooklyn apartment was about as big as he expected it to be, given the area. Clean, though, and meticulous in organization.

He liked that.

John found Siena sipping on a glass of water just a few feet away in the space between the open kitchen and living room. She had discarded his jacket, and her lips were back to their unpainted pink.

Compliments of his kiss.

She started it.

He didn't want to stop.

Siena's fingertips edged along the hem of her short dress, and his gaze

51

followed the path. A flash of creamy, shapely thighs, and his heart raced all over again.

His dick got hard, too.

Fuck, it had been *way too long*.

"Definitely not second-guessing anything," he told her.

Siena grinned, and hooked a finger at him. John took her silent gesture for what it seemed like, and came closer until he could take the glass from her hand. He set it aside on a small table beside the couch.

"I need a little help," she told him.

"With what, *bella mia*?"

Siena tipped her head to the side. "Getting this off."

John laughed a husky sound, and nodded once. He didn't mind helping her out with that at all.

It wasn't just her mouth that tasted like sweetness and sin, he learned. It was her jaw, too. The curve of her shoulder as he dragged her dress down. The spot where her spine met the back of her neck, and the dimples right above the swell of her ass. Skin so fucking soft, he couldn't stop touching her. Hair like curled silk when he drove his fingers in it.

A mouth meant to be put to use.

Sucking him.

Kissing him.

Begging him.

Siena's soft breaths echoed in John's ear as his lips ghosted over her jawline again. In just a couple of quick minutes, he had her standing in nothing but pink lace. In that same time, his mouth and hands had touched damn near every inch of her.

There was still so much more he wanted to find, too.

Explore …

Taste …

Darkening blue eyes met John's gaze, and Siena's bottom lip quivered when he tipped her head up to stare straight down at her. All it took was that one look—a silent, needy stare—that broke the haze for John.

Three years dry didn't make a difference then.

All he felt was need. A deep thrumming hunger that *burned*. A want so strong, it made his fucking bones ached.

Just because of the way she looked at him.

"Tell me you know how beautiful you are, Siena."

She blinked, but her lack of words said what she wouldn't.

"That's a shame," John murmured. "You are by far the most beautiful thing I have ever seen."

Another one of her sexy, sly smiles curved her lips. "Smooth talker."

"I don't do *smooth*."

"No?"

"Was never really my thing," he admitted. "I don't ever say things I don't mean, and sometimes that's the damn problem with me."

Siena swallowed hard. "Good to know."

"You have to tell me what you want next. It's only you calling the shots, sweetheart."

"My bedroom is the last door down the hall, John."

Good enough.

"Is there a condom in there?"

Because fuck him for not having one.

"A brand new box of six," she said, shrugging her naked shoulders. "Like a just-in-case, except just in case never actually happened."

He'd make sure the box was empty before morning came. Time to make up for, and all that.

John kissed Siena hard—harder than before, and yanked her to him with crushing force. She only sighed a happy sound, and parted those sweet lips of hers to silently ask for more. He didn't stop kissing her, or touching her, until they hit the bedroom floor.

Her hands worked far faster than his had to get rid of his clothes. They fell to the floor, forgotten, as her fingertips traced the hard lines of his naked abdominal muscles. With each touch, his nerves reacted. That wild feeling grew—the need he tried to shut off like it was a faucet of running water turned on, and cascading down.

A rush of feeling.

John just tipped his head back, and let her touch. He needed to let her explore. It was only when those teasing hands of hers slipped beneath his boxer-briefs that he look back down at her. Her fingers circled his hard dick—tightening and stroking, soft, yet fast.

"Christ," he grunted through clenched teeth.

"I bet it'll feel way better when I'm on my back, and you're inside me," she whispered.

Fuck.

"Yes to all of that."

Hell fucking yes.

Siena let him go just long enough to dig through the nightstand. Soon, she had a foil packet in her grasp, before she was tearing it open. He was the one to shove his boxer-briefs down and step out of them, but she rolled the latex down his cock.

John pinched her chin between his forefinger and thumb, and tipped her head back. Soft strokes of her hand circled up and down his length as he kissed her one more time, and then pushed her back to the bed. He climbed between her thighs, and hovered over her.

A kiss to her smirking lips.

Then her trembling chin.

Down over her throat.

Between the valley of her breasts still covered in pink lace.

The lower he went, the more she shivered. Those little breaths of hers picked up when his tongue struck out just below her navel.

"What other sounds do you make, *donna*?" he asked.

"Guess you're going to find out, John."

He grinned against her skin.

Yeah, he liked this woman a lot.

More than he probably should, considering her last name and all.

John's teeth nipped into her hip, and then he bit into the waistband of her panties. Siena let out a little squeak when he let the panties snap back against her skin. Just as fast, he bit into them again, and started pulling them down. Once they hit the floor, and all he could see was her bare, pink sex as she widened her legs, any desire he had to wait to prolong this was useless.

He couldn't do it.

She flashed her pussy at him, all wet and waiting, and he was done for.

John was back between Siena's opened thighs before she had blinked. Her hand guided him home, and he took her with one hard thrust. There was no hesitation to the way her pussy took him all the way in.

A wet, warm heaven.

Soaking him.

Hugging him damn tight.

She became like morphine to him, then. A shot of a drug he was addicted to, and hadn't gotten a good dose of in far too long. He was the fucking fiend in need of what she was supplying.

Those little breaths of hers turned in to gasps when he pulled back, and thrust in all over again. Those gasps turned in to the neediest moans when his hand slipped between their bodies to toy with her clit as he fucked her.

Siena's head fell back, giving him access to her throat, but it also let him see what he was doing to her. The way pleasure wrote heavily in her eyes, and in the shape of her lips when his name fell from her mouth.

So beautiful.

He hadn't lied.

She was perfect.

Her song when she came out high and broken with only his name. "*John, John, John.*"

She was like an ocean, he thought.

Like his mind sometimes was—large, wide, deep, and dangerous. Something he could get lost in, and something amazing to see. Frightening, too, but also too alluring to stay away from.

She could be the ocean.

He didn't mind drowning.

John listened for any sounds coming from Siena's bedroom as he dug inside the suit jacket he had discarded the night before. She was sleeping soundly, but he still took great effort not to make much noise while he searched for his pill case.

Just in case he wasn't home in the morning, he liked to bring along a smaller case that took care of his morning meds. Lithium, an anticonvulsant, and Zoloft. The final pill he set out on the counter was a mood stabilizer to keep the Zoloft in check with the rest of the pills. Sometimes one pill needed another pill to counteract the emotional or mental side effects it could have by mixing one with another.

Depending on the state of his current cycle, John's meds needed to be changed accordingly. He had become accustomed to knowing which meds he needed depending on where he was in his disorder. Any antidepressants during spells of depression meant no mood stabilizers, and no Lithium as they severely worsened and darkened his moods and thoughts to dangerous levels.

His new mix of meds—compliments of the therapist he had been seeing since his release—however, continued to leave him in a fog that he couldn't escape from.

Sometimes, it was a delicate balance. A balance that could easily be upset by things like a change in dose, or a new pill. Other times, it was an emotional upset that just couldn't be contained for whatever reason. Just like that, his balance would be tipped in a bad direction, and it only went downhill from there.

John had learned over the years not to fear that downhill slide. He could go months without having any kind of episode, be it manic, depression, or a mix of the two. He'd gone years without experiencing one once, but eventually, it would happen. Another manic cycle would start, and the mania festered until it got worse and worse.

It could be days.

It could stretch on for a couple of weeks.

Months.

And then the mania broke, and all John was left with was a blinding, crippling depression that coated his mind with blackness and dark thoughts. A depression that took all the euphoria-like feelings from the mania, and exhausted him emotionally and physically.

Still, he didn't fear the cycle.

He couldn't.

Not when it was just who he was.

Those four little pills he set out on Siena's counter—ones he took every morning—were just one of the many things he did to keep his disorder balanced. Despite his reservations about the new med regime, he opted to give it a fair try like the therapist wanted him to. There was still so much more to managing his disorder, too.

Medication. Diet. Exercise. Therapy.

Everyday.

Over and over.

Yet, he felt shame.

People heard bipolar and thought *crazy*. They thought, *highs and lows*. No one realized how much bipolar could vary between person to person. Or they looked at him like he was unstable, and might freak out any minute. The stigma around his disorder, and mental health in general, left him feeling very alone.

No one understood.

He didn't know how to explain it.

He couldn't be just Johnathan Marcello to somebody once they knew his little secret—he then became Johnathan who was bipolar.

That was every reason why he made sure to get up when it was still early enough for the sun to be down. Then, he wouldn't have to explain to a woman he had just spent the night with—but fuck, actually *liked*, too—why the first thing he had to do was slam back a cocktail of medications.

He couldn't be just John to Siena then.

He would have to be John and his bipolar.

It was selfish, sure.

Part of his therapy was being honest, and open about his disorder. Especially when it came to people he got involved with on an emotional level. Explaining his disorder and opening up to them was supposed to be healthy, and erase the stigma.

He often felt like it did the complete opposite.

Grabbing a glass out of the open shelf above the sink, John half-filled it with water. He scooped the pills up all at once, and tossed them back. A mouthful of water, and the pills were down. Some of them left a bitter taste behind if he let them linger too long on his tongue, so he just downed the bastards as fast as he could.

Breakfast, he told himself, looking around.

Food was also needed for some of the meds. They didn't mess with his stomach as much when he chased the pills with a meal, or even toast.

John didn't think Siena would mind waking up to breakfast, considering she had asked him to stay. Breakfast was one of the only damn things he could cook particularly well, too. It was a win-win all the way around the board.

He was still searching through the cupboards to find the things he needed to make pancakes when his cell phone rang.

Shit.

John damn near leaped over the table to grab his cell phone, and answer the call. It was still too early to be waking somebody else up because of his nonsense.

He put the phone to his ear with a, "Yeah, John here."

"Son, where are you?"

John stiffened at his father's voice, and the question. "What do you need?"

"Nice deflection, but I didn't miss it."

"I'm out."

"It's five in the damn morning."

John tried to keep his tone low and calm while he spoke. "I'm aware of what time it is, Dad. What do you need?"

"Somebody went over to your place this morning to grab you, but you weren't there. I need you to come to Amityville now."

"To your place, or the boss's?"

"Dante's."

Something was wrong. Nobody got called to the boss's home at this early in the morning unless something had happened.

"Dad—"

"I'll explain it when you get here," Lucian said. "I think it would be better to do face to face, all things considered."

Hesitation and concern slipped down John's ramrod-straight spine. He didn't like what he was hearing, or how defensive it made him feel. Like he couldn't be trusted or something with whatever his father had to say.

It wouldn't be the first time Lucian withheld things from John simply because he thought it was the better option. Sometimes, he understood why his father did it. Either way, every time it left him feeling the same thing.

Like his father didn't believe in him.

As though Lucian thought John was too unstable.

Again, John ... who was bipolar.

That fucking circle was vicious.

"Just tell me what's going on," John said. "I'm kind of in the middle of something ..." *To say the least.* "And I don't want to skip out unless it's important."

"You know that if one of us calls you and says something, it is important, Johnathan."

In the background, John heard his uncle, and boss, say, "Lucian, you need to trust your son. Explain to him what's going on because he asked."

Silently, John thanked Dante for stepping in like that. His boss didn't need to do that, but sometimes little things went a long fucking way.

"Lucia is gone," Lucian murmured.

John turned into a statue on the spot.

Cold.

Hard.

Unmoving.

"What?" he hissed.

"She took off last night—I thought maybe me and a few men could go out after them and bring her back before morning, but I misjudged how capable that young man is."

"Renzo," John said.

Just to be sure ...

"Yes," Lucian replied. "So, I need you to come here so we can—"

"I'm not going there at all."

In an instant, John's mind was made up, and his choices were done. He had gotten the chance to warn Renzo not to mess with his little sister, but the young man had just smirked at John, and walked away.

The Lucia and Renzo mess had been on-going for a good month now. His sister knew her parents didn't approve of the young man, but she didn't seem to want to back off. After John had privately approached Renzo, his sister practically cut off all contact with him, too.

She was supposed to be starting college in California for the second semester soon. She was smart girl—the good girl.

What in the hell was going on?

Fury slipped through John's veins.

"She's eighteen, though," Lucian put in, "and that makes things difficult."

"Not for me," John said. "I'll find her, and she'll be returned home."

And him.

John would find Renzo, and fix that issue, too.

Lucia was twelve years younger than John, but she was still the only sibling he had that actually gave a shit about him. His other two sisters barely spoke to him, let alone looked at him when they had to share a space.

Years of his disorder manifesting into outbursts, vicious words, broken walls, and spewed hate had ruined those relationships. He didn't blame Cella or Liliana a bit for how they felt regarding him.

But Lucia?

Lucia was not the same.

"John, you don't have to—"

"Yes, I absolutely do," John interjected, stopping his father from saying anything more. "Lucia trusts me more than anybody, and I know Renzo, his streets, and his people. I will find them. I will call you when I do."

John hung up the phone without another word. He quickly set the glass he used in the sink, and wiped down the counter.

Just like that, his mind had shifted.

He had a new task.

Things he had to do or wanted to do were shoved out to let the most important problem at the moment take over. That was just how his brain worked.

He shrugged on his jacket over his still-unbuttoned dress shirt as he stepped in the doorway of Siena's bedroom. She was still sleeping, and quite soundly.

He should have woke her up.

He should have said goodbye.

He didn't leave his phone number because he figured he would be back that night, or shit, at the most, a couple of days. An explanation later, and everything would be fine. Siena would understand what had happened.

After the night they had, surely she would know he hadn't just left her high and dry.

He should have left a note.

He should have … done a lot of things differently.

Problem was, his mind simply didn't work that way. It jumped from thing to thing—this to that—and he either got back to it, or he didn't. Siena was the same; she couldn't be any different.

John didn't realize, or even consider, that the next almost three weeks of his life would be spent chasing after his runaway sister, and her delinquent boyfriend.

A couple of days, he could have explained.

Three weeks?

John knew better.

He fucked that up.

He should have said goodbye.

Hindsight was always twenty-twenty.

SIX

Siena knew she was alone before she even opened her eyes. Maybe because each time she had woken up the night before, Johnathan had been holding her. Or even, pulling her closer, and into him.

Now, nothing held her.

And she was cold because of it.

She was so accustomed to waking up in an empty bed that the feeling should have been comforting. She didn't mind being alone, usually. It was mostly okay.

On this morning ... it wasn't.

Not at all.

Sure enough, when she opened her eyes and glanced over, she found the space Johnathan had occupied was now nothing but mussed sheets and a forgotten pillow. A pillow with an indent where his head had rested while he slept. For a long while, she just stared at the space, and did nothing. She didn't know what to do.

She wanted to give him the benefit of the doubt, sure, but a small piece of her knew better despite the hope in her heart.

Maybe he hadn't run off again.

Without an explanation.

For a third damn time.

The sheets still felt warm when she reached over and ran her palm over them. As though maybe he had only gotten up recently, and his heat still remained on the cotton. Another whisper of hope to bury into her heart, but would likely be ripped away all too soon.

She was a realist.

She dealt in black and white.

Still, a part of her held on.

A part of her hoped.

Johnathan's spicy scent still clung to the blankets ... and her. The smell of sex still lingered in the room, too. The feeling of his kiss still lingered on her mouth, and down her body where he'd spent far too much time kissing every single inch of her. As though she was the most beautiful thing to have ever graced his presence, and he needed to show her just how much.

It had definitely happened.

They had happened.

Except where was he?

She sat up straight in the bed, and used the bedsheet to cover her from the chest down. Not that there was anyone around to see her nakedness. Not a sound echoed from outside her bedroom.

Like she needed another fucking reminder.

Something akin to sadness stabbed in her chest when she looked for the clothes Johnathan had shed the night before. Her bedroom floor now only held what remained of her club dress, and the lace panties he had taken off with his teeth. Nothing of his were anywhere to be seen.

Fuck.

The contented thrum echoing through her veins—the kind of satisfaction one could only get from great sex and a hard sleep—should have been enough for Siena. It should have kept the anger and sadness at bay about having to wake up alone.

Still, she felt those things.

Still, she wanted to give him a chance.

Maybe he was still here.

Maybe he was somewhere in the apartment.

Siena got out of the bed, and snagged an over-sized sweater hanging off the dresser. One of her favorites for the colder months. She slipped it over her head, and sunk her arms in the sleeves. Folding her arms over her chest, the coldness slipping over her skin ebbed a bit as the sweater gave her a different kind of homey warmth. She needed everything she could get at the moment.

She didn't even bother to grab a clean pair of panties as she stepped over her crumpled dress, and forgotten things.

The sweater covered her ass, and that was enough for her to be satisfied. At least for the moment.

"John?" Siena called out.

Nothing and no one answered her back.

The apartment was still empty, although colder than it usually was when she spent time in it alone as she typically did. John was nowhere to be found.

All over again, Siena felt those stabs of anger and sadness.

A heavy sensation settled in her gut.

She'd thought, surely, their conversations and connection was not only felt by her. So why was she alone?

Why was he gone?

He hadn't left a note.

Nothing with his number.

No way to contact him unless she chose to seek him out again. Siena wasn't interested in that, not this time.

She found him once.

She would not be doing it again.

This was on him.

Siena Calabrese was not the kind of woman who continued chasing after a man who clearly did not want to be caught. She was not the type.

Who fucking knew if Johnathan was even worth the trouble?

Not her.

And he definitely wasn't worth the trouble when he pulled shit like this.

Her sadness swelled.

The anger grew flames.

Three strikes and you're out, John.

Siena went back to bed.

October ...

• • •

November ...

It was only the month of December that time actually began to slow for Siena. Or rather, the week of Christmas. Everyone just ... relaxed.

Finally.

It was just too bad that slowing down meant she had to spend more time with her family. It was the price she paid for less work.

Of course, it also reminded her of just how lonely she was considering all she had was the family that didn't feel very close at all.

She grabbed the rope of fir garland Coraline held out for her, and hung it the way her mother liked along the banister.

"Kind of late getting some of this up, aren't you?" Siena asked.

Coraline waved it off. "I didn't have much help."

Siena frowned. "You could have called me over, Ma."

"You're very busy, Siena."

That was true, too.

"Still ..."

Coraline flashed her daughter with a wide, brilliant smile. It was her mother's best defense, and one of her few distractions. Anything could be made better, or ignored entirely, with a single beautiful smile.

"You're here now, and the Christmas party will be lovely because of it," her mother said.

"Sure, it will."

Siena seriously doubted her mother's annual Christmas party would be any better or worse despite her presence, but she didn't argue the point. Whatever kept her mother happy and pleased, or so their father liked to say.

Usually a nice fur coat or diamond was enough to keep Coraline happy.

Or a good party.

"What did you get your father for Christmas?" Coraline asked.

Siena worked on weaving another fir garland through the banister. "A custom-made watch from the jeweler he likes."

"Is it ready?"

"I have to pick it up in a couple of days," she said.

"Cutting it close, Siena."

Like she needed to be told.

Christmas was only five days away now. The jeweler was cutting it terribly close.

"And your brothers?" her mother asked.

Siena gave her mother a look.

Coraline laughed as though she knew without needing to be told. "Money, then?"

"Money," Siena echoed.

It was the only thing her brothers loved more than their father, after all.

"Oh, you did that wrong … Here, give it to me." Coraline took the rope of garland, and shooed Siena up a couple of steps with a single wave of her hand. "It has to wrap around the top like this, Siena."

"Yes, Ma."

She wasn't even paying attention.

Everything she had already done, her mother would redo, anyway.

So was her life …

"So, have you been seeing anyone lately?" her mother asked.

Siena instantly said, "No."

She didn't consider mentioning Johnathan. She hadn't spoken to him since that night two months ago when they slept together. He didn't leave her with a way to contact him, and she left the rest up to him.

The whole three strikes thing, after all. He hadn't contacted her again, and he didn't try to seek her out.

Siena figured that spoke for itself.

Despite the way it hurt at first—rejection always hurt—the pain ebbed. She threw herself into work, and forgot the darkly grinning man with his lost hazel gaze.

She clearly hadn't been anything to him.

Why would she let him be something to her?

If only shit was that easy.

It never was.

"Shame," Coraline said. "You're going to be a lonely woman for the rest of your life at the rate you're going, Siena."

"Ma."

"I'm just saying. Why don't you go check on your father and brothers for me?"

"For what?"

"See if they would like a drink," her mother suggested.

"They can get their own drinks, Ma."

Coraline shot her a look. "Not in this house, Siena."

Great.

"Sure, Ma."

Men were the kings.

Women were meant to serve them.

Or, that's what her mother liked to believe.

Siena didn't wait on her brothers and father outside of this house, but if it gave her a chance to get away from her mother for a minute, she would do it. At least it gave her an excuse not to see every single one of her decorations redone.

The party was still a couple of hours away yet. She wouldn't be able to blend into the people until the house was full, and her parents stopped looking for her.

Same with her brothers.

"Nothing, you're sure?" she heard her father say down the hallway.

Siena headed to the kitchen where Matteo was discussing something with her brothers at the table. Like always, Matteo sat at the head of the table while her brothers sat on the right and left sides.

None of them paid her much attention other than a look.

Her father did make sure to say, "Make us coffees, Siena."

Like she had come in there to do anything else.

"Well?" Matteo asked. "Nothing?"

"Nope, nothing," Kev replied.

"And the one was definitely …" Matteo trailed off, and then said, "You know what I mean?"

"Yeah," Kev said. "It was definitely that."

Siena stayed out of their conversation as she made coffee just the way the three liked. A little bit more milk for her father, an extra sugar for her oldest brother, and all black for Darren. The three continued talking like she wasn't even there as she stirred the coffees.

"Maybe it's not a matter of not wanting to, but being unable," Darren said. "You know, the logistics or shit."

"Unlikely," Kev replied. "Just considering how it was, man. Think about it." Darren made a noise under his breath. "True."

"Can we not safely say we have passed the point of perhaps something being in the way? Perhaps it's more like Kev thinks, and it's done. We missed our chance to see something come of it."

Business.

It was always business in their house with the men. They never took a break, and didn't care who was around to listen.

Business was always the first discussion to have.

She wasn't surprised considering the Christmas party happening that night. A lot of her father's men would be there to celebrate. Matteo always got his plans set up before the men gathered, so he didn't look like a boss out of the loop.

Siena paid attention far more than her father and brothers thought she did.

Someday, it might save her life.

"So maybe something happened," Matteo added, and then grunted under his breath. "Well, shit. The better question is, can it be fixed?"

"You could … tip the odds to your favor again," Kev suggested.

"How should I do that?"

"There's a million ways, specifically one that would mean bringing the main goal close, you know what I mean?"

"This has always been at arm's length," her father explained, "and that's never changed. I don't think this would change that, either."

"It might not make a difference at all," Darren said.

"He's right," Kev agreed, "when you consider something preferred is right there to be taken, then anything is possible."

Silence echoed for a few moments as she walked her father and brothers their coffee. First, serving her father, the head of the house, and then going back for her brothers' mugs, too. None of them thanked her except for her father.

Matteo touched her wrist with his beefy hand—a gentle stroke that surprised her. "You're my good girl, huh?"

Today was not the day to piss off her father. For one, because she didn't want to listen to his nonsense. And for two, because it would seriously displease her mother.

"Yeah, Dad," she said with a smile.

He liked smiles.

They were the best distraction.

She thanked her mother for that lesson.

Matteo waved her off. "Go help your mother."

Of course.

Her father went right back to his conversation with his sons, and she was already forgotten. Shame, really.

Despite how festive their home was, how beautiful their family looked, they were really so far apart at the end of the day. People who spent a great deal of time together, but barely liked each other at all.

Even at Christmas time.

It was a lonely way to be.

A lonesome life to live.

Maybe that was why she had gotten so strangely attached to the infamous Johnathan Marcello without barely any effort at all. She had been lonely, and he was easy. Or … close enough to latch onto.

Two months later, and he still seeped into her thoughts like a fucking weed that kept on growing. And why? Because of nothing at all.

She didn't have any other reason, after all. Her stubbornness reared its head again, and she gave in to the instinct as it kicked her in the heart. She was going to hold true to the three strikes, and Johnathan was out of her life thing.

Even if a big part of her still wondered … *what if?*

What could that have been?

Siena was never going to find out now.

"Give me some time. This will be good for us; we need this." Matteo laughed, not even giving his sons a chance to reply. "For tonight, though, we enjoy ourselves. Merry Christmas, boys."

Siena was already heading out of the kitchen while their laughter echoed behind her. Soon, the house would be full of that sound, and clinking wine glasses, and Christmas music.

The place would still be as cold as hell in the morning.

It always was.

SEVEN

"So hey, do you want to talk to me today, or what?" John asked, leaning in the entryway to the living room of his parents' home.

Lucia didn't even look away from the flickering TV. "No."

Her tone came out flat, dry, and dead.

Ouch.

"I tried to call you while you were in California." John cleared his throat, and then added, "Every couple of weeks, actually."

"Maybe my phone doesn't work there."

"I think it does, Lucia."

"Then maybe that's a sign, John."

Damn.

She was not going to make this easy on him. His kid sister was pissed off at him, and maybe rightfully so. He had been the one to track her down months ago, and bring her home kicking and screaming the whole way.

Business picked up a lot after that, and John was given more responsibility. His boss, and uncle, seemed to think he could handle it, considering everything. Between his therapy once a week, sometimes more, the parole officer he had to keep up with, the public service hours he did every week, and business … John had no time to do anything.

He could barely breathe.

Lucia was home again, though, so he was trying to make time for her. He wanted to fix this rift he made months ago, but she wasn't having it.

Not at all.

"You've been back from California for a couple of weeks, kiddo. I thought—"

Her gaze turned on him—hateful and rage-filled in a blink. Eighteen, young-dumb, and angry. Those were the things he found in his youngest sister's eyes when she stared at him. It was not something John was used to with Lucia.

She was beautiful like their mother, sure.

She was also dark, vicious, and stubborn like their father.

"Don't ever fucking call me that again, John," Lucia hissed.

His spine stiffened. "What—kiddo? I've always called you that."

"Not anymore."

Her words stabbed at his guilt, and made it worse. Maybe he deserved it, after what he did.

"How's California?" he tried asking. "You've been there for a couple of months now."

Still, she ignored him. Her hazel eyes, ones so like his own, were hard and cold.

Lucia was the spitfire of their family. Young blood, and still learning the ropes of this thing they called life. She should have been out there having fun, but in a way, John had taken all that away from her when he dragged her home.

"You could at least talk to me, Lucy."

He used the nickname she hated just to get a rise out of her. She disliked Lucy even more than kiddo. Her response shocked him further.

"California is hot," she said.

"Yeah, I bet," he murmured.

"I start classes during the second semester. Next month after I go back."

"You're all settled in, though?"

"Guess so."

Everything about the conversation felt wrong and bad. Had this been one of his other sisters—Liliana or Cella—John wouldn't have thought anything of the cold demeanor and flat responses. Instead, it was Lucia.

His baby sister.

The kid he looked after since she was born, and he was twelve.

"You were supposed to be my best friend, John," Lucia whispered.

Angry eyes turned on him again, but now, they were filled with tears. She let one escape, and it made a track line down her cheek. With a quick hand, she wiped the tear away, and let out a harsh breath.

"You shouldn't have run off like that," he replied.

Lucia's cheek twitched—a sure sign she was clenching her jaw for all she was worth. Hiding that anger behind a stone facade and calm words.

Just like their father.

She wore her namesake well.

"I was hoping you might let me apologize, and we could spend some time together while you're visiting," John said. "But even at Christmas, you ignored me."

"Perhaps you should take a fucking hint, then."

"*Lucia.*"

He didn't get anything from that—not a damn thing. She didn't even flinch at his rough tone.

John tried a different direction once more. "What made you get mixed up with a guy like Renzo, anyway? Didn't I tell you not to mess with boys like that?"

Her laughter stung when it escaped her smirking lips. She turned on the couch to face him completely.

John should have took that as a warning, maybe.

"Like *him*?" she asked. "John, you and every other man in our family are no better than him. Except what? We've got money, and you guys wear nice suits and drive expensive cars. So, you've got a last name that gives you respect, and a family legacy that affords you privilege."

Lucia shook her head, never backing down for a minute as she continued with, "And guys like him? They come from the streets, and hustle every day of their lives just to survive. Did you know he was paying for his sister's private schooling? Nobody else paid for it. He was trying to let her *be* something when they came from nothing. Where do you think that left her? Or his little brother—his parents fucked off a couple years ago. Where does that leave the boy? Don't worry, I'm sure his sister—who can't go to school anymore—took him, or better yet, maybe a nice foster family picked him up."

John blinked, unsure and wary.

The contempt in Lucia's words were coated with bitterness.

He didn't know what to say.

"Fuck you with your guys like him shit," she snapped. "So, you've got money and a suit, but that's all you've fucking got, too."

Who was this girl staring at him like she hated his guts, and everything he stood for?

This wasn't the Lucia who fawned over expensive cars, and liked diamonds on her birthday. This wasn't his sister who was the quiet, perfect Marcello *principessa*.

No, this girl was entirely different.

"You come from the same privilege I do," John said quietly.

"Except I can own it now. Can you?"

John didn't know how to answer that. "I'm sorry, Lucy. Really, I am. I didn't think that it was all going to lead to him being put away for—"

"Shut up," Lucia spat. "I bet Daddy had that planned, and you knew about it, too."

"Dad didn't plan anything. I just came after you to bring you home. The rest was circumstance, and shit."

Lucia turned away from him, refusing to even grace him with her attention again. It burned, but John took it. Seemed he had managed to ruin the last good relationship he had with someone in his immediate family.

This time it wasn't even because of his bipolar.

Funny.

"Why don't we talk about you, John?" Lucia asked dryly.

Nope.

John didn't talk about him.

His defenses always flew up at the idea.

People probed, and it felt like needles swimming in his bloodstream.

"No, I'm good," he said folding his arms over his chest.

Without even looking at him, Lucia said, "Then we have nothing else to say here. Daddy and the rest of them are upstairs."

The rest of them.

He didn't miss the contempt in that, either.

John left Lucia to her thoughts and anger, though.

What else could he do?

"So that's it for us, then?" John asked. "You're going to go back to California in a couple of weeks, and you won't even bother with me at all while you're here? Nothing at all?"

"Don't take it personally, John. It's all of them, not just you."

Well, then …

John walked in the home office of his father to find there were more men sitting around the room than he expected. John's father, and Giovanni and Dante, his uncles. Andino, too, sat on the edge of the desk. A place Andino shouldn't be sitting considering Dante—the boss—was behind it.

It was sometimes strange and difficult to grow up in the world of Cosa Nostra. Made men with an entire family dynamic that was governed and controlled by the rules of the mafia sometimes created complexities that no one could understand.

John's father had never been able to be just his father, after all, not when he had also been an underboss. The same went with his uncles—Gio and Dante. They, too, had always held positions of power.

Family was family.

Cosa Nostra colored them up.

And now …

John gave Andino a nod, and a grin. "Don't you look comfortable, just like a spoiled little underboss should."

Chuckles passed around the room.

Had it been anyone else, John never would have disrespected the new underboss of the family with that kind of a joke. However, this was Andino. It wouldn't be normal for the two of them not to trade some kind of barbs with one another.

It was expected, really.

Andino was still kind of new to the position. A whole change that had come about over the last couple of months. Nobody was kidding around when they decided to move him up.

John still felt it was the right choice.

"Careful, I'm allowed to make *mistakes* since I'm so new and all," Andino threw back, grinning himself. "I would hate for you to be one of those mistakes, John."

"You could try."

The chuckles turned in to laughter, then.

For a moment, it was nice.

It never lasted long.

Not in Cosa Nostra.

Lucian looked to his son. "Did you talk to your sister?"

John scoffed. "Do you mean, did I let her rage at me? Because if so, the answer is yes."

Silence saturated the room, thick and heavy. It left a bitter taste behind in John's mouth, but it was what it was. It seemed like he wasn't the only one on the bad end of Lucia's moods since she had come home for a break from California.

"It's almost better when she ignores you, isn't it?" Lucian smiled sadly. "Never thought I would see the day."

"We all make choices we sometimes regret," Dante said from behind the desk. "And so, we have to live with those."

The boss of their family would probably understand that lesson better than anyone, considering the hell he had gone through with his own daughter recently. No family was perfect, John had come to learn. Not behind closed doors.

Those lessons were the hardest.

They hurt the very most.

"I don't regret it," Lucian said, "but I wish she wasn't so angry."

"More like … full of contempt, I think," John said quietly.

Nods passed between the men, and then it was right back to business as usual. Family only got so much time in before the mafia had to come out and play again.

So was their life.

Mostly, John didn't mind.

As long as they all had Lucia to worry about, they would not be getting on his ass for a while. It was a shitty thing for Lucia, sure, but silver linings were still quite silver.

"Lucian, are you staying or going for this?" Dante asked. "You're not required to being that you've unofficially stepped down, and Andino is here. The option is open, though."

Even in another man's house, sitting at that man's desk, the boss still owned the room. He directed the men, and where their conversation had to go.

Lucian passed John a look, and then went back to his brother. "I think I'll step out, actually."

Dante waved a hand as if to say, *go.*

John was surprised at that turn of events. Decades as a made man—and as the family's underboss beneath his brother—and Lucian just seemed … done with it all. Ready to move on.

"Find me after you're done here, son," Lucian said, clapping Johnathan on the shoulder as he passed him by. "Got it?"

"Yeah, sure."

For what, though, he didn't know.

Once the office door was closed, John gave his attention to his two uncles, and Andino. For the most part, Giovanni sat in the corner and worked on lighting his cigar. As the consigliere to the boss, it wasn't as though Gio really had to handle the men all that much. He was middle man for Dante in a grander sense.

John liked his uncle, though. Gio was the fun one, so to speak.

"How's the new crew going?" Dante asked.

"It's good," John replied.

"Just good?"

"Andino's crew might as well be a bunch of fucking saints, compared to some of them."

Andino chuckled darkly. "That's because I put the fear of God in to them."

Gio looked over the tip of his burning red cigar. "Not his crew, anymore. It's yours now, John."

John passed a look between his uncle, and then to his boss. "I was told this was temporary."

Dante smirked a little. "I wanted to make sure you could handle it again, John. It's been months since you were released from prison—you've done everything I asked you to do."

He had.

No messes.

No nonsense.

Business kept clean.

Attention low.

Dante's demands had been clear. John had even taken extra care with his disorder, and managing it because he didn't want to disgrace his family when they welcomed him home after everything he had done.

"It's not my crew, though," John said, gesturing at Andino. "It's his."

"The whole underboss gig keeps me busy," Andino replied.

Yeah, he bet.

"Or spoiled," John muttered.

Andino smirked, and flipped John the middle finger.

Dante continued talking like the interaction hadn't even happened. "I told you that the babysitting was only temporary, too. It's time to get back to being a proper Capo, Johnathan. It's what you're best at, *nipote*."

"It is," he agreed, chuckling.

Dante jerked a thumb in Andino's direction. "So, he's got a few dealings between crews of other families. Some schemes that get run on other territories, and things like that."

"A warehouse is shared on schemes that run between families to make it easier and keep the peace," Andino added. "You'll need to handle meeting up with the Capo of that crew. It's like a once a month thing or something."

"Who?"

"Darren Calabrese," Andino said.

John stiffened, but hid it.

Andino passed him a subtle look. "You okay with that?"

The question was loaded.

John shrugged. "Sure, don't see why not."

"Our history with the Calabrese family makes certain things tricky," Dante added.

"History—like their grandfather killing my great-grandfather, you mean?" John asked.

Giovanni coughed.

Dante cleared his throat. "Yeah, exactly that history."

"To be fair, Carl Calabrese is dead now," Andino said.

"That kind of shit doesn't wash out, Andi," John murmured. "They killed my family—even if Lucian was already adopted into the Marcello family—to take over, and nothing else. They wanted the seat, so they did what they had to do. My biological great-grandfather doesn't even have a proper grave. We don't know what they did with him.

"Bad blood like that doesn't wash out," John finished sharply.

"No, but we do put the stains aside for the sake of business," Dante said. "But we never fucking forget they're a bunch of snakes, John. There's a difference."

John didn't entirely like that, but it was what it was.

Siena Calabrese was a whole other issue.

She certainly wasn't like her brothers, and that made all the difference to him. However, he hadn't seen her in months. He meant to check in on her once he returned from finding his sister, but one thing after another thing kept coming up.

A new crew.

More business.

Family.

A cousin nearly getting killed in Cancun.

John wasn't even overstating it. He bet none of that shit would make a difference to Siena because like a prick, he had bailed on her.

Women took offense to that.

"Well?" Dante asked.

John looked to his boss. "I can handle the fucking Calabrese."

Andino snorted from his perch on the desk. "You can start by not calling them the *fucking* Calabrese, John."

Yeah, he would try.

No promises.

Johnathan found his father sitting in the small library downstairs. Lucian sipped from a neat whiskey while he flipped through a newspaper. He looked laidback, and entirely relaxed. Like the man who never stopped moving had finally taken a break.

It was an unusual sight.

"You wanted me to come find you?" John asked.

Lucian looked over the edge of the newspaper. "Seems the stock market is up two points."

John's brow furrowed. "All right."

"And some action movie is breaking box office records."

"Okay."

"Stop looking at me like my head is growing bigger, John."

He wet his lips. "We don't usually do this kind of small talk, Dad. That's all."

"Never really got the chance, did we? Cosa Nostra was always getting in the way, and putting up barriers that kept us apart. I couldn't only worry about my son—and the problems he constantly faced—when Cosa Nostra made me stay at arm's length."

John blinked.

Lucian waved at the chair beside his. "Come sit, and talk."

"I—"

"John, please come sit with me."

"All right," he said, his voice feeling like an echo.

He joined his father, and Lucian passed over a section of the newspaper.

"We're going to start doing this. You and me, I mean."

John stared at the paper. "So, doing nothing?"

"Not nothing. Being *normal*, John. Have I ever told you how proud I am of you, my boy?"

He had to think about it.

"Sure you have, Dad."

"Things I thought you wouldn't be able to do or handle because of the bipolar, you've done all of it and more. You still are. Expect me to tell you how proud I am more often now, John."

"Did you ever think that I liked the way we were?"

"Did you?" his father asked. "Like it, I mean."

No.

"I've done a lot of shit, Dad," John settled on saying, "to everybody—you included. Said a lot of things, you know. I burn bridges, but I don't usually fix them."

"And here we still sit, John."

"Darren," John greeted.

The Calabrese Capo shoved his frame off the barstool, and stuck out a hand for John to take. He did and shook Darren's hand, but made sure to keep a tighter grip than he normally would.

John had to do these meets and work with the Calabrese brother—or both, who knew, since the two stuck together a lot—but that didn't mean he was going to bow down to either of the fuckers. He didn't trust them with an inch.

"John, it's good to see you," Darren said with a smile.

John wished it felt welcoming.

It didn't.

"Care for a drink?" Darren asked, waving at the bar.

John used one of his old excuses to pass that offer up. "I don't drink during work time."

"You Marcellos are always so stiff with your rules."

"It's what makes us the best."

Darren's gaze flashed with something unknown, and John took that as a point to his favor. "Yes, well, sit. We can discuss how Andino and I have managed to have parts of our crews working together, and whatever else."

"He filled me in on some of the details."

"But not all, huh?"

John shrugged, and took a seat on an open barstool. "Better to jump right into it, I think."

"Sure."

John waved for the bartender, and asked for a water. Once he had the glass in front of him, he used it as a distraction to keep his attention focused rather than looking at Darren Calabrese. The longer he was near one of the Calabrese men, the more his old bitterness and rage grew.

It had never really gone away.

Not since he learned the truth about why their two families didn't have a lot to do with each other. He had been, oh, thirteen or so at the time when his father finally told him everything.

John thought he was a Marcello through and through.

Their blood ran through his veins.

The truth was dirtier—his father, the product of an affair with a *goomah*, had been the son of a murdered man. His biological grandfather, Johnathan Grovatti. And his great-grandfather, the former boss of one of New York's most powerful crime families, had been taken out because of greed, and nothing more.

72

By a bunch of Calabrese bastards.

John was still a Marcello, sure. In thought and mind, in body and spirit, he was every inch a fucking Marcello man. He spoke like them, lived like them, and *was* them.

But he knew now that he also had Grovatti blood keeping him alive. A whole family that had been wiped out without a thought or care.

So was the way of their life.

Or it was supposed to be.

That kind of shit was hard to let go.

So, when Darren spoke about a friendship between them, and good business, it made John's fucking skin crawl. It took every ounce of effort he had, all of his control, not to reach over and choke the life out of the cocksucker.

"What do you think, John?" Darren asked. "Is the deal up to spec with you?"

John had barely been listening.

He just wanted this first meeting over with.

Andino thought the next one would be easier, and so on. Well, John had a whole week to get used to the idea of working with someone from the Calabrese family, and he was still just as disgusted as he had been.

"Actually, it kind of seems like the Calabrese side of things might be getting a longer end of the stick," John said, "if you know what I mean."

Darren chuckled. "Come on, now. It's our warehouse, and most of our streets. Sure, the crew on the Marcello side does a lot of the work with the delivery and distribution of the shit, but—"

"I take it this deal was something to keep your business relevant," John interjected, cocking a brow before he took a sip of his water. "Am I right?"

"More money is always a good thing."

"Those streets—Dante handed them over to your family in a deal a few years ago at the Commission meeting, right?"

Darren nodded tightly. "Yeah, and we were owed them, considering the mess that went down between the guys."

"Except they're hard streets to work because your people don't have shit there. It was all built up by Andino's guys. I know because I used to work those streets with my cousin before I got locked up."

"Your point, John?"

John flashed a cocky grin. "Nothing, really. Just making it clear why it's like that. Even if the territory seems like it's yours, it's nothing without a Marcello crew backing it."

Darren sucked in a deep breath.

John smirked inwardly.

It was never good to make problems with someone whom you needed to do business with for the unforeseeable future. However, in this case, John absolutely wanted it clear that between him and Darren, he would always be the fucker coming out on top.

It was what it was.

That was just what Marcellos did.

"Good talk," John said, standing from the stool. "I'll be around the warehouse to chat with the guys, if you want to drop by. I'll leave my number with the girl at the front so you can, uh, give me a call when we have to do this nonsense again, Darren."

John stuffed his hands in the pockets of his slacks, and headed for the exit of the business. He didn't make it halfway across the floor before a much larger and more important Calabrese man stepped in his path.

Matteo.

The boss.

And … Siena's father.

"Well, well, if it isn't Johnathan Marcello," Matteo boomed.

Damn, the man was loud.

John gave a laugh, and tried not to let it show his irritation. He shook the boss's hand because fuck him, even if the boss was one he despised, he couldn't be rude. It was not the Cosa Nostra way.

Made men did not shun bosses.

"I heard through the grapevine that you're taking over Andino's business now that he's … stepping up, shall we say," Matteo said.

The man was as wide as a table.

Tall as a fucking tree.

Rings adorned all of his fingers.

His wealth, and his status?

It came from the blood running through John.

"Guess so," John said.

"Funny," Matteo murmured, "I always thought *you* were the second generation of the Marcello boys that would be stepping up, John. What happened to that, huh?"

The man reached out and patted John's cheek.

Inwardly, his blood boiled.

The touch was affectionate, and even … friendly. Like a family member might do.

John hated it, but managed to stay calm on the outside. "I don't think anybody thought anything about who was going where in the family, and I like where I am."

Matteo nodded. "Mmhmm, I bet, John."

"Is what it is, boss."

That word burned his tongue.

He said it anyway.

"Well, to have good vibes between our families, and this new arrangement with you and Darren, I think you should come over and have dinner."

John stilled. "I beg your pardon?"

"Dinner," Matteo repeated. "At my home with my family. It's the proper thing to do. Deals are best made over good food, John."

Not in the Marcello family.

Business was not had at the dinner table. Still, the rules his life were governed by banged around in his head.

Never shun a boss. Never, John. Even if he is not your boss.

John swallowed his pride, and the disgust weighing heavily on his tongue. Now, it just weighed down his stomach. "Sure, dinner. You let me know when, boss."

Matteo clapped John on the shoulder, and then moved on.

It was a strange encounter for more reasons than one, but mostly because John knew bosses didn't have their hands directly in the pot of business. They oversaw a lot, and directed people as to the business. They didn't, however, step right in.

It was almost like Matteo had been waiting for him.

John glanced at the beefy, tall Calabrese Don as he headed for the bar of the restaurant. Then, he turned back to leave the place.

He needed to get out of there.

The sight of someone far more beautiful coming in through the doors stopped him straight up. She was lost in the tablet she held in one hand, and the earbuds in her ears. Her hair was a bit longer, and darker like she might have gotten it tinted a bit. The knee-length dress and ankle-high boots she wore were far more conservative than the clothes he had taken off her that night.

Fuck.

He could still kind of taste the salt of her skin on the back of his tongue when he looked at her. He could hear those pretty little sounds she made in bed when she was underneath him, and begging for more.

Like music, really.

John slipped up because sex was supposed to be a no-go until his therapist gave the okay, but damn, Siena had been worth that. He was still a little bit tripped up on her considering he still hadn't found any female worth looking at since the day he saw her on the bus.

Fuck his life for being like this.

And then, Siena looked up—sea-blue gaze and still perfect.

John stared back.

EIGHT

"Johnathan."

Siena didn't miss how John subtly winced when she used his full name with a tone as sharp as glass.

Good.

He'd slept with her, and then fucked off like a coward before she could even wake up the next morning. All she got after that from him was nothing but radio silence. For three whole months. Who did that kind of thing to people?

This man, apparently.

She had done well trying to let go of that anger and hurt over the last while, but fuck him because now it was bubbling up all over again. At just the sight of him, looking so damn good in a fitted suit and a half grin, she was pissed. Like he didn't have a care in the world. All tall, dark, and handsome without even trying.

He probably didn't even know what he had done to her, and how much it stung. Maybe she was just one of many.

Siena resolved herself never to let it happen again. She attempted to move past Johnathan, but he stood too close to a table on one side, and people were eating at another table on his right. She had to slide in beside him, which only made her rub against him. His familiar spicy scent—like sex, man, and deliciousness—filled her lungs with one breath.

Fuck.

"Siena, wait," Johnathan said.

His hand came up to touch her shoulder. She stiffened; instantly frozen in place like a statue by his gentle fingertips sliding along the line of her shoulder. His touch grazed the exposed patch of skin where the neckline of her dress was open, and a shiver raced over her flesh.

Fuck.

Again.

Siena looked up at him, and all she saw was dark hazel staring back. "What?"

Her one word came out a hell of a lot quieter than she intended it to. She wished it had been that same sharp tone she first greeted him with.

No, instead he got her breathy and confused question.

Jesus Christ.

"Do you have a minute?" Johnathan asked.

Siena hardened her jaw, and schooled her features. "Not particularly."

And not for you.

"After work, then? I assume that's what you're doing."

He assumed right, but that didn't mean she was giving in. Or that she was going to make time for him.

"I'm kind of busy," she told him.

Johnathan nodded once. "Yeah, me, too."

"I bet."

He winced again.

Her sharp tone had found itself again.

Siena could see her father sitting at the bar with her brother. She was stuck between wondering why her father was even at the restaurant—he rarely showed up when she worked at one of her brother's places—and the fact that both men were very obviously staring. They made no effort to hide it.

Matteo and Darren had their gazes glued on Siena and Johnathan like they had found the most interesting show, and couldn't tear their eyes away.

It was unsettling.

She went back to Johnathan.

"Listen, Johnathan," she said, falling back to his full name, "I really am busy, and I have to get to work if I plan on getting out of here before dark."

Johnathan didn't look like he wanted to move at all. In fact, the two of them stayed locked in a staring contest, and his fingertips grazed her throat momentarily before he dropped his hand altogether. She thought there was something new to be seen in his eyes—usually she found a lost, wild glint there. Now, she saw something else.

A silent request, maybe.

A demand, possibly.

Siena didn't know.

She had learned through three months of silence that she really couldn't afford to find out much about Johnathan at all. Not when things like her feelings were in play, and he didn't seem to mind hurting them.

A weak woman she was not.

He would not make her one.

Still, Johnathan didn't move. He didn't say anything, either, but she could see he wanted to. He was holding back—maybe for himself, or for her. She didn't know, and she didn't really care, either.

"Excuse me," she said.

It came out like a whisper this time.

Soft, unsure, and barely there at all.

Johnathan still heard it because he finally stepped aside a little more to let her pass. Behind her, she heard him say, "I'm sure I'll see you around, Siena."

Doubtful.

She didn't answer him back, though.

She didn't even look over her shoulder.

Siena made a left before the bar to head for the back offices. Books to scrub and cook, after all. Her work never ended, and her life only seemed to revolve around what business her father or brothers needed her to do next.

Matteo calling her name stopped her. "Come sit with me, Siena."

She glanced at her father, and then at Darren who pushed off the stool behind him. The two men shared a quiet word as she made her way over. Darren left their father's side just as Siena came to stand beside Matteo.

"Pinot Noir—the dark red," Matteo told the man behind the bar. He looked to her. "That's the one you like, isn't it?"

"Usually," Siena said. "Not when I'm working, though."

It was not good to mix alcohol and numbers. Especially not when those numbers were fraudulent, but had to look better than real when the IRS looked at them.

Matteo laughed. "Oh, take a break once in a while, Siena. It's good for the soul. You can't work all the time."

What?

She only worked as much as she did because that's all they wanted her to do. They didn't give her any choice.

Siena said none of that, and instead, took the glass of red wine when the bartender offered it. She took one small sip, but kept her nose down in the glass as she swallowed. It gave her the chance to smell the wine, and ignore her father at the same time.

Heady fruits and the sting of alcohol filled her lungs, and coated her tongue. She wasn't a big drinker to begin with, but wine was the only thing she could stand to imbibe when she had to.

Red wine, specifically.

"Siena," Matteo murmured.

Damn.

"Yeah, Dad?"

She looked at him, but he was staring back across the restaurant. At the same exact spot where she had been standing with Johnathan only moments before. He was no longer there, or inside the restaurant at all, it seemed.

Thank God for small miracles.

Her heart was already a mess.

"Do you care to tell me what that was about between you and Johnathan Marcello?" Matteo asked.

"Not particularly."

"I'm sorry." Matteo chuckled. "I posed that question like you had a choice—you don't, Siena. Start talking."

"It's nothing, Dad."

"Is, or *was* nothing?"

"Both," she returned, and then took a much larger drink of wine. "There's nothing to tell. We met up a couple of times randomly on the street around where I get my books, and once on the city bus."

"And that's all?" Matteo pressed.

No.

She was not about to tell him that she slept with Johnathan. He was her father, not a fucking friend. The only reason she got away with occasionally having a boyfriend was because Matteo needed to keep Siena happy to a certain extent.

He needed her work with numbers. He needed her bookkeeping skills, and her understanding of how to cook his fucking books. A little bit of freedom in this life could go a long damn way.

Or so she had learned ...

"Yeah, that's all," she said, shrugging.

"He looked very uncomfortable when you wouldn't indulge his conversation," her father added after a moment.

"Perhaps that was because I didn't want to talk to him, Dad."

Siena knew that wasn't the right thing to say, but she hadn't been able to hold it back. Maybe if she got that out of the way, her father would back down on whatever he was trying to get at.

Unlikely.

"You know how I expect you to act around other men in this life, Siena. You're to treat them with the respect you give me, or your brothers. Should you run in to Johnathan again, I expect you to be your pleasant, sweet self. The good girl I know you can be, huh?"

Her father cupped her cheek, and patted it gently. A wave of bitter irritation swelled at the action.

She shoved it deep down.

What else could she do?

"I'll try, Dad," she said, offering nothing else.

Matteo smiled. "There is no trying. Not in this circumstance."

"All right."

The words felt like glass in her mouth.

Matteo chuckled deeply. "Oh, and we're having a dinner next week. I expect you to be there."

Even better ...

"Dad made this seem like it was supposed to be a big dinner," Siena said as she eyed the placements on the table. There were only six. Just enough for her parents, brothers, her, and one other person. "This isn't a big dinner at all, Ma."

Coraline rolled her eyes. "I think he means it's supposed to be an *important* dinner—a big deal, if you will."

"Why?"

Her mother didn't answer, but Siena's attention was distracted by her father and brothers roaring through the dining room. Their laughter carried through the space, and then followed them into the hall. The laughter echoed back, and muffled as the men headed into another room.

Siena turned back to her mother. "Again, why is this a big deal?"

And why the hell did she have to be there for it?

Coraline finished placing the cloth napkins on top of the plates, and gave Siena a look that scolded her. The kind of look she used to give her as a child when Siena was being too loud or whatever else.

"You know how this works—you're not new to this life, Siena," her mother said. "You don't get to ask questions. You follow the rules, and nothing else. Now, go find something to do, and get out of my hair."

Yep.

Just like a child.

Frankly, Siena didn't mind this time. It gave her the chance to get away from her mother who just kept redoing every little thing that Siena set out on the table, anyway.

She headed for the back of the house, and slipped in the sunroom. The space was fully enclosed, but had large windows that overlooked the backyard, and a door to exit out of should someone want to go outside. It was heated in the winter, and the potted plants in all the corners and on shelves gave the space an earthy smell.

Next to her old bedroom, this had been her most favorite space in the Calabrese family home. Barely anyone used the sunroom, except her mother to water the plants twice a week. Siena was almost always guaranteed some form of privacy here.

She sunk in one of the wicker chairs, and overlooked the brownstone's small, fenced in backyard. A recent storm had dropped a good half of a foot of snow on top of what little bit they already had. Now, covered in a heavy fresh sheet of pristine, sparkling white snow, it looked peaceful.

And cold.

Christmas was over now that it was a week into January, and all the decorations that usually warmed the place had long been taken down. The tree was gone, like everything else. Her mother had never liked to leave anything up for longer than she had to when it came to the holidays.

It was a good thing her mother hadn't been to her apartment in well over a month. Siena still hadn't taken her Christmas decorations down—what little bit she put out. Even the small five-foot-high fake tree was still lit up with the gold star twinkling on top in her living room.

Coraline would be aghast.

Maybe that's *why* Siena kept it up.

Who knew?

Siena wasn't sure how long she stayed hidden in the sunroom. Long enough that she wondered if maybe she had missed the dinner altogether, and someone forgot she was even there. It was unlikely, but she could still hope.

Her hope was for nothing.

"There you are," came a voice from the doorway.

Siena found her oldest brother standing there. Kev looked her over, and then peered around the room.

"You weren't playing with the plants or something, right?" he asked. "Dad won't be happy if you mess your dress, or whatever."

Siena scowled. "First, I'm twenty-five, not a toddler. Try to speak to me like an adult, and I'll remember not to use big words for you when I respond. Second, what do you want?"

"Time for dinner."

She waved a hand. "Yeah, I'll be right behind you."

"Siena, you could try to be pleasant tonight."

"No, what I could have done tonight, Kev, was stay at home on my couch under a blanket and watched the newest episode of my favorite show. Instead, I am here. Dressed and prettied up to show off Dad's beautiful family for whoever he's putting this show on for."

"And we're so awful, right?"

He flashed her a grin.

She smiled right back.

"Something like that," Siena said.

Kev sobered momentarily. "Seriously, what's up with you?"

"I don't know. Nothing in particular at the moment."

"But still something. I know how women work. You all say nothing is wrong, but in reality, you're stewing in some kind of shit inside your crazy heads."

And that, everybody, is one of many reasons why Kev can't keep a woman.

Siena didn't say that out loud.

But it didn't make it any less true.

"You going to tell me what's wrong, or what?" he asked. "Because I don't have all day, and they're waiting for us at the table."

She shrugged. "Don't you ever get tired of putting on airs for Dad and his people?"

Kev cocked a brow. "Siena, I am one of his people."

Yeah, shit.

She hadn't thought of that, but she should have. Her brothers never understood why she didn't enjoy being the child of a mafia boss the same way they did. Kev and Darren were revered as sons and made men, while she was the toss-away girl.

This conversation was going nowhere.

And fast.

Standing from the chair, Siena brushed down her skirt. "All right, let's get this over with."

"Smile," Kev said as she left the sunroom.

Siena flipped her brother off over her shoulder instead. *How's that for a smile?*

It only took a minute or two for them to get back to the dining room. Siena heard his voice echoing out from the space before she even stood in the entryway.

"Whiskey is fine," he said.

His voice came out dark and rich.

Like honey.

Fuck.

Siena's gaze drifted to where Johnathan Marcello stood beside her father and Darren at the small wet bar against the far wall. His stare found hers as Matteo passed him a three-fingered glass of whiskey.

He doesn't even drink.

Or, that's what he told her.

Siena was stuck between staring at Johnathan in his black on black suit, and wondering why in the hell nobody had thought to tell her he was the guest tonight. She felt tricked somehow, but she didn't know why.

After all, her father and brothers didn't actually *know* she had history with Johnathan. Or ... what one might consider to be a history.

Nonetheless, it was sure to be an awkward fucking dinner.

Johnathan still hadn't taken his gaze off Siena. Kev passed her in the doorway, however, and that allowed her to break the staring contest for a moment.

She took the chance to grab her chair at the table, and sit down. Fixing the napkin over her lap, she ignored the conversation happening between the men of her family and Johnathan. Soon, her mother was coming out of the kitchen with dishes in hand. She thought to help her mom, but Coraline was quick to tell her to stay put.

It was only once the table was full and wine had been poured that the men finally joined Siena and her mother at the table. Like always, Matteo sat at the head of the table, while her mother sat on the end. Darren sat beside Siena, while Johnathan sat directly across from her, and Kev sat at his left.

Every single time she looked up after grace had been said, he was right there. Looking at her. Talking to someone else, but passing her glances. Never calling her out directly for conversation, but still managing to get someone else to pull her in to it every once in a while.

Before Siena knew it, half of her plate was gone, and she had downed three glasses of a white wine that tasted like rotten grapes and old vodka.

The buzz was just enough to keep her from letting the growing butterflies in her stomach take over completely. Barely …

"Siena," her father said, "have we ever told you that Johnathan is connected to our family's history?"

She peeked up from her plate, and her gaze darted between a suddenly frozen Johnathan, and her grinning father.

Something in Johnathan's stiff as hell posture told her he was very uncomfortable. He picked up that whiskey glass he had barely touched, and tipped it up to his lips. Still, when he sat the glass back down to the table, the liquid level was still at the same spot.

He hadn't sipped on even a drop.

"No," she finally said quietly.

Matteo's grin grew wider. "His great-grandfather was once the boss of the Calabrese—"

"Grovatti," Johnathan interjected with a dull tone. "Then, it was called the *Grovatti* family."

"My mistake, John. You're right, but it's been our family for so long now that it's easy to forget."

Johnathan's grip on the steak knife in his hand tightened until his knuckles whitened. Siena again glanced between her seemingly oblivious father, and a very irritated Johnathan.

What was happening?

"Nonetheless," Matteo said, "Siena, your grandfather Carl took over after Johnathan's great-grandfather passed on. And that is how this organization came to be."

The silence that passed over the table felt thick with something Siena didn't really understand. Haughtiness from one side, she thought, and pain from the man across from her.

Johnathan hid it well, but for some reason, she could see it.

In his eyes.

There, he was hurting.

Siena downed what was left of her fourth glass of wine because she didn't know what the hell else to do. The bitter, sour flavor stuck to her teeth and tongue, but it was better than talking.

Awkward was not a good enough word for this dinner.

"I never did understand why Johnathan Grovatti's bastard son changed names after his father was killed," Darren said from beside her. "Lucian, I mean."

Johnathan's gaze darkened with a barely hidden hate as he looked at Darren.

"My *father* was adopted by Antony and Cecelia Marcello. That's why he took their surname."

"Even if he was birthed by a *goomah*, he was still a Grovatti."

Johnathan flashed a smile—cold and sharp in a blink. "We certainly are, and don't you forget it, either."

Siena hid in the sunroom the very second she was able to get away from the dinner table without earning herself a glare from her father. No one seemed to notice when she left, thankfully.

She toyed with the velvety leaves on one of the corner plants as she ran over the things that had been said at the dinner.

It still felt like a set up.

She still couldn't prove that it was.

"The information that your father neglected to mention was that your grandfather killed my great-grandfather."

Siena stiffened at Johnathan's voice, and then stood straight up. She spun on her heels, and found him leaning in the doorway of the sunroom.

"How did you know I was back here?" she asked.

He shrugged, and swirled the still-full glass of whiskey in his hand. "I skipped out on them by saying I had to use the bathroom. Apparently there's none on the bottom floor of this brownstone, so I'm going to pretend like I got lost."

Siena swallowed hard. "But you came looking for me."

Johnathan flashed a warm smile, and his hazel eyes drifted over her, unashamed. "Yep."

She refused to let this man in again. She would not let her walls down for him after the stunt he pulled on her.

Siena brought her cold demeanor out to play again. "Did I not make myself clear at the restaurant, or what?"

Johnathan looked down at the glass of whiskey, and then stretched his arm out to dump the contents in a potted plant on a shelf. "Shame to waste liquor and all, but I don't drink even for a boss."

"You could have refused."

His gaze cut back to her. "Made men cannot *refuse* any boss. I would not be here tonight, if I could."

Oh.

She heard what he didn't say.

"Was that the truth?" she dared to ask. "About my grandfather and your great-grandfather?"

Johnathan's lips curled at the edge—a sneer that roughened his handsome face, and gave her the answer before he even spoke it out loud. "Every bit of it, yeah."

"Huh."

"That's what you have to say?"

"What would you want me to say?" she countered.

Johnathan tipped his head back, and that intense gaze of his stabbed in to her with reckless intent. Like he had caught something he really liked in his sights, and he was ready to snatch it up.

It just happened to be her in his line of vision.

Fuck.

"I don't expect anything from you, Siena Calabrese," Johnathan said. "But I *hoped* you might let me say a few things."

"Like what?"

She knew better than to ask.

She wished she could take it back instantly.

The words were still out there.

Johnathan's throat bobbed as his tongue peeked out to wet his lips. "What happened a few months ago, for starters."

"Nope," she said.

Just like that, she was done.

Siena moved to push past him in the doorway and head back to where her family was, but Johnathan grabbed her wrist, and yanked her back. "Wait a damn minute, *donna.*"

In a blink, she was spun around and facing him. Dark hazel, and sharp lines clouded her vision. The hardness of his body fit perfectly against the softness of hers.

All she could see was him.

All she could smell was him.

It was bad, intoxicating, and addicting all at the same time.

"Just … wait a minute," he murmured softer.

"You don't *deserve* even a second," she replied, trying to level her tone.

"Maybe not, but will you give me one?"

"Why, so we can fuck again, and you can run off one more time? You didn't even leave me a note, or your number. I don't know if you expected me to chase you like this was some kind of game, John, but I don't run after any man. Ever."

He didn't even blink.

He barely moved.

She yanked her wrist out of his grasp, and took a step back. "So, no, I don't really want to hear anything you have to say."

Siena turned her back to Johnathan, and then quickly disappeared down the hallway. She grabbed her coat and bag from the hallway closet, and then headed for the dining room. Only one of her brothers was still there, and he was pouring yet another drink, it seemed.

Darren, that was.

"Let Dad know I'm leaving," Siena said as she dug through the bag for her keys. "I have work to do early tomorrow."

Darren snatched the keys out of her hands the second she pulled them from the purse. "Hell no. You've been drinking. You can't drive."

Siena glared at her brother, but didn't try to get the keys back. He towered over her, and she wasn't going to jump for the fucking things like a child. "Then call me a cab, or get Kev to drive me home. He barely drank anything at all."

"We're not your fucking chauffeurs, Siena."

Ouch.

Because she remembered more than one occasion when she had taken them home after dinners due to drinking.

The bastards.

"Listen, Dad mentioned you should probably stay the night anyway since you're supposed to be working with him tomorrow at the new dealership or something. You can just follow him in the morning since you don't know where it is."

Siena's irritation grew tendrils inside her heart and squeezed tight enough to kill her. "I want to go home."

Darren shrugged. "Too bad, I guess you're staying."

NINE

John headed after Siena, determined to get her to talk to him for more than five seconds. She disappeared into the dining room, and the Calabrese boss's oldest son stepped out of what appeared to be the living room at the same time.

"Here, let me take that."

John handed over the empty glass of whiskey he was still holding. "Thanks."

"You're not leaving yet, are you?" Kev asked.

John's gaze drifted toward the dining room, but went quickly back to Kev. "No, not yet."

But soon.

John wasn't about to tell Kev Calabrese that being in the brownstone was a special kind of hell for him. A constant battle between showing respect for the boss of the Calabrese Cosa Nostra, or defending the honor of a dead man.

"My father asked me to let you know he'll be waiting in his office to chat a little more," Kev said. "He thought you might have gotten lost or something."

John forced himself not to look toward the dining room again. Kev didn't mention having seen John following after Siena, and he wasn't about to make it obvious. He didn't know what the woman's family was like regarding her, men, and dating.

She didn't need trouble.

Not because of him, anyway.

"The office is on the third floor," Kev said gesturing at the stairwell. "Last door on the left—he usually leaves it open for us."

John nodded, saying only, "*Grazie.*"

Silently adding, *for fucking nothing.*

The very last thing John wanted to do was sit down with Matteo for longer than he already had. The dinner had been more than enough. Even still, he climbed the flights of stairs, and glanced over the family portraits hanging on white walls because the rules of their life happened to be a hell of a lot clearer than his wants at the moment.

Never shun a boss.

A boss is a boss is a boss, John.

He now understood—in a way—why the Marcellos tended to keep their distance where the Calabrese family was concerned. Friendships made from situations like these only led to men who did not actually like one another, but rather, made nice for the sake of appearances.

But when no one was watching …

That's when a man really had to worry.

John stood in the open doorway of the Calabrese Don's office, and tried to keep his posture as least defensive as he could. His arms stayed down at his side, and not folded over his chest. He kept his face expressionless, instead of the scowl he wanted to present.

Respect was not always easy to give.

"Johnathan," Matteo said with a wide smile.

Too wide.

John didn't move an inch. "Kev said you wanted to chat a bit more. In private, I take it."

Matteo nodded. "You guessed correctly. Come, have a seat."

The man waved at the chairs directly across from his large, cherry oak desk. Behind him, an entire wall was filled with old leather-bound books that lined the shelves. A skyline painting of New York hung on one wall, while a portrait of Carl Calabrese rested on another wall.

All over again, John fought to hide his discomfort.

It was getting harder to do.

John rested into one of the two leather chairs. His fingers clasped around the curved edges of the armrests, and he waited.

For what, he didn't know.

But *something* ...

Matteo gestured at a glass crystal filled with golden liquid. "Bourbon?"

John shook his head. "The whiskey was enough, if you wouldn't mind? I have to drive home."

Of course, he had to pose it like a question to Matteo. As though the man would get to decide whether or not John was done drinking for the night. He couldn't outright refuse the boss, so he had to try a different approach.

Matteo shrugged his large shoulders, and leaned back in the chair he dwarfed with his stature. "Yes, we wouldn't need you getting in trouble, all things considered."

John's jaw tightened. "Considering what, exactly?"

"Well, you've only been out of prison for what ... a couple of months?"

"Five at the end of December, actually."

Matteo pointed a finger at John, and wagged it. "Ah, see. And I bet you're still on some kind of parole conditions, aren't you?"

John stayed quiet.

The boss didn't seem to mind. "Mmm, I bet you are. If I remember correctly, your sentence was a five-year term. Yes, but you came out at, what, three years or so served before release?"

That time, Matteo did look to John for him to speak.

"Yes," John settled on saying.

Seeming satisfied with that line of questioning, Matteo came forward a bit to rest his beefy arms along the edge of the desk. He tipped his head to the side, and regarded John for a long moment before he spoke again.

And when he did speak, he completely changed directions.

"I heard some interesting information the other day, Johnathan," he said.

John cocked a brow. "What was that, boss?"

"Your cousin—Andino—has moved up in the Marcello family. An underboss, they told me. We didn't get the chance to properly speak about it at the restaurant. I'm expecting a meet with Dante and his new right hand soon, and it'll all be official then."

Typically, Cosa Nostra families didn't talk specifics about their respective organizations. It just wasn't good business practice. Despite the fact they all took the same oath, each family kept their secrets safely guarded.

For good reason …

Matteo didn't seem to need John's confirmation, however. "I did find it a little strange though, all things considered."

The man seemed to like that phrase a lot.

John didn't like it at all.

"Considering what?" John asked.

This all felt like one big circle. Matteo talked about what he wanted, and he led John exactly where he also wanted him to go in the conversation. It might have appeared like an open conversation from the outside looking in, but it definitely wasn't.

Matteo drummed his jeweled covered fingers to the desk. "Oh, come on, John. I'm sure you know that the Three Families in New York are always keeping up with the politics of the family next to them. It keeps us all in the loop."

"Sure, I guess."

John wasn't one-hundred percent sure why Matteo was doubling-down on this topic about his family, but he didn't like it. At the moment, there wasn't much more he could do other than sit there and listen to it.

Respect, and all.

"I think we all assumed it would be you moving up in the family when it came time—as I mentioned at the restaurant. You are the oldest, and your father is a very well respected made man. The longtime underboss to Dante Marcello—one of the most feared bosses in North America. And your other uncle—Giovanni—acting as a consigliere. That was the kind of structure and influence you grew up in. It just made sense for it to be you."

John didn't blink. "Andino grew up with those same people, and those same influences."

"So he did, I suppose." Matteo sighed, and looked to his left out the window at the dark sky. "But it's still a little odd that you haven't been given more control, John. A shame really. I don't think your potential is being put to work at its fullest. Not by a long shot."

"Maybe not, but it is what it is," John returned.

Matteo's lips curved at the corner. "So it seems, doesn't it?"

John chose not to answer that time.

John had his back turned to the entrance hallway as he shrugged on his jacket. He didn't see Siena coming for him until she had grabbed his jacket, and yanked him into the mudroom with her. She slammed the door shut behind them as he righted himself.

"What the *hell*, woman?" John asked.

Siena folded her arms over her chest, and refused to look him in the eye. "*Why*, John? Why couldn't you have just woke me up that morning? Knocked on my fucking forehead or something to make me wake up and say you had to run. You didn't even try to contact me after, and then out of the blue, you're here again like it's fine. It's not fine!"

John's brow lifted. "Are you usually this back and forth with your emotions? It's a little concerning, Siena."

She glared.

He shrugged.

"I thought …" She pressed her lips tightly together, as though she was refusing to say whatever had come to her mind.

"What?"

"That maybe you weren't like every other guy that tries to get me in bed, John. It turned out that you were exactly like every other guy."

John did stand a little bit straighter at that comment. "First, I was interested in you—still am. Second, shit came up, and I had to bolt. After that day, more things kept coming up that I had to deal with. I wasn't supposed to be getting romantically involved with somebody anyway, and I figured after I left you without fuck all the first time, you probably didn't want to see me again."

"You were right about that."

Her posture screamed defensive.

Her eyes shouted pain.

She was still lying.

"I don't want to be somebody's plaything," she told him quietly.

John nodded. "I don't want somebody to fuck with my emotions. So hey, I won't treat you like a toy, and you try not to give me whiplash with this kind of nonsense. It's a two-way street."

Siena still wouldn't meet his eyes when she said, "I don't know what to feel."

"Welcome to my world."

He felt like that all the time.

Either he had too many feelings.

Or he had none at all.

There was no in between.

Siena's tongue peeked out to wet her lips. "I *want* to give you a chance to apologize."

John barely hid back his smile as he inched closer to her. "Oh?"

"A little."

"So do that, *donna*."

She peeked up at him through dark lashes. "Something tells me you're kind of a risk, though."

"That instinct is correct."

"Maybe, but are you a risk worth taking, John?" she asked.

Well, that he didn't have the answer to.

"I'm sorry I took off," he murmured.

They stood toe-to-toe, now. He moved his pinky outward, and stroked the side of her hand with it, that's how close they were. If he leaned down just a bit, his kiss could graze her forehead.

John wouldn't do any of that unless Siena wanted him to. However, that didn't mean that he didn't want to do it. Because he did. A whole lot.

There was something about this woman that had kept her on his mind for months. Sometimes, she wasn't always the focus because he dealt with one thing at a time when it came to his brain. She was always there, though, buzzing and poking. Occasionally, thoughts of her would come back to the forefront to tease him.

She was right.

He was a risk.

But so was she.

A woman like her with a family like she had—not to mention the shit he dealt with being bipolar and how it fucked with his relationships—was a *huge* risk for John.

A mess he didn't need.

A problem he might not be able to fix.

Something bad.

Siena tipped her head back, and stared up at him. "Say it again."

"Hmm, what?"

"How sorry you are."

"Will it make it better?" he asked.

Siena grinned. "Probably not entirely, but it'll get us there."

"I *am* interested in more than sex, Siena."

"And if I asked you to take me home tonight ..."

John smirked. "I would not say no."

He might be sorry, but he was also very much a fucking man. She was all woman. Every single part of him knew it, too.

"So maybe we could do that?" she asked quietly.

John cupped her jaw and neck with his palm, and felt the way her heart raced under his touch. Or maybe it was her nerves from approaching him like this after everything. That risk she had mentioned.

"How about this," he murmured, "I will take you to *my* place, and if something comes up, you are more than welcome to stay until I get back. Because really, shit always comes up for me first thing in the morning. So hey, it'll be up to you if you want to take off on me as payback for what I did to you."

Siena nipped on her bottom lip. "Yeah?"

"Yep."

"I'm supposed to be somewhere for work around eleven, or so."

"I can take you there," he promised, "and cabs do go to where I live."

She laughed.

John waited ...

He'd been waiting months for this, after all.

He could wait a few more seconds.

"Do you have good coffee?"

John chuckled, and bent down to press a quick kiss to her grinning mouth. He let his thumb drag over her lips as he pulled away. "The best coffee, actually."

"Okay, your apology is accepted."

"Thought so."

"For now," she added.

John could deal with that.

Typically, when John woke up to the sound of his phone dinging, it automatically put him in a shitty mood. He didn't mind so much when he rolled over to grab the chiming device that morning because he was fucking *satisfied*.

Not at all tired.

Feeling damn good.

Yeah, satisfied.

He rolled to his back, and peered at the screen of his phone while he rubbed his palm down his naked chest. His hand rested just above where the sheet covered his semi-erection, and he scrolled through the text message update.

From the pharmacy, it seemed.

Prescriptions for Johnathan Marcello are ready to be picked up at—

John tossed the phone aside, already done with the message. He knew he had to go pick up his new dose of meds. He tried the higher dosage of Lithium with the mixture of antianxiety and mood stabilizer meds that the therapist wanted him to use.

His mind felt like a fog from it all.

The therapist had suggested she lower the dose of the Lithium. John hadn't bothered to tell her, but he had already started to half the Lithium every day, anyway. It was the only way he could break his mind out of the medicated fog it created.

He'd grab the prescriptions, but he still had a good three weeks' worth of his old meds before he had to worry about it. Then he would have to play the new pill game with the therapist while she tested yet another dose on him.

John didn't even need to roll over in the bed to know that the other side was empty. He'd felt the loss of Siena the moment she crawled out of bed about an hour ago, and had only gone back to sleep when he heard the shower turn on from the connecting bathroom.

He rested his arm behind his head as a makeshift pillow, and listened. Something metal clanged downstairs—a pot, likely.

Unlike him, Siena didn't seem to be a flight risk. She would have had every right to bolt on him even if she had promised to still be there in the morning after she dragged him into the bedroom.

He took that as a battle won.

Fucking that woman was like taking a five-mile run first thing in the morning. It woke him up out of the stupor that was his everyday life, and left him out of breath. She worked him good, made his muscles ache by the end of it all, but still feeling like another go 'round was a likely possibility.

A louder clang echoed from downstairs, and was followed by a loud cuss. John decided it was time to get up before Siena fucking hurt herself, or something. He pulled on a pair of sleep pants to cover his lower half, but nothing was hiding the half-mast of his dick pushing against the cotton.

91

Fuck it.

Soon enough, John was leaning in the entryway of the kitchen, and he watched as Siena balanced on a chair while she tried to pull a mixing bowl off the highest shelf in the pantry cupboard. Her wet hair hung in rivulets down her back, and he could see just a peek of her bare ass beneath the dress shirt she had thrown on.

His shirt.

It looked far better on her.

He didn't even mind.

Those bare legs of hers—all soft lines, and sweet curves—looked damn good as she tried to balance on one foot and stretch to reach the bowl high above her head. He was so caught up in staring at her that he didn't even mind she had seemed to tear his cupboards apart.

Anyone else, and John's odd tendencies about his place and things being just how he wanted them might have come out to play in a not so nice way.

But this was her.

And he didn't mind so much with her.

"Need some help?" he asked.

She must not have heard him coming downstairs because the shriek she let out damn near burst his eardrums. Not to mention, her body swayed on the chair, and she missed her step when she set her foot back down.

John bolted forward, and barely managed to catch Siena before she hit either the chair, the floor, or fucking *both*. Her brown hair created a curtain over her face, and she blew out a hard breath. A couple of strands puffed forward before Siena used a hand to push the hair back.

He'd caught her just a few inches from the floor. Lucky, really.

"Make some noise," she told him, glowering. "I almost killed myself."

"Thank you, John," he mocked, "for not letting that happen."

Siena pursed her lips. "And that, too!"

"Mmhmm."

She grabbed his jaw with one hand, pulled him in close, and gave him a kiss that made his dick go from half-mast to all the way hard. *Damn.* All it took was her teasing little tongue flicking against his lips, and then the promise of a taste of her, and there he was … ready to go again.

"I was trying to make breakfast," she whispered against his grinning lips.

"You needed the biggest bowl to do that?"

"Pancakes are messy, okay."

John nodded. "Sure."

"I kind of tore some cupboards apart looking for things."

"As long as you put it all back, I don't care."

Siena winked. "Deal. Will you get me the bowl?"

"You bet."

He straightened up, and put Siena to her bare feet. He didn't even need the damn chair that she had been trying to use to kill herself and get the bowl. All he had to do was lean up and grab the stupid thing out of the cupboard.

John easily snatched the bowl without trouble, and handed it to a scowling Siena. "Oh, don't look like that, now."

"It's not fun being short. Do you know how much it sucks to need a stool to reach anything? Nothing is made for my height."

"You're not … *short*. I mean, not for a woman. You're average."

Siena's mouth popped open, and then she took that bowl and smacked him in the arm with it. "Don't you call me average!"

John laughed, and rubbed his arm at the same time. Shit, that hurt. Her glare was also funny which only made him laugh harder. It felt strange and good. He couldn't remember a time when he had a morning like this. If he ever had one …

Siena pouted. "Don't laugh at me, too! That's doubly insulting, John."

Her downcast gaze was the only thing to sober him up. Instantly, he was reaching out to grab hold of Siena, and drag her to him. She softened against his chest, and tipped her head back to stare up at him. Those pretty pink lips of hers kissed the underside of his unshaved jaw.

"You're not an average woman," he murmured, kissing the top of her head. "You're beautiful and amazing, and you come in a slightly smaller package when it comes to height."

Her palm tapped against his chest jokingly.

"You're forgiven."

"Good." He dropped another kiss to her head. "Now, someone owes me breakfast. So, get on that, would you?"

John let Siena go, and smacked her ass as she passed him by. The cute little glare she shot over her shoulder at him only earned her a wink in response.

While Siena busied herself at the counter, John eyed the cupboard over the fridge. Nothing looked out of place on top of the fridge to say she had looked up there for anything. All his medications were kept safe, it seemed.

At least, for now.

If the two of them continued with whatever this was, John was going to have to bring up the topic of his disorder, and what it all meant. For him, and for her. It was the right thing to do, but the idea also left him with a heavy weight in his gut.

For more reasons than he cared to admit.

Would she bolt?

Would she look at him differently?

"Hey," Siena said from the island.

John glanced her way as her voice dragged him from his black mind. "What, *bella*?"

"Do you have honey?"

"For what?"

"It's better than plain old corn syrup. You don't have *real* maple syrup."

"Aunt Jemima isn't maple syrup?" John asked.

Siena arched a brow. "Are you serious?"

"It says maple on the bottle."

"It says *flavored*. It's corn syrup with flavoring added."

Huh.

"I have honey."

She gave him a look. "*Real* honey?"

"Yes, real honey."

Siena winked. "Good."

John turned to the pantry, and pulled the honey in question from the shelf. Still unopened, the jar was filled to the rim with golden sweetness. He strolled over, and set it beside the bowl where Siena was already starting to fill it with dry ingredients.

She peeked over at him. "Do you want to help?"

"I think I like watching you more."

Her smile teased him. "That so?"

"Yeah, love."

"*La dolce vita*," she said, grinning.

"The sweet life."

Siena nodded. "Every man likes to feel like a king in his home, doesn't he?"

John laughed a husky tune. "Some men certainly do."

"Are you one of those men?"

"I am right now."

Siena's floury hand patted his cheek, and left powder behind. "You're lucky I like you, Johnathan Marcello. I don't particularly care for spoiled men most of the time."

"Maybe you've been around the wrong kind of men, then."

Her blue eyes traveled over him once, and then twice.

"Most definitely."

John wasn't sure what did it for him—the way she was looking at him with those clear, honest eyes of hers, or the way her tone echoed with sin when it reached his ears. It could have been the way she looked in his shirt, too.

Whatever it was, it made the need for food come second to the need he felt for her.

John reached for Siena, and had her backside up on the counter before she even blinked. His mouth was on hers as his hands skimmed under the hem of the dress shirt covering her body. Soft, smooth skin met his warm palms while her tongue danced with his.

Something fell off the counter—the smaller bowl she had found, maybe. He didn't even care.

Her flour dusted hands left marks down his chest while her fingernails raked over the same spots. She widened her thighs as his hands slipped higher under the shirt, and found her pert tits. Hard nipples rolled under his thumbs, and then her teeth sunk into his bottom lip.

She promised.

She teased.

She gave.

She took.

Siena didn't have to say a thing, either. It was all in the way she touched him, how she kissed him, when she looked at him, and the way he felt from it all. The sensations clashed together like a wrecking ball coming through to tear down what little walls he had left for control, and there he was, pieces of a mess on the ground.

Her mess.

John yanked open the dress shirt to expose more of her body to him, and likely ruined three buttons in the process. Her skin heated and pebbled under his touch. She tipped her head back, and let him ghost kisses over her throat while his exploration went lower. The taste of her skin on his tongue was unlike anything else. He found one taste was not enough.

It never was.

Silky smooth, wet flesh met his fingertips between her thighs. Her little gasp when he stroked her sex with the pad of his thumb made him grin.

"So fucking responsive," he murmured against her throat.

Siena's throat bobbed with her hard swallow. "Something about you, John."

"That what it is?"

"Something," she echoed again.

He was more than happy to get her making more of those sounds. Nothing made him harder, or got him fucking hotter. Pulling back, he kissed her once hard.

"Don't move," he said.

"Promise I won't."

Siena stayed like a sexy little statue on the counter while John dug through the junk drawer on the other side of the island. Anything he had extra of, he just shoved it in there. Soon enough, he found what he needed.

A condom.

By the time he was back between the heaven of Siena's thighs, she seemed to have decided to take the lead. Her deft hands snuck beneath his sleep pants, and found his cock. The way her palm circled him, and stroked him even more awake was damn addicting. He handed over the foil packet when she reached for it.

Pants shoved down around his hips, and latex rolled onto his length, John figured he had waited long enough. He yanked Siena to the very edge of the counter when he first heard the phone ringing upstairs.

His cell phone.

The familiar tune—one he used for the boss—echoed in the back of his mind.

John ignored the call, and kissed Siena instead. The heat of her mouth tempted him while the wet slit of her cunt teased him. She rubbed the head of his cock along her pussy, and rocked her hips back and forth at the same time.

The phone call stopped ringing upstairs damn near to the second John flexed his hips forward. He found himself buried nine inches deep into Siena, and instantly without air. It all rushed from his lungs with the wave of relief that slid down his spine.

A heat like no other filled him.

A satisfaction like he'd never known slipped through him.

A want he had never known thundered inside him.

Her soft voice in his ear, and her fingernails dragging down his back urged him on. Every *please*, and *there, God, there* mixed in with her high and breathless cries. The prettiest music he had ever heard.

The phone started ringing again.

John was lost in something far better.

His fingertips dug into Siena's ass as he pulled her into every one of his thrusts. He could feel the tremor working its way through her legs when she tightened them around his hips. Her pussy squeezed him tight, and sucked him deeper.

It was in her eyes, though—a high, crazed look stared back at him.

He knew that stare.

It looked far better on her than it did on him.

Especially like this.

"Jesus Christ," she breathed.

John bit her jaw. "It's *John*, actually."

Siena's breathless laughter was interrupted by the clenching of her muscles. Her orgasm came on quick, and left her raking lines down his naked back.

John wasn't even close to being done.

"This better be fucking good," John grumbled when he walked in his uncle's office.

His steps faltered at the many men who waited inside the space. His uncles, father, and Andino. His gaze skipped to the most important man in the room because the boss was always the first one to be respected before anyone else—Dante.

"What's going on?" John asked.

Lucian spoke up first. "Have a seat, son."

John straightened his suit jacket. "Nah, I'm good. I kind of want to know why I'm here, though. I don't like to be interrupted, you know."

Those phone calls didn't stop coming until John forced himself away from Siena to answer one. His uncle said nothing except to get to the fucking mansion. Just like that—nothing else.

"Yeah, I bet," Giovanni muttered.

John gave his youngest uncle a look. "What the fuck does that mean?"

"John," Dante said, his tone thick with a warning. "Show some respect, huh?"

He checked his attitude, but not because he fucking wanted to.

"Yeah, all right." John gave the boss his attention. "I'm here—what's up?"

"You didn't think to tell any of us that you were going to be having dinner with the Calabrese boss and his family last night?" Dante asked.

"I was invited," John replied, shrugging. "Tell me how to refuse that without breaking the rules we live by, and I will do that next time."

"You still didn't tell anyone," his father said.

John didn't see why that mattered. "I didn't need to. It was a *dinner*."

"With the Calabrese *boss*. You know how the Marcellos feel about that family, John," Giovanni put in.

John's attention was still only on the boss. "I couldn't be disrespectful, and refuse. So, I went. It's over."

"You cannot trust a Calabrese," Dante murmured.

The familiar green eyes of his uncle bore into John. For some reason—not one he could pull forward right away—he didn't think Dante was only talking about Matteo and his sons.

"I don't trust the Calabrese boss, or his shithead sons," John countered. "I remember what they did to my father's family."

Lucian cleared his throat, but said nothing.

"Why didn't you answer my calls this morning?" Dante asked quietly. "You were fine with telling me you couldn't disrespect Matteo, and yet you made me call you ten times before you finally answered. What was so important this morning that you couldn't answer me, Johnathan?"

"I was busy."

His answer was not good enough.

He knew before he said it.

Dante nodded, and leaned back in the chair. "I know you took the Calabrese girl home with you, John. See, I found out about the dinner invitation, and thought just in case, you should have someone follow behind. I don't trust snakes like those ones in Brooklyn, and in no way will I allow a man of mine to confer with them without some kind of backup."

John only heard one thing in all of that.

One thing that made him enraged.

One thing that burned him like betrayal.

"You fucking had someone *follow me*?" he asked, deathly still and dark in his heart.

"I—"

"Someone tailed me?"

"John," Andino said, pushing off the edge of the desk. "He thought it would be best considering how the Calabrese are sometimes."

John's vision blackened.

His lungs ached with every breath.

All over again, he was left feeling like he did when he was first released from prison. Like a fucking wild animal that nobody trusted. Like he couldn't do his damn job because someone always had to be looking over his shoulder.

"Because I can't look out for myself or be trusted, right?" John asked. "That's funny, *boss*, considering the Calabrese didn't make any effort to hide fuck all about their intentions when they invited me to dinner. Except my own family does exactly that instead of just fucking asking me. But they're the ones I have to watch out for, huh?"

John let out a bitter laugh.

"It's not a big deal," Dante said, "and it's not like you're making it out to be, John."

"Or is it exactly that, boss?" he asked. "Have you gotten someone to follow me before this time, too?"

No one answered.

John didn't need them to at that point.

"Why?" he asked.

At least, his family was honest.

Brutally so.

"Andi mentioned you had an interest in the Calabrese girl," Dante said.

John's gaze flew to his cousin—bitter and full of anger. "What, you ran to tattle on me like a fucking baby, or something?"

"No, I—"

"Screw you, Andino."

Andino stepped forward, but John pointed at his best friend to keep the new little underboss back a step. A silent warning that Andino knew all too well.

John's father, on the other hand, had never cared. Lucian came closer, and John's jaw clenched so hard his molars might have cracked.

"John, they cannot be trusted, and you know that," Lucian said. "Not the men, and certainly not one of their women. No matter who she is."

That probably stung the worst.

They didn't even know Siena.

It was just her last name that colored her bad.

Like his disorder left them assuming shit about him.

It was all the same.

"Fuck you all."

The three words slipped out of John's mouth easier than he expected them to, and he let them escape before he really thought it over.

Dante stood from his chair.

Lucian came one step closer.

Giovanni didn't move.

Andino just frowned.

John shook his head, and turned for the door. He was done with whatever this was. He was done with them for today.

"Yeah, fuck every single one of you."

TEN

John's place was spotless ...

Siena kept that thought in mind as she finished up washing the last few dishes from the pancake mess she had made. A plate of pancakes sat on the cupboard, untouched and getting cooler by the minute.

She remembered the night before that Johnathan's bed had been perfectly made before they climbed in it, and messed it all up. Then, when he left this morning, he had taken five minutes to fix his bed again before he left the house.

For a bachelor who lived on his own, Siena expected Johnathan to be at least a little untidy. Like most men who lived alone were. A few clothes scattered somewhere. A floor that could use a sweep. Knickknacks or mismatched treasures spread out on shelves or tables. Nothing.

Johnathan had none of those.

His place was meticulously clean. His floors were shiny enough that someone could probably eat off them. She noticed that morning even the clothes in his walk-in closet were carefully hung by color, and arranged by each type of item.

It was all a little OCD-like, in some ways. Except ... Siena knew Johnathan likely wasn't struggling with Obsessive Compulsive Disorder. She only leaned toward that impression because she noticed him, too.

He didn't say a word when she went through his kitchen, or made a mess. He didn't have any strange rituals or compulsions, so to speak, for her to take note of. He washed his hands before and after he ate, and when he went to the bathroom, but that was about it.

Was it possible he just managed the disorder through tidiness and organizing every little thing? Sure, but she really didn't think that was the case at all.

Siena was also quite aware that OCD could not be simplified in to strange habits and a compulsive need to do very specific things.

She really shouldn't be speculating at all. It wasn't her place.

Those pancakes are going to be disgusting.

Siena scrubbed the massive bowl John had barely needed to reach for. She eyed the stack of three pancakes on the plate a couple of feet away.

She didn't know what to do with them because she didn't have the first clue when John was going to be back. The man had no plastic wrap in his house to put over food—she hadn't even found containers for leftovers.

Whether or not that was because John didn't eat leftovers, or perhaps it was something else entirely. Like the fact those containers always somehow magically lost their lids, made a mess in the cupboard, and were not at all very tidy despite how the commercials made them look. Who knew?

Siena had also noticed in her search of the kitchen that Johnathan tended to favor healthy foods. Organic seemed to be a favorite of his, like the eggs in the fridge, and the honey she had used on her own pancakes. However, that corn syrup in the fridge was not healthy at all.

Seemed he made a few exceptions.

Like the Oreos in the pantry.

Siena smiled to herself as she rinsed off the bowl. For as fit as John was, she couldn't exactly imagine him binging on a package of cookies.

But what did she know?

Siena went about drying the dishes and putting them all away. She opted to leave the big bowl on the cupboard beside the pantry where she had found it.

The clock on the wall said it was only nine, which meant she still had a couple of hours before she needed to be at her father's dealership. It only really registered to her in that moment that her phone had been dark all night and morning.

No calls from Matteo. No calls from her brothers.

None of them had even come downstairs when Johnathan left the night before, so she seriously doubted that they knew she had left with him. Except … her car was still at her parents' brownstone, so they must have suspected.

Yet, no calls.

No check-in to make sure she wouldn't be late today. Nothing.

The cupboard over the fridge caught Siena's eye. It was the only cupboard she hadn't gotten the chance to check while she was prepping to cook earlier.

Maybe a container or something would be in there to store the food until John got back. Pulling a chair out from the table, she pulled it over and stepped up onto it. The half of a dozen cards and papers pinned to the fridge made her pause.

One in particular made her stop altogether.

Dr. Amelia Goodane, PhD and PsyD, the card read. It had an address and phone number printed on the plain, white card. Under the woman's name, it said, *Psychologist.*

The appointment printed on the card was for January eighth, at eight o'clock in the morning. *Today.*

Siena glanced at the clock. Actually, an hour ago.

Had he blown off his appointment, or just forgot altogether?

Her gaze drifted back to the card as she took in the doctor's qualifications once more. John was in therapy—but for what?

Siena figured it didn't matter because it wasn't her damn business to begin with. Had he wanted her to know, then John would have brought it up.

Besides, it wasn't like they were a *thing*. They weren't anything where he owed her something, and certainly not an explanation about his personal business.

She put the card aside in her mind, and reached for the cupboards. Better to get the food put away, and deal with whatever else later *if* John decided it was something she needed to know about him.

The cupboard did not have containers or plastic wrap.

It didn't even have food.

Medication greeted her. Pill bottles with child safety orange caps stared back at her. She thought to close the door to the cupboard because this was—*again*—none of her business, but her gaze stiff drifted over the labels.

Johnathan Antony Marcello

His name was on every single one.

Lithium. Zoloft.

Another mood stabilizer. Antidepressants. Antianxiety meds.

It was a lot.

Some were obviously discarded meds, maybe ones he no longer used for whatever reason, considering the dates on the bottles and amount of pills still inside.

There were lots of rumors about the infamous Johnathan Marcello. Many of them passed Siena by because she only heard things from afar when made men gathered, and she happened to be around.

Some of them called John crazy. Some said he was just a little wild.

His arrest years ago that took him to prison had also led to lots of speculation about just what had gone down between John and his cousin in a restaurant. Apparently, some people that had been there said it was like John had fallen into a mental break or something.

No one knew for sure.

Siena had heard those rumors.

All of them.

She didn't entertain whispered gossip and stories. Not when it came from the mouths of men who would only say something behind someone's back, and never to their face.

And that was enough for her.

Siena instantly slammed the cupboard doors, and stepped down from the chair. She did it without thinking, and never having touched one of the bottles.

A huge part of her felt like she had just betrayed Johnathan in some way, even though she couldn't pinpoint exactly what it was. She hadn't been snooping, and in fact, didn't even leave the kitchen the entire time he had been gone except to use the bathroom once.

And yet, she still felt wrong.

Like she had done something wrong to him.

The purr of a Mercedes pulling in the driveway outside made her forget about it.

At least now for ...

"Ease up on the pedal a bit," Siena joked, "I'm not even late or anything."

John's white-knuckle grip on the steering wheel loosened ever so slightly. His gaze slipped to the clock on the dashboard, and the car slowed down subtly. "Yeah, sorry."

Something in the lilt of his tone caught her attention. Siena looked at him, but John's focus was only on the road ahead of him.

"Everything okay?" she asked.

John nodded. "Sure."

"Really?"

The bobbing of his throat as he swallowed hard did not escape her notice. Neither did the way his fingers tightened around the wheel again like he needed something to keep hanging onto. All of it felt wrong to her.

She just didn't know why.

"Did something happen?" Siena asked.

John chuckled. "Oh, something is always happening, *dolcezza*. Don't worry about it."

"You can tell me anything, if you want—"

"It's fine," he interjected quietly.

Siena let it drop.

What choice did she have at the moment?

"You sure we're going to make it to the dealership in enough time?" he asked.

Siena settled in the passenger seat. He had already taken her to her apartment to change, and freshen up. "We have lots of time."

She didn't bother to mention she might be a little late. Thirty minutes, or so.

The phone in her purse was still silent, though. No calls or texts from her father or brothers. It was like—for once—they didn't care at all that she was late.

Any other time, and her phone wouldn't stop until she walked through the front door of whatever business she was supposed to be working in.

John cleared his throat, and said, "So, I never thought to ask before ..."

"Hmm, what?"

"You do their books, huh?"

Siena smiled a little. "Something like that."

"What's what mean?"

"Someone does the main books for the businesses, sure."

John nodded. "Let me guess, you go in and clean 'em up."

"Something like that," she echoed.

His hazel eyes drifted to her, and then slowly looked her over. It was enough to make Siena heat up under the jeans, blouse, and tweed coat she had thrown on at her place. John wasn't even ashamed of his staring when he smirked, and then went back to staring at the road.

"I wouldn't have taken you for an accountant," he admitted.

"No?"

"Maybe a school teacher, or nurse. Something like that."

Siena snorted. "I like numbers, actually. I like *facts*. Things that add up, or work in the end. It's just how my brain tries to see everything, I guess."

"Yeah, I get that."

"My dad noticed that my grades in high school for math and sciences were high. I was taking college prep courses for those areas. Numbers make sense to me, if you get what I'm trying to say."

John laughed under his breath. "Numbers make sense to me, too. You know, when I can add more zeroes behind the first number."

Siena grinned. "I bet."

"Yeah, but keep going with your story."

"He had me doing books for some of the little businesses he owns when I was a senior in high school. He pushed me toward accounting degrees and whatnot after I graduated. I would have went in to something with math or science as a focus, anyway, but ..."

John glanced over at her. "Does it feel like you didn't get a choice?"

"Sometimes," she admitted.

"So, you're the one who handles the Calabrese numbers, huh?"

Siena wet her lips. "Not supposed to talk about business, John."

His eyes glinted with amusement. "How good can you scrub and cook a book, Siena?"

Well ...

"I haven't found a dollar amount yet that I can't hide, John."

He whistled low.

"Damn, *donna*."

Siena laughed right along with John. A second later, he reached over to find her thigh with his palm. He squeezed her inner thigh overtop her jeans, and shot her a wink. Then, just as quickly, his hand slid in with hers. Silently, he intertwined their fingers together, and held on tight.

John brought her hand up, leaned over, and pressed three light kisses across her knuckles. He didn't say a thing while he did it, but he didn't really need to, either.

It was such a small action.

A little bit of affection.

She didn't know what to make of it, but she liked it.

"What are we doing?" she asked him.

John didn't even think about it before answering. "I mean, whatever you want to do, Siena."

"Are we ... doing something now?"

"Like what, Siena? Right now, I'm driving you to work."

"No, I mean, you and me, John."

He cleared his throat, and shifted a bit in the driver's seat. "Depends on if you're still angry with me about taking off on you and shit."

"Blackmail, huh?"

John didn't even try to hide his grin. "I have to make you forget about that somehow, don't I?"

"I'm not ... mad," she said. "I might bring it up, but I'm not mad."

His laughter came out thick and husky.

A melody of sin.

"I see," John said.

"Anyway, I just ... want to know. If we are doing something, or whatever. So, I know from the jump what's going on here. I don't like games, John."

"We can be doing something," he murmured, his gaze drifting from the road to her, and then back again. "You might want to let me take you out properly or something, but that's up to you."

She hummed under her breath, very much liking the idea he proposed. "I will hold you to that."

"Noted. But you should know, I'm a terribly jealous fucker, and I don't like to share."

"Me, either."

John's lips curved sinfully at the edges. "Got it, love."

"You can't blow me off without an explanation ever again," she warned.

"I can't make promises, but I'll always be back."

Siena took that offer in, and said, "Okay."

"Sometimes, I'm not very easy to deal with," John said, keeping his gaze firmly on the road and anywhere but on her. "It's just a part of who I am, Siena. I don't mean to make shit difficult, but it happens, regardless."

She thought about the things she found that morning.

Even though she hadn't meant to …

He was trying to tell her something without giving it all away.

"Okay," she said again.

John finally looked over at her. "Just okay, huh?"

Siena shrugged. "I never really liked easy—I like things that make sense. Like romance novels with a happily ever after, or numbers that need to add up in a book. You, too."

His dark, low chuckles rumbled in the car. Unbothered, grinning, and looking like he didn't have a fucking care in the world, Siena thought John was the most beautiful man she had ever seen in her life. All over again, at the sight of him like that, she was stuck silent.

"Not sure I always make sense," John admitted after a moment.

Siena thought differently.

"Everything makes sense when you look at all the details."

John nodded. "Maybe you're right."

There was no maybe.

On that, Siena knew she was right.

All too soon, John was pulling the Mercedes over along the side of the road. An unfamiliar dealership awaited her—luckily, she had been able to pull up the address of the place from her emails.

"This the place?" he asked.

"Yeah, this is the place."

John gave her a crooked grin. "Give them my apologies for making you late, and you know, whatever else."

"Not really worried about it, John."

He gave her no warning before he leaned over in the seat, and kissed her. A hard, bruising kiss that took her breath away, and had her heart racing out of control. Every stroke of his lips against hers, and his tongue darting into her mouth to dance with hers, felt more and more familiar.

His hand cupped her cheek, and his thumb stroked her skin.

Siena smiled as John pulled away. "You still haven't even asked for my number."

"I do know where you live, Siena."

"Still …"

John smiled widely, showing off white teeth and sex appeal in a blink. "Give me your damn phone, *bella*."

Siena's week crawled by at the usual slow pace she had become accustomed to. One day was spent dealing with her father, and the next, Darren. She jumped between businesses from day to day finishing up last minute details before the taxes would have to be filed for each and every one.

It was mid-January, after all. The deadline for filing was looming. Technically, it was her busiest time of year. Most of the work was left up to her.

Normally, Siena didn't mind because it wasn't like she had much of a life to begin with. Except when she was supposed to be focusing on cooking the books and making numbers work, her mind was on something else entirely.

Or rather ... someone else.

John.

Sitting in the office of her oldest brother's favorite restaurant, Siena's gaze drifted between the three-inch high pile of documents she had just finished printing out, and the business accounts she had pulled up on the screen. While she electronically filed everything, she kept a physical backup just in case.

She still had things left to do.

Shit to go over.

Her finger hovered on the mousepad of the laptop. On the screen, the cursor rested on top of the web browser. She didn't use the work computers for personal business. Not that she couldn't, it was just the way she kept work and everything else separate.

Still, she clicked on the browser.

The office door was open, but the sounds of the restaurant filtering down the hall told her no one was coming. Kev had stepped out a while ago saying something about being hungry.

Siena still kept one eye on the door, and one eye on the Google search bar as she started typing in keywords.

Something had stuck with her for the whole week. Something just wouldn't let go of her mind. It kept going back there even when she tried to force it out for good.

She kept telling herself that it wasn't her business. The medications she had found in John's place was his thing to deal with, and he would tell her if he wanted to. And yet ... she wanted to know.

Siena typed in *Lithium*, and hit the enter button. The first thing to come up was the metal element, but she scrolled down past that, and clicked on the medical information. She already kind of knew what the drug was used to treat—mostly being that it was a psychiatric medication. Clicking on the link that directed to a medical page dedicated to the drug, she found a list of disorders that Lithium was specifically targeted to.

She clicked on the back button, and came to the Google page again. This time, she added *psychotherapy and Lithium* into the search bar, and then hit the enter button. The first thing to come up on the page was some article on the correlation of the medication lithium being best used in conjunction with therapy.

The following pages that came up in the search continued to use the same disorder again and again in the preview texts.

Bipolar.

Major Depressive Disorder.

Mania.

Siena clicked on a link, and read down through the information. Just as fast, she went back and clicked on another. And then another.

Back on the search bar, she added in new keywords—other meds she remembered from the cupboard. All over again, the information seemed to lead straight to a cocktail that suggested Bipolar.

A huge part of her wanted to close the browser down because none of this was supplied by Johnathan. He had not told her these things, and she didn't even know for sure if this was what he was dealing with behind closed doors.

Another part of her wanted to … understand.

If this was a part of his life, and something he was managing privately, she wanted to know more about it.

So, she went back to the search bar again. She typed in, *Bipolar*, and hit enter. She read through signs and symptoms, and how it was managed. Information came up on things like mania, cycles, and the depression that so often trailed those dealing with the disorder.

She found accounts from people who explained what their mania had been like for years before it was finally properly diagnosed. Not to mention, the things they had done to those around them during the spells, and the way their lives had been upended in the struggle for help.

Some of it was frightening. Some of it was uplifting.

A lot of it was hopeful.

A bipolar diagnosis for a lot of people seemed to be a relief. An actual confirmation that yes, they did feel things differently, and see the world and themselves in a different way. They processed emotional events or feelings at a different pace, and most of the time, at a far greater intensity. It didn't mean they were crazy, but rather, had to use different treatments and methods to manage the aspects of bipolar that negatively impacted them.

Siena just kept reading. She kept looking for more information, and a better understanding. She was a good thirty minutes into reading before voices directly outside the office finally made her blink away from the screen.

"So he's fine with letting all of that go on, then?" Kev asked.

"Guess so," Darren replied. "It's that opening he's been looking for, you know what I mean?"

"Yeah, it just might be."

Siena moved to click the exit button from the browser just as her two brothers walked in the office. She just got the browser closed as Kev rounded the desk, and jerked his thumb for her to move out of his chair.

His gaze darted to the accounts on the screen that had replaced the browser. Siena gave a silent sigh of relief that the browser closed in time. She didn't know how she would even begin explaining something like that to Kev.

"Move your ass," Kev said.

"I still have work to finish up, Kev," Siena told him.

Her brother shrugged like he didn't give a damn. "Take a break, or something."

Siena's brow furrowed. "Since when do you want me to take breaks?"

"Yeah, well, Dad reminded me to keep you fed," Kev grumbled as he began closing out the accounts on the screen. "There's a plate waiting for you in the kitchen, and somebody stopped by to see you, I guess."

"Who?"

"Just go find out. You've got an hour at the most, and then you need to get back to work."

She gave her brother a dirty look before leaving the office. There was a plate waiting for her, but the waiter simply directed her out onto the floor, but not before grabbing a second plate to carry.

It was John waiting for her.

He sat at a private table away from the rest of the diners. Blocked off by a partial wall, he stared out the window until Siena came to sit with him. The sexy grin he flashed had her pulse picking up. He looked damn good with his dark hair slicked back, a well-fitted suit tight to his fit form, and that goddamn smile.

Standing from the table, John allowed the waiter to sit the plates down, and then the man scattered. John reached for Siena, and pulled her in for a quick kiss. For the most part, all they had gotten to do over the week was text back and forth. She was too busy with work and everything else to go out, or stay over. He seemed okay with it, though.

"Sit, and eat with me," he murmured against her lips.

"This is why you texted me this morning to ask where I was going to be?"

"All you do is work, *donna*."

He kind of wasn't lying.

"So, is this …" Siena waved at the food, and then between them, "… like a date?"

John chuckled, and his smirk deepened. "Exactly that, yeah."

"And what comes after said date, Johnathan?"

"Whatever you want, Siena."

She laughed, and wagged a finger at him. "Smooth. Leaving the details up to me."

"Hey, I got over here today, didn't I?"

He did.

It meant the world to her.

Had someone asked her what she would like for a date, anything that didn't include being within five miles of her family would have been at the top of the list. Johnathan managed to keep her within thirty feet of her family, and she didn't mind at all.

All she saw was him.

John first.

Everything came second.

"How was your week?" John asked.

"Good."

"Anything come up?"

Siena could have asked or said a lot of things at that moment. The thing she knew, or the stuff she suspected. Yet, she didn't ask or say a thing. Not about any of it, and not because she didn't want to know, either.

John was John.

She saw him first.

Everything else was second.

ELEVEN

"Come on, Lucia," John muttered. "Pick up the damn phone."

He drummed his fingers to the leather-wrapped steering wheel, and glared at the form leaning against a car just ahead of his. At the moment, he had something else to focus on other than the fact Andino was following him around.

Like his goddamn sister, and the fact she wouldn't answer his calls. None of them. He'd called repeatedly since she went back to California, but he got nothing back. Not even a *fuck you* text.

It was driving him crazy.

John wanted to fix shit with Lucia, but he couldn't do that when she wouldn't even let him speak to her. Apparently, his sister was not messing around when she had told him after Christmas that she planned to have nothing to do with the rest of them.

Fuck.

"Call me, Lucia," John barked into the message when the phone beeped.

He shoved the phone in his pocket, and got out of the car. Staring at the warehouse across the road, he tried to relax a bit before he had to do business. He didn't need to go in there already in a bad mood.

"What, you're going to act like I'm not fucking standing right here or something?"

"That's exactly what I plan on doing, Andino."

To make his point clear, John slammed the door of his Mercedes shut, and crossed the street without as much as a wave at Andino. Grumbling something under his breath, Andino pushed off his own car, and headed after John.

"Wait a second, man."

"I have fuck all to say to you."

"Listen, I came all the way down to this part of the city to talk to you today, John. The least you could do is fucking listen to me for five minutes."

"No, the least I could do is what I am doing. Ignoring you, and not beat you into the ground for the shit you pulled on me."

"Hey—"

"And how the fuck did you know I was going to be here today, anyway?" John asked.

He never turned around.

Andino's footsteps kept following behind.

"Kev and Darren Calabrese do the same shit every month. Today is the day the crews get together with the Capos, and everything gets worked out for the next couple of weeks. I figured since you kept letting my calls go to voicemail, I might as well come here."

"Maybe you should have taken that as a goddamn *hint*."

And left him the hell alone. John wasn't asking for a whole lot.

A little over a week after the men of his family cornered him—or that's how it felt—and John was still not over it. In fact, he felt worse about it than he had that morning.

They didn't trust him. Not to get shit done. Not to make the right choices. Nothing.

To put the icing on that cake, they had to try and dictate his fucking romantic life like it was any of their goddamn business. It wasn't. He wouldn't allow them to think it was, either. That shit was never going to be on the table for them to meddle in.

Ever.

"Are you going to slow down and talk to me?" Andino asked.

"My legs are still moving. A lot like your dumbass mouth. Take the hint."

"Come on, let me explain, John."

The warehouse where he had to meet up with the Calabrese brothers was all but twenty feet away. If he picked up his pace, he could be inside and working in a few minutes. Andino's little show would be over and done with.

John couldn't do that.

Andino's words hit a damn nerve.

Spinning on his heel, John took one huge step forward, and came toe-to-toe with Andino. His cousin had a good thirty pounds of muscle on him, but they stood damn near eye level with one another. It wouldn't be the first time the two of them went to blows over something.

He wasn't scared of Andino. Andino wasn't frightened of him.

It was a bad combination.

"Say that again," John urged, his tone dipping low.

"What, that you should let me fucking explain what happened?"

"Yeah, man. Go on, tell me how you sold out my personal business to our fathers and Dante like you had any business doing so in the first place. Tell me how you not only put Siena in my path by inviting her to a club, but then went behind my back and told them I was involved with her, too. That's fucking shady, Andino."

John hit his cousin in the chest with a closed fist. Not hard, but firm enough that it made his point loud and clear. "Fucking. Shady."

"Get your hand off my body before I break it."

"You could try."

Andino's jaw clenched, and his green eyes darkened with anger.

Good.

He should be angry. Just like John was.

"It doesn't feel really fucking great when your family does shitty things to you, huh?" John asked.

"I didn't do what you think I did, John!"

John pushed his fist against Andino's chest again. "Fuck you. Thanks for the lesson, man. I needed it."

"What—"

"This conversation is over, Andi."

With that, John turned around and headed in the direction of the warehouse's entrance. Andino should have left it alone, but like the stubborn shit he was, he came after John. His cousin grabbed the back of his jacket, and pulled.

"John, you're going to talk to me!"

John spun around once more, and didn't even think about his next actions. He shoved Andino hard enough to send his cousin stumbling back.

Andino righted himself, and glared at John. He made a move like he was going to come forward at John, but didn't in the end. The two of them were left standing with ridged postures waiting for the other one to make a move.

"That's what you want to do?" Andino asked.

"No, man," John said, "but I will if you don't fuck off. I warned you, so figure it out before you force my hand here."

"I just want to explain."

"Your actions told me more than enough, Andino."

"John, we're Marcellos. The only people we have to trust in this life is each other. So fuck off with your mood, and give me a chance to tell you how this really went down. Give me that respect—don't you at least owe me that after everything?"

They'd been friends since Andino was born. His cousin always had his back, no matter what. Andino saved John from himself more times than he could count.

This still left a bad taste in John's mouth.

"When you were selling me out to Dante about Siena, did you think to mention that chick you're fucking behind everybody's backs?" John asked.

Andino stiffened, and his gaze hardened. "Excuse me?"

"Haven—right? That's her name. You think I don't know about her?" John smirked and nodded, saying, "Yeah, I heard you were seeing somebody they didn't approve of given your new position and all. Unlike you, I didn't go digging in your business, or mention that you were still running around with her despite the fact you're putting on a good show for them."

"You don't know anything about that, or her, John."

"I know enough to make it hurt." John pointed a finger at his cousin. "When, or *if*, I am ready to speak to you, then I will do that. Not one fucking second before. Get that through your thick skull, Andino. I decide when to see you, not the other way around."

"All right," Andino said.

"Good."

"One other thing, though."

John had all he could do not to punch Andino right in the throat. "What now?"

"You're ignoring your therapist appointments. Why?"

All over, John felt like someone had dumped ice cold water on him. "I beg your goddamn pardon?"

"You heard what I said."

"How in the fuck do you even know that?"

Andino glanced away, and shrugged. "I got a friend in with your parole officer. You miss an appointment, and the therapist has to report it. You miss three, and the parole officer has to write you up on it. What, are you trying to get your parole revoked, so you can go back in? Is that what it is?"

Again, someone was checking on his business. Again, someone was trying to stick their fucking nose where it didn't belong regarding John.

Again, he was shown how little faith they had in him.

"You know you have to go to those appointments, and not just for parole, either," Andino said. "I'm only trying to look out for—"

"Look out for yourself, and keep me out of it. You make me tell you that again, Andino, and we're going to have another incident like we did years ago. Only this time, I'll fucking finish it for good."

John didn't wait for his cousin to reply. He turned fast, and headed for the warehouse. This time, Andino didn't follow behind.

Inside the large building, John found the Calabrese brothers were already waiting for him. None of the crews from either organization had arrived yet, but he expected that. They showed up early to figure out any last minute details in private.

Kev and Darren Calabrese both sat on a table side by side in the middle of the warehouse.

"You two got nothing to do, or what?" John asked.

Kev shoved off the table with a chuckle. "Waiting on you, man."

"Sure, sure."

Darren ticked his chin up at John, asking, "Was that Andino I saw out there?"

John hesitated, and wondered just how much the Calabrese brothers had seen of his conversation with Andino. "Maybe. What about it?"

"Curious," Darren said.

"Curiosity kills men," John replied.

He headed for the corner where a white van had been parked. Inside the van would be some of the shit that needed to be dispersed between the foot soldiers of the three men's crews. Maybe if he got his hands busy with work, he could focus on other shit.

"Is that a thing for you, or something?" Kev asked.

John climbed in the back of the van, and wanted nothing more than to just get this work done. He had energy to burn. He was sleeping erratically, and very little when he did actually close his eyes.

"Is what a thing?" John asked.

He tore open boxes, and pulled out wrapped bricks of drugs. Weed, cocaine, meth, and more. A lot of pharmaceuticals. All hidden and packed in paper hay.

"Them babysitting you," Kev said, leaning into the back of the van. "Sending someone to check in on your business, and making sure everything is on the up. What, you can't handle your own shit, or something?"

All of John's irritations and misgivings about his family and how they treated him were being reflected in Kev's statements. A man who didn't know John, the shit he dealt with on a daily basis because of his disorder, or how that made his family treat him differently.

Yet, they could see it.

Kev saw how John was the weak link to the Marcellos.

Or, that's how it felt.

"I handle my shit," John said.

"Yeah, but do they really let you?"

"Or do they just make it seem like they're letting you?" Darren asked, leaning in beside his brother.

John shot the two men a look, and hated how unease and distrust burrowed into his nerves even more. Not for these men—he didn't give a fuck about the

Calabrese idiots. No, for his own blood; for his own family.

The things they were doing made him unsteady. In his heart, and in his life. It made for shitty days, and bad moods.

It screwed up his mind.

It messed with his emotions.

It fucked him up.

"I handle myself just fine," John said.

He wanted to get Kev and Darren off the topic of him and his family.

"Yeah, I mean," Kev said, "that's obvious, John."

"Except not to your people, I guess," Darren added. "Do you get what I'm saying, Marcello?"

Did he?

That was the million-dollar question.

"Johnathan?"

John cursed under his breath at the sound of his mother calling out for him. Still, he kept his attention focused on his tasks. Things he wanted to get done—it kept piling up, but he just worked through it, regardless.

The cupboards were stacked high with everything inside of them. Bowls he had placed by size. Glass and silverware that he wanted to change from one cupboard to another. The food from the pantry that needed to be reorganized because why in the hell had there been boxes with cans? And on the same fucking *shelf*.

It drove him nuts.

Nonsense.

He'd already ran through his office upstairs, took a five-mile run that morning, and reorganized his collection of movies and music from alphabetical to most liked through the most disliked.

And it was only …

John shot a look at the clock.

Ten in the morning.

It probably helped that he had enough energy to burn that sleep wasn't even a bother at the moment. An hour felt like three, and two hours of sleep felt like a whole night's worth.

His thoughts were scattered and erratic. Something he hated because he preferred a calm mind to one full of chaos. Unless he was focusing his attention on doing something—cleaning, working out, or working—then he couldn't get his thoughts to chill.

Siena, too.

His thoughts calmed when he put his focus on her.

"John, what are you doing?"

He found his mother standing in the kitchen entryway. Jordyn Marcello looked over the mess John had made with a carefully guarded eye, and a relaxed posture. John knew that look from his mother—it meant she was concerned about him.

"What does it look like?" John asked, wiping down the inside of another cupboard. "Cleaning and fixing shit."

"Is this all you've done today?" his mother asked.

"No, but it's the last thing I'm doing in this house today."

Jordyn took a couple of steps into the kitchen, and continued her perusal of the items scattered everywhere. She didn't reach out to touch anything, which John appreciated. He didn't want to fucking bark at his mother, but he didn't want her bothering things, either.

"You don't have to work today?" Jordyn asked.

Her tone came out calm and smooth. He recognized that, too. His mother only used that tone when she was trying to get something out of him, or needed to relax him.

John's defensive walls shot up—he didn't know what his mother was pulling. "I work, Ma."

Jordyn gave him a smile. "I meant, you didn't have anywhere to be *today*?"

"Yeah, later."

John offered nothing else, and Jordyn didn't press for more. Instead, she stood there rubbing her hands together while her gaze drifted between him and the mess.

He didn't have to be anywhere until after lunch. He had some drop-offs to make for business—people needed their drugs to sell, after all.

John didn't trust anybody to handle substance. He had to be the one to pass it off, and that way, he knew nobody was stealing from him.

"It smelled very clean in the hallway," Jordyn noted.

"So?"

Was it a problem that cleaning helped him to focus?

That keeping busy was a *must*?

That moving let him fucking breathe?

Jordyn just stared at her son. "When did you get up this morning, John?"

"What?"

"Just curious. The sunrise was nice," she added with a little shrug. "I wondered if you might have seen it, too."

Nothing on his mother's face spoke to the fact she might be lying to him. Her soft smile felt like safety and his childhood. Her familiar presence was calming in some ways.

At the same time, John was wary.

He didn't know why. He couldn't put his finger on exactly what it was.

Still, he hesitated in giving his mother the truth. Being wary was enough to add to his already growing paranoia about why his mother was even there in the first place.

The very second John felt any kind of paranoia that was it for him. He didn't indulge any other questions or conversation from anybody.

Not even his own mother.

"Well?" Jordyn asked quietly. "Did you see the sunrise, my boy?"

"Yeah, I saw it," John said.

Because he had been up since one after a two-hour nap that felt like ten hours of solid sleep. How in the hell else would he find the time to rearrange his whole house and clean it from floor to ceiling?

"John—"

"I'm kind of busy, Ma."

He looked over in just enough time to see Jordyn frown, but also hide it. She took one deep breath, and then glanced out the large kitchen window that overlooked the front of the Queen's house.

"Your father mentioned something to me, and I just wanted to check in on you." Jordyn took a couple of steps closer to where John was working at the counter. "Do you know when was the last time you came to visit me?"

"Yeah, you worry, I know."

"Johnathan."

He heard her call for him, but he was just lost in other things. The erratic, spinning thoughts in his mind. The shit he had to get done. The way he felt like he had suddenly been turned on high-speed for no reason at all.

"They're only looking out for your best interests, John," his mother said.

She had said more, but he only caught the last part of her sentence. It was enough to send a hot burst of anger shooting through his bloodstream.

Mostly because he knew exactly what she was talking about without even asking. His father, uncles, and Andino.

Watching him like he couldn't be trusted.

Acting like he didn't know how to do his fucking job.

Like he couldn't handle his shit.

"Fuck them," John uttered.

He picked up Dante's calls because he couldn't ignore the boss. Their conversations consisted of Dante asking a question, and John answering with yes or no. It never went deeper than that, though his uncle tried.

Anyone else, though?

His father, Andino, or even his uncle, Gio?

John ignored all of them.

"Maybe if you actually sat down and heard them out," his mother tried to suggest.

"What I want to hear is them saying they're going to stay the fuck out of my business, and let me handle my own shit, Ma. Nothing else. Pass the message along if you think they actually give a damn."

Because he didn't think they cared.

His whole life had been this nonsense.

"John—"

The cell phone on the island rang out with a familiar tune. John had gotten to the point where he added specific ringtones to certain people. That way, he knew who was calling without even having to look at the phone.

Jordyn made a move to grab the call, but John spoke up first.

"Leave it, Ma," he said. "It's just Andino."

Still, his mother glanced at the phone, but she didn't actually touch it. "Looks like he's called you ten times this morning."

"Came over last night, too," John said, "and I showed him how he could leave just as fast as he came."

Andino's visit damn near ended in the two of them going to blows—again. Like Andino promised a couple of days earlier, he came to check in on John. He should have just stayed away a while longer, and gave John some damn space.

John was still pissed at his cousin for spilling his personal business like it was public fucking consumption. Andino kept trying to say that hadn't been the case. The fucking proof was right there in black and white.

What more needed to be said?

He needed one thing from his cousin—something he gave to Andino without question.

Loyalty.

Nothing more, nothing less.

Being like John was, with the way his life sometimes spiraled out of control, he needed just one fucking person on his side no matter what. Andino was supposed to be that person, but it turned out, he was just like everybody else.

Loyalty was not promised.

John didn't have time for that, either.

"Come on, now," Jordyn said, "Andino is your best friend, and you won't even listen to him?"

"There's nothing to listen to, Ma. Now if you don't mind—"

The phone chimed again, but this time, with a new ringtone. Instantly, John pushed away from the counter, spun around, and grabbed the device before his mother could even look at the screen. He picked up the call, and put his back to Jordyn.

"Hey," John said.

"Hey, you," Siena replied on the other end.

Just like that, his day was better.

Just like that, he had something else to focus on.

"So, I am getting off early today because I finished up the details for this file, and it is getting sent off in like … five minutes," Siena said.

"That so, babe?"

"Mmhmm."

"What's that mean for me?"

She worked too goddamn much. He sometimes wanted to hide her away.

Life was a bitch like that.

"It means," Siena drawled, "that if you come pick me up, we could go see that action movie you mentioned was showing this afternoon. I mean, if you want to."

Hell yeah, he wanted to.

John didn't even think about it. He knew he had work, and places to be, but whatever. Siena and her time was already scant, and he could get back to business another day.

All that shit would still be there.

"Where you at?" he asked.

Siena rattled off an address.

"I'll be there in forty, love."

"See you."

John hung up the phone, and spun around to see his mother was watching him with curious, but guarded eyes.

"Got a date?" she asked.

John smirked, and pointed at the entryway. "I'm headed out, Ma. So, you can look around or whatever, but I won't be here. I'm sure Dad and the rest of them might like an update on the Calabrese situation—or, the Calabrese woman, because fuck them, they can't even use her name. Let them know I'm still good with what I'm doing, including her."

Jordyn cleared her throat, and glanced away. John simply headed out of the kitchen, and didn't bother looking over his shoulder to say goodbye.

He had fuck all left to say.

John brushed stray snowflakes from his leather jacket, and glanced up just in time to see Siena strolling out of the restaurant. Her grin bloomed into a full-blown smile at the sight of him waiting for her. He couldn't stop his gaze from wandering over her—it was strange how every time he looked at her was like the first time.

He kept finding new things to admire.

The way her eyes darkened when she peeked at him. How her lips curved just before she kissed him. How her hips swayed when she walked.

The wool dress she wore did little to hide the curves of her body. The knee-high leather boots she had on covered her legs up to where the wool dress ended just above her knees. Today, she'd left her hair loose in soft waves, and she wore just enough makeup to color her cheeks and lips, but not much more.

John liked her anyway he could have her.

It didn't matter to him. The girl was damn gorgeous.

"Don't you look nice," she said, coming closer.

He pushed off the car with a grin, and reached for her. Catching her hand with his, he pulled her in close enough to rest his hand at her lower back, and drop a kiss to her smiling, pink lips.

"Shouldn't I tell you how good you look?" he murmured against her mouth.

Siena winked. "Sure, but you do look good."

"I'm not even in a suit today."

"Maybe that's why I think you look … different."

John cocked a brow, and pulled back a little from Siena. "Different?"

"I don't know …" She looked him over, and brushed her hand along the cut line of his jaw. "Something about you is different lately. You're … laughing more, and whatever else."

"That sounds normal to me."

Siena hummed. "I didn't say it was a bad thing. Just different."

"You think?"

"Yeah."

"And you're sure that's not a bad thing?"

"Never," she promised him. "Did you end up getting some sleep last night?"

"Very little. I'm fine—wide awake, *bella*."

He tickled a hand up her side, making her giggle.

"I can see that." Siena gave him a look, and said, "And playful, too. Where's that coming from?"

"I can't be playful with you?"

"You can. You usually aren't, though. Serious to a fault. A bit intense."

"Give it a little bit, and I'll go that direction, too."

Siena laughed. "No doubt. But, you're sure that everything is good with you?"

"Yeah. So, my mood is little up."

Siena lifted a brow. "Just your mood?"

John's throat tightened with her suggestion. "Give me some time today, and we'll see what else gets popping up."

"I didn't mean it like that," she said, her cheeks reddening.

"I bet you did."

"Mmhmm. What were you doing when I called, anyway? Work again?"

"No, cleaning."

Siena's smile faded a bit. "Your house is spotless, John."

He shrugged. "Gotta do something to keep my attention focused."

"You could focus on me."

John laughed, dark and husky. His hand skimmed up her back, and tangled in the ends of Siena's hair. He tugged gently, and leaned in to capture her mouth with another one of his kisses. A hotter, and harder kiss. One that left his lungs aching with the need to breathe, and made her pupils blow wide while she stared back at him.

He pulled away. But not because he wanted to.

"Trust me," he said, "the only thing I plan on doing for the rest of today is focusing entirely on you, Siena. Whatever you want to do, and wherever you want to go. That's what we're going to do, love."

Her smile softened and sweetened. "Yeah?"

"Yeah."

"You are a little different today. Something, anyway."

John chuckled. "I have no idea what you're talking about, *donna*."

She winked, but gestured between her eyes, and his. "Just know, I've got my eyes on you. Don't you try anything cute on me."

"Hey, as long as somebody's watching out for me. That's all that matters."

Lately, he trusted her way more than anybody else in his life. The funny thing was that he knew her for a fraction of the time he knew all of them.

Still, something told him … Something inside said she was gold.

Precious.

Pure.

Priceless.

That couldn't be ignored.

John didn't know what exactly to make of it, or what it would mean for him. He would figure out all of that later.

Now wasn't the time.

TWELVE

Siena grinned when John dragged her closer, and engulfed her in his embrace. He rested his chin on the top of her head, while she buried her face against his chest. The busy theater ceased to exist for the moment. The long line they had been waiting in for thirty minutes just to grab snacks for a movie that had started ten minutes ago no longer mattered.

John's lips skimmed the top of her head when he said, "We could always pick a different movie, love."

"You wanted to see this one, though."

"What's the damn point if you miss the first twenty minutes of it?"

"We've only missed the first ten," she pointed out.

John's grip tightened on her, and his fingertips tickled up her sides. "Yeah, but by the time we actually get in there, it'll be twenty."

Probably.

Siena didn't care.

"The first bit of a movie is always an info dump and backstory, anyway," she said, tilting her head back to peer up at him. "It's like we'll go in and know nothing, and have zero preconceived notions."

John chuckled under his breath. "That's quite a way to sell a movie. Buy expensive tickets for something we're just going to drop you in the middle of, but trust me, it'll be good."

Siena poked him gently in the chest with the tip of her finger. She felt his muscles tighten and jump under the touch. "Maybe you just don't have a big enough imagination, John."

"Maybe not."

He was only half in their conversation at that point. She knew it by the way his eyes drifted over to something behind her, as though he had to keep a close watch on it for whatever reason. He had been doing that a lot lately.

John never outright ignored her when it happened, but she could tell he wasn't entirely present, either. Siena didn't know what to make of it.

Or a few other things …

There was something different about his eyes lately—the hazel was darker, and his gaze seemed sharper. Like the way he didn't let anything that moved around them go unnoticed. He was always looking from one thing, to another. Watching one person, and then the next that passed them by.

"Hey," Siena whispered.

John's gaze was back on her in a blink. "Hey."

"I'm here, you know."

She said the words quietly, and offered them softly. She didn't want him to take it as anything other than a quest to bring him back to her for a second or two.

"I know where you are," John murmured. His words made her heart pick up speed by a few beats. "I always know where you are, Siena."

"Oh?"

"If I don't know where you are, it's like some kind of itch under my skin that I can't scratch."

Siena's brow furrowed. "That sounds unpleasant."

John shrugged. "So be it."

She heard what he didn't say.

He didn't mind it. Maybe a part of him preferred it.

"Because it's me?" she asked.

John's slow smile curved those lips of his in the sexiest way. "Yeah, *donna,* because it's you."

"So, even when I tell you I'm here …"

"I'm already there," he said, winking.

"Hard to tell sometimes with the way your attention flips all over the place."

John lifted a hand and tapped a single finger to his temple. "No matter what, there's one part of this that will be—" He twirled that same finger over her head. "—always focused on that. Even if it seems like I'm not."

The heavy warmth that spread through Siena's veins at John's words was both comforting, and terrifying. A lot of things were like that with him—he barely had to try, and it felt like he was drawing her in, and warning her at the same time.

Maybe that should have been a sign.

She still didn't care.

Wordlessly, John dropped a kiss to the very tip of her nose, and then another one to her mouth. She felt his hands splay wide to her sides, and squeeze gently. All over again, the busy movie theater ceased to exist.

He was looking at her.

He was touching her.

Nothing else mattered.

Of course, as the saying went, nothing gold could stay.

John's phone rang not a second later, making his attention on Siena break as he pulled the device out of his pocket. He checked the screen, and then offered her a shrug.

"Have to take it, *bella,*" he said. "You good for a minute?"

"Sure. What do you want me to get you?"

John scoffed as he looked over the long line. "You'll still be waiting by the time I get back."

Probably.

He gave her a quick kiss, and then put the phone to his ear as he stepped out of the line. She kept an eye on him until his back disappeared around corner a few steps away.

Mostly, Siena tried not to worry about John as much as she could. It was made difficult by the fact she noticed the changes he refused to acknowledge when she asked about them.

Like his attention.

His lack of sleep.

His ups, and his downs—moments that came, literally, in a moment. Then, gone in the next.

Yet, those things were offset by the fact he was also highly productive. Upbeat, and constantly on some kind of move. He never stopped doing something.

Siena didn't know what to think. She worried that asking the wrong questions—ones that zeroed in on the medications she had found, and the disorder she suspected he lived with—might push him away.

No part of her wanted to allow that.

Except she knew ... the longer she kept what she had stumbled upon hidden from John, the more likely it was that he would feel betrayed or something worse.

She didn't want that, either.

"The line is moving."

Siena came out of her thoughts with a shake of her head to see that, yes, the line was moving. She gave the blond-haired, green-eyed guy a smile, and thanks. He winked back, which made his group of friends grin.

They all looked like they had walked out of a frat house.

No thanks.

Siena turned her back to them, and looked up at the signs overhead advertising junk food, and drinks. The guy's voice in her ear made her realize how close he had come when she turned around. Just a little bit too late.

"They make this crazy mix of popcorn, chocolate chips, and small marshmallows. They drizzle salted caramel and milk chocolate all over it. It's awesome. You want to try it?"

Siena turned slightly to give the guy a look, and make him back off. Thankfully, he did take a step back. He was probably harmless, but she also wasn't interested in finding out.

"No, thanks."

The guy shrugged. "Shame. You looked kind of lonely standing there all by yourself."

Siena didn't know if the guy and his group of friends had been standing behind her and John minutes ago, so she took him at his word. "I'm fine, really."

"If you're sure ...?"

"She's sure."

Johnathan's rough reply coming from her right made Siena stiffen. She couldn't remember a time when she had ever heard him sound like that.

Angry and cold.

Seemed he had come back from his phone call without her even noticing. She turned to face him, and slipped a hand in with his. Instantly, he pulled her in close, and rested one of his arms around the back of her neck.

The comfort came back.

Just like that.

"Sorry," the guy said.

John didn't even reply. He only grunted unintelligibly back.

"You good?" he asked her quietly.

His words murmured into her hair.

"I am now."

"Good, love."

John moved them subtly so that her back was facing the group of guys, while at the same time, he could watch them. Never once did his arm release her from the tight hold around the back of her neck and shoulders. Siena didn't even mind. She tipped her head back to stare up at him. The sharp line of his jaw showed a tic, and his gaze wasn't on her.

"Everything good—with the call, I mean?"

John didn't look down. "Yeah, babe. It's good."

"Fucking shame, man. Lucked out on that ass. Almost had it."

The ruckus of laughter from the group of frat boys, not to mention the one guy's words, had John stiffening.

"I hope you're not fucking talking about this girl," he said over her head.

Siena's heart leaped into her throat. She pressed her hands into his hard stomach to try and get his attention on her, and not on those fools. "Hey, it's fine, John."

Nope.

He didn't even look away from them at all.

"And what if I was?" the guy from earlier asked. "Chill, man, she's with you."

"Say something about her again, and see what I'll do."

"John," Siena murmured.

He wasn't hearing her at all. His blazing gaze was locked on a group of idiots, and yet, his hold on her hadn't loosened a bit.

"She isn't worth it, anyway," the guy said with a laugh.

It kind of sounded like he meant it to be dismissive. A way to back away from John's threats, and yet still keep some kind of pride with his friends.

Siena knew it was a mistake before he even finished talking.

She felt it in John's body.

Saw it in his eyes.

Heard it in the clench of his teeth.

"Don't," she whispered.

Siena barely got the chance to blink, and she was on the other side of John. She spun around in just enough time to see his fist crash into the face of the guy who had been talking to her. One single punch, and the man was down.

One of his friends moved forward.

John hit him, too.

Somebody's face was bleeding.

Somebody else wasn't moving.

Shit.

She was pretty sure John wasn't supposed to be getting in trouble while on parole. And yet, he didn't seem to think about that at all as his fists rained down, and another guy jumped into the mix.

It was like his judgement was gone, right alongside his inhibitions. Did he even realize that getting caught up in an assault charge would probably revoke his probation? Did he *think* about that at all?

Siena didn't know.

"John!"

He didn't hear her the first time, so she moved in to physically put her hands on him, and see if that would help. She grabbed the back of his jacket, and swore she could feel the way his muscles coiled tighter.

"John, that's enough!"

He spun around fast, and damn near knocked Siena off her feet. His gaze landed on hers—wild and pissed—but he relaxed. Not a lot, but just enough to take a fucking look around.

At the security coming closer.

At the girl behind the counter on the phone.

At the cameras up above.

"Shit," he hissed, "we have to get out of here."

Yeah, she figured.

"Siena," John murmured from behind her.

She ignored him as she unlocked the door to her apartment. Sure, she wanted to talk. Oh, she had *a lot* of things to say to him.

Just not right now.

"I'm sorry, Siena."

Finally, the goddamn door unlocked, and she pushed it wide open. Siena stepped into her place, and threw her bag aside. She couldn't get her coat off fast enough, but once she did it too was tossed aside.

Turning around, she found John was still waiting outside in the hallway.

"What are you *doing*?" she asked.

"I'm not sure."

"You're not sure?"

Her tone came out as a harsh hiss. John winced a bit, but still he didn't move an inch.

"I'm not sure if you want me to come in," he said.

Siena shook her head. "Well, I sure as fuck don't want you standing out there. I don't think my neighbors care to hear us talk, John."

"All right."

Taking careful steps, he came into her place. Yet, he didn't remove his shoes, jacket, and he didn't move beyond the entryway once the door was closed behind him. She wasn't sure if that was because he meant to leave, or perhaps he thought she was going to make him go.

Honestly, she didn't know what she wanted to do.

"They were just idiots making stupid comments," she said.

"Maybe," he replied.

He didn't sound like he believed it.

"What would happen if tomorrow someone knocked on your door because one of them decided to press charges against you, John?"

He stuffed his hands deep in his pockets, and glanced beyond her. "I suppose—"

"It would be a violation of your probation. I don't even need you to tell me the details of your probation to know that! Why would you do something like that?"

"A person can't let shit like that slide, Siena."

"Yes, you *can*!"

"Fine, then I can't let it slide."

Siena let out a harsh sigh, because at that point, she didn't know what else to do. His responses to hers were so flippant. Words he tossed out with an indifferent tone, as though it didn't make a difference to what had happened at all.

"You have to use a bit of judgement, John," she told him.

John's laugh came out dark and bitter. "Right, okay. I should let some fucking idiot come up on my girl, and then when he insults her, I should just use judgement to decide whether or not he needs his face fucking broken in. All right, sure."

For a long while, Siena simply gaped at John like a fool who suddenly forgot how to speak. Mostly, because she didn't know what in the hell to say to him.

John shrugged. "I get it, Siena, I crossed a line."

"No, I just …"

She couldn't figure out what she needed to say to make him understand. The words stuck to her throat like tar.

John came closer, and tipped his hands over like he was offering them to her. It took her all of a breath to reach back. Palms pressed tightly together, and fingers woven, he tugged her to his chest. He pressed his mouth against the top of her head, and held her tight. Neither one of them spoke, but she didn't have much to say, anyway.

Just like that, her anxiety simmered down to low, and she tried to let go of the rest. Because this—with him—was better.

"Maybe it scared me a little," she whispered.

John used a single hand to brush a few stray strands of her hair out of her face when she tilted her head back to look at him. "I'm sorry for that."

Siena frowned. "But not for the rest?"

"Shit like that can't slide, babe."

"It has to when it means worse things for you."

John's lips curved into a semi-sneer. "I'm not really concerned about shit happening to me, Siena."

"Well, what about me, then? Aren't you worried about what it does to me, or how I would feel if you were taken away?"

He hesitated, and his grip on her tightened. She didn't need him to reply, not when she felt it in the way he stiffened all over. Still, he gave her the *right* answer. In a way.

"I hadn't considered it," John said, "or thought about it like that."

It was something. She only needed something to make sense of the rest. Something worth it, anyway.

John was worth it.

"Think about it *now*," she urged.

John dropped a soft kiss to her forehead. "Yeah, I get it."

"Okay."

"I'm sorry."

"I know, John."

He cleared his throat, and asked, "Do you, uh, want me to go? I ruined the movie, and all."

"No, I want you to stay."

Amusement lit up his gaze. "That so?"

"Yeah. Besides, we can find something to watch here. And you can make me popcorn. I may even have chocolate for you to drizzle on it."

"I guess that sounded good to you, huh?"

"You guessed right. So, is that a deal, or what?"

"Deal," John said with a chuckle.

It was only later, once the sky had darkened, and they were halfway through a movie that both of them had already seen a few times over that Siena noticed something …

John was still keeping his distance. He sat across the couch from her, even though he had stretched his arm across the back, and played with the strands of her hair. He kept his gaze glued on a movie he clearly wasn't that interested in. His responses to things she asked or said were quiet, and short.

Like he was pulling away, maybe.

Is that what he does to others, too? She wondered, *is that how he protects himself … or them?*

Siena didn't like that at all.

"Hey," she said.

John looked over at her. "Hmm?"

She moved fast, then. Crossing the space between them, and climbing into his lap. She grabbed his face, and dipped down for a kiss as his hands landed to her waist and grabbed tight.

"You're too far away," she whispered against his lips. "I don't like that."

John's nose skimmed hers when he replied, "Sometimes, that's just easier."

"Don't pull away, John."

Something unknown warred in his eyes. She was seeing that from him more and more lately, and sometimes, she could hear it in his voice. She didn't know what it was, or how to fix it.

Then again, maybe it wasn't something that could be fixed. Or rather, it was something that didn't need to be fixed.

It was just another part of him.

"Siena—"

"Don't," she interjected. "It's okay, John."

"Is it?"

"It is. I told you it was. I'll never say something if I don't mean it."

His lips curved into one of her favorite grins. "Yeah, I got that. I'm never going to be able to let something like that go, though. Somebody insulting you, or fucking with you. I can't—they're lucky a beating is all they got from me. I can't change that, love."

"You could be more careful."

It was the best she had.

John just laughed. "Yeah, something like that."

She could still hear a lilt in his tone that suggested he still felt like he had to put up a wall between them. Keep the distance a bit.

Siena couldn't have that.

Not now.

Her next kiss came down hard on his lips. Demanding and wanting from him, and taking more when his lips parted to let her in. The squeeze of his hands against her side only urged her on. Like a shot of heat and lust straight to her veins, she only wanted more.

Always more.

She knew then that she had him caught—his focus and attention was all on her. His needs would tangle with hers, and lead them down a better path.

It took no time at all for their clothes to be removed, and discarded. His fingertips drifted over her cheeks, and down her throat while she climbed back into his lap. The foil packet he'd pulled from his pants before taking them off was passed over, and she tore it open.

John's mouth traveled a hot pathway under her chin, and down her throat. Her fingers shook while she slid cool, slick latex down his hardened length. He lifted her easily by grabbing onto her hips. She had his cock heavy in her hand, and hard between her thighs in the next breath.

Nothing was better than that first thrust. The way he filled her full, and took her completely. It was addictive—how he stretched her, and the way she soaked him.

Every single time.

It was always the same.

It was still so different.

Filled full of him, and feeling the way her sex clenched tighter as his hips flexed upward, Siena let out a happy little sigh.

"Love that," she whispered.

John's hand left her hip, so he could ghost his fingertips over her trembling lips. "What do you need, love?"

"*You.*"

His grin colored with sin.

His gaze only reflected her.

John pinched Siena's chin between his forefinger and thumb to draw her closer. Their lips grazed while he pressed his forehead to hers. Her hair made a curtain around them. It blocked out the rest of the world, like it didn't even exist in the first fucking place.

Just them.

Right there.

In that moment.

Together.

She only rode him when he asked for it, and came down harder on his cock when he pulled her into him. Every stroke of his length inside her brought her a little bit closer to the edge. It made the high already filling her mind that much better.

"Who's my sweet girl, huh?" John asked in a murmur. "You're all mine, aren't you?"

His husky, rough words slipped over her skin.

Like a silken promise with sharp edges.

It wouldn't hurt, though.

She knew that.

Pleasure snaked through her body, and assured bliss was soon to come. Every drag of her fingernails over John's broad shoulders only made his muscles twitch against her touch. The way her name rolled off his lips in a groan was beautiful.

"Are you mine?" he asked again.

"All yours, John."

At least, until he didn't want her to be.

And even then, she thought …

She would still be his.

Siena rubbed at her sleepy eyes with the back of her hand. She was unsure if the sight in front of her was real, or she was still stuck in a dream.

She blinked.

Nope.

John was still there, doing exactly what she thought he was doing. For another minute, Siena said nothing, and simply watched John as he placed books back on the shelf. One by one, with careful hands, he arranged each book and pulled the spines out to the edge of the shelf.

"John?"

"Hmm?"

He didn't even sound surprised that she was awake, and watching him. He didn't turn around to see her watching him from the hallway, either.

"What are you doing with my books?"

"Fixing them," he said.

Siena tipped her head to the side, and squinted. "Why?"

"Because they were a mess."

"But they're my books, John."

He shrugged. "Figured it gave me something to do."

"And that was what, exactly?"

John glanced at her over his shoulder, and then gestured to different shelves as he spoke. "I organized them by author—I take it the more you have by the same author, the more you like them."

Siena nodded. "I mean, yeah."

"So, your favorites are at the top, in alphabetical order." John gestured at the shelves down below. "And the rest are organized in alphabetical order."

"You know readers discover new authors who are favorites, but they only have one or two books, right?"

John gave her a look, and pointed at the third shelf. "Any books that seemed like you had thumbed through them a lot, or the spines seemed worn from being cracked open a few times, are here."

She didn't have any rhyme or reason to her bookshelves, and she wasn't really overly particular about what to do with them. It wasn't that it bothered her for John to reorganize something in her place.

Not at all.

It was something else entirely.

"When did you get up, John?"

"Two, or something. I took a run, too."

She looked down the hallway where a small window overlooked the cold, white outside. "Outside?"

"Where else?"

"It's almost the end of January."

And it was *cold*.

"I needed a run."

He said it so flippantly. His attention was already back on the books.

"And you're not tired at all?" she pressed.

"Nope."

He hadn't looked tired, either.

She remembered things about bipolar disorder that she had found on the web. Sure, she didn't think that it should be taken as gospel, but it was still concerning.

"Do you have to run over to your place this morning, or anything?" she asked.

John spun around to give her a smile. "Nope. I'm all yours today."

"Not for anything, John?"

Like his meds.

John gave her an odd look. "No."

"You didn't want to sleep, or what?"

"I had things on my mind."

"Like what?"

Slowly, John turned to face her. "Just ... some things."

Siena didn't want to push, or pry. She didn't want to do or say something that might offend him, or worse, make him throw up those walls of his. "You can tell me or talk to me about anything, John. You know that, right?"

"I figured that last night, yeah."

"Is there something you want to talk about?"

She hugged the blanket she had brought from the bed closer around her shoulders. It smelled like him, and her. It grounded her for whatever he might say next. She needed that.

John's easy smile drifted away, and so did his gaze. "There's something, yeah. I didn't know when or how to bring it up. I kind of have to, though. And if you want to tell me to go after, then I get it. Don't feel like—"

Siena held up a hand. "Can I just ... preface this with something?"

She had to be honest.

Especially if he was.

"All right," John murmured. "What?"

"Let me say first that it was accidental, and I wasn't snooping. I don't do that kind of thing to people because I don't want them doing it to me. I stumbled on it by accident, and different things that I had heard made me look up some things."

John's jaw tightened. "Heard about me?"

"People say things, and sometimes I overhear them. That's not what's important, though."

"Might be."

127

"Not right now, John."

His posture had stiffened, and he turned slightly like he wanted to put a barrier there between them.

"I was looking for something to put away the food I made at your place, and I found meds above the fridge. I didn't touch them, and I didn't go through them. I saw what a couple of them were, but that was it."

"Wait, you—"

"No," Siena said fast. "I didn't go through anything. I wasn't looking through your shit, or prying. I found them on accident."

"No, I meant, wait and go back. So, you found my meds and didn't think to mention it to me?"

"They're yours, John."

He blinked. "What?"

"The medication—whatever it's for. That's all your business, not mine. It's personal, okay. So, I figured if you wanted to tell me, or if you needed to then you would. It wasn't my place to get in your business, and demand answers."

John cleared his throat, but he still wouldn't meet her gaze. "And you, uh, said you looked some shit up?"

"It doesn't matter. This is about you, and if you want to tell me something you think I should know, then go ahead and do that. Do it because *you* want to do it, and because you feel like I should know. Don't do it because you feel like you owe me something. Not for what I found, or what you think I might know, or—"

"I was diagnosed with Bipolar I when I was seventeen."

Siena thought hearing him say those words might make her suspicions all too real, but if anything, she was just … proud of him.

"Do you tell people that often?"

John shook his head. "No."

"Why not?"

"Because of the way people look at me after—you can see it in their eyes. *Crazy*. You know, my family doesn't even use that word to me. Crazy, I mean. It's been pretty much banned in the context of saying it to me like it's a slur, or whatever."

"Yeah, I get that. I mean, before someone would have said bipolar and I would have thought, *high and low*. You know what I mean? Up and down constantly. I didn't really know much about it at all."

"Rapid cycling," John said.

Siena's brow dipped. "Pardon?"

"When someone goes from high emotions to low emotions like it's a roller coaster on a regular basis, it's called rapid cycling. It's actually more common in women than men. I mean, I have high and low moments, but I don't rapid cycle, and I fall more in spells of one or the other."

"Like a long bout of being high."

"Or a long bout of being low," he said, nodding. "Yeah, like that. My first episode came when I was thirteen. I never went into full blown mania back then, but the shit I did was sketchy. I was all over the place, and it was … a bad time for my family."

"Probably would be. You would have been, what, just going into puberty?"

"Just after, yeah," he confirmed quietly. "I went back and forth from what they call a hypomania to depression, and then back again. A cycle, but for a long spell with each, and not a quick up and down. Nobody thought something was wrong up in here."

He pointed to his head, and shrugged, adding, "Everybody just thought I was difficult, and a little too wild for my own good. It always felt like I was bulletproof. Nothing was ever going to hurt me, and I could do anything I wanted. And then it would change—I would be shattered glass. Broken with sharp edges, and cutting everyone who came too close."

"That's what it feels like?"

John laughed darkly, but sobered quickly. "No, only sometimes. Bipolar feels like … everything all at once. It doesn't give me time to process one thing before something else decides to wreck me. Mania is all of that, but times ten or more."

"I'm sure that word scares people, right?"

"Mania?"

She nodded.

John scratched at the underside of his jaw. "It's a good word for it, though. Manic—because that's what it's like. You just go, and go. The more you do, the better you feel. Sometimes my mania manifested physically. Things like fighting or sex. Sometimes it focuses on the shit around me. People I don't trust, or my work. It's a lot. It's everything. It's—"

"I get it," she interjected softly.

He frowned. "Then when the mania breaks, the cycle hits its peak before it goes way low."

"Depression?"

"Yeah." John sighed, and dragged a hand through his hair. "But I never went into full blown mania until I was seventeen. I disappeared for three weeks, and showed up in an ER. I had no idea how I got there, and I had so many different drugs in my system that I could have been a pharmacy. It was bad."

"But that's when you finally got diagnosed?"

"Around then, yeah. I found out after that there was someone else in my family history with the same disorder, so it showed a genetic link, too."

"Who was that?"

"She would have been my biological grandmother—my father's real mother. I'm named after my dad's father, actually. Johnathan Grovatti. Lina was my father's real mother. She was Johnathan's mistress, though, so a lot of stuff about her was destroyed after she was killed. It took some digging by my father to find the information on her."

"I'm sorry."

John smiled. "Don't be. I was in the height of mania when I went at my cousin three years ago—the whole shit that got me put away."

Siena's brow furrowed. "But if you were sick, then—"

"People can't know," John interrupted firmly. "Not in this life. Something like bipolar just makes me a fucking target, or worse, a stain on my family. So, I chose to go to prison instead of getting my disorder put on public record for anybody to know about."

Why wouldn't he look at her while he talked?

129

It bothered Siena in a way she couldn't explain.

"John."

He still kept staring at anything but her.

"John, look at me," Siena pressed.

He did.

She found pain there.

And fear.

"I don't want you to leave," she said.

John swallowed hard. "I would understand if—"

"I don't *ever* want you to leave. Not because of this. Okay?"

He didn't answer.

She didn't back down.

"Okay, John?"

Finally, he said, "Yeah, okay."

Siena moved closer until she could reach out and touch him. First, it was just her fingertips gliding up his taut arm. His muscles felt like fucking rocks under her touch. Then, she went higher to stroke the cut line of his jaw. Those hazel eyes of his never left her face, but his wariness remained.

"It's not an all the time thing," he said. "I've gone years without an episode as long as I keep up on my meds, and everything else. Don't think that—"

"You owe me *nothing*," she said, wanting to stop him from going further if he didn't want to. "Not anything, John. Not an explanation, nothing."

"It's a lot to take in, though. I know that."

"No, it's *you*. It's just another part of who you are, and nothing else. Don't be ashamed, John. Not with me."

John's gaze drifted over her face, and he gave her a little smile. "You're something else, Siena Calabrese."

"I'm pretty boring, actually."

"That's impossible. You can't be boring when you're amazing."

"Keep sweet talking me, John."

His grin deepened. "So, that's it, then? I thought this conversation would end far differently than it did."

A part of her heart broke for him.

How many people stigmatized something he had no control over? How many had hurt him with ignorant words, and ignorant minds?

She would not be one of them.

Ever.

"Thank you for trusting me," Siena said.

John stroked his thumb over her cheekbone. "You might be the only person I do trust right now, *donna*."

"I promise you always can."

"I might need a reminder. Just a warning."

Siena nodded. "Okay."

THIRTEEN

The blonde, tattooed woman to open the front door of Andino's brownstone was not who John expected to see. Tall and willowy, her smile came off soft and welcoming. John had only met the woman in passing a handful of times. None of them had been very deep meetings, and Andino didn't actively welcome his family around the girl.

"Johnathan, right?" she asked.

John could see why this woman would have caught his cousin's attention. She had a pretty face, and by all accounts the first impression was a unique one. She could certainly draw attention to herself. It was whether or not that attention was good that could be the problem for Andino, given his ... status in *la famiglia*.

John nodded. "It is. And you're Haven."

"I am." The blue-eyed woman glanced at the woman standing beside John. "He didn't say you were going to bring someone with you."

Siena stayed close to John's side even when Haven stuck out a hand to shake. She did offer her own hand, though. "Nice to meet you. I'm Siena. You're Andino's wife?"

John stiffened.

Haven gave a bitter laugh, and waved a hand. "No, see, I'm not appropriate enough to be a wife, Siena. I'm just ... something."

"Ouch," Siena murmured.

Still, she didn't bat an eye.

Haven smirked. "It's a work in progress."

Okay.

That was enough of that.

"Come in," Haven said, stepping back from the door and widening it further. "John, Andino is upstairs in his office."

"I'll be okay down here," Siena told him.

John hadn't even thought to leave her downstairs. "You sure, love?"

Siena shrugged, and smiled. "Yeah, I'm sure."

He dropped a quick kiss to her mouth, and left her standing in the hallway with Haven. Upstairs, he found Andino's office door open.

John stepped up to the doorway, and rapped on the doorjamb with two knuckles. Andino didn't even look up from his paperwork.

"You finally came around to see me, huh?" Andino asked.

"You finally decided to pull the underboss card and make me come see you," John replied dryly.

Andino glanced up with an indifferent gaze, and a posture that screamed *what's it to you?* His cousin had always been a complex person. Much like John, but without the mental illness to add to his different issues.

"Had you given me a choice, I still would have come over eventually," John said.

He was trying to forgive Andino, after all. Actually talking to his cousin would factor in there at some point.

"When would that have been?" Andino asked.

"Eventually."

"I sped it up, John. One of the perks of being the family underboss—nobody gets to ignore my ass."

John chuckled. "Yeah, lucky you."

Andino's amusement faded fast. "Well, the luck is debatable. Sit, John."

"I would rather stand."

"Why, are you going to fuck off if I say something you don't like?"

John tried to let that statement brush off his shoulders, but it was damn hard. "I see Haven is downstairs. Siena is chatting with her."

Andino's gaze narrowed. "You brought her here?"

"I was with her when you called. I promised to spend the day with her since all I do is work my fucking ass off. I owe her time every once and a while, don't I?"

"Sure, John, but you know how they feel about—"

"I imagine, the same way *they* feel about Haven, no?"

Andino tensed, and his broad shoulders stiffened. "Point taken."

"Yet, she's here, I noticed."

"You sound like a broken record."

"Give me something to give a shit about, cousin. It's been weeks, and all I've wanted to do is break your face. So yeah, give me something right now."

Andino glanced up, and cleared his throat. "Maybe I'm taking a page out of your playbook."

"Which is what?"

"Doing what I want."

John laughed. "That's not going to be an easy road."

Andino smirked. "No, definitely not. I didn't want to pull the underboss card to get you here, John. Honestly. I know you think I'm a fucking jackass right now, but I was fine with letting you come to me when you were ready."

"That so?"

"You felt like I crossed a line, and I get that."

John bristled. "You *did* cross a fucking line, man."

"They already had somebody watching you, John. I was approached because Dante had a guy trailing you, and he thought I might know something."

Instantly, John found the closest chair, and sat his ass down. He felt like that was going to be needed for whatever Andino might tell him next.

Andino leaned back in his chair, and steepled his fingers. "So yeah, Dante and your father came to me asking about the Calabrese, and whatever else. I thought if I tried to explain that Siena was really just a random encounter you had then they would leave it alone."

Anger simmered in John's gut.

Hot, heavy, and poisoned.

Somehow, he hid it.

"You didn't think to give me a fucking heads up that they were trailing me like that?" John asked. "And why the fuck can't they just *trust me*?"

Andino shook his head. "I get the intentions were good, or that's how Dante meant for it to be, but I warned him then that he was crossing a line with you. That kind of shit messes with your head."

John looked away.

Fuck yeah, it messed with him.

"I should have let you know, John," Andino said. "I'm sorry that I didn't."

John glanced back at his cousin. "They're never going to feel like I can handle this business without somebody babysitting my every move. It puts me on edge like nothing else. I fucking hate it, Andi."

"It won't be like that forever, John."

"Really?" John scoffed. "I've gone years without a major episode. I do everything they want me to do, and they still pulled this kind of shit on me."

Andino nodded. "I know, but it won't be forever, John. Trust me on that. I'll fucking make sure of it, man."

Now, he kind of felt bad for threatening his cousin.

Andino was good like that, though.

He knew John.

"Anyway," Andino said, hitting the desk with his palms, "the reason I had to pull the underboss card is because now, I am the one babysitting you."

Instantly, John's defenses were back in a blink. "Excuse me?"

"The boss wants me to keep an eye on you. Seems you're dodging your father, the boss, and even my dad."

"You know what they did," John said.

Andino waved a hand. "Doesn't matter, John."

"It does fucking matter."

"How's work?"

Just like that, Andino changed the subject.

John's irritation settled for the moment. "Work is work. I've got my crew handled. Money is coming in just fine. All the Calabrese work is going fine, as it should."

"Good," Andino said.

Confusion fluttered through John, and he eyed his cousin curiously. "That's it? *Good.*"

"Yeah, why?"

"You're not going to push and question me on every fucking aspect of everything I do?"

"Nope," Andino said. "If you say shit is on the up and up with you, then that's what it is, John."

He didn't know how to take that statement. No one ever simply took John at his word, and left it.

Then again, this *was* Andino.

His best friend.

Something clicked in John's head. "I see what you did there."

Andino smiled. "Did you?"

"I'm bipolar, but not crazy or stupid."

"I would never call you those things, anyway."

"I know."

"And I'm not going to treat you like the rest of the men in this family do a lot of the time," Andino said, giving his cousin a look. "I just want to make sure you're handling whatever you need to handle. Probation, work, and therapy. Anything else—who you're fucking, or the rest of that—is none of my goddamn business."

John cleared his throat. "You sure on that?"

Andino pointed to the ceiling, but kept his gaze on John. "As sure as the sky is blue, man."

"I still don't like it."

"Give them something, and they'll back off."

"But not about her," John countered. "Not on Siena, Andi. They won't back off a bit."

"You're really messed up on this woman, huh?"

John smirked. "How's that Haven thing working out for you?"

Andino returned his grin. "Yeah, I get it, John."

"But yeah," he added quieter, "I am, Andi."

"I guess nothing else matters, then."

No.

Not at all.

This entire meeting had not gone the way John expected it to at all. It wasn't a bad thing, but he had come here prepared for a war with Andino.

His cousin made peace.

Funny how that worked.

"You missed two appointments, and rescheduled three others," Amelia said.

John kept checking his watch because the goddamn time was not passing fast enough for him. "Busy, that's all."

The therapist tapped the tip of her pen against the pad of paper. It drew John's attention back to her for the moment. "Part of your probation involves therapy, Johnathan. Once a week, or more if I say it's needed."

"My probation says I need to attend therapy," he countered, "not that it needs to be with *you*."

And he wasn't entirely sure how he felt about his current therapist. She had a habit of fucking with his meds—leading him to screw with his own meds to counteract the way it messed with him physically and emotionally.

He felt like her test subject a lot of the time, and that didn't make for a good patient and doctor relationship. Regardless of how often he spoke up to say the new med regime she wanted to try wasn't working, or whatever else was the case, she consistently pushed him to continue on with it.

Like it would change.

Like the fog would lift.

Like it was *helping.*

None of it helped.

Ever.

He had done just fine using only Lithium and therapy while in prison, and then adding an antidepressant or antianxiety with a mood stabilizer when he needed it. His doctor, while in lockup, had allowed John to only use the medications needed to treat him at whatever point in his cycle he was currently at.

It worked.

He liked it that way.

Too many medications made him feel like he was constantly in a bubble. It wore him down, and made him tired. Too many medications mixed together reacted badly with his brain chemistry, and he knew it.

This bitch thought he needed all of them at once, or a change of dose when one didn't work to her satisfaction. He wasn't sure if she thought that he didn't understand his disorder, or if she believed she had a better handle on it. Whatever it was, John didn't like the way she handled his medication, therapy, or otherwise.

"Have you found someone else for your weekly therapy?" Amelia asked. "I would be more than happy to send your file over."

John kept his expression blank. He only needed to get through this goddamn appointment to satisfy his probation office, after all. Nothing more.

"Not yet," he settled on saying.

But he would look.

Soon.

"You seem distracted," she said quietly.

John's gaze darted between her, and the watch on his wrist. "Things to do today, that's all."

"Like what?"

"Work."

"Anything else?"

"People to see."

Siena.

His mother.

"You're awfully jittery, too. Bouncing your knee. That's new." The two of them stared at one another until the therapist moved on with, "What are your plans after you leave here today?"

John gave the woman a look, curious at where she was trying to go with this line of questioning. Usually, she tried to focus on how the meds were working for him—or not, typically—and his history, or his family.

"I have to be on one side of New York this morning, and on the other side tonight," John replied.

"Is that an everyday thing for you lately?"

John shrugged. "Can be. More often than not, it is."

"You must be exhausted."

"Not really."

"You're getting enough sleep, then?" Amelia asked.

"Enough."

"Like a few hours?"

"A couple," John said.

The therapist scratched something down on her pad with the pen, and said, "And you are keeping up with your medications, right?"

John lied, then. "Every single day."

He halved her dose of Lithium, and when that hadn't worked to stop the fog in his head, he got rid of the other three medications she put him on. She wouldn't agree to stop prescribing the anxiety and depression meds when he wasn't even battling those to begin with.

Sure, he made it look like he was taking the pills, but he didn't. He filled the prescriptions every month like he was supposed to. He didn't actually take them, though.

"*All* of them?" she pressed. "Did the fog you mention lift?"

John shrugged. "Not particularly."

He didn't offer more. Not even when Amelia stared at him like she was waiting for him to continue explaining.

"Do you find the meds helped with the anxiety and depression that took you up and down from day to day?"

Yes.

Mixed with two mood stabilizers and an anticonvulsant, they also made him feel like he couldn't think a coherent thought on a bad day.

"They did their job," he said instead.

"Are you getting a lot done?" the therapist asked after a moment. "Work wise, and whatever else."

"Always," John returned.

She continued on that line of questioning for whatever reason. She focused in on the things he did daily, and how he was spending his time. She asked him different questions about his family, and how they seemed lately. Not that he had much to tell her for that side of things.

John knew she was pressing for something—maybe trying to gage something with him—but he couldn't put his finger on it.

Whatever.

He let her dig.

Soon enough, his time was up.

"Do not reschedule your appointment for next week, Johnathan," his therapist said from behind him as he left her office. "Or I will report you for a third time to your parole officer."

Well … *shit.*

"Ma!" John called out.

The front door of his parents' Amityville home slammed closed under his hand. The female murmurings coming from down the hall quieted damn near instantly.

"In the kitchen, Johnathan," he heard his mother say back.

He kicked off his shoes, and shrugged off his jacket. Setting the items aside, he headed for the kitchen where the smells were already wafting from. Something sweet, with a hint of cinnamon. His mother could cook—goddamn, could she cook. His childhood had been filled with memories of things his mother made for him to eat.

Especially in more difficult times of his life, he could bring forth strong memories of Jordyn's sweets and other things she made just for him. It was a way she had gotten him to talk, or whatever else.

John found his mother sitting with his second youngest sister at the kitchen table. In her arms, Cella rocked a bundled-up baby. Swaddled in pink, this was the first time John had actually gotten a glimpse at his two-month-old niece.

She had not even been christened, yet.

"Ma," John greeted, crossing the space to drop a kiss on Jordyn's cheek. "How was your day?"

"It was good."

"Say hello to baby Tiffany," Jordyn said, waving at the baby.

John passed Cella a look, but his sister only shrugged. The two didn't even speak as he leaned over to tug the blanket aside with one finger. The sleeping newborn barely stirred at her uncle. Her cream skin, and long eyelashes were a sweet sight. One tiny fist had grabbed tightly to her swaddling blanket.

"She looks like you, Cella," John said. "She's beautiful. Congrats."

His sister smiled faintly. "Thanks, John."

Jordyn's gaze drifted between the two—her smile saying one thing, and her eyes saying another. He knew it hurt his mother that her oldest daughters were not welcoming to their brother. John knew that was never going to change. He had said too much and done too much in the midst of episodes where Cella and Liliana were concerned. Their issues ran too deep, and wounds like those never healed properly.

"I thought you were coming over a little later," Jordyn said.

He heard the question his mother didn't ask out loud. She wanted him to be there when his father was also at the house.

John had different plans.

The men of his family were no longer going to be messing in his business or life. Not if he could help it.

"Some stuff came up, Ma," John said, taking a seat at the other end of the table. A couple of chairs away from his sister, Cella finally looked like she relaxed a bit. Usually, his guilt would compound at the idea that being near his sibling caused her anxiety, but he simply brushed it off. What was done, was done. "I don't think Dad will mind."

"Your father was looking forward to having dinner with you tonight, John."

John shrugged. "If he wants information, Ma, he's got all sorts of ways to get it when it comes to me."

Jordyn outright frowned at that. "What are you talking about?"

"Ask Dad."

He wasn't going to hurt his mother like that.

Jordyn sighed, and reached over to stroke the top of the newborn baby girl's head as she spoke again. "Well, what came up, then? Because I was looking forward to having you come over tonight to eat, too."

"I'm here."

He would *always* make time for his mother. Sure, he had alienated himself

137

away from his family over the years. He put up walls, and made the distance grow as time went by. His mother *never* factored in to that. Ever. He would figure a way around anything that put up a roadblock when it came to his mom. Simply because he loved her enough to do it.

Jordyn had constantly loved him, after all.

Through everything.

No matter how awful he could be.

She loved him.

"I know you're here, John," Jordyn said as she stood from her chair, and headed for the stove that started to beep. "I also like to have you here when everyone else is, too. You're always coming and going when it's just me, but there's more than just me in this family, my boy."

Jordyn turned around to point a finger at him. "And your father loves you, too."

"Sure, he does."

He also didn't trust John.

How could the two ever repair the burned bridges when something like that came into play? He didn't explain that to his mother because she wouldn't understand. She loved them both—Lucian and Johnathan. Their faults were not something she liked to look at for very long.

"I also didn't forget that you avoided my question about what came up," his mother said.

Cella smiled at that, and looked down at her daughter. "She never misses a click."

"Tell me about it," John muttered. Then, louder for his mother, "I promised to take Siena to a new restaurant and bar in Manhattan, actually. I forgot that the opening was tonight."

He didn't forget anything usually, but it was happening lately. Little things—unimportant things. He figured as long as it didn't bleed over into business, it wouldn't matter.

Jordyn hesitated as she pulled a cake pan from the oven. "You forgot?"

"Yeah. She reminded me this morning."

His mother waffled in her gaze before she finally settled on asking, "Was she with you this morning?"

"Usually is."

He didn't offer more.

His mother let out a quiet sound, but said nothing else.

"Is that a cinnamon bunt cake?" he asked.

Jordyn gave him a smile. "It is—your favorite."

"I might be able to squeeze in some more time before I have to leave, then."

She laughed.

"So, you're still seeing her?" his mother asked as she worked at the counter. "The Calabrese girl, I mean."

"Please don't start with that, Ma. Don't be like the rest of them."

"Them?" Jordyn met his gaze from across the room. "For one, that's your family. Not *them*. For two, it's not the family that I worry about, John. It's *you*."

"I'm fine."

Cella cleared her throat.

John just ignored his sister, and kept his attention on his mother. "Really, I am."

"A relationship could possibly—"

"There's nothing to say, Ma," he interrupted sharply. "Not about me and her."

Jordyn nodded. "Sure. But what does she really know about you, John? Does she know everything? Have you been honest with her?"

John bristled at that comment. "If you're asking whether or not I told her about my disorder, then yes. I did."

His mother brushed her hands together. "All right. I just wanted to make sure. You should maybe bring her over for dinner on Sunday. Church, too. I assume she's Catholic."

John gave his mother an odd look.

What in the hell was she on?

"Do you think it's a good idea for me to bring a Calabrese to church and Sunday dinner with our family after I was told to stay away from her by Dad, and the rest of them?"

Jordyn shrugged. "You won't know unless you try."

She had a point …

"John!" Matteo Calabrese's voice echoed across the quiet restaurant. The heavy-set boss sat on a stool, and had what looked to be a glass of whiskey in his hand. "My boy, come over here."

John did his best not to bristle at the *my boy* thing. Matteo was always respectful, and John was dating the man's daughter, so to speak.

"Are you here for my girl?" Matteo asked as John came closer.

"I promised her dinner."

"Not here, I hope." The man gave him a look. "You can't call it a proper date when it's the same place she works."

"Not here," John said.

Matteo waved at the stool. "Sit, John."

He didn't have a reason to refuse, so John sat.

"I never get to sit and chat with you," Matteo said, grinning widely. "You're always running with my daughter, or working with my boys. You should stop and say hello once in a while. We're all friends, right?"

Friends.

Right.

If by friends, he meant two men who came from a long history of bad blood, then sure.

"Friends," John forced himself to say.

"Oh, I saw that father of yours the other day. Asked about you since I hadn't seen you in a while."

John stiffened. "That so?"

"He didn't have much to say about you. Kind of a shame, really."

John tried not to let that admittance sting him on the inside, but it kind of did. Seemed his father couldn't muster up a good word about John, unsurprisingly.

"Here, have a drink," Matteo said, waving at the bartender down the way.

Soon, two fingers of whiskey were sitting in front of John. He didn't have a reason to refuse, and he couldn't say no to a boss, anyway. So, he stared at the drink while Matteo nursed his and overlooked the patrons.

Before he thought much about it—he didn't really think at all—John picked up the whiskey, and tossed it back. The glass clinked to the bar when he sat it back down.

"Another," Matteo called, waving a finger between John and the glass.

He threw back three glasses of whiskey before he finally found Siena in the back of the restaurant working. She peeked up at him from the computer with a wide smile. Bending down, he pressed a quick kiss to her sweet lips.

Siena hesitated when he pulled away. "Were you drinking?"

"A couple with your dad."

"But you don't drink, John."

"Don't worry about it, love." It was just a drink. Alcohol wasn't great with his meds, but he was already fucking with those anyway. He jerked a thumb toward the door. "Are you ready to head out of here, or what?"

"Almost."

Siena went about saving all the files, and turning the computer off. She packed up her bag, and rounded the desk to come and stand beside John.

"So hey," he said.

He slipped two fingers under her chin, and tipped her head back to make her look up at him. Those blue eyes of hers darkened with lust when he dropped a soft kiss to her mouth. Her tongue teased along his when her lips finally parted for him.

"Hey," she whispered when he pulled away.

"I was thinking …"

"I thought you did that quite often." Siena winked. "Thinking, I mean."

"Cute. No, I meant about this weekend. How would you feel about coming to church with me, and then to a big Marcello dinner afterward? It's a regular thing."

"For them, or for you?"

John shrugged. "I don't go as often as I used to. You coming with me, *bella*, or not?"

Siena stood up on her tiptoes and kissed him again. "Definitely coming, John."

Something in the lilt of her tone sent a shot of lust straight through his bloodstream. John barely thought about what he was going to do next—his rationale entirely gone with a little smile and wink from her.

Lately, his grasp on good and bad decisions fell more to the reckless, stupid side of things. This would probably fall in that category as well.

John just couldn't find it in himself to care.

He was who he was.

Bulletproof.

Untouchable.

Invincible.

Especially with Siena.

He didn't care that her father was just twenty feet away. He didn't consider that this was a public place, or how disrespectful it might be to her family.

No, he just closed the door to the office, picked Siena up, and set her on the edge of the desk. She laughed breathlessly as he pushed her skirt up around her hips, and got down on his knees. The black cotton panties she wore slipped down her legs easily, and she widened her hips without even needing to be told.

She tasted like honey on his tongue.

A drug he wanted more of.

She muffled her cries with her hands. Every stroke of his tongue against her silken pussy, and hot little clit had her rocking into his mouth.

So perfect.

It was the recklessness of it all that got him off, next to the way Siena looked while he ate her out, of course. Still, the danger and craziness of it all made it that much fucking better. He couldn't deny the way the high slipped through his blood like a needle shot straight into his veins.

It was everything good and bad for John.

A part of him understood that—his life and actions lately were reflecting symptoms of his mania, and he knew it. From the lack of sleep, to the irresponsible decisions, and the wild behavior. The bigger problem was the part of him that recognized his spiral was quickly shut down, and shut out. Irrationality took control.

As quick as the understanding came …

It was gone again.

Forgotten.

He *felt* instead. He felt everything.

It was overwhelming.

It still felt like air, though. He just kept sucking it in.

No matter if it was poison.

Siena's cheeks were still blushed with a pretty pink when they left the office. John thought to say goodbye to Matteo as they left—for respect's sake—but the Calabrese boss was on the phone, and only eyed the couple as they left the business.

It was odd, but John figured it didn't matter.

He had what he wanted tucked into his side.

And she was still smiling.

FOURTEEN

Siena was not panicking.

She was *not*.

It was church. Sunday service. Mass.

She did this every week with her own family. She attended services every single Sunday since she could remember. Her first communion was one of her fondest memories. Church and God were a *must* for her family.

It wasn't a big thing. It shouldn't be a big deal.

So, why couldn't she just pick a damn dress?

Five church appropriate, Catholic service approved dresses rested across her bed. She had pulled out far more than five at first, but these were the ones she ended up with after discarding the others on the floor of her closet.

All had been spread out, so she could get a good look at them. She kept going from one to another, either finding something she didn't like about one, and then finding something she loved about the same piece.

They ranged in color—a white, off the shoulder number, another light green dress, one dark blue, a maroon red, and even a violet shade. All with designer names, respectable style, and modestly cut necks. Nothing too low, and nothing too short. All the skirts fell at her knees, or even an inch below.

And these dresses? That was all before shoes. Shoes were a whole other kind of hell. Siena was not ready for that hell.

This was not hard choice on any other day. Usually, Siena just grabbed a dress, and tossed it on. She didn't buy something if she didn't love it right off the rack.

The thing was, this wasn't any other Sunday. Her family would not be attending with her, and she wouldn't be going to her familiar church.

No, this was about John's family.

Other than Andino Marcello, Siena didn't really know any of John's family. Some of them by face or name, sure, because of her own family or things she had seen on the news over the years. That didn't mean she knew them on a personal level.

Not who they were beyond the last name. Not what they thought of her. She didn't know anything about the Marcellos. Nothing at all.

It made her so anxious, she was damn near ready to puke. And wouldn't that just be fucking fantastic to add to her problems. She could go to service smelling like a vomit factory, and two steps away from spilling what was left of her breakfast on a pew, or something.

Maybe she was being a little dramatic, but Siena figured it was better for her to prepare for the worst. Then, she wouldn't be all that shocked or disappointed if that was exactly what happened to her.

Her luck, it would.

The ding of a text on her phone drew her attention away from the dresses on her bed. She grabbed the device, and swiped at the touchscreen. A message from

John rolled across the screen, and made her anxiousness pick up a bit.

A lot. What was wrong with her?

Be there in twenty, his message read.

Siena let out a low breath, and tossed the phone aside. She put her hands to her hips, and eyed the dresses once more. She didn't have a choice but to pick a damn dress and get ready right now—John was nearly there.

At least her hair and makeup were done. That was one less thing to worry about. You know, on top of the mountain of other things she was already worrying about. Fuck her life.

The knock on her apartment door sent Siena's heart jumping in her throat. For a whole three seconds, she thought she had dazed out staring at the clothing, and lost time. Like that might have been John coming to pick her up, or something.

She quickly realized that wasn't the case when her mother's muffled voice carried through her apartment.

"Siena, I let myself in, darling."

Why was her mother here?

"In the bedroom, Ma," she called back.

Soon enough, Coraline was standing in the doorway of Siena's bedroom, and surveying the dresses on the bed. She acted like it was totally normal for her to be there, and not at all like she actually barely visited her daughter's apartment to begin with.

"Did you or Dad need something?" Siena asked.

"No," her mother replied. "I came to help you."

"For what?"

Coraline smiled widely, and gestured at the dresses. "To get ready for church, Siena."

Siena felt like she had swallowed a fly. "I know how to dress myself."

"Of course, you do."

So, why did it sound like her mother was patronizing her?

"It might not seem like a big deal to attend services with a family like the Marcellos, but I can promise you that it is," Coraline added.

She had not told her parents that she wouldn't be attending services with them that morning. She simply said something else had come up.

Sure, she had thought it was a little strange when her father didn't question her on it. Attending church was non-negotiable in their family, after all. She let it go and didn't press her father, thankful for one less argument.

"How did you know I was going to church with John this morning, Ma?"

Coraline stepped closer to the dresses, and looked them over. "At least you didn't pick anything black."

"Who wears black to church unless it's a funeral?"

"Siena, you would be surprised."

"I know black is a no, Ma."

"Good," her mother replied with a smile. "Also, the red one is a no. Catrina Marcello, the wife of the boss, prefers red. It's never respectable to show up in the same color as her, and since you never know if she's going to be wearing red or not, simply don't ever wear it at all."

Huh.

Siena blinked. "Ma."

"Yes?" Coraline moved to the white dress. "This one is nice—you have a pair of Valentinos that match the color, too."

"Ma, did John mention to Dad that he was taking me to church this weekend?"

"Siena, focus on the dresses. I know what time their Mass starts. You do not have time to be messing around with silly conversations."

Her mother was right. Siena put her attention where it needed to be.

The white dress it was.

John looked good in anything. Of course, he did. But a well-fitted suit, on an early February morning, grinning like he didn't have a care in the world, and looking at Siena? She thought he looked the best like that.

He brought their connected hands up from his side. Tucking her hand into his elbow, she was brought even closer to him while they climbed the stairs to the entrance of the cathedral-style church.

The gathering people at the top of the stairs couldn't seem to drag their gawking eyes away from the two. It was a little disconcerting.

"Ignore them," John said like he could read her mind. "Marcellos always seem to draw attention when it comes to church. Half of the parishioners think we shouldn't be allowed to attend, considering who we are, and the other half just like a good soap opera."

Siena swallowed her nerves. "Huh."

Then, the people parted, and several men came down the steps. One, she recognized. Andino. The others, she thought she knew, but wasn't comfortable enough to say. They met them half way up the stairs.

"John," the man standing beside Andino greeted. "Good to see you this morning."

"Uncle Gio," John greeted.

The oldest man—his face weathered with age—smiled at them both. "You don't come to church nearly enough, Johnathan."

"I'll rectify that, Grandpapa."

Antony, Siena realized.

The oldest Marcello. A man she had only heard people whisper about, or spoken with great respect in their voices.

"Where's my mother and father?" John asked.

"Inside," Andino said.

John gave a little laugh under his breath, and his gaze darted somewhere higher on the stairs. At the people gathered, maybe. "What, he couldn't come out and greet me or something?"

"You didn't really give him a choice about this," Gio said, his gaze darting to Siena. "You simply said this would be happening, and he had to make a choice."

"So, his choice is to make me walk into church alone?"

"You're not alone," Andino jumped in. "We're all here."

"Yes, but my father *isn't*." John shook his head, adding, "And neither is Dante—the boss. So, not only did my father shun my choice, so has the family's head. Someone could have given me a little warning about that, couldn't they?"

Siena felt like she had missed something important. Like maybe the traditions and customs in the Marcello family were a lot deeper than anyone actually knew. Surface appearances seemed to be important, but it went far beyond that, too.

The hurt in John's gaze—though he hid it everywhere else—was evident to her. Something about this hurt him, and she didn't like that. Not at all.

"It's like deja vu all over again," Antony murmured.

Everyone looked to the man. All of them wore masks of confusion. The older man simply chuckled at the attention turning on him.

"Oh, I get it," Gio said, grinning a bit.

"What is so fucking amusing about this?" John snapped.

All eyes flew back to him.

He was so up and down lately. One minute, he was light, carefree, and happy. The next, he snapped at somebody or at something. Never at her, though.

"I just meant," Antony said calmly, "that there was a time once when your father stood on these steps with a woman whom he too made a choice about, and this same thing happened to him. He took my lack of presence out here to greet him as a sign of my disapproval, and rejection. It was neither of those—I was being cautious, and had something else to deal with."

"Does he?" John asked.

"Hmm?"

"Have something else to deal with, Grandpapa?"

Antony smiled slightly, and his gaze drifted in Siena's direction before going back to his grandson. "We all have things to deal with at the moment. It's a part of being a Marcello, John. You shouldn't forget that, regardless of other things in your head or heart."

Gio cleared his throat. "We're going inside. Do you want to walk in with us, or not?"

The three men waited.

John sneered. "Nah, I'm good."

That was that.

Andino gave John a nod as the older two Marcellos turned and headed back up the stairs. Gio kept a hand on Antony's arm as the two navigated the icy parts. Andino stayed behind them both, and a couple of paces back.

"What was that about?" Siena dared to ask.

John shook his head, and gave her a smile. "Nothing, *bella*. Don't worry about it."

She didn't think it was nothing.

"Do they not want me here?"

"It's not that."

"What is it, then?"

"Bad blood," John murmured. "It's always been that way, and it's probably not going to change."

"You mean—"

"You're a Calabrese. I'm a Marcello. The history between those two names in this city is enough to make any man in my family cautious."

"Cautious," she echoed.

"Yeah, love."

"About me."

John coughed, and squeezed her hand tucked into his elbow. "Like I said, don't fucking worry about it. We're doing us, not them."

"Yeah, but—"

"I did what I did, and here you are," John said, giving her a look with hazel eyes that stopped her words, heart, and breath for a split second. "Now, come on. God doesn't like people to be late to Mass. Or, that's what everyone told me growing up. Apparently, He fucking takes attendance like it makes a difference or something."

Siena laughed. What else could she do?

"It's inviting them *in*," someone growled. "That's what this does, or at the very least, gives them the idea that's what we're doing."

"That's not necessarily—"

"The idea of it can be just as fucking dangerous, Lucian."

"Everyone knows that isn't his intention."

Andino's voice added reason to a conversation that only seemed to be growing louder the closer John and Siena came to the dining room of the large Marcello estate. A mansion that rested on six acres of land in Tuxedo Park, and belonged to his grandparents. Or, that's what he explained to her during Sunday service.

"The intention doesn't have to be known," the first man said again. "That's where the problem is, and we all know it. An idea is more than enough. I do not want even the suggestion that our home or lives are open to them. Not even her."

"Do you think *I* want them in my life, Dante?"

"He's your son, Lucian, so you tell me."

John's suddenly stiff posture straightened impossibly more at Siena's side. Yet, she kept holding his hand because for no particular reason, she thought it might ground him to her. His stress was obvious enough, and he didn't need more added on just because of her.

The two rounded the last corner of a long hallway, and came to stand in the entryway of a massive dining room. A chandelier the size of a small car hung from a vaulted ceiling overtop a table that was so big, it looked like it could fit three families in every seat.

Standing around the table, glaring at one another, or staring at the shiny oak top were several men. The same ones who greeted them outside the church, but also, the ones John had introduced her to after the services.

His uncles—Gio and Dante. Gio's son, Andino. His grandfather, Antony. And his father, Lucian.

Another man sat in the corner nursing what looked to be a glass of bourbon. Siena did recognize him, although he hadn't been at the church, and he definitely wasn't a Marcello. He did come from a family like theirs, though.

Cross Donati.

Like the Marcellos, Cross's family occasionally did business at arm's length with Siena's brothers. That was the only reason why she recognized his face. That was about all she knew regarding him.

Her introductions to John's family after Sunday services had been, at best, tense and short. Even his aunts, cousins, and mother had made sure to keep the conversation to the point, and respectful.

Nothing they did made her feel out of place or unwelcome at the church. At the same time, she didn't particularly feel their friendliness or care, either. They would smile at her, but it was guarded. They shook her hand, but little else.

Still, she could tell … She didn't need to be told. Siena was not a stupid girl. None of these people trusted her. All because of her last name.

At the sight of the two of them standing in the entryway, the conversation between the Marcello men silenced damn near instantly.

John laughed darkly. "Now, isn't that the kind of conversation we reserve for a weekday, and not in the dining room where any-fucking-body can hear it?"

Dante—who Siena now knew was the man heading the Marcello family—gave John a look, and it clearly voiced his displeasure without him needing to. "I can discuss issues with my family wherever I want to, Johnathan. You are quite aware of that."

"Except when anybody else does it on a Sunday, you're quick to shut them up."

"This isn't business. This is family."

"John," Lucian said, taking a step closer to his son. "Maybe we should go upstairs, and have a chat for a minute before dinner is served."

John shook his head, and tipped his head in Siena's direction. "No, I have a guest, so I'm going to settle her in. It's what a gentleman does. We don't leave anyone out to the wolves, right?"

At that statement, Dante stiffened.

"You think we would—"

"I think nothing at the moment," John interjected.

"Don't interrupt me, Johnathan. I am your—"

"Son," Antony murmured, his voice cracking a bit, "let him take the girl in, and have her meet Cecelia."

Antony's old gaze turned on Siena. "She had to help at the church after services, and so she didn't get to meet you properly, young lady. She would really like to say hello."

"Thank you," Siena said.

At her soft reply, the defensive postures in the room lessened a bit. John seemed to take that as their cue to get the hell out of the room.

Once the dining room was behind them, the conversation started up again. Although this time, it was a little bit quieter.

"She's just a woman," Andino said. "Did you hear her talk? She heard you insulting her, and she still spoke like a little mouse. How in the hell is she going to do anything to us?"

"It's not her," Dante said sharply, "it's where she comes from."

"I'm sorry," John murmured.

Siena shrugged. "They're probably right."

Who the hell knew?

Cecelia Marcello—with her dark hair snaked with tendrils of white, and kind eyes—shooed anyone in her kitchen out with a single whistle. All she had to do was see John and Siena standing in the entryway, and she made everyone else leave.

Johnathan's mother gave her son a quick smile, and a pat to his cheek as she passed him by. Her gaze barely drifted over Siena at all.

The rest of them followed the same suit.

She wasn't even offended, now.

"Grandmamma," John said, grinning wide, "what are you cooking?"

"Everything," Cecelia said, just as happy. Her soft eyes turned on Siena. "And you must be this Siena I keep hearing about."

"Nothing bad, I hope," she joked.

Everything was bad, she knew.

Cecelia let out a quiet laugh, and waved a hand. "It's a little awkward right now, Siena, but those are only details. You have to give these Marcello men a little room to figure out their nonsense. But me, on the other hand, is another story."

Already, Siena liked this woman with her wise words and her kind offerings.

Cecelia gestured at the dough in front of her. "Do you cook?"

"Of course."

"Then, come cook. I talk best when I cook, Siena."

"Watch yourself, love," John warned her. "Cecelia is a well-known tyrant in the kitchen."

Cecelia didn't even deny it. "And yet, you all come back every Sunday for more."

Careful conversation flowed at the Marcello dinner table. Siena couldn't help but notice how everyone made a great effort not to discuss anything too personal or behind the scenes when it came to their family. If someone did accidentally say something of that nature, Dante Marcello's gaze would dart in Siena's direction, and the topic would change.

She tried not to be offended.

She didn't want to take it personally. It still stung a little.

John kept one hand on her leg under the table while at the same time, discussing the upcoming opening of a new restaurant with Andino at his left.

Across the table, Lucian Marcello's gaze continued to drift between Siena, and his son. Lucian, maybe even more than Dante, was the most intimidating to

Siena. Where the others were loud and talked, he was still and quiet. His presence felt imposing. His words—when he did speak—were careful and delivered with a flat tone.

She didn't know what to make of him at all.

"You work with your brothers and father, don't you?" Lucian asked.

John's fingers squeezed Siena's thigh at his father's question. She, too, was surprised Lucian had engaged her outright in conversation. He hadn't done that yet, except to say hello earlier. Very little else.

Siena answered quickly. "I do."

"Doing what?"

"I handle all the bookkeeping and accounting for them."

Lucian's brow raised at that statement. She wasn't sure if it was surprise, disbelief, or interest. He gave nothing away. Hell, it could have been all three.

"For *all* their businesses?" Lucian pressed.

The chatter at the table had all but stopped. All eyes were on their interaction. John had yet to step in and speak, but Siena was grateful he didn't.

"All of it," she replied.

Down at the other end of the table, Dante spoke up. "I don't think you understand what my brother means when he says all of it, Siena."

She passed a look down the way. "I do know what he means. And yes, all of it."

Criminal. Legal.

She did it all.

Siena wasn't supposed to talk about those things outside of her immediate family, but she wanted that one thing to be clear. She didn't say things she didn't mean, and she understood exactly what these men were.

"Smart girl," said the redheaded woman beside Dante.

His wife. Catrina.

And she was wearing red, just like Coraline said.

"And how does your father feel about …" Lucian waved between Siena and John before saying, "This whole thing."

"Fine, I assume."

Lucian's lips curved a bit—not a complete smile, but not the expressionless, grim line he had been sporting. "You assume?"

"Matteo has no issues with speaking up about things he doesn't like," John said, finally coming into the conversation. "If he had a problem, he would let me know."

"You. Not her."

John stiffened in the chair. "That's what I said, Dad."

"That implies a friendliness, Johnathan."

Silence coated the room heavily again.

A second later, Antony said, "If everyone is finished eating, I think it's time we take this conversation upstairs."

"I agree," Dante said.

John looked to her—a silent question in his gaze. Siena patted his hand still squeezing her leg. "I'm fine."

"Now."

Their words were too quiet for anyone else to hear.

"I will be fine."

John nodded once. "All right, love."

Once all the men were gone from the table, the women started an entirely new conversation. Cecelia made every effort to bring Siena into the chats, and she appreciated it.

Down the table a couple of chairs, John's other cousin turned to Siena. Catherine, her name was. Beside her sat the only man who hadn't followed the rest—Cross.

"Are you really that good with numbers?" Catherine asked.

Siena laughed, and nodded. "Yeah, I'm really that good."

"I can make money."

"But you can't hide it, huh?"

Catherine smiled. "No, I can't hide it. I mean, someone does it for me, but it's always good to know more people."

Siena shrugged. "You know where to find me."

With that, Siena felt like she might have made another friend in the Marcello family.

Only another couple dozen to go ...

It was good half an hour later before the Marcello women stood to clean the table. Without being asked, Siena got up to help. She and Catherine ended up handwashing dishes while the others cleaned up the dining room and kitchen.

Cross poked his head in the entryway where there was only a couple of plates left. "Hey, babe, you want to come look at something for me?"

Catherine dropped the dishrag. "You good?"

Siena nodded. "I can handle the rest of this."

"Thanks."

Shortly after Catherine left, Siena realized she was all alone in the kitchen. She didn't really mind. It allowed her quiet time to go over the events of the day.

She was lost in her own mind when someone else saddled up beside her at the sink. She didn't realize Johnathan's mother was standing there until Jordyn Marcello picked up one of the washed plates to dry them.

"I thought we should talk, Siena," the woman said. "And since this is the first time my son has left your side, now seems as good of a time as ever to do it."

Siena wasn't sure why ... but that didn't sound good.

"What about?" Siena asked.

Jordyn set the dried plate aside. "My son. What else?"

"Considering you've barely spoken to me at all today, it's not a big surprise that I'm shocked."

The light laughter from Johnathan's mother was unexpected. Siena found herself smiling when Jordyn winked.

"I didn't mean to seem standoffish or cold, Siena."

Siena shrugged. "Yeah, well ..."

"But I worry about my son. All the time, and every single day. He's thirty, so he doesn't let me have any say now. I still worry. I wonder, though, do you?"

"What?"

"Worry about him?"

FIFTEEN

"I think we could have done this on any other day," Antony said as the Marcello men headed toward his office. "The no business on Sunday rule barely exists anymore, son."

"This isn't business, this is—"

"Family," Antony interrupted. "Except it falls in both categories, and you know how I feel about that, Dante."

"All right, Papa." Dante spun around on his heels in front of the two oak doors that led into the office. He pointed at his father, and then at Lucian, and Andino, too. "All three of you can stay outside for this. Gio can join me, but only because I think he's neutral."

John had no idea what his uncle meant, but Dante was the boss. He made the calls, not any of them. It was his choice to make.

"Dante," Lucian started to say.

"No, I don't want to hear it, brother."

"At least allow Andino in for Johnathan, then."

"No," Dante said simply. "He's another one that needs to learn a thing or two."

Andino's hard gaze settled on the wall, and his posture was stiff enough to be fucking ice. John saw all of those things, sure, but he didn't take them in properly for what they actually meant. At the moment, he was too pissed off to think about anything other than his own anger.

"It's *my* office," Antony said, his old voice sharpening with a warning.

Dante nodded. "And if this is going to be a problem, then I will move this discussion elsewhere. Speak now, or don't."

Antony said nothing.

Dante waved a single hand at John and Giovanni to follow him. John caught sight of his father shaking his head, and scowling just before the doors closed behind them—a sure sign of Lucian's disapproval. Likely with John, all things considered. Hadn't his statements at the table been enough to tell John that?

Inside the office, Dante headed for the desk. He stood behind it, but didn't take a seat in the large chair. "Choose some place to sit or stand, but do it fast."

Gio took a seat next to the window. John stayed standing in the middle of the room.

"I'm good," he said when the boss shot him a look.

"For now," Dante replied.

"What do you want, boss?"

Dante smirked, and looked up at the ceiling like he was sending out a silent prayer. "Where is this rudeness coming from, John?"

"I think after the little show downstairs, no one should expect me to be pleasant."

"And how about *your* show, huh?"

John straightened on the spot. "What show?"

151

"Bringing that woman to our church. Having her here for dinner with our family." Dante pointed a single finger at him, and then shook it with a laugh. "You didn't even consider for one second to call me and ask if that would be okay. No, you just did it. You know what kind of statement that is to bring a woman with you to church. We do not do that for just anyone, and—"

"She isn't just anyone to me," John replied.

In his chair, Gio cleared his throat. "That's a heavy statement to make, John. You've been seeing her for how long, now?"

"On and off after I was released—steady for a couple of months."

"That long?" Dante asked.

John shrugged. "Yeah, that long. But I guess we're going to pretend like you didn't already know that because you've had people watching me since I got out."

"John, that was my choice to do because of your history."

He didn't reply, simply scoffed with a nod. What the fuck else could he do? At every turn, someone else in his family had to remind him how little they actually trusted him. It stung like nothing ever had before.

"And I didn't know it was a steady thing," Dante countered. "It concerns me even more to know it, actually. Why any Calabrese woman would be crawling into bed with a Marcello man is concerning, all things considered about our families."

"Why, because she can't want me?" John asked. "Because it can't be just a me and her thing, it has to have something underhanded to go along with it, too?"

"Knowing them—"

John's thin control snapped.

It had been holding on by a thread.

"Jesus Christ," John exploded, "she is a fucking *woman*!"

Dante barely blinked at his rage. "A woman who apparently has a hand in the Calabrese business—albeit behind the scenes. Still, it would not be a stretch to think she is close to her father, or brothers. That perhaps her loyalty to them is far more than her loyalty to you, or even us."

John clenched his fists so hard that his fingernails bit into his skin, and broke the surface. It was better than punching his uncle like he wanted to do.

"That's what it comes down to—loyalty?" John asked.

"Her last name is Calabrese, Johnathan. She is their daughter—a woman from *their* family. How many times do I need to explain this to you before you understand it?"

Rage vibrated through John's bloodstream. A thick, beating thrum of hot anger that filled him up, and ate through his heart all the while. It had been a long damn time since he had gotten this angry, this fast.

Yet, he embraced it. He wasn't scared of it. Right then, he kind of needed it.

"You know nothing about Siena," John returned. "Nothing to make any kind of assumption that she is feeding them information, or fucking me over for them."

"Do *you* know?" Dante countered. "Would you know it if it were happening? Could you even see it happening?"

Damn. The sharp slice of betrayal stabbed John in his chest. Over and over. Every single word his uncle said only cut worse.

"Because I must be entirely fucking incapable at anything like that," John said, his voice quieting. "Paranoid, sure. Unstable, yeah. So much so, that you don't even trust me to be a capable made man. So fuck it, she's got to be one of those things, too. That's what it is, right?"

Dante tipped his chin up. "I did not say that, John."

"You said enough, boss."

"Your bipolar has—"

"Everything to do with me," John interjected. "It is everything that is me, and you know it. Except you use my disorder as a crutch—something to hold me back, or justify your shit. That stops, now."

"John, he doesn't mean to do that," Gio said quietly. "None of us mean to do that, honestly."

He ignored his other uncle.

Dante ignored Gio, too. In fact, the boss switched topics entirely.

"You have handled the Calabrese side of the business since December, haven't you?" Dante asked. He didn't give Johnathan a chance to respond before saying, "And you see, I know Andino barely did a thing with them. He didn't meet them for dinners, and have private chats with the boss. He spent as little time as possible with Matteo's two sons, and kept them at arm's length at all times. But what do you do, John?"

Again, he didn't give him time to answer.

"You date his daughter," Dante said, letting out a bitter laugh. "You work hands on with the Calabrese brothers when you could easily delegate the jobs to men on the crew. You're seen coming and going at all hours from Calabrese businesses, and I know you've had private invitations from that family."

For Siena, John held back from saying.

He did a lot of that for her.

"So," Dante continued, leaning forward with his hands splayed on the desk, "perhaps, John, you can understand why I am wary of how close you are getting to that family. Our history with them is long, and tainted. They are snakes—they cannot be trusted. Except you seem to be doing exactly that."

His uncle knew nothing.

John felt like that was the story of his life, though. He could talk, talk, and talk more. He could explain that all of those were either situations he had been put in to, or something involving Siena, but it would do them no good.

Dante would not care. Why?

John was a Marcello. Siena was a Calabrese.

"You don't know who she gives her loyalty to," Dante said, "and you can't trust her with it, Johnathan."

"So says you," he replied.

He refused to say much else, though.

"Marcellos will do a lot of things, but getting into bed with a Calabrese isn't one of them. Or, it wasn't. You may think that she's a woman, and she's fucking harmless, but the rest of them are most certainly not, John."

Siena wouldn't hurt a fly. Shit, she probably *couldn't* hurt a fly when it came right down to it. She was pure and good and gold. Everything that John wanted.

Dante didn't seem to care.

"You're telling me that she isn't going home tonight to feed her father information about us, and our family?" Dante asked. "Do you really trust her that much? You know how the Calabrese are, Johnathan. Do you know how very different your world might have been had a Calabrese not ruined it?"

John's nerves prickled with irritation. "I bet you probably would not be sitting where you are had things been different, actually."

Dante's jaw stiffened. *Point made.*

"Is it your loyalty that I have to be worried about, then?" Dante asked. "Not hers, but yours, John."

At that statement, Gio did stand from his chair. "Dante, come on."

John was over it. That one remark from his uncle had effectively ended the conversation for him altogether. Nothing else Dante said would make a difference to him, now.

"Nah, it's fine." John laughed, dark and hollow. "Fuck him."

"John!" Dante's roar hit his back.

It didn't matter. He was already gone from the office.

John headed down the hallway, bypassing his father, grandfather, and cousin. He didn't hear anyone following him, but he didn't care. All he wanted to do was find Siena, and get the fuck out of there. Do something else with just her …. Anything except being in this house, with these people.

"John, wait, son."

His father's words came just as he rounded the second floor's staircase. Lucian caught him by the back of his jacket, and yanked hard enough to spin him around.

"Look at me," his father said.

John found familiarity staring at him from his father's eyes. He also found a raised Marcello there, too. Not born, no, but *raised.*

"You're all the fucking same," John told his father. "Every single one of you."

"What are you talking about?"

"You know exactly what I mean."

Lucian looked upward in the direction they had come from. "Give Dante some time, John. Old habits die hard in this family and business—this is one memory for us that cannot be washed out in one run. You have to give it time."

"Like you give a shit. You couldn't have been clearer downstairs going on like you were with Siena at the table, Dad."

Lucian frowned. "I feel people out differently than my brothers do, that's all."

"Bullshit. Like I said, you're all the same."

"Don't you see—can't you see—I'm on your side, John? There's a reason he wouldn't let me in that office. Are you even listening to me right now?"

He didn't care. His perception of his father was colored heavily by his anger, distrust, and everything else that put distance between them.

Lucian said one thing, but John heard another.

It had always been this way. Neither of them could fix it now.

"Where's Siena?"

Catherine looked up from the tablet her boyfriend was showing her. "What?"

"Siena. She's not with everybody else in the theater. Where is she?"

"Probably still in the kitchen," Cross said, lifting a brow. "That's where Catherine left her."

"Did anybody think to ask if she might like to join them, so she wouldn't be alone?"

Catherine frowned. "I was with her—we were washing dishes. She's really nice, John."

"Quiet," Cross added.

John tried to soften his defensive stance a bit, but it was hard after the shit show upstairs. "Yeah?"

Catherine—his favorite cousin next to Andino—nodded. "Yeah, I really like her."

"Even if she is a Calabrese?"

Cross scoffed. "That old bullshit again?"

Yeah, that old bullshit again.

John only shrugged.

"So, the kitchen?" he asked.

"The kitchen," Catherine said before going back to whatever Cross had been showing her.

John left the two of them behind as he navigated the halls and rooms of the mansion. He never understood why his grandparents didn't sell their large estate. It was far too big for them, yet they held strong and refused to let it go.

He had hoped that by the time he found Siena, his anger from earlier would have lessened. That wasn't the case at all—more than ever, he just wanted to get the fuck away from his family. Quick, fast, and in a hurry.

John crossed through the dining room to get to the kitchen, but the sound of his mother's voice carrying from the kitchen made him slow down.

"You have to understand what he's like in those times," he heard his mother say.

"He's told me," Siena replied.

"John saying one thing, and actually experiencing one of his episodes are not the same thing."

"No, I get that, I just meant—"

"In his mania, he can be reckless in everything from his choices, to his behavior. He can blow through thousands of dollars in an hour, and the next day forget where the money went. We used to have boxes of things show up on the doorstep when he was a teenager because he would steal one of our credit cards, and order things online."

Jordyn let out a sigh, adding, "And relationships—romantic ones—can be difficult for him to navigate when physical attraction adds to his mania."

"I don't understand," Siena admitted.

John hated how quiet she sounded. Like the entire conversation had her backed in a corner, and she didn't how to fight her way out of it. He should have explained more to her, so that a conversation like this one didn't take her entirely by surprised.

155

It pissed him off, too.

How dare his mother do this? How dare she corner Siena and air out all of John's history like it was her right to do so?

It wasn't.

Siena could come to *him*.

Not anyone else.

The conversation in the kitchen continued with his mother saying, "Hyper-sexuality means physical expressions of attraction can often be confused for other things. And it only adds to his reckless behavior—like a high he chases. If he can't get high, he can do things that make him feel high. It's another way for him to self-medicate."

"He's not like that, though."

"Not *now*," his mother said sharply. "But I can see it—his father can see it. This is how it starts. Snappy conversations, and up and down moods. He seems productive. He bounces from one thing to another, and it looks like he's getting so much done.

"He rarely sleeps, and he focuses on the strangest things. This is how it starts, Siena. And I don't think you understand how it *ends*. It ends with the energetic him turning into a manic version of that—the snappiness and up and down changes into nastiness."

"He's not nasty—not to me," Siena said.

"Yet. Not *yet*. His sisters? They grew up fearing John, and his mood swings. He destroyed their things, and he would call them names. Threaten them, or worse. Now, they barely speak to him despite the fact those episodes were years ago. They can't let it go because it was awful for them. Apologies and ownership do not take away two decades worth of destruction that mania has caused in their lives.

"He becomes someone else," Jordyn continued. "A nasty version of himself that lashes out because he wants to hurt someone else. It's a dangerous game to play with him if you don't know what to look for, and if you don't understand what you're doing. And this is how it starts. All the signs point to where it's going, but you don't know that because you haven't lived an entire life with my son like we have."

"He's not like that right now," Siena said, repeating her earlier sentiment.

"*Now*," Jordyn echoed. "Are you helping him, or hurting him? Do you even understand the difference, Siena?"

"I—"

His mother didn't even give Siena a chance to reply.

"That's what I'm trying to explain to you. It's hard to tell with John because one thing he does may look like this to you—it may seem okay—but to him, it's something else entirely. It means something else entirely."

Silence answered Jordyn's statement.

John decided in that second that he had enough. This whole day had all been quite fucking enough for him.

He crossed the last few steps to the kitchen entryway, and instantly the two women inside noticed his presence. Siena looked as though she didn't know what to say. His mother only dropped her arms to her sides, and let out a soft sigh.

"Is this why you asked me to bring her to church and dinner, Ma?" John asked. "So you could corner her like this, and tell her all the reasons why I'm such a fuckup to you, and the rest of this family?"

"John, no," his mother said. "That's not what I was doing at all."

Her denials meant less than shit. He knew what he heard her saying to Siena, and he wasn't fucking stupid.

He looked to Siena. "Are you ready to leave?"

She nodded once. "If you are, sure."

"Let's go."

Siena darted for him, and discarded a dishcloth on the edge of the counter as she passed it by. "Sure, John."

"John, wait," his mother said.

John let Siena pass to exit out of the room before he turned and pointed at his mother. "Out of everyone, Ma, I trusted you the most. I didn't think you would do something like this to me."

"John, I was only trying to help." Jordyn stepped forward, but he took one giant step back. Siena had already passed through the dining room, and was gone. "I don't even think you realize it, but a lot of your behavior lately suggests you're slipping into another manic phase. I only wanted to warn her, so that she would understand and know how to help."

"You've got a strange fucking way of helping."

"You're not listening. That tells me I'm right, John. Listen to me."

"I am fine!"

"Are you?"

"Go to hell, Ma."

"John!"

Her shout echoed at his back. He found Siena at the front of the mansion. He helped her to slip on her coat.

"John, she meant no harm," Siena murmured. "She wasn't saying any of that to hurt you, I swear."

"It doesn't matter. They're all the same."

Siena frowned up at him. "What?"

"This whole family. They're all the fucking same. They talk about loyalty, but they don't know what it means."

"John."

Her whisper made him look down at her. Siena kept searching his gaze like she was trying to find something. He didn't know what.

"They love you, John."

Do they?

It was hard to tell when he was like this.

Siena laughed as John pulled her up the steps of a brownstone that was only a few blocks away from Fifth Avenue.

"What are we doing here?"

"Taking a look inside."

Siena peered up at the black brick of the home. "Who lives here?"

John flipped open a keypad, and punched in the numbers to make the door unlock. "A friend, but he's out of town. He's trying to sell the place, and let me know the code to get in, so I could check it out."

The door pushed open under John's hand, and he reached back to grab Siena, and pull her inside with him. He shut the door behind them, and Siena's laughter filled up the front hallway of the brownstone.

"Wait, shouldn't the realtor be here, then?" she asked.

John shrugged. "Who cares?"

"Because it's a break and entering charge, John!"

He only chuckled, and pulled her into his side. There, he could kiss her temple, and so he did just that.

She relaxed at the kiss. "At least you're in a better mood than you were earlier."

"Yeah, well, getting away from my family has its benefits."

Siena frowned, but didn't say more. John slipped his hand in with hers, and pulled her along. The first place he headed was for the stairs.

"I thought we were looking around?" she asked.

The two climbed the stairs to the second level, and then up to the third.

"Actually, there's only one part of this place I'm interested in," John said as they reached the top floor. It was an open concept space for what seemed to be an office on one side, and an artist's studio on the other side. "Look up, babe."

Siena did, and froze on the spot. "Holy shit."

John grinned as he looked upward, too. The entire ceiling was actually inverted for an indoor pool that had been built into the roof. The pool was surrounded by heated frosted glass walls that provided privacy from the neighbors. It didn't matter that it was February because it would feel like August inside the pool's walls.

"Let's go try it out," John said.

Siena followed behind him at a slower pace as they climbed the stairs leading to the roof. "Are we really allowed to be in here?"

"Who's going to tell, *bella*?"

She gave him a look. "Well, someone might."

"Have some fun with me."

"Kind of reckless, John."

"Not even close to being reckless, Siena."

She didn't respond except to tug on his hand again. John simply tugged back, and pulled her the rest of the way up the stairs. When he opened the door to the roof where the entire pool was closed in, he got the first whiff of chlorine.

"Are you seriously considering buying this place?" she asked.

John tugged his shirt off, and then kicked off his socks, shoes, and pants. "Maybe. Do you like it?"

"I like your place in Queens, too."

"That's a rental."

"I know, I just—"

"It's temporary," he added.

Siena gave him a look. "I like this, too, John."

"How could you not, babe?"

Her grin made him wink when he shoved down his boxer-briefs.

And then he dove in the pool a second later. The heated pool felt like a giant bathtub as he cut through the water, and then came back up for air. It was only about twenty feet long and ten feet wide. There was no deep or shallow end as it was eight feet deep all the way across except for a small portion on the other side that seemed to go from a couple of feet deep into a slope until it met the eight-foot limit.

John sucked in air the second he broke the top of the water. Shaking his head, water droplets flew all over the place that had been clinging to his hair. He found Siena watching him from the edge of the pool in that way of hers.

Like she couldn't stop.

Or she couldn't get enough.

He loved it.

"Are you getting in, or what?"

"Maybe," she said.

"Maybe?"

"Mmhmm."

John grinned, and waded closer to her. "Get in, Siena."

"I'm actually not a good swimmer."

He cocked a brow. "Seriously?"

"Yeah, kind of."

"*Donna*, everybody can float."

Siena gave him another one of those looks. "Yeah, but—"

John reached up out of the water, grabbed her wrist, and yanked hard. Siena fell in the water with a shriek, coat, shoes, white dress and all. He kept his hands on her waist as he pulled her high, and let her break the surface.

"Oh, my God," she growled at him, smacking his bare chest. "You ruined my coat!"

John kissed her lips, kept one arm around her back, and dragged the sopping wet coat off her arms. He tossed it aside to the side of the pool. "And I'll buy you a new one."

Siena sucked in a sharp breath. Her white, off the shoulder dress was almost entirely see-through now. Her wet hair stuck to her face. The caramel locks were darker when wet. John brushed them out of her eyes.

"I can't believe you did that," she said.

John smiled. "You have to be a little risky with me, Siena."

"I told you I wasn't a good swimmer, John."

"You're doing okay."

"Because you're holding onto me!"

"I always will," he returned easily. "You know that, don't you?"

Her anger melted away instantly. "Yeah, I do."

"Good."

Carefully, John moved them to the other side of the pool where it had that shallow slope for a good five feet. Siena rolled over to her back, and let the water lap around her while John sat beside her.

"I'm sorry about my mom," he said after a moment.

"Don't be. She really wasn't trying to hurt you, or scare me off, John."

"Doesn't seem that way."

"I wouldn't ever lie to you."

He looked down at her. "I know."

And yet, he still had the tendrils of distrust and betrayal where his family was concerned. It was disconcerting. Like his heart was being tugged in two different directions. A familiar war that fought back and forth with his thoughts and emotions.

Overwhelming, really.

"I am worried about you, though," she whispered.

John glanced down at her, and saw the truth in her gaze. He didn't want her to worry at all. Not about him. He had his shit handled.

Didn't he?

In a blink, he had rolled himself from his backside, to be hovering over Siena. She looked up at him through thick lashes, and gave him one of those sweet grins. He couldn't help himself but to lean down and catch her teasing little mouth in a kiss.

Against her lips, he murmured, "With you, I am always fine."

"Are you?"

Sea-blue eyes searched his gaze again.

"All the time, I feel like I'm drowning." John dragged a finger down Siena's parted lips and over the column of her throat. "Drowning in too much of everything. Responsibilities. Emotions. Reactions. People. Business. It never stops. Like I'm on my back in water, and it's getting higher by the second."

Kind of like her right then.

"But it doesn't feel that way with you," John admitted. "Or if it does, it's a good feeling."

"It's good to drown?"

"To drown in you, sure."

She reached for him, then, pulling him close again for a kiss that was harder, and deeper. Her tongue snaked into his mouth, and battled with his. Her hands slid down his naked, wet chest, and then her fingers slipped lower. His breath caught hard in his throat when her hands circled around his cock.

One stroke, then two.

Three, then four.

He was hard as hell in her palms, and she just kept stroking him awake even more.

"Fuck," he grunted against her mouth. "You're going to make me want something else, love."

"Please."

That was all she said.

Please.

His heart raced with want. His blood thickened with need.

He ran his hands down her sides, and grabbed a handful of her ass to grind her lower half in to him. She widened her legs even more, and hooked her heels at his lower back.

"Fuck, my pants are on the other side," he said, dragging himself away from her mouth.

His unspoken words clung heavily in the air. They didn't fuck without condoms. It was never a question as John always used them.

"I have the shot, John," Siena said, stroking a finger down his lips. "I get it on time, and I'm not with anybody else."

His gaze cut back to her. "I sure fucking hope not."

Her eyes lowered.

He realized his mistake instantly.

"Me, either, huh?"

Siena nodded, and her lips curved at the edge. "Good to know. It's fine, though. Just me and you, John."

Yeah, him and her.

The way it should be. The way he needed it to be.

John worked fast after that to drag Siena's white cotton panties down over her legs, and toss them aside. Like the rest of her, the panties were soaked. He fit himself between her thighs, and let her pull him close as his cock slid through the lips of her sex.

Her back came up out of the water in an arch when he thrust in. Every single fucking inch of her took him in, and hugged him tight.

She was wet, sure, but her pussy was something else. Warmer than the water, and wrapping all around him. A deep ache settled in his chest as he tried to stay still for a second—long enough to feel her, and just *be*. Without something between them. All bare, and feeling everything because of it.

Just like that, he was inside her, and everything was right again.

He was alive again. Breathing again.

Siena's fingernails made red lines down his back when he drew out, and slammed right back in. Her white dress slid up under his hands, exposing more skin for him to kiss, and taste.

He liked her throat the best.

How sounds crawled from it when his tempo picked up. How her muscles and tendons strained when he fucked her harder. How her pulse raced when his teeth cut into her skin and left a mark behind.

He liked those marks.

It meant she was his

"Oh, my God, John."

Her words were a light whisper in his hear.

Perfect and full of sin.

Blissed and high.

Fucking her did that to him, too.

Made him so goddamn high.

She came the first time with his name falling from her tongue. He flipped them over to get her on top for round two. He only let her ride him long enough to get that second orgasm, and then he was done for.

Nothing had ever felt better than coming inside her. He doubted anything would feel that good again.

SIXTEEN

"Yeah, Matteo here."

"Hey, Dad, it's me."

"Siena?" her dad asked.

"Yeah, would you mind if I took today off, and didn't come in to the restaurant?"

Matteo hummed a sound. "Well, you're supposed to be at the restaurant for noon, aren't you?"

"Yeah, I am," Siena said.

"Then, what's the problem here?" her father asked.

"Nothing's wrong. I just wanted a day off."

"It's a busy month, Siena. For both sides of business, if you get what I mean."

She did know what he meant, and her father was right. They were still in February. The tax deadline was coming up to have everything filed. While most of the businesses' books were closed for the previous tax year, there were still a couple left. Not to mention, the illegal side of business picked up in the new year, and that forced more work on her to scrub and cook books. Her books were ace, though.

It wasn't that she was concerned about. She really did just need a day off.

"I work all the time, Dad," Siena said. "I rarely ask for time off. Sometimes I'm working seven days a week. The least you could do is give me one day when I ask for it. And I don't ask for it very often."

"No, you don't."

"Exactly," Siena said.

"What were you planning to do today, then?" her father asked.

"I was going to spend the day with John."

"John." Her father didn't even sound surprised, simply interested. "And how is he lately?"

"He's … fine."

"Fine?"

"Yeah."

Matteo made a noise under his breath. "Your brothers mentioned that he seemed a little off last week. Not his normal self, or something of that sort."

"Off?" Siena asked.

"Yes, *off*." Matteo chuckled, adding "All men in our business get a little off sometimes. It's not unusual. They simply mentioned that he didn't seem up to par."

"He's fine with me. I haven't noticed anything."

Or rather, nothing that she was going to tell her father.

"Well, maybe that was just Darren and Kev."

Siena placated her father's assumption, but inside, she knew differently. After talking to John's mother a few days earlier, she was more observant of him. She noticed things that she might otherwise have overlooked. She paid closer attention to his behaviors, and the things he did when he thought she wasn't looking.

Sometimes, it was worrying.

What was more concerning to her was the fact that other people were starting to notice. Clearly, people were noticing. John's family. Her brothers, if this conversation with her father was any indication.

Siena was sure John would not want people like her father or brothers knowing anything was wrong, if something was.

"Nothing's wrong with John, Dad," Siena said. "He's a little tired lately. Like me, he works too much."

"Sure," Matteo replied. "Men like us always work too much."

Siena wished she believed her father. Something in his tone—a lilt she didn't recognize right away—felt like he was placating her. Matteo wasn't very good at hiding those things. Or most times, he didn't even try.

He was the kind of man who believed women should be seen, but not heard. Especially the women in his life. He would never expect Siena to ask him anything, or to call him out on his lies. She had not been raised to do that, but right then, it took every ounce of her willpower not to do it.

The only reason she didn't do it was for John. She didn't want her father thinking something was wrong. Or rather, that she knew something was, as he said, off with John.

The Marcellos didn't trust the Calabrese family. Unfortunately, that also included her. There was nothing Siena could do about that, except stay loyal to the one person that mattered the most to her. *John.*

Regardless of how John's family felt, Siena was going to take care of John. That meant watching his back and looking out for him. He needed somebody on his side, and she was that person. They didn't have to believe it—or like it—for it to be true.

As for her father … well, there had to be a reason why the Marcellos didn't trust the Calabrese. Knowing her family like she did, she didn't need to question *why*. They had done enough things over the years that Siena had seen from afar to know that they would do anything to get wherever they wanted to be.

And her father?

Her brothers?

They had always wanted to be on top.

Had they done anything to John? No. At least, not that Siena had seen. Nothing that she could point to and say, yes, this was directly related to harming John, or his family.

She had seen nothing like that.

She knew nothing like that.

Yet.

Because with the men of her family, it was hard to tell what they might do next if given the opportunity. She didn't trust them, and she definitely didn't like her father digging for things about John.

Siena asked, "Is it okay if I take a day?"

"I guess so," Matteo said.

"Great, thanks."

"And do let John know he can come to me anytime, if he needs something."

"Yeah, I'll let him know."

Except she wouldn't.

Not at all.

Siena hung up the phone, and set the device aside. On the countertop, the screen blanked out. She continued to stare at it long after the phone call was over. Something just wasn't sitting right with her. Not about her father, and not about John.

She was brought back to the things she had been noticing about John. Things she had overlooked before because the changes had come on slowly, and she felt maybe they were normal for him, considering. She didn't have experience with bipolar.

Only John.

Siena knew the truth was clearer than she wanted to admit. She was close to John. *Very* close. Her perception of him was tainted by her feelings. She was willing to turn cheek to certain things because she cared, and she didn't want to upset him.

She was worried she might not be able to do that anymore. Not if it meant his health—mental or otherwise—well-being, and safety was on the line.

There was no doubt in her mind that John was not aware of the changes he was exhibiting. If he knew, wouldn't he ask for help? Wouldn't he do something about it?

She thought so.

Siena didn't snoop. She wasn't the type, and she didn't want to betray anyone's trust by doing so.

Especially not John.

But at the moment, John had headed out for a jog because apparently he needed to run even though it was February. He was grabbing them breakfast on the way back, or so he said.

What that meant to Siena, however, was that she had a few minutes alone inside John's place. She could either confirm or deny some of her suspicions about his current state.

It made her sick to think about it.

It hurt her heart to consider it.

Yet, she knew she didn't have a choice. If John was in the midst of a hypomanic episode, or working towards a full-blown mania, then it would only hurt him to continue to ignore it.

She couldn't ignore it.

She had to know.

Jordyn's words had been playing on repeat every day since the dinner.

He seems fine, she had said. *He seems productive. He'll work and work. He'll deny if you ask because he really doesn't think anything is wrong. Sometimes he can recognize his problem, and sometimes he can't. It's a roll of the dice.*

For whatever reason, Jordyn had felt like she needed to tell Siena those things. A part of her was grateful because it gave her a better sense of what was really going on with John, and maybe how to help. A smaller part of her had been stuck in a constant state of worry since that night.

Because …

What would it mean if John was approaching a full blown manic episode? What would it mean if he was already there? How could she help him, then?

Siena didn't know, so right then, she opted to push those thoughts aside. She would deal with it later.

Walking through the small two-level Queens home that John kept meticulously clean, Siena took things in again with a new eye. No dirt could be seen, and nothing was out of place. The bookcases and shelves showcasing the movies in the living room were organized by what seemed to be his favorites. The black shelves didn't have even one speck of dust. She was pretty sure she could eat off the floor, not that she would try.

Every room downstairs was the same. Clean, organized, and looking almost like a showcase. Not as though someone lived there, but as if it was ready for a buyer to come in and have a look around.

Cold, in a way. A lot of John's personality was not actually on display in his home. Sure, he had things he liked here and there. Artwork, knickknacks, and different things. But little else. Nothing to say he had just spent a good eight hours walking around in his own home, and once again, cleaning it from top to bottom.

Eight hours, Siena knew, because yet again, John had not slept. Every time she spent the night at his place, or he at hers, she would wake up to find John roaming the halls. He might be scrolling through his phone, or watching TV. Sometimes he would be cleaning something, or staring out the window at nothing.

When she asked, he assured her that he wasn't tired. Nothing he did belied that fact. He was full of energy, he kept going constantly, and he never missed a click. There was no sign of exhaustion in his eyes. He never even yawned.

So no, she didn't think he was tired. At least, not physically.

Mentally, though?

Mentally he had to be exhausted.

And maybe that was the problem. Maybe his mind just wouldn't stop. Maybe he couldn't sleep because his mind wouldn't slow down enough to allow his body to rest.

She was upstairs looking through the meticulously organized closet when she heard the doorbell ring downstairs. Quickly, she made her way down to the main floor, and didn't bother to check the front door before she swung it open.

On the other side, a delivery man waited. He had a whole moving dolly full of boxes. Big ones, and small ones.

Siena did a quick count.

Fifteen boxes in all.

"Sign for these, ma'am," the man said.

He held out a tablet and pen for her to write on.

"Are you sure these are for the right address?" Siena asked.

"Definitely for this address," the man said. "I've been delivering here every day for the last week."

Siena stilled. "Every single day?"

"That's what I said, ain't it?"

Siena signed for the goods, then allowed the delivery man to roll the dolly in, and set the boxes of things in the hallway. She didn't even bother to say goodbye to the man as he left the house, and closed the door behind him.

She was too busy staring at the pile of boxes. This was the first time all week that she had spent the night at John's house. She had been busy with work ever since the dinner with his family the week before.

Siena didn't even think about it as she stared at those boxes. She didn't consider that it might be a betrayal of John's trust. She had promised him she wouldn't overstep his personal boundaries, but this was worrying to her.

His mother had mentioned one specific thing that really stood out. One of his behaviors when he was dealing with mania was spending money. A lot of money. Sometimes, he didn't even remember that he had spent it. The things he bought didn't have to be needed, wanted, or otherwise.

It just had to be things.

In the kitchen, Siena pulled out a chair from the table, and dragged it to the fridge. Climbing up, she opened the cupboard doors overtop the fridge. There, she found his medications. By the looks of it, more medications than what he had the last time she accidentally stumbled upon them.

But this wasn't like the last time.

Siena actually pulled out the medications from the cupboard. She looked them over. She read the prescription dates when they had been filled, and for some, she even opened up the bottles and counted the pills. One bottle had been filled a month ago, and according to how many pills had been prescribed, it should have been empty.

Yet, it was still half full.

Lithium, the prescription read.

Another prescription of Lithium she pulled from the cupboard had been filled the week before. And yet, it had not even been opened.

And another med that had just been filled was also not opened. Several, actually.

Siena knew it for sure then.

John was in trouble.

Siena was waiting by the door when John finally came up the walkway. His one-hour run, and the promise to bring home breakfast, had turned in to three hours. It was already closing in on noon. She tried not to be worried, but she was way past that point now.

She opened the door before he could even reach for it. His wide smile at the sight of her standing there said he didn't see a thing wrong. Not with her, or with himself.

Siena knew that was half of the problem. At least for John.

"What happened to getting breakfast?" she asked.

John laughed. "Shit, I forgot."

"Forgot?"

"Yeah, I got caught up with something else."

"And what was that?"

John shrugged. "Saw somebody I recognize from way back. Before I knew it, we had been talking for a fucking hour."

She stepped back, and he walked into the house. He barely even passed a glance at the mountain of boxes sitting in the hallway. It was like they weren't a surprise to him, but he wasn't interested in them, either.

"John, these came this morning," she said.

He waved a hand, and nodded. "Yeah okay."

"When did you order them?"

"Not sure."

Siena frowned. "Well, what's in them?"

"Shit, I imagine."

And just like that, John was gone from her view and inside the kitchen. The boxes were forgotten, and he had moved on to something new.

Siena tried to work up the nerve to bring up his medications as she headed for the kitchen. Inside, she found him pulling out a glass, and filling it up with cold water. She had been up with him since six that morning. Because of that, she knew he hadn't taken his medications. He took them at breakfast.

With food.

Always.

He hadn't done that this morning. She wondered when the last time was that he had taken his meds, or even had an appointment with his therapist.

In sweatpants, a sweater, and with a wool cap pulled down over the top of his head, he didn't look like the cold weather outside had affected him at all. Like maybe he didn't feel it.

"John—"

Siena's question was interrupted by knock at the front door. She looked out the kitchen window, but couldn't see who it was from there. John dropped a kiss to her cheek as he passed her by, and left to answer the door.

Siena slipped into the hallway just as John pulled open the front door.

A man Siena didn't recognize stood waiting with a folder in his hands. The color of blood, the folder stood out brightly against the black outfit the man wore, and the white of the snow falling down around him.

"Kent," John said. "What are you doing here this morning?"

Kent handed over the file. "Somebody ran this to me today, and let me know I needed to get it to you as soon as possible."

John took the file, and tapped it against his palm. "Thanks, man."

The man nodded. "No problem, John."

Kent turned on the stoop, and left without another word. John closed the door, and faced Siena.

"Who was that?" she asked.

"An enforcer," John said, still looking at the file in his hands. "One that works for a Marcello Capo on the other side of the city."

"He came all the way over here to give you a file?"

"That's his job. He does what he's told, not what he wants to do."

John opened the file as he slid past Siena in the hall. It took all of two seconds for his easy-going posture to change. He went from unbothered and calm, to as stiff as a board just like that.

"John?"

He was silent. His back stayed turned to her. She couldn't see his eyes, or judge from the expression on his face what was wrong.

So quiet.

Deathly so.

"What the fuck?"

That was all he said.

Siena was frozen to the spot. "What is it?"

"I … don't know. I mean, I do—fuck."

His outburst sent a sharp stab of cold dread piercing into her heart. The file went flying from John's hand, and crashed into a wall in the next second. Papers scattered everywhere. In the next breath, he grabbed the small table that held knickknacks and a decorative glass bowl, and overturned it with just a flick of his wrist.

Glass shattered all over the floor. John's curses reverberated through the house.

Siena was still frozen in place.

She didn't know what to do. Move, or stay right where she was. A fear settled deep in her gut. Not a fear of John, but of the unknown. Because she realized in that moment that she didn't know how to help him.

"John," Siena said, "are you—"

"Why would they fucking send me that?" John's fist crashed through the wall, crumbling plaster. He didn't even flinch. She didn't think he felt the pain. Turning fast, he faced her with wild eyes and teeth bared. "Like they think I don't already know what your family did to mine? Like I need a fucking reminder everyday now, or something?"

Siena didn't understand what he was talking about. She didn't understand what had set this off.

"John—"

No matter what, this was still John to her. *Her* John. Even angry, confused, and irrational. He was still her John. She saw his outburst, and faced it head-on.

"Tell me what's wrong," she said.

"Fuck."

One last curse, and one more thrown item to the floor, and John turned his back. As fast as he was in front of her, he was gone. She heard his footsteps echo as he headed up the stairs.

Yet, she was still frozen in place.

It took far too long for Siena to move again. Instead of going after John, she moved to the papers on the floor. She picked up one, and then another. Newspaper clippings, and items of a similar nature stared back at her. Her gaze drifted over the words, and the pictures attached.

Old newspapers. Old news.

It was still as clear as day.

The intention was obvious.

Marco Grovatti, one of the headlines read, *killed in his home.*

Another one … another headline… *Johnathan Grovatti, son of murdered mob boss, attends father's funeral with wife.*

Young Calabrese Capo suspected of murdering former boss.

Carl Calabrese takes over Grovatti family.

Over and over again.

Headline after headline.

Newspaper clipping after newspaper clipping. All sent to John. Apparently, by his own family, if she had understood him correctly.

All that bad blood between their families was suddenly staring Siena right in the face. She didn't know what to do. Go upstairs to John, or stay stuck in her fear?

She knew one thing for sure, though.

John still needed help.

"Andino."

Andino turned from the man he was currently going over paperwork with, and his gaze found Siena standing just a few feet away. The restaurant bustled with patrons, and employees. It was closing in on dinner time, and the place seemed filled to the brim.

"Siena?"

She brushed her sweaty palms off on her tweed coat. Her heart raced. At that moment, her nerves were out of control. She felt like she was going to puke. Every single part of her screamed that this was wrong, and bad. She shouldn't be here. She shouldn't be doing this.

Not to John.

But she had to.

"How did you find me?" Andino asked.

Siena took a deep breath. "I heard John mention something on the phone to someone. He said he might come see you later. He mentioned this restaurant."

"John hasn't been here. Not today."

"He probably forgot. He's been doing that a lot lately."

Andino frowned. "What, forgetting things?"

"That's one."

He cleared his throat, and nodded once to the man at his side. "Give us a few minutes. Find a table, and I'll come see you when I'm done."

Then, to Siena, he said, "Let's go to my office."

Siena didn't say anything, simply followed behind Andino. He strolled through a busy kitchen, and bypassed the bustling employees. Once inside the office, he closed the door behind them. He didn't take a seat at the big desk, but he offered a chair to Siena.

She shook her head. "I just ... kind of feel better standing right now."

"All right."

"I think John needs help."

In a blink, Andino shoulders dropped. It was a subtle action, and someone else might not have even seen it. His face gave away nothing. There, he was still cold, and emotionless.

"Help how?" Andino asked.

"Today, he got something. This morning, I mean. A file, I guess. He said it was from—or the guy was from your family. An enforcer." Siena hoped her rambling made sense because she had been dealing with more than enough, and this was just one more thing to add to her pile at the moment. "He threw the file, and had a fit. Broke things, and then he left. I've been trying to call him. He's not taking his meds."

"Slow the hell down," Andino said. "One thing at a time."

Siena was shaking. Her fingers trembled, and her shoulders felt heavy. She stuffed her hands in the pockets of her coat, trying to hide her nerves. Anxiety was most definitely not her best friend.

Not in this circumstance.

"I think John's manic," she said.

Andino sucked in a sharp breath. "Manic."

"Yeah."

"What makes you think that?"

"Why are you so calm right now?" Siena asked. "Doesn't knowing that he's manic bother you?"

Andino cocked an eyebrow. "This is how I am, and how I need to be. Now, what makes you think that?"

"Things he's doing. Things he's done. Today. Yesterday. Everything."

"And you said he's not taking his meds?"

Siena shrugged. "No, I don't think so."

"I don't deal with maybes when it comes to John."

"Definitely not taking his meds the way he should be," she said.

"And this file that was delivered to him," Andino said. "What was in it?"

"Things about his great-grandfather. The one that was murdered by my grandfather."

Andino folded his arms over his chest. "And you're sure it was delivered by a Marcello man?"

"An enforcer. That's what John said."

"Why come to me?"

All over again, Siena's nerves made themselves known. She wanted to be anywhere but there. She couldn't betray John, and yet here she was, doing exactly that. She no longer had a choice.

"They might take him away from me," she said.

Andino quieted for a long time. He simply stared at her, and said nothing. It only made Siena's nerves worse, but she figured in that moment, the truth was better than lying. She knew how much John cared about Andino, and how much he trusted him. Whenever John spoke about his cousin, it was with great respect and a genuine fondness. Something she had never heard John use when he talked about anyone else. Except for maybe his mother.

"His mother told me things at the dinner on Sunday," Siena said, "about his mania. Things that he does, and how to recognize it. She explained the way he acts, and what might cause it."

"Which can sometimes be the smallest of things," Andino added.

Siena nodded. "Yeah, but it made me stop, and pay attention. Things I was overlooking before, or whatever else. Maybe this is partly my fault, and I don't want them—they already don't like me—to blame me for this, and take him from me. Would they do that? I don't know, and I don't want to risk it."

"And so you came to me."

"Yes."

"You said he left?"

"In a fit," she confirmed. "He was really upset, and he wouldn't even talk. I don't know where he went, and he won't answer my calls."

Andino let out a harsh sigh. "Well, the most important thing to do is find him, get him calm, and then get him settled enough to actually talk."

"I don't know how to do that," Siena said.

"It's not an easy thing to do with John, and you kind of learn how to do it over time. You came to me, Siena, and that's the best you can do. That was the right thing to do."

"Is it?"

"Sure. Why would you think differently?"

"Because it feels like I betrayed him."

"Trust me," Andino said, "when this all blows over, the last thing John will ever think you did is betray him. It's quite clear where your loyalty is, woman."

What did that even mean?

SEVENTEEN

"JOHN!"

John heard his cousin's shout from behind him, but continued walking. His mind was entirely focused on one thing, and one thing only. He was just a few steps away from getting some answers. Or at least, something that would get him closer to finding out who exactly in his family had sent him that file.

Days later, and he was still looking for answers.

He'd been on the move for hours. Too many—he lost count. His phone wouldn't stop ringing in his pocket. Buzzing and buzzing, and only irritating him more. He ignored it every time it rang.

He only knew it was the next day because the sun was out, and nightfall had already left him behind. Not that he spent it sleeping because he didn't. He hadn't even gone back home after he left.

Not once.

"John," Andino called again, "wait up."

Once again, John ignored his cousin. He grabbed the handle on the pool hall's front door, and swung it wide open. The smell of liquor, and walls that spent years being coated in smoke from cigarettes and cigars smacked him in the face. Nobody could smoke in the place now, of course, but that smell just didn't wash out. Sometimes, it couldn't even be painted out.

"Jesus, John," Andino growled, "what the hell is wrong with you?"

His cousin was right behind him, but John's eyes were scanning the crowd. Men playing pool at the tables, and gathered patrons at the bar paying for drinks. It was only a little past noon, and already, it looked like quite a few of them were drunk.

Good, this would make things a lot easier for John.

Andino's hand clapped John on the shoulder, but he brushed the touch off. He heard his cousin saying his name, and trying to talk to him, but he just had other things on his mind. Other shit to do.

Other fuckers to take care of.

Quickly, John found the fucker he was looking for. A short, chubby twenty something year old at the farthest pool table across the hall. Drake was his name. Or something like that. A foot soldier in a crew belonging to the same Capo of the enforcer who had delivered the file to John the day before.

"John, will you talk to me for a goddamn second?"

"In a minute, Andino," John said.

He didn't think to ask his cousin how he had found him, or why he was looking for him. Those were details, and at the moment, they were not the details John needed to know.

John headed across the pool hall, his strides long and heavy. He recognized a face or two, and a couple even called out his name with a wave. A greeting he otherwise would have returned, but at the moment, he just didn't give a fuck. He was not here for them, and he had no interest in speaking to them. They would not help his cause.

Drake didn't see him coming. He was too busy bent over the pool table, aiming for his next shot. A winning shot, if he had made it. The five hundred dollars sitting on the edge of the pool table told John that the guy wanted to make that shot.

The guy didn't get to take the shot.

John grabbed Drake by the back of his shirt, and yanked hard. In one swift motion, John flipped the guy over, and smashed his back into the next pool table. Drake let out a shout, one filled with pain, but John only smiled at the sound.

A couple of the guy's friends stepped forward, but Andino moved in fast. He always had John's back. Ride or die, no matter what. His cousin was there, doing what he needed to do. Even if he didn't know why John was doing what he was doing.

"Hey, Drake," John said smiling coldly. "Looks like you and me need to have a fucking chat."

Drake's brown eyes widened, and words stumbled from his mouth. "About what?"

John chuckled. "Guess you're going to find out, cocksucker."

Uncaring about the people watching or those closing in around him, John kept a firm hold on Drake as he dragged him across the pool hall. Someone from behind the bar, a face John didn't recognize, stepped out like he was going to help the guy. John just pointed a single finger at the man.

"Fucking try it," John dared.

The guy held up his hands in surrender, and it only made John laugh. His face was recognizable. He'd been here before, but not to do this. Nonetheless, they knew who the fuck he was, and what he could do. They knew his last name, and what it meant in this city.

Nobody wanted to get fucking messed up with that mess.

Nobody wanted to get messed up with the Marcellos.

Soon, John had Drake out of the pool hall. The cold February air whipped around them. John didn't feel anything at all. Seemed he couldn't feel anything, lately. When he did feel something, it was just a mess. He couldn't process it. It was too much, and he didn't want to deal with it.

Drake didn't fight too much as John dragged him behind the pool hall. A dirty alleyway filled with dumpsters, and moldy cardboard boxes. It stunk like death. It looked like some animals had been chewing on shit, and digging through garbage.

Rats, likely.

New York was filled with rats in more ways than one.

John tossed Drake to the ground, uncaring that the guy landed in filth and wetness. Standing over him, John bent down to make sure Drake got a good look at his eyes. He needed to look somebody right in the face when he wanted to know if they were lying to him or not.

"Who the fuck gave you the file?" John asked.

Drake blinked rapidly. "The-the—"

"The file, you stupid fuck. Who gave it to you?"

"I-I can't remember."

John let out of scoff and rolled his eyes out words. "You can't fucking remember something that happened within the past couple of days? You can't remember who put a giant red file in your goddamn hand? Maybe if I cut your fucking hand off, it'll jog your damn memories, asshole. How about that?"

"Well, I ..."

The guy started to scramble back on the ground. His hands dragged through the wetness, and his clothes were now covered in the dirt and filth. He looked like he wanted to be anywhere but there. Like he needed to get the fuck away from John, and fast.

He was right. His instincts were on point. He did need to get away from John, but it was too fucking late.

"Who gave you the file?" John asked again. "One last time to tell me who gave it to you, and told you to give it to Kent."

Drake stumbled over his words again, trying to come up with some fucking excuse. He mumbled a name. Tim, or some other generic bullshit. There were a million fucking Tims in the city.

"Tim who?" John asked.

"Tim-Tim-Tim ..."

Fuck this shit.

John pulled out the gun hidden inside his jacket, took a step forward, and beat Drake in the head with it. Once, and then twice. Again and again until the man's face was a bloody fucking mess. The rage that swelled through John was addictive. Finally, an emotion he understood, and one that was not so overwhelming because he knew exactly what to do with it.

John blinked, and in the next second, Drake was dead on the ground. His face was smashed in, and bloody. No breath left his lips.

"Jesus Christ, John."

He'd forgotten about his cousin. Andino hadn't forgotten about him, it seemed.

John stepped back, and straightened. In a flash, Andino had taken John's gun out of his hand and kept it out of reach. John took another step back, and then another. Andino kept looking at him in that way of his.

"John," Andino said, "look at me."

He did, but he didn't like the sight looking back at him.

"What the hell are you doing?" Andino asked. "Coming here like that, making a fucking public scene, and dragging him out of there where anybody could see you do it, John? And now somebody's going to come back here, and find his dead body. Guess who they're going to call. Guess who's going to take the rap for it, John. *You.* Where's your judgement—you didn't know this was a bad idea?"

John blinked, and his fists curled in tight balls at his sides. "I'm trying to get some fucking information."

"About the file?"

"How did you know about the file?"

Andino glanced away. "Not important, but is that what it is?"

"It is fucking important. Was it *you?*"

Disbelief stared John right in the face.

"Do you seriously think it was me?" Andino asked.

No.

Still …

"Somebody from our family sent me that file. They want me to know—they think I forgot what the Calabrese did to my family."

"John, listen to yourself."

This was all bad.

All of it.

His brain raced, and his heart thundered.

"John, where are you going?"

He didn't answer his cousin. He was already at the mouth of the alleyway, and stepping out onto the street when Andino yelled for him again.

Behind him, he could hear Andino making a call.

"Yeah, I got a mess that needs cleaned." Andino rattled off an address. "No, don't let the boss know and don't tell my father, either. This is for me. Let's keep it on the low."

John was already gone.

John slipped through a restaurant that shouldn't be familiar to him because of who owned it, and yet it still was. He visited the business a couple of times a week just to spend time with Siena, but before her, he wouldn't have stepped foot near the place.

She was already waiting for him at a table. Standing, too. He could see concern in her eyes, but he didn't know why.

She outstretched her arms to him, and he took the embrace. Dropping one kiss to her forehead, and then a second faster one to her lips. Her sweet little smile made his grin grow.

"You didn't answer my calls," she said.

John shrugged. "Busy."

"For three days?"

He didn't like where this line of questioning was going, so his best defense was to simply ignore it. Apparently, she had been one of the people who kept blowing up his phone non-stop.

"Everything's fine," he told her.

"I didn't ask," Siena said.

John gave her a look, and then took a seat at the table. "You going to sit, or what?"

Siena did take a seat at the table, but she still had that look in her eyes. She was searching for something in him, but he didn't know what to tell her. He didn't know what the fuck she was looking for.

"I thought we were going to that show last night," she said. "An early Valentine's gift."

Shit.

"I forgot," John said.

He tried to wave it off, but he could tell she didn't want to let it go. He knew what talking would do. Talking would only lead to a fight. The last thing he wanted to do was fight with Siena.

Not now.

Not ever.

"I'll make it up to you," he promised.

Siena frowned. "And how are you going to do that?"

"Give me a little bit to figure it out."

"Maybe we don't have a little bit."

John heard her, but he was already waving to the waiter.

"Our usual," he called out.

The waiter nodded, and headed for the kitchen.

"John," Siena said. "Are you listening to me?"

"Yeah, I'm listening."

"Then, where have you been?"

"Working."

"Did you see your cousin?"

With one simple question, John's attention was entirely focused on Siena again. "What do you mean, see my cousin?"

"Andino."

John tipped his head to the side. "Did you talk to Andino?"

Siena's gaze darted away. "We ran in to each other."

Lies.

He saw her lies.

This woman never lied.

Not to him.

"Try that again," he told her. "This time, though, with the truth."

Siena swallowed hard. "I was worried about you."

That was all John needed to hear. In a second, his desire to have food, and even be near this woman was gone just like that. Andino had been following John around since he found him at the pool hall. Talking about John's frame of mind and shit he had no business discussing. Things John wasn't willing to talk about with anybody other than his useless fucking therapist.

"John, wait," Siena said, standing from the table.

No, he was done.

At least for now.

"I'll call you," he told her.

Siena sucked in a sharp breath. "John, I'm sorry."

Fuck that.

His back was to her in the next breath, and then he was gone. He never walked out of that restaurant so fast before. Unfortunately, the man he ran in to outside the business made his blood boil just as badly.

Matteo Calabrese.

"John," Matteo said. "I didn't expect to see you here. Siena again?"

"Actually, I was just leaving."

"Well, wait a second now. I hear the Marcellos are having a Valentine's party for the family."

John hesitated. "Are they? I wouldn't know."

Matteo nodded with a chuckle. "Guess you're not invited then, huh?"

The two men stared at each other as the busy street moved around them. Matteo, a Calabrese man who John both despised and distrusted with every fiber of his being. And John, the one Marcello who always seemed to be on the outside looking in when it came to his family.

Something Matteo always like to point out. Or maybe it was just something that the man recognized, when everyone else seem to want to ignore it.

"You know where I am, John," Matteo said, "if you ever need somebody to talk to. You know I'm always around."

Why did that feel like a hand to help him up as much as it did a threat?

The Marcellos were known for their parties. All through the year, the family threw events for nearly every holiday. Everyone in the organization was welcome to attend. It was always an open invitation. Made men, the wives, and their kids. John had become accustomed to these kinds of parties over the years.

Yet, as he strolled through the old Marcello mansion, passing by people he knew, and even his own family, he had never felt more out of place. Like mannequins smiling, waving, and talking to him as if they knew each other, like they were old friends.

Except, like mannequins, they seemed plastic. Realistic to look at, and yet still fake.

In the crowd he picked out his grandparents. Old in their features, yet animated and young in their cheer as they chatted with guests. In the corner, he found Andino drinking something dark red from a wine glass.

He didn't know if his cousin had seen him. John's attention was elsewhere.

Like always, the top men of the Marcello organization gathered in the same spot for these parties. The main room where they could see and talk to everyone, and also be the center of attention.

This party didn't look like it was anything different.

John cut through the people, and headed for the one man he needed to speak to. His father.

Lucian saw him coming, and stepped away from his brothers. "John."

"You didn't think to invite me?"

"You didn't think to answer your phone?"

John shoved his hands in his pockets, and stared hard at his father. The differences between them in that moment were a bright contrast, and easy to pick out. Lucian, in his fitted suit. John, in jeans and a hoodie.

"Have you been talking to Andino, or something?" John asked.

His father frowned. "Why would I talk to Andino?"

Did his father not know? Did none of them know what he had done to a man just a couple of days before in a back alleyway?

"I don't know if it was you, or Dante, or who the fuck it was," John said, "but I don't need any of you sending me shit like you did last week."

"What are you talking about?"

"Don't play fucking games with me, Dad."

Lucian took a step toward his son. "John, are you all right?"

John bristled at the question. "Is that all any of you ever think about with me? If I'm okay, if I can handle myself, if my shit is taken care of? I am fucking *fine*, Dad."

The level of John's tone drew attention. His uncles looked his way, and some of the guests. He saw his mother break away from his aunts, and come their way. John had no interest in talking with her, either.

"I only came here to make one fucking thing clear," John said.

Lucian held a hand up high when Dante stepped closer, as though he were going to step in on the conversation. It kept the Marcello boss from coming any nearer to them. Although, it wasn't like John gave a fuck either way.

"And what's that, son?" Lucian asked.

John smirked. "Remember, it's not my loyalty in this family that ever needs to be in question."

With that peace said, John turned on his heel and headed back into the crowd. People parted, letting him pass through. Their murmurs reached his ears, but he didn't really hear what they were saying.

His point had been made. People would talk.

John was not to be fucked with.

Not by his family. Not by anyone.

The grogginess in John's mind was so heavy that he struggled to stay awake as he peeled open his eyes. He wondered how long he had been asleep while he stretched his arms high above his head. He rubbed his palms against his face. The thickness of his facial stubble said it had been far too long since he had a shave.

He stared up at the familiar ceiling, but confusion filled his mind. He knew instantly where he was. It was as comforting as it was concerning.

He struggled to remember the events of the night before. A party for his family. He went, and made a scene. On his way out, he tossed back a couple of drinks. The frantic pace of his mind grew and sped up until he could barely take anything in at all.

Still, he pushed through the clashing and crashing thoughts to dig for more information as to how he got here. He left the Marcello mansion, and that was the last thing John could remember.

He struggled to bring back more memories. His chest burned like he had been drinking hard liquor all night long. The taste in his mouth said he likely had been doing exactly that. A deep pounding headache in his temples only confirmed it further.

But even drunk, or hungover, John wasn't one to lose his memories. He was not one to forget.

Yet, the space in his head was only a giant black hole filled with nothing, and giving him nothing when he tried to pull something from it.

"John?"

Her soft voice in the bed comforted him, and also made him stiffen. He looked over in the bed to see her staring at him with soft, familiar blue eyes.

"Siena," he murmured.

Her hand reached out. A tentative touch stroked his cheek, and woke him up further.

"How are you feeling?" she asked.

"The same way I did yesterday."

Out of control. Bulletproof.

Confused. Pissed off.

Too fast. Too slow.

Not right at all.

"When did I get here?" he asked.

Siena's brow furrowed, and she stroked his cheek again with her fingertips. "Showed up here around twelve."

"And you just let me in?"

"I couldn't just keep you out."

Something wasn't right with him. Everything was wrong with him. He knew it now more than ever.

"John—"

Siena's words were cut off by his ringing cell phone. The last thing John wanted to do was answer that phone, but he had been ignoring it for so long, and putting off too many things. Waking up with no memory and feeling like he was meant one thing.

He crashed.

Hard.

Now, he was scattered in broken pieces and wondering how he had gotten here to begin with.

Picking up the phone John put it to his ear and said, "Yeah, John here."

"What did you do?"

John rubbed at his eyes. "Andino?"

"The warehouse, John. Did you do it?"

John didn't know what in the hell his cousin was talking about. "What warehouse?"

"The Calabrese warehouse. The one your crew uses with them. It burned to the ground last night, John. Guess who is blaming you for it?"

John hung up the phone, and stared up at the ceiling. The deadweight settled in his stomach, and a burning dread drove into his heart.

Yet, his mind raced. Up and down.

Unstoppable.

He shouldn't have hung up the phone. He should have said he didn't do it.

Problem was, John didn't know if that was the truth.

EIGHTEEN

John shoved his legs into his pants. "You're sure I got here around twelve last night?"

Siena crawled out of the bed. "Yeah, around then."

She kept the sheet clutched to her chest. It wasn't like she was trying to hide her body from him, or anything. Most of the night before had been spent with them in bed together. He arrived at her place looking like he was out of his mind, and without a thing to say.

He didn't want to talk. He only wanted to fuck.

Siena hadn't been able to turn him away. As much as it killed her to see John like that, and to let him use her like that, she let him in. She had already let him into her heart, her bed, and into her life.

What difference would last night make?

None at all.

Fact was, Siena was selfish. She wanted John. She didn't care about the rest— those were details that they could handle at another time. She needed him close, and she wanted him with her. No matter his frame of mind, she just wanted him.

So, when he showed up at her door, she didn't ask questions. She didn't press him for information, or ask him where he had been. She didn't demand to know why he hadn't answered her phone calls or reply to any of her texts. He was there, and that was all that mattered.

"Did I smell like smoke?" he asked.

Siena frowned. "Smoke?"

"That's what I said!"

Siena straighten on the spot, and clutched the sheet tighter in her fist. "You don't need to yell at me, John."

"I didn't yell."

"You don't even hear yourself right now, do you?"

John hesitated when he grabbed his shirt. Instead of putting it on, he stared over at her. The two of them stood like that, staring at each other for a long while before one of them finally spoke and broke the silence.

"Have you seen your therapist?" Siena asked.

John's throat bobbed with a swallow. "Monday, maybe. Or Tuesday."

"You're not sure?"

"One of those days."

Siena nodded once. "When you *did* actually see her, have you told her that you haven't been taking your meds?"

John tensed all over. In a blink, Siena could see how his entire demeanor changed at her simple question. She doubted anyone had outright asked him that lately, if at all. Had he even been around anyone who would dare to ask him that question?

"Have you told her?"

"I've been taking my meds," John said.

"Have you?" Siena asked. "I've seen your meds, John. I counted the pills. They don't add up to the prescription and fill date."

His jaw hardened as his lips pulled back into a sneer. He turned on her with that look, and she knew something nasty was about to leave his mouth. A defense mechanism, maybe. Or it could have even been his mania still manifesting in a verbal form.

Siena really didn't know.

She couldn't let this go.

"Before you speak," she told him, "think very carefully about what you want to say to me. Consider if I am asking these things to hurt you, or because I care, John."

His posture softened.

As did his expression.

Siena took that as a good sign.

"My meds aren't important right now," John eventually said. "What I need to know is what happened last night."

"You showed up here."

"Nothing else? I didn't say anything? I didn't tell you anything?"

"No, all you really wanted to do was fuck, actually."

John shook his head, and pulled the shirt on. "I need to know what happened last night."

"I can't tell you."

"Then what fucking use are you?"

Siena sucked in a hard breath. His words stabbed at her skin, and cut out her heart. He might as well have just punched her in the chest, and ripped her heart out from between her rib cage. It would have hurt just the same.

"I'm sorry," John quickly said. "I didn't mean that."

And yet, even when he apologized, he was still getting dressed. He didn't look at her, or see how badly his words had hurt when they made their impact.

He didn't know at all.

His impulse control, judgement, and empathy was gone out the window. Entirely.

"I know."

And she did know.

But it still hurt.

It still worried her.

Then, John's words came out in a ramble. A mess of thoughts and feelings that Siena could only stand there and listen to, but not do much else. It was more than he had said to her in a long while.

Too long, really.

She thought it was probably the most honest thing he had said in a long while, too.

"The bitch kept messing with my meds," he said. "First it was I needed to try this, and then try that. Up this dose, and then lower that dose. If it wasn't one thing, it was another. All the meds put me in this goddamn fog that I couldn't get out of. I would be sleeping twelve hours a day, and I could barely think when I was awake. I told her—I told her again, and then I would tell her *again*, but all she would do was tell me to give it time. Like I had to let the fucking meds do what they had to do, and let them settle. She wasn't even fucking giving them time to settle."

John scrubbed a hand down his face. "She didn't seem to want to fucking listen to me when I said the one was enough. The Lithium worked for me for the last three years when I was in lockup. She kept saying this wasn't lock up. I felt like her fucking lab rat."

Siena came a little bit closer to him, being careful and mindful in her steps. She didn't reach out, or try to touch him despite how much she wanted to. And oh, how she wanted to.

Her heart ached for her to touch him.

Her fingers itched to feel him.

All of her wanted all of him.

Even like this.

"Back when I went after my sister, I was without my meds for a little while," he continued, shaking his head with a bitter laugh. "It's strange how your own head fucks with you—makes you think you're okay without the meds because you feel better for a split second. I got back after going after Lucia, and I wasn't in a fog. So, I started dropping the cocktail of meds the bitch kept feeding me."

"John," she said, "please let me help you. I love you. You know that, don't you? You have to know I love you."

John's hazel gaze drifted to her. "Do you?"

"You think that I can't?"

"I think that maybe you shouldn't."

"I do."

John reached for her then, and his arms wrapped around her. He dragged her close. There, in his embrace, she was happy again. They were fine again.

It would only last a moment.

It would never last forever.

It *couldn't*.

"I love you," he murmured against her forehead.

That was enough for Siena.

That was all she needed.

It made everything else worth it.

John kept Siena close to his side as they headed in a restaurant that looked to be in the midst of renovations. She didn't recognize the business, and since she was always aware of when her father or brothers bought a new business, she knew this one didn't belong to the Calabrese.

"Neutral grounds," John said, as though he could read her mind. "This belongs to a Donati man. They agreed to allow the Marcello and Calabrese families to gather here for this meeting. That way, no one is stepping on anyone else's toes here, so to speak."

Siena nodded. "Makes sense."

Inside the restaurant, she found more people than she expected waiting. She recognized almost all of them. Men from her father's family, and several people from John's side.

At the head of the room, her father and Dante Marcello stood toe-to-toe. The two men looked as though they were ready to brawl. She took that as a bad fucking sign.

At Siena and John's presence, the two men finally looked away from one another. She wasn't sure that she particularly like their attention on them, either.

"John, move to anywhere except where you currently are," Dante said.

John didn't move an inch. "No, I don't think I will."

Matteo look at Siena. "I've called you five times this morning."

Her gaze drifted between her father, and her brothers standing with the other men of the Calabrese family. She could feel their judgment, and their silent opinions searing into her skin. She didn't need to hear them say it, not when she could feel it.

"Busy," she said.

Matteo coughed as his gaze cut to John. "I bet."

"Why would you bring a woman here?" Dante asked.

"I brought her here because she asked to come."

Siena's fingers tighten around John's. She no longer wanted to let him go. Something felt like a thorn pricking at her heart. Her worst fear was that someone would take John away from her—because of this, or something else.

It didn't matter, because the end result would be the same.

John would not be with her.

Siena had barely finished getting dressed earlier when John's phone started to ring again. This time, it was not Andino calling him, but his uncle. *I'm eating*, was all he said.

He was to be there—at the meeting.

No matter what.

That was the order.

Siena didn't even think about what it would mean if she went with him to the meeting. She only knew that she wanted to go. John agreed, and so here she was.

"He burned down my warehouse," Matteo said, his gaze darting back to Dante. "You will answer for that, or he will. I do not care which one it is."

"You don't know for sure that—"

Matteo took one more step forward, the threat blazing in his eyes. "Who the fuck else would have done it, Marcello, *you*? One of your men, perhaps? Did you order it because you felt I was too close? You never did like it when the Calabrese get close to your men. Did you finally have enough?"

Dante's jaw hardened, but his face gave away nothing. Not an emotion, nothing at all.

"There's a reason why the Marcellos and the Calabrese don't mix business," Dante said. "And you know very well what that reason is, Matteo."

"And yet," Matteo said, "you had no problem with my daughter and your nephew."

"I had every problem with it."

Matteo sneered, and his eyes drifted to John once more. "Who's to say he didn't do it? Everyone in your family knows the man is unstable. Hell, anyone who spends time with him knows it."

John's stiffened beside Siena. She held tighter to him when she felt his muscles tense as though he was about to spring forward. His body felt like a winding coil about to come undone.

"John," she whispered too low for anyone else to hear, "it's okay."

It was like he didn't hear her at all.

"Say that again," John uttered.

Matteo gaze stayed firmly on John when he said, "It's no secret that you're crazy, John. The way you go on sometimes, and the shit you do … this isn't a surprise. What is a surprise is how long your family was able to keep it quiet."

Siena couldn't keep her hold on John after that statement. He ripped away from her side like a bullet shooting from a gun. He was a foot away from her father before someone was quick enough to step in and grab him.

Actually, several people.

And just like that, a meeting that had a possibility to be peaceful and calm was now chaos and violence.

"Say that again!"

John's words echoed above the shouting men.

Only a laugh answered him back.

Held back by his cousin, father, and uncle, they were barely keeping ahold of John. Matteo gave another one of his sneers. A signature look for her father. Something he always gave to someone when he felt above them, and he wanted them to know they were beneath him.

She was not surprised to see him use it on John.

"I think this meeting is done," Dante said.

Matteo turned away, and waved a hand to his men. "It was done before it ever began, Dante. We both know that. We're leaving."

Siena moved toward John, but she didn't make it far.

Kev grabbed her arm forcefully enough to leave bruises behind, and dragged her with him. Her protests, and her shouts to be left alone, went unheard. All she saw was the burning hazel of John's eyes before the restaurant door slammed closed.

Siena's heart felt as heavy as her feet. As though cement had been poured in both, and were now weighing her down.

She glanced back at the enforcer who stood with his arms crossed at the car. He kept an eye on her—a threatening eye—as she stood on the sidewalk. Her new best friend, as her father like to say.

She couldn't go anywhere without the enforcer either driving her, or following her.

Today was no exception.

The enforcer was just one new change in her life since the week before. Her father had also taken her cell phone away, and refused to provide her with a new one. The freedom she had been given with living away from home was suddenly ripped from her grasp. She had been relocated to her parents' home without any explanation.

Her days now consisted of waking up, working wherever her father told her she had to work, and going home to her parents' brownstone.

She didn't know where John was, and had not spoken to him in days. She didn't even know if he was okay.

"Are you going in?" the enforcer asked from behind her.

Siena gritted her teeth, and forced herself to be polite. There was no need to make the man run back to her father, and report bad behavior. All that would make for was another long night with Matteo raging on.

She didn't need that.

Nobody needed that.

She was struggling between keeping her father happy, and needing to know something—anything—about John.

"Well?"

Siena looked back at the enforcer. "Yeah, I'm going in."

"I'll be here waiting when you get out."

Unfortunately, Siena didn't doubt it.

She headed into the business, and was thankful that today, the restaurant wasn't as busy as it usually was. Instead of heading right for the back to an office to work, she went to the bar first. The blonde acting as the bartender for the day gave her a smile.

"Want a drink?"

Siena laughed. "A whole bottle would be great."

"Not sure I can do that."

"How about something to make this day worth it?"

"One of those, huh?"

Siena scoffed—the girl had no idea. "One of those."

The girl nodded. "Yeah, I got something for that."

Less than a minute later, the bartender slid three fingers worth of whiskey across the bar in a lowball glass. Siena eyed the drink, but didn't pick it up. She really wasn't a big drinker, but she also really needed something to get through the damn day.

"You don't like whiskey?"

"Not particularly."

"Throw it back fast, and hold your breath."

Siena did just that, but the whiskey still burned, and her chest felt like it was on fire when she sucked in a hard breath. At the same time, a deep warmth spread through her blood and body. It was enough to feel like she might make it a couple more hours today without a breakdown.

Anything to get through the damn day.

Siena pushed the glass back to the bartender. "Did you see my brothers come in yet?"

The woman nodded once. "Yeah, both of them. They're in the back."

Great.

Not wanting to waste any more time lest Darren or Kev get on the phone to her father, Siena headed for the back of the restaurant. She still walked a bit slower than normal to get that extra minute or two, so she didn't have to be in the presence of one of her brothers. What a sad mess her life had become.

She heard the voices of her brothers filtering down the hall the closer she came to the office. Kev first, and then Darren.

"The Marcellos are in a fit," Kev said.

"It worked, though," Darren replied. "Shame we couldn't get John to turn on them like Dad first wanted."

"Can only do so much. Move onto Plan B, when Plan A doesn't work out the way you want it to. Dad couldn't get John in close enough, so he pushed him on a little bit with the file. Still didn't get enough out of that, so we made it worse by burning the warehouse. See what all that did for us?"

"We're going to have to be careful for a little while," Darren said. "On the streets, I mean. I got word it's going to be all out war once we finish this off."

"Who would have thought the Marcello family gave that much of a shit about a fuck up like Johnathan Marcello?" Kev laughed. "As if being fucking crazy isn't enough of a disgrace for his family with the bipolar, now they're going to back him in this mess, too."

"You don't know that. You're assuming they'll back him here, but maybe this could be a last straw type of deal for them," Darren said. "How long has he been like this—how many messes have they cleaned up for him over the years? John's crazy. It didn't take very much for us to make it worse for him. I don't think he can count on his family as much this time around."

Kev's laughter came out louder the second time around. "Let's hope that's the motherfucking truth. Either way, they're all going down."

Siena couldn't stop her footsteps if she tried. Her heart filled with rage and hate as she stepped in the office doorway. Both brothers looked her way, but neither of them seemed very surprised to see her standing there.

"You're late," Kev said.

Story of her fucking life.

"I'm always late," she said. "It's nothing new."

"Yeah, well, you've got work to do," Darren said. "So get to it."

She had other shit to do now, too.

"How fucking dare you?"

Darren's gaze narrowed.

Kev's eyebrow raised. "Excuse me?"

Siena didn't bat a lash. "You heard what I said, and I heard exactly what you were just saying, too."

"Heard that did you?" Kev asked, waving a hand at her as if to flick her away from him. "Listen, Siena, you know enough about this business to know the Marcello family and the Calabrese family can't mix. The fact that Dad let you go on as long as he did with John should have been a hint that something was up."

Should it have?

She didn't think it should.

"How did you know?" she asked. "About John's disorder, I mean."

Darren smirked. "We had our suspicions. Rumors travel far and wide in this business, you know."

"And you forgot about this little thing called browsing history," Kev added.

Siena's heart stopped for a split second. She knew exactly what her brother was talking about without even asking for him to explain. The one time she had searched for information about her suspicions regarding Johnathan, she had used a computer in one of Kev's offices. Sure, she had closed the browser in time, but she should have known better than to trust her brother.

Privacy was an illusion for Siena. She wasn't actually granted any at all when it came to the men of her family. She should not have assumed otherwise. Look what happened.

Marcellos were right.

The Calabrese family was full of snakes.

And she was looking at two of them.

"Don't worry," Kev said, "this will all be over soon. Dad will get what he wants, and we can all move on. This has been a long time in the making, Siena, and you won't be the one to ruin it."

"And what does that mean?" she asked.

Kev shrugged from his position behind the desk, saying, "Well, the Marcellos are two seconds away from starting a war with the Calabrese. A war Dad thinks he can win. They just need a little shove."

"Might as well start with John," Darren added.

Siena's soul slipped from her body. She swore it did. Nothing had ever felt quite so painful before.

"You're a Calabrese, Siena," Kev said. "You should really start acting like it."

NINETEEN

"Amelia will see you now," the receptionist said.

John stood from the chair, and his father followed suit. The receptionist's gaze widened when the two headed for the office door.

"I'm sorry," she said, "but only John can attend his appointment unless the doctor has otherwise stated for the session."

"No," Lucian said, "I will be seeing her, too."

"I can't allow—"

"It doesn't matter what you can't allow," Lucian interjected fast. "It matters what will happen regardless of what you say."

John was only half listening. A part of him was there, and present. Another part of him was somewhere else entirely.

He followed behind his father as Lucian entered the office, feeling like a child again. It reminded him of all those times when as a young boy and teenager he had visited office after office, doctor after doctor, therapist after therapist with his parents. Each one offered something different as an explanation. He had been diagnosed as ADHD, and then ADD, and even by one, as on the autism spectrum. It was difficult knowing that none of those really fit, either.

His parents had never done that to harm him, or anything of the sort. In fact, it had been the exact opposite. They took him to person after person, desperately trying to help John when he was a child. They needed answers, not for them, but for him.

And eventually, they got those answers.

Bipolar.

He wasn't sure if that was the answer his parents had wanted, however.

Now, here they were again. John was thirty, a grown ass man, and his father was attending yet another appointment. To be fair, Lucian only came after he went through John's home, and found the massive pile of medications prescribed by Amelia, and then overheard as his son tried to deflect yet another scheduled appointment with the therapist.

John should have had this shit handled. Neither one of his parents should be involved. He didn't know which emotion to deal with first.

The guilt.

Or the irritation.

The way the two battled against each other was a poison to John's mind. It was hard to know that his anger was irrational when his mind came up with too many different reasons to justify it. The reasons didn't have to be good ones, of course, just *reasons*. It was even more difficult to deal with the guilt when the anger was an easier emotion to feed.

Yet, the two warred.

On and on it went.

Distracting him.

Sucking him in.

Taking him away.

"Johnathan."

At the sound of his therapist's voice, John realize that he was actually sitting in her office. Just like that, once more, he lost seconds. More moments gone from his day that he couldn't explain.

Time erased.

"How long have you known my son was manic?" Lucian asked.

"I'm sorry," Amelia said, "but I can't speak about my patient—"

"This is my son," Lucian interrupted. "And at the moment, what he needs right now the most, is the proper help. And I need to know if that is you, or if you are unintentionally hurting him."

"Hurting him?" The therapist stood from her chair, and discarded the clipboard and pen in her hand to the seat. "I've been treating John since he was released from prison. Yes, I have noticed that he was possibly entering a hypomanic stage, but—"

"But nothing," Lucian said. "At that point, the discussion ends. At the point you understood, or at the very least suspected that he was hypomanic, your job was to stabilize him. Nothing more."

"I—"

"Stabilize him," Lucian echoed again. "Not feed him more medications, or allow the hypomania to worsen into full blown mania by ignoring it."

"I did not ignore—"

Finally, John snapped out of his daze. He wasn't sure what did it—his father being his voice when he had suddenly stop learning how to be that for himself after all these years, or the therapist who was blatantly lying. John had tried to tell her for months on end what was happening with him in too many different ways to count.

"I said over and over again," John muttered, "that it was too many medications. I didn't need them. I need less, not more. I went through intensive therapy learning how to manage my anxiety and depression because I can't mix those medications with extra mood stabilizers. Putting them on top of medications I already take only puts me in a fog."

"Yes, but John—"

"But *nothing*," John said, sick, tired, and entirely over this whole charade. "I'm telling you right now what I need. I've dealt with this disorder. I've went through medication after medication. Not you. *Me*."

Lucian looked to John, and frowned. "He is his only voice—you are supposed to be the advocate for that voice, but you weren't. And for what? To suit your beliefs? Because you believed he didn't have a grasp on his disorder? What was it?"

Amelia didn't reply.

Lucian didn't back down.

"He came out of prison *stable*," Lucian stressed. "The most stable he has been in years."

"It's normal for those with bipolar to need medication changes!"

Finally, his therapist was able to get out one full sentence without being interrupted. Still, it was the wrong thing to say.

"But did he need it?" Lucian asked.

189

Amelia tipped her chin up. "I felt so, yes. I felt he could better manage other aspects made more present because of his disorder in this way. Like the depression, and the anxiety. Medication can help with all of that."

"Yet, he managed fine without extra meds before."

John glanced up at the clock. He was acutely aware of the ticking sound it made. For some reason, it felt like it was ticking inside his body. Something was counting down inside him, but he didn't know what it was.

"I stopped taking the other meds, and halved the Lithium to every other day just so I could think again," John said.

All eyes in the room turned on him.

Not for long, though.

Lucian turned back on the therapist in a blink. "You will hand over his files to whichever doctor's office contacts you for them. If you so much as breathe a word in his parole officer's direction that he is no longer having appointments here before we can find someone new, I will ruin you."

Amelia straightened on the spot. "Excuse me?"

"Have you ever seen a building this size burn?" Lucian asked. "I've seen them come down in twenty minutes or less. Oh, and your husband is an interesting man. He's thinking about running for the mayor next year, isn't he? I would hate for something to change that."

John's gaze drifted between the conversation happening in front of him, and the clock on the wall. The damn thing was still counting down.

But to what?

"And if you hand in your license to practice," Lucian said, "even fucking better."

"It's like a fucking pharmacy in here."

John heard his cousin, but he was too busy looking at the clock on the wall of his parents' kitchen. That tick-tick-ticking was still counting down inside of him. A count down that had not yet reached the end. A count down that he did not know what exactly was counting down.

He counted the numbers on the clock once, and then twice. He watched the second hand tick-tick-tick its way through another minute, and then two more.

Time was passing.

Time was moving.

John felt suspended.

Unmoved.

Frozen.

It was only when Andino sat at the other side of the table did John finally look at his cousin. How many days had it been since he last saw Andino? A few, maybe. Or could have been only one.

John had no clue.

Andino said nothing, simply stared at John for a long while. He didn't press John to talk.

For that, he was grateful. At the moment, he didn't know exactly what he would say anyway.

He remembered that over the last several months, Andino had been the one who stepped in time and time again to try and help John. He did so at the risk of himself, and without asking for anything in return.

Even after everything that happened between Andino and John years ago, his cousin was still one of the only people John could count on. No matter what.

And how had he repaid his cousin for that kind of loyalty?

John pushed Andino away. He dropped the ball, and left Andino holding it. His cousin had cleaned up his messes over and over.

The guilt growing inside John's chest only compounded at those thoughts. It darkened his mind, and grew like tendrils inside of him to clench around his heart and squeeze tight. Those brief moments of lucidity and clear thoughts were quickly interrupted by something else entirely.

It was easy then for words like *worthless* and *useless* to whisper through his mind. Those black, dark thoughts should have been a clue to John as to what he was now edging towards, but like everything else in his life, it was difficult to recognize.

Spread out on the table were all the medications that had been prescribed to John over the last several months. He hadn't realized just how many medications it actually was until his father dumped them out on the table.

It damn near filled the whole thing.

Three different mood stabilizers. Antidepressants. Antianxiety meds. A different dosage of Lithium for every month that he had been seeing Amelia.

Andino was right. It did look like a pharmacy.

"What is all this?" Andino asked.

He gestured at the bottles of pills.

John shrugged. "My meds."

Andino's eyes widened at the admittance, but otherwise he gave nothing away as to how he felt. "You take all of them?"

"No, maybe one or if it's going badly—a lot of shit happening, you know what I mean?—then I might add another just to settle it out."

"Then why is there so many?"

"Somebody thought I was a guinea pig."

Andino nodded. "Well, as long as it's settled now."

"Something like that."

John could see that Andino wanted to ask more. He probably wasn't satisfied with the lack of responses, or John's unwillingness to talk.

It wasn't exactly purposeful. It wasn't like John meant to be so quiet, or off-putting. At the moment, he simply had nothing else to say. He had other things to think about. He had memories that continued to stick to the back this mind like tar.

Impossible to get off or shake, and burning him over and over again. It wouldn't let him go, and instead, taunted him with the reality he had not been able to see before.

Memories of those he trusted, and those he distrusted, had muddled together overtime. He had mistook his paranoia and his raging emotions, and directed them in the wrong place because of his own bias. He had assumed wrongly about those who had never given him a reason to think that way.

It was a strange conclusion to come to.

Yet, he knew that no one around him would hear him if he tried to explain. It was hard to hear John when he was manic. The rational side of him was often lost to the irrational. In violent outbursts, and rambling admissions.

Who could make sense of that?

He understood. He didn't blame those around him. It wasn't their fault. They could only deal with what was presented in front of them because they didn't know what was hiding underneath.

"You know now," Andino said, "don't you?"

John looked up at his cousin. "Know what?"

"That you can't trust any of them."

"Not all."

Andino shook his head. "John, the Calabrese family has done nothing but try to ruin you, and the Marcellos. You see that now, don't you? We're damn near in an all-out war with them on the streets right now. This is exactly what they wanted from us. Matteo might as well have just fucking admitted it."

"Not all," John said again.

His cousin's frustration grew, and with it, John's irritation spiked up as well. It was another by-product of being in the state that he was. Conversations were not easy, and communication was made harder.

He could talk and talk and talk for days like this, but it would still lead them in the same goddamn circle. That's just how it was.

John knew it, and it made him less willing to speak in the first place. Besides, he had said his piece. He said what he meant, and he meant what he said.

He couldn't help if Andino did not—or could not—understand John's compromise. He didn't blame any of them, though. None of them understood what it was like to be him.

John couldn't explain it. No matter how hard he tried.

Mania for John was a vicious bitch. It manifested in so many different forms that it was sometimes hard to keep track. One day he could be highly productive, and laughing because he was almost high with the way he felt. The world seemed to move so fast around him on those days. The next day, he could be so low that the only thing he felt was right was lashing out at anyone he could reach.

It was violent. It was mean. It was nasty.

He knew after it was all said and done, and the dust cleared, that for those around him, his mania could be terrifying.

It was every reason why Cella and Liliana no longer made any effort to have a relationship with John. They had been some of the first people to experience the way his mania manifested in horrible ways. Like a tornado, he had ripped through their lives when they should have been doing anything but trying to hide from their older brother.

Instead of having happy memories of years that should have been good, they were tainted and colored dark. Too many moments of peace when John had been stable, and then bouts of chaos when his mania came out to play.

His sisters never spoke as adults about how their brother's episodes had affected them when they were younger; they simply kept a distance. They didn't allow him into their lives beyond the shallow surface, and they didn't intrude on his life, either.

It also taught others in John's family that when the mania darkened, it was better to step away unless they could handle what it might throw at them.

"John, listen—"

"I'm not taking those fucking pills!"

Lucian shot his wife a look from the side. Jordyn wrung her hands together from the kitchen's entryway, however, she didn't step in more than she already had. Her worry was as clear as day, but so was her fear.

Of what might come next. Of what John might do next. Of what her son might say next. This was not the first time. It would not be the last time.

It could never be the last time. John's brain was wired this way. He was who he was, and eventually, he always came back to this manic stage.

It would break, sure.

He would have moments of peace, yes. A long spread of time when he was right and good again. He always came back to this, eventually. It was the one thing he could bank on in his life.

"Jordyn, go."

Lucian's order drifted over deaf ears. John's mother didn't move an inch. Unlike a lot of the women in his life, his mother was one who was unafraid of him in his mania a good portion of the time. She always faced it head-on, but with soothing words and a comforting touch.

He heard her. He felt her. It just didn't help.

"I want to go home," John snarled at his father.

Lucian didn't blink in the face of his son's rage. "You can't."

"I've been here long enough!"

"You've been here a day."

John felt like someone had punched him in the throat.

A day. That was all.

A single day felt like weeks to John. Time was bleeding together, and he was missing it. Time was running out to fix the things he had somehow missed, and he was letting it.

"I'm not taking those pills," he repeated.

Lucian frowned. "They could help stabilize you a little more until we get you in with someone else."

No, they wouldn't. They would make his mania worse now.

Lithium had to be stopped when other antipsychotics were introduced. Otherwise, more meds needed to be added to the regime to balance out the counter effects of the mix. That only led John into the fog that had gotten him into this mess in the first place.

No, he wasn't doing that again.

"If you won't take meds, then I need you to stay," his father said. "I can't let you—"

"Because you don't get it," John hurled at his father. "You don't give a shit what it will do, or how it will change what's going on in my head right now."

He couldn't forget. He couldn't afford to forget anything right now.

"John, you have to let us take care—"

"I don't have to do fucking anything!"

Lucian stepped forward at John's rage, but all he saw was a threat coming at him. One that was meant to hold him back, and stop him from finishing what had started decades and decades before.

They would lock him in. They would hold him back.

He needed to do this. They wouldn't understand.

The second Lucian grabbed ahold of John, he snapped. What control he had over himself was gone. It had already been holding on by a thin thread as it was. He shoved his father hard, and didn't even feel the slightest flicker of guilt when Lucian slammed into the kitchen island.

He heard his mother's gasp, and his father's curse.

Still, he knew what he had to do. The clock was still ticking.

Tick. Tick. Tick. Counting down ...

John grabbed his jacket from the back of the chair before he darted past his mother in the entryway. Her shout echoed from behind him. His father's footsteps reverberated down the hall.

Lucian wasn't fast enough. He had never been able to catch John once his son made the choice to run.

John snatched the keys from the glass bowl on the table near the front door. Keys for a black Mercedes SUV belonging to his father. It wouldn't be the first time John had stolen one of his father's cars.

"John!"

The front door slammed behind him. He didn't even feel the cold wind as it wrapped around him. Inside, he was a fire burning out of control.

A raging devastation ready to ruin.

John was already pulling out of the driveway by the time his father had come out of the house. In the rearview mirror, he saw Lucian toss his hands up high. Exhaustion and wariness stared back in his father's eyes.

He knew that look well.

This could be a tiring state.

John was tiring.

The lights of the highway bled together. Like a scene from a fast-moving movie, it felt just as surreal.

John pulled the phone from his pocket, and turned the device on for the first time in he didn't know how long.

Too long.

He dialed a number. One he would have never called otherwise.

The man answered cheerfully. Like he had everything to be happy about.

"You said I could talk," John said into the phone. "Whenever, right?"

TWENTY

Siena's gaze drifted between the screen in front of her, and Kev sitting across the desk. Something on her brother's phone had become extremely interesting to him, but she didn't know what exactly it was.

Still, she couldn't ignore how heavy her stomach felt. Like a dead weight had come along to sit down and make itself at home. Nothing she did was getting rid of the dreadful feeling.

Her gaze darted to the landline on the corner of the desk. More than once since she had arrived at the restaurant, she had considered trying to make a call. Yet, every time she attempted to do just that, her efforts were thwarted by one of her brothers coming in the office.

Even when Darren had left for a couple of hours earlier, and Kev stepped out for a smoke, the enforcer came inside to sit with Siena while she worked.

For some reason, they were keeping a very close eye on her.

She couldn't breathe loudly without one of them looking at her.

What were they planning?

What was going on?

Nothing good, she suspected.

"What are you doing?" her brother asked.

Siena looked at Kev again. "Working."

"Then, why are you sitting there doing nothing?"

Jesus Christ.

She couldn't even be still without one of them suspecting something was up.

She knew it then …

Something was definitely about to happen.

Siena just wished she knew what it was.

"Do you want to stare at a computer screen for hours on end, and sit in this uncomfortable chair without barely moving at all? I can't take a minute to stretch my fingers and blink?"

Kev cocked a brow. "As long as that's all you do."

Asshole.

Siena kept her thoughts inside her head, but barely. If only she could get a couple of minutes alone, then she might be able to send out a call from the landline.

Something to warn John that her brothers and father were planning an attack on him. One that would push his family in to a war with the Calabrese.

Who else would tell them?

Kev stayed sitting in the chair across from Siena's desk. He wasn't moving an inch. The longer she stared at her brother, silently willing him to even get up and use the damn bathroom while Darren had stepped out, the more pissed off she became.

Siena's mouth opened to tell her brother off just for existing. Darren slid into the office, and stopped her from saying anything. The grin he sported was downright smug.

If not altogether evil.

"Well?" Kev asked.

Darren nodded. "Yeah, it's happening."

"How do you know?"

"Dad got a call. By tomorrow, this city is not going to know what hit it."

Kev returned his brother's grin. "About damn time."

"The Calabrese have waited a long time for this day."

Siena tried to remain calm as she listened to the conversation between her brothers. She didn't let a single emotion crack through her calm facade. If Kev or Darren thought Siena was planning something, or was even a little too interested in their conversation, she had no doubt they would lock her in even more than they already had.

At the moment, it was a risk she was not willing to take.

Sure, they didn't mention any names, and were careful about details. It didn't matter. It was enough for her to figure out something bad was going to happen.

Something between the Marcello and Calabrese families.

Something that probably involved John.

And she just couldn't allow that to happen.

"Does he want us to head over there just in case?" Kev asked.

Darren shrugged, and dropped into the chair beside his older brother. "No, he's sure he can handle it alone. He did mention something else, though."

"What's that?"

"I guess you-know-who is sounding even more unstable today."

Two pairs of blue eyes drifted in Siena's direction. Her gaze was firmly stuck on the computer screen in front of her, but she still saw her brothers' passing glance out of the corner of her eye.

That confirmed it.

Without any doubt.

They were talking about John.

They were planning something.

Tonight.

Siena's fingers drifted over the keys on the keyboard. Random letters and numbers appeared in the tables, but didn't actually make any sense. She only wanted her brothers to think she was working, after all.

The two continued talking, albeit quieter than before. It was hard for Siena to discern their conversation, so she opted to continue typing.

Not for long, though.

When she thought Kev and Darren were too distracted in their conversation, she took the risk of standing from her chair.

Neither one of her brothers missed it.

"Where the fuck are you going?" Kev asked.

Siena didn't hesitate. "To the bathroom. I have to change my tam—"

At just the suggestion she was on her period—she hadn't had a period since starting the shot two years ago—both of her brothers looked like she had smacked them in the face with a shovel.

Had it been any other time, she might have laughed.

"Go, then."

Darren scowled. "But hurry up and finish here, Siena. We have other shit to do tonight."

For the first time all day, Siena was out of her brothers' sights. The bathroom was at the very end of the hallway. There was a men's and women's, but no private bathroom for the employees.

The restaurant had closed about an hour ago, and Siena was grateful. She pushed a hand against the bathroom door as she passed it by to make it sound like she had gone in.

She didn't go inside, though. Instead, she went further out onto the restaurant's main floor. At first, she considered just leaving the restaurant while she had the chance. The enforcer still sitting in the car outside the place told her that wouldn't be a very good idea.

Siena let out a hard breath. Her gaze darted over the room, and then to the kitchen.

The phone in there, maybe.

It was worth a shot.

As long as she got a call out, then the rest didn't matter. She would deal with whatever came her way from her brothers.

She only needed to make a single goddamn call.

Siena darted for the kitchen. The landline hanging on the wall was a godsend. She picked it up, and dialed the only Marcello phone number she knew.

John's.

It rang and rang.

Her heart grew heavy.

Seconds passed.

The call went to voicemail.

Siena cursed, and tried again.

More ringing.

More nothing.

The sickness in her stomach damn near climbed up her throat, and threatened to spill out onto the floor. She tried one last time, but again, she got no response.

Siena didn't know if that was because John refused to take a call from her, or if he couldn't. The very thought of that almost made her puke, too.

She hung up the phone with a little more force than she meant to.

Think. You're not stupid, so figure this out.

Her thoughts taunted her.

The dark kitchen stared back at her. The chef made sure to clean his space thoroughly before leaving for the night. Hanging above the stainless-steel counter was a row of frying pans, skillets, and more. A deep-dish frying pan caught her eye.

Siena hesitated.

She was not violent.

She did not do this kind of thing.

But for John?

Rules did not apply.

She grabbed the deep-dish pan, and gave it a second look when she realized how substantially heavy it was in her palm. Really, she didn't have the time to second guess which pan to use. She headed out of the kitchen, and tried to keep her footsteps light as she crossed the main floor again. She had only rounded the corner nearing the hallway when she heard her brothers talking again.

"I don't know what this is," Darren said.

"These aren't even numbers. It's just a damn mess. Go get her."

"Yeah, all right."

Siena quickly darted into the women's bathroom. Holding that pan back as far as she could over her shoulder, she waited for the bathroom door to open.

When it did swing inward, she closed her eyes and let the pan go.

The sound it made when it cracked against Darren's forehead was sickening. It nearly matched the way his body slumped forward, and fell head first into the tiled floor.

"Darren?" Kev called.

The bathroom door wouldn't shut completely. Darren's body—he was knocked out entirely—was in the way.

Siena stepped over her brother, not sure if she should be happy that he was still breathing, and moved into the hallway. She took a couple of steps until she was just outside the office.

Kev appeared in the doorway.

She swung the pan again. Kev wasn't like Darren. She had to hit him twice before he stayed down. She didn't bother to check if he was still breathing, too.

Siena made sure to grab both of their cell phones, and cut the wires to the landlines before she left the restaurant from the back exit.

How much of a head start did she have?

That was the million-dollar question.

Siena had too much riding on it to lose.

The taxi driver glared when Siena tossed a handful of bills over his shoulder to pay for the ride. She wasn't even sure if it was enough money to pay the man. She didn't particularly care at the moment, either.

"Don't leave yet," she said. "I may need you again."

His shout echoed at her back when she jumped out of the back of the car, and to the sidewalk. She took the stairs leading into the entrance of a familiar restaurant two at a time.

Andino Marcello's restaurant.

The place looked like it was closed. The business hours hung from a sign on the door, taunting her further. Not one single light was turned on inside, and she could see the tables had been cleared. The chairs were all upturned on the tops of the tables, too. The front door was locked when she tried to pull it open.

Shit.

She yanked and yanked on the door until a sob broke through her chest.

Fuck.

Why did it have to be like this?

Why couldn't one single thing go right for her tonight?

"Siena?"

Siena turned fast on her heels to face a blonde she recognized. Haven. The woman climbed the restaurant steps quickly until she was just a foot away.

Salvation stared Siena in the face.

"What are you doing here?" Haven asked.

"Where is Andino?"

She didn't have time for small talk.

She didn't have time to explain.

"He was here working in the office," Haven said. "But he got called out a while ago."

"Where is he *now*?"

Haven glanced away. "Why?"

Siena could tell just by the look in Haven's eyes that the woman didn't want to give up any information about Andino. Maybe she had been told not to, or something.

It really didn't matter in that moment.

"Let me guess, you're not supposed to trust me either, right?"

"Well—"

"I don't have time for this," Siena hissed, heading back down the stairs. "John is in trouble."

"John?"

Haven's quiet question made Siena's footsteps falter. She hesitated, and glanced over her shoulder.

"Yeah, John."

"Andino is a couple of blocks away. I guess John's father called. He took off."

"John did?" Siena asked.

Haven nodded. "Yeah. Earlier."

Oh, God, no.

Siena didn't have time to go somewhere else yet again. She couldn't chase people all over the city in hopes that she would finally find someone who would actually listen to her, believe what she said, and help.

Her brothers had said it. Tonight was the night.

They didn't say John's name, but what they had said had been more than enough to make Siena believe that's who they meant.

Which meant he was probably heading to her father's place now.

Siena turned back on Haven. "Please, tell them John is at my father's home."

Haven swallowed hard. "Why would I do that?"

"Because if you don't, Andino will never forgive you when they finally get John's body back from my family."

The blonde stilled in place like a statue with a gaze full of ice.

Siena was already heading back down the stairs. "I can't chase them. I have to help John instead."

Behind her, Haven called out, "Don't make me regret this, okay?"

Siena laughed.

The only thing she regretted at the moment was being born a Calabrese.

Siena didn't recognize the black Mercedes SUV that had been left running on the side of the road in front of her parents' brownstone. The taxi driver pulled away from the curb, still pissed that this time, she had all but thrown a handful of credit cards at the back of his head.

Her mother's car was not parked in the driveway beside Matteo's tan-colored Suburban. She wasn't surprised about that. Her father often sent her mother away for the night when he planned to do business inside the brownstone.

Coraline never questioned Matteo.

She never refused him.

The perfect little mob wife.

Siena found the brownstone was unlocked. She opened the door with a careful hand, not wanting to make more noise than was necessary.

She had no idea what she might walk in to. She didn't know what to expect just beyond the front door.

Surprisingly, she found the foyer and front hallway empty and dark. Her father's boots and coat rested in their usual spot, while her mother's belongings were missing. Further proving her belief that Coraline was not home at all.

Even the kitchen and living room were dark and lifeless. The counters were spotless, and nothing was out of place. It almost made her wonder if her mother had been home at all as it didn't look like someone had even cooked supper.

Siena didn't go to the back of the house on the bottom floor because she didn't hear anything coming from that direction. Nothing was really back there, anyway, and her father always had his meetings in his office upstairs.

Would he kill Johnathan in his home?

Would he risk doing something like that where his wife might come home and see?

A memory stood out to Siena. One deep in the recesses of her mind from when she was just a child. A loud noise had woken her from bed one night when she was barely five, and scared her to death because of the moaning that followed.

The next morning, she remembered watching her mother cover a reddish-brown stain on the living room carpet with another decorative carpet. Before the day was out, the carpet had been ripped up and replaced with hardwood flooring. Any carpets in the home had been replaced as to not have a similar incident occur.

No one ever spoke about it.

No one ever explained what happened.

Siena figured she knew.

And it answered her own question.

Yes, her father would kill here.

No, he would not care.

Siena was on the second floor of the brownstone when she first heard their voices echoing from one floor higher.

Her father.

And John.

"Of course, you can trust me," her father said. "I wanted you to understand, Johnathan, how they see you. Like the dirty little secret they have to hide. I didn't hide it. Doesn't that say you can trust me?"

John's answering words made her heart miss a beat. "More than them?"

"Far more than them, Johnathan."

No, he couldn't.

He couldn't trust Matteo at all.

Siena picked up the pace, and took the last stairwell two steps at a time. She was sure her footsteps would be heard, but that was exactly what she wanted.

Maybe ...

God, maybe, Matteo would not kill in front of her. Maybe her presence would be the one and only saving grace for John.

She didn't know.

But she had to try.

More conversation drifted down from the office, giving Siena a bit of hope that she still had a few seconds left to spare. Siena ran from the top of the stairs, and down the hall when her father's voice rang out first.

"Loyalty is hard to come by in this life. You need to take it from those who have always proven they're willing to give it to you."

"Every Marcello knows loyalty doesn't come from a Calabrese," Johnathan replied. "You forgot that even though I bleed Grovatti blood, I've always been a Marcello man."

Bang.

The gunshot was so loud that Siena flinched. The scream caught in her throat as she rounded the doorway to her father's office.

She thought for sure ...

Every part of her believed ...

A gun fell from John's hand.

Her father bled out as his body slumped over the desk. Blood trickled in a thick stream from the circular wound in his forehead.

John looked over his shoulder.

Siena stared back, unafraid.

"I'm not sorry."

Didn't he know?

"You don't ever have to be, John."

He never had to apologize to her.

Not for himself.

Siena stayed close to John in the bed. His features were relaxed, telling her that he had finally slipped into a deep sleep.

She had never seen him so out of it before.

It had only been those brief few seconds in her father's office when he had seemed lucid and understood what was happening around him. And then as easily as his mind was clear and right, he was lost again to some place she couldn't bring him back from.

It had only been his father and cousin's arrival minutes later that saved John from doing something else he might have regretted later.

Siena made only one demand.

Take him to his own home. Let him wake up in his bed. Somewhere he would recognize instantly. A place that was comforting and familiar to him. He would have chosen his own home, she knew.

Lucian had agreed to bend to that one demand. He didn't give her much else, though.

"You know," came a voice from the doorway, "it isn't usually this exciting with John."

She found John's father standing there watching her. She didn't care how she looked resting beside John while he slept, and stroking his face.

This is where she wanted to be.

So, she didn't move.

"Oh?" she asked.

Lucian chuckled dryly. "No, these episodes have become less and less frequent over the years, and not nearly as severe as they once were. Maybe that's why when they do happen, they take us all by surprise."

"When was the last severe one?"

She thought she knew the answer.

But she wanted to be sure, too.

"Over three years ago." Lucian leaned against the doorjamb, adding, "And before that, four years. Sure, he's gone into a hypomanic stage—the hyperactivity, lots of energy, and highly productive—but recognized what was happening and got it under control before it worsened. I think this was a mixture of a lot of things for John. Too many changes in his life at once, and trying to push through it regardless.

"One part of it, anyway," Lucian continued. "His family plays a big role. Maybe more than some of us want to admit."

"How so?"

She felt like these were important things for her to know. Her only goal after this was to be the one thing—the one person—whom John could depend on, no matter what. No one would ever hurt him or do to him again what had been done to him this time.

She would make sure of it.

"He often says we smother him, or make him feel as though he can't take care of himself," Lucian said, shrugging his broad shoulders. "We do things that seem as though we're taking away his control, or managing his life for him. We know he can handle it—he's been on his own since he was eighteen. Still, we're always waiting for that next episode, and I think he knows that, too. And so, he pushes away from us, and stays on the outskirts of our lives where we can't come close enough to touch his. We have things to change, too."

Siena nodded. "I can understand that."

"Does that ... bother you?"

"That this sort of thing is a possibility?" she asked back.

Lucian shrugged.

"No, it doesn't bother me."

John's father stared at her for a long while before he nodded, and then pushed away from the door. "I have to make some calls, Siena. We're downstairs if you need us."

Alone with John again, Siena settled back into the bed. She tucked her body in closer to his, and wished sleep would take her under, too.

Reality kept her wide awake.

What was going to happen now?

How would things change for them now?

Siena didn't know how long she had been lost to her thoughts before another form darkened the doorway. This time, it was Andino.

"Siena."

She glanced his way. "What?"

"Someone is here for you."

She straightened in the bed. "Who?"

"I assume he's one of your father's men. Or, was. Either way, he says Kev has sent for you."

Andino's dry, flat replies bothered Siena in a way she couldn't explain. Her heart thudded hard in her throat.

"Understand," Andino said, "that we don't have a choice but to hand you back over to them right now."

Her eyes prickled with tears.

"But why?"

Andino stared hard at the floor. "We're unprotected at the moment. We thought about John, but didn't prepare for anything else. We don't have a choice."

Siena's gaze drifted from John, and then back to Andino. "What will happen if I don't go?"

"They have several vehicles outside at the moment. We can safely assume each one has a driver, obviously, but likely more. What do you think?"

No.

Her heart broke all over again.

"I'm sorry," Andino murmured.

Siena shook her head, and quickly wiped away the tears that slipped down over her cheeks. "No, it's okay."

It really wasn't.

She could only imagine what life was going to be like for her once she left this house. She had not only attacked her brothers in order to help John, but also betrayed her own family. They had probably found her father's body by now, and put things together seeing as how they found her with John.

This was bad.

For her, it was going to be really bad.

Moving off the bed, Siena headed for the door with slow steps. Every single inch of her screamed to turn back around, and hide in the bed with John.

At the door, Andino stopped her with a hand on her shoulder.

"This isn't over," he told her. "Know that this is only temporary."

"I don't know anything, Andino."

All she wanted was John.

Andino nodded once. "We'll finish this."

She didn't ask how.

She didn't want to know.

"How fast?" she asked.

"That, I don't know."

Siena looked back at John. "They can't ever hurt him like that again, Andino. No one can ever hurt him or use his own mind against him ever again."

The man stared at her for a long while, saying nothing. Like maybe he had found something he hadn't even been looking for.

Siena knew what it was.

Loyalty.

Like him, her loyalty was sparse and carefully hidden. She didn't offer it freely, and only to a select few.

John was one of them.

He would always be.

"Ever," Siena repeated.

"Never," Andino agreed.

TWENTY-ONE

John stumbled from the bed. A muddy sensation filled up his mind. A medication-induced fog had nothing on a manic break. The exhaustion that came on a person when the mania finally left was unlike anything else.

A hell he would wish on no one.

Not even his worst enemy.

It was like a thousand pounds of rocks had slipped into his body to replace his muscles and bones. Cement had been used in place of his blood.

Walking was a chore.

Breathing was too much work.

Being alive was troublesome.

John moved down the stairs of his home, grateful that somehow, he had been brought home—or made his way—to a familiar place. It made this process so much easier to understand. He felt less out of place, even though not a single thing in his life currently felt right.

He took the stairs carefully, navigating one after the other with heavy feet while he held onto the banister. The quiet chatter coming from the kitchen drew his attention in that direction.

He recognized the voices. Andino, and his father. However, there was one voice missing. One voice that he wanted to hear the most.

In the haze of his memories of the week and night before, John distinctly remembered one person standing out the most above all others.

Siena.

Where was she?

Why wasn't she here?

He was sure that she had been in bed with him the night before. His eyes had cracked open, though they felt like someone had taped them shut, and he had seen her lying next to him.

That had not been his mania.

He had not imagined her there.

So, where was she?

John stumbled into the kitchen. Instantly, the gazes of his father and cousin darted his way. Lucian stood from the table first, and then Andino quickly followed suit.

"John," his father said. "How are you feeling?"

In Lucian's eyes, John could see the questions his father didn't ask. Things about his mind, and what was currently going on up in there.

John didn't know what he would say if his father did ask. His thoughts were slower, and his mind was not warring between emotions, and trying to process them. He did not have so much shit muddling up his brain, even if it did still feel muddy in ways.

It was better.

Not like it had been.

"Where is she?" he asked.

Lucian looked at Andino, and then back to John. "Who, son?"

"You know who."

He was not playing this fucking game with them.

Andino took a step forward. A hesitant step. He had a right to be hesitant, John knew. After the weeks and weeks of mania, anyone had a right to look at John in that moment with a little bit of hesitancy.

"Siena?" Andino asked.

Is this twenty fucking questions?

"Where is she?"

Andino swallowed hard. A nervous tic his cousin tried his best to hide, but never quite succeeded with his family. "John—"

"Where is she?"

His roar reverberated through the home. The sound made his head ache even worse, and his heart hurt like nothing fucking else. His soul was slipping from his fingertips, and he couldn't grab it. He couldn't hold on to it.

All he wanted was to hold on to it.

"Where is she?"

"We had no choice," Andino said.

"No choice," John echoed.

What did that mean?

What did that mean for her?

What did that mean for him?

What did that mean for them?

"They sent for her," Andino said.

"We had no choice," Lucian confirmed, "unless we were willing to have them come in on us unprotected, and we were not. Not with you in the midst of a mental break, John. We wouldn't have been able to get some kind of backup here in time to help."

John nodded, but the action felt robotic. Just an action his brain told his body to do, but not something he had actually wanted to do.

Silently, he turned around and left the kitchen. He wasn't quite sure how he made it back up the stairs, but he did. Soon enough, he was in his bed once more. The blankets suffocated him, but he liked it just fine that way. He brought them tighter around himself, until he could barely breathe at all.

The darkness seeped in through his mind, and spread through his body like poison.

He didn't want to move.

He didn't want to breathe.

He didn't want to see.

He didn't want to feel.

He didn't want to be.

This was what the mania was like when it finally broke.

A dark nothingness that settled deep within John's body and psyche. A harsh emptiness that left him lonely, and so out of touch with everything, and everyone. His body ached, and his mind screamed into blackness.

A depression that almost nothing could fix.

Or, that's how it felt.

John wasn't sure how long he stayed like that before he felt a hand touch his shoulder over top the blanket. The blanket was tugged away just enough for him to see his father looking down at him.

Lucian tried to give him a smile, but it didn't feel true. Nothing could be true.

"It'll be okay John," his father said. "Another one of those things for us to figure out."

"Will it?"

How could it be?

"We'll handle it, John. We always handle it."

John thought about how easy it would be to fix this problem forever. How simple it would be to take away the one issue that constantly brought his father and the rest of his family so much heartache, and so much trouble.

Him, that was.

He thought of the gun in the bedside drawer. He knew what gun metal tasted like. It wouldn't be the first time he tried to swallow a bullet.

Wouldn't it be easier?

He thought so.

He also knew those thoughts—those self-harming thoughts—were not entirely his own. And if he didn't speak up to deal with them now, they would only get far worse.

John looked up at his father. "I'm sorry I hurt you, Dad."

With words.

With violence.

With more …

Lucian shook his head. "You always see these things far differently than the rest of us, John."

Maybe.

"Tell her I'm sorry I had to go again."

Lucian frowned. "What?"

"Siena. I'm always leaving her with no explanation. I promised I wouldn't do that anymore."

"We'll fix this, John."

"Sure."

For now, though …

He had to fix himself.

"Are you not interested in talking with me at all today, Johnathan?"

The white-haired, bespectacled therapist rarely ever sat down during his sessions with John. The man liked to move, and it was a little disconcerting for him. Especially considering John liked to look at people when he talked to them. See their eyes, and gage their words when they spoke.

His therapist at Clearview Oaks Facility was everything John was not accustomed to. And yet, John looked forward to this hour every day with Leonard.

"I don't know if I want to talk, no," John admitted. "I haven't done much of that today."

He hadn't talked a lot at all since he voluntarily admitted himself into the place. That was three weeks ago.

The first week was hell.

Suicide watch all the way.

They didn't put him in a padded room or anything, but they did the next best thing. They took everything and anything away from him that could be used as a tool to harm himself. Shoelaces, plastic, bed sheets, and more. They even gave him clothes with double sewn hems and no elastics so that he couldn't pull them apart. When he ate breakfast, someone had been sitting beside him, and he was forced to use a spoon.

For everything.

Even a steak.

All in all, the facility was nothing like a psych ward at a hospital. It was more open, and the staff was welcoming. The grounds were beautiful when he had finally been allowed outside on the second week. His time was spent between his private room, therapy, and roaming between different activities. The expensive facility toted everything from a spa, to a state-of-the-art gym.

"I've noticed you don't rapid cycle," the man said.

"No, I'm not a rapid cycler."

"Ever?"

"In mania, maybe."

Leonard nodded. "That would make sense. In general, though, you don't find yourself rapidly cycling between highs and lows daily or even weekly?"

"No, not generally. That's more common in bipolar women, isn't it?"

"Typically, but I have seen it in men, too. I was curious. Give me a one to ten on the depression today," Leonard said. "One being good, and ten being the worst. As always."

"A four, maybe."

"We don't deal in maybes, John."

Of course, not.

"Five."

Leonard nodded like that was more the answer he expected. "Good. Another couple of days and we'll start weaning the antidepressants away."

And begin a new mood stabilizer regime.

John knew how this worked.

What he liked the most about this facility was that his therapist listened. He looked over files from John's history, and saw the facts staring him in the face. He didn't deny those facts, or try or push too many different choices on John.

He didn't need a constantly changing martini of medications. His disorder was most stable when he only had to take one or two.

"So," the therapist asked as he rounded the couch, "are you going to talk with me today, or not?"

"We talk," John said.

Leonard tapped the top of his nose, and then pointed the same finger at John. "Safe topics, sure. But not what brought you here, or the things that drove you into your latest manic spiral. You have to deal with all of that so then the next time—"

"I'm prepared."

"Yes," Leonard said with a smile. "Exactly."

"Do I have to?"

Today was just one of those days for John. He was tired, and would much rather be in bed than doing anything else. That's why he settled on a five and not a four for the depression.

"I think today is a good day to talk, John. You see, you have a visitor coming. I was forewarned by your father during our last phone call that you would greatly like to see this woman who is coming later today. So, I am absolutely not above using the means I have at my disposal to get you talking."

He had no reason to believe it was *her*, and yet, something inside knew it absolutely was her.

Siena.

John's throat tightened at the thought.

"Blackmail, you mean," John said to Leonard.

The therapist chuckled. "Well, that's a language you understand, isn't it? Men like us always understand the language of blackmail."

Men like us.

Criminals.

Living in shades of gray, and never black and white.

John knew there was a reason his father suggested this facility, and pushed his son to take the opening when it was offered. Something other than the prestigious name, expensive price tag, and privacy it offered.

"Talk?" Leonard asked.

"If I answer one, can I ask one?"

The white-haired man smiled. "I can't promise to answer, John."

"Yeah, me either."

"Tell me, I know you struggled to agree to voluntarily check yourself in this facility. Why is that?"

John swallowed the knot in his throat. "Because everything I have worked to keep from the public would be exposed."

"Being bipolar?"

He only gave a nod. "My turn. Who are you?"

The man raised one thick eyebrow. "A man who used to be someone entirely different, John."

"And my father knew who you were before?"

"It's my turn."

Shit.

"Yeah," John said, "I guess it is."

"Why hide your disorder?"

"Would you want to be known as the disgrace of your family?"

Leonard coughed gently. "Is that how you see your disorder?"

"Bit self-deprecating, isn't it? That typically isn't my style."

"And yet …"

John shrugged one shoulder. "It's my one thing."

"Have you ever taken a good look around at your family, Johnathan? Have you looked at the structure of support and unconditional love they've built around you? Do you know that your father calls me every day just to make sure you have had *one* single good day? I know that it is sometimes easier to alienate yourself away from those you love because it's simpler."

"I hurt them. All the time."

"Not all the time."

That was up for debate.

And not one John wanted to have.

"My turn," he said.

"Go ahead."

"Mafia, or otherwise?"

The therapist flashed a grin that spoke of years long gone, and a younger man. "Otherwise."

"Hmm."

"Your father tells me you've met a woman—love, he said. He believed you to be in love."

"Just how much have you talked to my father?" John asked.

"More than you care to know. Old friends, so to speak. You don't recognize me at all, do you?"

John's gaze narrowed. "For business, or otherwise?"

"I diagnosed you, Johnathan, after your first severe manic episode."

Jesus Christ.

John could do nothing but stare at the man. Leonard simply stared right back, unmoved. He wasn't quite sure how he felt knowing that he was staring at the man who had changed his life forever with a simple diagnosis. He didn't know whether to be grateful, or something else entirely.

"It's been over ten years," the therapist said, tipping his head to the side a bit as he eyed John, "and of course, you were in a very bad place. They opted not to treat you in a facility back then, and so I referred them to someone who would go in-home."

"It's been a little over thirteen years, actually, and I begged them not to put me in a place."

"I know. Now, about the woman."

"Siena," John murmured. "Yeah."

"Do you think the change in your emotional circumstance and just her in general might have … had an impact on edging you toward the hypomanic stage?"

"No."

"Not at all?"

"If anything, she held me back for longer," John admitted. "I feel like I fucked up at the end with her—that she's going to feel like I didn't do enough to keep her with me after everything she did for me. At first, when I realized they had sent her back to them, I was still in a state of suspension; between the manic break, and the heavy depression. I should have gone after her. I should have—"

"Should or could?"

John met the therapist's gaze. "I wish I had."

"You checked yourself in here being suicidal, and low functioning. You were fresh off a mental break, and certainly not in any position to be going to war with anybody for a woman, John."

"How do I tell her that?"

Leonard raised one thick brow. "I don't think you'll have to tell her anything. If she is a good woman, she will understand your situation."

"She is."

"Pardon?"

"A good woman," John clarified.

Leonard smiled. "Then, you've talked yourself out of that problem. Haven't you?"

"Maybe."

A bit.

"Hmm," Leonard said. "Your turn."

"Specialty?"

The man smiled widely, clearly understanding John's question without further details. "Cocaine, actually. Smuggling, specifically. See, I am a hobby pilot, John. I think you might call that a—"

"Side-hustle. Nice."

"It served me well over the years. On you, though, how do you feel about this … Siena?"

John barked out a laugh. "Her, or love?"

"It has to be both, doesn't it?"

Leonard was right, of course.

John knew it.

"It's hard to grasp the concept that someone loves me the way she loves me," John said quietly.

"Self-deprecating again."

John shook his head. "No, I just never thought that was going to happen. I didn't look for it—this disorder ruins so many things for me when I bring people close because they can't handle it, or I shove them away."

"And she …?"

"Kept coming back."

"And what does that mean for you?"

"My biggest fear with people is that once they know—or see what this is really like for me—it becomes John *with* bipolar. She just sees me."

"John."

"She only sees me."

Leonard ticked a finger in John's direction. "Well done, John."

"My turn?"

"Your turn."

Siena's gaze was only on John as she entered the facility after being checked in by one of the nurses. The white dress she wore made him think she looked like some kind of angel gracing his life.

Funny.

She had always been like that for him.

A saving grace.

Right up until the end.

The rules of the facility were clear when it came to patients and visitors. Hugs were okay, but any romantic displays were not appropriate or encouraged. Patients were there to get healthy, not go on a date.

Even knowing it might be a mark against him, or another long chat with Leonard about walking the right lines, John grabbed hold of Siena the second she was close enough for him to do it. He dragged her close, wrapped his arms around her, and kissed her hard.

The way her lips curved into a sweet smile sent his racing heart slowing down to a more settled tempo. All those nerves finally drifted away. She was still his peace, it seemed. His one place of calm inside a continuous storm of chaos.

He had been worrying nonstop since he found out she was coming. He knew in that second that his worries had been for nothing.

"John," she whispered.

He kissed her nose. And then her eyelids. Finally, her mouth again.

Someone cleared their throat nearby.

The warning was clear.

John ignored it.

Siena cupped his face with her hands, and she drew him in close again. Not to kiss, but just to stare in his eyes for a moment.

"You look better," she said.

He laughed.

Damn.

It felt so fucking good to laugh.

"I feel better," he admitted.

She smiled.

A bright, beautiful smile.

Lighting up his life just like that.

John had a million and one questions for Siena, but the nurse that was closing in said he needed to put a bit of distance between them. It'd be a fucking shame if they took her away from him before he even really had her again.

"Come sit down with me?"

Siena nodded. "Of course."

The visiting area was not closed to just the indoor areas. They were allowed to go outside, but the heavy snow falling down didn't look particular warm today.

Siena took a seat next to John on the white leather couch. Her fingers found his, and wove tight.

He had done so much in a very short period of time. He had done so much to her.

"I'm sorry," he said.

Siena peered over at him. "Never do that, John."

"What?"

"Apologize for being you. I never want you to do that with me."

"You do understand everything that happened, and what I did, right?"

"I know."

"So—"

"John," she said, leaning in close so all he saw was her, beauty, and life. "You know I love you, don't you?"

Yeah, he knew.

"How could I not, now?"

Siena nodded. "I always will."

"I'm still sorry."

Not for killing her father, but for everything that came before.

Matteo got what he deserved.

Simple as that.

Siena patted his cheek. "Let's talk about anything other than all of that. I don't have much time. It was hard enough just to get the time away to be here, John."

"Yeah, about that."

"What?"

"How?"

He had been told—during the one visit from Andino—that Siena was being heavily controlled by her brothers. His cousin hadn't explained much more, only that he had a line of contact occasionally.

Siena smiled slyly. "I took up yoga. It gives me an hour or two a couple of times a week to get away. I sneak out the back."

"How tight of leash do they have you on?"

Her brothers, he meant.

Siena frowned. "So tight it's killing me."

He appreciated her honesty, but ... *fuck*.

"It's okay," she added quickly. "It's not forever."

He didn't know how.

He didn't know anything that was happening beyond these walls. His father and Andino made sure to keep him in a place where he was simply dealing with himself, and nothing else. John knew they were making the right choice in that regard.

If he didn't take care of himself first, then bad shit happened.

And what happened leading up to this moment could never happen again. Or, he was going to try his hardest to make sure it didn't happen again to this severity.

"How bad is it?" he dared to ask. "The streets, I mean. The families."

He didn't know if she would tell him.

He wouldn't blame or push her if she didn't.

Siena's eyes drifted down to their connected hands. "It's bad."

"How bad?"

"It's war, John."

DISGRACE

JOHN + SIENA, BOOK 2

ONE

Stifling was not a word Siena Calabrese used often, but at the moment, it was the one that best fit her life. Hot, stuffy mid-June air blew through the hallway of her oldest brother's brownstone. It reminded her that it wasn't only the two men looming at her back making her feel like she was roasting with suffocation. Even the muggy weather had hot, sticky hands around her small throat.

So was her life, now.

"Greta, Giulia," Siena greeted.

The two teenaged girls stepped into the brownstone with guarded eyes. As they always did. As they *should*. There was nothing in that house—but for Siena, perhaps—that could be trusted, and the girls knew it.

Every time they were faced with their half-brothers, Siena highly suspected Greta and Giulia wondered about their fate. Or rather, what their fate might bring for them today.

Greta more than Giulia, likely. She was, after all, closing in on eighteen faster and faster. Giulia, on the other hand, was only fifteen. She still had a few years of safety under her belt.

Not even the girls' mother had been able to save them.

Not when it came to Kev and Darren.

"I like the red," Siena said, reaching out to play with a few strands of Greta's long, wavy hair. Her half-sister only offered a slight, yet still awkward, smile in response. "I thought you were thinking about something darker?"

Greta shrugged. "Ma liked red."

Silence saturated the hallway. Both of Siena's half-sisters refused to look up from the floor, not even after Kev cleared his throat, and Darren let out an exasperated sigh.

"Too bad she won't be able to see it," Siena said.

She was only forcing herself to talk because every part of her felt like Greta and Giulia. As though she should hide away somewhere, and avoid drawing attention to herself. That would be for the best—that was what would be the safest for her.

Siena couldn't do that.

Not now.

Not after everything.

It would be like throwing these two young girls to the wolves. Those wolves being their own half-brothers.

It wasn't like any of the Calabrese daughters—not Siena, being the only legitimate daughter, or her half-sisters, born to her dead father's equally dead mistress—could trust their brothers to have their best interests in mind. Kev and Darren had proved over the last few months that their interests were solely tied up in one thing, and one thing only.

Moving higher.

Ruining the Marcellos.

Taking over New York.

Siena's mind drifted over the months that had passed since her father's murder, and then John going into a facility. A little bit of February, March, April, May, and now here they were in the middle of June.

Her father was still dead.

John was still gone.

And yet ... so much had changed.

So very much was different.

Kev had taken over as the boss in lieu of their father's death. Darren was, of course, Kev's right hand man. If only that was all ...

A failed marriage arrangement. A missing half-sister. Two others, now orphaned. A war on the streets. Bodies piling up.

Siena shook those thoughts out of her head. She could not afford to get lost in them today, and certainly not right now. It didn't help that Kev and Darren were at her back damn near constantly. She couldn't move without one of them knowing about it.

Again ... so was her life.

But for these two girls?

For her little sisters, so lost without their own big sister to guide them, Siena was present. She forced herself to be present and to do what she needed to do, so they saw a smiling face, and someone they could trust.

Because fuck Kev and Darren.

They would not do to these girls what they had tried to do to their missing sister. Well ... to Greta and Giulia, Ginevra was missing. Siena knew the truth—and while right now, the younger Calabrese girls hurt, it would not last forever.

Missing did not mean dead. Someday, they would know that little fact, too.

"Are we all going to linger in the goddamn hallway all day, or have lunch?" Kev asked. "I'm starved."

Greta and Giulia kept their gazes locked on the floor. Neither of them answered their brother, but frankly, they had learned rather quickly about Kev and Darren. When the two men asked a question, they weren't actually looking for a response, but rather, an action.

They only wanted well-behaved women.

Very little else.

"Are you hungry?" Siena asked the girls.

"A little," Greta said.

Giulia dared to look past Siena, and her familiar blue eyes narrowed. "Not particularly."

Siena let a little smile slip through at the youngest girl's barely hidden contempt. "I cooked, though."

The girl's gaze darted back to Siena in a blink. "Did you?"

"Your favorite."

"Oh, well ... okay."

"I'm hungry," Kev repeated.

"Then, go sit down in the damn dining room," Siena barked over her shoulder.

The warning that flashed in both her brothers' eyes was enough to tell Siena she was toeing a very thin line with them. Before her father's death, she used to get away with a hell of a lot more than she did now.

Kev and Darren barely let her breathe. Apparently, even breathing was wrong. Or rather, *Siena* breathing was wrong.

"Let's grab some food," Siena told them.

The girls nodded, and then followed in front of her when she urged the two forward. Greta and Giulia passed by Kev and Darren without saying a word. Siena didn't miss how the two sisters' lips curled a bit in their disgust at being close to their brothers.

That could happen when a person was forced to watch brothers you barely knew do things like try and force your older sister into an arranged marriage, not to mention, how they found their mother one morning.

All by Kev and Darren's hand.

Siena tried her fucking hardest to ignore the awkwardness as the siblings settled into the kitchen together. What else could she do at this point? What else could she possibly do for these two girls—both fighting invisible battles, and confused?

At least, she thought, Greta and Giulia had some freedom even if it was just an illusion. The two lived with an aunt, although the woman was largely paid and happily so by the Calabrese brothers. The sisters weren't forced to be in Kev and Darren's presence every single day of their lives. Usually once or twice a week, instead.

Siena, on the other hand …

Well, it all went back to the stifling thing again.

Her brothers were the worst.

She was rarely able to escape them.

It was a couple of hours later before Siena saw her half-sisters off. Shuffled into the back of a black town car driven by a Calabrese enforcer, Greta and Giulia were taken away once more. They were packed up like prized beauties to be brought out and dusted off for showing on another day.

Siena knew it.

The girls knew it.

A fucking shame, really.

"You're late, Ma," Kev grumbled.

"I had things to do, son."

"Things like what, exactly?"

"A friend called."

Kev scoffed. "Sure, Ma."

As the footsteps of her mother and older brother came closer to the kitchen, Siena tried to relax the tension in her shoulders. The anger she felt toward her mother reared its ugly head whenever the two were in a damn room together.

Today was not going to be any fucking different.

How could it?

"I really did have other things come up, Kev," her mother said.

The two were just outside the kitchen, now. Siena didn't care to eavesdrop, but that had kind of become a part of her job.

So to speak …

"We are *trying* to put on a united front," Kev reminded Coraline. "It is the most important thing right now. I'm quite aware of how you feel about Greta and Giulia, but you need to forget about it, Ma. Put it aside for now, so we can all handle our business in this city."

"Mmm."

"What?"

"Handle business," Coraline said. "I suppose we're going to pretend that another Calabrese Capo was not killed last week, are we?"

"No one is pretending—"

"Well, we can't forget about that *united front*, Kev."

"Ma."

"I said what I said, didn't I?"

Kev let out a harsh sigh. "We have a plan—an attack coming up. A few days after the funeral. One of their warehouses on the west end that they think we don't know about. An answer to the Capo's death. Darren thought it would be appropriate that we wait until after. Respect to the man, and all that."

"Sure," Coraline said. "Your father never would have *waited*."

"I am not my father, Ma."

"Obviously."

Siena didn't even bother to look up from the dishes she was washing as her mother and brother slipped into the kitchen. Coraline moved toward the island where a plate of hot food had been left to sit out for her, and looked it over.

"Really, Siena, chicken alfredo?" her mother asked.

Siena kept her attention on her work. "It's Giulia's favorite. I was trying to make her comfortable."

Coraline made a noise under her breath.

It sounded a lot like disgust.

"It might have helped had you shown up like you were supposed to for dinner," Siena added. "They were looking forward to having an actual conversation with you, Ma."

Siena did turn around and chance a glance at her mother, then. Coraline looked like something awful had been shoved into her mouth. Horrified, displeased, and disgusted all at the same time.

The last thing this woman wanted to do was greet, be nice to, or handle anything about her husband's mistress's children.

It wasn't like it was the girls' fault. They hadn't asked to be born, or for their father to be an unfaithful bastard. Yet, here they all were.

Coraline had been perfectly fine, pleased, and pampered in her life before Matteo's death. She had not minded turning cheek to her husband's behaviors, and dalliances with women. She even pretended like she didn't know her husband's mistress had once lived in a bigger house than she did simply because she birthed him the same amount of children that Coraline had given to Matteo.

No, none of that had mattered to Coraline *before*.

Now, with Matteo dead, and the girls' mother dead, Coraline had no choice.

Despite knowing it might cross one of her brother's many lines, Siena didn't mind reminding her mother of her place at the moment. Sometimes, it was the only thing that actually worked where Coraline was concerned.

"It would not look very good for you to shun the only Calabrese *principessas della mafia*," Siena murmured, letting her finger edge along the line of the island as she spoke. "Even if those mafia princesses are illegitimate daughters born from a several decades-long affair. You know this, Ma."

Coraline scowled.

Kev passed a look between the mother and daughter, but said nothing.

"They are not the only *principessas* of this family," Coraline said, smiling in that cruel, cold way of hers. "And don't you forget that, Siena."

Dread slipped down Siena's spine.

A cold fear met it with open arms.

Siena knew all too well how open and vulnerable she was to her brothers' games. She could just as easily be used as fodder for her brothers' plans as her half-sisters.

And shit …

Maybe better her, than them.

Siena didn't show her fear, or her weakness. Not to a woman like her mother. Coraline ate that shit for breakfast.

"Maybe that's what bothers you the most, Ma," Siena said, shrugging. "That one of the illegitimate daughters will be used before I ever am—the only legitimate daughter. *Your* daughter. What a fucking shame that would be, huh?"

Coraline's gaze narrowed.

A silent threat.

A vicious promise.

"Legitimate in name and birth *only*," Coraline hissed right back. "We all know how you've betrayed this family with all you have done to us, Siena. None of us will ever forget the disgrace you are. Marrying you off to get you off our hands, or getting rid of you by some other means would be a *blessing*. Nothing more."

Kev chuckled. "She's got a point."

What a life this was.

The disgraced one.

Siena wished she cared.

The church quieted as the Calabrese family slipped inside. Siena stayed firmly behind her older brothers, yet still in front of her mother. Appearances were everything, and even how they entered a space was now a well thought out event.

Kev stayed a half of a pace ahead of Darren. A subtle, yet still clear, message about which of the two men now ran the Calabrese show. Darren never seemed to mind, as his brother's right-hand man, seeing as how he still had quite a bit of control himself.

Siena was always made to be in between her brothers and mother—a clear indicator that she was both protected, and watched. Enforcers trailed behind them all. One for each person, and sometimes more.

Somedays, it felt as though Siena couldn't breathe. Every direction she looked, someone new was watching her. Someone else would be reporting back to her brothers on her latest behaviors.

She found it easier to be compliant and complacent, but inside, she was a raging monster battling against the walls of her cage. A prison cell that no one else could see, sure, but that she was all too aware of when it came right down to it.

Siena's gaze drifted over the people already sitting down and waiting for the funeral to start. She didn't linger on one person for any length of time, and she didn't even give them a smile. What would be the point?

She was only there for show.

Much like her brothers.

At the front of the church, standing at the closed casket of a now-dead Calabrese Capo, was the family of Arty Moretti. Siena stayed back beside her mother as Kev and Darren greeted the dead man's wife first, and then his oldest daughter, and one son. Both of the man's children were adults—Siena counted that as a blessing in disguise when it came to this war between the Calabrese and Marcello families.

At least this way, the two were not young children now left without a father. They were already adults into their own lives, and would not be left feeling abandoned and alone. Or … that was her hope for them.

She suspected it still hurt them, of course. Grief was a lot like the ocean—wide, sometimes clear and sometimes murky, and always dangerous. It could swallow someone whole, and drown them in pain.

Siena stepped up to the family when her brothers moved away. As Kev and Darren moved to speak with a couple of their men gathered close by, she and her mother took to comforting the family.

It was also their job.

Another one added to the pile.

And what did they say to these poor people?

"We're so sorry."

Sorry our family has taken from you.

"We're here for you."

So long as you are here for us.

"He is with God."

And more men will soon join him.

Because that was the way of war, and that was all that could be guaranteed for these people, and their pain. More deaths would follow, and it would be all the Calabrese family's fault.

Why?

Siena's gaze drifted to her brothers again. Sure, they looked as though they fit the part of mafia *principes* turned kings in their black suits, shined shoes, slicked back hair, and straightened postures. Their cold eyes held little warmth, and their tones delivered orders with a sharp flatness that could both chill, and slice at the same time.

Matteo—during the years that he lived—had certainly trained her brothers well. They stepped into the positions they needed to without hesitation, and without batting an eye. The rest of the Calabrese organization didn't think to question the brothers when they moved up in power, and replaced others that might have been a better fit. No one said a thing when they first tried to strong-arm the Marcellos into a peaceful deal, and then turned on them when said deal went sour.

Fingers pointed.

Bullets were readied.

Blood spilled.

The city tasted like war now.

Nothing could stop them. Kev and Darren were obsessive in their desire and assurance that the Calabrese family would soon be the one running New York City with an iron fist.

Well, that's how it felt, anyway. They still had to get the little issue of the Marcellos out of the way. The Marcello family made it very clear that would not be an easy task.

Siena patted the hand of the Capo's widow, and offered her a smile. A forced smile, sure, and one that didn't reach her eyes, but who could tell? It was a funeral, after all. No one was supposed to be *happy* or *true*.

"Anything you need, I promise," Siena repeated.

The woman nodded. "Thank you, Siena. You're such a sweet girl. Your brothers must be so proud of you."

Siena smiled a little more honestly at that statement. Bitterness coated her tongue with the taste of bile, and she patted the woman's hand once more.

"You have no idea," she murmured.

As quickly as Siena had greeted the woman and her adult children, she turned away from them, and followed behind her now-moving brothers. Kev and Darren weaved through the group of men who had come to talk to them, and made for their designated seats.

Only because this was not their family's funeral, and this was not their church, did they sit in the pew directly behind the family. Unfortunately, while sitting, there was no chance for Siena to hide her displeasure or discomfort behind her brothers' backs. She was forced to take a little more care with her appearance, and the mask she put forth.

Darren looked over at her. "Did you really have to pick a purple dress?"

"It's a dark color."

"*Black* is appropriate."

"I'm fucking sick of black, Darren."

All she ever seemed to wear anymore was black.

Once this was all over—she had not forgotten what Andino Marcello told her months ago when she was ripped away from John, after all—she was never going to wear black again. Not unless someone fucking forced her into the color.

This won't be forever.

Those words rang and rang.

They echoed and echoed.

She kept them close.

What else could she do?

A few minutes before the service was supposed to start, murmurings passed between the people in the pews. Heads began to turn in the direction that the whispering started. Hot, humid heat from the outside slipped up the church's aisle.

Siena turned, too.

She wanted to see, too.

There, at the back of the church dressed in black on black and standing in a close line of at least ten men, were Marcellos.

The boss. His men. John's father.

Dante Marcello—the boss of the family—smiled and ticked a finger forward. His men moved behind him as he took a step forward, and then another. Slow, purposeful strides. A confident, uncaring stroll.

Beside Siena, her brothers and mother hissed back and forth between one another. Clearly, they had not been expecting this move.

Siena was kind of impressed.

"How fucking dare they?" Kev asked.

"Stop sitting there—do something," Darren snarled.

"What should he do?" their mother asked. "He *cannot* make a scene in this church."

No, Kev certainly couldn't.

Once again, it looked like her brothers were bowing down to the Marcellos. It seemed as though not every battle was started and finished with bullets, blood, and funerals. Some battles were won with killer smiles, and a simple show of power.

Siena was starting to believe she should keep score.

Calabrese family—zero.

The Marcellos—one.

It was almost funny how one simple action could change all kinds of circumstances. Suddenly, the enforcers that rarely left Siena alone when she was outside of her brothers' sights were now fully distracted by the show happening inside the entrance of the church.

With the funeral over, it seemed Siena's brothers had finally decided to take action with the Marcellos.

Better late than never.

Siena hung back behind the crowd—her interest in watching men verbally spar over their growing feud was nonexistent. None of this would do her or the cause she was silently fighting for any good at the end of the day.

She kept one eye on her mother as Coraline edged along the crowd. Her mother's eagle eye was fully pointed on Kev, Darren, and the Marcellos.

Siena never would have taken her mother for a woman who involved herself in mafia politics, or the business of men. And yet, there Coraline was on a daily basis. Doing exactly those things with her sons, and never thinking twice about it.

Who knew why.

The name she carried.

The man—now dead—she had married.

The legacy behind her.

The promise of one ahead of her.

Siena didn't know.

It wouldn't matter when this was over.

A form slid in beside Siena. She stiffened a bit at the man's presence, and the scent of his familiar cologne. He wouldn't typically be so bold, but it seemed like everyone around them at the moment was currently distracted.

Andino smiled a bit when Siena looked at him. "What do you have for me?"

This little game of theirs had started months ago. It started with nothing more than a single sentence in passing from Andino—*perhaps you should take up a hobby ... like yoga.* Back when there had seemed like a chance of settling this feud between their families with something like a marriage was possible, he had given her that line, and she ran with it.

Yoga it was.

It was the only time—two hours twice a·week—that her brothers allowed Siena any kind of privacy and peace. The enforcers stayed outside the complex. She slipped out the back. Andino was always waiting.

John's cousin was fighting this war in a far dirtier way.

Siena respected him for it, really.

"Well?" he asked again. "What do you have for me?"

"A west end warehouse," Siena said. "An attack in a couple of days. Retribution for Arty's death. That's all I know."

Andino's face cleared of emotion, and his gaze hardened. "All right. You don't know what, or how many—"

"I would tell you if I did. You know that."

Andino's hand touched her shoulder lightly. "I know."

She glanced back at him again. "I miss him."

John.

She always missed him.

She hadn't seen him in months.

Andino nodded once. "I know that, too. Soon, Siena. I know he'll be getting out soon. He made the choice to stay in the facility for this long because of his own health. He *chose* stability. That's the thing about John, and being bipolar. I don't think he's ever really chosen stability before now. And with that comes taking a hard, long look at a lot of things in his life. I don't think he felt it was good for him mentally to try handling his personal business while dealing with everything outside of it, too."

"I want him to be good."

She wanted John to be healthy, and happy.

Safe.

He was not going to come out to stability, or safety.

Not now.

"He's going to be fucking great," Andino said with a grin, "as long as you're still waiting for him when he's ready to come back, then nothing else matters."

"Of course, I'll be waiting."

She loved John.

Nothing was ever going to change that.

Andino nodded. "So, hey, what's the thirtieth looking like for you?"

"Of this month?"

"Yeah."

Siena shrugged. "Yoga."

Andino chuckled. "Thought so. I'll be waiting. We should really go visit John."

"Really?"

"Yeah, girl, really."

That made everything so much better.

"Okay, go before someone sees you with me," she said, flicking her hand at him.

Andino rolled his eyes. "Trust me—they're all too stuck up their own asses to even think about you right now. You didn't seriously think this whole show was just about fucking with their heads, did you?"

"Well ..."

Yeah, kind of.

Andino smirked. "I will always find a way to get my message in, Siena, no matter how protected they think you are. Do you have a new phone?"

"Yeah, Kev changed it again last week."

"Same old, same old."

Siena nodded once. "Random wrong numbers, I know."

"This whole thing isn't forever, remember. Soon, you'll have what you want."

Not what.

Who.

She reminded herself daily that this wasn't forever.

No, it was just for right now.

Forever was going to be far more beautiful.

TWO

The red circle around July twentieth both taunted and promised Johnathan Marcello. It was just a date—a single date among many on the calendar. One of the nurses at Clearview Oaks had given him the calendar months ago when he first arrived. Each month showcased a different picture of the facility's grounds.

The older nurse had suggested that crossing off dates on the calendar would give him some sort of satisfaction. It hadn't, of course. Not until he knew his release date.

Now, every little black X in permanent marker felt like another chain coming undone from his body. And yet, the closer he got to that big red circle, the tighter the invisible rope became around his throat.

Strange how that worked.

"Nervous, John?"

He spun on his heels to find his therapist leaning in the doorway of his private room. Patients weren't allowed to have their doors closed unless the doctor was also in the room, and only if the patient was nonviolent. On a suicide watch, the door was never closed. Ever.

"Well?" Leonard pressed.

"For what?"

"Your chosen release date is coming up. Three weeks away."

John passed the calendar one more look. "I like how you posed that as if *I* chose when I could leave, when actually—"

"You did choose."

Leonard smiled when John glanced back at him.

"You made it clear you didn't think I was ready to go," John said pointedly.

The older man shrugged. "Yes, well, you weren't. Every little medication change sent you into another round, and we had trouble getting you settled with the right dose of Lithium. Never mind the actual therapy, John."

"I am, though. A little nervous, I mean."

"All normal, considering."

"I'm looking forward to it, too."

"As you should," Leonard replied. "I'm curious, though, what has you the most nervous."

John laughed under his breath. Running this fingers through his hair, he once again turned to face the calendar. Leonard had a way of pushing John into talking about things beyond the surface of what he presented to the world. The therapist had no problem with really digging into the crux of John's issues.

About life.

His family.

Being bipolar.

Out of the many, *many* therapists John had gone through in his life, Leonard was—by far—the best for him personally. Sure, he didn't always like what the older man had to say. He didn't particularly appreciate being forced to drag out old issues and dirty laundry to reexamine. That didn't mean Leonard's tactics were useless.

They weren't.

They worked.

They worked especially well for John.

What more could he ask for?

"Well?" the therapist pressed when John stayed quiet. "What has you nervous—reentering life, integrating with your family again ... *her*?"

John swallowed hard.

Her.

Siena.

John chuckled. "Not her. Never her."

Leonard returned John's smile. "You haven't seen the woman in ... well, almost four months, now. You sound very sure of that statement, though."

He was.

It wasn't like he had a reason to be.

He also didn't have a reason not to be.

John shrugged. "It's not her."

"The rest, then?"

"It's a mixture of the rest, I think."

Leonard closed the door behind him, and stepped further into the room. He waved a hand at John, and then gestured toward the seating area next to the windows. So was the therapist's way when it came to a session. He liked to make John sit, while he remained standing, or pacing. Sometimes Leonard would also sit, but it wasn't particularly often.

John's private room was more like a very expensive, yet also clinical-feeling, bachelor pad. He had his own small kitchen with a two-person table. A double bed, and private bathroom. A sitting area with bookshelves and a flat screen television. The walls showcased photographs of mountains and colorful flowers set in clear frames. The floor was a marble stone that somehow never felt too cold in the mornings.

If anything, it was comfortable. Clean, which he appreciated. Simplistic in design, and catered to his private needs. He had a private phone line to make calls out if he needed to or wanted to, but other than a few calls to his mother, he had not used the phone a lot. After all, he was here to get better, and to focus on himself. Besides, the person he wanted to talk to the most—Siena—he had not been able to. For whatever reason, her old number was dead. No one had given him a reason why.

John had been able to make his room at Clearview Oaks feel somewhat like home in different ways.

John opted to sit in one of the white leather recliners next to the window. Leonard leaned against the wall beside the flat screen, and gazed out the window. Next to the backdrop of crisp white walls, the therapist blended in with his stark white hair and jacket.

"Let's talk, John," Leonard said.

"You are aware I know why you like to stand and pace while I stay sitting, right?"

Leonard's gray eyes cut to John with amusement dancing in his thick, lifted brows. "Oh, do tell."

"When you sit, then I can zone out. I know exactly where you are, and I feel safer to focus my attention elsewhere. The wall, or the clock. Maybe a picture. My hands. Whatever it is, then I don't have to keep an eye on you because you're no longer moving around and keeping my attention on you."

"Keep going."

"When you move, the kind of man I am, means I have to keep an eye on you constantly. I can't let you move behind me, or too close to my side. I need to see your hands, and what they're doing. It takes up a great deal of the focus in my brain, and that makes my mouth vulnerable to letting things slip. If I *can* zone out, I am far less likely to talk. Or if I do, it's ... as you say, surface things."

"What people see, not what really *is*."

John nodded. "Although, if you would sit, I would talk, too. For you."

The man's smile softened a bit. "Would you?"

"I would, Leonard."

"I thought so," Leonard replied as he moved to take a seat across from John. "And well done on figuring that strategy of mine out. It only took you ... a few months."

"A couple," John shot back. "I knew about a month in."

Leonard chuckled, and wagged a finger at John. "Talk, now."

"It's different."

"What is?"

"Here, to there. Being *inside* here, and then going back into the outside. One of the first things you told me was that I had to choose stability. Not just for now, or for a while, or even for a few years. I had to choose stability for the rest of my life."

Which meant meds, even when they made him feel like shit. It meant choosing to get up every single day and take medications regardless of how he felt about it until a better medication could be chosen. It also meant never excusing himself because of being bipolar, but accepting and being honest about it. It meant being honest to those in his life about what was happening inside his mind, and keeping himself accountable.

Stability was a choice. Because he could just as easily choose to refuse meds, to self-medicate, or to live his life in a constant spiral of hypomania, full blown mania, and depression. A vicious cycle that would continue to hurt him, and those around him.

John chose stability. He didn't expect it to always be easy.

"Because in here is routine," John said, glancing out the window. "Here, I know exactly what time the lights are going to come on, and when I can go outside. I know which channels will be on the television, and what the menu looks like for the next week. I know which meds are coming, and which ones need to change. I just ... know everything."

"Your life is also pretty structured outside of here, too," Leonard reminded him. "You have made a great effort to set up personal routines that you like to follow, from what time you get up in the morning, to how you clean your house. You're not leaving an environment like this and walking into pure chaos, John."

John nodded because the man was right. "Sure."

"But you have the factor of the unknown out there that we don't provide in here."

"Exactly."

"I understand why that's a little unsettling."

"It might help if they told me more," he said.

John didn't say who, specifically, but the therapist understood what he meant. The only people who came to visit him—his choice, not others—were his father, and Andino. His uncle, Giovanni, had come once as well, and got the bottle of booze he brought along confiscated. It was, by far, one of the most amusing days since John entered the facility.

Still, when the men of his family came, they didn't talk about business. They never told John what was happening outside of these walls, or what he could expect once he left the facility. It was a little unsettling because he wasn't quite sure what that meant.

Were they hiding something from him?

What was it, if they were?

Leonard also knew some of the private details of John's life that he didn't share with outsiders. Or rather, the illegal side of John's life being that he was a made man, and fully engrained in the way of Cosa Nostra.

It certainly helped for these talks.

John didn't need to skip details, or dance around them in some way. He was able to be honest with his therapist, and because he too knew things about Leonard's personal life, he did not feel as if it might get him in trouble simply to talk. All good things.

"I think they intend for you to focus on yourself, and not … the business," Leonard murmured.

"Funny."

"What is?"

"I've been focusing on the business a lot lately."

"Because you don't know what's happening?"

"Mostly."

Leonard nodded once. "You're going to do fine, John. Regardless if you leave here and it is sunshine, rainbows, and puppies, or if it is hellfire, chaos, and anarchy. The unknown can only really threaten your stability if you allow it to dig in a bit too much, if you get what I mean."

"I do."

"Good." Leonard stood, and brushed invisible lint from his pant legs. "I also have another proposition for you before I give you some good news."

John smirked. "How about you give me the good news first?"

"Nice try. I make the rules."

Asshole.

"What is the proposition?" John asked.

"You need a therapist when you leave here."

John stiffened. This was not a topic he wanted to discuss because it was a sore spot for him. He didn't like the idea of leaving Clearview Oaks only to need to find a new therapist to see. He was not about to trust someone after the last debacle.

"I can physically *feel* how much discomfort this is causing you," Leonard said.

"Yeah, well, what can you do," John said through gritted teeth. "Nothing, apparently."

"I would take your file on as a patient outside of this facility. Twice weekly. One weekday, and one day on the weekend."

The tension in John's body bled out slowly. "Would you?"

"Sometimes," Leonard said, "it is more about the patient finding the right doctor, than it is about anything else."

"Twice weekly, then."

"Do you want the good news, now?"

John nodded, and stood from the chair. "I almost forgot about it with the whole new therapist thing, actually. What is it?"

"You'll have visitors tomorrow. Your cousin—Andino—and a couple of people he's bringing along. Ladies, apparently, if the information he provided is to be trusted. Unlike his father, Andino doesn't tend to be disruptive when he comes here."

John only laughed. "My uncle, Giovanni, makes it his first and only goal to have fun."

"This is not the place for fun."

"Mmm."

"You didn't ask who Andino is bringing, by the way," Leonard said over his shoulder as he left the room.

Fuck.

He hadn't. Too late now.

"John, my man. You're looking good."

He heard his cousin's greeting, and felt Andino's firm hug, but John's gaze was locked on the dark-haired beauty standing just a few feet away. After all, it was kind of fucking impossible for him to pay attention to anything when the love of his life was once again gracing his presence. She was the only thing that ever mattered.

Siena wore the brightest smile that matched the flower printed summer dress accentuating all of her curves and height. A dress that showed off all kinds of leg, and the four inch heels on her feet. She had let her long, dark hair down in soft waves. One of his favorite styles on her because he could wrap his fingers in the silky strands, and get lost. She'd painted her lips a striking red, and those blue eyes of hers never left him once.

Damn.

What had Andino just said?

John didn't know. His attention was somewhere else entirely.

"What?" he asked Andino.

His cousin only laughed, and the man's green eyes looked John over. In his usual suit and shined shoes, Andino made John miss the fact he hadn't worn proper Armani in months. Instead, he'd dressed down with jeans and T-shirts.

"Shit, you didn't hear a word I just said, huh?" Andino asked.

John's gaze drifted to a very patient, quiet Siena. "Not really, no. Sorry, man."

Andino clapped John's cheek with a gentle pat as he chuckled. "Nah, it's okay. You've got a good reason to be off your game today. I guess they didn't fill you in on who I was bringing along to visit, or what?"

"Leonard has his odd ways."

"Sure, sure."

"It's good, though."

So good.

John wasn't the type who appreciated surprises, but this was far more than fine. Surprises were unknowns that he couldn't prepare for, and he much preferred to prepare for an unknown. This, though? He didn't mind this surprise *at all*.

"Anyway," Andino said, turning to stand beside John. His cousin gestured in front of them. "I said, I hope you don't mind that I brought someone else to properly meet you. I mean, I know this place is supposed to be sacred for you, and all. Focusing on you, but I might not get another time to do this before you come home."

Yes. The woman standing at Siena's side. *Haven.*

John had noticed the woman, of course, but his mind always tended to focus in on the most important things first, and then everything else second. Siena was, by far, the most important thing standing on the walkway in that moment when it came to John and his life. And shit, he had been counting down the days until he would get to see Siena again. Not that he had known today would be the day.

No offence to Haven. Or Andino.

John said none of those things out loud.

"You don't mind, do you?" Andino asked again.

John shook his head. "No, man. Of course, not."

"Good. I want you to meet the girl I'm going to marry, you know. Properly fucking meet her, John. Not hear things about her from someone else, or see her in passing. Actually meet her *with* me. Take some time to sit down and have a real conversation with her. I talk about you all the time, and she's a little out of the loop about me and you. Kind of a big fucking deal to me, and everything."

John's brow rose high as he took in his cousin a second time. Andino never looked more nervous than he had in that moment. His cousin scrubbed a hand over his unshaven jaw, and his gaze kept darting back to Haven like he didn't want to take his eyes off her for even one damn minute.

Huh.

John knew that look. He had that look.

Every time he looked at Siena, that was.

It was kind of strange for John to see his cousin so off-balance in this way. And *marriage*? Genuine, honest to God, going to settle down *marriage*?

John never thought he would see the day. Not where Andino was concerned, anyway. His cousin just wasn't the type to settle down into a monogamous relationship where something like forever and love might get thrown in the conversation. Not to mention, Andino was usually the guy who liked to poke fun at a man who did get his dick tied into a knot over a woman.

This was a whole one-eighty. So yeah, John did a double-take.

"Seriously?"

Andino nodded. "Yeah, man."

"I thought ... I mean, the family didn't have a high opinion of her a few months ago, and all. I thought they had made it clear she wasn't acceptable, or some shit. You kind of gave me the impression you didn't know what the hell you were doing about them, her, or the rest."

"It's not about them."

Fact.

He knew that all too well. Sometimes when it came to their family, the best thing a man could do on the personal side of his life was shut the fuck down. Keep everything closed up tight. Make it clear nothing was open for discussion.

John didn't know if that's what Andino had done when it came to Haven, or not. It also really didn't fucking matter.

Good for Andino.

Whatever it took to get what the man wanted.

John laughed, and clapped his cousin on the shoulder. Dragging Andino in for a quick, tight one-armed hug, the two men's laughter colored up the front yard of the facility. Andino hugged John back with a firm hold.

Some of John's unease about leaving the facility started to drift away in those few seconds. Despite how his disorder often colored up his impressions and perceptions of his family, he still found himself reminded time and time again of their loyalty and love for him.

No, he didn't mind at all that Andino brought his girl along. He appreciated it, really. He would make sure to take time and speak with Haven while she was there because it was what she, and Andino, deserved.

Besides, the woman had to be something interesting to catch Andino Marcello's eye, and steal his fucking heart.

But for now ...

"Give me some time with Siena," John said quietly as he pulled away from his cousin. "It's been too long."

Andino stepped aside. "You got it, John."

All John needed to do was hold his hand out in Siena's direction, and she instantly darted forward to catch it with her own. The second her warm palm fitted in his, and her fingers wove around his own, John's world tilted back to its proper axis once more.

Strange how that worked.

It had been months since he looked at her—*talked* to her—and yet it took only one single touch from her to settle him. His restless heart calmed, and his tight chest relaxed. Everything that was right and good in his world was currently holding his hand. It was just a gesture. A small act of affection, but it was everything and more to John, too.

Siena's blue eyes met his, and her sweet smile grew a little more. Her olive-toned skin flushed with a happy pink when he bent down and caught her lips in a quick kiss. Maybe he should have asked if that was okay with her, but the way she kissed him back said it was just fucking fine, anyway.

He had a million and one things to ask.

About her. Them. The outside. The families.

Business.

The war she had alluded to the last time she was there with him.

So damn much.

And yet, all John wanted to do was kiss her. He only wanted to drag Siena closer, wrap his arms around her, and breathe her in. All her familiar warmth, scent, and love. All of her.

The world ceased to exist. Nothing else mattered.

Unfortunately, the facility had goddamn policies about public displays of affection, and that forced John to pull away from the kiss far sooner than he wanted to. Siena only grinned and kissed the pad of his thumb when he stroked her bottom lip.

"Damn, I missed you," he said.

Through thick, lowered lashes, she watched him. "Did you?"

"Every day."

"Every *single* day?"

John smirked. "First thing on my mind in the morning."

"What about at night?"

"Last thing I think about before I go to sleep, *bella*."

Siena's love colored her happiness. John knew his wasn't always as easy to see because he made a great effort to keep those vulnerable parts of himself well hidden from the world. It had become such a habit that he worried now whether or not the people who deserved to see his love could actually see it.

People like Siena.

She had her ways of reminding him everything was just fine. Her palm came up to cup the side of his face, and her thumb stroked his cheekbone.

"I missed you, too."

"Walk with me," he demanded.

Siena nodded, and tucked in close to his side as they moved off the main walkway, and headed onto the cobblestone path that led all over the facility's private, protected grounds. John took a quick look over his shoulder, and found Andino was still standing side by side with Haven. His cousin hugged the woman in close, and kissed the top of her head when she laughed about something.

Yeah, John most definitely knew that look his cousin sported.

Siena's quiet little hum brought John's attention right back to her. Glittering eyes looked him over, and she reached up to stroke his face once more with her fingertips. "I wish I had more time today."

John tried not to frown, and failed. "Andino didn't say anything about you leaving."

"I only have a couple of hours before I have to be back. Yoga ends at two, so."

"Yeah, still doing that, huh?"

Siena let out a hard breath, and looked away from him when she spoke again. "It's the only way I can get out of my brothers' sights for more than five minutes. Or hell, one of the enforcers they're always sticking me with."

He didn't like the sound of that. Not at all.

"So what, they haven't figured out that you sneak away when you're supposed to be at yoga, yet?" he asked.

"No." Siena shrugged. "But I've only done it when I need to do something, or meet someone."

"Meet someone?"

"Andino, mostly. Sometimes it's someone else."

"Meet them for what?" he pressed.

"Not important."

John tugged on his girl's hand, and the action made her look at him. "It is important, *amore*. Why are you meeting people behind your brothers' backs, and what's happening that people aren't telling me about?"

"A lot."

"Like what?"

Siena glanced over her shoulder, and back down the path. They had gone far enough that neither of them could see Andino or Haven any longer. John doubted his cousin would leave him alone for very long, especially not if the visit wasn't meant to last.

"Andino doesn't want me——"

"Fuck what he wants," John said. "It's *me* asking right now."

Siena looked down at the path. "There's a lot of stuff that's happened over the past little while since you came here. At first, the families tried to avoid a feud between them with more peaceful means. When all that went to shit, the violence really got started."

"You said war before."

"That's the impression I got from my brothers."

"But was it?" he asked.

Siena shook her head. "Not like it is now. It's bad now."

Fuck.

"No one's mentioned this to me when they visit," he said.

Siena cleared her throat. "You have to focus on *you*."

"I'm aware, but——"

Quick as a blink, Siena had turned on her heel, and stopped John from walking any further on the pathway. Her hands came up to press against his chest, and her fingernails dug in just enough to make him suck in a sharp breath.

She tipped her head up, and pressed a fast kiss to his lips. Just like that, everything he was worrying about was gone in an instant.

The girl had many talents. Distracting him was just one.

"I promised Andino I wouldn't tell you," Siena whispered against his lips. "Please just focus on you for the time you have left here, John."

"I am," he assured her.

His hands cupped her face, and he kept her close enough that she was forced to keep her eyes on only him. Nothing else but him.

He needed to see her, too.

"They mean well," she said. "You have to trust them."

He heard her. He understood.

It still was hard.

THREE

Siena stepped out of the cool complex into humid July air. It made the lingering wetness from the quick shower she had taken to get rid of the workout sweat stick to her skin. The smell of chlorine from the complex's pool vanished with every breath of fresh air she took in.

The day was beautiful, and the streets were quiet. A clear sky, and a bright sun that suggested no rain was on the horizon, despite the humidity. Siena couldn't complain about that. Nobody wanted rain in the summer.

Then, as quickly as her happiness came, it fled just as easily at the sight of the man waiting for her next to a running Mercedes.

No, not her enforcer.

Her brother.

Darren pulled the aviator sunglasses he wore away from his face as Siena took the steps of the complex slowly. The longer she didn't have to be in his presence, or talk to him, the better. He gave the simple black dress she wore a curious look, and his gaze narrowed on the bag she carried. She was barely within reach of her brother before he snatched the bag from her shoulder, and opened it up.

What the hell?

"Hey," Siena snapped. "Give me that back, Darren."

"In a sec."

He didn't even look up at her as he dug through her bag. His hands pulled out her personal effects without any care at all. All that was in there were her workout clothes, a bathing suit if she felt like using the pool when she came to the complex, the cell phone her brothers provided, and her wallet.

Nothing more.

Nothing less.

Still, he kept looking like he expected to find something.

He wouldn't.

Siena was not dumb.

"Why are these clothes damp?" Darren asked.

"Because working out makes people *sweaty*," Siena said. "Which you know, gets on the fucking clothes you wear while you work out."

Not that her brother would know anything about exercising. The older Darren got, the rounder he became in his middle. Pear-shaped when it came to his body, while his hair was thinning at the top of his head. Sometimes, if she turned too fast, she was struck by how much he looked like their father.

She figured that was probably a lot of Darren's problem where his health was concerned. He had been spoiled too long by their father. He had become accustomed to eating whatever he wanted, and never cared for his body. He much preferred to sit behind a desk like their father had taught him to do, and issue orders, instead of doing something himself.

So far, Kev had avoided behaving that way, too. He was still quite a spoiled, demanding man, however.

"That's disgusting."

Darren made a face, and handed the bag back to her as though the item had suddenly turned diseased. *Screw him.* Siena snatched it from his grasp with a dirty look, and slung the bag over her shoulder.

"What in the hell was that all about?" she demanded. "I don't go through your stuff like I have any business doing so."

Darren gave the complex a look, and then his sharp gaze cut back to Siena just as fast. She didn't like the way his eyes glinted with something unknown. She couldn't trust her brothers with a goddamn inch, to be honest.

"It's strange—that's all," he said. "Every time you come here, your enforcer says you come out wearing the same shit you go in with. Problem is, Kev and I both know you pack clothes to work out in every time you go."

Siena barely hid her frown.

Her brothers were looking into her business, and that spelled bad news. It made her uncomfortable as hell to think that either one of her brothers were starting to get suspicious about anything she did. Especially if that meant they might take away her one opportunity for her to actually get away from them.

She had to think … and *fast.*

"Do you want to wear the same clothes you work out in for the rest of the day?" Siena asked. Pulling her bag from her shoulder, she offered it to her brother. "Here, take it again and smell the clothes in there. Do you think sweat smells like fucking roses, or what? Jesus Christ. Get a grip, Darren."

Darren made that same disgusted face, and refused to take the bag. "I get it, Siena. Chill your hormones out, all right."

She wasn't one hundred percent satisfied that she had got her brother to believe that she wasn't doing anything at the complex but working out. For now, it would have to do. Unless she got another goddamn idea, or they forced her hand.

"Just yoga today?" Darren asked as he opened the door to the car.

Siena passed her brother a look as she slid into the passenger seat. "Today, yeah."

"You didn't see anyone you recognized in there, or whatever?"

Jesus.

"No, not today."

Siena tried to close the car door, but her brother held strong. He leaned down to stare Siena right in the face as he spoke again.

"Have you seen anybody you recognize here since you started coming to the place?"

"Just my enforcers."

Lies.

Siena had never been much of a liar, but she had become especially good at it over the last few months. Maybe she was just as bad as her family—maybe she owned her last name the same way her brothers did.

The thing was, Siena wasn't doing it for the Calabrese name. She wasn't doing anything of this for her brothers, or even for her dead father.

No, she was doing this for someone else entirely.

For her.

For John.

For them.

"You're sure?" Darren pressed.

Siena tried to find what her brother was reaching for as she searched his eyes, but came up with nothing. For as good as she was with hiding things, so were Darren and Kev. It was a little unsettling when she didn't know what their game was. Besides, it was far easier for her to beat her brothers at their own game when she knew what was coming.

Even if that meant cheating a little ...

Her last meeting with Andino had been the previous week when they visited John at Clearview Oaks. She had barely managed to get back to the complex in time once they left, as she dragged her feet too much while they were there. She hadn't wanted to leave John when she didn't know the next time she was going to be able to see him. In fact, she was so late getting back that her enforcer had just entered the building to come search for her as she passed by the receptionist's desk.

Sure, the guy hadn't seen her coming in through the back entrances. She had been a little sweaty from running through the back parking lot, and the building to get to the front. Her hair had been mussed, and her face clear of makeup when she scrubbed it all off during the drive back.

Nothing was out of place. Nothing for the enforcer to mention. It had still been a little too close for comfort.

Maybe that's what had Darren's suspicions up.

Who fucking knew?

"I'm sure, Darren," she said. "Now close the damn door. It's hot outside."

She barely even got to finish her sentence before her brother did just that. Siena moved her fingers out of the way in the last second to avoid getting them jammed. She shot him a dirty look through the window, but Darren only smiled in response.

Fucking asshole.

All too soon, Darren slipped into the driver's seat, and without even looking over his shoulder, pulled out onto the road. He kept quiet for a long while, and hell, that only made Siena even more unsettled. Like he was trying to think about what he wanted to say, or something.

Everything about her life, and her brothers, was now a very carefully thought out process. Nothing was said without it meaning something, and they very rarely told her things unless it was to demand something, or announce something.

Shit.

She wished they would talk to her less, actually.

"Someone mentioned they might have seen Andino Marcello around this part of Brooklyn a couple of times," Darren said. "Kev wanted me to ask if you had seen the fool, too. You know what he drives, right? Black Mercedes, kind of like this one."

Actually, Andino drove two vehicles. One was a white Porsche, and another was a black Mercedes SUV. And it was nicer than her brother's.

Siena swallowed hard. "No, I haven't."

And by *someone*, she suspected her brother meant one of her enforcers. She didn't bother to ask if that was actually the case, though. Too many questions from her, and it would drive Darren's suspicions even higher. She didn't need that trouble right now.

Siena kept her gaze on the sidewalks and people they passed by. Many of the shops were taking down their Fourth of July decorations as the holiday had now passed. It gave her a chance to keep her attention on anything but her brother.

Maybe then, he would get the hint.

She wasn't up to chat.

Darren never did care. "We've got to keep a better eye on them, that's all."

Well, that piqued her interest.

"The Marcellos?"

"Yeah."

"Why?"

Darren shrugged. "Things are happening in that family, that's all. It's important we keep up with it, and act appropriately to it."

"Things like what?"

She was pressing too hard.

She seemed too curious.

Darren was too focused on the road to notice, it seemed. That, or whatever he was caught up with regarding the Marcello family had him distracted. "I guess the Marcellos announced Andino's engagement to some chick—let everybody know at their Fourth of July party. Shit, they're not even waiting, really."

"I don't understand."

He passed her a look. "To get *married*, Siena. They're not waiting to get married since they just announced it and all. Fuck, keep up. You're not usually this dumb."

Ouch.

She let that insult roll off her shoulders.

"When are they getting married?"

"On the twentieth."

Wait …

"Of *this* month?" she asked.

Darren nodded. "Yep."

"And they just announced it?"

"Like I said, they're not waiting. Sounds to me like someone wants to move little Andino up in the family, and he needs to position himself appropriately for it."

"He's not really little, is he?"

More like a fucking linebacker.

Darren scoffed. "You know what I mean."

"I don't know what any of that—him getting married, or whatever—has to do with us, though."

Her brother smiled. "No, I wouldn't expect you to, Siena. You're only a woman."

Only a woman.

That insult was not as easy to ignore, but she forced herself to, anyway. Someday, her brothers would think twice before thinking because she was only a woman, she could not hurt them. Hell, they should have already realized it.

Look what happened to their father. Sure, that hadn't been her, but she hadn't stopped John from killing Matteo, either. She didn't even apologize for not trying to stop him from doing it. She didn't even cry at Matteo's funeral.

Her father didn't need her tears. He wouldn't want them.

She had always been *just a woman* to him, too.

Besides, she had something better to consider at the moment. Andino getting married so soon likely meant he had a lot on his plate, and that was probably why he hadn't shown up to talk with her today at the complex. Sometimes, that happened.

Andino was Johnathan's best friend, and vice versa. There was no way in hell Andino would get married without John being there, too.

Siena knew, then. She had a date to count down to for when John would finally be out again. They were one step closer to finishing this forever.

Her forever was almost there …

For the first time in longer than Siena cared to remember, she sat alone in the church pew.

Well, not *totally* alone.

Just down the way on her right side sat her mother. On her left, a few seats away, sat her enforcer. Her mother's attention never left the priest speaking at the altar, while the enforcer seemed more interested in the phone in his hands than on the service.

Siena took the few moments she had to check the screen of her phone without the enforcer or her mother looking over her damn shoulder. She didn't get that chance very often. The date on the home screen stared back at her.

July twentieth.

She had counted down the days. She had paid way too much attention to the calendar on her wall every single day she woke up, and then again before she went to sleep.

The day was finally here.

John was getting *out*.

Siena only knew for sure that he was getting out today because of a *wrong number* call from someone. The call came to her cell phone like it always did when Andino sent a message. Some random person asked for the wrong name, Siena would apologize and say it was the wrong number. Then, the person on the other end of the call would quickly deliver whatever message needed to be said before she hung up without a second thought.

That way, should anyone be near her when she picked up the wrong number call, no one would think anything was amiss. And should someone else pick up her phone when the call came in, like Kev had done once, they would only have the person on the other end apologizing for calling the wrong number.

Today, the message had been clear.

Three o'clock. Waldorf, Manhattan. Room 403. Room key will be waiting at the desk.

Siena knew that time coincided with Andino's wedding. The location for the event hadn't been given when it was announced in the society rags, but the date and time had been mentioned. Not to mention, Kev and Darren had gotten information, too.

Siena eavesdropped far more than was safe.

She was kind of betting her life on it, at the moment.

This morning, however, no one had been around to hear her wrong number call. No one had been around since the night before when Kev and Darren each packed a bag, and slipped out of the house. They didn't tell her anything about where they were going except to say they wouldn't be back until the next day or sometime after, and her enforcer would be close by.

They also made it clear she was to attend church with her mother.

Well ...

Siena was here.

So was her mother.

She couldn't promise to stay, though. Not when she knew John was just within her reach, and so was the taste of freedom. Even if that bit of freedom wouldn't last for long.

It didn't matter.

The opportunity was too good to pass up.

Siena passed another look at her enforcer as she slipped the phone back into her purse. The man's attention was still firmly stuck on the phone in his hand. It looked like he was playing a game of some sort.

She swore she could hear the clock ticking down in the back of her mind. It was getting louder by the second.

Taunting her, even.

Goddamn.

She forced her attention back to the priest. His sermon on faith and love to one's family was entirely lost on her. Or perhaps, she just didn't have the right family at the moment to give those things to.

Soon, the service was over. People stood from the pews, and Siena followed suit. She had been at least able to drive herself to church in her Lexus, which was one less thing for her to figure out at the moment.

She only needed to get away ...

"You should come over for dinner," her mother said behind her.

Siena stiffened. "Not tonight, Ma."

Turning, she faced Coraline. Her mother reached out to fix a stray curl, but Siena quickly stepped out of Coraline's reach. She was not interested in entertaining the woman's false affections. Besides, her mother's love was dependent on how well-behaved and loyal Siena was to their family.

"I do miss spending time with you," her mother said.

Siena nodded, and smiled. "I'm sure you do, Ma. Tonight, I have other plans."

"Like what? I know your brothers are out of town. You must be bored in Kev's brownstone all by yourself. Surely, you're not entertaining ..." Coraline trailed off, and nodded in the direction of the waiting enforcer. "Neither of your brothers need *that* kind of trouble, Siena."

God, no.

She didn't even hide how disgusting the idea made her feel.

"No, not that, Ma," Siena muttered. "I just meant I wanted a quiet night. Me, my book, and maybe some wine."

Those were most definitely not her plans, but as long as it got her mother off her back …

Coraline's bitterness was back in a blink. "Well, don't say I didn't *try*."

"I would never, Ma."

Because she didn't try.

Neither did Siena.

This was just another game.

Siena allowed her mother to kiss her cheeks, and offered the same in return. She watched her mother step out of the pew and into the aisle before she turned to face the waiting enforcer. The man looked like he was ready to leave.

She had news for him.

"I need to speak with my priest for a few minutes," she told him.

The enforcer—a young twenty-something whose name she hadn't even been given—scowled. "Didn't you listen to him enough today?"

"You're not a very good Catholic, are you?"

"I go to church."

"Do you make use of confession?"

The man coughed. "Well, no …"

"I do. Excuse me."

She heard the enforcer's sigh echo out from behind her, but all she could do was smile. Shooting a look over her shoulder, Siena found the enforcer had sat back down in the pew, and dragged his phone out to look at it once again. He wasn't even paying any attention to her at all.

Good.

That's exactly what she wanted.

In their life, very few things were held sacred. And for her, a woman who had disabused her family, and misused their trust, even less things were sacred for her.

Certainly not privacy.

Except, of course, when it came to confession.

Siena would disappear out one of the back doors, and be long gone in her Lexus before the enforcer even realized what was happening. He likely wouldn't know she was gone until he figured out how long he had been sitting there waiting for her.

Besides, confession could take a long time.

The phone in her pocket burned a hole as she headed past the last few people. A part of her wanted to pull out of the phone, and make one single call. She knew Andino's number—she could let him know that she would be there today.

The smarter part of her brain knew that probably wasn't a good idea. Her brothers crawled through her phone history on a regular basis. She couldn't even delete shit without them finding out. She didn't need that kind of trouble when they got back.

She left the damn phone where it was.

Their priest didn't have a particularly large congregation, but it was a decent size. He often allowed confession to be open after every Sunday service, just in case someone in the church wanted to make use of it.

He held confession in the back of the church, behind the altar. A private room set up with rich tapestries, and two chairs facing one another. Sometimes, it made confession a little awkward when a person was forced to look someone in the face when they admitted to some of their deepest, darkest sins.

The comfort of the room often helped, though. It certainly didn't look like the old confessional booths in movies. Actually, Siena didn't think she had ever used one of those kinds of confessionals.

None of that mattered.

She wasn't going to be attending confession at all.

At least, not today.

She was banking on the fact that the enforcer was rather new to watching her, and quite young in the grand scheme of things. She hoped that those facts would keep him from calling her brothers to let them know she had skipped out on him, if only because he was one of the many men in their family who had a healthy fear where Kev and Darren were concerned.

He wouldn't want to get in trouble.

Not for *her*.

Siena slipped into the back hallway that led to the offices, and the private room used for confession. The priest was already greeting a man standing outside the private room, and gestured for the man to go in.

He didn't even see Siena.

He didn't see her take a sharp right, and head out the exit, either.

Siena glanced down at the peach-colored dress and matching pumps she wore. Even the peach hat on her head was Sunday services appropriate. And wedding appropriate, although she wasn't sure if she would even be attending the wedding.

That invisible clock in the back of her mind only stopped ticking down when she slipped inside her Lexus, and turned on the ignition. She was no longer counting days or minutes or seconds to when she would see John again.

To when he would be *out* again.

She was finally in the fucking homestretch. Even just a few days of not seeing him was far too long.

Whatever trouble might find her for this …

So worth it.

FOUR

Leonard sat beside Johnathan on the bench just outside the entrance doors of Clearview Oaks. Up above, the sky was a pale blue, and cloudless.

Despite the beautiful day, the humid heat was enough to make John wish he was not wearing jeans at the moment. The thick material stuck to his skin, and made him hotter. He pulled out the collar of his T-shirt, and waved it a bit to create the illusion of cold air.

His attention to the weather did not escape his therapist's notice.

"Quite hot out," Leonard noted.

"It's been like this for a while. Going through a spell, I think."

"Better hot, than cold."

John nodded. "Truth."

Leonard passed a look at the brown paper bag resting beside John's thigh. "It didn't take you very long to pack up your things, did it?"

A smile passed between the two men. Even John couldn't help but chuckle when Leonard shook his head.

"I didn't come in with very much," John admitted. "I had everything packed before breakfast this morning, actually."

"And I suppose you didn't ask for anyone to bring you very much while you were here, either," Leonard said. "At least, you never asked me to make that request on your behalf to someone in your family."

"No."

"Shame."

John cocked a brow. "What is?"

"Sometimes packing up your things and leaving a facility can be just as cathartic as anything you find comforting—or even, a great satisfaction. Something you completed. Or even, a goal you achieved. A challenge in your life that you bested, and your reward, so to speak, is packing up your things."

"It still felt … rewarding."

Maybe that wasn't exactly the right word to use, but it was all John felt like offering at the moment. Packing up his few things to leave Clearview had felt a lot like when he left prison almost a year ago. Different circumstances, sure, but the emotions and how he felt them were still very much the same in a lot of ways.

Relief as he pulled the few photographs off the wall, and anxiety as he exited out of the bars that had kept him locked up for years. Anticipation, too, at the idea of freedom, but knowing he wasn't quite sure what to do with it.

This time had been months.

It also wasn't prison.

Yet, those same emotions plagued him. Those same worries about the *outside*, life, and even his family were forefront in his mind. Like little needles sticking in his brain, and staying like that for far longer than he wanted them to.

No matter what he did, he could not remove that strange sensation. At the same time, he wasn't sure that he wanted to, either. Although uncomfortable, it was still comforting in its familiarity.

No, Clearview hadn't been a prison. Leaving the place was still very much a variable unknown to John.

Funny how it still felt the same.

Leonard pulled out a form from the inside pocket of his white lab coat, and waved it in the air to catch John's attention. "Your probation is all set again. Of course, we had to pull some strings when you were first admitted as to not break your probation."

"Yeah, thanks again for that."

"No thanks needed."

Leonard handed over the form, and John opened it up. Looking the document over, it seemed that Leonard had finally been listed as John's official registered therapist for the unforeseeable future. Well, for after his release from Clearview.

The form listed approximate appointment dates, and Leonard's signature was heavy and bold on the bottom of the paper. A sign of the doctor's agreement to follow the letter of the law where John's probation was concerned, and report him to the probation office should he stop attending his appointments.

"Would you really report me?" John asked. "If I didn't show up to my appointments, I mean."

Leonard chuckled. "Should I, John?"

He looked over at the therapist. The man simply raised a thick, white eyebrow in response, waiting for John's answer. Leonard was too good at this shit, but frankly, John was more grateful to this man than anyone could possibly know.

"Thank you for giving my parents an answer all those years ago," John murmured. "I imagine it can't be easy to tell someone that their kid is—"

"Not crazy. Not in need of a cure to be *curable*. Don't say those things."

"I wasn't."

"Then what?"

John smirked. "I was just going to say bipolar, actually."

Leonard nodded, and the man's gaze turned pensive for a moment. "I know you may have felt like I sentenced you to something you did not want back then, John, but I hope in a way that you found relief in having the right answer, too."

"I did—it took a while."

"Sometimes it does for those with bipolar."

"But thank you."

Leonard waved a hand high, and settled back into the bench. "No thanks needed."

"You didn't answer my question, by the way. I'm emotionally unstable sometimes, but not dumb or stupid."

The older man laughed hard and loud, and his sharp gaze cut to John in a flash. "Which question—whether I would report you or not for missing appointments with me?"

"Yes."

"Well, you didn't answer *me*, John. Should I report you?"

John really didn't have to think about his answer. It wasn't an easy answer, sure. The thing was, nothing about his life or his disorder was easy. It couldn't be, and it was never going to be. That was something he was taking away from this place, and because of the man sitting beside him. Yet another thing to be grateful for.

For some reason, John had a sneaking suspicion that there was going to be a lot to be grateful for over his lifetime where Leonard was concerned. At least, during the period that Leonard was his therapist.

"I'm choosing stability," John said after a moment.

"You are."

"And so yes," he added, "you should report me."

Leonard reached over and clapped John firmly on the shoulder. He wasn't really the touchy-feely-type, but he was getting better at it. He had learned that sometimes a hand on his shoulder was meant to praise him, and not simply break through his personal space barriers.

He had spent almost five months at Clearview Oaks. For some people, that would seem like a ridiculously long amount of time simply to reset, recharge, and get their shit figured out. At first, it had seemed like a long time to John, too.

Sometimes, mental health couldn't be fixed with new meds, a couple of chats, and a pat on the back. Sometimes, mental health was so much more than the disorder a person lived with, and the outlook it gave them.

Mental health could not be timed.

It could not be wished it away.

It took patience.

John had needed this.

Damn, how he *needed* this.

"Seems your drive has arrived," Leonard said.

John's gaze drifted from Leonard's smile, to the black Mercedes pulling up next to the Clearview welcome sign. He had thought a lot about who might come to pick him up, but that was not the person he considered. "Huh."

"Not who you were expecting, I suspect?"

"Actually, I can't say I'm surprised," John admitted as the man exited the car, and came to stand on the other side. "Unexpected, yes, but not surprised. I thought my uncle, Gio. Or maybe even Andino."

Leonard chuckled as he stood from the bench. "Mmm, I am sure both of those people fought tooth and nail to be the one here today."

"Likely."

"Someone else fought harder, clearly."

Leonard waved a hand at the waiting man.

Lucian waved back in kind.

"Nice to see you again, old friend," Leonard called.

"And you, Leo," John's father replied.

Leonard looked down at John. "Don't keep people waiting for you—it's rude."

Goddamn.

John got his ass up, and took the hand that Leonard offered to shake. "Thanks."

"I will see you next week, John. Bright and early. Be there."

"Of course."

John's father had barely pulled the Mercedes out onto the road, before his hand reached for his son. Lucian's palm cupped John's cheek, and then slid around to grab the back of his neck. John blinked, and he was pulled closer to his father.

Lucian never looked away from the road when he laughed, gave John a quick pat on the neck, and brought him close enough that their temples touched.

"You look good," his father said when he finally let him go.

John smiled. "You think?"

"Happy, John."

"I am."

Or, as happy as he could be. Sometimes, happiness meant feeling settled and stable. It did not have to be overwhelming joy and pride. Happiness was as simple as feeling and being good inside his head.

It was the little things, after all.

"I thought Andino might come today," John admitted.

Lucian waved a hand before placing it back to the leather-wrapped steering wheel. "He's a little busy, that's all. Everyone is, but they all bickered for hours about who was going to come and get you."

"Hell, I could have taken a cab home."

"Not my son."

That was all his father said.

Maybe, it was all Lucian *had* to say.

John still heard the meaning beneath the simple words. "Thanks for coming to get me, Papa."

Lucian shot John a look, and nodded once. "I'm always going to be here to get you when you need me to, my boy."

"My birthday is in ten days—I'll be thirty-one."

He didn't finish his statement. He figured he didn't really have to.

Lucian only shrugged. "Always my boy—my *only* boy, John."

"I suppose Ma wants to see me."

"Among others," Lucian agreed. "We have to make a trip to Tuxedo Park, before we head into the city. Manhattan, specifically."

Damn.

John just wanted to relax.

"*Have* to?"

"It's a big day," Lucian murmured, shooting his son a grin.

"What does that mean?"

His father cleared his throat. "Well, a lot has happened, John."

"And that's why we're going to drive all over New York today?"

"Kind of."

"Papa."

Lucian chuckled at the tone of John's voice. "You sound just like Antony

245

when you do that. Your grandfather would be proud as hell."

"I bet. What aren't you telling me?"

"A lot, and nothing at all. Where do you want to start?"

John looked over his shoulder, and noted a freshly pressed tux resting in a see-through garment bag. A peach-colored vest, tie, and pocket square was also inside the bag. "Let's start with why there's a tux in the back."

"It's for you to wear."

John's brow dipped low. "With a vest and tie that looks like it belongs in a wedding?"

"That's because it does." Lucian reached over, and pulled out a small box from the glove compartment, and handed it over to John. A ring box, it seemed. He opened it up to find a set of rings inside—one female, and one male. "You're going to need this, too. Keep a hold of it, and don't lose it. It's really your only job today."

John blinked. "What the fuck?"

Lucian laughed darkly. "Yeah, that's a good start. You're Andino's best man. You need a tux, and it's your job to keep an eye on the rings, and hand them over when the priest asks for them. You'll stand at the altar where you're told to stand, and leave when you're told to leave. There's really not much else to it—Andino and Haven did not want a lot of fanfare for this day, and we didn't exactly have a lot of time to work with."

His father passed him a look, quickly adding, "They are being married at Antony and Cecelia's estate, and the dinner and party will follow at the Waldorf Astoria in Manhattan. You see, we're having trouble keeping out of sight lately. We don't want to stay gathered—at least, not the whole family—in one place for too long where we might be attacked in some way. And so, we are having the wedding with a very limited amount of guests in our private home, and the larger party where people are less likely to attack in a very public setting."

Lucian ticked a finger into the air, saying, "Of course, still *highly* protected."

"Wait, Andi's getting married today?"

"I said that, yes."

"*Today.*"

"Yes, John."

"He didn't tell me—"

Lucian's gaze cut to John's, quieting him instantly. "He asked her the day they came to visit you, and only announced it to us a couple of days later. They did not want to wait to be married, and everyone has agreed to this. Andino did, however, want to wait for you."

John looked down at the rings again. "A best man, huh?"

"You're not really surprised, are you?"

"Fuck no."

Lucian let out another one of his hard laughs, and then reached for his son again. John let his father bring him close, touch their temples together, and pat his neck with affection he had denied his father for years.

Then, John had another thought.

His mind had been so caught up in the revelation about Andino getting married today that he hadn't stopped to think at all about the other information his father offered to him. The mention of moving the family from place to place because of protection. How they were planning in order to prevent an attack that they believed might come.

"It's the Calabrese, isn't it?" John asked quietly.

"How about today, we—"

"How about you just answer me, Papa?"

Lucian nodded with a dry chuckle. "All right. Yes, it is the Calabrese."

"How bad is it?"

Sure, Siena had given John a bit to go on, but that's all it had been. A little bit of info—a tease, if you will. Something to make him stay up at night and ponder, but not enough to chew on and really understand what was happening.

He needed more.

He needed it now.

"Dante wanted this feud between our families to be settled peacefully," Lucian said.

"Someone mentioned that to me already. I'm not sure what methods he used for that, though."

"An attempt to arrange a marriage, actually."

John stiffened in his seat, and his gaze flew to his father. "What?"

"You heard me,"

He didn't like what that implied. There was really only *one* Calabrese woman worthy of marrying into the Marcello family, or rather, one woman that Dante would consider worthy in the grand scheme.

Siena.

"He didn't—"

"It was not your woman," Lucian muttered. "Relax."

John did not realize how stiff his body had become in those few seconds, or how firmly he had gritted his teeth until relief flowed through his body. Sweet like sugar, the sensation washed through his bloodstream. His molars ached when they released from the tight clench. He found crescent shaped marks on the insides of his palms from how tightly he clenched his fists together, too.

Jesus Christ.

"It was not Siena," Lucian repeated. "And the details do not matter, honestly. What matters is that the deal failed, and the violence escalated from there. We had in good faith information about an attack that would happen on one of our warehouses, but it did not happen."

"That's a good thing, then."

"It is, except when one does not go through, it is usually because another bigger, better one is coming. The only major event we have going on as a family right now is—"

"Andi's wedding."

Lucian nodded. "Exactly, son. Mind you, we have been very careful about releasing details regarding the wedding. The main event is not an open invitation to *famiglia*. The party afterward at the Astoria is, but it's very public, there will be a large crowd."

"And you said it's well protected."

"That, too, yes."

"But you're still concerned."

"We all are," Lucian said quietly. "These are dangerous days, John."

And for what?

Because of him.

John still didn't regret what he did when he killed Matteo Calabrese. He would never regret any of that, but he hadn't wanted this. He didn't want his family to suffer again because of him.

"I'm sorry."

"You have absolutely nothing to be sorry for, and this is only a passing moment in all of our lives. We have lived through worse, and we will live through this. There is always something beautiful waiting at the end. What is it you want when you get to the end, John?"

Well …

"Siena," he admitted. "But that's a little fucking impossible, isn't it?"

Lucian looked over at John. "Keep your fucking chin up, and your eyes on the prize, John. Marcellos don't look down."

"Not unless we're looking down on somebody, right?"

Lucian's chuckles echoed once more. "Right, my boy. Chin up."

"You couldn't fucking let me in on the little secret, or what?"

John's question—his tone coated with amusement—quieted the whole room of men. The one person he had directed his question to was the first person to find him and Lucian standing in the doorway waiting.

Andino grinned widely. "John."

"Hey, cousin."

"About fucking time you showed up. I was starting to get nervous."

John smiled. "I might have lost the rings, so, yeah."

"You didn't."

"No, I damn well didn't."

John flashed the box in question. Slung around his arm was the garment bag with his tux safely hidden inside. He still had to get dressed, but he had a few other things to take care of first. Like his family—Andino, mostly.

"Come here," Andino said.

John crossed the room, and took the tight hug his cousin offered. Andino smacked John on the back twice, and then let him go with another one of those signature grins. His cousin patted his cheek, and nodded.

Quietly, Andino said, "I really didn't want to do this day without you, man."

"Yeah, I kind of got that. Congrats, huh?"

"Hold off on that. We still need to get Haven to the altar, and everything."

Chuckles lit up the room, reminding John once again that they still had a bit of an audience. He didn't mind—it was just his family, after all.

His grandfather was the first to approach them. Antony took his time looking

John over, and then the older man clicked his tongue. His weathered face cracked with age when he smiled, and shook his head.

"You're not properly dressed, Johnathan."

John held up the garment bag. "Working on it, Grandpapa."

"Work faster. We're all a little late today."

"He's not lying," Giovanni said as he stepped in beside his son to clap Andino on the back. He gave John the same attention. "Good to see you home, *nipote.*"

"Glad to be back," John replied in kind.

"I bet."

And then, the one man John might have been dreading speaking to just a little bit stepped closer. His uncle, Dante. The boss of their family—the patriarch who John had, without a doubt, disobeyed, disrespected, and more before he entered Clearview.

He didn't know what to expect from Dante.

He didn't know what to say.

Dante only smiled.

Not a cold smile, either.

"Boss," John said.

Dante's grin deepened a bit. "Not for long, John."

John's gaze darted to Andino, who only smirked. No, he supposed someone else was getting ready to take Dante's place, now.

It was appropriate.

All reigns eventually came to an end.

Even a Marcello King's.

"I certainly hope you're ready for this day, and what comes after," Dante said, eyeing John with a careful eye. "Are you?"

He didn't know what the hell his uncle meant.

He didn't care, either.

"Of course, I am," John replied.

Dante nodded, and reached out a hand. John took it, only to then find himself dragged into a quick, tight hug from his uncle. Dante let him go, and smiled again in that way that reminded John of when he was a young boy, and idolized his uncle to the ends of the earth and back.

"You have ten minutes to get dressed," Dante told him with a smack to his cheek. "Hurry the fuck up—nobody here wants to make Andino wait longer than he already has for this girl of his. Isn't that right?"

Laughter colored up the room.

Everybody agreed.

John made quick work of getting dressed in a separate private room, and had only took one step out before his mother damn near tackled him in a hug. Well, his mother, grandmother, and both aunts. Lips found his cheeks for kisses that were then quickly wiped off to avoid lipstick stains, hands patted his cheeks with sweet affection, and Italian words filled his ears.

Nipote.

Bambino.

"Let me breathe, *donnas,*" John heard himself say with a chuckle.

The women didn't really let him do anything.

John didn't really mind.

Soon, though, his aunts and grandmother dispersed to leave John alone with his mother. Jordyn checked him over, ran her fingers through his hair to slick the longer length of the high fade back further, and smiled in a way only a mother could when she was staring at her child. Those blue eyes of hers lit up with love, and John smiled back.

"Hey, Ma."

Jordyn let out a happy noise. "I missed you, my boy."

"I know, Ma. I didn't mean to scare you."

"Never, John. I only worry. You've certainly made my life interesting when things seem boring, though. Big day today, huh? You kind of ended up thrown in the middle of the whole shebang."

John shrugged. "I don't mind."

"Not when it comes to Andino, right?"

"Right."

"Come on," Jordyn said, tangling her arm in with his. "I will walk you to your spot. It's my job to make sure you know what to do today."

John didn't mind indulging his mother—she loved him so very much, after all. He chatted away with her as she walked him through the large Marcello mansion, and to the main ballroom where the chairs and decorations filled the room. Outside would probably have been nice for a wedding, considering the weather, but he didn't even ask why they hadn't bothered.

He already knew.

It was open.

It made them targets.

Protection be damned.

Jordyn led John to his position at the front, and he gave his mother a quick kiss on her cheek before she darted off. Probably to find one of his sisters—who he had not seen in months—or his father.

It wasn't too long after that before Andino took his place beside John. The priest was there, too. Likely paid off considering the man was marrying them outside of a church, and on a very short timeline that did not allow for couple's counseling.

Funny how the church worked.

When the music started, Andino said to John, "Watch this, man."

John waited.

He watched.

Dante Marcello walked Haven down the aisle.

It was as good of a show as any. For the few guests invited, it meant a hell of a lot without ever saying a damn thing. The woman—regardless of heritage or bloodline, or history—was a Marcello. Accepted, brought in, and protected.

Respected.

John could only think of one person he wished would get the same respect: Siena.

"Walk a little slower, would you," his father joked.

John laughed as the two navigated the halls of the Waldorf hotel. "I'm supposed to be downstairs, all right. The party isn't even over yet, Dad."

Lucian shrugged. "For you, it is. At least, down there."

"What?"

His father didn't answer. A floor later, and Lucian handed over a room key. It matched the number on the door that the two stood in front of.

"What, are you putting me to bed like a fucking kid, or something?"

Lucian smirked. "Or *something*."

"I should be downstairs with Andino."

"Sure, but we all kind of pulled some strings hoping this would work out for you today, and it was just our luck that it did." Then, his father reached out and smacked John's cheek lightly. "Or shit, maybe it was *your* luck, huh?"

"I thought they used to call you Lucky."

"It's been passed down," Lucian replied. "From me, to you. And you'll pass it on, too."

Well, John didn't know about that. He wasn't sure if he was every going to pass anything on to children from his blood, but this wasn't the time for that discussion, either.

Lucian tipped his head toward the door. "Go ahead. We'll all be here tomorrow. Breakfast with your mother and sisters. They'll like that."

He didn't know about his *sisters*, really. His mother would like it, for sure.

"You really fucking took me from the party to put me to bed, didn't you?"

Lucian only grinned. "Just open the fucking door."

John gave his father a look, but did as he was told. He slid the keycard through the slot, heard the lock beep, and then the tumblers roll. Pulling the handle down, the door opened easily under his hand.

He expected the room to be dark.

It was lit up.

He expected the room to be empty.

She stood there waiting.

Siena.

"John," Siena greeted with one of her sweet smiles.

He was just ... stuck.

Speechless.

Stupid.

Happy.

Awed.

All day, he had listened to whispers from his family about the Calabrese family, and the war raging between their organizations in the city. He heard them call them snakes, and untrustworthy. He listened as they made more plans to get rid of them entirely. There was no love lost between the Marcellos, and the Calabrese organization.

This war was apparently one of the bloodiest, and messiest the city had seen in a long while. There was not one person in John's family who had any issue with saying openly and proudly how wonderful it would be once the Calabrese legacy was gone forever. Not to mention, how great it would be for the Marcellos to be the ones to do it.

Poetic justice after all the history, and bad blood.

And yet …

Here she stood.

In front of him.

Everything his family hated right now. Everything they were working to destroy, and to remove from their lives forever.

Except, his father had alluded to everyone working together to have Siena here for him. As though they were working with her in some way. As though, perhaps, they trusted her in some way. At least, enough to bring her here.

For him.

John really wanted to know what in the hell was up, and what he had missed out on, but not right now.

Right now …

"Your mother kept her company for a while today," Lucian said, "and I figured she had probably had enough of being alone, and missing out. She can't come downstairs, of course. We wouldn't want our best asset at the moment being photographed with the rest of us, now would we?"

"No, we definitely wouldn't," Siena said.

John still had not found the right words to say.

His father didn't seem to mind. With a clap of his hand to John's shoulder, Lucian gave his son another smile, and a nod.

"Enjoy your evening, son."

FIVE

Siena caught sight of the smile Lucian directed her way one last time before John stepped into the room, and colored up her vision entirely. Nothing else mattered nearly as much as he did when he was in her presence.

"You should close the door," she told him, grinning a little.

John still seemed a bit stunned at seeing her there. Not that she blamed him. "I should, shouldn't I?"

Siena nodded. "Yeah. I mean, who knows what's going to happen now that you're finally up here. We wouldn't want to give the rest of the floor a show, right?"

His tongue snuck from his mouth to touch his top lip as he grinned in the most salacious way. A smile that spoke entirely of sex and sin, and how dangerous this man could be for her body and heart.

Goddamn.

She loved him.

Still.

So much.

John reached back, and swung the door closed without ever taking his eyes away from Siena. Like maybe he thought if he blinked, she might suddenly disappear on him. It was almost comical.

"Look at that," she said.

John's eyebrow quirked up. "Hmm, what?"

Siena waved a hand between them. "We match."

He looked damn good in the fitted tux he wore. It hugged all of his strong lines, showcased his broad shoulders, and only added to the tall, dark, and handsome thing he had going on. The peach vest, tie, and pocket square as accents to his tux perfectly matched the color of the dress she had picked for church that morning.

John's gaze traveled over Siena's body, unashamed. He didn't even try to hide the way he lingered on her legs, and then his gaze skipped back up to her face just as fast. "I suppose we do match. Was that part of the plan, too?"

"What plan?"

"You being here."

"That was the only plan," she said. "And really, I don't even think they knew if this would work out, John. Sometimes, I get a message to try and be somewhere at a certain time, and I just can't make it work, so I don't go. It happens. Today could have been one of those."

"Except it wasn't. You're here."

"I am."

Siena offered him another brilliant smile, but John only stood there, still as stone, and staring at her in that way of his. A way that put her entirely off balance, and yet grounded her at the same time. She didn't want to move, yet she wanted more than anything to reach out and drag him closer to her.

"I'll have to leave in the morning. Early, likely. I have to be at one of Kev's restaurants tomorrow, so the enforcer will need to see me leaving the house like he always does. I can't risk staying any longer than that."

John nodded. "And where are your brothers that they're not looking for you tonight? I assume that's why you were able to get away today. Or was it just the right circumstance kind of thing?"

Siena laughed, although the sound came out a bit hollow. "It's always when the right circumstances happen, John. I live with Kev, now. Occasionally, they let me go back to my apartment to grab some things, but someone is always with me."

He frowned. "Oh."

"My life revolves around them—it's not new, though. My life was always about what they wanted or needed me to do, and the small illusion of freedom that I had before was just that, and nothing more. An illusion."

John's jaw ticked—a sure sign of his irritation. "Circumstances were right today, then?"

"Something like that. I don't know where my brothers are at the moment. Out of town for a couple of days. That's all they told me when they left last night."

"Out of town," he echoed.

Siena shrugged. "I was at church when I got the chance to sneak away, and so I took it. My newest enforcer hasn't been on the job long, and I don't suspect he'll want to get himself in trouble by telling one of my brothers that I got away from him. I assume he likes being alive, and all that. Kev has killed enforcers for far less—the fear in them is real. Small blessings, you know."

There was a question burning brightly in John's eyes as he looked her over once again. He came a little closer, and then closer still. Until finally, he was close enough for her to reach out and touch him.

So, she did just that.

Her fingers stroked the strong line of his jaw, and then her hand cupped his neck. She felt the way his pulse quickened under her touch, and how his muscles jumped when her fingertips pressed a little harder into his skin. The slight bit of stubble tickled her palm, and she smiled at him when his hand came up to cover hers.

"Tell me," he murmured, "are you working for my family?"

Siena stilled, and John's hand tightened around hers. "And if I was?"

"What are you doing for them, Siena?"

"It's complicated right now."

"Why is that?" he asked.

"Because I'm not really sure what I'm doing at the moment, I only know what my end goal is."

Him.

Nothing else.

Just him.

John cleared his throat. "Are you just feeding them information?"

Siena used her other hand to reach up, and tap a single finger against his lips. "Let's talk about all of this tomorrow, okay. Not tonight. You can order me breakfast, and feed me, and then I will tell you all the things I haven't been able to."

John didn't agree, or disagree.

She took that as a good sign.

"Hey," she whispered.

John came closer again, wrapping his arms around her. "Hey."

"I know you don't like surprises."

"This was a good one. I'll deal with this one."

"But any others in careful moderation, huh?"

John chuckled. "Exactly that, *bella donna*."

"Did you have fun today—Andino got married, right?"

"He did, and it was busy, but good."

"I bet something looked good," she teased, toying with his lapels, and then the peach-colored tie. "Too bad I missed it."

"You didn't miss it, babe. I'm here."

Siena smiled widely as she looked up at him. "You are."

The very second those words left her lips, John closed the small bit of distance left between them. His lips crashed against hers, and took her damn breath away. Their two short meetings over the past few months had been careful, and not at all affectionate in the physical sense. She got the impression that the facility did not approve of that sort of thing.

John was making up for it tenfold in that moment. His tongue struck out against the seam of her lips, and teased her without ever saying a word. She granted him access to her mouth with a grin, and a little sigh. His tongue slipped in to war with hers, while his hands slid up her sides, and then cupped her neck.

He drew her closer.

So much closer.

His body fit against hers perfectly. The world just didn't exist anymore when they were like that. All she could see was dark hazel drinking her in, and that was just fucking fine.

She didn't need anything else.

All too soon, John pulled away. He dropped quick, soft kisses along the seam of her lips, across her cheekbones, over her chin, one to her forehead, and then another to the tip of her nose. Siena's smile only grew more and more until her cheeks hurt.

She hummed a happy, soft sound under her breath.

John kissed her mouth once more.

"I love you," he murmured.

Siena nodded. "I know, John. I love you, too."

His lips skimmed her cheek, and ghosted along the shell of her ear. She heard his words whisper along her skin as she buried her face against his chest.

"Do you hear that?" he asked.

She listened.

All she could hear was his heart beat.

"I hear you," she replied.

John pulled her back a little, tipped her head up, and winked down at her. "No, the music. Can you hear it?"

Siena gave him a look, but indulged his question. She quieted, and listened hard for this music he spoke of. Sure enough, in their stillness and silence, the softest hum carried through the walls and floors.

A slow, lovely beat.

"Someone is waltzing," Siena said.

John smiled charmingly, slid one arm around her waist, and captured her hand with his. "Dance with me?"

Siena laughed. "That's what you want to do right now?"

"Right now, yeah. So, dance with me?"

How could she deny him?

"Lead away, John."

Siena found herself drifting across the large floor of the hotel room. Swaying softy together as John drew her closer, and she pressed her forehead against his. The way his smile deepened made her own grow wider. He kissed her lips, and then her cheek.

She could barely hear the music now.

Not overtop her racing heart.

Siena didn't mind.

"Who taught you how to dance?" she asked.

John laughed a husky sound. "My mother, and then my grandmother, and then my aunt, and finally my other aunt."

Siena's giggles echoed. "What, it took that many for you to get it?"

"No, none of them thought the other one knew what they were doing. My family is both large, and strange sometimes."

"I think they're wonderful."

John blinked, and the two of them stilled in their dance. "Yeah, they kind of are, huh?"

"They love you very much, John."

"I know."

Siena leaned up, and pressed a kiss to John's lips. She intended for it to only be a quick kiss, but he pressed his hand against her lower back with a firm touch, and wouldn't let her go. She didn't mind at all, and soon, their kiss had once again deepened into something far hotter than how it had first started.

"I don't want to dance anymore," she whispered against his lips.

John's smile turned sinful. "Me, either."

His skillful hands made quick work of unzipping her dress from the back. Never once did his lips leave hers, and if they did, it was only long enough to kiss her chin, or down the column of her throat. She loved the way the taste of him lingered on her tongue. A heavy, heady unique-to-him scent and flavor that always left her a little wet between her thighs, and hot on her skin.

Cool air hit Siena's body as John dragged her dress down. His warm palms slid over her curves, and he finally pulled back from their kiss long enough to let his gaze wander over the black lace panty and bra set she wore.

While his attention was on her, she started undoing his jacket, and vest. John let her pull the items off, along with his tie. She was working on the buttons of his dress shirt when, without warning, he dropped to his knees.

He didn't give her much time to think, or react. No, he simply grabbed the waist of the lace panties, and yanked them down her thighs with a hard tug. The material pulled against her skin, making her release a sharp breath.

John's husky chuckles echoed.

Siena looked down.

She only saw the flash of his hazel gaze, and that was it. Suddenly, his face was buried between her thighs, his tongue was assaulting her clit in the best way, and the rest of her thought process was gone.

Just like that.

Poof.

It was like time hadn't separated them. Space hadn't been between them. The seconds, hours, days, and months away no longer mattered. He knew her body, and just how to love it in the right way to get her hot, shaking, and falling over that blissful edge in barely any time at all.

Siena gasped when John's mouth left her sex. She wanted to refuse, and pull him right back, but his quick, dark order came too fast for her to speak.

"Open up more for me," she heard him demand. "Now, babe."

Two sharp taps of his hands to her inner thighs had her legs opening wider. He was back between her body in a flash—his tongue on her clit again, but this time, his fingers joined the effort. Two inside her pussy fucked her hard, and then widening to stretch her open as he drew them back out of her sex.

She could hear how fucking wet she was.

She could smell her own sex.

Her noises echoed.

Sweet, breathless sounds.

"Come on, come on," he growled against her inner thigh. "Give me that honey of yours, Siena."

Jesus.

She came so hard.

It took away her sight for a brief second.

Her breath, too.

It was glorious.

Siena had only blinked, and John was rising from the floor. His hands trailed over the backs of her naked legs, her thighs, and ass. He let her step out of the panties that had bunched into a useless pile at her heels. The second the garment was gone, his hands pressed at her back and ass again, and she found herself lifted from the floor.

The room spun.

John was all she saw.

Siena's back hit the bed, and his hands did that goddamn wandering thing again. Stroking her skin, and memorizing her with touch. Her back arched as his weight came over hers. A substantial weight that left her feeling breathless and oh, so high.

She fumbled with his belt, and the pants until he could pull them down, and kick them off. Soon, his shirt was gone too, and then the white boxer-briefs. He pulled at the hook of her bra connecting the two cups together, and freed it from her body. Nothing was between them but skin, and the hardness of his cock pressing into her thigh.

John's lips were at her throat again. His teeth nipped into her pulse point, and his tongue tasted her skin. His words crawled over her in the best way—soft, yet harsh at the same time. Like the promise of a hard fuck that would leave her sore, but so satisfied, too.

"Get those fucking legs open for me, *donna*," he said.

His voice was a rumble.

Thick and dark.

Siena widened for him, and he fit between her perfectly. Just like he always had. She only felt his hand between her thighs for a brief second, and then the head of his cock was at her slid. Rubbing, smearing her juices, and teasing her.

Begging was easy.

With him, it was too easy.

"Please fuck me," she whispered. "Oh, my God."

She missed him.

Too much.

It couldn't be healthy.

She didn't care.

John's hands found her hips, his fingers dug in hard enough to leave marks behind, and she sucked in a sharp breath. The waiting was a killer—the knowledge that it was coming, but not yet there was enough to drive her crazy.

And then he was.

If that first thrust was heaven, the ones that followed were unaltered sin. A bliss like no other. He stretched her wide, his cock filled her full, and her nerves sang.

He fucked her crazy.

Until her lungs ached from panting so hard, and her lips were numb from his kisses. His teeth left imprints behind, and her skin heated beyond compare.

Siena's fingernails dragged lines over the flexing muscles of John's back with each push and pull of his body into hers. Deeper, and harder he came. Hitting the right spot every single fucking time, and then dragging every inch of his cock against it as he left her once again.

She couldn't get enough.

Not of this man.

Or of them.

It was never going to be enough.

"More," she demanded.

He gave her that, too.

Warm sunlight danced over Siena's naked shoulders, but the sensation was nothing compared to John's kisses dotting down her spine. He kissed all the way down, and then back up again, only stopping at her neck.

"Get up," he murmured against her skin.

"But it's so comfortable."

"It's morning, Siena."

"Quite aware, John."

And if she woke up, she would have to face the day. Or rather, face reality. Which meant leaving the comfort of this bed where she had spent all night relearning and loving a man she had been separated from for far too long.

It would mean leaving him again.

Who knew for how long?

It meant going back home.

Siena didn't want to do any of that at the moment—never, really—so she stayed firmly stuck on her stomach, and refused to even roll over for John when he demanded it. She should have known better, though.

John was not a patient man.

Soon, she found herself flipped over. The soft white sheets tangled in her legs as she laughed breathlessly, and her vision swam. John hovered over her with one of his sinful, signature grins that made her want to get down on her knees for him.

"That was mean," she told him.

John only shrugged. "I told you to get up."

"But I don't *want to.*"

"I ordered food."

He said it as though he were dangling an offer he knew she couldn't refuse. Her stomach just had to go and growl at his declaration, as if it had heard him make the offer, too. She didn't even bother to try and look sheepish when he raised a brow at her.

"Will you feed it to me in bed?" she asked.

John's smile softened. "Whatever you want, babe."

"Remember that."

"But it is time to get up. I didn't forget what you told me last night, and the last thing we need or want is you getting into trouble with your brothers. You have to get back home, right?"

Fuck.

"Why did you have to go and ruin the moment with that nonsense?"

John frowned. "I don't live in delusions, Siena."

"Sometimes, reality is not a fun place to be."

He didn't reply, simply pushed off the bed, and turned his back to her. She felt bad, then—it hadn't been him who ruined their moment at all. It was her, and her shitty morning attitude.

"Sorry," Siena muttered.

John looked over his shoulder, and winked. "No worries. Get up. Let's have a few minutes before you do have to go. I would have let you sleep, but then you would have needed to run as soon as you woke up."

"Ah, so this was more for you than it was for me. I see what you did there."

John only laughed.

As much as she didn't want to move, Siena forced herself out of the bed. She found her discarded clothes from the night before, and carried them into the bathroom. She winked on the way past John. The man had no shame—naked and staring at her like he was.

She made quick work of using the bathroom, washing her face, and pulling her hair back into a simple, messy bun. She was stuck using her finger to brush her teeth with the small tube of toothpaste the hotel provided, but whatever, as it did the trick for now.

Slipping the clothes back on from yesterday, she was grateful nothing had been too wrinkled or ruined in their haste the night before. She smoothed down the front of the dress, and then zipped up the back, too.

Siena wasn't really a high-maintenance woman when it came to her appearance, and that came in handy for the moment. Her half-assed hairstyle worked, and she did just fine without makeup for the most part.

John held out her small clutch as she left the bathroom. "Didn't know if you needed something in it."

"Just my phone."

Which she had turned off the night before.

Siena decided she should probably turn it on, and check if she had missed any calls. The phone came to life under her hand as John went to the door when a knock echoed. She checked her phone over while he directed the man in with the cart of food.

"Well, shit," Siena muttered.

John was at her side, and pressing a soft kiss to her temple once they were alone again. "What, something bad?"

"No, actually."

She showed him the phone.

"No calls from my brothers," she explained.

John cocked a brow. "So?"

"So, the enforcer did what I thought."

"He didn't call them."

Siena nodded, and grinned. "Nope."

"Any calls from the enforcer?"

"A text," Siena replied.

She hadn't even bothered to open it, but she did when John prompted her to. *Where the fuck are you?*

And then another, later that night saying, *I will be outside the brownstone at nine when you should be leaving. You better fucking be there, Siena. I am not getting my ass killed for your stupidity.*

"He doesn't seem happy," John mused.

Siena laughed. "No, I guess not."

She typed out a reply for the enforcer. Nothing to excuse herself, or explain where she went. *I'll see you at nine.*

No reply came.

Siena looked at John. "Lucky me."

He kissed her temple again. "Something like that."

Well, either way …

"This was worth it," she said.

John nodded. "Yeah, but it still makes me fucking edgy, babe."

So was their life, apparently.

At least, for now.

Siena wanted to get her mind, and John's, far away from all of that nonsense. Well, for as long as they possibly could, anyway.

"Let's eat," she said.

John let her go with a grin, and moved toward the cart of waiting food that was still covered on silver platters. "There's a spread, so whatever you want. You made the orders, and I will feed you like I promised."

She preened. "You better."

"*No!*"

"Cella, it's—"

"*No.*"

John's head whipped in the direction of the door, but no one came busting through despite the shouting that suddenly filled the hallway outside. Still, he left their food, and grabbed his clothes hanging off the back of the chair. Pulling on the items, he moved for the door, and opened it up just in time for the yelling to get louder. More voices joined the chorus.

Siena heard pain.

Disbelief. Grief. *Anger.*

"Not my husband—not my *husband!*" Cella screamed. "You're lying, Daddy. Why would you lie to me like that?"

John's gaze cut back to Siena, and then just as fast, he disappeared out into the hall. She should have stayed where she was—after all, a lot of his family didn't actually know that she was even there to begin with. The whole point was for her to stay low, and leave out the back quietly where she wouldn't be seen.

Siena didn't stay in the room. She left instead.

"I'm sorry," Lucian said, the words coming out repeated and sadder with every one. "I'm so sorry, Cella."

The young, dark-haired woman—one of John's sisters—fought with her father in the middle of the hallway. Her fists slammed into his chest when he tried to hug her, and tears stained her face as sobs ripped past her lips. People surrounded them. Confusion echoed as questions were asked.

Still, Siena heard the explanation given to John when he finally found someone who knew what in the hell was happening.

"William had taken the baby to grab some things from their place—I guess they forgot a bag," Jordyn told her son. "Cella was sleeping, and he told Lucian he didn't want to wake her, so he took the baby, too. His car was run off the road, and shot up. We got the call a little while ago."

"Is she—"

"We don't know about the baby," Jordyn interjected.

"And William?" John asked.

"*Why, Daddy?*"

Cella's pain coated the hallway. So thick, and heavy. Like a blanket of agony that no one could escape. Siena didn't think John really needed his question answered, not when all he needed to do was look at his sister, and hear her cries.

"I'm sorry, *bambina*, I'm so sorry."

Lucian finally got his daughter in a bear hug that she couldn't escape. Jordyn must have felt safer to move closer, and so people parted to let her through. Siena heard people murmur about the hospital, and needing to go.

Someone else mentioned waking Andino, and his new wife.

What a morning after that would be.

A beautiful wedding, and a horror in the morning.

"Was it them?" someone asked.

"It was, wasn't it? The Calabrese."

"No one's claimed it—but we suspect, yeah," Giovanni Marcello said, confirming Siena's worst fears to the questioning family.

She realized then that perhaps her brothers did have a motive for leaving the city. Something they had put into motion that she had not known about beforehand. She wondered if William had been personally picked as a hit, or if he had simply been an opportunity given the circumstances.

Those were not answers she had.

Siena wasn't able to think on it for long.

"Why is *she* here?" Cella demanded.

Siena snapped back at the venom in the woman's tone. Cella—younger than Siena, maybe, or possibly the same age—stared at her with growing hatred in tear-filled eyes. She didn't blame the woman, but it still hurt.

She stepped back.

John stepped in front of her. "Cella, she didn't do anything."

"*Why is she here?*"

This time, it was a scream. A stabbing accusation.

"You just had to fucking go and get in bed with that fucking family full of snakes, John," his sister shouted. Despite being pulled down the hallway by her parents, Cella continued on. Her rage spilled out—hurt and confusion following. "You don't *care* what it means, do you? You don't even *know*—"

"Cella, that's enough," Lucian snarled.

Sobbing echoed, and then the girl was gone, along with her parents. A few people followed them, mentioning the hospital again.

Siena was left standing in the middle of the hallway, feeling oh, so fucking cold and unsure. It wasn't like Cella had been wrong, though she directed her words at the wrong person. John had not deserved those statements and accusations.

It was not his choices that did this.

It was not his family who took from her.

"Hey, babe. It's okay."

John was there in front of her before Siena had even blinked. His hand came up and touched her face with the softest stroke, but a line of tears still fell. She didn't bother to wipe them away. He did it for her.

"It's okay," he repeated.

She didn't think it was. Not at all.

"She should have known," someone said. "Isn't she the one fucking feeding the boss information?"

Siena looked at the man who spoke, but she didn't recognize him. "I didn't know."

Giovanni—Andino's father—stepped in front of the man to block him. "Nothing at all, Siena? They didn't say anything? You didn't hear anything about something like this?"

She shook her head. Nothing. She knew nothing. She fucked up.

"I'm sorry," she mumbled. "I'm sorry."

SIX

John was pulled away from Siena by his uncle. Giovanni cut through the people gathered in the hallway with a low curse, and a shake of his head. It wasn't hard to figure out that his uncle was pissed, especially when Gio waved at the men following him to get inside one of the hotel rooms. Once they were all inside, he then slammed the door hard enough that John thought the wood might have cracked.

A couple of more men slipped into the room not long after the door had closed. Once most everyone was there—barring a couple of important people—gazes drifted between one another. It was almost as though they were silently asking who wanted to speak first.

John didn't know what to say.

He didn't have all the details.

Instantly, all the men started talking at once. The Marcello Capos that had been invited to the dinner and party portion of Andino's wedding, and had stayed overnight like the family did, made a catacomb of noise inside the hotel room.

John tried to take everything in.

"Has someone told the boss?"

"Dante is awake, and aware," Gio answered. "He has something else to handle with someone else, and then we will all sit down with the boss and figure something out after we chat here. Not before."

"What about Andino?"

Gio's gaze cut to the man who had asked that question. "Someone has gone to wake him up, as well. I should have been the one to do it, but here I am instead. I don't expect him to be very pleased, all things considered."

"Shitty way to wake up from your wedding night."

Wasn't that the fucking truth?

John figured his cousin was—in some ways—ready for this sort of thing. Andino would have to be, considering he was making big steps to take over their uncle's position as the boss. No man went into that job with rose tinted glasses on. Trouble always came when you least expected it to, and even when you did expect it.

Andino had to be ready for that.

That didn't mean a man wanted to have to deal with this kind of thing on what should be one of the happiest days of their life. Some shit just shouldn't be touched in their life—women, children, and so forth. Only fucking cowards attacked made men and their families during vulnerable times like weddings, births, or even Christenings.

Those days were supposed to be sacred.

Nothing was sacred anymore.

Then, another voice joined the chorus. An older Capo—closer to John's father's age, who flat out refused to concede his position to a younger man. Sometimes, that shit happened, but it didn't always make for good business.

Nathan was the man's name.

"We're supposed to believe that the Calabrese woman being here in the morning after what they did to us today is nothing more than coincidence?" Nathan asked.

Gio's gaze darted from a suddenly stone-still John, to Nathan. "Well—"

"You honestly think she doesn't know what the fuck happened, or that it was going to happen? I heard there was some kind of behind the scenes action with someone inside the Calabrese family, but I didn't realize we were using a fucking *woman* to get it."

John opted to speak up, then. He really didn't need to, and God fucking knew they didn't need more problems at the moment, considering everything. It probably would have been a smarter idea for him to just keep quiet, and let Giovanni handle the questions and explanations for the men.

He couldn't do that, though.

Not when Siena's name was brought into it. Not if it meant letting someone drag her through the mud, or stain her with accusations she wasn't warranted, and could not defend. That kind of shit was not okay, and he would never allow it.

"Do you have a fucking problem with Siena Calabrese?" John asked Nathan.

The older man stood a little straighter in his bathrobe and cotton sleep pants. Nathan was the type that figured his age gave him some kind of edge, or even a heavier respect, than those younger than him in the family. Bullshit. The least he could have done was thrown on a fucking shirt before leaving his room, but here they were.

"Yes, I damn well do," Nathan replied.

"And what is it?"

"Her last name, for starters."

John scoffed. "So she's good to feed you information, but the second someone knows it's her, she's not good enough, huh?"

"I didn't know it was her."

"Fact remains the same, Nathan. If you're going to run off at the mouth about Siena, I suggest you do so where I cannot hear, or where she is ready and capable of defending herself. Otherwise, I'm going to make you apologize to her for acting like a goddamn prick, and I can promise that you will not like the way I fucking do it. Got it?"

"It is a little concerning that she's here," another man put in.

"She was here for me," John snapped over his shoulder. "She didn't leave my room all day yesterday, or last night. She was kept company by several people while she waited for me. And if you have a fucking problem with who I involve myself with, then you can bring that issue to *me*."

"John makes a valid point," Giovanni said, stepping in between the men. "And right now, the important topic is not who is involved with who, but what we need to do next to lock this family down, and protect anyone who needs protection."

"And what, ignore the fact he's sleeping with one of the goddamn snakes?" Nathan asked.

Jesus.

John had done *so well.*

He hadn't let his anger or frustration overwhelm him for a long damn while. His new med regime really helped with the sometimes heavy swings of emotions that he experienced. At the very least, it gave him some time to think shit over before he outright reacted to something. But sometimes, shit just could not be helped. This was one of those times.

Rage swelled through John like a fucking tsunami coming to destroy hallowed ground. Rage was often his favorite emotion as it was the easiest to understand, and to feel. It certainly wasn't the easiest to control, but he wasn't concerned about that at the moment. He had other things to handle.

He swung around, despite seeing the warning flash in his uncle's eyes, and took aim at the idiot who smirked at him. Good.

Wiping that off would be greatly satisfying.

John reared back, and let his fist crash into the face of the Capo. He didn't hold back for a second, and he put every bit of his weight behind the punch. He swore Nathan's nose broke under the impact as the man's bones flattened with a sickening crunch damn near instantly. That sound was quite satisfying, really.

Blood poured.

Someone swore. Someone else moved closer.

"John," he heard his uncle warn.

John didn't need anybody to step in. He knew exactly what he was doing, he was perfectly in control, and he had this shit handled. He had *himself* handled.

John pulled back, stood straight once more, and fixed his fucking jacket. Another time—another day in his life or another person he disliked a little bit more than Nathan—and he might have beat the guy to a bloody pulp because he couldn't fucking control himself, and it would have felt divine.

Today was not that day.

John only needed the one hit to make his fucking point clear. He looked over Nathan as the man covered his broken, bleeding nose with one hand, and nodded when the Capo glanced up at him. Bleeding and holding onto his face, Nathan muttered a garbled apology when John cocked his brow at the man.

He hadn't even needed to ask. The Capo just knew. So was their life.

Pointing a finger at him, John said, "And you fucking remember how this shit went down the next time you put Siena's name in your goddamn mouth, too."

Turning fast on his heel, John looked to his uncle. What had been concern and a warning in Gio's eyes before was now only a slight amusement, and shit, maybe even pride. It was hard to tell with Gio sometimes. His mind was all over the place, and really, he was usually the first man in their family to step out of line when it came to rules and whatever else.

John figured he was good to go. And even if he wasn't, that one punch had been worth it, all things considered.

"We don't assault other made men," Gio said quietly.

"Let him act that way toward your wife, then."

Gio raised a brow. "Siena is not your wife, John. Therein lies the difference, and you're quite aware of that."

Yet. She was not his wife yet.

John didn't say that out loud, only shrugged. "I said what I said."

"Can we finish our discussion, now?"

"Sure," John murmured, "but somebody might want to get Nathan a towel. He's ruining the rug, and that's a damn shame."

"They said nothing to you?" Dante asked. "Nothing at all?"

John's defensiveness edged a little higher at the sound of his uncle questioning Siena. It wasn't that Dante Marcello was a bad man—he wasn't. In fact, the current patriarch of their family was known to be incredibly kind and giving to those he allowed beyond his hard outer shell.

To someone on the outside of their family, however, Dante was also known to hold nothing back. He could be cold, and extremely callous. He had no qualms with removing what he perceived to be threats against his family and organization.

Maybe it was the way Dante had treated Siena months ago that left a bad taste in John's mouth now. He was not willing to allow anyone to treat her with anything less than absolute respect, including his uncle.

John leaned in the doorway that separated the main living quarters of his hotel room with the small kitchen section. Dante and Siena sat at the small two-person table. His uncle drank a coffee. Siena picked at food on her plate.

Dante's gaze caught John's, but he chose not to move. He simply wanted his uncle to know that he was there, and *listening*. That was the most important thing

"Nothing," Siena said. "They left last night, like I said. Darren came over, and Kev had a bag packed. They said they might be gone a couple of days. I hadn't heard anything before that to suspect something."

"You didn't think you had any reason to tell us they left?"

"No."

Dante sighed, and leaned back in his chair. "And you've gotten no calls from them since you've been here?"

"No," she repeated.

"If this happens again—where they up and go without explanation—I will need you to let someone know however you can. I know it's a little ..."

"Dangerous, yeah," Siena filled in.

Dante nodded. "I know, but it's important."

John took a single step into the room, drawing their attention his way. Siena tried to smile, but he could plainly see it did not reach her eyes like it usually would. He didn't like that at all, and he didn't like some of the shit he was hearing.

"Someone needs to explain to me what in the hell is going on with her," John said.

Dante cleared his throat, and his gaze drifted between Siena, and John before he finally spoke again. "You know I'm not required to give you any sort of—"

"You will tell me, or someone else will. Clearly, she's feeding information to the Marcellos. I got that fucking much at least. But I thought it was just Andino, or maybe even my father after he was the one who let me know she was here last night. But now you're mixed up in this scheme, too? What switch got flipped when

I was away, huh? What changed your mind?"

Dante chuckled dryly. "There was no *switch*, John. I have always done whatever I needed to do for this family and organization. That's never changed in all my years."

Fair enough. John still felt uneasy about a lot of things.

"I still need some answers," John said.

Dante's gaze fell on something—or someone—behind John. The man nodded, and then stood from the table. He looked to Siena at the same time Andino slipped in beside John. His cousin had gotten rid of the tux he wore the night before, and replaced it with dark wash jeans, and a white T-shirt.

Andino didn't particularly look pleased to be there, but John couldn't exactly blame him for that, either. The man should have been spending his morning with his new bride. Like any man would want to do.

"Siena, why don't I introduce you to my wife," Dante said. "You've met Catrina before, but I think you'll appreciate her a little more with a personal conversation."

John didn't want Siena going anywhere. "She can stay—"

"We should talk," Andino interjected. "Just you and I, John. Let her go with Dante."

Andino's statement offered no room for argument, and also, hinted at something he didn't fully explain, either. John thought back to the day before, and how a simple gesture of Dante walking Haven down the aisle for Andino would have been seen as a big deal.

"It could help her case a lot," Andino added quieter, "just to be seen with the boss. Having others trust her is of the utmost importance right now, man."

John nodded. "All right."

He didn't let Siena by without pulling her in close enough for a quick kiss to her temple, though. Her smile grew the longer he held her there, and she gave him a nod before disappearing out of the small kitchen behind Dante.

"Talk," John demanded once he was alone with his cousin. "And give me something worth chewing on while you're at it."

Andino folded his arms over his chest. "You know, I could be fucking my wife—"

"You'll get back to that. Talk."

"On your one question—Siena has been feeding us info for months now. Shortly after you went in, actually, I had the chance to give her some direction. She took my advice, and I used it to my advantage."

"How so?"

"She goes to yoga a couple of times a week. I either meet her inside, or she slips outside and fills me in on things."

"You said us, but that sounds like just you."

"Your father was involved behind the scenes, but he stepped in. My dad, too."

"And Dante?"

"Came in later," Andino said, smirking. "You know, when I didn't give him a fucking choice. It's like this—Dante wants me to take over this family, and I am going to do that. But I will do so on my terms, and how I want to do it. He didn't want a war with the Calabrese, and I am never going to bow down to those fuckers for anything. Not after what they did to us decades ago, and not after what they did to you. I wouldn't betray you like that either, frankly."

Andino shrugged, adding, "I'm going to remove them from this city altogether. Her information, when she has some to give, helps a great deal."

John cleared his throat. "So what, you take over their organization, too?"

"That's not important right now."

"I think it is. You're putting Siena in a lot of fucking danger, Andino."

"No, John, she is."

John straightened on the spot. "I beg your fucking pardon?"

Andino shook his head. "She is the one putting herself in danger. I neither need her for information now, nor to end this when the time is right. She's helped me more than enough, and got me what I needed the most—for a real war to be started in this city. For a reason to get rid of them once and for all."

"You used her to start a fucking war?"

His cousin laughed in that dark, dry way again. "John, you helped, too, but she's the one who pushed them over the edge with me. And now, she is also the one who has chosen to continue on when she knows she could step back now. She is doing this because she has something to gain, too. *You*, man. Or did you forget about that?"

"Andi—"

"She's doing this for you, John. No one is ever going to manipulate you again. No one is ever going to get to you after this. She won't let them."

"I still don't fucking appreciate you using Siena as a means to further yourself in this city, Andino."

His cousin stared hard at him for a long while before Andino dropped his arms to his sides, and pushed away from the kitchen doorway. He shook his head, and gave a little sigh.

"You know what, John, you don't get it. That's fine. There will be a hell of a lot of days ahead of us yet for me to get this through your thick skull. Today, though? Today I have other shit to handle—a new wife, and a dead cousin-in-law. A war to finish, and *win*. Either get with the fucking program, or shove off."

Andino didn't give John the chance to reply before he left the room. John heard the hotel room's door slam shut a couple of seconds later.

So, that's how it was going to be?

John wished he could be surprised, but he really wasn't.

Instead of following after Andino to demand more answers, or tear his cousin a new one, John opted to take a seat at the small table, and fucking relax. The entire morning had been too much—from one damn thing to another.

He hadn't got the chance to breathe. He needed to think.

Too much stimulation was not a good thing for John, and he recognized that for what it meant when it came to himself. He did not need to be adding more shit to his already overactive emotional state and mind.

John was so lost in his own thoughts that he didn't hear the hotel room open and close. He didn't even realize he was no longer alone until Siena's arms wrapped around him from behind. She hugged him tight—so fucking tight.

He needed that. He needed her.

Siena's lips pressed to the top of his head, she hugged his neck even tighter, and then she kissed his temple, too. A sweet, yet lingering kiss.

And all was right again.

"I have to go," she told him.

John nodded. He knew that, too. Didn't like it, though.

"Yeah, I know, babe."

"We'll figure something out," Siena whispered against his skin. "Us, and the rest of this stuff. We will figure it out, John."

He didn't know when he was going to see her again, or how long that would be. He didn't know *how* he was going to see her again, considering how controlled her life seemed to be under her brothers' demands, now. It was a mess.

John didn't say any of that out loud, though.

Not while she was there. Not while she hugged him.

Everything—for a moment, anyway—was perfect.

"John?"

"In the kitchen, Ma."

John popped open the blister packaging for his pills. Leonard opted to have John's prescriptions filled as a daily intake, and not a whole bottle that left John managing his meds for months.

Jordyn slipped into the kitchen, and offered her son a smile. It didn't reach her eyes, but he wasn't surprised.

Too much shit had happened over the last day.

"Come to fill me in?" John asked. "On Cella, and whatever?"

That's the only reason his mother would be there. Their family had been taking care of shit, and dealing with the mess the Calabrese attack left behind. John had taken the day after the wedding to settle back into his rented Queens home. He reminded himself to thank his father for keeping up the rent, and having someone come in to clean the place. He tossed his pills back with water.

"Yeah, I'm here to fill you in. Your father was going to come, but Gio showed up, and Tiffany needs someone to look after her."

"Cella can't look after the baby, or what?"

"Not in her state."

"How is she?"

Jordyn cleared her throat before taking a seat at the table. "Heavily medicated tonight."

John winced. "That bad, then."

"That bad," his mother echoed. "You know, when I first married your father, I thought we would have some day in our lives to enjoy … well, life. Things would slow down, and we would not be so on the go, so to speak. Not everything would be bullets, blood, and *famiglia*."

He gave his mother a look. "Bit naive of you, don't you think?"

Jordyn shrugged one shoulder. "I did not say that I don't absolutely love our life because I do, John. I simply meant I hoped there would be a time when for once, Lucian and I could focus on being a family, and not *the* family."

"Made man for life, Ma."

"So it seems."

"Tiffany is good, then?" he asked.

Jordyn nodded, and smiled a bit as John came to sit beside her at the table. "Yeah, she's good. A couple of scratches from the glass, but nothing too bad. Nothing that can't heal."

"Unlike her father."

His mother frowned. "Yes, unlike William."

"If you need any help with the baby, or Cella, just let me—"

"Actually, that's one thing I needed to chat with you about."

John leaned back in the chair, and stared at his mother, waiting. "Go on."

"Cella is … still very angry, John. She needs someone—something—to blame right now, and she's shooting for the easiest targets she can find."

"Me, you mean."

Jordyn blew out a shaky breath. "She doesn't mean the things she says, and she's so confused with how she feels."

"Of course." John shrugged. "Her husband is dead—a violent death. She's left with a young baby to take care of alone. Hell, she married a man unaffiliated to the mob, and even that wasn't enough to keep her from being punished for this life. I get it, Ma, really. I'll keep my distance, and let her grieve. I don't need to be showing up and making her uncomfortable or anything. Don't worry about it."

"You don't have—"

"It's *fine*," he said firmly. "Really."

Jordyn smiled, and nodded once. Reaching over, she patted the top of John's hand with her own. "Someday, your sisters will see the man you are now, is not the boy you used to be, John. It's been hard for them to separate their emotions from all the things that happened while they were growing up. Give them time, okay?"

John shook his head. "I don't think they'll ever be one hundred percent good with me, Ma. And that's okay—I get that, too. I wasn't good to them, and you can't shake that kind of shit off. It's a long history to work through, and they might never work through it. I don't expect anything from my sisters."

"I do, though," his mom said.

John smiled, leaned over, and cupped his mother's cheek. She smiled at the affectionate touch, and he felt guilty that he had not asked for his mother to visit him more during his time away. She loved him so much—she always had.

"I know you do, Ma, but don't push them to do something that they can't. I understand, and that's what's most important."

Jordyn sniffed, and patted her hand over top John's gently. "I'm happy you're home again."

"Me, too."

"I'm proud of you, John."

"You're always proud of me, Ma."

Jordyn laughed. "You still need reminders."

He did. He loved her for that, too.

SEVEN

"Kev and Darren aren't going to be following us around all day?" Greta asked.

Siena gave the older of her two half-sisters an amused look. "You know, it would benefit you greatly to tone down the attitude when you use one of their names. Not because you *have* to like them, but because a little respect will go a long way with those two."

Greta cocked a brow. "But I don't respect them."

"Yeah, I got that. Me, either."

"I don't get your point, then."

Siena grabbed her bag from inside the hall closet, and skipped over a light cardigan or jacket. It was still boiling hot, even at the end of July. She didn't need to be adding extra layers at the moment.

Turning to face the seventeen-year-old, Siena said, "But you like having a little bit of freedom, don't you?"

"You call being taken from my school, and shoved into a private school freedom? Or losing my mom, and being forced to live with my aunt freedom? How about the fact I can't even go to the movies with friends because one of them is a *guy*? That's not freedom, Siena."

No, it wasn't. Not *normal* freedom, anyway.

That was part of the whole problem neither of her two half-sisters realized. Nothing about their life was normal, and it was a damn shame, really. They had grown up almost entirely removed from the life Siena had lived as a *principessa della mafia*.

Maybe that had been because their mother demanded it from Matteo—that he already had one legitimate family to use to further his mafia agenda. Or, it could have been because her dead father didn't believe his illegitimate daughters would do anything for him in the grand scheme of things.

Siena really didn't know. Frankly, none of that mattered, either.

Not now.

"Matteo is dead," Siena said.

Greta flinched. "I *know*."

It was strange to Siena in a way to see someone—other than her mother and brothers—grieve over her father's death. It seemed, somehow, that her half-sisters had a different opinion from hers on the man who helped to give them life.

They loved Matteo. They talked fondly about him.

Siena couldn't say the same.

"And your mom, too," Siena added. "She's also dead."

"Do you think I don't know all of this?"

Greta's angry tone was matched only by the red flush covering her cheeks. Siena had hit a nerve, but that was exactly her point.

Someone had not properly sat these girls down, and explained what their life was going to be like from here on out if they didn't hurry up, and *do something*. What that something was, however, depended on the girl.

"Exactly," Siena murmured, staring her half-sister in the eyes, and refusing to look away. "They are dead, and so everything that they promised you for your life will no longer happen. You want to go to college, Greta? Will it further the family—will it further Kev or Darren somehow?"

"Well—"

"Or better yet, will college or something else make you a better house wife when they find a man to marry you to like they tried to do with Ginevra?"

Greta's mouth slammed shut.

Siena nodded. "Yeah, you get it, huh?"

"Will they really do that to us?" Giulia asked from behind Siena.

It was the first time the girl had spoken since the two had been dropped off for their day with Siena. Something was keeping the two very quiet, and sometimes, she could drag out of them what that something was. Today had not really been one of those days. The girls didn't seem interested in talking—unless Greta's attitude could be considered talking.

Siena turned to face the fifteen-year-old. "If it furthers their agenda, and they think they can get away with it, then do not put it past them."

"I don't see how respecting them will—"

"Because, Greta," Siena interjected, tossing a look over her shoulder, "if you think the more you irritate them will make them want to keep you around, or give you anything that you want, you are sorely mistaken. And until they're gone, your best bet, is to give them what they want."

"Until they're gone, huh?"

Siena cleared her throat. *Shit*. That had been a slip of the tongue.

"Pretend you didn't hear that," Siena said. "Now, are we going out, or not? I thought you two wanted to go swimming at Jacob Riis Beach, and then grab some gelato?"

Greta didn't move, and instead, put her hands on her hips. Siena had never met the girl's mother, but goddamn, when she did that, Greta looked just like Matteo. Tall, formidable, and un-fucking-moveable. Even the look in her eye was the very same. Like she was daring Siena to come closer, and try to move her.

Good luck Kev and Darren when you go toe-to-toe with this one, she thought. Her brothers deserved the trouble, anyway.

"You were the only one with Ginevra on the day she was supposed to get married," Greta said.

"So?" Siena asked.

"Kev and Darren were *very* mad at you."

"Listen, they're always very mad at me, okay? Depending on the day, they don't even look at me. There's a reason they call me the stain on this family."

Greta's gaze narrowed. "They only really started that after Ginevra went missing. They say she's dead. Is she?"

Siena cleared her throat again. Dammit.

It felt like a giant knot was forming there, and she couldn't get it out. The uncomfortable sensation only grew the longer she tried to come up with an acceptable response for Greta. Nothing was ever simple, or easy.

This answer couldn't be, either.

"A lot of things happened on Ginevra's wedding day," Siena tried to say. "And a lot of things happened after. You have to consider—"

272

"Is she alive, or not?"

"I can't tell you that," Siena said.

"Why not?"

Greta might as well have stomped her foot, too.

"Because it wouldn't be safe for me to," Siena explained.

"I won't tell, and neither will—"

"It's not you or Giulia that I am worried about. It's Ginevra. Do you know what would happen if she suddenly wasn't missing anymore?" Siena asked.

Greta blinked. "No. What?"

"Let's just say you should be grateful that Kev and Darren's anger and hate is focused on me now. Being called the shame of this family is moderate and pleasant compared to what they would do if your older sister suddenly showed back up. So, she won't. Not today, anyway."

"Someday, maybe?" Greta whispered.

"Maybe."

Giulia frowned as she pushed past Siena, and her sister. "Okay, can we go now?"

"Yeah," Siena said, never taking her gaze off Greta, "we can go."

Outside at the bottom of the steps, was the enforcer who Siena had skipped out on the week before when she went to see John. The man still wasn't very pleased with her, but as far as she could tell, he had not yet run to her brothers about what she did.

Actually, Kev and Darren still hadn't come home from wherever they went.

Like cowards, they were hiding out. Likely hoping that the Marcellos would have gotten all of their violence and retribution for Cella's husband's death out of their system, or something like that.

Problem was, this couldn't end so easily. It was going to continue. It would grow. So was the way of war.

"Where to?" the enforcer asked, moving to open the back door of his black town car.

Siena gave the man a look. "I will be driving *my* car, thank you."

She didn't get to use her Lexus very often, anymore.

"Your brothers prefer—"

"I am taking my car," Siena said. "And when Kev and Darren get home, I will go back to riding with you. Okay?"

The enforcer's jaw tightened before he muttered, "Your ass, I guess."

The most her brothers would do was yell. Siena cared little about that. Yelling she could handle, and besides, their focus was elsewhere at the moment.

Plus, they weren't even home.

"Could we get gelato first?" Giulia asked as she slid into the backseat. "Before the beach?"

Siena nodded. "Actually, that sounds great."

Greta glared at the enforcer before she slipped into the car, too. Siena smirked to herself, and closed the door to the Lexus, shutting the girls in.

Poor kid. Greta just couldn't help herself. She was a lot like Siena in that way. Hopefully, it never came back to bite her.

It wasn't long before Siena had navigated the streets of Brooklyn, grabbed them all some gelato, and headed for Jacob Riis Beach. The three sisters sat in the parking lot of the beach with the doors of the Lexus thrown wide open while warm wind blew through the vehicle.

Silent, mostly. They people watched. Kids squealing, and parents chasing. Water flying, and music blasting. It was both nice, and sad.

For a moment, they could pretend to be normal people, doing normal things. And yet, they were far removed from all of that.

This was just another illusion. One soon to be shattered.

"Are you jealous that we got a good dad?" Giulia asked suddenly.

Siena looked back at the younger of the two sisters. "You mean, about Matteo?"

Beside her in the passenger seat, Greta stuck a spoonful of gelato in her mouth. The older girl looked both interested and kind of worried what Siena's response might be.

Giuia shrugged. "Yeah, I mean, I see what your face does when we say something nice about Daddy, and stuff."

Siena didn't realize her face *did something* at all.

She wasn't surprised, though.

"No," she said after a moment, "I'm not jealous. Happy, if anything."

"Happy seems strange," Greta muttered around her spoon.

"I can't be happy that he was a good father to you two? That you have fond memories of him, and loved him?" Siena smiled faintly, and peered back out the windshield at the playing children, and relaxing people. "I am happy that you will have good memories of him to carry you through life. I can't say that I have the same—I wouldn't wish my memories of him on you two at all."

"Oh."

Giulia's quiet response was only echoed by silence. Really, Siena no longer had anything to say about it. Not Matteo, or her life as his daughter. She meant what she had said about her half-sisters lives with him, though.

Out of the corner of her eye, Siena saw the enforcer approaching the car.

"What?" she asked him. "Jesus, we only got here a few minutes ago."

"We have to go," the guy said, offering no room for argument, "right now."

"But—"

"Now, Siena. Your brothers' homes are burning to the fucking ground. We don't have time to argue. Leave the Lexus here—someone will come get it later. I've been ordered to deliver the girls to their aunt, and take you to your mother's place."

Siena straightened in the driver's seat. She heard everything that the enforcer said, but only one thing really stood out the most. "*Both* of their homes?"

"Guess so."

"Burning?"

"Looks like it," the man uttered.

Well, fuck. Where was she supposed to live, then? Oh, was Siena supposed to care that the Marcellos finally attacked back at her brothers after what they did to them? Because she didn't.

Siena stood on the side of the street, and watched as workers began the process of cleaning away the mess left behind from the fire at Kev's brownstone. Two days after the blaze, and the smoldering and smoking bits had finally been completely extinguished.

The heat hadn't helped.

Neither had the lack of rain.

Large dumpsters had been brought in to contain the rubble and ashes covering the space between two other brownstones. It would take them a couple weeks to clean up, or so they said, and then once the investigation was finished on the fire, Kev could rebuild if he wanted.

Siena didn't know if that was her brother's plan, or not.

At least the fire department had been able to save the homes connected to Kev's. They contained the blaze enough that very little damage had been done to the main walls connecting the other brownstones, and the supports needed to rebuild.

The firefighters had made it their main focus to save the other buildings once they realized the fire was containable to the one brownstone.

Kev's place, however, was gone entirely.

Nothing but a pile left behind.

The workers placed a large tarp along the bit of charred grass, and then began dressing in their safety gear. Apparently, they would place anything they found in the rubble on the tarp for Kev to look over. Anything that might have made it through the blaze.

By the looks of it, nothing did.

All of it was gone.

A few feet away, Kev and Darren hissed between one another. As usual, their conversation was not quiet enough to keep their words just between them. They still didn't know the meaning of fucking privacy.

Not that she was surprised.

"Look at it," Kev snarled.

"Well, there's not really much to look at, Kev," Darren replied.

"Oh, you got fucking jokes today, huh?"

Darren sighed. "My place is gone, too, man. What do you want me to say? We put a hit out on one of their people, it went through, and then what? You expected them to sit back, and do fuck all about it?"

"Well, no—"

"This is what they did," Darren interjected, his voice a rough murmur. "Now, we answer back, or figure something else out."

"Something else, huh?"

"What do you want to do, Kev? Focus on a place that means nothing to you? What did you have in there other than some documents, guns, and clothes? It's not like you had anything you gave a shit about in there. Rebuild, or go buy somewhere else."

"That's not the point!"

"Well, if you want to get into semantics about all of this, and whose fault it really is that our places got burned down, let's start with you, brother."

Kev glared. "Me?"

"Yeah, you."

"Why the fuck *me?*"

"You were the one who said it would be best if we dropped low for a while after the whole hit thing, you know what I mean? Maybe if we hadn't ducked out for a week, this wouldn't have happened. We would have been more present here, and whatever else. Kind of hard to burn a place down when you've got someone going in and out of it all the time, or somebody watching it. I mean, you didn't really do that, and neither did I."

"There was somebody here—*Siena.*"

Two gazes drifted in Siena's direction. She quickly looked away as if to make her brothers think she was not paying any mind to their conversation at all.

She still needed to feed Andino and the rest of the Marcellos whatever information she could, after all. Kev and Darren were constantly predictable in the way they never looked at her—they never even considered she was smart enough, or had enough guts to be the one fucking them over.

Their mistake.

Her gain.

Darren stared hard at the empty space where Kev's brownstone had once stood tall and proud. A sharp red brick against the brown bricks of the other homes on the block. It was more than just things lost, sure, but Siena wondered if that was only part of her brother's problem.

Maybe Kev was starting to realize he had bitten off far more than he could chew where the Marcellos were concerned. Or hell, maybe not.

"Maybe we've gone about this the wrong way with them," Darren said.

"Who?"

"The Marcellos—who the fuck else?"

Kev scrubbed a hand down his jaw. "I'm listening."

"I mean, their control over this city has always been the fact they have connections, and so much territory. Not to mention, *men.* The largest Cosa Nostra family in North America, right?"

"What's your fucking point?"

Ouch.

Even she could hear the jealous tone in Kev's voice.

"Don't get pissy at me," Darren said. "I'm just saying. Anyway, we've got at them from the front, so to speak. We've attacked them, and caused violence on their streets. Brought attention to them, and whatever else. Figured it might make them take a step back, or reconsider their usual way of handling these kinds of issues."

"And it did none of that," Kev muttered.

"Nope."

"So, what is your grand fucking plan now?"

"Well, that wasn't *my* plan to begin with. It was yours—it didn't work really well for us."

"Keep taking those shots at me, man."

Darren rolled his eyes. "I mean, let's go at them from a different direction. From behind, in a way. Make it hard for them to do business. Rough up the streets where their Capos have control. Step in between their contacts keeping things under control."

For a long while, silence stretched on between the two brothers.

Then, Kev spoke. "I like it."

"Thought you would."

"You know, I got word someone saw Johnathan Marcello around here shortly before the fire started," Kev said.

Darren cleared his throat. Out of the corner of Siena's eye, she saw Darren look in her direction before going back to the conversation at hand.

"That so?" he asked.

"Apparently."

"Anything else?"

"So far, the investigator agrees an accelerant was used, and they've called it an arson."

"Just like my place," Darren muttered.

"But hey, we know who probably did it," Kev said.

"Yeah, I guess so."

"We'll get him."

"Among many," Darren agreed. "For now, though, where do we *live?*"

Kev laughed dryly. "Well, Ma wants me over there. You, too."

"For a while, that's fine. But you know how it is."

"That won't work with Siena, though," Kev put in. "She's the one handling Greta and Giulia, you know what I mean?"

"Ma won't have Dad's bastards going in and out of her house all the time. She puts on a good show, sure, but—"

"She'll only take so much."

"You could just say fuck the girls for now," Darren offered. "Focus on everything else."

"I need them compliant, just in case."

"Sure, sure."

"Siena's enforcer said she did well while we were gone—never acted out of line."

Siena smiled at that—faintly so it couldn't be seen. All the while, she never looked away from the men cleaning up the mess that was once her brother's home.

Good things were coming her way.

She could tell.

"She's still got her apartment, too," Kev added quietly. "A couple of months there with an enforcer looking after her won't be a big deal. I even got the guy to check on the building—there's an apartment available two doors down from hers."

"You're going to send her back to her place?" Darren asked, incredulity coloring his tone. "After everything she did with Johnathan, and even after Ginevra?"

"We don't know that she helped Ginevra—"

"Suspecting is more than enough in this case, Kev! You're fucking crazy to let her out of your sight, and you know it."

"I have to," Kev grumbled, "for now, anyway."

Siena smiled wider.

That time, she hid it by looking up at the bright sky.

Good things *had* come for her.

Siena's fingers ached from typing all day, and her neck and shoulders felt like rocks from sitting in an uncomfortable computer chair for hours upon hours. The last thing she wanted to do was climb stairs, but freedom was just a few steps away.

Her apartment, that was.

She had been back at her old place for a couple of days. Nothing was better than closing the front door to her apartment, and knowing that her brothers wouldn't be hanging around a corner or something.

Sure, it left her out of the loop.

She didn't have information to pass on.

You win some, you lose some.

Siena still kind of considered this winning. At least for her.

She ignored the ache in her feet as she climbed the stairwell, and opened the hallway door leading down the row of apartments on her floor. Behind her, the enforcer still tasked with looking after her followed close behind.

He didn't speak.

He rarely did.

At her door, Siena pulled out her key, and stuck it in the lock. Like always, the enforcer opted to wait behind her until she had opened up the door, and slipped inside the apartment. She caught sight of his nod before he headed further down the hall.

The guy had gotten that extra apartment, after all.

Siena never left her place without the enforcer waiting outside her door. He drove her to and from work, and to wherever else she needed to go.

Now, with her brothers back, the guy didn't let her have an inch. Likely because he knew Siena would turn around and take a mile back from him.

Smart.

Siena locked the front door behind her, kicked off her heels, and reveled in the cold floors pressing against her aching soles. She dropped her bag in the corner, and picked up the contemporary romance paperback she had left sitting on the stand on her way out that morning

Thumbing through the pages of the book, she went back to the spot she had left her bookmark. The heroine was getting ready for a date with a guy she despised, but felt she had no other choice given her circumstances.

Siena was so focused on her book, that she damn near rammed head-first into the tall form standing in the middle of her living room.

She knew it was him before she looked up.

Before he even spoke, she *knew.*

"John," Siena whispered.

Her eyes found his, and John smiled sinfully.

"I see you're distracted again," he said.

Familiarity comforted her. Love wrapped around her.

Hope held her.

Still, Siena's gaze darted over her shoulder to the door. "How in the hell did you get in here?"

John shrugged. "Used the back door when someone was coming in, and picked your lock. I'm buying you a new one, by the way. No one else has a key, right?"

"The enforcer who watches after me."

His gaze narrowed. "Yeah, I saw that prick, too. Is he fucking decent to you?"

"He's okay."

She wasn't lying.

John nodded. "Can you change out his key?"

"Probably. Sometimes he's leaves them sitting in the cup holder when he runs into a place."

"Good enough for me."

Siena shook her head. "What are you doing here, John?"

His grin deepened. "Do you not want me here, babe?"

How could he possibly think that?

"Of course, I do, but it's danger—"

John interrupted her protests by grabbing her wrist, and yanking her in to him. Her book fell to the floor the second his lips crashed against hers. The kiss was enough to quiet her worries, make her wet between her thighs, and remind her of all the reasons why she loved this dark-in-his-soul man.

"They saw you," she whispered against his lips.

John hummed a low note. "Saw me, what?"

"Around Kev's place the day it was burned down."

He stiffened.

Siena shrugged. "Was it you?"

"Yes—someone else, too. But they were there to keep a look out."

"Because of what they did to Cella's husband?"

John shook his head, and kissed her lips again. "Nope—maybe partly. But mostly, no."

"Then, why?"

"Did you think I was just going to wait until I could see you from afar by chance again?" John laughed darkly, and kissed the tip of her nose. His affection was a bright contrast to how cold his voice and words were when he spoke. "No fucking way, *bella.* I am all in on this. Us, I mean. I tip hands to *my* favor, not the other way around. I needed a way to get you out from under their thumbs a little bit—now you are. See what I did there?"

Siena blinked. John grinned.

Well, damn.

EIGHT

"I have a surprise for you," John said.

Siena blinked up at him, happy and sweet in the next breath. "For what?"

"It's not much."

"I don't care. It's from you. Anything from you is wonderful, John."

He had no doubt she was telling the truth. He could see it in her eyes, and feel it in the way her fingers curved around his wrists to hold on tight.

John had come to figure out that Siena was somewhat of a cornerstone in his life—long term, and short term. He had regaled himself to the belief that everything he did for them now was so that they *could* have a future. He also got through the darker moments in his days by thinking about her.

She got him to the next breath. A thought about her smile made him wake up in the morning. Memories of them got him looking forward to the next week.

So, yeah.

Long term.

And short term.

Siena was all of it for John.

"It's in the kitchen," he told her.

Siena pressed her palm into John's, and wrapped their fingers tightly together. With a soft laugh, she pulled him along to the kitchen. She came to a sudden, full stop when the item on the island counter caught her eye.

"You didn't—"

"Thought I forgot, did you?" he interrupted her.

Grinning, John pressed a kiss to Siena's temple.

"Never, babe," he added.

Siena let out a little sigh, and her gaze drifted from him, to the item on the counter. A single cupcake, decorated in white frosting, and sprinkled with edible sparkles. The one candle inserted into the top flickered with a flame—he had lit it when he heard the lock jiggle in the door.

"Did anyone tell you yet today?" he asked.

Siena shook her head, and wetness gathered along her bottom lashes. "No, but I suppose it's not very important in the grand scheme of things."

Jesus.

Why would she ever think that?

Or *feel* that way?

"Siena, everything about you is *most* important—especially to me, *dolcezza.* Every part of you will always be important to me. You know that, don't you?"

Her hand came up to cup his cheek, and her thumb stoked his skin with a soft touch. It was enough to chase away the chaos that had been John's mind lately. So much had been piling up, and he took just a few minutes away from it all today, so he could be with Siena.

She took the rest away, too.

God, he loved this woman.

"Thank you," she said.

John slid a hand around the back of Siena's neck, and pulled her in for another quick, hard kiss. Her grin formed against his mouth, and he whispered, "Happy birthday, my sweet *donna*. Do you want me to sing it for you, too? I will."

Her fingertips patted his cheek. "I believe you, but you don't have to."

"Blow out your candle, then. Before wax gets all over your cupcake."

Siena laughed, and John let go of her. She reached for the cupcake, and pulled it from the counter. Holding it in front of her, she eyed him over the flickering flame. He could see the question burning brightly in her blue eyes.

"What, love?"

"So, I guess we're just going to act like yours doesn't matter, then."

John cocked a brow. "My what?"

"Birthday. A couple of days ago, right? Thirty-one."

"It's another day, and I spent half of it sitting on a sofa talking to a therapist."

"I bet your mom made you cake, though."

John flashed a smile. "She did, too."

Siena frowned.

He couldn't have that.

Stepping closer, he slid a hand along the curve of her waist, and pulled her a little bit closer to him. She kept the flickering candle at a safe distance as to not burn either of them while she looked up at him.

"What is it?"

"Sorry I missed your birthday," she said.

John kissed the tip of her nose. "It's fine—next year."

"Will we have a next year?"

"I'll make sure of it."

Siena's little smile came back. "Will you help me blow out the candle?"

She offered the cupcake between them with a little shake that made the flame flicker dangerously. Like an offer he couldn't refuse, not that he would refuse her anything.

"Anything you want, babe," John said. "Do we make a wish, too?"

"Is that too juvenile for you?"

"Not if you want it."

"A wish, then." Siena held the cupcake higher. "On three."

"One, two …"

"Three," she said.

The two of them blew out the candle together, and John made his wish. He didn't say it out loud, and he didn't even *think* it, really. Looking at Siena, he figured his wish was kind of obvious, anyway.

All he ever wanted now was her.

"This was great," Siena said as she pulled the paper from the bottom of the cupcake. Setting it and the candle aside, she pulled a chunk out of the cupcake, and offered it to John. He took the bite with a wink. "Thank you, really."

She swept a dollop of the frosting onto her finger, and sucked it between her lips.

Jesus Christ.

That one action was enough to kill him.

John tried to keep the huskiness out of his tone when he said, "Don't even mention it. This was so little compared to what I would have done in different circumstances."

"This was *perfect*."

She sucked another dollop of icing off her finger.

"Siena."

"Hmm?"

She looked up at him.

Innocent and blue-eyed in a blink.

Goddamn her.

"You need to stop sucking on your finger like that, *donna*."

"But it's good frosting."

She swept her finger through the top of the cupcake again, and offered it to John. Not even thinking about it, he took her finger into his mouth, and let his tongue do the work of cleaning off the digit. He felt the shiver race through Siena as her gaze met his.

"Yeah, okay," she said. "I get it."

"Good," John murmured when he released her finger.

And then she did it *again*!

Siena pulled her finger from between her pink, wet lips with a grin. She knew exactly what she had done, and John's control was all but gone. He snatched that cupcake from her hand, and ignored her shriek of disappointment.

She wouldn't be disappointed for long, after all.

John swiped his own finger through what was left of the frosting at the same time he pulled Siena up onto the island counter. Her legs opened for him, and let him fit in between. A perfect fit, really.

It never failed to amaze him.

His gaze was stuck on her pretty little pout, and how sexy her lips looked in that moment. All pink, and wet from her tongue sweeping along the seam.

"You know, the only time your lips look better than they do right now is when they're wrapped around my cock," he told her.

Siena sucked in a sharp breath, and her gaze darted up to his. "Is that so?"

"Very much so, yeah."

"Maybe we can do that later."

"I think you could clean me off once I'm done with you."

Her smile turned sexy.

So fucking sexy.

God.

This woman made him *crazy*.

John took that bit of frosting on the tip of his finger, and smeared it along Siena's bottom lip. He didn't even give her the chance to clean it off before his mouth was on hers. He used his lips, teeth, and tongue to take away the frosting. His teeth nipped into her bottom lip, and pulled gently. She rocked her hips as he pressed closer, and it only made his growing erection grind into her center.

His tongue felt numb from their kiss, and her taste. Sweet from the sugar, and goddamn hot from her.

Siena's tongue battled with John's. Her fingernails cut into his jaw line when she pulled him impossibly closer. Shit, all he could think about now was getting his cock buried nine inches into the heaven that was between Siena's thighs.

It had been too long.

He couldn't wait—patience was not his friend, and it had never been.

Yanking up the skirt of her dress, and never breaking their kiss, John pulled Siena's thong down her legs. The forgotten material fell somewhere to the floor as Siena's lips left his, and trailed down his throat.

One kiss. Then another.

His breath caught in his throat when her lips sucked at his jaw. The breath came out in a rush when her teeth cut into the same spot.

"Fuck," he groaned.

"We're getting there," she promised. "You should probably hurry up, John."

Laughing, John grabbed Siena by her throat, and tipped her head back. He stared into deep blue, and watched how her pupils blew wide from his rough handling. She was loving this—she always seemed to love whatever he did to her.

To the outside, Siena was sweet and innocent. Her appearance, with her gentle smiles and wide eyes, made people think she was nothing more than a doe-eyed woman. Harmless, entirely honest, and pure.

Those people didn't know a damn thing. Not about Siena, anyway. This girl was sin. His sin. John liked that just fine.

"I make the demands," he told her, "and not you."

"Sometimes me, too," she said, pouting.

John kissed her pout just because he could. "Sometimes you too, yeah."

He had to give her something, after all.

His hand snaked between her thighs—wet, hot flesh met his fingertips when he stroked her pussy. Bare and soft, he knew she had been waxed recently. He loved when nothing was between them. Loved the feel of her entirely naked against him.

He let two of his fingers sweep through her sex again, taking wetness from her slit up to her clit. One circle around the throbbing nub, and then a second, and Siena's legs trembled against the pressure. She was staring down to watch John play with her pussy, but he couldn't have that.

A slight tap of his hand against her sex made her gaze fly upward.

"Eyes on me right now," he said.

Siena blew out a breath. "But I want to—"

"Eyes on *me.*"

He punctuated that statement by letting his two fingers slip inside her sex. Instantly, he curled his fingertips into her G-spot hard. His thumb slipped up, and rubbed at her clit at the same time.

It didn't take long before her fast, short breaths turned into low, sexy cries. Her legs trembled more, and her inner walls clenched firmly around his fingers.

"Right there, huh?"

Siena's gaze never left his. "Right there, yeah."

Her orgasm came on fast. Her pupils expanded again just before she came, and her legs widened a little bit more. Her lips made that perfect O shape, and he caught her mouth in another kiss to swallow all her sounds.

He loved her sounds, sure.

He still didn't want to draw attention to them.

Siena's hands fumbled with John's jeans as he kissed down the column of her throat. Salt and sex met his tongue. Her heart thundered under his teeth at her pulse point. He didn't help her at all because she had things covered.

Soon enough, his length was in her tight little palm, and she was stroking him awake even more. Not that he needed it—his dick was already painfully hard, but her firm tugs gave him a little bit of relief.

Not nearly enough. He needed to be inside her for that.

"Don't you want me to fuck you?" he asked in her ear.

Siena shivered.

John chuckled.

"Don't you want to come again, Siena?"

He didn't need to tease her more. She fit him between her thighs, and her warm wetness coated the head of his cock while she stroked his dick through her slit.

Once. Then twice.

She brought him down to her entrance again, and John flexed his hips forward. She was so damn wet that she took all of him in with no hesitation at all. Her cunt soaked him, tightened around him, and took away his ability to breathe for too many seconds.

It was still fucking wonderful.

"Jesus Christ," he grunted into her throat.

Siena's breathless laughter coated his senses. Addicting and sweet.

"Fuck me," she urged.

His hand slid along her throat, and pushed her head back again. He needed to see her eyes—wanted to look into them and see all the chaos he caused for her like this.

He loved that, too. Love stared back.

His love lived inside this woman.

"Gonna kill me," he said.

John felt like a broken record with her sometimes.

It didn't make it any less true.

"You'll meet me at the warehouse, then?" John asked.

"I don't think you need me there, son," his father replied on the other end of the call.

"Maybe not, but I want you there. It helps, you know."

"What does?"

"When I have someone to keep me in line."

Lucian cleared his throat. "And that's me, is it?"

"Sometimes Andino. Leonard suggested I be more open to you, though."

"I do like Leonard."

John rolled his eyes upward. "Not news, Papa."

"I will be at the warehouse. Say in what, an hour?"

"Or two. I have to grab the fucker first."

"I thought you already did that."

"I got distracted."

John's gaze drifted to Siena's sleeping form, but he didn't mention to his father where he was. He didn't want anyone concerning themselves about his choices, or what he was doing on the personal side of his life. They kept telling him to have patience, but things were not always so simple for him.

Especially not Siena.

Siena was not simple at all.

"I will see you in a while, John," his father said.

"All right. Thanks."

Hanging up the phone, John gave Siena his attention again. He had been up for a good hour—compliments of his internal clock that didn't know how to let him sleep in. Not that he could afford to do that today, anyway. He'd taken a quick shower, pulled on his clothes from the day before, and swallowed down his meds before calling his father.

He only had a few more minutes before he needed to leave. Soon, Siena's enforcer would be probably getting up, and making his way over to check in on her. She let John know the guy's usual schedule for her in the mornings.

Running his fingers over Siena's naked shoulder, his gaze traveled to her nightstand. He'd left a burner phone for her there, and a hastily written note.

It wasn't much. He would never leave her without an explanation, now. He promised.

Keep the phone out of sight. I'll only call early in the morning. I had some business to do early, and didn't want to wake you up. I'll call tomorrow. Love you. —J

Duty called.

John gave Siena one more look, and then he was gone.

John backed his Mercedes through the opened bay doors of the warehouse. Darkness cloaked his vehicle, and as soon as the front of his car was entirely inside, the bay doors began to close. John only got out of his car once the doors had closed completely.

He found his father standing by the switch used to open and close the bay doors. Lucian said nothing as John moved to the back of the Mercedes, and popped open the trunk.

Still unconscious, the enforcer John had picked up shortly after he left Siena's place was bleeding like a gutted pig all over the damn trunk. That was going to need to be cleaned, for fuck's sake. There was nothing he hated more than bloodstains.

"Fucking mess," John muttered.

Uncaring that it would hurt the man, he reached into the trunk, and dragged the man out by his already broken arm. That had happened in the struggle of John wrapping a wire around the guy's throat, and dragging him across a concrete parking lot. Shit, the guy should have just come with no fight.

That was always easier.

"And which one is this?" Lucian asked, coming closer.

"Kev's man, specifically," John answered.

He let the guy fall to the floor of the warehouse. The thump of the unconscious man was almost sickening, in a way.

"Brad, or some shit," John said. "He's the one Kev uses whenever he wants something done. I've watched him for a week, so I feel pretty good we'll get something useful from him."

"As long as you don't kill him first."

There was that, too, yeah.

John reared back, and kicked the unconscious enforcer in the side of his chest. Likely breaking a rib or two. Brad's hazy eyes flew wide, and his mouth opened with a shout. The guy coughed, and clutched at his chest as he rolled over to his side.

He didn't seem to know where he was, or what the fuck was happening.

This could be a little confusing.

"Where's the fucking hose?" John asked.

Lucian nodded to something over John's shoulder.

"Keep him awake," John said.

His father started nudging the groaning enforcer with the tip of his shoe in all the sensitive spots. Like his aching chest, and his broken arm. John found the hose, turned on the water, and headed back to Brad.

Lucian stepped back from the man at the same time John turned the hose on him. Ice-cold water blasted Brad right in the face, and then the rest of him, too. John didn't stop until the guy was fully awake, and soaked to the goddamn bone.

Sometimes, cold water could be as good as torture.

It all depended on the man.

"Stop, fuck, stop!"

John lowered the hose. "Who did Kev have make the hit on my sister's husband?"

Brad blinked up at John from his back. Water coated his eyelashes, and dripped from his cheeks. "You think I'll tell you that, Marcello?"

To his father, but never looking away from Brad, John said, "In the back of my car—grab the black bag, thanks."

"You got it, son."

"I think you're going to tell me quite a bit, actually," John told Brad. "I mean, by the time I'm done with you. And don't think that just because you give me information means I won't kill you in the end. No, that's not the case. I will kill you regardless. How fast I kill you depends on the kind of information you give me. Do you understand?"

Brad sneered. John smiled.

Soon, Lucian had dropped the black bag at John's feet. Bending down, John upended the bag and let the contents spill out where Brad could get a good look at them.

Just to make the point of each thing clear, John went through all of them. "A couple of knives—I like to watch people bleed, you know. Small ice picks because when I drive them up under your fingernails, you'll choke on your own vomit. A stun-gun. We all know what that does, right? It'll be better, though, because you're soaked with water, now. Vice grips—they're great to pull out shit. Teeth, whatever. And a gun."

John smiled at the man again, knowing damn well he looked cold. "Take your pick."

Brad stumbled over his words.

John nodded. "Yeah, we're not playing games now. You need to start talking."

Like most fuckers, Brad was stubborn. John used the stun-gun first, and watched the foolish idiot jump halfway across the warehouse floor before the shocks finally stopped running through his system. He let the guy bleed a little bit when he drove a knife into his kneecap, and then sighed—annoyed—when Brad *cried* when the ice picks came out to play.

Bending down in front of the now bound, soaked, bleeding, and soon-to-die Calabrese enforcer, John tipped his head to the side. Maybe his father was right.

Maybe he hadn't needed somebody to keep him in line after all.

"I just want information, Brad," John said, "and I have all day. We would really like to give my sister something to make her husband's funeral a little bit better. You could help us out here."

"Y-y-you fuck—"

John stabbed the stun-gun into Brad's neck for a couple of quick seconds. It was another minute before the guy stopped jerking all over the place.

"Next time," John told him, "I am going to shove this fucking thing down your throat, and stab your eye out with the goddamn ice pick. See, I would have taken information for my sister about William, and probably called it a day. You couldn't make shit easy on me, though, could you? Now I'm going to expect a hell of a lot more."

Brad swallowed hard.

John nodded. "Yeah, I told you I wasn't fucking playing around, asshole. Start talking."

The enforcer would still die, though. It was just how shit worked.

John slipped into the third pew behind his sisters and mother. He didn't want to impose his presence on them right now, considering everything.

At the front of the church, William's black casket rested high enough for everyone to see it whether they were standing up, or sitting down. The silver accents and bars shined brightly under the flickering candles.

"When do you think you can come over again?" Siena asked.

That burner phone he left for her was coming in handy. Talking with her early in the morning gave John something to get through the day, really.

"Not sure," John replied honestly.

He knew that wasn't a good enough answer for her, but it would have to do. After all, they had delivered the dead enforcer's body to the doorstep of Kev Calabrese's new place of residence—his mother's brownstone. It had only been a few days since John extracted information from the guy, and then killed him, but he kept him on ice to keep the body from going into decomposition.

He hoped Kev liked their present.

"I'll try to figure out something soon," he said. "But I have to go. This funeral is about to get started."

"Don't forget to tell Andino about Kev and Darren for me."

"I won't forget to tell Andino, love. Relax."

"Okay."

"*Ti amo*, Siena."

"I love you, too, John."

He hung up the call, and at the same time, Andino came to sit beside him in the pew. Ahead of them, Lucian sat down next to Cella who was currently holding onto her eight month old child like Tiffany was the only life line she had left in life.

Maybe the baby was. Who knew?

"Tell me what?" Andino asked.

"Siena—I guess the Calabrese brothers are planning to make work and life a special kind of hell for us. They figure if they can't get to us with violence and whatever else, then picking away at business will do the trick."

Andino scowled. "Fucking bastards."

"They're not even worth all of this, Andino."

Not the death of their family members. Not his sister's pain.

None of it.

Andino felt differently, apparently. "Anything can be worth something, John. It's all about what you get in the end from it, really. Take that as you may."

Maybe that was part of the problem.

John saw one thing. Andino saw another.

"I take it you met up with Siena somehow?" Andino asked. "I didn't get the chance to get over there last week during her yoga time."

John shrugged. "I had a way in. I took it."

"Don't blame you."

Ahead of them, Lucian murmured something to Cella which caused John's sister to break in to tears. More tears. The woman hadn't stopped crying.

John's guilt increased. He knew what his father told her. William's killer would be dead tonight. They had a name. They knew who did it.

She could thank John for that, but he would never expect it from his sister. He only hoped that someday, she did not feel like she did right now. He hoped that someday, she would be happy again.

His part in it made no difference. He didn't want recognition.

"It's almost over," Andino said beside John. "We'll get them. We'll end them. Soon."

NINE

Siena was beginning to hate the passage of time. Or rather, how time no longer passed by for her the way it used to. Before all of this had happened—before John came into her life, and was then taken from her—she never paid much attention to getting through her days, or how slowly they crawled by.

None of that ever seemed important before. She got through the days by focusing on her work, and getting lost in books. By using the black and white simplicity she applied to her love of numbers, and the little joys she got in her private moments alone.

Back then, she had yet to find something that was worth counting her seconds, minutes, hours, and days for.

It was no longer that easy.

Now, time felt like a snail sliding ridiculously slow across ice. No amount of work could keep her distracted or focused enough, and she worked all the damn time. *Still.* Her eyes continued to travel to wherever the clock was on the wall, and she often found herself counting down.

It had become a game of sorts.

Twenty days since I last saw John.

Twelve hours to John's next phone call.

Three days until yoga.

Whatever she had to tell herself to get through the fucking day, and into the next, that's exactly what Siena did.

Problem for her was, that method only went so far, and her distractions were not without some kind of consequence. Mostly, her work.

Siena blinked, and rubbed the heels of her palms against her eyes. The numbers on the screen might as well have just bled together for all she understood of the mess in front of her. She wasn't even sure where some of these goddamn numbers had come from, or how she got them to this point.

Her bottom line number in the Excel spreadsheet lit up bright red. A sure sign that the total had ended up in the negative, which meant nothing good because that wasn't where those numbers were supposed to be. Not even close. That told her she had done something wrong at some fucking point.

But where?

How?

Which account had the mistake?

Siena sighed, and pressed her fingertips into her temples to relieve some of the pressure starting to form there. A migraine from eye-strain and stress, likely. She was getting them far more often than she liked lately.

In her head, she started going back through numbers, accounts, and their individual books. She had worked on at least fifteen different accounts for Kev's restaurant today—a pretty average day, all things considered.

Still, she needed to find that error.

The books couldn't ever be filed in the red.

She was paying heavily for her distractions. More hours at a computer fixing books she should have already had done a week or more ago. A sore back, and stiff fingers from working so much because this shit had to be done, and she was the only one doing it for her brothers' businesses.

"You're still not done yet?"

Siena quickly glanced up from the numbers on the screen to find Kev standing in the doorway. He stared back at her, seemingly unbothered or unknowing of her troubles. She couldn't decide if that was a good thing, or not.

"No, I'm not done yet," she finally said.

Kev looked at the watch on his wrist. "It's almost five, Siena."

"I'm aware, Kev."

She had been watching the clock, after all.

"Jason had shit to do today, Siena. He's been waiting on your slow ass all day."

"Jason?"

Who the fuck was *Jason*?

"Your enforcer," Kev said as though he were talking to a small, dumb child.

"You know," Siena replied, "that's the first time someone has ever told me his name. And that includes him."

"Huh." Kev shrugged. "Guess it wasn't important for you to know."

Nothing ever was.

"I won't be much longer," Siena said, waving a hand and going back to the computer screen. "Tell him a half hour, at most."

Or she would make it that long.

One or the other.

"I told you—he's got shit to do," Kev said. "Just go. It's not like you can't pick up where you left off tomorrow, or something."

Except that's not how Siena had been taught to do things, and work. It was not the proper way to do things. What accounts she opened and started in a day, she had to finish inputting and calculating numbers.

That way, there was less chance of more mistakes should she come back to it, and forget her place. In her business of cooking and falsifying books, she could not afford very many goddamn mistakes before it became noticeable.

Numbers were unforgiving that way.

Kev didn't understand.

Arguing wouldn't help.

Siena decided to take this small blessing for what it was, anyway. There was no way her brother would take her request for a break seriously. He would just laugh, and refuse while telling her she didn't need a fucking break.

She could be having a stroke, and he would still want her to show up to work the next day. So was her goddamn life.

"Fine," Siena said heavily as she pushed up from the chair. Quickly, she closed the books out. She didn't even bother to save the work she had done for the day because it all needed to be redone, anyway. Then, she looked at Kev with raised hands. "I'm done. Happy?"

"I will be when you get out of my office. Jason is waiting in his car outside."

Good for him.

Kev plopped his ass down in the chair as soon as Siena moved out of the way. He had already put the phone from the desk to his ear by the time Siena stepped out of the office. She closed the door behind her, but it wasn't enough to hide Kev's conversation. Like their father's voice had once done her brother's also carried through walls.

Siena took the second or two she had to lean against the hallway wall, and press her fingers to her temples once more. Without the unforgiving brightness of the screen in her eyes, the pounding in her head subsided just enough to make the oncoming migraine a little more bearable.

At least, for now.

Behind her, she could hear Kev talking on the phone. She only knew he was talking to Darren—wherever he was today—because Kev used her other brother's name.

"When it comes to this, Darren, no news *is* bad news," Kev snapped.

Somebody needed to give her brothers' lessons on privacy. Neither of them understood how loud their voices could be.

It was sad, really.

"You're telling me that not one effort we've made to fuck with the Marcello family's business on the streets—or otherwise—has worked? Not one fucking thing?"

A beat of silence passed.

And then, "Then we're going to go back to my way—*yes*, exactly that, Darren."

Siena should move, as her enforcer was waiting for her, and Kev might come out of the office soon. Still, she stayed right where she was.

"Your way isn't working either," Kev snarled. "At least with my way, we were knocking them down. Even if it was one by fucking one. Let's try my way one more time—something a bit more violent. It's my choice, and I made it."

Shit.

That didn't sound good.

Kev's conversation continued on with Darren, but Siena only listened for long enough to learn that he wasn't giving anything about his plans away. Nothing that she could use to tell John, or Andino.

The vibration of the cell phone made Siena quickly step further away from the office door, and dig around inside her bag to answer the call. She put it to her ear, and asked quietly, "Hello?"

"Is Meghan there?"

Siena smirked a little. "Wrong number, sorry."

As she pulled the phone away a little, she heard the guy say, "Andino is in the back alley of the restaurant. Ten minutes, at most."

Click.

Siena dropped the phone into her bag, and looked between the bustling restaurant just down the hallway, and the back exit that was just a few feet away. It wasn't the back alley, but it would lead her to the back alley, plus give her a way back in.

Kev's conversation was still going full force behind her. It was a risk. But frankly, everything she did lately was risky.

Siena slipped out the exit door, and tried not to roll her ankles as she ran toward the back alley behind the restaurant. Sure enough, she found an unknown red car running in the back alley parked between two other businesses.

Andino didn't drive a red car, but he was behind the wheel of the vehicle. Siena slipped into the passenger seat without thinking about it.

"New car?" she asked.

Andino laughed. "Borrowed, actually. Your brothers' people know my shit."

"Oh."

"I have a favor to ask."

Siena looked over at the man. "Sure."

"It's not going to be easy."

She scoffed.

"Nothing in this life is ever easy, Andino."

"Fair enough," he murmured.

"By the way, Kev is pissed that nothing they're doing to the Marcellos is working at the moment, so he's decided to go back to his old ways."

Andino scowled. "Violent means."

"You could say that. He didn't specify what or who, though."

"Shit."

"Sorry."

Andino shrugged. "No worries. I'm hoping this plan I have for you will end a lot of it. Or shit, at the very least, make your other brother stop and reconsider some of his fucking options at the moment."

Siena's brow furrowed. "You're going to have to explain that to me."

"How much do you care for your brothers?"

All she could do was dead-stare Andino right in the face. She had no appropriate response because none would be good enough. Her care and concern for either one of her brothers was so low, it couldn't even be measured.

Hate was not a good enough word.

Truly.

"Let me guess," Andino drawled, "if you don't have anything good to say, then say nothing at all."

"Something like that," she replied.

"That makes this easier. How opposed are you to murder?"

A lump formed in her throat instantly.

His suggestion was blatant, and cold.

Still, Siena barely had to think about it at all. "It's all for him, right?"

For John.

For *them*.

For forever.

"I need Kev gone." Andino passed over a small clear bag with one tablet inside. "Arsenic pressed into a pill. It'll dissolve quickly in something like liquor, or anything with a good amount of acid."

"Like juice, or soda."

"Exactly."

Siena nodded. "That's a terrible way to die."

Andino laughed. "Fuck, you know what, if I wanted easy right now I'd have blown up his restaurant once I knew you were gone from it. Unfortunately, that draws a lot of attention, and I'm trying to follow some kind of rules at the moment."

Jesus.

That lump was still firm in her throat.

"Make sure there's a lot of people around, and not only you and someone else. You don't want suspicion being drawn to you on this, either," Andino said.

"Definitely not."

"You don't have to let me know when it's done, either. I'll get word."

Siena glanced down at the pill in the bag. "John won't like me doing this."

Hell, even *she* was struggling with the idea of actually being the cause of someone's death. She wasn't quite ready to use murder in context with everything, but she was not so naive that she didn't realize that's exactly what it meant.

John would understand why she dirtied her hands in this way eventually, sure, but that didn't mean he would like it.

Not at all.

"Well," Andino murmured, "we're just not going to tell him until after."

Yeah.

Shit.

"I should go before someone notices me gone."

Andino nodded. "Yeah, go."

Siena barely blinked, and two weeks passed her by just like that. As though she hadn't even been a part of it at all. It was strange how when something was weighing on a person's mind, everything else in their life became inconsequential. Nothing else mattered but that one thing they couldn't seem to shake.

Not long ago, she had been wishing for time to speed up, and make life a little more bearable. Oh, sure, she could absolutely see the irony in it. Now, here she was wondering where in the hell those two weeks had gone, and how she managed to spend them entirely lost to her own mind.

She felt like she was in a bubble, of sorts. All the time, and never ending. Floating high above everyone else, and looking down on them while they continued living their lives. The world kept moving, but she was frozen— suspended.

She could hear their conversations, and see their expressions and gestures. Yet, everything still felt a little cloudy and muffled to her. She was sure this was what people called an out-of-body experience.

Was it supposed to last this long?

Was it supposed to be this confusing?

Siena didn't know.

If anyone noticed her disengaged attitude, or distracted behaviors, no one mentioned anything to her about it. Not even John when he caught her zoning out during their early morning phone calls.

For that, she felt most guilty. She couldn't explain to him, though.

Andino was clear.

Siena just needed to get this done.

And by *this*, she meant killing her own brother.

Strolling through her mother's brownstone, Siena saw far more faces than she cared to count. Many, she recognized, but there were a few whom she couldn't place. Her brothers' men, their families, and friends.

All the people who should gather for a party when there was something worthy to celebrate. Today, they were celebrating Kev's birthday. Apparently, a new boss should always have his momentous events celebrated by his men.

Siena didn't know if that was actually true or not, and she really didn't care at the moment. Kev was simply celebrating something only to never see it through. He wouldn't see the end of his birthday—he wouldn't wake up the morning after being a day older than he was right now.

She had to make sure of it.

She was going to make sure of it.

The filled-to-the brim brownstone was exactly the kind of circumstance Siena needed to get this done. Andino's warning about making sure many people were around when she did the deed had not been simple. She always figured out ways in her mind about how the murder would be linked back to her.

Not tonight, though.

Balloons, streamers, and banners hung from the ceilings, and decorated the stairwell. A bit juvenile for a grown man, really, but their mother didn't know how to tone it down when it came to her sons.

A gold and black theme, it seemed. Even the cake had black frosting piped with gold trim. God knew Siena didn't want any of that overly sweet shit—she would probably throw it back up.

She already felt like puking. Her nerves worked overtime. She wasn't sure if it was because her anxiety was acting up, or due to the action she was about to take against her family.

Once again, betraying them. Once again, proving she was exactly what they all said.

The shame.

The disgraced one.

It was just too damn bad that none of those thoughts really stopped Siena's resolve to get this whole thing done and over with.

"Siena!"

Coraline's sharp bark made Siena hesitate as she tried to pass by a group of gathered men. Turning, she faced her scowling mother standing in the entryway between the hallway, and the living room.

"Yeah?"

"Your brother is going to blow out the candles on his cake, and cut it for everyone to have a piece."

And that meant what exactly to Siena?

"So?" she asked.

Coraline cocked a brow. "Please have the catering people come in and bring the food into the dining room. They can set it out on the table, and everyone can pick what they want like a buffet."

Siena wondered if this was her chance ...

She didn't have time to think on it.

"Sure, Ma."

"Well, hurry up!"

Jesus.

Siena made her way into the kitchen where a catering team had taken over the space. It looked as though they were mostly done with their preparations for the dinner, and wouldn't need much help moving things into the dining room.

Behind her, Siena heard her mother calling out, "Everyone to the dining room to wish Kev a happy birthday, grab some food, and have a piece of cake!"

People moved through the kitchen to the dining room. More simply used the hallway. Either way, Siena was acutely aware that people were leaving her alone, and she didn't have anyone looking over her shoulder at the moment.

Winning.

"Excuse me," Siena said to the lead caterer.

The woman wore the only white hat amongst the rest. She smiled at Siena, asking, "Yes, what can I do for you, Miss Calabrese?"

"We would like the food moved into the dining room as a spread—buffet-style, if you wouldn't mind."

"No problem at all."

One sharp whistle, and the catering crew was moving fast. Soon enough, they had almost everything moved from the kitchen in one go.

On the second round the servers made to the kitchen, Siena slipped out, and headed for the wet bar in the dining room. At her back, people sang Kev happy birthday. She kept her back turned to the people, and her brothers.

No one approached.

No one saw a thing.

She pulled the sleeves of her dress down over her fingers, and worked to open up liquor bottles, and set up the glass. The little pill she dropped into the screwdriver drink dissolved with three quick twirls of the spoon inside the glass.

Siena took a deep breath, and then another. It didn't help to settle her nerves, but for some reason, her racing heart had slowed down just enough to make her think she was in some kind of control of her emotions.

It was an illusion.

She would freak out later.

Break down later.

Not now, though.

As soon as the happy birthday song was over, Siena turned fast, and slid through the crowd of people already beginning to swarm the table and food. No one seemed to pay her any mind as she pushed through to the head of the table where Kev had decided was his permanent seat for the night.

Her brother had stood to accept a plate of food from their mother. He didn't see Siena set the glass down next to his napkin, still not letting her fingers touch anything lest she leave something unintended behind. She was grateful she had chosen the long sleeved dress that night instead of the other one she waffled on.

Nobody saw her do a thing because like always, she blended in far too well. She was the forgotten one—the useless daughter who nobody thought to watch.

Here, Kev was a king.

Or, he thought so.

He expected people to wait on him—his men, sister, mother, and even his brother. It's what he had seen his father expect from everyone around them for his whole life, and Siena really didn't expect Kev to be any different in the grand scheme of things.

He was spoiled.

He was demanding.

He was excessive.

Siena was already at the other side of the dining room and picking up a paper plate to begin filling it with food by the time Kev sat back down in his chair. Not food she would eat, but something she could pick at until the action really got started.

Kev sat his plate of food down in front of him, and laughed at something Darren said beside him in the next chair. He picked up the screwdriver—his favorite drink, as everyone should know—like he expected it to be sitting right where it was … as he was the boss.

Everybody always catered to the boss.

Siena watched Kev down half the drink in one go. He ate a bit—finished the drink off right after. He didn't make it through a quarter of the way through his plate before he started foaming at the mouth.

Fuck.

Siena had been right.

It *was* a horrible way to die.

The hospital bustled with movement and people. In the corner, Siena found her mother sobbing as Darren tried to console Coraline.

It was pointless.

She couldn't be consoled. One of her prized things were gone.

Kev was dead.

"Are you listening to me, ma'am?"

Siena turned her attention back to the cop taking her statement. She had tossed the small bag the pill had been in on their drive to the hospital—the enforcer had been too busy barking to someone on the phone to notice her getting rid of evidence.

The cop had already swabbed her hands—and everyone else's, too. Not that any of them were very pleased about that. No one in their business particularly liked to be involved with cops in anyway, but it was difficult to refuse police when something like murder came into play.

Her fingers had never touched the pill, or the items used to mix the glass. She wasn't the least bit worried about being found out.

Everyone was either too confused, or too scared to realize she had been the one to set the glass in front of Kev just a few hours earlier.

"Ma'am?"

"I'm listening," Siena said.

"And then what happened after the song?" the cop asked.

"I got my plate ready like everyone else was doing."

"You didn't see anyone approaching your brother, or leaving something for him?"

"I saw him talking to my other brother. My mother brought him a plate."

"Think harder."

"There was no one," Siena said.

Her eyes were dry—no tears to be seen. She tried to conjure up some kind of emotional response to make this cop think she was in a state over Kev's death, but it was kind of pointless. She couldn't do it.

The man seemed to think it was something else entirely. He touched her shoulder with soft affection, and leaned in closer. "I know it's a shock—you'll process all of this in time. I'm sorry for your loss."

"Thank you."

Maybe she should have felt like the biggest piece of shit for pulling this stunt—for doing this to her family.

Yet, she didn't.

All she could really think about was ... getting out.

The cop turned to talk to his partner, and Siena's gaze drifted over the people in the waiting room. Her brother and mother were still fully distracted with each other, and the people surrounding them.

Siena's enforcer was another one distracted by barking into his phone. He'd been doing that all damn night.

She finally had a chance to get out. Five minutes to breathe alone. All she could think about was John.

No one noticed her standing there alone, dry-eyed.

No one noticed her leave, either.

Siena used the key John kept hidden in a safety box on the back deck of his Queens home to get inside his place. She hadn't called to let him know she was coming over only because she didn't dare use the phone given to her by her brothers.

She left the burner phone from John at her place, hidden in a spot where it wasn't likely to be discovered.

Quickly, she slipped through the dark, quiet house. Upstairs she went until she found John sleeping in his bed. His house was usually locked up tight—she had spent enough nights with him to know the slightest sound or creak would wake him up.

The fact he didn't move at all as she crossed the bedroom was a testament to how busy and stressed out he must have been. So much so, that sleep was probably his only escape from everything.

She didn't want to wake him.

She didn't want to sleep, either.

"John," Siena whispered.

His name barely left her lips before his eyes flew wide open. Dark hazel darted right, and found her standing next to his bed. He blinked once, and then twice, like he was trying to make sure it was actually her standing there.

John didn't saying anything.

No, he simply grabbed her and pulled her into the bed with him.

Siena's sudden laughter was muffled by the hard kiss John leveled to her mouth as his hands gripped fiercely to her sides. He rolled to his back and took her with him. Never once did they break their kiss.

She couldn't help herself but touch him. In nothing but boxer-briefs, she had all the access to his body that she wanted. Hard lines, and muscles that strained with every movement. The dark dusting of hair that led from his navel to the waistband of his boxer-briefs called her name.

John didn't say a word—only groaned—when Siena kissed down his throat, over his chest, and kept moving lower. He pushed his lower half against her body when she wrapped her fingers around the waistband of his boxer-briefs, and started to tug them down.

Already, he was hard.

Already, she wanted to taste him.

Soon, she would have to go again. Before the sun was up, likely. Before either of them could possibly talk properly, or get their fill of one another.

It sucked.

But that's just how it was.

For now ...

Siena's fingers wrapped tightly around the base of John's cock, and she took the head of him into her mouth. The unique taste of him and his precum burst along her taste buds. He flexed his hips upward making her take damn near all of him into her mouth at once.

Her eyes watered.

She loved it.

Siena stroked him at the same time she sucked him. She let her teeth work magic as they grazed the sensitive skin of his shaft, while her tongue flicked at the head of his dick every time she came back up to the top.

She could feel his heartbeat in his shaft.

Racing. Thumping. Out of control.

So close, so close ...

"Fuck, fuck, fuck," John groaned.

She looked up through her lashes, and he was already staring at her. Dark hazel met light blue, and Siena was lost for those few seconds.

Frozen.

Perfect.

So happy.

John brought her back from that bubble following her around with one loud, sharp shout of her name. He came hard, held her tight to his cock, and blew his load down her throat. She took every bit of him in, cleaned the rest of him up with her tongue, and then kissed her way back up his chest.

"Jesus fucking Christ," John muttered into his hand.

Siena kissed the back of it. "Hey."

He peeked out at her. "Hey. Nice way to wake up."

She grinned. "Couldn't help myself."

"Don't help yourself more often."

"Noted," she said with a laugh.

John cleared his throat, and love reflected back in his eyes as he stared at her "What in the hell are you doing here? Almost got yourself killed, Siena."

"You would not have done anything to me."

Silently, he reached his hand under his pillow, and when he slid it back out, a gun came with it. "We're a shoot first, ask later kind of family."

Yikes.

"Next time, I'll call."

"Please." He pulled her down for another quick kiss, then asked, "Seriously, though, what are you doing here? Don't they have you on lockdown, or something?"

"Usually. They're all kind of … distracted tonight. Being at the hospital, and everything."

John raised a brow high. "Something happened?"

"Kev, yeah."

"Siena."

She looked away, but John's hand grabbed her chin, and turned her back to stare at him. He wouldn't let her go, either.

Andino did say *after*.

Siena couldn't lie to John.

"Kev's dead," she whispered.

John stiffened in the bed. "How? Shot, or something?"

She wasn't surprised that was the first thing he thought of. A lot of the warring between their families had been violent and bloody.

"No, he was poisoned at his birthday party tonight," she said quietly.

John blinked, and stilled. "Poisoned."

Siena shrugged. "Yeah."

"That's a very specific way to die. How do you know he was—" John's words cut off abruptly when Siena glanced away again. The truth was in her eyes. She wanted him to see it and figure it out much more than she wanted to explain it. "Siena."

She wouldn't look at him again. He said her name again.

And again.

"Siena," John murmured, his hands grabbing tighter to her waist than before. "Don't tell me you were the one to do it."

"I did what I was told to do."

It was what she was best at, after all.

TEN

"You fucking asshole!"

Andino looked up from the papers on his desk, and narrowly missed John's oncoming fist by ducking. "Shit."

It didn't make a difference. John landed a punch to his cousin's jaw on the second swing, anyway.

The hit connected hard enough to send Andino's head flying to the side. John was already bracing for the impact that was sure to come back at him. Andino didn't disappoint. His cousin pushed out of the chair faster than he could blink, and came at him.

John was quick enough to duck the first swing Andino aimed for his head, but forgot that his cousin was a south paw, and sneaky as fuck. Ducking like he did only gave Andino the chance to land a hard punch against John's fucking kidney.

Jesus Christ.

That hurt.

Andino shoved John into the office door. John went right back for more. He shoved Andino hard, too, knocking his cousin into the chair, and desk. Not that it kept Andino down, or anything. He came right back for more, too.

So was their way.

Soon, the two cousins were pounding fists into one another on the floor of Andino's office, while the employees in the kitchen worked on like nothing was happening. Just another day working for Andino Marcello, apparently.

This wasn't the first time the two had gone to blows over something, and it likely wouldn't be the last. Sometimes, this was just how they dealt with any kind of shit between them, but this time, it was different for John.

He was pissed.

Really fucking pissed off.

Where in previous fights he would make sure to keep his punches clean, and not hit Andino somewhere it would do lasting damage—like his face—John just didn't care. He needed to get some of his goddamn anger out, and since Andino had been the cause of that anger in the first damn place, here they were.

It didn't take long before Andino figured out John was not going to calm, or back down. He tried holding John down, but that didn't do anything for either of them. Andino got his own hits thrown in, too, but John barely felt them at all.

Maybe after the third or so punch John landed to Andino's head did the trick—he didn't really know what it was—but his cousin figured out this was not like every other time they went to blows.

Either way, Andino pulled back, and rolled away from John. He laid to his back on the floor, and stared up at the ceiling. It took all the willpower John had not to roll over, and start fucking up the man again.

Outside the office, dishes clattered. Footsteps echoed just beyond their space as the employees continued to work.

It would be comical.

If it wasn't so fucking sad.

"So fucking lucky Snaps wasn't here today," Andino snarled under his breath.

John let out a hard exhale, and scrubbed his now-sore hands down his face. "Where is he?"

"Haven took him to the spa."

Side-eyeing his cousin, he said, "The fucking *spa*."

"He likes it, okay. They rub him down, bathe him, and give him treats. It's their thing—she takes him once a week."

"He goes to the spa once a week. Are you serious? He's a dog."

"A dog that would have ripped your face off for this bullshit."

Fair enough.

"Fuck," Andino muttered, touching the spot above his eyebrow with his fingertips. "I think you cracked something in my face."

"Not going to apologize for that."

"What the fuck is wrong with you?"

John's jaw clenched so hard, his goddamn molars ached. The anger that had damn near controlled him for the entire day before, and this morning, was still entirely present. Apparently, there was no getting rid of it.

He tried using one of Leonard's techniques, which meant John had to make a conscious choice to put his reactive nature aside when something got to him. Whatever it might be—anger, or something similarly overwhelming. He needed to try and give it some time to settle, and then handle it appropriately.

Clearly, that had not worked.

Here he was.

"They change your fucking meds, or something?" Andino asked.

That hit a nerve.

John's fist came out like lightening, and landed hard to Andino's kidney. His cousin's air came out in a sharp whoosh, and then a low *fuck* followed right behind. Sweet satisfaction curled through John.

"Don't take cheap shots at me about being bipolar, or my meds. You fucking asshole."

"All right, all right. I kind of deserved that one," Andino grumbled through pants of air. "Jesus Christ, that hurt."

"You deserved it a little more than kind of, prick," John replied. "You're putting her in a lot of fucking danger, Andino."

"What, who?"

Oh, so now his cousin wanted to play dumb?

John wasn't up for that.

"*Siena.*"

"Shit, John—"

Quick as a blink, John rolled over, got to his knees, and then stood from the floor. Andino stayed right where he was on his back, and looking up at John. In a way, it gave him the feeling that his cousin was the weaker between them for the moment.

In a sense.

It didn't matter who was the weaker one between them. Either way, John still had shit to say, and he needed it to be heard. He needed Andino to fucking *hear him*, and get it. Really fucking get it. He wasn't playing these stupid games anymore, and he didn't want Siena to be playing them, either.

"Siena showed up at my place the night before last," John said, "you know, after Kev Calabrese croaked at his birthday party. Somebody poisoned him, huh?"

Andino lifted a single brow. "Word made rounds, yeah. What about it?"

"That's how you want to play this?"

"John, come on, now."

"You had her do that job, Andi."

Andino sucked air through his teeth, but his cold gaze never wavered from John for a second. "It needed to be done, and I couldn't trust anyone else to do it. Who the hell else is that close to those brothers, John?"

"Any one of their fucking men, Andino!"

"Couldn't turn one. Or rather, I couldn't trust one to turn them. That's not my goal in this—that's not the job I need to be concerned about at the moment. I just need those goddamn brothers out of the fucking way. That's it."

John didn't have the first clue what his cousin was talking about. "You're trying to ruin that family, but you don't want the task of controlling them once you've done that?"

Andino rolled his eyes. "She got it done. What else is there to say?"

"Stop putting her in these fucking positions, that's what. At first it was just getting information from her which was dangerous enough considering how controlled she is by that family—now *this*?"

"Is it because you think Siena is too innocent to kill a man, or because you don't want her dirtying up those pretty hands of hers?"

John forced himself not to kick Andino as hard as he could in the guy's ribs. It took a hell of a lot more effort than he thought it would. "You're purposefully being an asshole right now, and I don't appreciate it."

"Because you're acting foolish, and letting your feelings cloud up what you should already know about a war like this. We do what we need to—use who we can use—and get it done. Finish it. We finish them. That's all that matters."

"Not to the sacrifice of *her*!"

"You assume she'll be a sacrifice because she cannot handle herself, or something like that. Maybe that's something you should handle with yourself, John, because Siena has her shit covered. She's gold. She knows exactly what she's doing."

He heard Andino.

He still didn't like it.

"Darren Calabrese is not a stupid fuck like you might think. Is he a little screwed up or distracted right now because Kev is dead? Sure, but that means *nothing*. If you don't think they weren't already suspicious that someone inside their circles were feeding us information, then you're delusional, Andino."

"I—"

"Darren, or somebody else who will let him know, is going to figure out what is going on. They will figure out that it is her. The more info from her you use, or the more you get her to do, the worse it will get for her. I won't have you putting her in that kind of danger, Andi. I just won't."

"Are you going to fucking let me talk, or what?"

John fixed his jacket, and gave his cousin one last look. "I said what I had to say, actually."

"Shame—you're missing out on the bigger picture entirely."

"Your picture isn't *my* picture, Andino."

After all, John's bigger picture showcased Siena. It seemed like Andino's only showcased ruining the Calabrese.

"Get the hell out," Andino mumbled.

Fine by John.

"John," Leonard barked.

John glanced away from the clock just long enough to give his therapist a look. "What?"

"You're all over the place."

"I noticed that, too."

John's father slipped through the living room of Leonard's home. Lucian now made it his job to occasionally show up at John's appointments. He tried to put his reasoning under the umbrella that Leonard was an old friend.

Frankly, John saw that guise for what it was.

"When was the last time you slept?" Leonard asked.

John sighed. "Last night."

"How long?"

Good catch, Doc.

"Enough," John replied.

"That's not a good enough answer for me," Leonard said. "Try again, and give me the truth."

"Four hours."

"One long stretch, or in total?"

"Total."

Leonard nodded, and stood from his chair. Strolling to the window, he looked out at the clear September sky. "Tell me about work, John."

John glanced at his father.

Lucian only shrugged as he sipped from a glass of bourbon.

"It's busy," John said.

"Dangerous, I think," Leonard countered. "I watch the news. I keep up with things. Seems the Marcello organization is in a major feud with the Calabrese faction at the moment. Three deaths this last week alone between the two."

"Two were theirs—Capos."

"A foot solider for us," Lucian put in. "Replaceable."

"Your woman—Siena."

John stiffened on the couch "What about her?"

"She comes from their side, doesn't she?"

"Yes."

"How often do you see her? Or even, when was the last time?"

John cleared his throat, and just as quickly as his father had slipped into the room, Lucian left it the same way he had come in. When privacy mattered in John's sessions, and his father was there, Lucian knew when it was time to step the hell away.

He appreciated it.

"The beginning of the month."

"Almost two weeks, then," Leonard supplied.

"Yeah."

"I suppose you're concerned about her."

"It's a lot more than just her, but yes, I focus on her a lot, too."

Leonard turned to face John with a pensive expression. "You're going too much, and not taking enough time for up here."

The therapist tapped his temple.

John got what the man was saying.

"I don't really have a choice at the moment, all things considered."

"You're going to put yourself back into a hypomanic phase, John."

"I have it under control."

Leonard stared hard at John.

It made him edgy.

"What?" John asked, irritated.

"Choose stability."

"I *am.*"

"How structured have your days been since you left the facility, John?"

Well, that one, he had to stop and think about. It was not an easy answer because at the moment, his entire life just felt like one giant ball of chaos. One thing after another thing, after another thing. It never ended.

"I'm structured in the areas that need to be handled," John chose to say.

"Your bipolar. Managing it, you mean."

John nodded. "That's what's important, right?"

"Take that away, though, John. Remove your twice weekly appointments, your strict regimes for diet and exercise, and the other routines you have in place to manage your disorder. Is that the *only* thing keeping you on track right now?"

"Somedays, it's the only thing keeping me sane at the moment, yeah."

"You're playing a dangerous game with that."

"Not sure how to correct it right now, either."

Leonard tapped his watch with one finger, but never took his gaze away from John. "You allow me to do that for you. Sometimes, a break is good for you. I'm the one who—regardless of what is happening in your life—makes you take a moment to step back, objectify things around you, and relax."

"I don't find our sessions very relaxing."

Hard.

Sometimes irritating.

Often, invasive.

Leonard smirked. "Then explain to me why you've just spent the last fifteen minutes in a far calmer, less jittery place than you were when you walked in."

Shit.

"Well …"

"It's fine to say that this is your safe place, John. We all have one, you know? Mine tends to be high in the sky, amongst the clouds."

"You're not my only safe place," John said. "I have others."

"Who?"

"My cousin, for one."

"Andino."

John's lip curled back at Andino's name. Clearly, he was still sore over their fight a few days before. Leonard didn't miss it.

"Is there trouble with your cousin?"

"I think he's causing problems to further his own agenda, and I'm not very fond of the way he's going about it."

"And so, you're too irritated with him to let your emotional guard down."

"You make me sound pathetic."

Leonard chuckled. "Far from it. I could not imagine what it must feel like to be you, John. To be constantly stuck in a high-intensity emotional headspace twenty-four-seven. To feel things much faster, and more extremely, than those around me. And yet, you do it every day, and handle yourself all the while. That's admirable, not pathetic."

Well, then.

"Mmm, your woman, too, I suppose," Leonard added after a moment.

John scrubbed a hand down his unshaven jaw—making a mental note to shave. "What about her?"

"She's a safe place for you, too."

"More so than anyone else."

Understatement.

"So you do have places you can go where you do not have to be on edge at every waking second," the man said.

"She's not around very much at the moment, so no, I'm stuck with—"

"Me," Leonard interrupted with a grin.

Again, the man tapped his watch. John didn't know what he was getting at.

"We'll add an extra hour onto the two sessions a week you already do, and add a third session on Wednesdays to break up your week."

John groaned under his breath. "I don't have time—"

"You will make time because you need to."

Fuck.

Leonard waved a finger at the doorway where Lucian had disappeared. "Go let your father know you'll both be here for a bit longer."

"Wait, you mean we start the extra hour today?" John asked.

"I did not stutter," Leonard murmured.

John found his father sitting on the front steps of Leonard's quiet Brooklyn home. Lucian alternated between sipping his bourbon, and smoking a cigarette. He offered the pack to his son, and John took one out.

Maybe a smoke would calm his nerves.

Who fucking knew?

John didn't smoke very often, now. Just whenever the urge struck, or he needed a bit of stress relief. That first drag off the cigarette burned his lungs like nothing else, but also felt like calm swimming through his veins.

"Are you done for the day?" Lucian asked.

"Not entirely. Another hour, or so."

"Okay."

John glanced over at his father, but found Lucian didn't seem the least bit bothered that he couldn't leave. In fact, Lucian seemed perfectly content to sit right where he was, and wait for his son.

"Thanks, Papa."

Lucian looked up from his seat. "For what, John?"

"This."

You.

Lucian seemed to understand, and only gave his son a nod in recognition. John was coming to learn that maybe he had more than a couple of safe places—in many ways, his father was becoming one, too.

"I didn't mean to overhear," Lucian said, "but I heard what you said regarding Andino."

John's irritation flashed through his gut.

Hot and poisoned.

Damn.

He wished he could let that go.

"He's putting Siena in danger again and again," John said. "And for what? Nothing."

"Not nothing, son, to—"

"Take over the Calabrese. He'll absorb the Calabrese Capos, streets, and their crews into the Marcellos, which will only make his organization bigger when he finally takes over Dante's position officially. So, that compared to Siena's life? *Nothing,* Papa. That's what."

Lucan looked over at John, and his familiar hazel gaze flashed with something John didn't recognize. "He's not explained this to you at all, has he?"

"Explained what?"

"You've got this all wrong, John."

"Again, wh—"

John's question was cut off by the sight of a black sedan with tinted windows slowing down in front of the drive leading up to Leonard's home. He saw the driver's side front and rear windows roll down a few inches, and gun metal glinted in the light.

"Shit," John hissed.

He grabbed his father, and took them both to the ground with enough force that he was worried he might have broken something.

Bullets rained down.

Relentless.

Violent.

Deafening.

John kept his father covered.

Fucking Calabrese.

More people were going to have to die for this.

Shame.

John scrubbed a hand down his face in frustration as more people flooded into the hospital room. Jordyn snapped at anyone who came too close to her husband while the nurse gave Lucian his first small dose of morphine.

Getting two ribs broken could be painful, after all.

"Give me the run down," Dante said, moving in beside his brother's bed.

Sweet Jesus.

If there was anyone's glare who could rival the Devil's, it was John's mother. Even his uncle couldn't help himself but take a quick step back when Jordyn leveled it on him. John held his chuckle back, but barely.

"Jordyn, it's—"

"Not fine, Lucian!"

John's father passed his two brothers a look, and gestured one finger toward the door. "And take my son with you when you go. Let Ma through when she gets here."

Italian men and their mothers …

It could not be a joke when it was the truth.

Dante waved a hand, and John followed behind him and his other uncle. Giovanni looked John up and down, and nodded to himself.

"What?" John asked once the door was closed behind them. "That look—what the fuck was that for?"

Dante cocked a brow, but said nothing.

Gio shook his head, and glanced away. "Nothing. I was thinking, at least one of you made it out unscathed, I guess."

"I'm the one that broke his ribs," John pointed out. "I took him to the ground too—"

"You did fine," Dante interjected firm and fast. "You did *right*."

John quieted at that, and nodded. "Where's Andino?"

"Trying to settle people into safe places tonight," Dante explained. "He wanted to come, but I know the two of you are having some issues at the moment. Better for him to be elsewhere."

"He could have come."

Dante gave John a hard look. "Andino knows when to step back for someone else."

Fine.

John was not going to argue the point further. He didn't think it would get him anywhere. Looking back at his father's room, he saw one of his sisters slip inside.

Cella.

She still wouldn't look at him.

She never talked to him.

John shook it off, and went back to the conversation at hand. "The run down?"

"Yeah, give it to me."

"They caught us on the porch. Did a quick drive-by. Black sedan. Didn't even get the make or model as I wanted to get Dad down. By the time I looked up again, they were gone. I mean, we know *who* ordered it, right. There's no question there."

"Definitely no question," Dante agreed. "We still have to figure out what to do about these fucking foolish idiots."

"Maybe stop fucking around with them like Andino has been doing, and challenge them head-on. If it's a proper street war they want, then—"

"There is a method to Andino's madness," Giovanni said, stepping into the conversation only to defend his son. Or so it seemed. "Don't shit on his way of doing things just because you have a different opinion about how it could be done."

"Had I started something like this," John shot back, "I would have fucking finished it shortly after, too."

Dante cleared his throat, and moved subtly in between the nephew and uncle. "All right, that's enough. Take a fucking breath, and lower your damn voices. We're not here to give the hospital staff a show, huh?"

"Sorry," Gio muttered behind Dante.

John still gave his uncle a look that spoke volumes without him needing to say anything at all. "I stand by it, though."

"You can't be that fucking entitled, John." Giovanni shook his head, and smirked in that irritating way of his. "You think the rest of us are putting our asses on the line for this plan because Andino *thinks* it's a good idea? Are you really that selfish in your own head that you can't see he's—"

Dante turned around, and shoved Gio on his shoulder. Pointing a single finger to the hallway leading out of the hospital wing, he said, "Go wait for Papa and Ma, Gio."

"Dante—"

"*Go*, I said."

Andino might have been the boss in waiting.

Dante was still *the* boss.

Giovanni moved past Dante, but pointed a finger at John as he went by. "Clean up your fucking shit, John. You think going on like that is going to suit a man in your position once this is over? I don't think so."

John's brow furrowed. "What in the hell was that supposed to—"

"Excuse me?"

Dante spun around on his heel at the quiet voice. John found a young nurse standing there with a yellow bubble mailer in her hands. She offered it out, but neither of the men moved to take the item from her.

"What?" Dante barked.

The woman shrunk a bit.

"This was dropped off at the nurse's station in the next wing, and we were directed that it be delivered to a Johnathan Marcello. Apparently, his father is being treated in *this* wing. It must have been a mix up."

Dante passed John a look.

John reached for the mailer. It was only once the woman was gone that he turned to his uncle, concern writing heavily along his brow. "Open it, or no?"

"She was holding it pretty firmly, and she moved from one wing to another with it. I don't think there's anything explosive in it, otherwise it would have went boom already."

"Nice."

Dante shrugged. "Here."

John took the knife his uncle offered. "Thanks."

"Open it from the back end, just in case."

He did just that.

Papers and photographs spilled out.

John's throat closed up at the images staring back at him, and the information now freely available to anyone with the right contacts, and deep enough pockets.

Information about him.

His disorder. On record admissions to a mental facility. Somehow, a fucking patient record. Photographs of him on the grounds of the facility.

It was everything that stabbed John right to his core.

Everything he didn't want people to know.

His one weak spot.

Crazy.

The word was scrawled across several photos.

Disgrace.

Another word written in thick, red ink.

Why was he so calm all of the sudden?

It wasn't even the calm that scared him.

No, it was the darkness seeping into his mind at seeing his disorder exposed and mocked like this. It was knowing his family would be ridiculed for the things he had done, and how they protected and shielded him.

How much more could they take?

Was he really worth this kind of shit?

"Who else do you think got a package like this?" John asked.

"Let's hope not very many," Dante replied.

John doubted that would be the case.

ELEVEN

Jason beat the sole of his shoe against the hallway floor with more force than was necessary to get his point across. Siena shot the enforcer a glare over her shoulder, but he only cocked an eyebrow back at her in silent response. He didn't move as she flipped through the keys on the ring to find the right one for her apartment door.

Asshole.

Apparently, she was taking too much time unlocking her door. The same way she took too much time to get into a car, or cross the goddamn street. Or getting to and from places. Even eating in front of a window took too much time.

Anything.

She just took too much time lately. According to Jason, anyway.

Siena knew what the issue really was. Nobody in the Calabrese family felt safe ever since their attack on the Marcellos the week before. And rightfully so, likely. Siena only heard about the attack because the shooting was on the news, and the anchors had named names regarding the *victims* involved.

She wasn't exactly sure John would appreciate his father and him being called victims and then criminals in the same goddamn sentence. Just the victim portrayal would be enough to piss him off.

Nonetheless, no one in the Calabrese family felt very safe at the moment. They were back to violence and bloodshed by Darren's command, and yet, the Marcellos had yet to respond to this latest attack.

Everybody was on edge. What would they do? Who would it be?

How? When?

Siena was often shuffled from place to place before she could even sit down and think about where she currently was. She might spend a half of a day in one place to work, and then be moved to another place before she could even finish.

She wasn't allowed to stay out very long in public, and heaven forbid she stop on the side of the street. Her enforcer was closer than ever, including driving her all over the place because she couldn't even use her car.

It was stifling. Suffocating. She was *dying*.

Finally, Siena got her door unlocked, and pushed it open. Turning as she entered the place, she gave Jason a wave and said, "See, there, all safe. Bye."

The guy opened his mouth. Siena closed the door in his face.

It wasn't like the guy would run to Darren and tell on her for misbehaving, or anything. Darren was too caught up in his own bullshit to care very much about Siena at the moment. It was a blessing in disguise, really.

Opening up her door not long after she closed it, she peeked down the hallway to find that Jason was just closing his apartment door. The slam echoed.

Siena smiled.

Quietly, she shut her door again, and headed through her small apartment. Another benefit of Darren being caught up in Kev's murder, and trying to plan for the next attack from the Marcellos was that he had yet to move Siena from her

310

place. Shit, maybe he even forgot that it had been him who was so outspoken about letting her move back.

Who knew? Who cared? Not her.

All that mattered was she was still in her place, and that gave her a little bit of freedom to move. At least, where John was concerned.

In her bedroom, she bent down and pulled out a shoebox from under the bed. Flipping off the top, she dug through some magazines to find the item hidden beneath. She dug out the burner cell phone John had provided, and turned the home screen on. Instantly, her heart dropped.

There was no messages. No missed calls. Nothing.

Today marked one entire week since John had contacted her. The last time had been the morning of the shooting—he mentioned he would be going to his therapist's, and if he could, would call her that night.

He hadn't called. Not then. Not since.

Siena was started to get worried. It wasn't like John to break his word, and after everything that was going on between their families and on the streets, she really needed him to check in with her.

She needed to know he was okay. Something. *Anything.*

Was there a reason he went off the radar?

Siena didn't know that, either. The last time she had spoken to Andino was weeks ago, as it seemed he no longer needed information from her, or rather, knew she would pass it through Johnathan, anyway. She didn't know if she could get any information from him about John, either.

She dialed John's number, and put the phone to her ear. It rang and rang, but no one picked up. She tried again, and then again. She sent a text message, and waited five minutes to see if she would get a response.

Nothing.

Her worry picked up a notch. Her anxiety thrummed deep.

Siena glanced out her bedroom window to find the sun was still high, and bright. It wasn't even supper time, but Darren didn't want her out in public too much. Someone might come after her, apparently.

She didn't think anyone was coming for her.

Siena knew better … It was a huge risk.

She shouldn't leave when it wasn't even dark. Someone might see her, or follow her. It was a dumb move to make, and yet, her heart screamed louder than the warning bells ringing over and over again in her head.

Still, she sent one last text to John letting him know she was coming over, and to expect her. She kept an eye out when she left her apartment building and hailed a cab. She glanced up and watched the windows of Jason's apartment, but never saw a single curtain move as she left the place. It all seemed good.

She thought she was in the clear. She didn't see anybody …

But that didn't mean nobody saw her.

"Your front door is unlocked."

John didn't look up from the things he had spread out on his bed. "You said you were coming over. I left it open for you when I got home."

"You couldn't call me back? Send a text?"

"No."

That was all he offered.

No.

Siena could see in the way John's gaze narrowed as he fingered the edge of a piece of paper that something was weighing on him. On his mind, likely. Maybe it was the slope of his shoulders, too, or how he wouldn't look at her.

She came a little closer.

"What's all this?"

It looked as though he had dumped out a bubble mailer if the empty package tossed to the pillow was any indication.

"My latest surprise," he said dryly.

"What?"

John looked up from the stuff on the bed.

Pain stared back at her.

"I keep getting these—this shit," he said, waving at the papers on the bed. "It's like they want to remind me how easy it is to dredge shit up from my past. It feels like they're telling me they can put my life and business on display. I don't know how they keep finding this shit, Siena."

She grabbed a document on the bed, and looked it over.

A police report, it seemed.

A sixteen year old Johnathan Marcello had stolen a neighbor's car, and crashed it on the interstate. He tested positive for two different kinds of drugs, and had a blood alcohol level slightly over the limit.

Holy shit.

Siena understood that this event that had been documented in John's life— when he was younger, of course—was shortly before the time his bipolar disorder had finally been properly diagnosed. It was likely one of the many manic episodes that had led up to the final diagnosis.

"This accident was brushed under the rug," John said, taking the paper from Siena. "Or it was supposed to be. My family paid people off—got serious about trying to figure out what in the hell was going on with me, then."

"What happened to the case and file?"

John shrugged. "Should have been destroyed. Some went on record—few hours of probation, some fines. I once spent sixty days in a juvenile detention center for other shit. Of course, none of them ever actually had my disorder on record. That was all before I got diagnosed, and then even after, we were careful about keeping it off record when shit went down."

He gestured behind him to other opened bubble mailers on the floor.

"What is this?"

"Me," John said. "Me and bipolar."

Siena blinked, and then looked at John. "Someone is sending you these?"

He nodded. "Every day, usually. I come home, and one is on my doorstep. I come out of a place, and one is stuffed under the wiper of my car. I'm not the only one to get a package, either. Some of my people—my family, too. Associates of mine."

"John—"

"It makes people look at me differently, and that irritates me like nothing fucking else. Like I might blow up, or freak out. They don't trust me, or something."

"Or is that just how it makes you feel to have other people know," she said. Siena didn't even pose it as a question.

John didn't respond.

She figured it was probably a bit of both, really.

"They're fucking with me, and I don't like it."

"Darren's people?" she asked.

She didn't really need to ask.

She already *knew*.

John looked up from the stuff on his bed, and finally met her gaze. She didn't like what stared back, or how distant he seemed. She knew that John didn't rapid cycle from high to lows all the time, but things could tip him one way or the other.

High, or low.

Good, or not.

Manic, settled, or depressed.

She wondered how low he was right then.

How low did he feel?

How dark was he in his mind?

"None of this is important," she told him, grabbing one of the papers, and shaking it hard. "Not to you, or your family. You know it isn't important. None of this has ever made any difference to them, John."

She tossed the paper away, grabbed another, and then did the same thing. She continued until all the crap was gone from the bed.

John never moved, or said a word.

Siena felt marginally better, but she doubted John did. "I'm worried about you, John."

"I'm sorry I didn't call."

"You haven't called in a *week*."

"It's nonstop lately."

"What is?"

"This," he said, waving at the mailers, "and this."

He pointed to his head.

"So *call me*," she said.

"I'm trying to handle it, Siena."

"Alone?"

"There's enough going on without me—"

Siena heard enough. She moved around the corner of the bed, and stepped in front of John. She put her body between him and the bed to make him look away from the spot that had been filled with things he likely regretted, and events that made him ashamed.

She knew what he had been doing.

Going over everything.

Reliving mistakes.

Wishing for different things.

Eating guilt like a second meal.

Fuck all that noise.

Siena reached up and cupped John's face. His hazel eyes locked on hers, and for a second, that darkness dimming his gaze disappeared. He focused on her, and nothing else seemed to matter to him.

She wished she could be here more.

Give him more.

Do more.

"Stop giving my brother and his people what they want by getting messed up over all of this," she said quietly. "You know that's their goal—don't do it, John. Nothing else matters but right here, and right now. Everybody else around you is going to tell you the same thing. You have too many other things to worry about right now."

He couldn't be off his game.

Not now.

The risk was too high.

She wondered if anybody else had told him that.

Did anyone else even know his state of mind?

John's fingers circled around Siena's wrists, held tight, and then he kissed her. A soft, quick kiss that didn't stay long, and yet still lingered once his lips were gone from hers. He gave her a crooked smile, and she gave him one back.

"Thank you," he said in a rough murmur.

He never needed to thank her.

Not for loving him.

"Don't worry me again."

He nodded. "I was just going to jump in the shower, and got distracted. I was out for a jog before I came home."

"To another mailer?"

"Yeah."

Fuck Darren.

"Go have your shower," Siena said. "I'll still be here."

"Better be."

John let her go, and Siena tried not to show how the loss of him made her heart heavy all over again. She watched over her shoulder as he disappeared into the connecting bathroom. She took a seat on the edge of the bed as the shower turned on, and eyed the mailers on the floor.

Her anger grew.

She wanted to kill Darren, too.

How much longer was this going to last?

The silence echoed from the bathroom. Siena looked over her shoulder to see the curve of John's naked back, but he wasn't moving. The shower continued raining on, and while he was naked, he didn't make a move to get in the water.

She was inside the bathroom before she had even really thought about it. John stayed stone still as she slipped in behind him, and let her hands travel over his naked back. A soft, light touch that eased some of the tension in his muscles.

"It'll pass," he murmured.

His mood.

This nonsense.

Everything.

Siena nodded, and pressed a kiss to the spot between his shoulder blades. "It'll pass, John."

"You probably shouldn't have come over here today."

"Probably not. I needed to see you, though."

"Worrying you, huh?"

"Yeah."

"Sorry, *mia cara bella*."

Siena smiled, and pressed her forehead to his warm back. His muscles jumped from her touch that time. "I always have you on the back of my mind, John."

"Always have my back, too, huh?"

"Forever."

"*Sempre.*"

And always.

John stepped into the walk-in shower, and Siena decided she didn't like him being that far away in those moments. She wanted to be close to him for as long as she could. Quickly, she shed her dress, and undergarments. Stepping into the shower, she found herself tugged into John, and then his arms wrapped around her.

Water pounded down.

Steam wrapped around them.

The world stopped.

That was just fine, too.

It took only an innocent kiss to her forehead that led to another kiss on her lips which started an entirely different fire. One that stroked her from the inside out, the same way his fingers felt stroking her pussy when they slipped between her thighs.

Before she even knew what had happened, Siena was backed against the shower wall, and lifted from the floor. Cold tiles met her back, but she barely felt it at all. She was too focused on the way John's mouth felt slipping down her throat. The way his tongue lapped at her skin, and his breath came out harder when his cock rubbed against her center.

One of his hands tangled into her hair, while his other kept her held up under the curve of her ass. His fingertips dug into her skin in the best way—a shock of pain that swam through her blood, but only made her want more.

"Love me, *love me*."

It was as good as *please, please* to him.

She didn't need to say more, or ask for anything else. It was only a quick shift of his hips, and her hand sliding between their bodies to line his cock up with her center. She took in one good breath before his cock filled her full.

She needed that breath.

He took the rest while he fucked her.

John kissed her again, then. All tongue and teeth warring. A hard kiss that left her lips numb, and her tongue tingling. She found he kissed the same way he fucked.

Deep and fast.

Unforgiving, and passionate.

A sweet dance she had come to crave.

Constantly.

John buried his face into her neck, and his teeth left marks behind on her pulse point. Each thrust of his cock brought her a little bit closer to the edge. Every time he withdrew, his length dragged across every single one of her most sensitive spots. Her heels dug into his back while her words urged him on, whispered fast and low into his hair.

There, there ... almost there.

"Come on, give it to me, love," she heard him grunt against her neck.

His fingers dug deeper.

Her nails drew lines across his shoulders.

The orgasm came on swift, and left her a mess in his arms. John didn't seem to mind. It was only then that his pace slowed, and he went back to kissing her. Her mouth, cheeks, the tip of her nose, and down over her jaw. His thrusts came at a leisurely pace. He took his time getting himself to where he wanted, and Siena didn't mind at all.

She wanted to do this for the rest of her life with him.

Calm him.

Love him.

Have him.

Someday, someday ... someday.

Her mind chanted it.

Someday soon.

He would be all hers, then.

John came with a shaky exhale, and his eyes locked on hers. His thumbs trembled when he stroked them over her jaw, and then her lips.

One softer kiss to her lips ...

A quiet, "I love you, my girl."

And then the phone rang.

Reality was always waiting to call them home.

He would be so angry with you for this.

Siena's inner voice taunted her, but she pushed it aside to deal with her current task. There would come a day in their life when she would no longer have to do something like this. There would come a day when John would have her every single day—he could come to her, and never have to worry about needing someone else to have his back like she did.

That's what she kept telling herself, anyway.

It made this easier.

She had almost talked herself out of it, but ended up just doing it. Dialing a familiar number before she could think twice, she put the phone to her ear, and waited the ringing out.

One ring. Two. Three.

She thought it might go to voicemail.

Thankfully, it didn't.

"*Ciao.*"

The Italian greeting almost made her smile.

"Lucian?"

A beat of silence passed before John's father asked, "Siena?"

"One and only."

Her joke fell flat, but she figured that. Sometimes, shitty humor was the only way she knew how to deal with things that stressed her out.

She had way too much stress lately.

"New number?" Lucian asked.

She laughed. "A burner from John, actually."

"Ah, I see."

Siena wasn't exactly surprised that Lucian didn't quite know what to make of her call. Sure, she had been given his number from Andino in case she needed another way to get ahold of him while John was in the facility. Lucian had periodically got messages through to her about John while he was away, too.

Still, their conversations were short, and to the point. He wasn't, however, rude to her or anything. Always respectful, and kind, but never personal. Siena kind of got the feeling that was just how Lucian approached people, and how he handled them.

She didn't take it personally.

"What can I do for you?" Lucian asked.

"Check on John for me, that would be great."

She didn't mention that she was at John's place, or that he had taken off shortly after she arrived because someone called him away.

"Why do you need me to do that?"

"He hasn't called in a while."

Not a lie.

"Oh?" Lucian asked.

"Usually, he calls every day."

"He's been a little off lately," Lucian said.

Good.

Someone had noticed it. Someone was taking note. Someone could help.

Siena wasn't entirely comfortable with outing John's business to anyone, even if it was his father. That's why she chose to hold off on telling Lucian that she suspected John was in a rough place because she *saw* him in a rough place.

John wouldn't want her bringing that up, either. His lines in the sand about his disorder, and how he wanted to handle it with those close to him were clearly drawn. Siena was not about to cross one of those lines.

Still …

She had to do something.

John needed *something*.

This was the best she could do—a call, a suggestion, and a simple request. No information, and no personal details that crossed a line. John would get someone to check in, and talk to him more than he had talked to her.

It was the best she could do. It was all she could do right then.

Siena hated that.

"He's keeping up with everything, right?" she asked.

Her unspoken question hung heavily between them.

His meds? His therapy? Everything else?

Lucian seemed to understand what she didn't say. "He is."

"I hear a *but* in there."

"But," Lucian said, chuckling dryly, "he got some unsettling things thrown his way lately. I don't think he handled it well. That's to be expected."

Siena's gaze drifted to the packages in the corner. It looked like John had gotten more than *one* unsettling thing thrown his way, actually.

Did Lucian know about those?

She hated her brother for doing that to John. She had made a promise months ago that no one would ever use John's own mind against him again, and yet, here they were.

It was happening.

Again.

"Could you check in on him for me?" she asked. "Just don't mention I asked. I know everything is all over the place lately—I need to know he's okay, that's all."

John loved his family. Siena saw in his expressions when he spoke about them, and heard it in his voice when one of their names were brought up. John was careful in the way he talked about others, sure, but he couldn't hide anything from Siena.

He loved his family so much.

"I will," Lucian promised. "I was going that way tomorrow."

"Great. Thanks."

"Be safe, Siena. This war is almost over."

"I'm trying."

"That's all we can ask."

Lucian said a quick goodbye, and then hung up the phone.

Siena pulled a pad and pen from the nightstand next to John's side of the bed. She scribbled a quick note for John as she looked around his empty bedroom.

Call me. Love you. —S.

She had thought to stay and wait for him. Maybe he would get back before she had to leave again, but that didn't seem to be the case. She needed to get back home just in case someone dropped by, or shit, Darren decided to call her away from her place.

She couldn't afford to be caught stepping out of line right now. Who fucking knew what Darren would do?

Her heart felt heavy as she slipped out of the room, and headed down the stairs, and left his house. She still kept an eye out for someone she might recognize.

Nothing seemed out of place.

That didn't mean it was safe.

TWELVE

John stepped out of his car, and tightened the neck of his leather jacket to keep the cool mid-September air away from his body. Only part of his mind was on the warehouse in front of him. The other part was back with Siena where he had left her at his place.

He figured by the time he got back, she wasn't even going to be there. She mentioned she would need to leave as to not be noticed missing.

It sucked.

It was their relationship in a nutshell.

Fuck.

She didn't know it, but she had helped him more than he could explain just by showing up to his place. Over the last little while, his mind had disintegrated into darker thoughts and places. It was a dangerous game for him to play because it meant nothing good was to come.

Depression was a bitch.

It could claw its way into John's mind and life before he even realized the whore was there. And once she was in, she didn't let go.

Siena's presence was enough to filter through all the noise swimming in his mind, and the darkness thickening his blood. There was something about that woman keeping him from getting too deep into a headspace that he wouldn't be able to get out of.

She fought for him.

She loved him.

She had his back.

What more could he want?

What more did he need?

Her.

He needed her.

Forever. To wake up to her every morning, and keep her close at night. He wanted her laughter filling up their house, and her warmth in his bed.

He didn't want an hour here and there when it could be fit in when someone wasn't looking. He didn't want to sneak in and out of her life. He didn't want it like this.

And yet, this was all he had.

John needed to take what he could get.

For now.

John tightened his jacket more, and jogged toward the warehouse. A white car drove by, but because of the speed and the clear windows, he didn't think much of it as he crossed the street. Inside the warehouse, he found one of the Marcello Capo's crews hard at work.

None of the fourteen guys noticed John step into the place. They were too busy taking apart what seemed to be a truck of electronics. Flat screen televisions, mostly, but some other high value shit, too. It would sell damn well on the streets—a sort of gray market for stolen goods, and a fast way to get rid of hot items.

The guys worked quickly to unload the truck, separate the goods, and destroy anything that might be trackable. They worked as a team, which was a sign of a good crew, and a nod to the Capo that ran them, too.

Speaking of the Capo …

John bypassed the working guys, and headed to the side of the warehouse. He moved up the metal spiral staircase, taking them two at a time. He didn't bother to knock on the office door upstairs—the only room up there—as the Capo who had called him earlier left it open.

"Marky," John greeted.

The man—who would usually be working behind his desk—was pacing from one side of his office, to the other side. He passed John a quick glance, and a nod but continued his pacing.

"You said something was up?"

Marky nodded. "I got a call—friend of a friend down in Brooklyn."

"All right. What about?"

"Supposedly, my associate overheard some talk. Apparently, the guys are in with the Calabrese people. Not deep involved, mind you."

"Not made, you mean."

"Yeah."

"Go on."

"He said they mentioned a new job. Burning some warehouses. One mentioned was one down this way. The only one down this way is mine, John."

Shit.

"Going back to that again?"

Marky shrugged. "It's concerning. Listen, we've gone through this nonsense with them—burning shit, and shooting up whatever they can. I can't afford to lose another business because of the goddamn Calabrese family."

"Don't blame you."

Their Capos were hemorrhaging money at the moment with all their losses. It didn't have to be the loss of life. The loss of a safe business, or place to do business, was just as bad in the grand scheme of things.

"I figured you're in close with Andino and Dante, and neither of them are very easy to reach at the moment."

"Truth. You know how the boss is, though. Dante has Giovanni for shit on the streets, and messages get relayed back depending on importance."

"Exactly, but this might not be considered important. It's only *talk*, John. My friend didn't even know the name of the guys, and shit, he was in the back of a strip club throwing dollar bills at a girl shaking her ass in front of him. It's not someone's solid word. I can't take that kind of shit to the boss, his underboss, or his consigliere. He doesn't like—"

"To have his time wasted, yeah. I got it."

John glanced around, and back at the opened door. He could still hear the men working away downstairs. Some of their murmurings and laughter climbed up high to reach them in the office.

"Do you think it's a smart idea to have your guys working in a warehouse at the moment, considering?" John asked.

"I don't have much of a choice, unless you could help me along there until this shit blows over."

"How so?"

"Like I said, you're in close with the boss, and Andino. I mean, sometimes it's Andino running the show, and sometimes it's Dante. Whoever makes the calls, I guess. Point is, if they want me to keep bringing in money and *safely,* I need a place to do that."

"I can try to work—"

John's words cut off at the scent of something reaching the doorway behind him. A strong smell that burned his nostrils with every sniff. An unmistakable smell. He sniffed again, and then took a step closer to the doorway.

What the fuck?

"John?"

"You don't have gas or anything in the warehouse, do you?"

"A tank in the back—the guys use it to fill up every once in a while. I keep it full for them to make sure they have gas if they're running low on cash, or whatever."

"A tank."

"Yeah, an above ground one."

Shit.

The smell was stronger, now. John left the office altogether, and leaned over the banister. He could see the guys of Marky's crew were hard at work, and seemingly oblivious to the fact something bad was going down.

"Bay doors at the back of the warehouse?" John asked over his shoulder.

"Yeah, why?"

"Get all these guys out," John said. "Now."

"What, wh—"

John shouted down to the guys working. "Get out of the warehouse! Go through the front, not the back! Get the fuck out now!"

Marky came out behind John just as the crackling started. The guys on the floor ran for the front, and John headed for the stairs. The smell of gas increased, and so did the smell of fire.

The tank in the back exploded just as John pushed Marky out the front door of the warehouse. The place was flattened by fire in less than five minutes.

It never stood a chance.

The fire department never even made it in time to try.

Beside him on the street, Marky watched as fire fighters shot their hoses at the smoldering pile of rubble. "That truck was a good hundred grand payout."

"Truck isn't worth the life of your crew."

"I won't have a crew if I can't keep them working, John," Marky muttered.

Shit.

Yeah.

"Let me call the boss," John said. "Enough is enough with this shit."

"About time someone else thinks so."

"Son."

John stiffened a bit at his father's voice traveling in from the front door. "In the kitchen."

Soon, Lucian's footsteps echoed closer until they stopped altogether. John continued on with his work.

"What are you doing here?"

"I wanted to stop by—check in. I can do that, can't I?"

"I suppose."

"Were you working last night?" Lucian asked.

John kept his back turned to his father as he finished dumping in bubble mailers and other shit into the garbage can. "Another attack."

Lucian sucked air though his teeth so hard, it whistled. "Shit."

"No one was hurt this time around."

"Small blessings."

If you wanted to call it that.

John turned to face his father, and found Lucian standing in the kitchen entryway. "I called Dante last night to let him know what happened before someone else did, and he directed me to Andino before I could even finish speaking."

"His right to do, I suppose."

"Andino told me not to counterattack."

Lucian didn't blink at that statement. "His right too, I guess."

And that was the whole fucking problem.

"Who is really the one running this family?"

"Pardon?" Lucian asked.

"Who is running the family? Andino, or Dante? Which one is it? Nobody seems to know right now, and that makes shit dangerous."

"Officially, it's Dante. Unofficially, it's Andino."

"Why doesn't everyone else understand that—*me*, for example?"

"They've made the choice to do it this way for their own reasons. I suppose to take other organizations by surprise when the time comes, but also, you know how this business and family goes, Johnathan."

Yeah.

"Don't question a boss."

"Exactly. There is method to their madness. You have to respect their right to make the final decision."

"The Calabrese tried to burn out one of our warehouses from the back last night. The Capo had a whole crew of guys working in there to get rid of a boosted truck full of electronics. The Capo never could have handled that situation by himself, and the crew probably would have been lost had I not smelled the fucking gasoline in time. The time for games is over—we need to start acting more than we have."

"We act when we need to," Lucian replied calmly. "Not every action a Marcello answers with is violent, or straightforward. That's where the Calabrese differ from us."

John was getting nowhere with this conversation, but he wasn't surprised. Everything his father was saying had been repeated to John for three decades—his entire life. He knew all of this was the truth, and yet, he was antsy and edgy.

Something needed to be done.

Soon.

"Shit, maybe ..."

"What?" Lucian asked quietly.

"Maybe a large part of my problem is that I'm just ... impatient," John muttered. "Tired of waiting for this to end. Tired of being fucked with all the time."

Lucian lifted a single brow. "Tired of being made to wait for her?"

That hit a nerve.

A good one—an honest one.

It still hit it.

John had never quite realized how well his father actually knew him, but the truth was, Lucian saw more things in John than he ever admitted out loud. Perhaps that was because his father loved him more than John understood, or even maybe Lucian just had a way about him that allowed him into other people's perspectives.

He really didn't know what it was.

"Siena is definitely a reason for my impatience," John admitted. "The longer I have to wait, the further away she seems."

"Good things come to those who learn how to first wait for them, John."

"Impart that wisdom on someone who gives a damn. At the moment, it isn't me."

Lucian chuckled. "So is the way of a Marcello man when it comes to his woman."

"Yeah, well ..."

The two remained quiet as John turned back to compact the evidence of his former misdeeds deeper into the garbage can. He didn't realize his father had come to stand beside him until Lucian's hand snaked into the trash bag, and pulled out one of the documents.

Lucian stayed deathly quiet as his gaze drifted over the crumpled documents, and took the words in. It was the record of an event he should recognize.

John, at newly turned seventeen, had taken off for a little over three days in a hypomanic episode, and damn near killed himself with liquor and pills while he chased a rush. It ended up being the first of many hospitalizations leading up to his first full blown manic episode, and final diagnosis.

It took all of John's willpower not to snatch the paper from his father, and shove it back where it belonged. In the goddamn garbage. He forced himself to remain still, and let his father take in the paper.

Lucian dropped it back down into the bag, and grabbed another. Then, another and another. He took his time reading each one until he seemed satisfied enough to know that everything in the bag was the same.

All about his son.

All about his disorder.

"What is all of this?" Lucian asked.

John stuffed his hands in his pockets. "Me."

Lucian gave him a look. "It is not *you*. It is moments in your life during darker times. Moments in which you were not entirely yourself. Moments when you still needed help you were not getting."

"Yeah, I know."

And he did know that now. But it took several fucking days looking at this shit for it to really sink in that all of this garbage meant nothing to John at the end of the day. These events in his life had passed long ago, and he no longer behaved this way.

"I thought there were only a few of these packages sent out to people you know," Lucian said quietly. "What did you do, go and collect every single one of them from everybody?"

John laughed.

Hard and bitter.

"No, these are all mine. All sent to me."

Lucian stilled, and his gaze darted to John. "Oh, I see."

"Another reason I am so impatient to get this over with when it comes to the Calabrese family," John muttered.

"You know," his father murmured, "growing up, everyone liked to tell me that my son was the wild one. He came from you, but he acts like a young Giovanni."

John chuckled, knowing some of the stunts his uncle had pulled growing up. Of course, Gio had not been bipolar, or anything of the sort, simply … a wild child, and far too free spirited for his own good, according to everyone.

"And then you got older," Lucian continued on, not letting John speak at all. "We learned you were not like Gio—you were you, and you had your own set of obstacles to overcome. Yet, you were so focused, John, even on your worst days, and in your darkest moments. You had a goal that never changed in your life, and I wasn't sure whether to be proud, or terrified because of it."

John knew exactly what his father meant. He was living that dream now. "Being a made man."

Lucian nodded. "I worried how *la famiglia* might treat you, considering everything. I worried that something would happen to forever brand you in Cosa Nostra. Once a man ruins himself in this life, he is done."

John cleared his throat. "I kind of did do that, though. The Andino episode years ago. Matteo a few months ago. No man in control of himself would—"

"Except none of those events have ever pushed you out of the family, or affected your ability to do exactly what you do best in this business. Men still want to work with you—you still make *money*. They still respect you, and hold a healthy amount of fear for you at the same time. You earned all of that and not in spite of your bipolar, but because of it, John."

Lucian clapped his son on the shoulder, adding, "Nothing the Calabrese fools might release about you or your history is a shock to anyone who knows you, or has watched you grow up, John. Old news, that's all. The men of our family may not speak about it at the dinner table, but they have seen enough and know enough, and yet, we are all still one."

True.

Sometimes, John needed things pointed out to him. It was easier for him to see the bigger picture when he had been focused on only one piece of it for too long.

"I misjudged our *la famiglia*," Lucian said. "And that was my fault. Don't make my mistakes, John. We may be bad men, but we are also good men, too."

"Yeah, I won't."

"Good," Lucian said, patting him on the shoulder once more. His father turned to head for the counter where the electric kettle sat waiting. "Coffee?"

"Sure. You know, that was my biggest fear growing up."

Lucian looked back at him. "What?"

"Being the shame or disgrace of this family. I figured, how far could I push, and how many people did I have to hurt before it was all over for me? I kept getting one more chance. No matter how far I alienated myself from everyone, I still had to be close enough to the edge of the family to see inside. I didn't feel right, otherwise."

"Of course you did. We just gave you time."

"You completely disregarded what I first said."

"No, I didn't," Lucian said, prepping a mug for instant coffee. "You're not a disgrace to this family. You could never be, John. That's it, that's all."

"I like how everything is black and white for you."

Lucian smirked over his shoulder. "Far from it—my life has been lived in shades of gray, son. Much like yours. Now, have a coffee. We have a meeting to get to."

"What meeting?"

"Andino called it. He's decided on a course of action."

"Finally."

Lucian gave him a look.

John shrugged. "I can't help how I feel. That's part of this whole being bipolar thing, all right. I feel what I feel, and I feel it much more than any of you ever do. I can't help it."

And right then, he was feeling really fucking irritated with his cousin.

"I know, but you can be quieter about it."

Fair enough.

John did not expect to see what he found waiting for him in his uncle's office. Instead of Dante sitting behind the desk—where the boss always sat when a meeting was held—it was only Andino.

His cousin waved a hand at the chair across from the desk, saying, "Sit, John."

John stayed standing. "Shouldn't Dante be here? His house, office, desk, and family."

Andino smirked a bit. "The pretenses about who is running this show is just about over. Are you going to sit, or not?"

"Made men should never appear level with their boss. Stand for respect, or sit when he's standing to allow his voice to carry. We all learned these things, Andi."

Andino nodded. "Except, you and I have always been on equal ground, cousin. Never one higher than the other."

"You are now."

"In appearance only." Andino pointed at the chair once more. "Sit."

John dropped his form into the chair, and only glanced back over his shoulder when the office door was closed behind him. "We're the only ones here for this, or what? Not a good sign for you, Andi."

Andino chuckled. "Keep poking my nerves, man."

"I kid."

"I know." Andino shrugged. "No one else is needed for this at the moment, John. You had some issues last night, huh?"

"Another burned warehouse."

Andino's expression turned pensive as he turned his head a bit to look out the window. "Shit, like we can fucking afford another loss like that."

"My thoughts, too."

Sighing, Andino looked back at John. "Unfortunately, I need you to stand down on all of this. Do not respond to that with another attack, just like we let the drive-by shooting on you and Lucian go unanswered, too."

Irritation simmered through John's blood.

"Seriously? What are you trying to—"

"The Calabrese need to believe we are subdued in every aspect, from business to family. By not answering them back, it will slow their violence. Give them the idea they have possibly strong-armed us into a corner. Regardless, it allows me to put feelers out, which I need at the moment. I have an end goal here, and I want to reach it soon."

Andino smiled coldly, "It's time to put the last part of this plan into motion, John. I can't afford for anything to ruin it. So, no attacks, no threats, no anything. I need quiet streets until I get the Calabrese into the position I want them in."

John tried to swallow down his rage, but it was damn hard.

If not downright impossible.

"And your goal is what?" he asked sharply. "To make the Marcellos look weak—incapable, easily manipulated, and broken by a few attacks? To let them think we've backed down, and that they've scared us?"

"Yes, that's exactly what I would like for them to assume."

Andino's admittance took John by surprise.

John straightened in his chair. "What kind of fucking boss does that make—"

"A very smart one," Andino replied. "A boss that they won't see coming, as they still don't know I am the boss. Think, John, they know I will be taking over, but not *when*. As of now, it is still assumed Dante is running the show. Perhaps Dante is too old—too tired—to keep up with this kind of nonsense. Consider *Dante* gives them a way out of this that would satisfy their need and want to have more control in New York."

Andino leaned forward, and steepled his fingers together. "Consider, cousin, that their greed and ignorance will put them in a position where they open up to us. Where we finally get our in to remove the issue entirely. Where they are the ones who are weak, manipulated, and *broken.*"

John took in Andino's words.

He liked them.

And he didn't like them at the same time.

"I knew this was your plan all along," John murmured. "To take over that family, I mean."

"Wrong. Oh, I do want to reorganize and make it a faction of the Marcello family, yes," Andino said, giving John a look from the side, "but I have no intention of absorbing it into this family. It was never ours to begin with. It belonged to someone else."

Andino gave John another pointed look. "It has *always* belonged to someone else. Aren't you ready to take back what was rightfully yours, John?"

A heavy realization fell on John.

A weight on his shoulders.

A birthright denied.

A promise …

For a long while, John and Andino only stared at one another. John decided to be the first one to speak between them.

"That's why you had me sit—why we are equal," John said quietly.

Andino nodded. "We have always been equal, cousin, and we always will be."

"You didn't think to let me in on this bright idea of yours, or what?"

"I needed to position myself where I could not be challenged," his cousin admitted, "and while this plan of mine is for you, it is also for me. I married a woman not up to the standards Cosa Nostra demands—I have effectively guaranteed the line of Marcello bosses will end with any sons I have, if I do. But there's always you."

Andino smirked, tipping his head in John's direction, "There is always you in one of the Commission seats who will not deny my position, or my wife. There is Cross Donati as another boss—we know he'll marry one of our cousins—and because of that, will be unwilling to start a war for the sake of his own family. And there is Chicago—too far away, and too caught up in controlling their own city to worry about us. Vegas, too, but my uncle still runs that syndicate, so I felt comfortable enough to push that line there, too."

"But had the Calabrese been sitting in that seat …"

John let his words trail off.

Andino cleared his throat, and sat back in the chair. "It would have been an opening for them. A weak spot in the Marcello chain to pick at until it broke. I love Haven—I wasn't giving her up for anything, or anybody. Not this life of ours, and not this family. You understand, don't you?"

John thought about Siena.

He thought about her.

About *them.*

"Yeah, I understand."

Andino smiled, although fainter than before. "Then let's finish this."

THIRTEEN

Siena didn't start in fear when someone crawled into bed with her before the sun had even properly come up in the sky. She didn't have to be scared when she knew who it was without even opening her eyes. His presence was like a tangible aura to her. Something that sunk deep into her senses, and made itself at home there.

She felt him.

Smelled him.

Loved him.

"Go back to sleep," she heard John murmur.

Siena reached for him the second John was close enough to grab, but he seemed to have other plans. His arms tangled around her—like strong, steel bars keeping her close to him, protected, and hidden from the world. He dragged her closer in the bed, tucked her head under his chin, and refused to let go.

Siena could have fallen back to sleep like that. It would have been easy given how comfortable and tired she was. Instead, she dared to tip her head back on the pillow, and look up at him. Dark hazel stared back—familiar eyes that hid so much from the world, but showcased nothing more than a beautiful soul to her.

She was happy to see he looked better than the last time they were together. Less darkness in his eyes, and fewer lines of worry and anxiety on his face. His voice hadn't held that same low, unsure quality as it had before, telling her that his mind was likely in a far better space than before.

It helped *her* anxiety that hadn't left since she took off from his place to know that he was doing better. She didn't need to know the reasons why, or what pushed him back in the other direction. Just knowing he was there was more than enough for her.

Ten days ago.

Yeah, Siena was keeping count, now. It was yet another way she had found to get through her days without John, and the time in between seeing him again. Marking off days in her mind was like a challenge of sorts—could they see each other sooner this time around than the last time?

Silly, sure.

It kept her going.

"When did you get here?" she asked.

Siena had the slightest feeling he had been there for longer than it took him to wake her up, and crawl into her bed.

"Long enough to make a coffee, and take my meds," he said. "It's four in the morning—go back to sleep, *amore.*"

"Did you pick the lock again?"

Because he hadn't changed it like he said he would. This was the first time he had actually gotten back to her apartment since that first time after he got out of the facility. Things were always getting in the damn way.

So was their life.

"Yes," he said, "and I came in the back way with the extra building key you gave me. Now, stop talking, and go to sleep."

"But when I wake up, you're going to have to go."

"Sleep," he said again. "I'll be here."

Surrounded by John, his warmth, darkness, and soft sheets, Siena really didn't need to be told again. John's fingers stroked a gentle path up and down her naked spine, which was enough to make her close her eyes. The sensation sent her off to dreamland in seconds.

John's voice followed right behind. "I'll be here."

The next time Siena woke up, sunlight had filtered through the bedroom through the break in the curtains. Warm rays streaked lines over her naked back, and dust particles danced in the stream of light; her gaze followed the amusing sight.

"I need to dust," she said.

The form she was resting on started to chuckle. The sound rocked them both on the bed, and made her smile even wider.

"Did you pull me onto you, or did I climb on?" Siena asked.

"A little bit of both," John replied in a murmur.

"Huh."

"And you do need to dust."

Siena laughed, and tipped her head back to stare at John. He had sat higher on her bed to rest his back against the headboard. He looked entirely relaxed sitting there watching her—like this was the one place he was meant to be, and the only place he wanted to be.

Siena supposed it was.

Or she hoped it was.

And maybe, had the circumstances been different in their lives, they could have already been well into the start of their own life.

Together.

She pushed those sad thoughts away. It wasn't the time for them, and it wouldn't do her any good. Besides, she had John with her right now, and that was all that mattered to her. It was all she needed to make her whole day brighter.

"I've been busy," she admitted, "and for the record, I didn't even live here for *months*. Nobody lived here. I only got to come here once in a while if I needed to grab something specific, and I wasn't allowed to stay. Kev and Darren didn't want me getting any ideas about coming back to my apartment, you know."

John's gaze hardened momentarily—it always did that whenever she brought up how controlled her life was—but he still managed to offer her a smile. It didn't reach his eyes, but he tried. "I guess you can be excused, then."

"Geeze, thanks."

His hands squeezed her ass firmly. The action made Siena laugh.

She pushed up higher on her knees, and crawled up John's body where she stopped just a breath away from his lips. His gaze zoned in on her mouth, and his pupils dilated as he watched her lips curve into a grin. His tongue peeked out to wet the seam of his lips.

Then, the corner of his mouth quirked up in a half-assed smirk that instantly made her wet between her thighs. She found herself wondering what she might have to do to get him to put that tongue of his to work on her pussy.

Yeah, she went to that dirty place fast. All because of him, too. He didn't have to even try. He barely did a thing!

Goddamn.

This man was terribly sexy.

More than he could possibly know.

"Are you going to kiss me good morning, or what?" John asked.

Siena's gaze drifted to the clock on the nightstand. A time flashed back at her, and made her frown. Like she thought when he first woke her up, they wouldn't have very much time together. Life would come along to separate them all too soon.

"As long as that's all we do."

John's fingers dug into her backside even harder than before, and he grinded her lower half against his. He didn't even try to stifle the groan of her name. "That's unfair, and you give me more credit for my control than I actually have."

Siena laughed, and then pressed a fast kiss to John's lips. Her innocent gesture soon turned into something much hotter. Heated coals coaxed into a raging flame with every graze of their lips, and tease of his tongue. She loved the way he urged her to kiss him deeper with flicks of his tongue against hers, and then the way he bit her bottom lip just hard enough to take her breath away.

She found herself rolled over on the bed in a single breath, and John hovered above her. The hard lines of his body were like a canvas of art for her—unblemished and mostly unmarked. She could stare at him all day, and never be bored.

His fingers tangled with hers, and pressed them into the pillow above her head. He fit perfectly between her widened thighs, and she could feel his erection growing harder against her naked thigh with every shift of their bodies.

John dropped a kiss to her nose.

One to each eyelid.

A path across her jaw.

Dotted kisses to her cheeks.

It was so sweet, that all she could do was smile when he finally came back to her lips. For the moment, the two could pretend like a war wasn't raging outside their small bubble. That nothing was wrong in their life.

They could be *normal*.

"I missed you," he said quietly.

His words grazed her lips like his kiss had. A soft-spoken promise that only brushed along her surface, but somehow managed to reach deep into her heart, and grab tight. An assurance that would never let her go.

She couldn't let it go.

"I missed you, too," she said.

John grinned. "I figured I had the chance to come over, so I might as well take it."

"Not complaining."

"Didn't think you would."

All over again, she was struck by how at ease John seemed compared to the last time. "You look a lot better—headspace-wise, I mean."

"Do I?"

"Mmhmm."

John's lips curved a bit at the edges. "Choosing stability means being honest when I'm having trouble. Not to everyone, mind you. It's not about them—this is all about me, and my mental health."

"Absolutely."

"Leonard—the new therapist—dropped the mood stabilizer for a bit and changed it to an antidepressant until I level out again. Might take a couple weeks. Might be a month. All depends."

But ...

John had gone and done that.

Asked for something different.

Acknowledged something was offset.

Knew he needed a change.

It was *huge*.

"It's not a big deal," he said at the sight of her growing grin.

"You know it kind of is, John."

"It's a good thing, yes."

"That, too." Siena looked over at the clock again. "I've got a little while before Jason will be knocking on my door again."

John's happiness was soon gone with those words. "Mmm."

"Kev's funeral," she explained.

"Ah. Shame."

"It is. I would rather stay in bed than go and put on yet another farce for him, even if the bastard is dead."

John stilled and quieted as his gaze traveled over Siena. She could hear his silent questions without actually needing him to ask them. She could feel the unspoken words burning between the two of them.

They hadn't talked about what she did.

Not *really*.

Seemed that silence was over.

"You don't regret it at all, do you?" John asked.

Siena didn't flinch. "Not when it's for you—for us."

"He was still your—"

"Nothing. He meant nothing."

John cleared his throat. "Jesus, woman, don't be so cold. I don't like you cold."

Siena smiled, unable to stop herself. "Never cold to you, John."

"Better not be."

He let go of her hands, and Siena used that freedom to cup his jaw, and pull him in for another lingering, burning kiss. That flame he created was now a devastating inferno, ravaging her insides in the best way.

"Do you ever think about the future?" she asked.

John—so close she could see the flakes of gold in his hazel eyes—smiled. "I do when I feel like punishing myself. Nothing is ever really guaranteed, you know."

She did know.

"Doesn't matter to me," Siena told him. "I still think about it. I need to. It helps."

"What do you think about, then?"

"Us."

John's smile deepened. "Be specific."

"Everything. A wedding. I'd go for ivory, likely. In a church, maybe, but I wouldn't be offended if it wasn't, too. I wouldn't want to walk alone, though."

"No?"

"You could walk with me. Be different."

John laughed. "I would absolutely walk with you, *donna*. You never have to be alone."

"And I think about what comes after all of that, too. Life, kids—"

Siena's words trailed off when she felt John stiffen above her. She met his gaze, but could plainly see the way he tried to hide his discomfort.

"What?" she asked.

"Kids is kind of touchy topic for me," he said, shrugging.

John dropped to the bed beside her. He used a hand to rest his head on as he stared at her, waiting for a reply. Siena didn't really know *how* to reply.

"Why?"

"It isn't obvious?" he asked.

"No."

John waved a hand toward his own body. "This, Siena."

"I'm lost."

"I didn't wake up one day *with* bipolar—I didn't catch it like a sickness, babe. I've had it in my genetics from the day I was born, and puberty was the switch turning it on for me. There's no cure for it, either. You learn to manage it, and to stay at relatively stable levels that still fluctuate no matter what you do. There's a genetic component. Something in my DNA that was there from someone else in my family. Passed on, you know?"

"John—"

"Having kids means continuing this on—or possibly. You don't know for sure, right? My parents had four kids, and I was the one that found the barrel of the gun in the game of genetic roulette, so to speak. I'm not sure I want to do this to one of my kids. I know what it felt like to be confused for more than half my life, and to constantly feel like I was drowning."

"But there's nothing wrong with you."

John gave her a look.

Siena only gave it right back.

"Siena," he said, a little too patronizing for her liking. "I didn't say something was *wrong*. There is something different, though."

"You don't want kids at all?"

"I didn't say that."

"You're not saying differently, either."

John frowned, and scrubbed a hand down his jaw. Rolling to his back, he stared at the ceiling. "I never gave it a lot of thought—settled myself on the idea it just wasn't going to be something I moved forward with."

"See, that kind of sounds like a strong *no*."

He looked over at her. The intensity of his gaze made her still in place.

Siena still managed to speak. "This is a hard line for me, John. I want children. I have *always* wanted children."

He nodded. "I never did."

Ouch.

"Until this, and you," he added in a murmur.

Relief so sweet it was almost poisonous swept through Siena's insides. "Oh?"

"Mmm." John sighed, and went back to staring at the ceiling. "Like everything in my life, I can't go into something like that without planning for it. It's a huge change, and—"

"I get it."

Quickly, Siena crossed the space between them, and crawled back on top of him. She straddled his waist, tangled their fingers together, and looked down at him.

"But there isn't, by the way," she said.

John cocked a brow. "What?"

"Something wrong with you. There *isn't.*"

"It took me a long time to figure that out, though, Siena. I'm thirty-one now. I still wake up some mornings and think, *why can't my brain work like everybody else's?* I wonder why I have to struggle with emotions, and processing them, not to mention everything else that comes along with being bipolar. It took a long time to figure out nothing was wrong. It was hell."

"But you did. That's what matters most *today.*"

John didn't deny it.

Siena felt like that was a battle won for him.

Siena's attention drifted between her brother saying one last goodbye to the closed casket keeping Kev's body hidden from view, and the sunlight streaming in through the colorful stained glass windows. She should have been more present, or at least, made the effort to seem like she gave some kind of damn.

She couldn't do it.

At least, she had managed to put on a proper black dress, sweep her hair into a simple chignon, and brush her face with a bit of makeup. It wasn't the effort she would usually put into getting ready for church or a funeral, but it was the best she could do for today. Anything more, and it might seem like she cared.

She didn't.

Darren nodded to one of his men when the guy came closer. It seemed like her brother had more of those—men to do his bidding—than she cared to count, now. Unlike Kev who only worked with a couple of people, and kept Darren the closest, her other brother was entirely different. He kept many men at his side, and handed out orders like a tyrant who was unwilling to be questioned or challenged.

The change had happened instantly.

Practically overnight.

Siena supposed she now understood what her father had meant when he once told her that while many bosses came into the position by chance, far more bosses in this life were simply made that way. Men born to be in a position of power because they had the temperament, control, and mindset to do the job.

Her brother was not the man born to do the job, but rather, one who had come into the seat by chance, and was making the best of what he had to work with. Sometimes, it was a fascinating show to watch, and other times, it was incredibly disconcerting to Siena.

Darren was a chameleon—able to change the exterior he offered to someone depending on the situation at hand. He might not be a boss on the inside, but he was fully capable of presenting the image of a boss on the outside when he needed to.

Unlike John.

A man who Siena thought would suit a position like a boss's seat far better than Darren. John, who commanded attention without needing to change his image to suit the needs of others in order to make his position and demands clear.

John was who John was.

Darren, on the other hand, wasn't quite sure who he was at the moment, but rather, only knew who he needed to be.

"Get up."

Siena glanced over at her mother's sharp order. "What?"

Coraline waved at the aisle. "Come on, we have to follow behind the casket. Stop acting like a daydreaming, foolish girl, Siena."

Jesus.

She pushed out of the pew to quickly follow behind the casket carrying her brother. Darren was one of the pallbearers, along with a few other men he had chosen to do the job with him. She kept her head down as she walked toward the entrance of the church, entirely uninterested in meeting the gazes of those who had come to say goodbye to Kev. The scent of the priest's incense clung heavily all around them.

Almost over.

She would soon be able to take off her mask again.

Be *free* again.

Siena's mother slid in beside her as they continued their trek behind the casket and procession. Coraline's mask of grief was all but gone in that moment, and instead, a cold, expressionless, and unfeeling one took its place.

For a second, it took Siena by surprise.

Her mother didn't give her the time to question it before she started talking. And when she did talk, it scared Siena to death.

"You should have been more careful with your business," her mother murmured. "And by business, I mean Johnathan Marcello."

Siena swallowed hard, and looked forward. She kept her gaze locked on the back of the shined, gleaming black casket with its gold-plated bars and details. "I have no idea what you're—"

"Don't play stupid with me," Coraline hissed low. All the while, her mother's face remained impassive. Her voice stayed too low for someone else to overhear, and her expression gave nothing away as to their conversation. Siena could not say her face looked the same. "I will not allow you to ruin what your brother is working so hard for simply because you cannot control your stupid little *heart*."

Her mother said the word with so much disgust, that Siena flinched.

"You think this little issue with the Marcello and Calabrese families is *new*?" Coraline scoffed low, and shook her head subtly. "No, Siena, it is far from new. Years—*decades*—in the making, really. It started with your grandfather, and then was passed onto your father. He passed it onto your brothers, and finally ... Jesus, *finally*, we have the chance to finish this. To either take a controlling portion, or ruin the Marcello family for good. Except here you are, getting in the goddamn way with that man."

Coraline sneered, but quickly replaced it with a sad smile when she waved to someone who reached out to touch her arm as she passed. Out of the corner of her mouth, her mother said, "Darren has the Marcellos where he needs them to be— soft, and pliable. Backed into a corner, so to speak. I love you, Siena, and that is the only reason I was willing to turn my cheek about what I knew you were doing, but if you don't stop, I won't be able to pretend anymore."

Siena's throat tightened more.

Her mother nodded. "And you do know what your brother would do to Johnathan should he find out you have been entertaining the man behind his back, don't you? I am sure you would hate for your crazy boyfriend—if you could even call him that—to die because of your stupidity."

"Ma—"

"Shut up," Coraline hissed.

The two walked out into the sunlight, and quieted for the moment. Siena took the second she had where her mother wasn't talking to suck in a deep gulp of air. It felt like the breath had been ripped right out of her lungs, and her chest was crushed.

How did her mother know she was still with John?

How had she known *anything*?

Siena was careful—she had to be. She made sure not to leave anything lying around where someone could find it. She was back at her own place which meant she didn't have to worry about someone listening through the walls, or just outside the door.

She didn't take risks.

She didn't dare.

Except ...

She had.

Once, or twice.

Kev's casket was pushed into the back of the hearse by the pallbearers. The men all slapped the back of the casket with their palm—a final goodbye.

Siena's mother turned to her once more. "You are my daughter, Siena, and I do not want to see you become fodder to a man's games or plans. Play this right with me, and you could have far more than you ever dreamed of. Johnathan—is he *really* your highest bar to reach? He is what you really want? Why? You could have much more, darling."

She didn't reply.

Her mother apparently wasn't looking for one.

"The Marcellos have called a meeting with your brother. Darren expects it will either lead them into a peaceful resolution that puts the Calabrese higher, or it will dissolve into more violence that will lead them into a longer war. Either way, it will be happening soon. Should you do anything to cause your brother to call off that meeting—say, get caught with Johnathan—you will *not* like what I do."

It was always men who planned.

Men who played games.

Men who manipulated.

Siena learned in that moment that men often forgot women were the flies on the wall. Women were the ones who needed to be watched because they held more information than anyone possibly knew.

Women were the dangerous ones.

Women like her mother.

"How did you know?" Siena asked.

"About you and the Marcello man?"

Siena only nodded.

Coraline turned to face Siena with a cold smile. "I was coming to visit you a while back, but you rushed out of your place like a bat out of hell. Your enforcer didn't trail behind, so I thought I should. I saw where you went, and I saw you leave his place. I thought … maybe I should keep a closer eye on you. I am glad I did."

Fuck.

Nothing was ever safe.

Not in their life.

"You see," Coraline said, "your brothers are a lot like your father—or *was*, for Kev. They're stupid in the way they believe that their word is law, and because they have said it, us women will automatically follow it. I know better. Do you think I stumbled upon my marriage with your father because I loved him, and wanted to marry him?"

"I don't know why you married Daddy, no."

"Because I was told to, but not because I wanted to. I have learned over the years to make sure the men in my life take everything I give them at face value and never feel the need to dig deeper. I loved Matteo, I *did*—it took years, but I loved him. And I will not see everything he worked for ruined because one of his children cannot manage to step in line with the rest."

"I will stay in line, Ma."

Only long enough to watch the Marcellos ruin this family.

After that, it was fair game.

"You better, but should you think to do something to force my hand," her mother warned, "you will not like what I do. I will make my arranged marriage and carefully sheltered life look like a cake walk compared to your future after this, darling. I do not want to hurt you, but I absolutely will."

What could she possibly say to that? Nothing.

So she didn't.

Coraline moved down the stairs, calling over her shoulder, "Keep it in mind, Siena."

FOURTEEN

The conversation filtered down the main hall of the large Amityville home as John strolled through the front door, and closed it behind him softly. He took quiet strides, following the conversation until muffled voices were much clearer.

"It'll take time," he heard his mother say.

"That's what everyone keeps telling me," Cella muttered heavily.

"It's okay to not be okay, Cella."

"Is it? I think it's easier to pretend, Ma."

"But you *shouldn't*."

"Yeah, I know."

John used two knuckles to knock on the wall as he stood in the entryway to his mother's living room. He didn't want to interrupt the conversation happening in the room between his sister, and his mother.

At the same time, he also didn't want to be caught eavesdropping on a conversation he knew really wasn't any of his business. Cella would not like to think that John was stepping in on her personal shit—mostly *because* it was John.

"Hey," John said when the two women looked his way.

"*Mio ragazzo.*" Jordyn smiled. "Come in, John.

John took a step in the room as Cella cleared her throat, and dropped one of the items of clothing she had been folding back into the basket on the couch. She wouldn't meet his gaze, but he didn't take it personally.

"Cella," John greeted.

"John."

Well, his name was better than nothing, he supposed. It was more than he had been getting where his sister was concerned.

Jordyn didn't look all too surprised to see John standing there, but then again, she had known he was coming over. After all, he had sought out his mother's help to try and make some kind of amends with Cella over what happened to her husband.

Jordyn had been all too willing to play the go-between in that regard. She always disliked how John's sisters—mostly Liliana and Cella—were not willing to close some of the distance between them. John understood why, of course, given their history. It was not a good history shared between them. He was once known to burn bridges with harsh words.

Here he was trying to fix a bridge instead.

Funny how that worked.

Sure, William's death was not done by John's hand. It had not been him who pulled the trigger, and took the man away from his wife and child. Nonetheless, it had been—in a way—John's involvement and subsequent dealings with the Calabrese that started this feud between the two families.

So, maybe, it was his fault.

Shit.

He felt far too much guilt.

"John," his mother said, "I will go make you a coffee. Your father is upstairs having a nap, too. I'll let him know you're here."

Keeping a firm grip on the gift bag in his hand, John nodded to his mother and came closer to the couch. He didn't set the bag down, step in his sister's way, or even get in her personal space. John wasn't here to upset Cella in anyway, just ... try to apologize.

If he could.

If *she* would let him.

"Don't bother Dad," John told his mother. "Let him sleep. I bet his ribs are still sore."

"A little," Jordyn replied. "But he won't admit it."

John figured.

Lucian was too proud a man to tell someone he was in pain, or that someone had bested him in a way that kept him down for the count. That, and Marcello men just didn't talk about that kind of shit when it came to pain, or injuries. Weaknesses were not publically acknowledged as to not give someone a vulnerability to pick on.

So was their life.

So was their ways.

He gave Jordyn a quick kiss to her cheek, and let her pat the side of his face with her warm palm. He was trying to be more affectionate with his mother—affectionate gestures did not always come easy to John because a lot of the times, they just made him feel awkward and out of place.

This wasn't the same thing.

It was his mother.

He loved her.

He should show her.

"Thank you for trying," Jordyn murmured too low for Cella to hear. "Regardless of the rest, that *matters*, John."

He nodded once. "I know, Ma."

She patted his cheek once more, and then darted out of the living room. He knew she probably wouldn't come back, despite her declaring she was going to make him a coffee. He would likely have to go find her after this was all said and done.

"Do you have a minute?" John asked his sister.

Cella shrugged, and probably just to keep her hands busy, grabbed the item of clothing that she had previously discarded. A baby onesie. "I guess. What do you need?"

"Very little, actually."

"Not sure I'm the right one to help you then, John."

Probably not.

He was hoping to help her, maybe.

John eyed the baby onesie she folded with careful hands. "You're staying here, huh?"

Cella nodded. "It's easier. Ma helps me with Tiffany, and Daddy gives me someone to rage at when it's all ..."

"A little too much," John finished for her.

"Basically."

"Dad's good like that."

"He is," Cella agreed. "And besides, it's hard being home. Seeing things, and being around things. I cleared a bit out because someone said that might help—it fucking didn't."

"People don't know anything about this kind of grief, Cella. Nobody really knows what it's like to lose someone—your spouse, I mean. They're well-intentioned, but a lot of the shit they say still sucks. I know you probably don't want to hurt anybody's feelings, but you can tell them to stop when you need them to fuck off. It's okay to do that."

Tears gathered in his sister's eyes, but she kept her passive expression turned down on her work. "So I am learning."

"And I'm sorry."

Cella's hands froze in her work. "Pardon?"

John shrugged when she shot him a look. "You blame me for things, and I get it. I didn't pull the trigger, but I'm a catalyst in a way to William dying."

"Are you?"

"The Calabrese, and Siena. I know my place—I know my choices. I know what they did. You weren't wrong when you said what you said, but you said it in the wrong way at the time. You were angry, though, so I get it."

"Do you love her?"

"Siena?"

Cella shrugged one shoulder. "Daddy says you're still seeing her sometimes."

"It's complicated given the situation, but yeah, I love her."

"She seems nice."

"She is wonderful." John scrubbed a hand down his jaw, and decided to just get this over with. Say the hard shit—stuff he hadn't ever said to his sister, but she still deserved to hear all the same. "I've taken a lot from you—and Liliana, too—over the years. Safety in your own home. Peace and quiet. Possessions. I've said a lot of shit, and done a lot of shit when we were growing up. It should have been a good time in your life, but I turned it into chaos. I recognize that, Cella. I know I can't change it, but I am sorry."

A single tear made a traitorous line down Cella's cheek. She didn't try to wipe it away, or even acknowledge that it had escaped.

"I do love you, John," Cella whispered. "I just have to do it from afar."

"Yeah, I know. We all have to do what we have to do for ourselves, so don't think I expect anything more from you than what you're willing to give."

"Thanks."

John placed the large gift bag on the coffee table, and took a step back. White tissue paper overflowed from the top. "Ma helped a little bit. I hope it helps you, and the baby, too."

Cella glanced at the bag, and then back to John. "Nothing really helps, John."

"Yeah, I got that. I'm sorry, Cella."

"I know. I wish it helped."

John headed out of the room when Cella went back to folding clothes, but didn't touch the gift bag. He didn't want to push or pressure his sister for anything. She was going through enough shit as it was.

He found his mother in the kitchen. She already had a cup of coffee waiting for him, and a seat open at the table.

"How did it go?" Jordyn asked as he sat down.

"Uh, well, she didn't tell me to fuck off."

"That's good."

John smirked. "She didn't say much else, either."

"Did she like—"

"She didn't open it with me there," he interjected.

Jordyn nodded, and took a quick sip from her coffee. "Oh, I see."

"It's got to be at her speed, Ma. On her time."

"You're right, John." His mother reached out and cupped his cheek. "You're good that way, my boy."

Something like that.

He stayed with his mother until he finished his coffee, but quickly got up to leave once it was done. He had business to do, and Andino to meet.

Things on the Calabrese side of business were starting to move forward. John was anxious as fuck to put it all to rest.

"I'll see you later, Ma," John said, dropping a kiss to the top of her head. "Tell my father I'll call him."

"Don't forget."

"I won't."

A quick *I love you* to his mother later, and John headed for the front entrance of the house. He had to pass by the living room on his way to the front door. The sight of his sister sitting on the couch stopped him for a minute.

She was holding his gift—hugging it, actually.

And crying.

John had managed to get one of William's T-shirts from Jordyn when Cella cleaned out some things. A soft, cotton T-shirt with one of the man's favorite band logos on the front. He'd sent it to someone his mother suggested, who made it into a throw pillow, of sorts. Something for Cella to keep, or hug. Something for her daughter to have when all that was left would be pictures, and dusty knickknacks.

John had nothing else to offer.

He didn't have the right words.

He *did* hope it helped.

Even if just a little.

"John."

Andino greeted John with a hand already outstretched to take his. The two shook before Andino sat down at the table. John fixed the lapels of his Armani blazer before he too sat down.

Waving two fingers at his empty placement, he said to the passing waiter, "Water, but put ice in it."

Andino smirked. "Always making it look like vodka, huh?"

John shrugged. "Do what I got to do, man. I'm not late, am I?"

"Right on time, actually."

Andino didn't explain more, instead standing from his seat. John looked over his shoulder to see a familiar man walk through the front door of the restaurant. At the sight of a familiar District Attorney, John stood from his seat to greet the man, too.

It paid to know people.

It *really* paid to use people.

"I thought it was strange that you didn't want to do this meeting in your own business," John said under his breath.

Andino nodded. "You know how these button-up-types are."

"Yeah. Can't be seen in the place of a mobster."

"I hate that fucking title."

They all did.

People used *mobster* or *gangster* like they were slurs. Especially people who fancied themselves firmly on the right side of the law. They didn't truly appreciate what it meant to be a *Mafioso*, or how the mafia had come to be the rock-solid foundation it was today.

Not that any of them cared to explain.

It was what it was.

"Arthur Lorde," Andino greeted, holding out a hand to shake.

The D.A. gave the place a look as he shook Andino's hand. "Shit, Andi, you couldn't make an effort to get us a better table? One that might not be so goddamn close to the windows."

"Relax," John said, "we don't use this place, either."

Arthur didn't look entirely convinced, but he nodded nonetheless. John didn't offer his hand to shake, but that was mostly because Andino had been the one to call this meeting. It was his job, and his show. John was just there to take attendance, and know what the hell was going on plan-wise.

Because he didn't know shit.

Not at the moment.

Andino gestured at the table. "Sit, Arthur, and we'll chat."

Arthur glanced at his watch as he sat down. "I don't have a lot of time here, Andi. I am running shorter and shorter on time lately."

"This won't take long."

Once all the men were sitting at the table, the waiter came back. He had John's water with ice ready, and a glass of what looked to be whiskey for Arthur.

"Still your preferred drink, right?" Andino asked.

Arthur nodded. "It is when we do business. What do you need, Andino?"

"Always to the point."

"I have to be with you and your father."

"I need quiet streets," Andino said. "Peaceful business. Less attention from the media, and officials. I would like for the detectives to quit calling my lawyers five times a day trying to get me in for different interviews. Do you get what I am getting at?"

"Don't you think you and your father have called in enough favors with me?"

Andino smirked. "I mean, you call them favors, but we call it repaying a debt.

You know how this works Arthur."

The D.A.'s face reddened.

Andino nodded like he expected that. "Or blackmail. That works, too. You see, we would really hate for information to get out on that dog fighting ring you had going on. Dad keeps impeccable records when it comes to his people, though, so something could still accidentally slip out should it need to."

Arthur cleared his throat. "There's no need to go down that road, now."

"So you keep saying."

"Andino—"

"And yet you give me trouble every time I need something from you," Andino interjected with a calm, cold tenor.

It was almost amusing to John how his cousin often reminded him of their uncle, Dante, at times like this. Giovanni—Andino's father—could, of course, be cold and harsh when needed, but this was something altogether different.

This was a strange kind of detachment that Giovanni—no matter the situation he was put in—just could not achieve. He was like John in the way that he reacted based on emotions, and it was often that same thing that worked to his benefit when it came to making a point, or getting what he wanted.

The cold detachment, though?

That was Dante Marcello all over.

"Maybe that's because you need things from me far too often," Arthur responded heatedly.

Andino kept his demeanor, unruffled and unbothered. "And I will continue to need things from you until you are useless to me. At the moment, you are not useless. Maybe you should count that amongst your good traits because once someone becomes useless to me, you would not be pleased to find out how I dispose of them."

John smiled to himself.

This was amusing.

He was glad he showed up.

"Jesus Christ." Arthur took a long sip of his whiskey, and then set the glass down a little harder than was necessary to the table. "You're fucking relentless, Andino."

"I have to be in my business."

Arthur pointed a finger at Andino, and shook it. "I almost prefer to walk into a meeting, and see your father sitting in a chair rather than you."

"As you should. Giovanni has a far greater tolerance for nonsense than I do."

"What do you need?"

"I told you—less attention, and peaceful streets."

"I don't understand what exactly that means."

"It means," John said, stepping into the conversation just because he could, "that things will be heating up soon between the Marcello and Calabrese families. As it is, we already have enough attention on us because of their little tricks. You like a quiet city—you prefer we Marcellos keep our business clean, and out of sight. We are trying to do that, but they are making it very difficult."

"I don't see how I can help you with that problem."

Andino chuckled. "I just need your word, Arthur. Nothing more."

"My word for what, exactly?"

"When the time comes, you will make every effort to help the Marcellos go back to their previous position in this city. Business that does not make headlines every other day, and so forth. We will make the streets quiet again."

Arthur sighed heavily, and cleared his throat. "Tell me, then, how I am supposed to help your family go back to the edges of society with the rest of the—"

"Careful," John murmured.

The man passed John a look.

John smiled coldly in response.

"You have the floor," Arthur said to Andino.

"I want a guarantee of freedom," Andino said. "For my men, and me. Whatever we do to quiet the city again, and make the streets safe, we will do it. And in return for giving you a peaceful city, and you know, not exposing your dog fighting history to anyone with a screen in front of them, you will make sure any and all attention or charges from officials can be either put away, or disabused in whatever fashion necessary. Not enough evidence. Destroy statements. Burn a goddamn police station to the ground. I really don't care—you will make it happen."

"You are asking for a lot," Arthur said.

Andino nodded. "And you have a lot of contacts in this city to make it work."

"What exactly are you planning to do that you need this kind of guarantee, Andino?"

Andino looked to John.

John responded for his cousin. "Watch the news. You'll see."

Andino flashed his teeth in a wicked smile. "It'll be a blast."

The lead up to anything should always come with a palpable feeling. Be it dread, excitement, or something altogether different. It should make a man's heart race, and his palms sweaty with the knowledge that everything he wanted or waited for was finally there.

It was finally happening.

It should thrum through his veins, and beat with his heart. He should be left awake in the night from the anticipation of *almost, almost.*

And yet, the one moment John had waited for had finally arrived, and there he was, entirely calm. Eerily so, even. He felt nothing but a confident assuredness that this was everything he had wanted to see come to fruition, and it was almost over.

Maybe that was it.

Maybe once this was finally done with, he could get that rush of excitement and relief that he had been missing for so long. Maybe once all of the things that had been standing in his way were finally gone for good, he could celebrate.

John would just have to wait and see.

An enforcer stepped up to his door as John pulled his car to a stop at the curb. The man opened the driver's door, and waited for John to exit the vehicle. He handed the keys over, but gave the enforcer a severe look.

"Only move it a block," John said. "No more."

"You sure?"

"Just keep it out of the immediate zone. I need to drive home, but I don't want to walk a damn mile to get my car after this is over."

"All right."

John turned to find his cousin was also getting out of his car. Two Marcello Capos had also been invited to the meeting of the bosses. Andino allowed Darren Calabrese to pick the venue of the meeting because really, it wouldn't make a difference.

It was all going to end the same way.

"No one else is coming?" John asked as Andino approached.

"We don't need anyone else."

John nodded. "Your call."

"Soon to be yours, too."

"Don't get ahead of yourself."

Andino clapped John hard on the shoulder, and turned them both to face a rundown restaurant that looked as though it had been out of business for a while. "John, I already told you. There's a boss's seat waiting for you, and that's right where you're headed. There's no argument. It's already been done."

Well …

Almost.

"Hey," Andino snapped. "Be careful with that fucking thing, you foolish fucker."

The enforcer carrying a blue crystal vase full of colorful tiger lilies damn near missed a step at his boss's shout. The man straightened up, and held the vase a little more carefully, and took his steps a bit slower as he crossed the road.

Across the street, another enforcer stood waiting. He was the one who took the flowers from the first man, albeit with a hell of a lot more care. John watched the exchange with an amused fascination.

"Fucking idiots," Andino grumbled. "They're going to end this before I can even begin it."

"Give him some credit. I still can't believe you went with *flowers*."

Andino shrugged. "Haven thought it was a nice touch."

John smirked. "There's something cold about your wife."

"I know. It's what I love best about her. You ready?"

"Are they inside?"

"According to our men, yes," Andino said.

John nodded. "Then yes, I am ready."

The two cousins crossed the street without as much as a look around them. They didn't have a reason to be concerned until they got inside the restaurant, and even then, it was only because they needed to get out alive afterward. Neither of the two were very concerned about an ambush of sorts from the Calabrese for several reasons.

For one, the Calabrese *needed* this meeting to go well. Darren was out to get something from the Marcellos—be it more control, power, or influence in New York—but he needed an actual agreement to get it. And he needed to be alive, too. Earning himself a grave would do absolutely nothing for his end goal.

For two, killing John and Andino wouldn't achieve very much for Darren, anyway. In the grand scheme of the Marcello family, John was only a simple Capo. Two other Capos had come along, too, although they would remain outside in waiting vehicles until the others left. Killing a Capo would mean nothing except more bloodshed.

As for Andino?

He was just one of three high-ranking men in the Marcello family. Killing the underboss—as no one outside the family was aware that Andino had taken control of the Marcello organization—was not going to cause the family to crumble. There were still two other men with heavy influence and control.

Darren was greedy.

He made rash decisions.

He was violent.

Stupid, though?

No, he wasn't stupid.

The one enforcer stayed back a step, and kept hold of the flowers as Andino and John stepped up to the entrance of the rundown business. The other enforcer—the one Andino had snapped at—came to open the door of the place, and let John and Andino inside.

John let Andino go first, as a boss should, and then followed right behind. He was entirely unsurprised by the ripped up floors, overturned tables, and wires hanging from an exposed ceiling. Who knew who owned this place, but John was grateful for the venue. It didn't look like the place had been used in a while, or that anyone had worked in it for God knew how long.

It meant less clean up.

Less lives lost.

Small blessings.

Darren Calabrese stood in the middle of the floor flanked by three men. He kept his hands folded at his back as he stared expressionless at John and Andino. None of them moved until the other two Marcello enforcers had also entered the restaurant, and stood waiting behind their respective boss.

It was all about the respect in Cosa Nostra.

John doubted that would ever change.

"I'm happy to see you can follow direction," Andino said dryly. "Three men to you, and three to us."

"Inside," Darren agreed.

John smiled. "We're aware of your men outside, and how many there are. We had a three block radius scouted before we ever even came within five miles of this place today, Darren. We're not stupid."

Darren's cheek twitched, but otherwise, he gave nothing away. "I can assume the two of you brought a small army of your own, then."

"You can," Andino said.

"Where is Dante?" Darren let his arms fall open to his sides, as though he were asking for some kind of gift to be handed to him. "I thought I would be dealing with the boss today, and not his underboss, and a useless Capo, too. What good does that do me?"

John let the insult roll off his shoulders. It wasn't meant to do anything but be fucking offensive, anyway. "It wasn't very fucking long ago that you too were nothing more than a Capo, Darren. It would do you well to remember that."

Darren altogether ignored John, not that it was surprising. After all, the asshole had spent a whole week sending John package after package detailing how much of a shame he thought the Marcello man was.

"The boss?" Darren asked Andino again. "Where is he?"

"You *are* looking at the boss of the Marcello family," Andino said, smirking just enough to look self-serving *and* smug as fuck at the same time. It was a look to be respected and appreciated, really. "I can't help it if you're unable to keep up with the politics of families outside of yours, Darren."

The enforcers flanking Darren passed looks between one another. Darren, to his credit, barely blinked a lash at Andino's admission. It didn't matter—John knew the truth. The damage was done for Darren with his men in that moment. He had likely assured them that this would all go exactly according to his plans because he knew all there was to know about the Marcellos.

The truth was clear now.

He knew nothing.

It was simple, but effective.

A man needed all the faith and trust from his men that he could get in this business. It was the one thing that might save his life, or end it at one point or another. It was a good lesson to learn, and one of the first John had ever been taught when it came to being a made man navigating this very dangerous life.

"Then you misrepresented to me what this meeting would be," Darren said, taking a step forward. "This is a farce, and I can't say that I want to continue—"

"Are you interested in settling this feud once and for all, or continuing on with the bloodshed?" Andino interrupted with a cocked brow. "Because I know which category the Marcellos fall under, and as I told you when I asked for this meeting, we are willing to do whatever necessary to finish this *appropriately*."

Darren hesitated in his next step. "Anything? You're absolutely sure about that?"

"I said what I said."

"And we don't repeat ourselves," John added for his cousin.

Darren passed John a look that lingered for a beat too long before he said, "I want him to leave, then."

"John stays."

"You're making this very difficult for me to want to work with you, Andino."

At that, John scoffed.

All eyes turned in his direction.

"Work with us?" John asked.

"Him, not *you*. I have little interest in working with a dishonored made man, regardless of which asshole is his father, or which bitch pushed him out into the world."

John's lips curved into a wicked smile. "Too far, Darren. You went a little too far with that one."

"Deny any of it is true."

"I don't have to do anything for you, and frankly, if you thought *I* would ever work with you after the things you've done, you're the one who was mistaken."

Andino looked to John, and nodded.

John looked back to Darren. "You were right—this was a farce. A fake meeting. Nothing could ever come from it. Much like you being the boss in your organization. A little prince playing pretend in a king's throne, Darren. That's all you are."

He turned his back to Darren, adding, "And I will greatly enjoy taking that throne, and your crown from you."

"I'll kill you, Marcello!"

Darren's worlds stabbed uselessly into John's back.

They meant nothing.

One of the enforcer's followed John out, while Andino stayed a bit behind in the doorway with the other one.

"Shame," Andino said behind John, "as this could have gone down far differently. Or … not. Here, a gift, Darren. We thought you might appreciate a kind gesture from us."

John didn't look back to see what happened, but he knew what the plan was. The flowers would be set directly in front of the door—carefully, of course, as to shake them or move them too much would set off the chemical mixture inside the vase. The door would be closed, and Darren would need to move the vase before he could exit the place.

A seemingly innocent vase.

Innocuous flowers.

All harmless, really.

Until they weren't …

"Move your ass," Andino barked at the enforcer.

John finally looked over his shoulder.

Through the front window of the rundown restaurant's door, he saw Darren kick the vase of flowers. The explosion was beautiful.

Not as big as they had hoped, but enough to blow the windows out.

Enough to knock them to the ground.

John wasn't sure how long he stayed like that—prone on his back and staring up at a clear early October sky—but the sound of laughter brought him back down to reality.

It took him a minute to realize it was his own laughter.

He was the one laughing.

He finally felt that relief.

It was glorious.

FIFTEEN

"Pass me the bowl of flour, and I'll show you what to do if it seems like the dough gets a little too sticky," Siena said.

Greta pushed the bowl across to Siena, while Giulia hoisted herself up on the edge of the counter. The two girls watched silently as Siena added just a tablespoon of flour at a time to the bread dough before she rolled it and kneaded it again and again.

"You have to make sure it mixes all the way through—you don't want one part of the bread to have too much flour while the other parts don't have enough. Always make sure you knead it really well after you add any extra in."

"What would happen if the dough was too wet when it cooked?" Giulia asked.

"Depends, really. It might be too dense—it might not rise high enough. It could still be doughy in spots, and it'll have that dough-ish taste."

"You can't just … cook it for longer?" Greta asked. "Make up for the difference, or something?"

"No, it doesn't work that way, unfortunately. Bread has to be made just so— even the dough has to be the right consistency every time to make it perfect. If you add something, or take something away, you have to account for it somewhere else. If your kitchen is hotter than normal, you need to account for that, too."

"Ugh," Greta groaned.

Giulia echoed her sister's sentiment. "This seems like a lot of work for just *bread*."

"Sure, but if you master bread, then the rest is kind of easy at the end of the day. And we Italians do love us some bread."

"Truth," Greta said.

"It's really that particular, though?" Giulia asked. "I feel like I should have been taking notes from the start, or something."

Siena laughed a little, and gave her half-sister a smile. "The only thing more fickle than a man on this earth, is bread."

Greta and Giulia passed a grin between one another. Their girlish laughter filled up Siena's apartment. She took the moment to slow her kneading of the dough, and soak in their happiness. So much had been taken from these two young girls, and she wondered how much they would have to sacrifice before they could finally get their own happily ever after.

She was the one left caring for them a lot of the time. Sure, their useless aunt gave them a home to live in, and beds to sleep in. The woman fed them, and kept them clothed—*mostly*. That was the extent of their aunt's involvement in their lives.

She didn't care for them on a deeper level. They had no woman to go to when they needed a private chat. They had no voice to be their reason, or to give them direction when they needed that, too. They were, essentially, alone.

"Ma tried to teach me how to make bread once," Greta said.

Siena passed the older of the two girls a look. "How did that turn out?"

"I wasn't paying attention the way she wanted me to. She got mad. I got mad. We yelled a lot, and she kicked me out of the kitchen. I guess ..."

"What?"

Giulia picked at her nails, avoiding everyone's gaze and looking all kinds of awkward for the moment. It wasn't very often the girls talked about their mother. They buried all their feelings, and memories of their mother somewhere deep, and kept them locked up tight where no one could reach. Siena didn't think that was very healthy to do, honestly. Someday, they were going to have to deal with the murder of their mother, and the things that preceded it.

Right now, though, they couldn't do any of that. It wasn't a topic that Kev or Darren had wanted them to chat about, really. It might upset Coraline, after all.

Not that Siena's mother made very much of an effort to be around the girls. Because she absolutely didn't if she could help it.

"I guess," Greta continued after a long stretch of silence, "I wish I had listened now. Been better that day—on a lot of other days, too."

Without even thinking about it, Siena pulled her hands away from the bread, and reached out to her half-sister. She touched the girl's cheek with a dough- and flour-covered hand to give Greta a gentle pat. It left fingerprints of flour behind, but Greta didn't seem to mind.

"Your ma loved you, Greta. Regardless if you were terrible, or wonderful. She's your ma, so you know what that means, right?"

"What?"

"That she loved you just as much on your best days as she did on your worst days. That's what good mothers do. And I know you have a whole bunch of good memories to think about, but sometimes the bad ones slip through, too, right?"

Greta shrugged. "It makes me feel guilty sometimes."

"Don't. Okay? Just don't. Focus on all the good because you are going to have more than enough bad moments in your life to focus on at a later date. Right now, just focus on all the good you remember."

Her sister nodded. "Okay."

"Back to bread?"

Both girls agreed.

Siena made quick work of breaking the dough into three chunks. She passed a piece to Greta and Giulia before pushing the bowl of flour over, too.

"Put a little on your hands, but not too much," she said. "Keeps it from sticking. We'll knead it a bit more, and then put them in bowls to rise for thirty minutes to an hour."

"Okay," the girls echoed.

Siena continued chatting with her half-sisters while they worked just to keep them occupied in a verbal way. At least then, she hoped their attention would not go back to darker places in their thoughts.

Or ... that was her hope.

In the background of their work, the television played through breaking news on the major news network Siena liked to keep on daily. The news was always depressing, but in some ways, it also reminded her that her life could be a hell of a lot worse in ways.

Unfortunately, she also kept it on for another reason. Her family—and

John's, at times—seemed to be the focus of New York related news a lot lately. Organized crime was making a comeback; not that it ever went away, the idiots. The streets were bloodier than ever between the crime families, and rivaled the Chicago War from two decades earlier.

Attention was never good in their life.

It hindered business.

Siena slowed in her work as a shot of a street came into view on the television.

"Some sort of explosive device was detonated on …"

Siena blinked at the reporter's words. Not because of what the woman said, but because of what she saw on the television. She recognized the street they were showing—a Brooklyn street full of small businesses. Mostly restaurants, but a few other vendors, too.

And then the shot changed to a building. Windows blown out, and a door ripped off the hinges. The front charred from fire, and smoke still billowing out from the broken, gaping holes of the business.

Explosive device.

"A restaurant that was undergoing renovations and owned by—"

"Darren," Siena said quietly.

Her sisters looked to her, and then back to the television screen. They, too, stopped in their work to take in what they were seeing on the news.

The reporter continued talking. "Sources tell us prior to the incident, they had witnessed several men entering the restaurant at different times. The police have, so far, suggested it looked to be a meeting of sorts between the Calabrese and Marcello crime families. As you know, Gordon and Marney, there has been quite a bit of news about those families lately."

The shot switched back to the anchors at the station. A man and a woman with their makeup pressed with powder, and their hair perfectly coifed back with not a strand out of place. Siena always thought they looked sort of like dolls in a way.

Fake, and unrealistic.

Unmoving, and unfeeling.

"We have reports of deaths on the scene, too, don't we?" the woman asked.

"At least two."

Siena held her breath.

She *wondered* …

She *feared* …

Her hands started shaking against the counter top.

Please give a name … please, please, please give a name, but don't be his name. Don't be John's name. Give me a name.

"Others were apprehended at the scene," the reporter on location stated. "Of course, the police were unwilling to release the names, as they have not yet stated what or *who* was the cause of the explosion, but we did get word elsewhere of the names of suspects apprehended."

Siena gripped the edge of the countertop so tightly that her knuckles turned white from the pressure. She didn't dare look away from the screen for fear she might miss something important. Her stomach had all but climbed up into her throat, while her heart had altogether stopped beating for the moment.

"Several members of the Marcello family—Andino and Johnathan Marcello being the two most recognizable figures apprehended at the moment," the reporter continued.

Siena felt like her fucking knees gave out, though somehow, she managed to stay upright. Her stomach dropped back down into place while her heart began a slow beat once more.

Not dead, not dead … not dead.

Just in custody.

A knock echoed on Siena's apartment door, but she was only half paying attention at that point. It took Greta poking her in the shoulder when the knock echoed a second time for Siena to snap out of her daze.

As she crossed the space to answer the door, she kept reminding herself that apprehended and in custody did not necessarily mean arrested. It simply meant they were with police, and likely being questioned.

Was it good?

Fuck no.

It was still *workable.*

This life taught her that.

Siena was still looking over her shoulder at the television when she opened the door to her apartment. She didn't even get the chance to turn around and greet whoever was at her door before a form flew at her.

"You little *bitch!*"

Siena first felt her mother's fingernails rake down her face before Coraline slapped her. The surprise attack—and the sting of the pain—was enough to set her off-balance. Her vision swam as she put her hands up in front of her face to defend whatever might be coming next, but it did no good.

Her mother hit her again.

And then again.

Unsteady from the surprise, Siena lost her footing as she quickly tried to back away from Coraline's attack. Her back hit the floor hard enough to take her breath right out of her lungs, but she didn't even have enough time to recover from that.

"How *dare* you?" Coraline screeched.

The sharp points of her mother's heels hit her body. Her sides, and her temple.

"Ma, stop!"

"You knew, didn't you? You knew what they were going to do! I warned you, Siena, I *warned you!*"

Another kick landed to the side of Siena's head.

She was not a weak girl—not an incapable woman. She could and would defend herself, but something made her turn away from her mother's attack, and simply *protect* herself instead of fighting back.

Maybe because it was her mother. She had once loved his woman. She thought Coraline loved her, too.

It was painful to be wrong.

So very painful.

"Stop!"

"Leave her alone!"

Greta and Giulia's voices filtered through the ringing in Siena's ears. That last kick to her head had done a number because her vision was fuzzy, and everything sounded like it was under water.

Siena blinked in just enough time to see one of her half-sisters fly at Coraline. She wasn't sure which one, but the other girl came right after her, too.

Coraline landed on her back as she was shoved away from Siena's prone form. It took another few seconds, and more shouting, before Siena finally gained enough of her bearings to try and move. She rolled over to her knees, and coughed painfully as she clutched her head.

"Little whores," Coraline spat, standing up slowly. "Just like your mother."

"Say that again, and I'll cut your fucking tongue out," Greta hissed.

Siena looked to the side to see Greta wielding a knife. One of the kitchen knives Siena had used earlier for their lunch.

"What are you going to do, little girl?" Coraline taunted. "Do you honestly think you could use that on me?"

"Try me," Greta urged right back.

This was getting worse by the second.

So bad.

"Ma, *leave*," Siena whispered.

Goddamn.

Her head pounded.

It hurt ... bad.

"Leave," Siena said louder. "Now!"

Siena looked at the floor, and the lines of the hardwood seemed to swim. She only heard the slam of the apartment door before her sisters were at her side again.

"It's all right, it's fine," Siena tried to assure them.

Greta touched the side of Siena's face, and her fingertips came back red. "You're bleeding."

"It's fine."

"Giulia, get something frozen from the freezer for her head," Greta barked.

"Okay!"

"I'm *fine*," Siena said.

Then, she promptly vomited all over the floor.

Yeah, that wasn't good.

Greta made Siena look her in the eyes. "She kicked you really hard in the head. A lot. Maybe you should go to the—"

No.

She had to stay.

What if John came?

What if ...

"It's fine," Siena repeated.

She was becoming a broken record.

Greta frowned. "I'm sorry you don't have a good ma, either."

Yeah.

Siena was sorry for that, too.

"There's a phone under my bed in a box," Siena said, struggling with every word. "A shoebox—it's black, like the phone. There's a contact. John. Just … call until he answers."

"John?"

"John," Siena echoed.

And then everything went black.

Siena was alternating between icing the lump on the side of her head, and pressing the frozen bag of mixed vegetables to her cheek where Coraline had scratched her viciously. The scratches felt like they were on fire whenever something cold wasn't being pressed against them to level out the heat.

At least, her vision had cleared and her head had stopped pounding. That only took a good six hours. She probably should have listened to Greta, and took the young girl's advice to go to the hospital.

Siena likely had a concussion, and needed to be looked at. Still, she stayed at her apartment. Neither Greta, nor Giulia left, either. In fact, they stayed right by Siena's side the entire time to make sure she was okay. They wouldn't let her sleep, or even close her eyes for more than a couple of seconds at a time.

They were sweet girls.

Good girls.

They did not deserve the hell that had been brought down on their lives by their half-brothers. Siena was never more aware of that fact than now.

"Greta?"

"Hmm?"

The girl looked over at Siena with worry creasing her brow. Siena instantly wanted to take that away. Greta was only seventeen. She didn't need to be worrying herself with the problems of the adults around her.

This life made girls grow up too early.

It always did.

"Ginevra is in Canada," Siena said quietly.

Greta stilled. "What?"

"On the day she was supposed to get married, a gift was sent to her private room when it was just me and her in there. That was intentional—planned ahead of time. The gift was a letter with instructions, new identification documents, and a way to get out of the country."

Tears filled Greta's eyes.

Giulia had fallen asleep on the chair across from where they sat on the couch.

"So, she's okay?" Greta asked.

"She is great," Siena said, "as far as I know now. I haven't gotten any information on her since she left. That was kind of the deal."

"Will she come back?"

"Maybe."

"When could she come back?" Greta pressed.

"When it's safe."

When all the men threatening her safety and life are gone from this city. Siena didn't say that out loud, though. She knew they were one step closer after today to finally getting Ginevra back to her younger sisters.

Kev was gone.

Darren ... might be, too.

Siena didn't really know at this point. She had been watching the news, and waiting for any snippet of information that might give the names of the two men deceased from the explosion at the restaurant. Nothing had come up yet.

Her mother had not come back for round two, thankfully, but that also meant she couldn't get any information out of Coraline, either. The enforcer who had dropped the girls off earlier that day had yet to come back and get them.

Siena figured that was because too much was going on outside of her apartment at the moment. A whole world of new trouble had just popped up for all the men of the Calabrese family, and it was all about damage control right now.

They needed to get this situation under control before they even considered dealing with something less important. They had better things to deal with than two *principessas* who needed nothing more than to be returned to their aunt's home.

Greta and Giulia likely didn't even mind.

Neither did Siena.

"Okay."

"I'm sorry I didn't tell you months ago," Siena said softly.

Greta shook her head fast, and wiped her eyes with the heels of her palms. "No, it's okay. I understand, really. Thank—"

The front door of Siena's apartment opened with such force that it smashed into the wall. The noise made Siena jump, Greta duck, and woke a very confused Giulia up from her sleep.

Jerking in surprise was not a good thing for Siena's current state. Pain swelled in the side of her head all over again, and made her double over on the couch. She pressed the frozen bag of mixed vegetables harder to her temple in a shitty attempt to relieve some of the sudden pressure. Her stomach threatened to revolt all over again.

"Oh, my God," she groaned.

"Siena? Shit ... babe."

John's voice was the only thing that felt remotely *good* in that moment. Siena didn't even have time to lift her head up before he was in front of her. Kneeling down, his hands found her thighs, and his gaze locked on hers.

Warm hazel.

True love.

Calm and beautiful.

For a second, her vision focused, and Siena was good again. At least, for a moment.

"Don't move," she told him.

John's brow furrowed. "Why would I move?"

"Just ... don't. If you move, I might get dizzy again, and I don't want to puke."

"What happened?"

His harsh demand made her flinch. He didn't miss it.

"Shit, sorry. Sorry, babe. I would have been here sooner after I got the messages on my phone, but I wasn't even given my phone until they released me once my attorney got there. Here, let me look at you."

Soft fingertips drifted over her face. The sensation was such a stark contrast to the pain and heat coursing through her head. He peeled her fingers away from her cheek, and then convinced her to drop the frozen bag, too.

Siena watched John's gaze drift over her face, and injuries. His fingers followed the same path—careful not to press too hard, or hurt her as he checked her out. As the silent seconds ticked on, she could plainly see his rage growing.

He hid it, sure.

She still saw it.

"What happened?" he asked one more time.

Calmer.

Quieter.

Still as stone.

"It's okay," she told him.

John made a grunt under his breath—dismissive, yet heated. "Nope. Try again."

"Her mom," Greta said. "She came over, yelled at Siena, and hurt her."

John's gaze darted to the girl beside Siena. "And who are you?"

"One of Matteo's other daughters," Siena muttered.

To his credit, John didn't blink a lash at that. Nor did he out the fact he had been the one to take Greta's beloved father away, either.

"Well ... hello," John said. "You were the one that called me?"

Greta nodded.

"Thank you."

"Siena looks after us," Greta said as though that explained her loyalty.

"Who are *you*?" Giulia asked.

John glanced over his shoulder at the girl. "Johnathan."

"Johnathan *who*?"

"Marcello."

The two girls passed looks between one another like that explained *everything*. Their silent conversations could sometimes be annoying, but in that moment, Siena had other things to focus on.

John, mostly.

Always John.

His hands cupped her face, and he brought her in closer. He pressed a soft kiss to her lips, and a tear escaped the corner of Siena's eye. He made quick work of wiping it away, though.

"I saw the news," Siena whispered.

John nodded. "It went well."

"Could have told me."

"This wasn't really my show. More ... Andino's."

Siena nodded once. "Oh, I see."

"Your head has one hell of a knot on it, and those scratches look really bad." John looked her injuries over *again*. "I don't like the looks of this—you should go get checked out."

"I'm fine."

"You're not fine."

"I *am.*"

"Siena, I am taking you to—"

"I can't leave, John," she said. "I don't have an enforcer with me, and it'll only cause problems. I wanted you here because I was scared."

A small smile edged at the corner of John's lips. "You can do whatever the fuck you want to do. Don't you realize what happened today?"

"A lot happened."

And she was still trying to figure it all out. She supposed her scrambled head wasn't really helping her case at the moment.

"Darren is good as dead, Siena," John murmured, holding her face so she couldn't look away from him. "The cops let it slip when they were hounding me— he's on life support until someone pulls the plug, and he's not coming out of it. This is almost over. We're so fucking close, love."

A small swell of relief threatened to drown Siena.

Reality was a quick bitch, too.

Darren wasn't *dead*.

Not entirely.

Not yet …

"Everything is going to change," John said. "Starting now. I promise."

Siena stared down at the prone form resting in the hospital bed. Monitors beeped, displaying heart rate, oxygen levels, and a non-existent brain function. Stiff, white blankets that had been warmed before being brought in were tucked firmly around Darren's form.

According to the nurse, the blankets were new. Over seventy percent of Darren's body had suffered severe burns in the blast, and being covered was typically considered a major no-no. However, the lack of brain function, and the stress his body was under meant Darren had not been placed on the burn victim ward.

There was no point.

John had been right.

Darren was not coming back from this.

A tube down his throat attached to a respirator kept him breathing. His heart only continued to beat because of the oxygen being pumped into his body. His brain was not working, and thus, not allowing his body to breathe on his own.

CT scans, MRIs, and reflective tests all showcased the same thing for Darren. He was, entirely, braindead. He was not going to wake up one day, and he was not going to get better as time passed on.

Ever.

The nurse and doctor moved quietly throughout the room. They worked in tandem which was interesting to watch. As soon as the doctor reached for something, the nurse came right behind him to finish what he left behind. Or better yet, should he need something, the nurse was already there to fulfill his unspoken request.

It was only once their attention turned back on Siena that she straightened a bit more, and waited for their next move.

"You can wait to sign the documents, if you so choose," the doctor reminded her.

"My lawyer was clear. We went through the proper channels. Darren has no wife, no children, and at the moment, no parent we can make contact with. I am— according to the law, and the judge that signed off on my lawyer's petition— Darren's only next of kin. And I made my decision."

She said all of this with a cold detachment that likely didn't escape the doctor or nurse's notice. At the moment, it was the best she could offer them. She *had* gone through a lawyer to get this finished—it only took about a week when her mother couldn't be contacted, and did not appeal the decision to make Siena her brother's next of kin capable of making life or death decisions for his person.

Who knew where Coraline was?

Siena had no idea.

"Could we get started?" Siena asked.

The doctor cleared his throat, and nodded once. "Yes, sure, of course. Once you sign the documents, and witness us turn off the machines, and remove the tube, you will not need to remain in the—"

"I will stay."

The man gave her a look. "Many don't prefer to stay and watch, and it can take a while."

Siena stared back, unaffected. "I will stay."

Until the bastard's heart stopped beating.

Until he couldn't hurt them again.

Until she was safe.

Her sisters.

John.

Siena would fucking *stay*.

"Okay," the doctor murmured. "Let's get started on these final forms."

The next several minutes were a blur. Siena checking boxes, and signing her signature on too many dotted lines to count. It was all the same thing over and over again, simply reworded a different way, and on a new page.

Did she understand ...

Does she agree ...

No liability ...

"And here," the doctor said one final time.

Siena scribbled her name a little harder than before.

Done and done.

She stepped back, and found a chair in the corner of the room to make herself comfortable for the next little while. For all the machines and wires hooked up to Darren, it took only a couple of quick minutes to remove them from his body.

"Would you leave that one on?" Siena asked.

The doctor hesitated as his hand hovered over the monitor. "You want me to leave the heart rate monitor on?"

She needed to know.

She *had* to.

"Yes, if it's possible."

The nurse and doctor shared a look before the man nodded once at her. "Yes, I can leave it on. It might be upsetting, however, and—"

"I can assure you it won't be."

And it wasn't.

When his heart stopped …

When it was still …

When it was silent …

Darren was dead.

Siena only felt relief.

Siena stepped out of the hospital room to find the enforcer that had been placed at the door before she went in had not moved an inch from his post. The man greeted her with a kind smile, and a nod.

"Siena," he said.

Respectful.

Caring.

Soft-spoken.

This enforcer—a man who introduced himself by name, with a smile, and a handshake the first time they met—was not like any other guard Siena had ever had. He did not treat her like a piece of property to *la famiglia* that he was simply protecting.

He was not a Calabrese enforcer.

He was a Marcello enforcer.

And he was hers, now.

John had said everything would change the day the bomb blew a week before, and he had not been lying.

Everything was different.

"Pink," she greeted.

Yep.

That was his nickname.

Pink.

Siena didn't know how he got it, and she didn't care to learn. It just made her smile every time she used it.

"You're the only one who can't say my name with a straight face," Pink said.

"Come on, it's *cute*."

"I've heard all the comments, Siena. They don't surprise me or bother me anymore. Come on, the boss is waiting for you."

"Where did John go?"

"To grab a coffee downstairs."

"Oh."

"He's waiting for you—figured he would get back up here by the time you were done," Pink explained.

Siena shrugged. "It's okay. I don't mind chasing after him."

She had all the time in the world to do that, now.

Pink guided Siena through the upper level of the hospital, and then down to the main floor where John had apparently gone. They did not find him at the coffee shop, but rather, outside surrounded by several men.

Most of which, Siena recognized.

They were her brothers' men.

Or ... they used to be.

John, in his tweed coat and black Armani suit, with a hand flicking outward to showcase a diamond encrusted Rolex in a dismissive gesture, looked entirely at ease. Despite, apparently, the stiffened postures and angry expressions of the men around him.

"You seem to think you have control now," John said, "or even that *dead* men have control of this family now, and I am not very sorry to inform you that you are all mistaken. Your first—and *last*—mistake with me will be to ever underestimate or question my authority."

"We don't answer to you, Marcello, not now, and not—"

"You will address me as your boss, or as the Don, or you will address me from your broken knees with my gun in your mouth. *Try again.*"

Pink kept Siena back a few steps by holding onto her shoulder with one beefy hand. She saw a few gazes of the men drift in her direction, but they quickly went back to John.

"So, that's how it is, then?" another one asked. "The Marcellos are just going to come in to our organization, and clean fucking house like this?"

"I'm not cleaning anything," John said, "this is *my* house. It has always been mine. Someone else was looking after it for a time. Mind you, they did a shit job about it, but you've got a new boss to correct that issue now."

"This is not your *famiglia!*"

John pointed a single finger at the man, and then looked over at the guy who had driven him and Siena to the hospital earlier while Pink followed behind in Siena's car. "He will be the first to learn. Tonight, don't stall."

"Yes, boss."

The man in question made a move like he was going to come forward, and John didn't wait for him to make the choice. Instead, John was the one to go forward himself until he was standing toe-to-toe with the man.

"Do you have something to say?" John asked. "Now would be the time."

The man swallowed hard. "You're a fucking lunatic. Crazy—a *shame*. No Calabrese man will ever accept you as their boss. You don't have what it takes, and they'll ruin you, Johnathan. Mark my fucking words."

For a brief second, Siena's heart clenched for John. He had been right—

everything was changing for them. Starting with the Calabrese family. He and his men had slid into the organization, and within a week's time, made it abundantly clear there was new leadership in charge.

That didn't mean it was easy.

Or that the men were agreeable.

She knew that everything that man had just thrown at John were some of his worst fears being laid out on the ground in front of him to see, and for everyone else to dissect. That he was not good enough—that he would never be.

But they didn't know him.

Not like she did.

Siena caught sight of John's slow, cold smile starting to grow. His next words came out calm, and sure. The most sure she had ever heard him speak.

"This is no longer a Calabrese family—there's a Marcello running this shit now. Keep calling me crazy, and your wife will get you back in pieces. I don't have what it takes? You think this position just *came to me*? You think this isn't mine to take?"

John took another step closer, crowding the man and smiling wickedly all the while. "Check my bloodlines, motherfucker. I was made by men—and raised by men—you can only dream to be. My bloodlines? They're written in fucking red. Grovatti blood. My life? It's written all over this city. Marcello legacy. You'll understand what all that means really soon. It's a promise. I don't break those."

Good God.

She loved this man.

360

SIXTEEN

"Jail gray looks like shit on you," John noted.

Andino looked away from the clock on the wall to showcase one of his usual easygoing grins. "Right? But fuck, it was this, or the suit I was wearing last week when they threw me in here."

Yeah, fuck.

"What are you still doing in jail, huh? You should have been out by now, Andi. Arthur Lorde clearly isn't doing what he's supposed to be doing. You're still fucking in here. They've filed charges, man."

Andino shrugged. "But what do they have?"

"Andino—"

"No video surveillance. Darren Calabrese made sure he picked a spot where there were no cameras around to spot us going in and out. No witnesses to say I did anything except *be* there. No *live* victims—the other enforcer Darren brought along died yesterday. They couldn't even hold you and the other guys, John. They have nothing. Arthur is likely just biding his time."

John sometimes wished he could have the same bright optimism as the people around him, but his mind didn't work that way. He first went to the worst place imaginable, and then worked back from that to get to a relatively decent place.

"You're forgetting details," John pointed out.

"Do tell."

"The detectives are hounding everybody. My lawyer's phone won't stop ringing. They're threatening charges on us still, even though they released us. The only reason they're holding you is in hopes they'll get someone else to roll for your sake."

"Maybe someone will do just that," Andino said. "It would be a win-win all the way around the board. I'll get out of this shithole, and they'll get someone to eviscerate on the news, so they don't have to lose face."

"You're missing the point, Andino."

His cousin sighed, and his green gaze drifted to John's. "I'm not, man. I get this is not going the way I planned. You're right, too. I should have been out of here by now, but at the moment, it is a waiting game. This whole life is one giant waiting game, anyway. I can wait for one more thing, surely."

John knew that feeling.

At first, a little boy waited to grow up, so he could be the same as the men around him. Then the grown-up boy waited to be made. Being a made man only took a man to waiting for several different things—money, honor, death, or jail time. Funny how that worked.

"Haven is …"

Andino's gaze darted to John again. "What?"

"Your wife is very upset."

Putting it lightly.

361

Haven Marcello was in one hell of a fit. Damn, the woman wasn't even Italian, but she knew how to raise hell like any good old Italian woman at the end of the day. She was a nasty thing when she thought something or someone was fucking with her life, and her husband.

Not that John blamed her. This shit was bad.

"You'll figure it out," Andino told John.

"Was that part of your plan, too?" he asked.

Andino smiled. "What, leaving you to hold the ball for me?"

"I suppose you could put it that way."

"Man, I have held the ball for you time and time again in our life. I didn't mind doing it, either. No, it wasn't part of the plan, but here we are. I have all the faith that you'll do whatever you need to do, so we can get back to controlling this fucking city like we were always meant to."

John nodded. "Ride or die, right?"

"Since the days we were fucking born, John."

Yep.

It wasn't long before the damn jail guard came around to knock his baton against the metal table to signal it was time to wrap up the visit. John didn't know if that was some kind of shit the jail had worked out with the detectives or not, but they didn't allow Andino's visitors to linger for too long.

Mostly because the bastards couldn't stay too close. Certainly not close enough to overhear their conversations—the man was allowed privacy, after all, even if said man was a fucking criminal in jail on suspicion of murdering a handful of people with a simple explosive device.

"Tell my wife—"

John looked at Andino, noting the way his words cut off. "What? I'll pass whatever along. I know taking your calls upsets her."

So was the way with women married to a man like them. Those ladies fought tooth and nail for their men's freedom, but at the end of the day, they were still women looking down a long, hard road that might just lead them straight to hell.

It was a big undertaking. It wasn't for the faint of heart.

"I was going to say you could tell her to relax," Andino said, grinning a little, "but I don't think you could handle Haven in one of her moods. She's not like Siena, you know?"

"Definitely not as mild-mannered and sweet, no."

Andino smirked. "She can be. You just have to stroke her the right—"

"Thanks for that, but no thanks."

His cousin's laughter lit up the visitation area. "Tell her I love her, man."

"Will do, Andi."

It was the best a man in this life could offer to a woman he loved. His faith, and undying loyalty. He could hope for forever, but promising it was never really a guarantee he could keep. She could share his life, but John wasn't sure the life was ever really theirs to actually *have*.

"I'll be seeing you around," John said, fixing his Armani blazer as he stood.

No goodbyes. Those were too final.

"Of course you fucking will."

John was collecting the items he had been asked to hand over coming into the jail when a familiar detective saddled in beside him. He only knew who the detective was because the guy was giving his best effort to put Andino behind bars for a twenty to life sentence. He was also the same asshole that had been the one to release John as he taunted him about his cousin.

He shoved his phone, wallet, and a roll of cash into his pants pocket, all the while, ignoring the detective. He wasn't speaking first. Made men didn't talk to cops of any sort if they could help it.

"No greeting for me today?" Detective Rosencauld asked with a shit-eating grin. "Not even a *go fuck yourself* for good measure, John?"

"What do you want?"

John checked the time on his watch, and then headed for the entrance of the jail. Rosencauld followed close behind at the same time, never missing a step with John. It was both amusing and annoying.

"Your visit with Andino didn't last long. Your cousin didn't have orders to give today, or what?"

"I don't take orders from Andino," John replied, opening the doors and heading out into the mid-October day.

Taking over his own organization as a boss meant John answered to only himself, which was something he hadn't realized he needed in the grand scheme of things. It was simply easier when he was the one calling the shots for his own people.

Not that the Calabrese fools made it easy.

"Is that because he's family, or …?"

"That's because none of your fucking business," John said.

Waiting at the side of the road was a black town car. One of John's enforcers—one of several men he had brought over from the Marcello side to help control the Calabrese organization—waited with the door already open to the car. Smoke puffed from the tailpipe, telling him the man had kept the engine running during his visit.

"Have a good day," John said to Rosencauld as he slipped into the back of the car. He went to close the door, but the detective grabbed it at the last second. John gave the man a single look—promised violence silently for stepping in his way. "Do you have something else you need?"

"Just one thing, John."

"Which is what, exactly?"

"No matter who steps in to try and shut this investigation down, I am not going away. Papers can go missing, and witnesses can recant, but I'm still going to be here at the end of the day. Don't forget it."

John only smiled. "Keep reaching. You might actually grab something. Heath."

At the call of his name, the enforcer stepped in to crowd the detective away from the car, and further from John. Heath was a bull of a man—as wide as he was tall, and all muscle, too. He slammed the passenger door shut, and stood in front of it until Rosencauld backed off entirely, and headed for the jail again.

"Fucking asshole," John muttered.

But his mind had found that goddamn detective to be something worth thinking about, apparently. His focus zoned in on the things the man had said, and everything he suggested. Even as Health climbed into the car, and chatted away while he drove, John was still laser focused on a few passing comments from Rosencauld.

No matter how many times John tried to shake the comments, or forget the man who really couldn't do anything to him or Andino as long as everything went right, the thoughts wouldn't leave.

It wasn't even so much the detective as just everything about this whole situation in general. Andino didn't know, but John *had* been working to get his cousin out. He didn't stop—from morning until night. He was sleeping maybe three hours a night, and running all goddamn day, too.

He didn't feel it, though. Not exhaustion, anyway.

It was everything else that he felt too much of lately. It was everything else that kept his attention obsessive, and unwilling to let him go. He had been taken out of the deep swell of depression, and thrown into the hyper-focused, fixated state he was now.

That probably should have been a sign.

John's gaze zoned in on the clock as voices echoed around him. Leaning back in the kitchen chair, Siena moved around the arguing men like their raised voices and irritation didn't bother her in the least.

She dropped a kiss to the top of John's head as she passed his chair at the head of the table. It was the only thing to break his focus away from the clock, and the countdown he had begun silently in his head.

"Coffee?" she asked him.

John shook his head once. "No, thanks."

"Cake?"

He smiled, because *fuck*, here she was in his house, and making cake. It was everything he wanted and so much more, but at the same time, he wished that was all they were doing together at the moment.

Instead, they could not focus on the fact they were actually together. That she was with him—had been with him, and waking up in his bed every morning for over a week. No, they had to let other things take center stage in their life at the moment, and deal with it first. They came second.

"Not right now," he said to her offer of cake.

Siena nodded, and patted his cheek before heading off to the island again. John's attention went back to the clock while the men around him raged on. His family—uncles, and his father.

"Has someone updated Haven today?" Giovanni asked.

John held up a single finger. "She yelled a lot."

Lucian frowned at his son. "I'm sure she's having a difficult time."

"Didn't say I blamed her."

"What about that goddamn deal Andino put in with the District Attorney?"

Dante asked. "Arthur, or whatever the fuck his name is. Why hasn't something come of that yet? The boss of the Marcello family cannot remain in lockup for very long. It's *dangerous*."

Gazes drifted to John, but he was still staring at the clock. He felt them looking at him, though, and waiting for a response. He didn't have very goddamn much to give them right now. He knew as much as they did, honestly.

"We're quite aware of how fucking dangerous is it for him to be in there," Lucian snapped back.

John did look away from the clock at that statement. It was very unlike his father to be sharp in his words or tone, but especially to his brothers. Lucian Marcello had long since perfected the art of cold words, and a detached delivery. Even when it came to family. It was how he managed to distance himself from an argument with people he cared about.

"I'm just saying—"

"I know what you're not saying, too, Dante," Lucian muttered. "I don't think we have to worry about someone putting a hit on Andino while he's in lockup. That's not the kind of issue we have been having lately. John has a bribe in with two of the guards as well, so he's being fucking watched as much as we can watch him."

"Scum has a way of surfacing when they think they have a chance to be overlooked, Lucian," Dante replied.

Lucian opened his mouth to respond, but John stepped in to save his father the trouble. He knew his father was speaking for John, in a way. He rarely ever did that, but John's distraction at this meeting was not going unnoticed, either. He couldn't exactly help it at the moment.

Talking would do nothing. Talking *had* done nothing.

John needed to do something.

"I will figure it out," John said simply.

Dante looked at John, and so did Giovanni. John's father, on the other hand, only leaned back in his chair like he knew the discussion was just about over with entirely. Lucian was smart that way—he could recognize when John had found his limit of politeness for the day. John had found his limit.

"And just how—"

"I will let you know," John said, standing from his chair. "I shouldn't have to make this clear, but this was a plan Andino put into motion. It was his choice to make, and he knew the risks. It was a plan he brought me in on for obvious reasons."

John's gaze drifted to where Siena was wiping down the island counter. She kept her gaze on her work, but he had no doubt she was listening to him. The woman was smart like that, and he appreciated it.

"So that means it's our issue to clean at the end of the day," John continued, giving Dante and Giovanni a look. "Let us do that without stepping in where you're only stepping on my fucking toes."

"John—"

He held a single hand up, and then just walked away from the table and conversation altogether. He left his father, and his uncles behind.

John had said his peace. He gave his order. He meant it.

"Where is he going?" Giovanni demanded.

"We're not done talking, John," Dante called.

"Actually," Lucian said, "he is done, and he can be done whenever he wants to be, brothers. Benefit of being the boss—a benefit you used all the damn time, Dante. A boss is a boss is a boss, even if he is the boss of another family. He said what he said. It's done. Let it be done."

"John?"

"Hmm?"

"What are you doing?"

"Looking for the fucking cake, Siena."

"What?" she asked.

Her sleepy confusion might have been cute any other time if John wasn't so goddamn fixated on finding the cake she had mentioned the night before. He felt her come closer as he peered into the fridge again, and moved things around.

There wasn't even that much in there. It wasn't like the fucking cake had got out, and walked away or some nonsense.

"Did you put it in the cupboard or something?" he asked.

Because it wasn't on the counter in a dish, either.

Standing, he shut the fridge door, and turned to face Siena. She had leaned one hip against the kitchen island like it was going to keep her standing. Her droopy eyelids spoke to how tired she was.

"You want *cake*?" she asked.

John shrugged. "Yeah, the chocolate cake. You had it out yesterday when everybody was here. Where is it?"

He had pretty much gone through his office, and then the living room on a cleaning spree. Everything was meticulously shiny again. There was no dust to be found, but he only felt marginally better, really.

"You want the cake," Siena said again.

John just stared at her. "That's what I said."

"Holy shit, John, it's ..." Siena looked at the clock on the wall, blinked twice, and then looked at the watch on her wrist. "It's three in the morning."

"Is it?"

What did that matter?

"I still want the cake," he told her.

Siena shook her head, and rubbed her hand against her eyes. Finally looking a little bit more awake than before, she took another look at him, too. "When did you go to bed, John?"

Well ...

"I didn't."

"Why does the living room smell like bleach?"

"I cleaned."

Siena smacked her tongue against the roof of her mouth, and nodded. "You didn't sleep last night, either. I saw the shelves on the way down the stairs, too. You moved everything around again."

"I didn't like the way it was."

"Yeah, I bet." Siena tightened the belt on her thigh-high, white silk robe, accentuating her tiny waist a bit more. "You just, what, suddenly wanted cake?"

"Listen, I'll just go drive around until I find fucking cake, Siena."

"It wasn't a big cake, John. They finished it off. I'll make you one tomorrow."

No, he kind of wanted one now. And when he fixated on something—like cake at the moment—he was willing to do just about whatever he had to in order to get it. It was not as simple as a promise of *eventually* getting what he wanted.

"That's not going to work," John said.

Her blue eyes showed no surprise, and little concern at that point. "Do I have to take your keys from you?"

"Why would you—"

Siena started ticking things off her fingers in that calm, sweet way of hers that always lulled John into a sense of comfort. "You're not sleeping. You're fixating on different things. Your energy is through the roof. If and when you sleep, it's maybe an hour at a time. You're watching clocks like time is the only thing tangible to understand at the moment. You're distracted at every turn unless it's something you're obsessing over. You're not quite nasty—*yet*—but your moods are flipping up and down depending on who's around at any given time."

John cleared his throat, not bothering to deny anything Siena just said. None of it was a lie, and he knew it. "It'll settle."

"Likely not at the moment," Siena countered. "Leonard has had you off your stabilizers for the antidepressants for what, a couple of weeks or more?"

"Something like that."

"I think you need to get him to switch them back over now, John."

John's ability to rationalize emotions and his situation at any given time was often hindered by his current phase of bipolar. The more hypomanic he became, the less concerned he was over his behavior and actions. He gave it all very little thought because that was just how his disorder worked. Right and wrong became whatever he could get away with a lot of the time.

All over again, he was reminded of how difficult it was to live his life, be a made man in the utmost control of himself, and manage his disorder.

"It's all right," Siena said like she could read his mind. Her hand came up to stroke his jaw, and she pulled him close until the two of them were just a breath apart. Damn, he loved his woman. "We can call Leonard in the morning, and get the meds switched back around."

"Always have my back, huh?"

Siena flashed him a smile. "You know it."

"People *know* now—about me, I mean," he said.

"Yeah, I know."

"But they can't know this shit, too. They can't know these things, too."

"They won't."

Her words felt like a promise. She didn't break promises, he knew.

"It'll always be just you and me for this," Siena told him. "We'll handle it. It's your life—your business. Those doors are shut, John."

"Where did you come from, *bella donna*? You seem a little too good to be true when it comes to us."

Siena laughed. "I came from Brooklyn. And you know damn well I was made for you, John."

He gave her a quick kiss and said, "Damn right."

"Are you still thinking about the cake?"

John grimaced because, yeah, he kind of was. He really wanted some of that, and it wasn't just going to go away because he knew he was being irrational. "I can't—"

"Help it, yeah. I know. How about I distract you instead?"

Her tone dripped with sex. It couldn't be missed.

John grinned. "I'll give you a head start."

Siena cocked a brow. "A head start?"

"Mmm, make it to the bed, and I'll bend you over. Let me catch you, and you'll suck me off and get fucked right then and there."

Her eyes widened, and glinted with lust. "That sounds like a win-win for me."

"Me, too. You get three seconds. *Go.*"

John's attention switched from chocolate cake to sex just like that. All it took was Siena darting away from him with a sexy, teasing wink thrown back over her shoulder. Her robe flicked outward as she spun around the island, and gave him the briefest peek at the swell of her bare ass.

Damn.

"You're not wearing panties?" he called after her.

"Nope."

Sweet and sexy all at once.

John groaned. "That's unfair. Had I known that, I wouldn't have given you a head start, Siena."

"Too late!"

Her voice echoed to him from outside the kitchen.

"Fucking tease."

Then, Siena's head popped back in the entryway of the kitchen. "Better make it worth my while, John."

Just as fast, she was gone again.

"Yep, time's up, babe."

Only her laughter answered him back.

John discarded clothing as he headed after Siena. He didn't really have that much on, anyway. A cotton shirt, and sleep pants. Like her, he hadn't pulled anything on underneath his nighttime clothes. His shirt hit the kitchen floor, and by the time he got to the staircase and could see Siena just reaching the top, he had shoved his sleep pants down, too.

Siena left her robe hanging off the bannister. He caught sight of her bare tits as she turned at the top of the stairs, and then quickly disappeared. But not before she graced him with a sensual smile that promised all kinds of sin.

Jesus.

"You're going to kill me, *donna*."

"I love you too much for that."

John rounded the top of the stairs only to be tackled from the side by Siena. Her unexpected attack came out of nowhere. He expected her to be down the hall in the bedroom, but apparently, that was not her plan.

He lost his footing, but somehow managed to keep ahold of both of them as they tumbled to the floor. His dark laughter lit up the hallway, but it quickly turned into a low groan when Siena's lips found his throat.

Her kisses trailed lower over his chest, and down to his stomach. Her fingernails dragged soft lines down his skin, making his nerves come alive, and his skin heat under her touch.

She barely had to do anything at all to drive him crazy. A simple touch. A quick kiss. A lingering look. One of her softly whispered words. Sex was one thing.

Sex with Siena was something else entirely for John.

"Jesus Christ," he grunted when her hand snaked around his cock. A firm grip answered his harsh words, and then she stroked him as she leaned back up over his body at the same time. Her lips hovered over his, and her blue eyes locked with his gaze. "I think you like this, babe."

"Hmm, what?"

"Getting the upper hand on me."

"It doesn't happen very often."

"Do me a favor, huh?"

"What's that?" Siena asked.

"Get your mouth on my dick before I fucking explode."

Siena flashed him a smile, and without another word, she moved lower again. His fingers tangled into her hair as her mouth hovered over the head of his dick. Her tongue snaked out to strike against the tip, and taste him.

"Fucking tease," he told her again.

"*Barely.*"

That was all she said before John lost his ability to breathe or speak. She took his cock in from the tip all the way to the base. He felt her throat muscles contract from how deep he was in her mouth, and then her lips closed around him.

Silken lips. A rough tongue. Hot wetness.

Christ.

"Love your fucking mouth," he mumbled.

John swore he saw Siena try to grin around his cock. He lost sight of her eyes as she dipped her head back down and swallowed his cock again. He loved the feeling of her mouth tight around his dick, and the way her tongue stroked his shaft as she pulled him out of her mouth once more.

Still, he needed to see her.

"Look at me, Siena."

Instantly, her eyes were back on him.

Blazing blue. Raging lust. Brimming love.

John tugged on Siena's hair with one hand, and grabbed her arm with his other. Yanking her up, he pulled her into his kiss with bruising force. She straddled his waist, and let her fingernails rake over his pecs hard enough to leave stinging red streaks behind. Her wet cunt grinded against his erection in the best fucking way possible.

"Get on me, girl," he growled against her lips. "Stop this fucking teasing,

Siena."

She didn't need to be told again. Her hips shifted just the right way, and he positioned his cock where he wanted to be the very most. She fell down on his length with a sigh that melted into a satisfied moan.

"You like that?" he asked. "The way I fill you up, babe?"

"So much, John."

She rocked her hips, and fit her body even tighter against his. Every little flex of her inner muscles hugged him tight. He could feel her honey coating his shaft—he bet he could get her even wetter before they were done, though.

"You gonna ride me?" he asked.

"Yeah."

"You gonna fuck me, my pretty girl?"

"All night, if you want me to."

John grinned. "You better."

Her pace was frantic when she started riding him—a fast, hard rhythm that drove him insane. She tossed her head back, and her hair fell in a wavy, wild curtain over her tits. His hands cupped her breasts, and his thumbs tweaked at her hardened nipples.

"Come for me, Siena, and let me taste that cunt of yours."

"*Fuck.*"

He loved that.

Loved how she swore when she fucked him, and how good she sounded doing it. Not to mention, the way she *looked.*

Good God.

Siena's eyes flew wide, and found his. Her body tensed, and the broken cry that resounded matched the way her cunt squeezed him tight. He pulled her off his cock, and grabbed onto her ass to pull her higher.

Siena's hands slammed into the floor right above John's head as he yanked her down onto his mouth. He was right—she was fucking soaked.

Tart, hot, and slick.

Her arousal flooded his tongue as she finished her orgasm. He wanted to feel her coming again, though. Feel her shaking, and get her skin heating up under his touch all over again. His tongue struck out against her clit over and over.

Relentless. Fast. Unforgiving.

Siena trembled and shook as he ate her pussy until she came a second time.

"Again," he heard her whisper above him.

John kissed the hood of her clit, and looked up to find her watching him. "Whatever you want, babe."

John ticked his finger over his shoulder, and Pink followed behind at his boss's unspoken request. The enforcer was good like that. All the while, John continued chatting on the phone with the fucker giving him the most trouble at the moment.

"You mean to tell me there's nothing you can do at this point?" John asked.

"My hands are tied," Arthur Lorde said. "Unless you come up with something tangible enough to put reasonable doubt on the table, Andino is stuck where he is."

"The fact nothing ties him to the bomb—"

"It is now wide knowledge he is running the Marcello organization, Johnathan. He was there, in a business with men he was known to be having issues with, and they died. It is not a stretch for them to put two and two together to get four."

"Except you're talking a lot of circumstantial shit right now."

"They're putting things together."

"You agreed to help clear—"

"He did not say he was going to bomb a fucking restaurant in the middle of broad daylight in Brooklyn!"

The fucking bastard on the other end of the phone was lucky that John had been taking his mood stabilizers for a few days. Had they had this conversation a while ago when John's rationale was all but gone, he would have made a quick trip across town to break the motherfucker's teeth out of his head.

"Something tangible, you said?" John asked.

"Enough to cast a bigger shadow for reasonable doubt, at the very least. I need something *more*. Give me that, and this will go away."

"It'll be in your hands by tonight."

John hung up the phone without as much as a goodbye, or a fuck you.

Pink had stepped in front of his boss, and grabbed the door handle of a rundown warehouse in the heart of lower Brooklyn. He pulled it open, and let John walk into the dank-smelling, dark space.

John pointed to the side. "Go turn on the light, and then get your camera ready. Put the bag of shit aside, too."

"Got it, boss."

The second John spoke, the mumblings started from within the darkness. A sorrowful, terrified yammering that instantly made John's irritation spike a little bit higher. He shoved it down, and rubbed his hands together as he took a couple of steps into the darkness.

"No, no, please … no," it continued on.

John sighed. "Hurry, Pink. It's been a while since he's seen any kind of light."

"Gotta find the fucking switch, boss—oh, there it is."

Instantly, the warehouse was lit up by huge overhead lights that were almost as bright as the goddamn sun. It even made John squint a bit, and he knew what was coming. In the middle of the warehouse, sitting in a pool of his own piss, excrement, vomit, and water that had been thrown on him occasionally was the Capo from the hospital.

The same man who had dared to speak out against John when he could have just as easily stepped back into his place. He was sure the Capo thought John just planned to kill him, but nothing was ever that simple.

At the bright lights overhead—the first time the man had seen any kind of light since that day a week ago—the Capo withered away from the brightness. He still wore his soiled clothing he had been brought in with, although, now also with the added accessories of chains that kept him locked in a spread eagle position on the warehouse floor. In that pile.

Shit. Piss. Vomit. Water. It was undignified, really.

Well, he *had* called John a disgrace. John just figured the Capo would appreciate a better understanding of what it felt like to have his dignity taken away altogether. The man had not been touched. Not beaten, or otherwise. Not yet.

"Jesus, just *kill me*," he mumbled from the floor.

"Stop being dramatic, Roy," John murmured. "It's just a little light."

That probably felt like needles stabbing into the man's eyes.

"Why won't you just kill me?"

"This is better—more amusing," John supplied. "I was curious how much I could take away from you before you finally broke. I refused you light, food, and other than the warehouse, you have no real shelter. I took away your voice, as you can no longer communicate with anyone who will listen, or anyone who cares to. I removed your dignity the first time you pissed yourself, and I took your honor when you begged to be killed. Welcome to the land of the disgraced, Roy. We're a very pleasant bunch. I assure you."

"You're ... you are ..."

"Come on, find a noun or even an adjective to use. Pick one."

The man stammered on more.

John only nodded to himself.

Almost over.

Stepping back a few paces, John bent down to dig through the bag Pink had set aside. He pulled out a few items—a knife, ice pick, and two small handguns. John much preferred something a little heavier when it came to guns. An Eagle was perfect, but these would do the trick.

Keeping the items hidden at his back, John moved closer to Roy again. "I will let you clean up, and give you clothes. You will sit in a chair, and say exactly what you are told to say. And should you disobey, or fight, I will start with the ice pick. It will remove your ability to walk when I break it through your kneecaps before I start removing the tips of your fingers with a knife. Do you understand?"

Wild, terrified eyes stared back at John from the floor. He only smiled.

"Wh-what?" Roy stammered.

"You will do as you are told, or for the unforeseeable future, this will be your life now. Darkness, humiliation, and pain. I won't kill you, no, but I will have someone come in everyday to remind you of why you should have simply listened to me in the first place. I will feed you just enough to keep you alive, and then make you wish you would die every single day for the rest of your life. You can choose allowing your wife to get your remains back a battered, unrecognizable mess, or something far easier to understand."

Roy gaped.

"Do you understand?" John asked, bringing the ice pick out to swing it back and forth. "Well?"

Weak men were predictable. Roy was a weak man.

"Y-yes, I understand."

Just a little longer, Andi.

SEVENTEEN

"Do you want the good news first, or the good news last?" John asked.

Siena grinned. "Well, where does the bad news fit in?"

"That's the thing—there is no bad news."

Her laughter drew the attention of the other guests eating with them at the restaurant table, but John paid his family no mind.

"Just tell me," Siena said.

"Ginevra is coming back to the city this weekend—Greta and Giulia will be the first to greet her."

For a split second, Siena thought her heart had stopped. But no, the beats just took a chance to recharge before picking up an even faster pace.

"Really?"

The girls would be *ecstatic*.

They had been asking … and asking more.

Siena didn't know what to tell them.

"Really," John said.

Not even thinking about it, she leaned over to give him a quick kiss. She planned to pull away just as fast—no need to give everybody else a show, but John held her there for an extra beat in time.

"Since you're sharing news, what do you have on Andino?"

Siena frowned when John's attention drifted away from her momentarily to deal with the men who had filed into the restaurant moments before. His uncles, and his father, each took a seat at the table.

"Good morning to all of you, too," Siena said.

John shot her a sly smile. The rest of them had the decency to at least look a little bit sheepish.

"Our apologies," Lucian said, shrugging. "John is not very good at keeping people updated, and so, we have to chase him around to find out things we need to know. Isn't that right, John?"

John gave his father a look. "I update you all when there are things to report."

"Are there things to report?" Dante asked.

The quietest of the three men—Giovanni, Andino's father—rested back in the chair with a passive expression. It was almost like he didn't want to give off the aura of hope, lest karma come around and see it, only to knock him back down again. Still, the conversation held his attention, and he didn't look away once.

"Good news," John assured.

"How good?" Dante pressed.

"You really didn't think I would get this handled for Andino, did you?"

The three men quieted as they passed looks between one another. Siena cleared her throat, feeling just enough awkwardness to want to move to another table, maybe. John hadn't asked her to do that, though, so she stayed.

Finally, Giovanni spoke first. "We absolutely thought you could—"

"And would," Dante added.

"—get this done for Andino," Giovanni finished. "What we were concerned about was the fact you chose to keep us out of the loop, and went forward with your plans alone. That's not how this family works. We have always been a unit working together."

"Except that's not how *I* have to work," John replied.

Lucian grinned at his son. "And they know that now, too, John. Really. Changes like that take some adjustment, though. I think all things considered, they did pretty well stepping back as much as they could, and giving you faith."

John's jaw ticked—to Siena, a sure sign that his emotional currents were flip flopping back and forth. He was good at hiding when his high to low swings came on strong from others, but he still felt them. She couldn't imagine how hard that must be for him on a daily basis. The kind of struggle unique to him in his circle as no one else could possibly understand what it was like for him.

But his family was learning.

It seemed like they were getting it.

Finally.

Progress was progress. Whether John wanted to admit it or not, that progress would mean the world to him at the end of the day. He often alienated himself from his family, and his history with them kept him at arm's length a lot of the time.

Siena wanted to change that for him. He so loved his family, and they loved him. Look at all they had done for him.

"I think you will find," Dante said, leaning back in the chair, "that this business will be far more accommodating to you, John, once these changes become permanent."

"Which changes are those?" John asked.

Because there were a lot, Siena knew.

John had a good point.

"You controlling your own faction, and answering to yourself," Dante continued. "Andino—someone you trust and are close with—running his own faction, and answering to himself. I think, in ways, you will also … help Andino in a way."

Giovanni looked to Dante. "How do you figure?"

Lucian laughed. "I think I might know."

"Go for it, then," Dante urged with a flick of his hand.

"John is the only person Andino wouldn't go to war with. Consider how Andino is, Gio … you know it, and we all know it. His concern and care for others is fickle. He's just as quick to remove his loyalty from someone, as he is to promise it if it suits him. He is a *good* boss, but he is also a volatile one, too. You've seen his games—he manipulates, and he does whatever he needs to in order to get what he wants."

"Except with me," John murmured.

The men's gazes drifted to John again.

"Except with you," Lucian agreed. "With Dante's daughter marrying into the Donati family at the end of next month, you taking over the Calabrese faction, and Andino heading the Marcellos … we are unlikely to ever see another war between the three Cosa Nostra families controlling this city. That's unheard of."

Giovanni chuckled. "Everything our father always wanted, in a way."

"It only took three generations to get there," Dante added with a smirk.

"You know, I haven't *officially* taken over the Calabrese family," John said.

Siena decided maybe then she should get up, and go to the bathroom. Or something to get away from the conversation. It wasn't as though any of the men made her feel unwelcomed, but her upbringing had taught her that this was not the sort of thing women were allowed to be a part of.

"I'm just going to go—"

"You can stay where you are," John said, giving her a look.

"It's business, and you know women don't entertain business, John."

"They do in this family," Dante said, "or they have started taking an interest over the years. You're fine to sit."

"See," John pointed out.

Fine.

"It's a matter of semantics," Lucian said, "as they know who their new boss is, and what's expected of them."

"Sure, but I still have to make a show of it, too. Drive the point home."

"We could help with that," Giovanni offered, grinning, "if you would like us to."

"How so?" John asked.

Before any of them could answer John's question, the restaurant door blew open, and with it, bringing cold late-October wind. Siena didn't recognize the disheveled looking man wearing a trench coat, and glaring, but the other men at the table seemed to. Their postures stiffened as the man came closer to their spot.

"Detective," John greeted.

"I don't know what you fucking did, but this isn't over," the man hissed.

"Now, Rosencauld—"

"Who did you pay, huh?" the detective spat out. "Who did you blackmail, or threaten? How did you do it?"

John only smiled up at the man from the side, and never once showed concern or irritation at the intrusion. "I didn't need to do anything. The evidence was on our side."

"Evidence like this?"

The man threw a tablet down on the table, and a video was already playing. On the screen, Siena saw a man she recognized—a Capo from the Calabrese family, although she had never had a real conversation with the man. The same Capo who had spoken against John outside of the hospital the day she pulled the plug on Darren's life support.

He stumbled through his words on the video, tears filled his frightened eyes, though he sat straight and proud on a chair. Darkness rested behind him, and nothing else.

He admitted to the bombing, and to setting it up. He admitted to killing *both* Siena's brothers, and to encouraging the feud between the families to worsen the peace in the city. He admitted where evidence could be found to connect him to everything he confessed. And then he killed himself with the gun sitting in his lap by swallowing a bullet.

Rosencauld pointed a shaking finger at John. "This isn't over."

John laughed. "Oh, it's been over for a while, detective. Have a good day." The lesson was clear.

Don't fuck with the Marcellos.

"Andino will be out soon," John said after the man left. "*Very* soon."

Siena carefully maneuvered between the men sitting around the table. It was not her first time being in this spectacularly large home—the Marcello mansion— but she bet it was probably the first time for a lot of the Calabrese made men.

The fact they couldn't stop staring, wide-eyed and enraptured by the blatant show of wealth in status covering every inch, gave credence to their amazement. A few of the men had nodded to her in polite greeting as they were directed inside the home for the meeting, but more than a few wouldn't even look her in the eye.

It was going to take time.

They *would* give respect.

That was just how Cosa Nostra, and made men worked. They did not have to like the situation they currently found themselves in, or even agree with the new boss in charge. They did, however, have to offer respect at every turn.

It was that, or their life.

For most, it was an easy choice.

"Thank you," the last Capo at the table said when Siena set his glass of vodka down beside him.

"You're welcome."

She gave him a smile, but little else. She didn't linger to chat, either, instead heading for the front of the dining room where John had asked her to sit once she was done. She hadn't needed to be present for the meeting—probably shouldn't have been, anyway—but he asked for her to be there.

Siena didn't know how to refuse John.

Not really.

Still, she wasn't there to entertain the Calabrese men, or make nice with any of them, either. She was simply there for John, and so he could make his point clear with these people about where they now stood, where he positioned himself against them, and even Siena's place in the family.

As *his*.

All semantics.

Theatrics of the mafia.

It was what it was.

Sitting on a chair that was not pulled into the table, but set far enough back to make it clear Siena was not joining the men, she only took her attention away from their conversations when John came into the room. Despite the room being full of people waiting on him, he only looked at her.

Coming to stand at her side, his fingers drifted through her loose waves, and he quickly dropped a kiss to the top of her head. At home, in private, John dressed for comfort, or whatever he was doing that day.

Tonight, though, he wore one of his black Armani suits—black shirt, black vest, and black tie underneath. Black on black on black. It was quite a striking sight, and she thought he looked *most* handsome like this.

Sexy, too.

But she would save that for later.

"You good?" he asked her.

Siena nodded. "Of course."

"Good."

One more stroke of his fingers along the line of her jaw, and he turned to greet the men in the room. A wave of his hand to them, and their voices hushed.

John took the chair at the head of the table, and sat down. Glanced passes between one another, and Siena saw the arch of John's brow when he cocked it in challenge.

"You stand when a boss sits unless he has directed you otherwise," John murmured, "so move your asses."

It took a beat.

And then another second.

Chairs scraped as the men slowly rose to their feet. A couple of them grumbled under their breath, but didn't dare voice their complaints much louder than that. Once everyone was standing, John leaned back in the chair, and surveyed the men with his thumb and forefinger resting against his jaw.

"I thought you all might want to see what success in the criminal underworld really looks like," John said, waving his other hand at the opulence of the dining room.

The chandelier was bigger than a small car.

The table?

Flaked with gold.

"You could all learn a thing or two by accepting your fate of a new boss, and a new path for this family, but I assume there are some of you who plan to make this hard for me. Nonetheless, I brought you all here so you could have your *vote*. As we all do—we put in nominations for positions, and vote on them. This is no different. So, we will vote on the boss."

The men's gazes darted fast to John, and then between one another.

"Vote," one of the men echoed.

"That is what I said," John replied calmly.

"Yet, you present yourself as the boss, so where is the vote really?"

John smiled coldly. "I am giving you the illusion of a choice, and then I'm going to make my point very clear."

He lifted his fingers high, and snapped them twice. Siena stayed put on the chair with her hands folded in her lap, and quiet as could be. She knew what was coming, and it didn't shock her like it did the rest of the men to watch a good twenty more men file into the dining room.

Marcello men.

Enforcers.

Capos.

Trusted people.

Each had a gun in hand, though they kept the weapons lowered, and pointed to the ground at their front. Each man came to stand behind every standing Calabrese man, though they didn't speak, and in fact, didn't even look the other men in the eyes.

"I really don't mind wiping a family out and starting over," John said, shrugging. "It actually seems like the easier thing to do, but this takes work, too. Building a family, and working the streets takes time. I figure it will be far more beneficial for all of us to simply … accept what's going to happen, and move on to better success."

"You can't be fucking serious," one of the men said.

John's gaze drifted to the Marcello man standing behind the Capo who spoke up. His head subtly moved to the side, and the man lifted the gun, and put it to the back of the man's head.

"You will, from this day forward, refer to me in only the best of ways, and with the utmost respect. You will stand when I enter a room as you should do for your boss, and you will behave as proper made men should in a family. Should I find out you even breathed a slur against me—call me crazy, inept, or anything—you will quickly find your way into a grave."

John smile, and leaned forward as he pointed a finger at the men. "You are *all* replaceable. Never think different. I do not care how long you have been a made man, or what got you to this point. You will respect me, or I will be forced to teach you how to respect me. I would much rather leave it to you to figure out."

Then, John looked over at Siena, and gave her a brief smile. "And my girl—Siena. You will see her quite frequently. With me, or at my home. She is an important presence in my life, and she is to be treated as such. She is to be treated with the same care and respect you would give to your mother, sister, or even your wife. As you want other made men to treat the women in your life, I expect the same. She is not your pet, or your servant. She does not answer to you, and what she does choose to do for you, you are to thank her each and every time you are graced with her presence.

"I intend for her to be my wife, and I expect you to treat her accordingly," John said with a wave of his hand.

Siena's throat tightened at those words. Of course, she wanted to marry John. She wanted to be with him forever—but he not used that word with her. He had not yet asked her, but still, happiness slipped through her veins like a drug.

"Do not make me regret choosing this way with you," John said. "Do not make me think the easier route would have simply been cleaning house one by one. That option, by the way, is still very much alive."

Instantly, every man but one sat when John stood from his chair. Siena could not hide her smile, but her concerned gaze drifted to the one man who had stayed standing.

"Do you have something to say?" John asked the man.

"I will not—"

John swept his hand in a sharp motion, and the sound that followed was both deafening, and morbid. The Marcello man standing behind the Calabrese Capo had raised his weapon faster than Siena could catch the move.

Now, the Capo was dead. His body slumped over the beautiful, large cherry oak dining table. His blood from the back of his blown out head mixed in with the ruddy brown of the shined table top.

John sighed, and then waved at the rest of the men. "Shall we start, then?"

Sometimes, a forceful show was the way to go.

Siena couldn't be prouder.

Siena made a run for the front door, and grabbed the bowl of mini chocolate bars on the way. "I got it this time, John!"

"I like to see them, too."

He slid in behind her with a grin just as she opened the door to showcase three little boys and one little girl in various ninja costumes. They were by far some of the cutest that had come through for Halloween.

Bending down, Siena held the bowl out for the kids to pick their favorite treats from the mix. "Go ahead, boys … and girl."

The little girl with the pink and black ninja costume preened at Siena. "I's can be a ninja, too!"

"You can be whatever you want to be," Siena told her.

John chuckled in the doorway, and helped her to say goodbye to the kids. Once they had darted back down the steps to where their parents were waiting, she and John headed back inside the house.

"Okay, those were my favorites of the night," she declared, setting the bowl aside.

John's laughter followed her into the kitchen. "You've said that for every kid that knocks on the door tonight."

"I can't help it. Look at them."

"So hey, my sister is coming down from California for a week or two," John said.

Siena turned to find he was leaning against the island. "The youngest one?"

"Lucia, yeah. She hasn't met you yet, and I was hoping we might be able to do something with her, or … try. Then she can get to know you, or something."

"Why try?"

John shrugged. "She's still pissed at me for shit that happened a while back. Maybe rightfully so, but it is what it is. I can't change the past, you know?"

Siena smiled softly. "I'm sure she'll forgive you—whatever it was."

"Yeah, maybe. Anyway, you wouldn't mind, would you?"

"Of course, not."

One of her favorite pop songs started to play from the living room, and Siena couldn't help but dance a little to the beat. She went back to working on the food for dinner that she had discarded when the kids knocked.

She could feel John's eyes on her as she moved, and it kind of felt like butterflies beating inside her stomach.

It was strange in some ways how much had changed in such a short amount of time. Her sheltered, carefully controlled life was gone, and she was *happy*.

Sure, things were still a little shaky in a lot of ways. John taking over the family. Her mother was still missing.

Siena was still happy.

She only had one person to thank for that, too.

"Siena."

She spun on her heels to face John at his call of her name, but she had to look down. He was down on one knee, and had one hand outstretched toward her. He opened up his palm, and sitting inside was the prettiest princess cut diamond resting on a thin, interwoven gold bands.

Her heart thundered.

Her muscles froze.

Her breath caught.

John smiled. "I'm sorry it took so long for me to do this, babe."

Siena shook her head. "Never apologize for you, John."

"I love you, Siena. You know that, don't you?"

God, he had to ask?

"I love you more than life itself, John."

"I know—look at all you've done for me. My father used to tell me that everyone has one person who is their person. One single soul meant for theirs. I didn't really believe that until I met you."

She quickly wiped the one tear that escaped from her eye. "You're my one person, John."

"And you're mine, *mia amore*."

"Hurry up and ask."

John laughed. "Siena, will you be my wife?"

"*Yes.*"

He was up off the floor before she had even finished speaking. His lips found hers as he pulled her impossibly close to his body. Love thrummed through her soul. Happiness buzzed through her mind.

Unfortunately, Siena knew …

Reality was never far behind in her life. She never seemed to hold onto happiness for very long before something came to take it away.

She hoped that wasn't the case this time.

God.

She hoped …

EIGHTEEN

John leaned back against the bar, and grinned wide at the sight of the man coming through the front doors of the Brooklyn pub. Andino brushed invisible dirt from his black tweed jacket as the door swung closed behind the three men who followed him in.

Andino's gaze swept the floor—a predatory gaze, in ways—as he looked for the fucker who had demanded a meeting with him for no other reason than because *they said so*. A meeting that needed to happen this very day. On Andino's release from jail. There couldn't be another time.

John hadn't given any other information about the meeting, either. Not that it was him who called it, or why he thought he had any kind of clout to call in a meeting with a Cosa Nostra Don. Knowing his cousin like he did, John figured Andino would show up just to make a point to whatever dumb fuck called him in that he answered to absolutely no one.

Seemed he had guessed right, after all. His cousin didn't look very pleased. John smiled wider.

Finally, Andino's gaze found John leaning against the bar, and for a split second, his posture softened. His cousin took him in standing there once more, and raised an eyebrow from across the floor.

It was as though Andino was silently asking, *Really, John?*

"Hey, we have to get our kicks from somewhere, man."

Andino let out a laugh, and crossed the floor. His hand came out fast, and struck against John's already outstretched palm to clap, and then shake. Despite not being a physically affectionate kind of guy, John still pulled Andino in for a one-armed hug before he let him go again.

John took his place leaning against the bar once more as he flicked his hand at the two enforcers of his lingering close by. "Go have a drink, *cafones*. Relax a minute. We'll be staying a while before we move onto the next thing."

"You got it, boss."

Off the men went without a look back.

Andino, too, gave the two men who had followed him inside the bar a quick wave and a, "Scatter."

They *scattered*.

"You look good," John said, smirking. "I guess jail did something decent for you after all, huh?"

Andino flipped him the middle finger before taking one of the many stools at the bar. He gestured at the bartender with two fingers, and said, "Whiskey, neat."

Then, his attention was back on John.

"I can't believe you hauled my ass down to this dirty fucking pub for a drink *hours* after I get released."

John shrugged, and tipped his glass of water up for a drink. "Hey, I let you have some time with your wife. Mostly because she threatened everyone who even suggested they wanted to be at the house when you got home, but that's a story for another day. Bet you used and enjoyed every fucking minute with her, too."

Andino didn't deny it. "Yeah, and then I get a call about some arrogant, stupid fuck demanding a meeting with me like he's got some kind of right to."

John chuckled. "I knew you would come here just to beat someone's skull in."

"That's exactly what I was going to do, yeah."

Figures.

"Also," Andino said as he grabbed the glass of amber liquid from the bartender.

"What?"

"Thanks, John."

John nodded. "About time I save your ass for once, I guess."

Andino laughed hard. "Let's not make it a habit."

"You are the one with the level head."

"You've got your good qualities, too," Andino replied in kind.

Turning their backs to the bar, both men overlooked the quiet pub in comfortable silence. John enjoyed this—kind of needed it, really. It had been too long since he just sat down with Andino and did *nothing.*

"You must be busy as hell lately," Andino noted, shooting John a look.

"Christ, you don't even want to *know.*"

"Try me."

"The Calabrese organization is a mess. Mind you, it's a mess I can handle, and one I am handling just fine. It's still a goddamn mess at the end of the day. I suspected a lot of the men would be difficult, and they are at times, but they're coming around too."

"How many did you have to kill to get them that way?"

John cleared his throat. "Half a dozen, or so."

"Better than I thought."

"Funny," John drawled. "It's not even the men, really. It's more than that. Their business is shit, Andi. They've depended on their affiliations with other families, and small time gangs to keep their crews moving product, and making money. I don't know if some of the younger made men even know how to go out on the streets, and hustle up a dollar. It's fucking outrageous. Imagine being the boss who drove your organization to that kind of breaking point. They're a goddamn shame."

Andino smirked.

John didn't miss it. "What?"

"Wasn't it you and Siena they called the disgrace of your families? Seems they had something to be hiding in their own closets. Makes sense why the brothers were so adamant about trying to get in more on our business. A slice they could take and claim for themselves, I suppose."

He scowled. "Yeah, well, now I'm left with what's left of what they were trying to hide."

Andino nodded. "Yeah, but you were always one of the best Capos the Marcello *famiglia* ever had, man. Those men have the best to learn from, John. You're going to do fucking fine, and be raking in all the money."

He couldn't help but smile at that. "Better be. I don't need to be wasting my time—I'm trying to live my life, for Christ's sake, not spend the rest of it working the streets as a Don."

"You'll get it straightened out. I have no doubt. I see you're all fucking dressed up, too."

His cousin reached up, and flicked one of the silver buttons on John's blazer.

"Armani," Andino said, cracking another smug smile. "The boss only wears the best."

"I've been wearing Armani since I was sixteen," John said, shaking his head. "The thought of wearing different brands when I know this one fits me well, and doesn't bother me, makes me want to stick an ice pick in my temple."

Andino's brow lifted high. "That's a little ... over the top."

John shrugged again. "Being bipolar sometimes is."

And he had his habits for a reason. Things he ate, and the stuff he did. The clothes he preferred to wear, and even the brand of shoes he had bought for years. He was always going to be a little particular, picky, moody, and obsessive.

It was just who John was.

"So what are you doing today?" Andino asked after another minute of silence.

"Taking a break from work to pester your dumb ass."

Andino shook his head, and grinned. "*After*, I mean."

"Taking my fiancée to meet Lucia."

"Bit that bullet, did you?"

"I waited long enough," John murmured. "I was not waiting one second longer."

"Not really by choice that you had to wait, man."

"Yeah, I know."

"How do you think little Lucy is going to be with Siena?"

John scoffed. "Siena, she'll love. It's me she hates, Andi."

"Not forever."

"Right now is hard enough."

Andino tipped his glass high. "Truth. Consider, though, that she feels so strongly in a negative way about you at the moment because she felt just as strongly about you in a positive way. That means good things—the bridge is not yet burned."

"Actually, that just makes me feel like even more of a piece of shit. She trusted me, and I took something away from her that she cared about."

"Give it time. Better days are ahead, John. Far better days are ahead."

Sure.

But for how long?

John stayed a few paces behind Siena and Lucia as the two navigated The Annex. Usually, he liked the market because it was yet another place where he could be surrounded by people, but he didn't need to engage them at the same time. He was all for anything that put him in a crowd, but didn't make him the center of attention at the same time.

He was only good with that when *he* wanted it.

Today, though, John was starting to feel like a third wheel as he watched Siena and Lucia chat, and laugh together. He was not privy to their conversation as he didn't want to intrude, mostly. Lucia had barely given him a hello when he picked her up earlier, but she took to Siena damn near instantly.

Small blessings.

He was counting those up.

"John, you're out of that jam you like, right?" Siena asked over her shoulder.

Lucia's gaze drifted to her brother when Siena mentioned his name, but just as fast, hazel fire turned to dark ice in a blink. She looked ahead once more, and didn't grace him with anymore of her attention.

John sighed.

Siena didn't miss the exchange, and frowned. Had his youngest sister not been standing right there, he would have reassured Siena everything was fine. He couldn't do that, so instead, his love was left to try and fix things.

John had come to learn that about Siena.

She was a *fixer*.

"We can grab some of the jam on the way out," he told her. "Don't worry about it, *bella*."

He meant for her not to worry about more than just the jam, and hoped his unspoken message got the point across. He seriously doubted that it did, though. Siena just didn't work that way when it came to John.

Always looking out for him.

Always having his back.

"No, I can make a trip around. I need to grab something else that way, too. You and Lucia keep going. She wants to grab—what is that, again?"

Lucia didn't look at John as she said, "Some bagged tea."

"Yeah, so take her," Siena said, dropping his sister's arm and giving him a pointed look. "And I will meet you at the entrance on the way out of the market."

John tried not to scowl as Siena dropped a quick kiss to his lips and murmured, "Stop pouting, John."

He was *not* fucking pouting.

"I will meet you at the entrance," John grumbled.

"Good."

Her hand patted his cheek affectionately, and then she was gone. Quickly disappearing into the crowd of people. Just as fast, one of the two enforcers that were following along, but also keeping their distance, split away from his partner without needing to be told. He followed behind Siena without her ever realizing he was even there.

That left John.

And Lucia.

Alone.

Together.

Fuck.

"Well, come on, then," Lucia said with a cool tone and a dismissive wave.

"It's cold, and I don't want to freeze out here for too long."

John chuckled dryly, but followed along behind his sister. "You didn't mind five minutes ago when Siena was here."

He saw Lucia's shoulders stiffen from behind.

"Yeah, well …"

Time to bite another bullet.

"What do you need me to say, Lucia?" John asked quietly, speaking to the back of her head because she still wouldn't even look at him. "Tell me what to say so that we can move on, and I will do that. Sorry isn't going to be good enough—I get that. So what will do it for you?"

For the briefest second, his sister's posture softened. She stopped walking, but the people continued to blow by them in the market. No one around them seemed to feel the tension biting pain passing between the two siblings.

Slowly, Lucia turned around to face him. The coldness in her gaze had finally left, but he wasn't all too sure that he liked what replaced it, either. A line of watery tears that were damn near ready to fall, but somehow, she held the floodgates back.

"You're right," Lucia said quietly, "sorry *won't* be good enough, John."

"But I am sorry."

She nodded. "*Now.*"

"The day it happened. The day I found you. The day Renzo was taken away. That very second, Lucia, I was *sorry*. That was not what was supposed to happen."

Her jaw hardened, and goddamn, she looked so much like their father in that moment, it was unreal. Only their dad could hold back his emotions with a hardened jaw, and clipped words.

Lucia didn't do that, though. "Did you know he hated me?"

"Who?"

"Renzo," Lucia said. "At first, he thought I was just some little rich bitch with an air-filled head, and a pretty face. I didn't know what it was like to be poor, or to struggle. I didn't know the streets, or how hard they are on people like him. I didn't know what it was like to come where he comes from, or how to survive without a trust fund."

"Lucia—"

"He was right, too. And maybe I should have thanked him for making that obvious to me, you know? He woke me up. It took thirty days to change my life, and *seconds* to make it worse all over again."

John scrubbed a hand down his jaw, and glanced away. Silently, he dug in the inner pocket of his jacket, and pulled out a piece of information he had been keeping hidden for a while. He always planned to give it to Lucia, sure, but at the right time.

Now seemed like that time.

"Here," John said.

Lucia eyed the folded up piece of paper. "What is it?"

"A better apology."

His sister plucked the paper from his hand, but never took her gaze off him all the while. It was almost like she thought he was going to jump out and snatch the paper back, or some kind of nonsense.

Lucia unfolded the four squares of the paper, and silently read over the information. He saw the way her gaze flicked back and forth—how her fingers tightened to crumple the edges of the paper, and the way her eyes filled up with tears all over again.

"You don't have to say anything," John told her. "Not thank you, or fuck you, or anything, Lucia."

"Does Dad know you got this for me?" she asked.

John shook his head. "Nope. It's also not about Dad. It's about us. Sometimes, I think Dad just worries too much about us. He wants us to be safe, and happy, and fulfilled. In the process, his protective nature sometimes smothers us, too. And that's just Dad—he is who he is, and we have to love him regardless, Lucia."

"I do love Daddy, but—"

"You're angry with him, too."

A single tear dropped down Lucia's cheek, but she didn't move to wipe it away. "So fucking mad, John."

"It's cliché, kiddo, but what's meant to be, will be, and fuck the rest." John pointed at the paper, and said, "There's your lifeline, Lucia. You want to talk to Renzo—you want to *know*? He's right there. I'm sorry it's not more."

Lucia clenched the paper harder, and looked up at her brother. "This is perfect, John."

He smiled. "That's all I wanted to—"

His words cut off when a scream filled The Annex. A terrified scream that was accompanied by several other shrill shrieks. People began to scatter like horrified rats shoved in a very small space. One shoved John, which caused him to ram into Lucia. He grabbed hold of his sister with a fucking death grip to keep her from being shoved to the ground.

"What is happening?" Lucia asked.

John had no idea.

Another shrill scream echoed.

Someone shouted, *"She's got a gun!"*

John's blood ran cold. He didn't have any reason to think this was an attack on him, or Siena, but for some reason, he just … knew.

It had to be.

His luck had run out.

"Don't fucking move," he told his sister when he shoved her behind a vendor tent.

"John!"

"Don't move!"

John didn't look back as he darted in the direction that everybody was now running from. The same direction that Siena had went in earlier to get his fucking jam.

Jesus Christ.

For *jam*.

He would be lucky if he could ever put the shit in his mouth again after today. At the moment, it only made him want to vomit at just the thought alone.

John rammed through the oncoming people—he barely heard their shouts of terror, and he faintly registered the fear on their faces. He was laser focused on one thing, and one thing only. He didn't care about anybody else at the moment.

Siena. Siena. Siena.

His heart thundered her name. The organ practically jumped into his throat, and beat even harder there, too.

"You *ruined* us, you little bitch! Everything our family worked for, you ruined it! You disgraced our name, and our legacy and for what? So you could spread your legs for some Marcello—"

"Ma, put the gun down. Please, put the gun down. You're scaring people."

John pushed through the last few people, and came to an abrupt stop only fifteen feet away from the entrance of The Annex. Siena stood in a cleared circle with her mother only a couple of steps away.

Coraline Calabrese.

That fucking bitch.

John hadn't been able to get a lead on the woman once she disappeared after Darren's death, but he hadn't been too worried. He thought—stupidly, clearly— that the woman was just that ... a *woman*. Not one with any power, or capability to hurt them. She could go away and lick her wounds about her shattered family in private, and maybe come back to beg her daughter for forgiveness in the future.

He had been wrong.

So wrong.

They were going to pay for it.

Siena held up her hands, and in one, held the jar of jam John liked. A bright red, sweet mix of raspberries and strawberries. Her position almost looked resigned—she spoke so calmly, and without fear.

John reached for a non-existent gun at his back at the same time Coraline pulled back the hammer on the revolver. He didn't have a gun on him; it wasn't safe given his position, now. He had too much attention from cops and detectives, and his probation said he couldn't have any firearms on his person, legal or otherwise.

That's why he kept the enforcer's close.

Where the fuck were they?

Coraline's gun lit like a sparkler on the Fourth of July when she pulled the trigger. Another gunshot rang out right after.

John was already darting into the circle. His arms were already opened to grab Siena ... or in this case, to catch her.

He fell with her.

On damp pavement.

On cold ground.

Unfeeling.

So numb.

The jar of jam shattered—spilling sweet red all over the ground. It mixed in with the blood pumping from the love of his life in his hands, and the woman resting face-first on the ground with a blown out skull.

Siena stared up at him from his lap as red bloomed over her chest. It soaked through her white, off-the-shoulder dress in the most morbid way. "*John.*"

Panic and rage and fear and pain washed through John's senses all at the same time. He had never been very good at handling this kind of thing.

He raged.

Roared at the man who had shot Coraline.

Shouted at Siena, too.

"John," she breathed.

Dots of blood peppered her lips. Losing pink, and gaining the wrong shade of red, he thought.

"Look at me," he heard himself say. "Keep looking at me, my girl."

She did.

And then she didn't.

The noise in John's mind and emotions became impossibly louder. It became far more painful. It couldn't be contained.

He raged on.

"They were only trying to *defuse* the situation, John," someone said.

"Which is exactly what enforcers are taught to do," someone else added.

"You don't want them going out with guns blazing all the damn time—that's not how we fucking work, and you know it."

"They did their job, son," was the next sentence flung his way. "Coraline is dead—he took the shot the second he knew he had no choice."

Over his shoulder, John hurled with venom, "A fucking second too late!"

Silence answered him back.

His emotions were up.

Then they went *way* down.

Like a fucking swinging pendulum. One he couldn't possibly control no matter how much he tried to hide his issues.

He knew it was because today had just been too much—too much stimulation, and too much happening. His meds were not meant to combat these kinds of mood swings caused by traumatic events.

He tried to force himself to be quiet so his outbursts lessened.

John went back to staring at the clock.

Three hours in surgery …

Three more hours to go.

Or, that's what the nurse said when she came with an update.

Siena's heart had been nicked by the bullet. It ricocheted off a rib, punctured her lung, and grazed her heart. She'd been drowning and choking in her own blood while she laid in his lap, and that *killed* him.

He was never going to forget that.

Nothing was going to take that image away.

"And you want me to fucking let them go without punishment?"

His snarl echoed back in a silent waiting room.

He had tried to be quiet again.

He failed.

"John?"

He blinked as he stared at the clock. Every ten seconds, on the dot, he blinked again. Like a fucking robot. He heard them talking—his family, and his men. He heard their words and their justifications.

Part of him knew they were right.

Part of him didn't give a fuck.

That part was the one with bloodstained skin, and hatred in his heart. That part was the one who wanted to punish every stupid fuck that had failed to protect Siena today. That part was dead and dying and full of a rage so hot, it could only be the color black.

Like his mind.

Tar black.

"John?"

He looked to the side as someone tugged on his jacket, and found Lucia staring up at him. Her red-rimmed hazel eyes were a stark contrast to his dry, blazing gaze.

"Is she okay?" Lucia asked.

John shrugged, but even the action felt like it took too much effort. "I don't know."

"John, we need to talk about the enforcers—"

He found the men staring at him over his shoulder again—his father, uncles, Andino, and his own men.

They wanted to *talk*.

He wanted to *kill*.

John looked back at the clock. "I don't need to do anything at the moment."

Besides, his choice for those enforcers had already been made.

She lived—they lived.

It was that simple.

It was in God's hands now.

John's hands were tied.

NINETEEN

Siena cracked aching eyelids open to see white stucco tile staring back at her from the ceiling. A strong antiseptic smell burned her lungs with every breath. The low, rhythmic beeps made her head pound. Something hurt like fucking hell in her chest.

She coughed.

Oh, God.

Yeah, shit, that hurt way worse.

Still, she refused to close her eyes and go back to sleep, no matter how much she wanted to do just that. She could tell she was in the hospital, but it was only after a few seconds of being lucid that she remembered why she had found herself there.

Her mother shot her.

Her own mother.

Siena blinked again.

"Look into this light for me, sweetheart, and follow it," she heard a man say.

That statement was quickly followed by a snarled grumble in the corner of the room—an angry, heated hiss of words that both worried her, and comforted her. Siena's bed was propped up higher, and her gaze found the person in question.

John.

His hard-set jaw, and blazing eyes would have nailed the doctor to the wall had the man been looking at John. He clearly didn't like the man using pet names on Siena, and while it was cute, she didn't even think she had the energy to smile at the moment.

"Follow the light, not the angry Marcello in the corner," the doctor said, grinning just a little.

Apparently, she could smile.

It didn't take that much effort after all.

"Sorry," she rasped.

"Johnathan," the doctor said, "I think the patient could use a bit of water. Three quarters of ice, one quarter of water, please."

"The nurse—"

"They are all busy at the moment. Siena will be fine for the entire forty seconds it will wake you to walk across the hall to the machine, and fill her a cup of water."

John looked like he struggled the most just to get up out of that chair. His blazing gaze flitted between the doctor, and Siena momentarily before settling on her. The anger there quickly bled away when she offered him a dry-lipped smile.

Or the best she could give.

"Please?" she asked him.

John nodded, but he didn't tear his gaze away from her until he was out of the room entirely.

"He's very protective of you," the doctor noted, still moving his light.

Siena followed it with her gaze as she had been instructed to do. "He can't really help it."

"He scares my nurses sometimes."

"Yeah, he can't really help that, either."

The doctor chuckled low, and clicked the button on the end of his mini-flashlight. The bright light turned off, and then he shoved it into his breast pocket.

"All in all, you're doing remarkably well. We expected you to wake up within a few hours of your surgery," he explained, "but maybe your body felt you needed the extra rest, as it's been twenty-four hours since you came out of the OR."

Siena almost felt like a sludge hammer had come and beat her right in the chest. "A whole day?"

"Your surgery took about five hours. There was a lung to repair, and a small piece of heart. Once in there, I found fragments from the bullet had embedded into different places. I didn't want to leave those in, so what should have been three hours turned into five. I suspected six—sometimes we all win."

Siena coughed, and pain followed all over again. Blinding, aching pain deep in her chest cavity that then spread throughout her entire nervous system. As though it was her body's way of trying to numb the pain a bit by spreading it out.

Still, it fucking hurt.

She pulled back the hospital gown to see the bandages wrapped around her chest. She suspected there was going to be a mighty scar left behind, but it was only details in the background of far bigger thoughts.

She had survived.

She was alive.

"How long is it going to feel like this?" she asked.

"Hmm, like what, sweetheart?"

"If he doesn't like it, then you probably shouldn't call me that."

The doctor grinned, saying, "You're probably right."

"It feels like I am breathing in acid."

"Ah. Well, until the wound in the lung heals, I imagine. You're breathing without a respirator, and came out of surgery like that, so it won't be long. You are young, and healthy. All good things. I suspect you will be discharged in a couple of weeks, and by then, you probably won't need the bandages. Your nurses will be in twice a day to check the surgery incision, and change the bandages when needed."

The doctor shrugged, adding, "You were incredibly lucky. Had the bullet been even a couple of millimeters to the left, your heart would have been useless. You'll need to take it easy for a month or so. No strenuous activity—nothing more than walking from one room to the next."

That sounded fun.

"I will make sure she rests," John said from the doorway.

John gave Siena a sexy wink, and crossed the room with a cup of ice water in his hand. The doctor gave her one last order to get some sleep, and keep the excitement to a minimum for the first couple of days, and then he left.

The sliding ICU doors closed shut behind him. It was only her and John left, then. The curtains covering the glass windows blocked out the outside world. John used a dial behind her head to turn down the lights in the room.

Another button quieted the machines.

Silently, John climbed into the bed with Siena. She hadn't even gotten the chance to ask him to do that—he already knew what she wanted.

The second he was there with her, and she was wrapped in his embrace, nothing else mattered. She cried because she was sad, and she was happy, and she was terrified. She was all of those things at once, and it was overwhelming.

John rocked her while his lips pressed against her forehead with a soft kiss— comfort, affection, and assurance all rolled into one. Next to the heartbeats between them, she couldn't hear anything else.

She didn't want to.

John tipped her head back, and used the pads of his thumbs to wipe away the tears from her cheeks. He quickly pressed one kiss, and then another just as fast to her smiling lips. All the worry he had shown earlier was gone for the moment. Sure, there was still a bit of concern flashing in his eyes, but nothing like before.

"I'm sorry," she said.

John's brow furrowed. "For what, *amore?*"

"Between us, I'm always the calm, levelheaded one. I know this probably upsets you. I'm sorry."

"*You* don't upset me. Ever."

His statement was so small, and yet firm and sure at the same time. As though it wasn't at all up for argument, and he didn't want to entertain it further. She chose to let it go because it didn't really matter.

John kissed her again—lingering longer the second time, and letting his tongue tease at the seam of her lips. It was not nearly as innocent or sweet as his first kisses. Siena's heart picked up the pace.

"You're not supposed to *excite* me," she whispered.

John laughed darkly. "My bad."

Then, she had another thought. "Is my mom—"

"Dead."

Flat. Dry. Cold.

His tone was all of that, and more.

Siena sucked in a shaky breath. "Yeah, okay."

"Sorry," he murmured. "I know that probably hurts."

"A little."

She was still her mom.

Coraline had given her life.

She simply hadn't cared about it.

"But probably not for the reasons you think," Siena added.

"I think—"

John's words cut off when a knock against glass echoed. Siena could see through the one sliding glass door with no curtain that people were waiting. A new family for her. People who loved her because John loved her.

His family.

"So much for no excitement," John muttered, climbing off the bed.

"They'll be good, and quiet."

"They're Marcellos. They don't know how to be good *or* quiet."

He was right.

But she had needed all their noise and love.

Just like she needed him.

Six weeks later ...

The front door to the Queens home Siena now shared with John slammed shut, and she cursed under her breath. She didn't even have the time to hide the laundry basket she was hauling up the stairs before her lover came around the corner.

John's gaze drifted to the basket in Siena's hands, and then to where she stood halfway up the stairs. His eyes narrowed, and he gave her *that* look. The one a parent might give their child when they caught them doing something naughty.

"Oh, my God," she grumbled, "it is *just* clothes, John."

"You're not supposed to be doing anything but resting, Siena."

He came closer, and she shook her head.

Nope.

She was not doing this with him anymore. She was fine, and he was just going to have to let his overprotective nature down a little bit.

Holy fuck, she was lucky she could wipe her own ass the way he went on sometimes. The most she had gotten to do since leaving the hospital was attend Catherine Marcello's wedding to Cross Donati.

And even then, John barely left her side, or let her do anything more than walk a few steps before he told her to sit down. She knew he was concerned—he didn't want her to push too far, and hurt herself.

Siena was *fine.*

John was going to have to deal with it.

"Siena, put that damn basket down and go read one of your books, or something," John said, his foot landing to the bottom stairs.

She knew he was pissed.

How?

He hadn't taken his shoes off at the front door. There was nothing he hated more than dirt being tracked through the house because people didn't take off their shoes. The fact he was the one tracking dirt meant his focus was somewhere else entirely.

All on her, apparently.

"No," Siena said, turning her back to him.

"*Siena.*"

Her name practically yanked from his lips in a growl. A warning, if she ever heard one. John was not playing around, but neither was she.

Siena picked up her pace, and climbed the last few stairs without even losing a breath. She hoped that would be a clue to John—because her last three appointments had apparently not done that for him.

John was right behind her all the way. She made it to their bedroom, and dropped the basket on the floor beside the bed when he rushed into the room, too.

"What in the hell is wrong with you?" he asked.

"You."

John snapped back like she had struck out at him.

So, maybe she could have presented that statement a little bit easier than she had. Still, it needed to be said, and John needed to *hear* it for once.

"You hover, and you nitpick at every little thing I do," she told him. "You even get frustrated when I want to have a shower instead of a bath because I might be on my feet for too long. I couldn't even dance at your cousin's wedding—I wanted to dance with *you*. In case you forgot, I also have a job. Or I did, before you know, my brothers were killed. But now *I* own those businesses—they're mine, and I have to take care of them. I need to get out, and do shit, John. Work. Walk. See the goddamn sun."

He stared at her, unmoved and quiet.

Siena continued on, saying, "It's a laundry basket with a half of a load full of clothes. It weights six pounds at most. I can carry it from the downstairs, to the upstairs, and put it away without a problem. I am *fine*."

"Fine," John murmured.

"That's what I said."

"And I am your problem."

Siena pressed her lips together before saying, "I didn't mean it like that, and you know it, John. I just meant … I know what happened was traumatic for you, and it scared you. You're not going to say that, though, because it's you. But I *know*. I do."

John glanced away, and scrubbed a hand down his face. "I don't want you to push yourself too hard, that's all."

"It's been six weeks. I am cleared. I can resume normal activity. You know this."

"But what if—"

"No."

"Siena, you have to—"

"No."

"You can't—"

"Nope."

John let out a frustrated grunt, saying, "Let me finish a sentence, *donna*."

"Unless that sentence is something about getting me on my knees, I really don't want to hear it. Because you know what, that's another thing. You won't even fuck me for fear I might get out of breath. That's kind of the point of *sex*, John."

"I know what sex does!"

"That is not the thing I want to hear," Siena said in a singsong fashion.

John gave her a look.

Another unspoken warning.

Siena wasn't having it.

"Killing me here," John muttered under his breath.

Siena grinned wickedly. "What if I helped you along, then? Do you think that would snap you out of this nonsense?"

"It's not nonsense. It's—"

John's words cut off when Siena pulled the straps of the dress she was wearing down over her shoulders. Without the straps to hold the flimsy fabric up, it simply fell down her body, and landed in a heap at her feet.

She wore nothing underneath.

No bra.

No panties.

This was planned.

She had a goal.

She was going to get it.

John made a noise under his breath, and then said, "What are you doing?"

Siena gave him a wink over her shoulder as she moved toward the bed. "What do you think?"

"You seriously want to fuck right now? We're having a discussion."

"No, you're having a discussion with yourself. I told you what I told you, John."

She bent over the bed to reach for one of the pillows, and pulled it toward her chest. Her scar had healed, but it could still be a little tender. Having something soft to rest on would help that little issue.

"Jesus *Christ*," John said low and husky.

Siena looked back at him.

She knew exactly what he was seeing—her bent over, and her bare ass high in the air. Given her legs were a little spread, he could probably see a peek of her pussy, too.

John's gaze lingered on her backside.

Siena smiled.

Good.

"Killing me here," he rumbled, moving closer with every word. "I know what you're doing, Siena."

Dark.

Rich.

Sinful.

His tone promised sex.

Siena's body hummed in anticipation. "Do you?"

She jumped—heating shooting through her body—when John's warm, rough palm slid from her ass to the top of her spine. His other hand landed a soft slap to her backside. Not enough to hurt, but just enough to *sting*.

It made her sigh.

"I am fine," she said, looking back at him.

John's hazel gaze found hers. "So you say."

"I am."

"Mmm."

He just needed a little more pressure applied, apparently.

Siena could do that.

She pushed her ass back into his groin before he could think to stop her. At the same time, she slid her hand between her thighs, and let the tips of her fingers run through her sex. Dampness met her fingertips, and she used that wetness to help her fingers slide in fast circles around her clit.

Jesus.

Already, her body was revving to go. Already, she was wet between her thighs. It had been too long for this, and she was not waiting one more fucking second.

"Siena," John murmured.

She kept playing, knowing damn well he could hear the sound of her fingers sliding through her arousal. "You should help me out here."

How was she already breathless?

How?

"Well," John drawled in that rumbly way of his, "I think you should get yourself off first, and then we'll talk about what comes after that."

Siena's eyes widened, and she found him grinning behind her. He lifted a single brow as if to ask her to challenge him while he shrugged off his suit jacket, and began unbuttoning his dress shirt.

Her fingers stopped working between her thighs. He didn't miss it.

"Don't stop now, Siena, you started this little game."

"But … but I want *you* to—"

"I know what you want, and you can wait."

Fuck.

She as not a dumb woman.

She could see how this turned around on her.

His palm came down on her ass harder than the first time. The harsh, yet still lovely, sting sent her flying up to her tiptoes with a gasp.

"Play," John ordered. "And don't be fucking cute about it, either, or you'll wait longer, babe."

"Fuck you," she whispered through a laugh.

John flashed her a grin with teeth. "And we will be talking about the other shit you brought up after."

"Whatever," she said, working her fingers faster against her clit with every passing second. "I got what I wanted."

"Or you will soon," he countered.

"You know it, John."

"Widen those beautiful legs of yours. Show me that pussy—I want to see your fingers nice and wet. It's all mine, so let me see it."

Damn.

His filthy words flamed her desire higher.

Siena did what she was told, and made sure to let him see two of her fingers press deep into her sex before she dragged them back up to her clit. "You like that?"

"Just worry about you, babe."

Because yes, he did like it.

Siena heard the fabric of his shirt ruffle as he yanked it off, and then tossed it aside. She looked back at him again at the rustle of a buckle just in time to see him shove his pants down over his hips, and free his already hard cock from the confines of his boxer-briefs.

Not once did John's eyes drift away from where her fingers worked between her thighs. She saw lust glint there—a pure, carnal love at what he was seeing. That only made her hotter, and already, she felt like she was going to combust.

Her nerves sang.

Her skin hummed.

Her clit ached.

"Almost?" he asked.

"God, *yeah*."

"God does not live in this bedroom, babe. It is just you, and me."

The spiral of her orgasm came on fast. A shot of cold down her spine, and a wave of heat in her gut. Pleasure started from somewhere in her center, and radiated outward until it reached the tips of her fingers and toes.

"Holy shit," Siena breathed into the pillow.

Intense, but not quite enough.

Wonderful, but it could have been more.

Good, but the relief didn't linger.

She couldn't make herself come like John could. It was sometimes strange to her how this man knew her body even better than she did.

John proved it in those seconds by letting one of his fists tangle in her hair, and sliding his hard length into her clenching sex before she had even finished panting her way through the orgasm. She felt him flex, and he was seated in deep.

Stretching her open.

Filling her full.

"Christ, I love the way you soak me," he said behind her.

His body fit perfectly against hers. So deep, her muscles hummed from clenching around him so tight. She vibrated all over.

She could feel that promise of another release—a better, stronger one—just beyond her grasp. She wouldn't be able to reach it herself.

No, he would have to take her there.

"Ask me for it," John murmured against the back of her neck.

His other hand slid around her throat. Long fingers wrapped along the delicate column, and held tight. She still had her breath, sure, but it caught in her throat a little with every exhale and swallow. His fingertips danced along her pulse point.

"*Ask me for it, Siena.*"

"Please fuck me."

"Hmm? I didn't hear you, babe."

His lips grazed her neck, and then her ear. His words slipped over her skin with damningly sinful intent.

A wicked promise.

"Please fuck me, John," she said a little louder.

Not much, though.

She was airless.

Her mind muddy.

Her body needy.

"Please, *please* fuck me."

He either got the response he wanted, or he felt bad for teasing her like he had. She didn't even get the chance to take another breath, or prepare for him to take her again. He simply pulled back, and flexed forward all in the same second.

A hard thrust that sent her back up to her toes, and pushed her further into the pillow. She was right—the softness of the pillow cushioned her chest enough to keep the tenderness at bay.

She didn't even think about it at all as he pounded into her from behind. She couldn't think about anything except for his cock driving into her over and over again, and the way he held onto her hair and throat at the same time.

His pace was brutal.

Unforgiving.

So relentless.

John didn't slow at all when Siena's cries became a little higher, and her breaths came out shorter. He fucked her through the second orgasm, and then kept on going until she was shouting her way through a third.

Nobody owned her like he did.

Nobody loved her like he did.

Nobody could ever possibly be him to her.

"One more," she heard him say, his words mumbled into her hair. "Give me one more, babe."

"I can't—I *can't*."

She didn't think she could come again.

John had a different opinion. "You sure fucking can."

It took longer for the fourth orgasm to come. It took her fingers toying between her thighs, while he fucked her hard enough to make her bones ache in the best way. It took two of his fingers stuffed into her ass while he yanked her hair back, and whispered the dirtiest things in her ear.

God.

She loved all of it.

She didn't hurt a bit.

She really was just fine.

"Fuck, *yeah*."

She heard John's grunt through her mindless, pleased haze a second before his warm cum painted her back. His hand pressed hard against her shoulders, and she could feel the tremor working its way through his body just from the pressure alone as he tried to keep himself upright.

Siena laughed.

John chuckled, too.

"I still said what I said," she said, tasting sex and love on her tongue. "And I meant it—I am fine, John."

"Don't push me, Siena."

"Who else will?"

TWENTY

John laughed as the men crowded him into a hotel room. His father followed in behind his uncles, cousin, and grandfather with baby Tiffany on his hip.

"Come on," John said, "I am sure I can fucking dress myself, now."

"We have to make sure you don't run," Giovanni joked.

"And we have to have at least one drink before you head down," Andino added.

He gave his cousin a look. "I'm not drinking."

Dante gave John a light slap to his cheek as he passed. "One drink will not hurt you—we'll make it a beer."

Fine.

A beer he could do.

"Here," Andino said, throwing the garment bag at John.

"Christ, that's a four-thousand dollar Armani suit. Be easy, Andi."

Andino pointed a finger at his cousin. "Get your ass dressed."

Lucian gestured at the attached bathroom. "Get ready in there. We'll be waiting when you're done."

The rest of them were already done up, and waiting on him. Frankly, they had kept him running and on his feet from the moment he woke up to a splash of cold water being dumped on his face that morning.

Fucking Andino.

"I hope you all did this to Andi on his wedding day, too," John threw over his shoulder.

"Nope," someone called back.

"Assholes."

He shut their laughter out by closing the bathroom door. Finally, he had some kind of silence for the first time all day.

John stood there and soaked it in.

Soon, nothing would be quiet. A room full of guests.

A dinner. A party after.

It was a lot of stimulation, and probably the only thing about this whole day that had really concerned John. Still, anticipation curled heavily in his gut, mixing with the lingering longing that hadn't left him since he knew he loved Siena.

He was getting married to the love of his life today.

Nothing else mattered.

"All right, I'm fucking dressed," John said as he left the bathroom.

Surprisingly, only his father and Andino were left in the room. Well, and little baby Tiffany sleeping over her grandfather's shoulder.

"Where did everybody go?" John asked.

"To get the drinks," Andino said, flashing him a grin. Coming close to John, his cousin pulled him in for a one-armed hug. "You look good, man."

"I better."

Andino laughed. "Don't pump that ego up too big, huh?"

"Too late."

"It's a Marcello thing."

That was the excuse they all used.

Nothing ever changed.

"I have to go grab something from Haven, but I'll be back," Andino told him.

John nodded. "Sure, man."

Once Andino was gone from the room, John took a seat beside his father. Lucian gave him a small smile all the while patting his granddaughter's bottom in a rhythmic fashion to keep her asleep.

Things with Cella weren't necessarily better, but they weren't horrible, either. At least, his sister could stand to be in the same room with him, and didn't make it her second job to glare at him. She was still grieving, though, and so John opted to keep his distance.

Time would heal wounds.

After all, time had healed *his* wounds.

Well, time and Siena.

"You know I'm proud of you, don't you?" Lucian asked quietly.

John nodded. "I know, Dad."

He reached over and stroked the sleeping baby's cheek.

"She's precious," Lucian said. "I thought very little would compare to when my children were born, but let me say, grandchildren are something else entirely. I look forward to having more, and *soon*."

His father gave him a pointed look.

John rolled his eyes. "Not even trying to be sly."

"I have moved beyond that stage in my life. It doesn't get me what I want."

"Children are not on the table for a while."

Lucian frowned. "Why not?"

John shrugged, but didn't offer any information as to how much the thought of children terrified him to his core. He still struggled with the idea of passing on a life that sometimes felt like a punishment, rather than simply a difference.

"Ah," Lucian said like he could read John's mind.

John cocked an eyebrow. "What?"

"You still think about that genetics test we did years ago, don't you?"

"And the information you found about Lina."

Lina being his father's biological mother.

Lucian cleared his throat. "And yet, despite the fact she was bipolar, all I remember about my mother is how beautiful, loving, and wonderful she was,

John."

"Perhaps your perspective is colored by the fact she died when you were like seven, or something."

"Perhaps, but I don't think it matters, either." Lucian smiled faintly again. "You should never—*ever*—be afraid to have a child just like you, son. You were an amazing boy who grew into an incredible man. You were perfect—more like me than your mother, but with just enough of Jordyn to color you up. You made your mother and I better people, John. You made us better parents. We learned to stop and take account of ourselves, and of others. We learned not to be ignorant in our thoughts and feelings about things people suffer with, and often suffer in silence."

Lucian shrugged, adding, "You were, and still are, one of our greatest gifts. And if anything I have ever done makes you afraid to be a father, then I am sorry."

"You are the best father."

"Who still makes mistakes sometimes," Lucian said.

"That's what humans do."

It had just taken him a long time to realize that.

"Please don't be afraid to have a child like you, John. Don't ever be afraid to become a better man because of it, either."

John stood at the end of the makeshift aisle. Silk and tulle and bushels of white and pink flowers covered the place in light colors, and floral scents. Guests had already filled the fifty or so white chairs set up—their ceremony was small, but their party would be massive.

Siena liked the harp, so a woman dressed in purple played one in the corner. An ordained minister waited behind John and Andino, ready to begin whenever those doors at the back opened.

They could have had this ceremony in a church, as would have been better for *la famiglia*, but John refused to wait. He would not spend time on useless couple's counseling when he already knew what he wanted for the rest of his life.

He didn't need a priest to confirm it.

Siena was his.

And he was hers.

Andino's hand clapped John on the shoulder. "You ready?"

John nodded.

Sweet Jesus.

He had been ready for his whole life. It just took three decades to finally meet her. Because that's what Siena was to him—his life.

"Yeah," John said.

Andino nodded to someone in the back, and the waiting man stepped up to the doors. He swung them open, and took a step back to get out of the way.

There, waiting, was Siena.

In her A-line, ivory lace wedding dress that swept the floor, and trailed behind her with a four foot train. Her veil kept her face hidden, but not quite enough. He could still see the way her painted red lips curved with love when his gaze landed on hers.

She was beautiful.

So perfect.

He was going to spend the rest of his life loving this woman, and making sure she knew it every second of every single fucking day of their lives.

She had been his catalyst.

She had been his saving grace.

She was his everything.

Loving her forever was the least he could do.

"Your turn," Andino said.

Yeah, it was his turn.

He promised, after all.

She wouldn't walk alone.

John made his way down the aisle in a quick stroll. Siena stayed still at the very end, waiting for him.

He probably should have waited until the end of the ceremony to do what he did.

It was the custom.

Tradition.

John didn't care about any of those things. The second he met her at the end, he bunched her veil up, flipped it back, and kissed her hard.

Laughter lit up the room.

Siena's smile curved against his.

"I love you," he told her.

"I love you, John."

"Are you ready?"

Siena nodded. "I have been ready."

They turned to face the now-standing guests.

A future was waiting.

Finally.

EPILOGUE

Three years later ...

If there was one thing—above all things—about her marriage and John that Siena thought was most important to remember, it was that surprises were not welcomed. Especially if said surprise meant a huge change in their lives, or something that could cause a massive emotional upheaval.

For other people, a change could be a good thing. A little stress, and a bit nerve-wracking, sure. They would, however, roll with the punches and accept the change.

For John, though, a change that could and would impact his entire life often led him to overthinking, panicking, and more. It almost guaranteed a hypomanic episode would be on the horizon, and once that was controlled, a short bout of depression to battle.

Siena never blamed him for these things.

She never wished for anything different.

Oh, she loved John.

Every part of him was hers to love.

So as she sat on the edge of the tub in their master bathroom, and stared at the little strip of plastic in her hand ... she couldn't help but think of what this would mean, and what would come of it.

The pregnancy test flashed with the word *pregnant.*

Over and over.

It had been flashing that for thirty minutes now. Her heart was so full— happiness, trepidation, and joy. A love so fierce, she could hardly breathe. Already, she loved this baby. A child she didn't know, and would not see or hold for months. A child whose gender was still unknown, and whose name was yet to be picked.

And yet ...

God, she loved this baby.

Still, the hesitance she felt was also very real.

Long ago, she and John had decided that children would be a very carefully planned event for them. When both of them were ready, and when everything was handled, then they would move forward *together* on having children.

This had not been planned at all.

Certainly not carefully.

A bout of a terrible chest cold that left Siena with a nasty infection, and led into pneumonia that she couldn't shake caused her to miss an appointment for her shot. She had been stuck in bed, and then in the hospital for two weeks when the pneumonia got really bad.

John had barely left her side, of course.

Once she was better, her doctor recommended she wait until her cycle started at least once—as she hadn't had a period in years since starting the shot—before they started the birth control again. They had been advised to use condoms as a backup method.

Yeah, well …

Her cycle never started. She and John didn't know what a fucking condom was considering they hadn't used them since the start of their relationship years ago.

They both knew better.

She knew better.

This was bound to happen.

Siena had promptly vomited every bit of the eggs and bacon mess John had left for her in the oven before he left for his morning jog. She had been keeping a pregnancy test hidden in her purse … just in case.

A part of her already knew.

Siena tapped the test against her palm again.

Pregnant, it flashed.

She was still trying to figure out a way to tell John and not surprise him, so to speak. She knew it was going to be practically fucking impossible. There could be no cute reveal that she secretly recorded, and then posted for the world to see. There could be no baby shoes in a gift box for him to open and be surprised.

None of that could happen.

She had to take away that element of shock so that this did not feel as though something John was not ready for in the first place.

Easier said than done.

Children had been his one sore topic for years. Not because he didn't want to be a father, but because she knew he worried that he was going to pass on the same genetics that had been given to him. Whatever it was in his DNA that left him with a disorder that clouded and colored his life, thoughts, and emotional processing a little bit differently than everyone else.

It didn't matter.

Children had always been non-negotiable for her. And she knew without a doubt that John would be the best father.

There was nothing wrong with him. There had never been anything wrong with him. Just like their children—nothing would ever be wrong with them, either. Regardless, they would be perfectly *them*. Little babies made by people who loved each other, and would love them.

They *would* have kids.

It was simply when.

Siena figured that time was now.

"John?"

"Hmm?"

He leaned over the top of her, and kissed the top of her head. In the vanity, her smile grew the longer his kiss lingered against the top of her head.

John's fingers tangled into the waves of her hair, and held firm. "Love you."

Siena reached up and patted his cheek—three day scruff tickled her fingertips. "I love you."

"What did you want, babe?"

"I was thinking …"

"Keep going."

He straightened a bit, and she kept an eye on him in the vanity mirror. In sleep pants that hung low on his waist, and his chest bare, it was a little distracting.

Siena forced herself to pay attention to the topic at hand. "I was thinking about the bedroom across the hall."

"The empty one."

"We kept it empty for a reason."

John's fingertips drifted over her bare shoulder. "For the *someday* nursery, you said."

"Yeah, for that."

"What, did you want to turn it into a private office or something?"

She usually worked out of the house, and if she did work inside, she used his office. John never minded, or if he did, he never said anything about it.

"Or something," she replied.

John met her gaze in the mirror, and amusement stared back. "Okay, what, then?"

"What do you think about pastel green?"

"For a color?"

"Like paint," she said. "It's neutral."

"So is beige."

"But beige doesn't really fit for a nursery, John."

Momentarily, she saw him stiffen. Just as quick, though, he relaxed.

"No, I guess it doesn't."

"I would really like to start getting the nursery set up, John."

"Would you?"

Siena shrugged, and all her worries drifted away the second John bent down to kiss the top of her head again.

"All right," he murmured. "I think we can do that."

"Because we'll need one."

John's eyebrow arched a bit as he tipped his head up, and found her gaze in the mirror once more. "Will we?"

"What names do you like?"

His next swallow echoed.

The silence stretched on.

Siena waited John out.

"Luciano for a boy."

"For your dad," she said.

John nodded once. "And for my grandfather, yeah. Johnathan for a middle name."

"What about for a girl?"

"I don't know."

Siena grinned. "You better figure it out, don't you think? We'll need to know."

John sucked in a quiet breath, and his hands tightened on her shoulders. Not to a painful point, but a feeling that made her calm in an instant.

"That so?" he asked.

"I know this isn't happening the way we talked about it, and—"

"Nothing is ever as I plan, Siena."

"Are you happy?"

"And terrified," he admitted. "But so happy."

So happy.

That was all she needed to know. The rest, they could deal with. Just like everything else in their life.

They faced it together.

Head-on.

Unafraid.

Unashamed.

Unbroken.

Four months later ...

"Your turn," Siena whispered to John.

He laughed, but she heard the stress in the sound. He smiled for their gathered, waiting family, but she saw the tension in his shoulders.

The further along in her pregnancy she became, the more changes she saw in John. Never toward her, but just him in general. She recognized his lack of sleeping, and his up and down moods. She saw his methodical cleaning, planning, and organizing even when he tried to hide it.

She wished he wouldn't hide it.

It was so much harder to settle him back when he hid it.

Leonard would be at their house when they got back—waiting for John, as the man always did. Twice a week, and sometimes more if John felt it was needed, his therapist came for an in-home session.

They never opened up discussion about John's mental health to anyone who asked. They didn't talk about his meds, his therapy, or anything.

Their choice.

John's choice.

Leonard, however, would be there tonight because Siena had made a call and asked for him to come, not John. Sometimes, she needed to do that. Sometimes, she had to be the voice when John was not letting his come through loud enough.

John took the one cupcake Siena offered to him—the only one left. Everyone else around them already had one, and now they were just waiting on him, too.

"My turn," John echoed.

Siena nodded, and smiled. "I love you, John."

"I know you do."

She always would.

"Everybody at the same time," Siena said, directing her comment at the room, yet never looking away from John. "Okay?"

"You got it, babe."

"Now."

Everybody bit into their cupcake, and blue frosting colored up the middle of the sweet cake. John stared at the sweet in his hand for a long while, and Siena reached over to wipe a bit of blue frosting from his bottom lip while cheers lit up the room.

"It's a boy!"

"A boy!"

John barely blinked as his father crossed the room to clap his son on the shoulders, and congratulate them. Jordyn followed behind Lucian, and did the same. Siena and John took a moment to take the congratulations, and the ones that followed from everyone else.

But soon, the room settled, their family faded as John looked at Siena, and it was just them once more. No one else.

He had wanted this gender reveal.

For his family.

To allow them *in*.

Sometimes, he still found it hard to let them in.

The pregnancy was one thing he continued to try to open up for them, but especially for his mother and father.

"Luciano, then," John said.

Siena smile wider. "Luciano Johnathan Marcello. And he will be perfect, John."

So perfect.

Just like his father.

Luciano Johnathan made his way into the world loudly. He made damn sure his mother felt every pain, and he didn't let her rest in the labor for even a single second.

Siena didn't mind.

Once that hazy-eyed, dark-haired baby that looked so much like his father was placed in her arms, the rest was forgotten. Nothing mattered but little Luciano.

And then his father got a hold of him, Luciano's eyes opened wide and found John's. Siena knew in that moment, she was probably never going to get him back.

Not entirely.

"Oh, my God," John murmured. "Look at this boy, Siena."

She had.

And in those few seconds, she memorized him.

"He looks just like you," she said.

He chuckled. "And you."

But not nearly as much as Luciano took after his father. Siena didn't mind.

John's finger traced the line of the baby's nose. Soft, gentle, and sweet.

"Everybody's waiting to meet you, Lucky," John said.

Everybody could wait, too.

The baby blinked, and his tiny little fingers instinctively curled around his father's thumb.

John smiled. "Yeah, I'm your daddy, *bambino*."

At the same time he spoke to their son, he reached for her. His palm cupped her cheek, and his thumb stoked her skin.

Even while falling in love with his child, he never forgot about her.

He still loved her.

Their forever was now.

And it was beautiful.

JOHN + SIENA
EXTENDED

JOHN + SIENA, BOOK 3

ONE

"Damn, how much did you lose?"

"A solid five-K," Michel muttered to John's left.

Andino laughed hard. "I told you that was *not* the team to bet on, man."

"Yeah, fuck you, too."

At the other side of the table, Lev—also known as Pink to almost everybody who didn't know the man personally—smirked as he reached for the creamer sitting in the middle of the table to add to his steaming black coffee. "I mean, *everybody* told your stupid ass not to bet on that team, Michel, and yet …"

"I favor the underdogs, that's all."

John chuckled. "Just because, at one point in time, you were the underdog doesn't mean every other underdog will always win."

Michel sighed, and turned to stare out the window. He knew better than to keep engaging the conversation between his cousins—and Pink, who was just a friend. Well, Lev was an enforcer for Andino who now moved between the main Marcello faction and John's side of the business in another part of the city.

Sure, John could have easily used one of the men who had shown they were— *mostly*—trustworthy from the handful of original Calabrese Capos instead of taking one of Andino's most favored, and *loyal*, men to keep his faction under control. But hell, sometimes it was good to have someone a man could trust inexplicably to call on when shit needed done or someone had to be watched.

Pink was that guy.

"You know what," Michel said, drawing John back to the chat at the table, "don't you have somewhere to be, man?"

John shrugged, resting back in his chair with a warm mug of the best coffee this side of Manhattan between his palms. "Not for another …." He made a show of checking his watch before giving his cousin a grin that he knew would irk Michel like nothing else. "Well, I'll have to leave in ten minutes or so to make the meeting and not be terribly late. That's more than enough time for me to annoy you a little more. Besides, I can stretch it a bit."

Andino flashed his teeth in a grin. "Nobody says shit to a boss when they show up late, anyway. Everybody else is just early."

He pointed a finger at his cousin. "Yes, that right there. Exactly that."

"Fucking hate you."

"No, you don't."

Laughter rung out over the table, and likely drew in the attention of other patrons of Andino's restaurant. Every single morning, this was where John came. Sometimes, it was just him and Andino having breakfast or a coffee. Other times, it was all of them. Just like they were right now. Either way, it was a good start to John's day.

He needed that.

More than people understood.

Routine was still the thing that kept John moving from one thing to the next day after day without spiraling into a chaos of his brain's making. Sure, the routine had changed a bit from what it used to be—and for the better, if he were being honest—but it still did the same thing for him regardless of what it was.

There was something to be said for the nostalgia of sitting down with old friends for a drink and good conversation. It was something Johnathan Marcello tried to do more often because, next to when he was home with his wife, this was one of the only times when he could actually relax and be *himself*.

Something that was easier said than done, considering everything. He figured … well, he'd probably earned many of the titles that people called him behind his back. Some were to his benefit, of course, because being the boss of the new Marcello faction—the old Calabrese Cosa Nostra—meant he constantly dealt with men who didn't know John beyond his last name and the way he'd taken over their *famiglia*.

They called him *crazy*.

Unstable.

Not to be crossed.

Before, some of those things might have bothered him. Now, John knew it was better people feared the unknown about him than the things they *did* know. Everyone else in his life—the people who really mattered like the ones sitting at the table with him or his family spread out across the city—they saw the *real* John.

He liked that just fine.

"You know what, I *was* going to come and run interference with you for those bunch of assholes on your side of the city," Michel muttered under his breath, "but I don't think I will now. Should let you listen to their whiney asses all on your own."

"No, you won't," John said assuredly, "because Gabbie is in court all day, you're supposed to be on vacation from the hospital, and you have nothing else better to do with your day. At least with me, you get to play *mafia*."

"I don't *play*, John."

Well …

"Yeah, that's fair," John replied. "You're still welcome to join me, though."

Michel made a noise under his breath. "Probably will. I have nothing better to do."

Exactly as I thought.

John didn't say that out loud, however.

"Careful with that," Andino decided to speak up. Once again sharing a warning he'd already said more than a dozen times to Michel and John since the two started doing business together after he took over the Marcello faction. "You start stepping into a *famiglia*, Michel, and people might think you want to stay there. Don't get your place confused unless you're ready to change it in this business, you know?"

Michel passed John a look.

He said nothing to his cousin.

Shit, he'd been telling Michel this for a while, too. After years of saying he didn't want to be a made man, it seemed Michel did find *something* he enjoyed doing in the mafia. That just happened to be running interference between people or showing up in places where John didn't want to be when the time called for it.

A lot like a *consigliere*.

Did it mean something?

Maybe.

"We got time to figure it all out," John said, standing from the table, "but I need to leave, or I'm going to be more than late. You coming?"

Michel nodded at the question, also standing.

Pink stayed sitting.

This time.

Another meeting or situation, and he probably would have got up and went with John, too.

"If you'd just pick an underboss and consigliere from the family," Andino murmured, picking up his own coffee after letting it cool for most of their breakfast like he usually did, "then you wouldn't need Pink and Michel to be your go-between, man."

John gave Andino a look. "It's handled. It always is."

"Right. That's what you keep saying."

"Because that's what it is, Andi."

And that's how it would stay.

John would make sure of it.

TWO

Siena was dying.

She was sure of it.

Okay, maybe that was a *little* dramatic, but the thing was, she never got sick. *Ever.* Colds and flus were practically nonexistent to her. She'd always been too busy to get sick—not that being busy stopped her from catching anything, but she never did.

Until now.

She regularly got her shots and took vitamins every morning to help give her immune system an added boost. Whether or not those things actually helped to keep her from getting sick, she didn't know.

Apparently, it didn't help this time around when a morning cough and a stuffy nose turned into a full-blown chest cold that no over-the-counter medication would help. Only, the chest cold lingered which gave her a throat infection like nothing else. She swore every time she swallowed, it felt like she was swallowing knives.

God.

For the last week and a half, Siena's bed had become her best friend. Work was out of the question when she couldn't focus on the computer screen in front of her for long enough to get anything done without her head starting to pound and feel as though it would explode from the pressure building in her sinuses.

Instead, she stayed at home. That killed her a little bit too, if only because she knew that meant work would be constantly piling up for her until she finally got back to it. Then, who even knew if she would be able to get through it all?

Jesus.

Willing the lamp on the bedside table to shut off without her needing to reach over to do it—she didn't even have the energy for *that*—as she started coughing *again*, Siena pulled the blanket tighter around her head. At least then, she could block out the light.

Mostly.

"Still not feeling any better?" came a soft question from the other side of the room.

The very fact Johnathan had returned home without Siena even realizing he was there told her a lot of things. For one, an entire day had passed her by without her even realizing it had happened. A part of her still thought it was far too early in the morning and that's why the room felt as hot as hell because the morning sun did that to their master bedroom. No wonder she was exhausted—had she even slept, or did she just lay in bed open-mouth breathing and staring at the wall while the time passed?

"Hey," she heard murmured.

John had crossed the bedroom. Now, he hovered above their bed looking down at her. She could see the concern in his gaze when she didn't smile or greet him the way she usually would. But frankly, she didn't even have the damn energy for *that*.

413

"I feel like I'm dying," she croaked.

His brow dipped. "Are you hot?"

"Yes and no."

"What?"

"It comes and it goes."

Sometimes, it seemed like she was never going to stop sweating. Other times, she had the chills so bad she could shake the damn bed.

Kneeling at the side of the bed, John pushed the blanket away from Siena a bit so that he could get a better look at her. She wished she could wipe away the worry in his gaze, but even that would take energy she just didn't have. His palm found her forehead with a soft touch before he stilled, frowning.

Usually, when John came home, it was Siena's favorite part of the day. The two of them could shut the rest of the world out and pretend like it was just them and nothing else. She needed that time as much as he did. Lately, they hadn't even been able to have that. While he didn't say anything about it one way or another, she knew it had to be bothering him.

Hell.

It bothered *her*.

"Have you checked your temp?"

A rattling cough left Siena. "No. The last time I got out of bed was to pee, and even that took me a half hour. I wasn't going all the way downstairs just for a thermometer to tell me I am sick and have a fever, John."

"Babe, you're *really* hot."

And yet, she felt cold.

Funny how that worked.

"Being sick *sucks*," she whispered.

"I think maybe we should make another trip—"

"No, I don't want to go to the hospital again. They'll make me wear a mask while I wait, and there's always a whole roomful of people staring at me. I hate it."

And she did.

So fucking much.

No, Siena would just sit in her bed, fever and cough whatever this hell was out, and deal with it that way. All they would do at the hospital was shove more medications down her throat that wouldn't help and send her home to battle her sickness alone.

Why bother?

"Siena—"

John didn't even get to finish his statement before she started coughing. This time, the hacking fit didn't stop in a few seconds. After a half of a minute, John helped to sit her up in the bed while he reached for the glass of water—who knew how long that had been sitting there—on the bedside table to get her to drink.

Except she couldn't stop coughing to drink.

Wonderful.

Her husband had also had enough, it seemed.

"That's it," John muttered, "you're going to the fucking hospital."

Siena couldn't refuse again.

She was still coughing her guts out.

THREE

Pneumonia.

Fucking *pneumonia*.

Apparently, it wasn't all that uncommon for a bad cold to travel into the lungs, but when someone couldn't expel the fluids ... well, that's when shit became dangerous. John kicked himself again and again over the fact that had he just decided enough was enough a couple days earlier than he had, then his wife wouldn't have needed to spend time in the hospital taking antibiotics, maxi-mists and getting IVs.

Jesus.

The thing about John that no one really knew was that he liked to indulge Siena a little too much. No matter what she asked for or wanted, he would give it to her if he was capable. And if he couldn't do it, then chances were he could find someone who would. The same went when she got sick. She didn't want to go to the hospital, so he didn't push her to go. He kicked himself in the ass for that now.

It didn't matter that the rational part of John's brain told him this wasn't his fault. Not that Siena had gotten sick, that she was stubborn as hell, or that he was so busy for the last couple of weeks that he'd been willing to not fight with his wife and let her battle through the illness at home instead of taking her into an ER. None of it was his fault, and he knew that. Still, it didn't stop the part of him that continued to berate himself internally. Until it was all he could hear.

Fuck.

A knock on the private hospital room door had John lifting his head from his palm. The last thing he wanted to do was take his gaze from Siena's sleeping form in the bed that he *knew* was damn uncomfortable—considering the amount of times he'd been chained to one of those goddamn things in his later teenage years while they worked to diagnose his bipolar, and he'd been at his worst. Still, he turned to see who had come to the room.

A nurse, he thought.

Maybe a doctor.

All their visitors had come and gone pretty regularly. His parents, siblings, and Siena's friends. Even his cousins had come to sit with him or their wives came along to bring Siena something to make her smile. Hence why the room was full of fresh flowers and balloons. And yes, every single one made her happy.

So was his wife.

Sweet as could be.

Instead of hospital staff, John was surprised to find his therapist standing in the doorway. Leonard tipped his head down, a silent *hello* as his gaze darted to the sleeping woman in the bed. He raised a single white eyebrow at John, then; more silent conversation. It never failed to amuse John how well he and Leonard worked together—or rather, how well his therapist seemed to know and understand him without John ever needing to say a thing.

He bet that wasn't common. Most doctor and patient relationships didn't go beyond a hospital or counselor's chair. Leonard, however, made an active effort to involve himself as more than just John's doctor. He now counted him as a friend.

And God knew he was grateful for the man.

Incredibly so.

"Heard visiting hours are over soon," Leonard said quietly, mindful of not waking Siena up, "so I suppose I made it in time to see you."

John chuckled. "I missed a session, hmm?"

"Well, that's not why I'm here, of course."

No, that was probably because John hadn't called. Leonard only really became concerned that something might be wrong when he didn't get a phone call. Most times, John made every effort to make each session with Leonard because that was also just a part of his routine. One he enjoyed because for an hour or two a couple of times a week, he was able to sit down and simply focus on nothing but himself.

For someone like John, that had value.

"I just wanted to check in, actually," Leonard said. "I heard Siena was sick, and made a call to your father to see if I could be of any help. He mentioned you hadn't left the hospital after she was admitted, so I thought I would come down and speak directly to you instead of about you. I know how you prefer that."

John grinned. "That I do, and thank you."

Leonard glanced Siena's way again. "How is she?"

"A lot better."

Thankfully.

"Good to hear. And you?"

John sighed. "Feeling like a fuck up."

"Because she's sick?"

"Because I ... well, a lot of reasons."

Leonard nodded. "And you know it's not *your* fault she's here, yes?"

"I do."

"And yet ..."

John shrugged. "My brain does what my brain does."

"Well, try not to beat yourself up too badly. I stopped at the nurse's station. The doctor on rotation tonight—he's an old friend. Siena will be discharged tomorrow, I heard."

"That's the plan."

"And then you'll finally get some sleep, I assume."

Another smile stretched over his lips. Leonard truly did know John better than he even knew himself sometimes. The man didn't even have to ask if he was sleeping—he knew he wasn't.

"Once she's home," John murmured.

"And your meds?"

"Andino brought them in."

Leonard nodded. "What about work—how's that?"

"Are we condensing a therapy session down to a three-minute conversation now?"

"I do what I can, John, when I can and with what I can. This is me doing a check on you—all points of your life that I know tend to crumble first when you're not in the best state. However, by all accounts, you seem good at the moment. I still want to check."

Yeah, John knew.

"Andino is handling business—my other cousin and another man step in when needed, too. Everything is fine. For now, it's all about her."

"Right," Leonard murmured. "Well, had you made it to your session this week, there was something I wanted to speak with you about, but it can wait until our next one. And of course, you know how to reach me should you need something. Don't hesitate, John. I'm only a phone call away."

"I appreciate it."

"Say hello to Siena for me. I owe her a lunch date."

John chuckled. "She'll be sad she missed you."

It wasn't a lie.

Everyone in John's life thought Leonard was the best thing—next to Siena, that was—to ever happen to him.

And frankly, they weren't wrong.

FOUR

"So, how are you feeling?"

"Really good," Siena answered her mother-in-law honestly. "The first week after I was discharged was … long seems like a good word."

Which wasn't at all a lie. She spent the entire first week mostly in bed. Although this time, without the coughing and inability to breathe. It was as though her body and mind decided to shut down and *make* her recover. Not just from the illness, but from the stress of it all. Honestly, Siena truly needed the break.

Her second week out of the hospital had been a great deal better, thankfully. She was out of bed, actually eating three meals a day that were not made up of some kind of soup or broth, and she could make it through an afternoon without needing a two or three-hour nap. Although *really*, who didn't need a good nap once in a while?

Naps were life.

It didn't matter how old she was.

"You were still tired, probably," Jordyn said.

It brought Siena back to the conversation at hand. Other than a few visits to see if there was anything in the house that needed done, or phone calls to check up on her, most everyone had left Siena alone to recover. She didn't mind; it's what she needed.

"All the time."

Jordyn laughed. "Sickness has a way of doing that to us women. And then when you become a mother, it's even worse because guess what? You don't get time off. It doesn't matter if you're on your deathbed, someone *is* going to need you, and you're just going to have to suck it up. But you understand … you have your younger sisters and all."

Siena sighed. "Yeah, I know."

"But what matters is you're out of the hospital and can finally get back to normal. Which means *we* can also figure out what we're doing for your sister's birthday—"

The opening of the front door had a smile growing on Siena's face. The last thing she wanted to do was seem rude to her mother-in-law, but she didn't think Jordyn would mind when she interrupted her to say, "We can plan that another day—John just got home, I think."

"Ah, then yes we can. Say hello to him."

Siena smirked. "And I will make him call."

He didn't do that enough. In fact, his least favorite thing to do was talk on the phone. People would get a better response out of John if they just texted him because that was easier and faster than him making time to sit down and chat. Oh, he tried—definitely. Sometimes, though, life just became too much and John disengaged from everything. And more often than not, that meant taking a step back from others.

Including family.

At least now, Siena thought the people around them were better at recognizing that's what John was doing and not purposely trying to cut them off. Occasionally, he needed to take time for himself to recharge. Just because he did it in a different way than someone else might do it for themselves didn't mean he *shouldn't* do it.

"I have the *best* daughter-in-law," Jordyn mused, the smile in her tone clear.

Siena laughed. "I am your *only* daughter-in-law."

"And yet, that changes nothing."

"I'll get John to call."

"Thank you, sweetheart. Have a good night. We'll chat soon."

"Sounds good."

Siena had just hung up the phone and tossed it aside on the couch when footsteps approached her from behind. Tipping her head back, she smiled at John as he shrugged off his suit jacket and came closer. Without saying a word—not even a *hello*, although that was fine with her considering the way he did greet her—he leaned down and kissed her. Those teasing lips of his moved smoothly against her own, coaxing them open until he could get the taste he was so clearly looking for.

Then, his mouth traveled over her chin. The sweet kisses dotted over her skin, leaving sparks every single spot that they landed.

God.

She loved this man.

All too soon, though, John pulled away with a teasing grin. "Missed you today, babe."

"Did you?"

"Mmhmm."

Nerves climbed higher in Siena's throat. Not that John made her nervous, but rather, something she had to talk to him about. She'd given it two entire weeks after her hospital discharge before even broaching the topic if only because her husband was who he was—and he could be *overly* protective of her for it, too.

"Well, you'll be seeing me more during the day soon," she told him.

At that, John straightened to his full height and placed his hands to the back of the couch. "Oh, why is that?"

"I was thinking ... I should probably get back to work. I mean, it's been two weeks since I got out of the hospital. I was given the all clear yesterday, and we both know those numbers don't work themselves."

"I had someone—"

"Doing *all* the numbers?" she asked.

John chuckled and tipped his head to the side. "I could find someone to do *those* numbers, too, Siena."

Yeah, he probably could.

Didn't matter.

Siena was the only one who really knew all the illegal facets of John's business when it came to money. She could hide it, wash it, and more. The idea of someone else having access to those files and numbers made her sick to her stomach. It would only take *one* mistake. One misstep—a single error—for the IRS to be up their ass seven ways to Sunday. Which would only leave her husband arrested, likely.

And her.

Siena wouldn't have that.

"I want to get back to work," she said simply.

John smiled softly. "I figured."

"Did you?"

"Yeah. You get stir-crazy."

She scoffed, but really … he wasn't wrong.

"And I planned for it," John added, his right hand leaving the couch to skim over her throat and down her chest. His wandering hands came to a stop at the neckline of her over-sized sleep shirt. He fingered the fabric of her shirt, every graze a tease to her senses. Did he even know how much just his touch could affect her? "A driver and shorter workdays to start back—how's that?"

"And no argument otherwise?" she replied.

With less air. His fingers had just danced over her throat again, after all.

"Did you think I would argue about you wanting to go back to work?"

Siena swallowed hard. "Well, you *do* worry."

"Not right now," he murmured, a glint in his eye as his gaze traveled over the shirt she'd pulled on after a shower.

She grinned back. "Not now. So, does the way you look right now mean you're done treating me like a china doll?"

"First of all, I have *not* treated you like a china doll."

"Actually, for the entire time I was sick. Like you thought I would break if you looked at me the wrong way, John."

His tongue peeked out to wet his lower lip before he smirked sinfully. The sight alone made Siena a little more breathless. *God.* He was beyond sexy when he grinned like that—did he even know what it did to her; how *wet* it made her?

"*Secondly,*" he added, as though she hadn't said anything at all, "how do I look right now?"

"As though you're going to fuck me all night."

That time, he flashed his teeth with his smile.

She couldn't breathe at all.

"Do I get to start with having you on this couch?" he asked. "Because you know I love the way my name echoes in this room when you scream it."

"I certainly hope so."

With his next laugh—one that rang dark and *pleased* and wicked—he dropped his blazer to the floor. Siena still hadn't managed to catch her breath before he was rolling over the back of the sofa to fall on top of her. She didn't think it was possible to get one's clothes off in mere seconds, but somehow, she and John managed it.

Yeah.

It had definitely been too long.

John gave her what she wanted, too. Fucked her until she was screaming his name and it bounced off all the walls. He worked her body like a fine instrument that he'd spent his entire life learning to play with the best kind of love.

And then he took her upstairs to their bed to do it again.

FIVE

"Listen to the two of you—bickering like *babies*."

Pink scoffed hard and loud. "Babies don't bicker, man."

"Nah, they whine and cry," Andino returned just as fast, "and your whining and crying is getting on my damn nerves."

"Everything gets on your fucking nerves."

"Starting with *you*."

"Yeah, but it keeps you at your best, Andi," Pink returned.

"That's debatable."

"Or true," Michel added, joining the conversation. "Otherwise, why would you have kept Lev around for this long, anyway? Someone else with his mouth and bullshit, and you would have put them in a shallow grave before anyone knew what happened. That's facts."

"That's what *I've* been saying for years."

John had to agree with Pink and Michel, but unlike them, he knew better than to point it out to Andino. That would likely lead to a whole other discussion that would only make his cousin feel defensive. Andi didn't like to admit when he cared for people, never mind when he *needed* somebody around. He much preferred for everyone to believe he was the cold asshole with a heart of stone.

Frankly, John understood why.

Mostly.

"You know what," Andino muttered, "you're both working my nerves now. Lucky I fucking like the two of you."

Laughter filled the restaurant's rear office between three distinct men as John approached. The chef behind the prep station lifted his head and nodded at the passing man; he returned the gesture to Andino's employee. One of the few that he actually liked but that was mostly because the man could cook like nobody's business. He had an attitude, but most people who were successful at something were a little too cocky for their own good.

Even John.

"Who's bickering about what now?"

John's question at the three men in the office turning to find him standing in the doorway. When one couldn't find Andino doing business *outside* of his favorite restaurant, and the man also wasn't eating at one of the tables or the private section, then he could always be found in his rear office. It was probably supposed to be for the manager of the business but seeing as how this was where Andino did the majority of all his work—well, the manager likely made it work elsewhere. John never cared to ask.

"And that's my sign to get going," Michel said, standing from his chair with a chuckle where he had been sitting beside Pink. "I have to drop Antony off to Ma because Gabbie won't have time today."

John stepped aside in the doorway to let his cousin pass. "You're handling that issue today for me, aren't you?"

"The Capo with the racket trouble—it's on my list."

"Thanks, man."

Michel clapped John on the shoulder as he passed and then waved two fingers over his shoulder to say goodbye to the other two men he left behind in the office. With a nod from Andino, John closed the door behind Michel and shut out the rest of the restaurant. Not that any of the employees would have anything to say about the business and discussions they likely overheard day in and day out, but one couldn't be too careful in this life. Andino had great employees that he vetted like nobody's business, not to mention paid *very* well to turn their cheeks to his activities, but still …

No chances.

"How's Siena?" Pink asked, standing from his chair before removing the coat he'd set along the back. "Feeling any better?"

John grinned at the thought of his wife. "Much better."

"Good to hear. I'll be out in the dining room when you're ready to get a start on the day, John."

"Sounds good. Leonard is coming—let me know when he gets here. I promised him breakfast and a chat before I do anything. You don't mind waiting for that, do you?"

Pink shrugged. "Not at all."

"Multitasking?" Andino asked after Pink exited the office.

John sighed, and took a seat opposite to his cousin sitting behind the large desk. Beside the furniture slept a dog who hadn't even perked his head up at John's arrival or the exit of the other men. Then again, Snaps was so accustomed to the three of them coming and going from his master's office that he no longer cared.

That was, unless Andino wasn't *in* the office. Then, Snaps became something else entirely, and he behaved as though he didn't recognize them at all. Nonetheless, the ruddy-colored Pitbull slept happily, snoring away.

"Getting things crossed off my to-do list," John replied. "And you know, getting everything back the way I like it after my break."

Andino nodded. "I had everything handled."

"Not like I handle it, though."

That had his cousin chuckling.

"No, I suppose not, John."

"No offense," John added quickly.

Andino shrugged his broad shoulders and leaned back in his chair to fold his arms over his chest. He'd rolled his dress shirt up to his elbows; a sure sign that the man planned on doing very little for the rest of the day and was ready to relax. That's always what it meant when he removed his blazer and rolled up his sleeves.

"No offense taken," Andino replied. "It's better we understand now that you and I aren't the same men, and we're not going to handle our business the same. Although, it seems you might have finally figured out what to do about the whole underboss and consigliere thing, no?"

"I'm not following, and Leonard's going to be here soon for a session, so—"

"Michel and Pink."

Ah.

"Listen, it's not been explicitly said or anything," John explained, "but they do what they do, and it works for me. I know they're not made men—"

"They don't have to be. They just have to be *your* men. There's been many bosses who had right-hand men that weren't *in* with the family in one way or another. Associates, or whatever the case may be. No one is going to think less of you or them because they're not made men."

"Might it cause trouble, though?"

Andino smirked. "Well, we'd handle that, yeah? *Easy.* Same way we handled it when you took over the Calabrese faction. It's really that simple."

But was it? John didn't know.

"It's not just everyone else," John told his cousin. "It's also *them.* Lev and Michel, I mean."

"What do you—"

"I haven't asked *them*, Andi."

"Michel is spending his afternoon picking up his son before making a trip to see your Capo, and Pink is waiting for your therapist so that you can take your breakfast in peace without interruption while you have a session. What more needs to be said?"

John stared hard at his cousin. Andino looked right back, unbothered.

Nothing new to see here.

"I don't know," John murmured.

Andino nodded. "Yeah, me either."

His conversation with Andino lingered in John's mind long after it finished. He was halfway through his breakfast and chat with Leonard before he'd blinked, and yet his mind kept going back to his cousin and what he'd said.

"John?"

"Hmm?"

Across the table, Leonard smiled at him. "You seem distracted."

"Work."

"Oh—bad things?"

"No, just things to think about," John returned.

"That happens. That thing I'd mentioned—I was hoping you might make time to meet with someone for me."

That had John's full attention.

"Who?" he asked.

"A friend," Leonard replied. "I think he could help you with things that perhaps, I cannot."

"You help."

"I might not always be able to, though."

John took more than a few seconds to reply to that. "Why?"

The silence grew longer. *Heavy.*

It wasn't like Leonard. John didn't like it at all.

Eventually, his therapist said, "I'm sick, John. Bladder cancer. My first treatment was two weeks ago, but I wanted to wait until everything was settled with you before I brought it up. I hope you understand."

Why—when everything in his life seemed to be going *so* well—did the world have to come crashing down around him?

SIX

Apparently, Siena's first day back at work—which just happened to land on a Friday—was also welcome Siena back day with a constant stream of visitors. Everyone from John's mother to his sister came to say hello and drop her off a little something.

Candy.

Coffee.

Flowers.

She loved it all.

But she also wanted to work.

After the third visitor who knocked on her office door, however, Siena simply settled herself on the fact that she would not be getting *anything* done. At least, not today. So, she shut down her laptop, ordered a round of drinks and sides from the kitchen, and made her way out to the dining room to sit down and enjoy her friends and family.

"I'm not too late, am I?" Haven asked, tossing her bag to the floor before dropping into a chair. "I had some things to handle, is all. Sorry."

Across the table where she sat next to John's mother—because Jordyn decided today was the best day to go over the plans for her sister's birthday party—Siena laughed and shook her head. "Listen, after Ginevra left when Alessio came to pick her up and Catherine called to say she would be here around supper, I gave up *any* hope of getting work done today."

Haven grinned widely. "*Aww*, you have friends who love you. *Shame*, that."

"I'm not complaining."

And she wasn't.

Truly.

"But you all could have spread out the love over several days, maybe," Siena said. "I just caught a bout of pneumonia—I didn't die."

Haven, as serious as she could be, simply stared at Siena. "*And?*"

God.

These people.

She loved them, though.

"How's Val doing in Toronto?" she asked.

"Rose gold or gold and silver?" Jordyn asked, peering down at her phone. "Although, there's this cute black and rose gold theme I'm really liking. We could make that work."

"Rose gold and black," Siena returned. "Definitely. She will *love* that. I swear since Ginevra moved in with Alessio and Corrado, they've both bled into the girls more than anyone knows. One is all class and screams wealth—the other is all dark and moody … it's like two entirely different people. Which they are. I don't know how she does it." Then, back to Haven, she added, "I haven't seen Val in forever."

Never missing a beat, Haven said, "Really well. I don't get to see her as much as I like, but we figure it out and do what we have to so that we get time together. Or you know, I bitch *a lot* to Andino, which he can't stand, and then he gets mad enough to call Chris and do his thing. We make it work."

"Your husband can be kind of horrible."

Haven smiled again. "I know—it's why I love him."

Good thing somebody did.

That's what counted.

"But seriously," Haven said, giving Siena a look, "how are *you* feeling?"

"A lot better."

"Yeah?"

"Less dead," Siena replied honestly. "That's an improvement, trust me."

Laughter passed between the three women at the table. They quieted when one of the servers made her way to the table to refill Siena's coffee, bring Jordyn another glass of lemon water, and then took an order from Haven as well.

"And John? How's he doing with … all of this, I mean? I know he gets a little on edge whenever something is going on with you. I imagine he must have been something else for the past few weeks, huh?"

That made Siena pause.

Just for a second.

Haven didn't mean any harm by asking. And nothing that she said was a lie, either. It was no secret that John could become just a touch unbearable when something was wrong with his wife. Snappy, difficult, and moody … those were just a few of the things that anyone in direct contact with John had to deal with during times that put him under a lot of stress.

At the same time, they were *so* private. They didn't share a lot about what was happening in their personal lives because it was one way that John felt like it kept his mental illness a closed book to anyone who wasn't his parents or wife. It wasn't that he didn't want to share, but without meaning to, people often projected their own assumptions or beliefs about how John should deal with it even when they knew nothing about it.

It was easier to just … well, *not*.

"He's fine," Siena said. "You know John."

Yeah.

That seemed like a good way to say it.

Or *deflect*.

But hey, if Haven was offended that Siena didn't get deep into the details about how John had handled her sudden illness and short hospital stay, the woman didn't know it. Not that it stopped Siena from still feeing like she had to be defensive of her husband, and their choices *not* to discuss anything that even remotely touched his bipolar disorder or might even bring it into the conversation.

It was only after Haven's order came in, and her phone rang with a call that she stepped away from the table to take that Siena turned to her mother-in-law who was still busy making an entire inspiration board for her younger sister's birthday party.

"Is it always going to be like that?" she asked.

Jordyn lifted her head. "What do you mean?"

She sighed.

And took a second to *think*.

Maybe feel, too.

If there was anything that being with John had taught Siena, it was that there was nothing wrong with taking a moment to handle yourself before someone else. It was a good lesson to learn because everyone had to look out for themselves first whether that was for their mental health or whatever.

"John," Siena eventually said. "Will I always feel like—when it comes to other people—I have to defend him or protect him … you know, without offending everyone who asks about him or me or *us*?"

Jordyn smiled softly. "Do you feel like you have a reason to be defensive about John—or rather, has *he* given you a reason to do that?"

Siena didn't even have to think about it.

"No, he doesn't. It's just … I don't want anyone else to, either."

"Well, that's your answer, then. And if you don't allow them to, then they can't. What's to be offended over about that, Siena?"

She had a good point.

Siena would remember it.

SEVEN

Rosewood Central—a new park located outside the city limits and popular for those living in the upper scale suburbs—was quieter than it would usually be on a Wednesday. John would know considering he spent every Wednesday walking through this park with Leonard because it was what his therapist liked to call a *middle ground* for them both. Instead of a session at Leonard's office or the man's house, or even John's, the two of them met here.

Very few joggers passed John by on the pathways. Only a handful of dog owners had been milling in the dog park section. He wouldn't complain about the lack of people, however, considering the man he would usually be meeting here would not actually be showing up today, though the plan had been for him to be here, because—

"Johnathan, you're looking well. It's been what, a few years since we last spoke?"

John found the source of the question sitting on a nearby bench under a rather large oak tree which provided a good spread of shade for anyone sitting underneath its heavy branches. Cara Guzzi smiled his way and that alone felt welcoming even if every inch of him radiated with hesitance and wariness. It wasn't because of her—or her presence, really—but it just was.

New things could be … tricky.

Especially for John.

This would certainly be that.

"A few years for sure," John replied, making a careful effort to keep his tone pleasant and measured. He didn't want Cara to feel uncomfortable at being the middleman here—as Leonard liked to say—because she was simply doing a friend a favor. "Are we—"

"Come sit," Cara said before he could say another thing. "And we'll have a chat for a minute before we do anything else."

John dragged in a burning lungful, filling his chest to capacity before letting the air out just as fast. If the woman on the bench noticed his discomfort and stress, she didn't say anything one way or another. He was grateful.

Taking a seat on the right side of the bench and leaving lots of space between him and Cara, John busied himself with undoing the two buttons on his Armani blazer while he peered down the pathway leading toward the small lake. "Quiet today."

"Oh, is this not the norm here? Shame, I liked it."

"Well, it's never overflowing," he replied, "so it's quiet enough that you can enjoy yourself."

"Hmm." Cara passed him a look, adding, "And I'm sorry Leonard couldn't make it today. Seems his chemo ran later than usual, did it?"

"Apparently. Things happen, though."

Life had taught him that.

John rarely expected anything to go as planned regardless of how much he wished for that to be the case. Things in his world would be far easier to process if everything was exactly how he wanted it to be. And yet, *he* was the one who still learned daily how to adapt to the fact that nothing was perfect. Including himself.

It was a process.

As were most things.

"Has he discussed his illness with you?" Cara asked. "Since I was the one who made the call to Cree, and both he and Leonard knew you and I were acquainted, Leonard thought you wouldn't mind me being here. I hope he was right. I wouldn't want to make you feel out of place, John."

"You don't. Mostly. The whole day does but that's not unusual for me." John swallowed thickly. "And Leonard and I spoke briefly about the cancer—the important parts and what's happening now. How it looks, and all of that. I think he realized I was not taking it well and decided it was better we didn't get too particular about it."

A soft smile stared back at him.

"You consider him a friend, yes?" she asked.

"One of the few I do have." John clasped his hands in his lap, needing the tight control of his fingers wrapped around one another to keep his tone level when he added, "And I haven't discussed the fact he is sick or in treatment with my family yet. Not even my wife."

"Why not?"

"They'll worry. Partly. It's just ... Leonard is sick. It's *him*. And he's my therapist, not theirs. So, these aren't issues of theirs. They're issues of mine, that's all. I would like to keep them as my issues to handle and not theirs."

Then, John turned to her and asked, "So, Cree, hmm?"

Cara nodded. "Yes, Cree. I think you'll like him."

"Oh?"

"He's ... an unusual breed in our business. Let's just say meetings with—well, he doesn't call people patients, I guess—but his meetings don't take place in offices or parks. That's not really his style."

Right.

Because that's why John was here.

To meet his *secondary* therapist.

"So, where are we meeting him?" John asked. "And when?"

"Not far from here, and whenever you're ready to go."

A lot of things about this day made John want to go home, crawl into bed with his wife who he was sure he could convince to take a day off, and pretend like nothing else existed. But the thing was, he'd signed up for the long haul with Leonard, and the man's ways when it came to treating John and his bipolar disorder. Including this because right now, it was needed.

"I'm ready anytime."

Cara smiled brightly. "Wonderful. Let's go."

John wasn't sure what he expected this *Cree*—who apparently had a major hand in a venture in Las Vegas that included training and auctioning assassins with a partner—to look like or anything. Leonard hadn't given John much to go on when he said he wanted the two to meet so that he could consider working with a secondary therapist alongside his preferred one, but he didn't expect the man who waited inside a boxing ring.

Wearing nothing but loose shorts, with his hands already taped up as though he were ready to fight, and his long, black hair plaited into a single rope down his back, Cree grinned at John.

"That suit isn't going to do in here," Cree said.

John arched a brow and stared up at the man. "You think I'm getting in there?"

"I think by the scars on your knuckles, we're not going to pretend like you've never thrown a punch, Johnathan."

"I prefer John."

"Do you? Interesting."

Was it?

He didn't sound like it.

John passed Cara a look over his shoulder, but she simply shook her head and looked away with a smile. "So, Cree?"

She laughed under her breath. "Cree—he can take a bit to get used to. Give it a moment to warm up. That was my husband's suggestion."

"I do not need a moment to *warm up* to," Cree returned. "I am simply an acquired taste that very few have been lucky enough to try. And I will accept no other description."

John gave the man points for confidence.

"I promise he's ... give it a chance," the woman said as though she knew personally. Hell, maybe she did. Cara shrugged at John's questioning stare before saying, "Everyone, even men like you, John, living the life you do, need safe places, spaces, and people. Leonard does know what he's doing—Cree simply does it differently. We all do."

Right.

He'd try to remember that for this.

"Take the blazer off," Cree called from the ring. "I'm sure you can spar in the rest. Next time, less formal clothing."

Well, that was that.

EIGHT

Everything was about to change.

Again.

That was most certain, and it also seemed like the only thing Siena could be sure about in her life, now. Her and John would just become settled into some kind of a routine in their marriage—it happened over and over again in the last three years since they said *I do*—and something would come along to give them a new normal.

Except this couldn't be the same.

Not at all.

If there was one thing—above all things—about her marriage and John that Siena thought was most important to remember, it was that surprises were not welcomed. Especially if said surprise meant a huge change in their lives, or something that could cause a massive emotional upheaval.

For other people, a change could be a good thing. A little stress, and a bit nerve-racking, sure. They would, however, roll with the punches and accept the change.

For John, though, a change that could and would impact his entire life often led him to overthinking, panicking, and more. It almost guaranteed a hypomanic episode would be on the horizon, and once that was controlled, a short bout of depression to battle.

Siena never blamed him for these things.

She never wished for anything different.

Oh, she loved John.

Every part of him was hers to love.

So as she sat on the edge of the tub in their master bathroom, and stared at the little strip of plastic in her hand ... she couldn't help but think of what this would mean, and what would come of it.

The pregnancy test flashed with the word *pregnant*.

Over and over.

It had been flashing that for thirty minutes now. Her heart was so full—happiness, trepidation, and joy. A love so fierce, she could hardly breathe. Already, she loved this baby. A child she didn't know, and would not see or hold for months. A child whose gender was still unknown, and whose name was yet to be picked.

And yet ...

God, she loved this baby.

Still, the hesitance she felt was also very real.

Long ago, she and John had decided that children would be a very carefully planned event for them. When both of them were ready, and when everything was handled, then they would move forward *together* on having children.

This had not been planned at all.

Certainly not carefully.

The terrible chest cold that left Siena with a nasty infection, and led into pneumonia that she couldn't shake caused her to miss the appointment for her shot. She had been stuck in bed, and then in the hospital when the pneumonia got really bad.

John had barely left her side, of course.

Once she was better, her doctor recommended she wait until her cycle started at least once—as she hadn't had a period in years since starting the shot—before they started the birth control again. They had been advised to use condoms as a backup method.

Yeah, well …

Her cycle never started. She and John didn't know what a fucking condom was considering they hadn't used them since the start of their relationship years ago.

They both knew better.

She knew better.

This was bound to happen.

Siena had promptly vomited every bit of the eggs and bacon John had left for her in the oven before he left for his morning jog. She had been keeping a pregnancy test hidden in her purse … just in case.

A part of her already knew.

Siena tapped the test against her palm again.

Pregnant, it flashed.

She was still trying to figure out a way to tell John and not surprise him, so to speak. She knew it was going to be practically fucking impossible. There could be no cute reveal that she secretly recorded, and then posted for the world to see. There could be no baby shoes in a gift box for him to open and be surprised.

None of that could happen.

She had to take away that element of shock so that this did not feel like something John was not ready for in the first place.

Easier said than done.

Children had been his one sore topic for years. Not because he didn't want to be a father, but because she knew he worried that he was going to pass on the same genetics that had been given to him. Whatever it was in his DNA that left him with a disorder that clouded and colored his life, thoughts, and emotional processing a little bit differently than everyone else.

It didn't matter.

Children had always been non-negotiable for her. And she knew without a doubt that John would be the best father.

There was nothing wrong with him. There had never been anything wrong with him. Just like their children—nothing would ever be wrong with them, either. Regardless, they would be perfectly *them*. Little babies made by people who loved each other and would love them.

They *would* have kids.

It was simply when.

Siena figured that time was now.

So, she took a moment to absorb how different everything would be now. Then, she stood up, shook off the overwhelming emotions, and began planning how she would tell John.

NINE

"Sorry, sorry," John muttered as he entered the master bedroom of their home. "I didn't mean to be this fucking late."

"It's all right."

But was it really?

Already, Siena was sitting at her vanity, a silk robe tight at her waist as she removed her makeup for the day and prepped for the night. It wasn't like they'd had plans today or anything, but he did promise to be home for supper and yet …

It was dark outside.

Even the streetlights were on.

Which meant he undoubtedly missed supper with her because she probably waited for him and when he didn't even call—because he got caught up in everything else—she just packed it away and readied for the evening. He bet, if he went downstairs to look, he would find a container of food waiting for him in the fridge.

Because that was his wife. She never complained.

Fuck.

John stood just beyond the doorway with his blazer half on and half off, and sighed. He gave Siena a look from the side where she watched his reflection in her vanity mirror. There was no disappointment or anger staring back, but he didn't have to see it from her. He felt enough of it for himself to last them both a lifetime.

Nature of the beast.

"I'm sorry I didn't call," he said. "I didn't think about it, really."

"It's okay. I kept busy."

He had the greatest urge to go to his wife, wrap his arms around her, and hide them both away from the world for the night so that he could remind her of each and every reason that he loved her. But most importantly, for the patience and understanding she constantly showed him.

"Get ready for bed," Siena told him.

John chuckled, passing another look at the window behind their bed and the darkness outside. "Yeah, I better."

She tipped her head toward the walk-in closet, and he followed her unspoken order to go. Inside the closet, he changed out of the suit that felt like a second skin a lot of the time. It was only inside his home and on lazy days when he knew he would be doing absolutely no work that he was able to wear anything that wasn't a fucking suit.

Pulling on a pair of sleep pants, he heard Siena speak from the bedroom.

"Where were you today, anyway? You didn't even show up for lunch at the restaurant?"

"Therapy," he muttered, "and then work."

Which wasn't a lie.

John hadn't quite decided *when* he was going to tell Siena about Leonard—and now this new development of Cree—but he would. Soon. Mostly, he wanted to have everything all figured out for himself and how he felt about it before he brought someone else's opinion into it, even if it was his wife. Siena would understand regardless if he told her now or two months from now, although he didn't think he would wait that long.

He just … needed some time to process.

What was so wrong with that?

"And everything is good?" Siena asked.

John hesitated before he came out of the walk-in closet. Just long enough to consider his wife's question and how he wanted to answer it. Was everything *good*? He couldn't quite say that and because he didn't lie to Siena, he settled on replying, "It's getting there."

"Good."

"Yeah."

Back in the bedroom, John headed for the bed and pulled the blankets back. Then, he rounded the end of the bed and moved to stand behind Siena as she finished her work at the vanity. It was his favorite part of the day, though he'd never told his wife that, to watch her do literally *anything*. Even if it was something like prepping for the night. While their life had become busy and chaotic over the last three years, John found peace in remembering the fact that he would soon be home with her—just them together—doing things like this.

He needed that.

Needed *her*.

"John?"

"Hmm?"

He leaned over her from behind to kiss the top of her head. In the vanity, her smile grew while his kiss lingered on her hair. He breathed in the sweet floral scent of the shampoo his wife loved so much, and the vanilla perfume that always kissed her skin.

John tangled his fingers into her hair and held tight *just because*. He wasn't quite ready for her to move yet. "Love you."

Siena reached behind to pat his cheek and the three-day scruff he'd yet to shave—but desperately needed to. "I love you."

"What did you want, babe?"

"I was thinking …"

"Keep going."

He stood a bit straighter, but she kept a lock on his gaze in the vanity mirror. Although, when her gaze traveled down his body, taking in his bare chest, and the way his sleep pants hung low on his hips, John gave her a quick wink.

She enjoyed looking.

So did he.

They could get to *that* part of their evening soon.

"I was thinking about the bedroom across the hall," she said.

"The empty one."

"We kept it empty for a reason."

The skin of her shoulder felt like silk under his fingertips. "For the *someday* nursery, you said."

"Yeah, for that."

"What, did you want to turn it into a private office or something?"

"Or something," she replied.

John took his attention off the silkiness of his wife's skin to meet her gaze in the mirror again. Besides, *soon*, he'd have her in bed with him and then he could touch her as much as he fucking wanted. "Okay, what, then?"

"What do you think about pastel green?"

"For a color?"

"Like paint," she said. "It's neutral."

"So is beige."

"But beige doesn't really fit for a nursery, John."

That took John a second.

Then, two.

He relaxed a bit as he thought to himself, *is she trying to tell me something?* The topic of children had only come up a handful of times between them. Mostly that they wanted kids, but John had his own reasons for wanting to wait. Some of those reasons dealt with the business he found himself in, and others were because of his genetics that caused him pause.

Not that it mattered because he knew, *someday*, children were in his future. They just didn't talk about it a lot and he was fine with that.

"No, I guess it doesn't," he eventually said.

"I would really like to start getting the nursery set up, John."

"Would you?"

Siena shrugged, a soft smile curving her lips. That grin of hers was enough to make him want to kiss her again, so he leaned over and pressed another to the top of her head, murmuring, "All right, I think we can do that."

"Because we'll need one."

John arched an eyebrow and watched Siena in the mirror. "Will we?"

"What names do you like?"

He swallowed hard. The silence stretched on. He didn't really have to think of a name. One was already at the tip of his tongue, and he'd always wanted to carry it on, if he could. "Luciano for a boy."

"For your dad," she said.

John nodded. "And for my grandfather, yeah. Johnathan for a middle name."

"What about for a girl?"

"I don't know."

Siena grinned. "You better figure it out, don't you think? We'll need to know."

Sucking in a quiet, quick breath, John tightened his grip on Siena's shoulders. Maybe he should have paid more attention to what his wife was saying because *yes*, he realized as he kept watching her in the mirror, she was trying to tell him something.

Something *important*. God. This was not at all what he expected to find when he came home tonight, but it was still amazing all the same. Scary because he understood how much their life would change, but still wonderful.

"That so?" he asked.

"I know this isn't happening the way we talked about it, and—"

"Nothing is ever as I plan, Siena."

"Are you happy?"

"And terrified," he admitted. "But so happy."

Again, the silence came. He didn't mind.

Siena turned around on the vanity's chair and pulled John in for a kiss that set his heart on fire. How she was able to do that for him, he would never understand. He would always love her more for it, though.

"I'm going to be a dad?"

His question whispered against her lips. Siena smiled along his when he kissed her again and she replied, "You are—we're having a baby, John."

TEN

Eight weeks later …

"Oh, my *God*, John," Siena breathed. "We have to get ready for our dinner. Everybody will be here at—"

"No," her husband replied, his voice gruff and thick in her ear. "What I need is for you to come again. And then maybe *again*, but if you keep squeezing my dick like that with your pussy, you're going to make me bust a nut before I can get you off a third time."

Shivers raced all over her body. Thrusts accompanied every single one of his words. He fucked her from behind, bent over his desk, with her hands wrapped in one of the two silk ties she'd brought in for him earlier.

Siena knew exactly how this moment happened—those damn *ties*. Or rather, just the one. She brought him in two options to choose from to wear for the dinner they were throwing for his family where they would announce the pregnancy. She dared him to do *anything* but a solid color, and he dared to ask if he could just *do* anything with the tie instead.

So, here they were.

Not that she was going to complain about this. *Fuck*. She loved nothing more than when John let go of all his control and let loose on her.

Really fucked her.

Just like he was doing then.

It wasn't entirely the fault of the tie seeing as how it seemed like the moment her husband knew she was pregnant, he just couldn't get enough of her. John could be insatiable on his good days, but this was something else entirely.

She loved it.

"Yeah," John muttered behind her, "one more time, or maybe two."

"*God.*"

Her moan melted into a high whine.

"Just John tonight, babe."

He would kill her like this.

It'd be a glorious death, though.

"You don't have to rush. Have a seat and let me plate some food. There's no reason for you to run yourself ragged over a *dinner*, Siena. I can help. I know how overwhelming this family can be to cook for when we're all in the same house."

At the same time Siena's mother-in-law tried to get her to relax, the doorbell for their home rang yet again. She passed Jordyn a look and added on a sigh for good measure. *Just because.* As if pregnancy didn't make her exhausted enough—good *God*, could she sleep any more than she did now?—this dinner so she and John could announce their pregnancy to their family as a whole was going to have her sleeping for a good day or more. She could tell already.

Not that Jordyn knew she was pregnant.

Not yet, anyway.

Soon.

"Thanks," Siena said to Jordyn as the noise picked up in the living room and the dining room at the same time. The Marcello family really was huge when they all got together in the same space. One didn't notice as much when they were spread out, but John and Siena didn't have a mansion in the hills to give a bit of space. Maybe they should, though … "But I knew what I signed up for with this. If you could plate some more food while I get that door, however, I would be forever grateful."

Jordyn laughed and nodded where she stood behind the kitchen island. "I can definitely do that. No worries."

"You're a life saver."

"No. Just your loving mother-in-law."

Siena grinned. "I did get kind of lucky with you, huh?"

Jordyn shrugged. "Well, we wives had a good role model of our own, to be honest. Go get the door—I promise the kitchen is handled."

"Perfect."

Siena left the kitchen in as much of a hurry as she had come into it. Maybe her nerves had a part to play in why this dinner made her so anxious. Not that anyone made her feel that way—hell, they didn't even *know* about the pregnancy yet, but still … it gave her pause. Their family only ever asked things out of love, but sometimes the way they asked it didn't come out as positive as they meant for it to.

Would some ask if they were ready? Or about *John*? Perhaps his mental health or the current state of it?

Questions like those would undoubtedly dampen the happiness of the day, and it worried Siena. More than she wanted to admit, although she hadn't told John any of that. It wasn't like it would help him at all. It was bad enough that she worried about it constantly. He didn't need to get the ideas stuck in his head, too.

Thankfully, it seemed John had grabbed the door before Siena even got a chance to reach the end of the hallway. She joined her husband who was currently greeting his therapist with a handshake and a nod. She didn't hear what the two men said before she arrived, but she caught the tail end when John said, "And thanks for coming today."

"Of course, I came. It's what friends do." Then, Leonard turned on Siena with a smile when she wrapped one arm around John's waist. "And Siena … how have you been?"

"Good. Tired, but good."

Leonard smiled. "As long as you always end with *good*, then that's what counts."

"You're looking well," she noted, taking in the man's tailored suit; something he didn't wear frequently as he usually settled on slacks and a dress shirt.

"That's a good sign, then."

A good sign?

"For what?" Siena asked.

"John!"

The newest arrival of a guest had Siena's attention drifting behind Leonard to where Andino, his wife Haven, and their toddler and baby—one in each parents' arms—waited. She didn't get the answer to the question she asked Leonard because John had them promising to talk more later and moving forward to greet his cousin and the man's wife and kids.

That was fine.

They had time.

ELEVEN

Usually having his house full of people—even if those people were his family and friends—would put John on edge. He'd find himself balancing between wanting everyone there and at the same time, being two seconds away from snapping at them all to get the fuck out. It wasn't that he didn't like having them there, but his home had always been the one place where he hid away from the rest of the world. Even those who cared for him.

A part of him wondered if they came because they wanted a peek at the inside of his life that he kept most private, but he also knew that was just his paranoia making itself known and nothing more. All of these people—at one point or another—had been inside his home for a visit. But not all of them at the same time.

And he *did* want them here.

Hell, he suggested this dinner to Siena as a way for them to announce the pregnancy to everyone at the same time so that no one felt left out or had to learn late. So, instead of focusing on the negative thoughts poking at the back of his mind—those bastards never truly left; he simply learned to handle it in healthier ways—he put his attention back on the table and the people sitting around it with conversation flowing while they devoured his wife's food.

That alone made John smile.

He knew how hard Siena worked for this.

Speaking of which …

Beside him, Siena's hand found his thigh under the table. She squeezed and tipped her head in his direction, shooting him a look from the side. He knew what she was doing—testing the waters, checking on him to see how he was doing with all of this. Crowds were never his favorite thing, and it had a way of spiking his anxiety like nothing else ever did. For her, though, he grinned and gave a wink. Just like that, his wife's smile bloomed a little wider and she nodded.

"Love you," he murmured low.

Leaning in close, she pressed a sweet kiss to his lips, replying, "More than you will ever know, John."

Nah.

He knew.

Better than anyone.

Pulling away from their kiss, Siena asked, "Should we tell them now?"

Apparently, that question wasn't quiet enough for no one to hear because just two seats down beside his wife, Andino tipped his chin up and demanded, "Tell us what?"

Fucking Andi.

John smirked his cousin's way. "Mind your business."

"Tell us!"

Now, everyone at the table looked their way. Another time or day and that might *really* mess with John's head. Like crowds, he also didn't like the attention of many to be on him. But with these people—his parents, cousins, siblings, aunts and uncles and more—he just smiled back for the moment.

They could deal with the rest later.

Surely.

"Siena?" John asked.

Beside him, she laughed. "You say it."

"Say what?" his father asked.

He did want to tell them. He also wanted to kiss his wife again. So, he did both at the same time. Grabbing Siena's jaw, he pulled her in for one more kiss and then turned to the rest of the table to say, "We're going to have a baby."

The cheers from the rest of the people at the table would linger in John's ears long after his family had gone for the evening.

John was three hours into a deep clean of their house—not that it needed it between the three-day-a-week maid that came in, Siena cleaning, *and* him—when all at once, he dropped everything in his hand and stared down the dark hallway of the downstairs. The dinner party was long over, the kitchen and dining room had been cleaned … his house was quiet, and his wife had been sleeping since eleven.

Without him.

Because John couldn't sleep.

At all.

His mind raced from one thing to another, and it seemed like all at once, John's brain made a list of every single thing they would need to do or have done before the baby arrived. It didn't matter that his wife was still early in her pregnancy or that they had a while to go yet before the baby would come because eventually their child would be there.

And they were not ready.

Nothing was.

It took him far too long to realize that what he was doing might not be … *good*. The last thing he wanted to do was wake his wife because she needed her rest. Usually, he would call his father and talk shit out with Lucian, but it was far too late—or early, depending on how one looked at it—to do that, either.

John sat on the couch and reached for the phone he'd discarded on the coffee table earlier. Looking at the black screen, he went through the list of who else he could call. Leonard was almost always his first option because the man would pick up a call from John no matter the time or day. Except … despite Leonard being at the dinner and looking well, the man was still undergoing treatments and needed his rest even more than anyone else did.

So, he ended up calling someone else.

Cree.

"John," the man said, rather cheerfully, when he picked up three rings later. "Isn't it three in the morning there?"

"Quarter after three," John replied, "but who's watching the clock?"

"You, apparently."

Fair point.

"Don't you sleep?" John asked.

"Don't you?"

"Not when I feel like this."

Cree hummed under his breath. "Are you *up*? Your cycle, I mean."

"Feels like it. I'm not usually this aware."

And after he went up, John always had to come down.

For now, though … "I'm going to be a dad."

"Well, then."

"*Yeah.*"

"Babies are terrifying," Cree muttered.

"I'm not really scared of that."

"Then, what are you scared of?"

Everything else.

Every single thing else.

TWELVE

"Listen, I told you last week that I was going to need those profit reports for last quarter, and now here I am, ready to do these spreadsheets and guess what I don't have? And actually, I told you the week before last to start prepping them for me, right?"

The man on the other end of the line grunted under his breath, already getting his nasty retort for Siena ready. She never understood why people went into a career they knew they wouldn't like—such as accounting. See, she *loved* numbers. Her day wasn't complete if she hadn't turned on a computer and played with calculations. Not everyone was like her, however, and they didn't find fulfillment in the same thing she did.

The guy on the phone was one of those.

He was also her go-between for the company she used to manage John's overall investment profile for his legal side of business. Everything that had to be cleaned, cooked, or otherwise were numbers only *she* got to touch. At least then, when she sent the numbers off, she didn't have to worry about anything being wrong.

Not when she didn't make mistakes.

Not those kinds, anyway.

Maybe Siena was a bit short with her temper lately, too. Normally, she could handle more bullshit from other people than she was capable of lately. She blamed that on the pregnancy, the fact she wasn't getting enough sleep, oh and because her morning sickness had yet to wane. That shit was all a lie, too, because it wasn't only in the morning.

It was all the time. *Whenever.*

"I will have it—"

"You'll have it ready by this evening," Siena said, sighing while she rubbed at the tension headache starting to form in her temples. Or was that a stress headache? It was probably all the fucking same because it sure felt like it lately. "In my email— that's where it better be when I check later. All right?"

"Yes, ma'am."

God.

Now she was a *ma'am.*

Perfect.

"Thank you," she muttered before hanging up the phone.

It wasn't like she had anything else to say now. As long as those damn reports were in her inbox before she left the office for the day, then she wouldn't have anything more to say, either. Although, now that she didn't have those reports, she also didn't have anything to *do.* Which wasn't a bad thing because it meant she could take the rest of the afternoon off, but it also meant that tomorrow, she would have double the work to finish.

Just wonderful.

"Knock, knock." The man who poked his head in Siena's office doorway smiled kindly. "You busy?"

"Michel, what brings you to this part of the city?"

Johnathan's cousin stepped into the doorway and shoved his hands in his slacks pockets. "I was in the neighborhood—actually, I was wondering if you had talked to John at all today?"

That was ... unusual.

"Yeah, this morning," Siena replied. "Before he headed out for the day."

"But not since?"

"I mean ..."

Siena didn't quite know what to say to that because it wasn't strange for John to be wherever he was doing whatever he did for most of the day without checking in with her. It was part of his routine, and sometimes he called or he didn't. Other days, he might show up to have lunch with her at the restaurant where she did the majority of her work.

Like today. He was supposed to come today for lunch.

For the first time in God knew how many hours, Siena checked the clock on the corner of her computer screen. That's how she realized John was an hour late for their lunch date.

"Something wrong?" Michel asked.

Siena passed him a look, careful in her words when she replied, "I don't know, is something wrong?"

"It's not like John to go MIA, that's all."

Or was it?

John *did*, in fact, go off everyone's radar when he wasn't in the best place. He often opted to turn his phone off and simply do what he needed or wanted to do without much thought or care for those who might be concerned about him.

Siena didn't point it out, however. She also hadn't noticed anything different about John lately. Usually, she tried to keep a handle on his schedule and routines because that was typically the first place to go downhill when something was off.

"He had an appointment after lunch," she told Michel. "And he turns his phone off then. That might be why you can't get a hold of him."

"We were supposed to meet up a couple hours ago. And Pink said he didn't show up to their meeting yesterday. I was going to call Andino—"

"Or you could just let John come to you," Siena suggested. "We're busy, you know?"

"Right, but—"

"I'll let John know you were around, Michel."

It was all she could offer. Now, she had to worry about her husband. Everything else came second.

After Michel left the office, Siena reached for the phone on her desk. First, she called John's cell phone, but he didn't answer. She didn't bother to leave a message because for the most part, he didn't check those anyway. The second call she made was to Leonard—the person John had an appointment with after what should have been their lunch date. The therapist also didn't answer the phone.

Well, then ... Siena never went to the worst-case scenario first. It wasn't her style, and she'd learned to trust John. She was concerned, yes, but she would also give her husband the benefit of the doubt. She had to. That's how their entire marriage worked.

THIRTEEN

John was surprised to find Andino's house quiet when he arrived later in the day. Even though he was supposed to meet up with his cousin at a restaurant in the city like they usually would, business simply caught up to him and plans had to change. He hadn't thought Andino would mind all that much if only because the man could appreciate and understand how business sometimes piled up and took over everything. So was their way.

He expected to hear the kids running around and find Haven in the kitchen as she would normally be, but for the most part, the house was empty.

Except upstairs.

There, he found his cousin. With his other cousin. And Pink.

John stayed far enough back from the office doorway to hear the conversation happening inside. Well, mostly it was just Andino questioning Michel and Pink while the other two man stayed mute. Which wasn't at all what John expected to find when he came here. He couldn't say he particularly liked it, either.

That wasn't good for his nerves.

Or his fast temper.

"So, you're telling me he hasn't been in touch but neither of you have anything to tell me about that? He's not seemed a little *off* lately, or …?"

John's gaze narrowed.

Was Andino asking about *him*?

"I know you two can fucking talk," Andino snapped.

John decided, before his cousin could act like an even bigger asshole than he already was, to speak up and find out exactly what was happening. Although just by the looks and sound of it all, he already knew. "What the fuck is going on here?"

All at once, three pairs of eyes in the office turned on John standing in the doorway. He didn't pay the two men sitting in the high-back, leather chairs much mind. Instead, he leveled all of his attention on the one behind the desk.

Andino, that was.

"John," Andino started.

Nope.

He wasn't doing that.

Not the tone, the attitude, or the arched eyebrow Andino turned on his cousin. All of it felt like the man intended to chastise John, and he wasn't doing that shit with people anymore. He was a grown fucking man—closing in on his mid-thirties—not a child that needed constantly watched. That's kind of what it felt like Andino had just been doing before John spoke up.

"I asked a question," John said.

Andino sucked air through his teeth, replying, "How about, where the fuck have you been all day, huh?"

"Busy."

"Doing what?"

"You demand updates about my whereabouts and business now?" John asked.

"Let me remind you, Andi, that you're not my fucking boss. I don't have to answer to you or keep you updated about anything. When I choose to do that, it's because I want to, or we're doing something in business together that requires you to know. Otherwise, it's none of your goddamn business, and I think it would do you well to remember that."

Andino's jaw tightened at that statement; his narrowed gaze swung toward the men on the other side of the desk. "So, we're going to pretend like you don't have these two running like crazy for you? So much so, in fact, that I have to go through them just to get to you?"

Well ...

That had John smirking.

Just a bit.

"Don't all bosses work that way?" he asked.

"Sure," Andino said, "but not us. Hell, I even had to call people working for you to come to me to get any kind of information on you."

Oh, was that how Andino wanted to play this?

Fine.

"I had business on one side of the city and ended up on an entirely different side today," John said, "because apparently, the only person who gets to be taken seriously in this fucking city is *you*. Right? Because if even you can't fuck off and let me work without watching over my shoulder constantly, how in the hell is anyone else going to do it?"

The silence coated the room heavily.

John didn't mind a bit.

"Anything else you want to know?" he asked his cousin.

Andino stared hard at John. "Maybe I'm just worried about you."

"Maybe you can ask me instead of whatever the hell you were doing here today."

In the chair closest to the window, Michel cleared his throat. "Sorry, man. He already had Pink here when I showed up after getting a call, too. I let it slip that you missed your lunch date with Siena and all."

"Maybe I mentioned I hadn't talked to you in a couple days," Pink added.

Andino sighed.

John simply nodded at the other two. "No worries."

They were honest.

That's all he wanted.

As for Andino ...

"Give me a call when you figure out what the fuck we're doing here," John told his cousin. "Otherwise, keep my name out of your mouth entirely. You hear me?"

"John, I was just—"

"It's my business. All of it. Any of it. That's for *me* to handle."

He was a bit flaky lately. Not entirely off his game, but only because he was *way* on it instead which meant he still missed shit because he focused too much on one thing or another instead of everything as a whole. He stayed awake more than he slept. Remained high more than low. Not that it mattered because it was still for him to handle, and not anyone else. Which he was dealing with. But he also didn't feel like he had to explain any of that to anyone.

Including Andino.

Better his cousin be aware now.

Right?

"And if we're going to keep working together," John said to Pink and Michel—because he wanted all of this to be crystal fucking clear from here on out—as he pointed a finger at them both, "then let that be a lesson to the both of you. My business is *mine*. I don't care if you haven't spoken to me in weeks. You don't take it anywhere but to *me*. Got it?"

Pink, to his benefit, nodded. "Yeah, man."

Michel, on the other hand, gave John a look. "I'm not a made man, John. I don't answer to anybody but myself."

"And this isn't a game. You don't get to play when you want to and quit when you don't. You're either in with this, Michel, or you're out." He shrugged, adding, "Figure it out. Both of you. Then, we'll all know where we stand in this business, yeah?"

FOURTEEN

Siena glanced up from the glass of water she had cupped between her palms. She'd been holding it for so long that now her fingertips were numb from the coldness. Even the condensation dribbling down the side of the glass had left wet spots on her gray sweatpants, but she couldn't find it in herself to care when she had other things on her mind. Hell, she needed to drink more water according to her doctor.

Yet, she couldn't bring it to her lips.

Well, at least she filled a glass to carry around with her heavy thoughts. That was one step in the right direction. Maybe once she got rid of the concerns weighing her down, then she could get back to focusing on what counted.

Like her pregnancy.

And drinking more water.

Right now, however, her gaze focused on the entry hallway and the front door. The shadowy figure behind the front door moved closer, and the lock jiggled. She could only see her husband on the front stoop of their home because she'd left the porch light on.

Did he know what time it was?

That he'd missed supper?

Jesus.

Siena should be in bed—it was closer to twelve than she wanted to admit. God knew she hadn't wanted to let someone else's worries about her husband get in her head, but here she was doing exactly that. Wouldn't she know if something was up? After all, she lived with John. Spent most of her days with him. They slept in the same fucking bed and woke up together. Surely, if something was wrong, she would notice.

Wasn't that how it was for them?

She was his *person.*

She looked out for him—had his back.

Always.

No exceptions.

Now, she found herself wondering if she had failed at that.

Siena didn't move from where she sat on the staircase when John finally opened the front door. With the rest of the house dark and quiet, he made as little noise as possible while he kicked off his shoes and shrugged off his blazer. Putting the items where they went, he turned to face the rest of the hallway and came to a stop when his gaze landed on her.

"Why aren't you sleeping?" he asked.

Siena swallowed hard, taking in the lack of tiredness in her husband's gaze—despite the late time—and the high note of his tone wasn't lost on her, either. "Do you know what time it is?"

"Yeah—almost twelve."

"And that you missed our lunch date?"

John made a face. "I got caught up on the other side of the city."

"You didn't call."

"Someone else got in the way, Siena."

"Leonard didn't pick up the phone when I called, either. Did you miss your appointment with him this afternoon, too?"

That had John standing a little straighter. "I did miss that, but—"

"I don't usually miss these kinds of things with you, John, you know?"

"Babe."

Siena shook her head and stared down at her glass. "I got worried."

"Don't be."

"That's not how it works, John."

"You don't have to be worried about me. I have everything handled, Siena."

He usually did.

Still …

"I know you do, but when you don't even call and, I have to just sit here and wonder, it makes me—"

She didn't even get to finish her rambling word vomit before John had crossed the entry hall and had kneeled in front of where she sat on the stairs. One of his hands took the glass of water from hers, setting it aside to the step. Then, both of his hands found her face with the softest touch that reminded her exactly why she loved this man as much as she did. He tipped her head up, those fingers of his tangling into her hair, before he kissed her.

Once, then twice.

A third time, too.

It was only when his tongue teased the seam of her lips did she open up for him, letting him deepen the kiss just enough to get her hot and breathless. At the same time, the sweetest relief floated through her because John *was* fine. Or shit, maybe in his mind he wasn't entirely great, but it was okay because he was here. They could handle it.

The same way they always did.

John pulled back from the kiss, but stayed close enough to her that his lips grazed hers with every word that he spoke. "Let me take you to bed, hmm? You should be *sleeping*."

Siena grinned. "You think you can kiss me like that and then tell me I have to go to sleep? *Really*?"

"Well—"

"Take me to bed, *love me*, and then we'll talk."

John didn't even think about it.

Not really.

He kissed her again.

"Deal," he murmured.

FIFTEEN

After the kind of day John had, the only thing he wanted to do was come home and lose himself in his wife. Whether that meant watching her read, or holding her while she slept, or *even better*, getting to fuck away his worries and problems with her. She offered the latter sitting on those stairs.

He wasn't about to refuse.

John understood once they came out of this haze together, he was going to have to revisit the shitty day *and* answer all the questions he found staring at him in his wife's eyes. He would get there—he'd handle that, too, just like he managed everything else.

Not right now, though.

For the moment, he lost himself in the sight of Siena riding him to a slow finish in their bed while she still trembled from her orgasm just moments before. Those dark waves of hers fell over her naked shoulders. She used her hands on his wrists where he kept his palms flat to the small—barely noticeable—swell of her abdomen to work him with every lift and lower of her body. All those breathy, sweet sounds that crawled out of her were music to his ears.

He'd never get enough.

Not of her.

"*Come*," she whispered.

Once, and then twice.

His name on her lips teased him.

When he did finally reach his peak, it came in strong and fast despite her steady, but slow pace. She took him deep and held him steady as he groaned out his approval for her while his cock jerked inside her snug, wet pussy.

This was what he needed.

So badly.

He bet she knew it, too.

After, with their sheets still smelling like them, John rested with his back against the headboard of their bed while Siena snuggled on top of him. With his palm flat to her stomach, and his other tight around her back, he finally felt more settled than he had in a long while.

Funny how that worked.

Her fingertips traced soft lines along the grooves of his chest while her breaths came out even and steady. Had she not been touching him, then he might have thought she fell asleep. Which, frankly, would have been easier. Then, maybe she would forget he promised to talk.

Except …

Well, he didn't hide things from his wife.

Or he tried hard not to.

"Leonard has cancer," he murmured.

Siena's touches stopped all at once before her head darted up. Those wide eyes of hers met his own, and John gave a small shrug at the sight of her concern. "What?"

"Yeah, I found out right about the same time we learned you were pregnant. He's been doing treatments and you know how fucking chemo is, Siena."

She gave a small sigh. "*Hard.*"

And tiring.

No, *exhausting*.

"He wasn't always going to be feeling well enough to do my sessions," John muttered, "and so he decided to get me working with someone else."

Siena's brow dipped. "Who?"

"You don't know him—better you don't. Cree's methods are ... not at all like Leonard's but honestly, I like the difference. One pushes me in a different way than the other does. And you know, Leonard had a treatment yesterday—one of his last—so that's probably why he didn't pick up your call today. He called to let me know he wouldn't make it but that Cree was in town if I felt like I needed to sit down."

Or rather, meet up with the man at a gym and get the piss beat out of him while at the same time, getting his thoughts and feelings picked apart by a man that John couldn't hide shit from. Because yeah, he'd learned that about Cree since he started seeing the man regularly. If Cree thought something was up, he became a dog searching for a bone. And he didn't forget shit. It didn't matter if John randomly mentioned something in passing, the guy kept it locked in the back of his mind for future use.

Sometimes, it was annoying.

Other times, it helped.

"Why didn't you tell me?" Siena asked.

John let out a heavy breath, his arm tightening around her while he stroked her stomach with his other hand. "I just ... I figured, you're pregnant, you got a lot of shit on your plate, and I'm handling my business. There wasn't any reason to give you something else to obsess over when you already do that with everything else, babe."

She didn't even deny it.

Strangely, though, out of all the people in his life, Siena was the one and only— next to his therapists—that could call out his shit, or see it for what it really was, and he didn't get defensive about it. John didn't put up walls with people who were there to protect him, his wife included.

It made him vulnerable, yeah.

He worked through it.

"Anyway," John said, "that's what got in the way today. Cree's meeting places are unconventional, and when Leonard canceled today, I had to go elsewhere. I keep up with my sessions no matter what—I promise. But we shut the phones off. It's a thing. I lost track of time, that's all. I do that a lot with Cree."

Siena cleared her throat. "That's not a bad thing, though. It means you don't mind being there with him, right?"

"I guess. After, I had to run over to Andi's place because I missed shit with him today, too, even though I had business handled elsewhere. Except he was a fucking prick overstepping on me, and I had to let him know it."

There.

He'd told her everything.

Basically.

No, he hadn't given Siena all the details, but she also didn't need them. She only needed the important bits so that she knew what was going on and why shit might seem different lately with him.

"Still could have told me," his wife whispered. "And that doesn't seem like Andi."

"He becomes an asshole when he's worried."

John hated it.

He still saw it for what it was, though.

Once his cousin had gotten some shit through his thick skull and came back ready to apologize, then the two of them could sit down and properly hash all of this out. Simple as that. Right now, however, John needed some time by himself.

"When I start to feel like I'm not good enough to be where I am," he said, letting one of his darkest thoughts finally come out of his mind, "the last thing I need is for those around me to think the same thing."

It was funny—he hadn't been able to tell Leonard that's how he felt lately. Or even Cree. Yet, with his wife, the words came out *too* easily.

"Why would you feel like that?" she asked.

John swallowed hard. "I've just ... been really *up* lately. It's not bad, but it's noticeable. I'm not bouncing back and forth or being irrational but it's still there."

"Not medicate-able, you mean."

"That's not even a word," he said, chuckling.

"But *still.*"

He nodded. "Yeah. Thing is, when I go up, I always gotta come back down. I keep thinking about you and the baby and—"

"We're *fine*, John."

He met her gaze, and she held strong.

"We are," she promised. "And so are you."

Leaning in, she closed the small bit of distance between them to take a kiss. John let her. The rest of the evening and all his worries, well, they didn't exist when they were like this. Siena would never understand how grateful John was that she could do that for him.

He'd love this woman forever.

She didn't give him a choice.

SIXTEEN

Siena should have been more involved in her current conversation with Johnathan's aunt, Kim, but she was a little busy with scanning the room to find her husband. Not that Kim was saying or doing anything to bore Siena, but she felt like her other job tonight was a bit more important than chitchatting about the weather at the moment.

"He just headed into the kitchen," Kim said to Siena's left.

Trying to laugh her distraction off, she turned towards the woman at her left only to find Kim was smiling at her as though she didn't mind at all. "Sorry. I'm being rude, aren't I?"

Kim shrugged. "I always wanted my eyes on Gio all the time, too. Sometimes, because I thought he was too on edge to be doing these dinners. Other times, it was just that I didn't want to look away—what if I missed something? I get it."

Well ...

That had Siena nodding.

The woman wasn't wrong.

Then, Kim asked, "But everything is good, right? I mean, with the baby and you two?"

Usually, questions like those would feel like someone was asking specifically about John's mental health. Which, of course, would make Siena defensive because she didn't care to answer those questions. This time, however, it didn't feel like that at all.

"We're great," Siena replied.

It wasn't a lie.

She and John *were* great. The baby was still looking and sounding perfect with every appointment she had for the pregnancy. Soon, they would find out the gender of their first child, too. By all accounts, on the surface anyway, things looked fine.

Perfect, even.

But it was what people didn't know—and the things Siena and John didn't share—that told another story. Like the fact her husband's mood had started to severely drop over the last week. He wanted to spend more time standing in a shower or lying in bed than he did doing anything else. He had little to no interest in sex. That only meant one thing when it came to John.

The depression was coming.

Fast.

Well, that was partly a lie. The depression had already arrived. It simply had yet to reach its peak, and Siena wanted to be there when it did. Whether it happened tonight, tomorrow, or next week. John never explicitly said so, and while he talked a hell of a lot less when he was like this, she knew it was easier on him when he did have her and others around that he trusted when he found himself dark with thoughts and feelings that made him believe he was worthless.

Something he could never be.

Not to her.

For Siena, her husband was worth the world.

And more.

Leonard knew. A med change from his therapist had her husband irritated and quick to snap at others and wishing he could sleep more than he had to be awake. Not that he meant to, but it was a real possibility all the same.

Which was every reason why Siena was trying to keep an eye on her husband at this dinner party. Although, for most of the night, John seemed perfectly content and fine in the old Marcello mansion surrounded by his family and friends.

She still wanted to be sure.

Careful.

If someone did mention his mood or the way he whipped back and forth between being up and down—sometimes, it could happen all in a single conversation—and John didn't want to handle the conversation that would surely follow, then Siena could.

But it was hard to do when he was in the kitchen, and she was in the dining room talking with his aunt.

"Do you mind if I go find him?" Siena asked Kim.

Waving a hand, Kim replied, "Not at all. We can catch up later."

"Thank you."

Siena found John's reason for being in the kitchen. With his back turned to her, he chatted with his mother who was currently readying a dish of cheesy scalloped potatoes. Next to Jordyn, John's father tried to sneak a piece of shredded cheese but ended up with his hand slapped by a wooden spoon.

"*Fuck my life,*" Lucian snarled under his breath. "You're going to break my knuckles, woman."

Jordyn smiled. "Keep your fucking hands out of my food. You know better than that. I know because your mother taught you better."

John chuckled, and when Siena stepped in beside him, his small grin turned on her. It was harder to see the blank emptiness in his eyes when he was smiling. She found that most disturbing. Not John, no. But the fact something like depression could be so easily hidden by something like a smile.

She realized then just how carefully her husband had perfected hiding his problems. At the same time, he also didn't mind asking for help when he needed to now.

It was a give and take.

A constant learning process.

"Hey," she whispered.

Pushing up to her tiptoes, she pressed a kiss to his jaw.

"Hey," he murmured back.

She gave him a questioning look—a simple raise of her brow that asked *you good?* John winked back, and tried to smile a little wider for her but it didn't quite reach his eyes. She knew then that he was probably ready to head home and call it a night. Hell, dinner hadn't even been served yet, but at least no one could say he didn't make an effort to come.

Wasn't that what counted?

She thought so.

"So, Lucian and I were talking," Jordyn said, drawing Siena's attention away from her husband for a moment, "and we were wondering if you both wanted to do a party after you find out the gender like a surprise for everyone. We could throw it and—"

"I don't know," Siena said quickly, wanting to give John the choice to say yes or no to that before anyone else became too attached to the idea. Just in case he really didn't want to do it because then he wouldn't feel required to agree. "We haven't really talked about it."

"Why not?" John asked. "We could figure something out. It doesn't have to be a big thing, right?"

"No, of course not," Lucian said. "We could even do dinner for just family if you wanted."

"Yeah, I think—"

John's words cut off when a familiar guest came to stand in the back entryway to the mansion's large kitchen. He lifted a hand and tipped his head to the side, a silent invitation for John to join him. Andino didn't make it seem like he was demanding anything, though.

Probably a good idea, considering everything.

"I'll be right back," John said to Siena and his parents.

Lucian cleared his throat when he glanced over his shoulder to see what had caught John's attention. "Sure, son."

John pressed a quick kiss to the top of Siena's head and pressed his palm flat to her stomach before stepping away from the conversation entirely. That just left her and his parents to plan a gender reveal. If they noticed that something was off with John, well, they didn't say. Then again, his parents rarely did mention that sort of thing now. They would much rather let Siena and John handle it alone, but they were always there if they needed help.

"Well," Siena said, giving her in-laws a smile, "I guess we're planning a gender reveal."

SEVENTEEN

John followed Andino through the old mansion in silence. Side by side, the two men took their time heading to the upstairs office where—far more than once—they had both been dragged to in order to get yet another lecture about the importance of their last name and maintaining the dignity and respect of being a Marcello.

Now, he couldn't forget it.

He didn't think their legacy weighed as heavily on Andino's shoulders as it did for his own, but John couldn't say for sure, and he'd never thought to ask. Better he didn't, maybe. They all had their own things to handle.

Nonetheless, the mansion brought back a lot of memories for John. Colored with nostalgia in every single corner, the past was never far from his mind when he was here. Every step he took inside the place, he could relive five different memories from years long past. He looked forward to the many more they were sure to make with their own children here.

The legacy lived on.

Once the two were inside the old office that didn't get nearly as much use as it used to, John closed the door behind them.

John was the first to speak. "Do you remember how they used to drag us into this office every single time *any* of them had something to say to us?"

Andino laughed under his breath. "Seriously, every time we came to this mansion. At least fifty percent of the time it was because I kicked somebody's ass for talking shit about you behind your back. Man, I fucking hated when they did that."

He grinned.

Because it was true.

"I worry," Andino said, turning to face John with his hands shoved into his pockets. He shrugged his broad shoulders and glanced to the side as though he might find something interesting to stare at on the far wall. John understood the need to look away—it was always easier to admit your wrongs when you didn't have to look someone in the face while you did it. "And you know, Haven likes to tell me I can become an even worse asshole in that case."

John cleared his throat, rocking on his heels while he replied, "You certainly can."

His cousin sighed.

The silence raged on.

John simply waited it out.

Sometimes, in this life with men like them, it was all about the waiting game. And the thing with Andino and John was the fact they were best friends. Always had been and always would be. Until the very fucking end. From the time the two of them were put together when they were still wearing diapers, they'd forever had each other's backs.

Yeah, sometimes shit happened. Sometimes, they had moments like these. They always came back, though. Just had to wait it out.

Andino turned back to John, meeting his cousin's gaze as he said, "I'm sorry."

John nodded. "For being an asshole, or questioning my ability to do what I need to do?"

"Fuck, do you know Haven does that shit to me all the time? Makes me explain *every single reason* I'm sorry, what I did wrong, and why it was wrong. Drives me crazy."

"Her right to do so. She is your wife."

"Yeah, but—"

"I'm fucking with you," John said, laughing under his breath. "I don't need you to explain shit, Andi. Although, if not for your wife, you'd be a lot less tolerable, let me just say. I hope you know that woman really is your better half, man."

"She is. I'll never deny it."

At least Andino knew it.

"Same for your wife," Andino added quieter.

"I know."

All too well, really.

"And I talked to Pink," Andino said, shifting from foot to foot. The only show of his nerves. He had so few tells, but growing up alongside him had allowed John to know every single one of them. "Seems he's fine to stay right where he is working with you—he makes a good underboss, doesn't he?"

John swallowed hard. "We'd not talked specifics."

"I did. He was my man—hand-picked. I'll never have another one like him."

"Are you pissed I took him from you?"

"Not really. You need him more than I do."

"Good point," John muttered. "Like Michel, though, he's not a made man."

"Doesn't have to be. You're a small family—and the faction works from Marcello business now, so it's all on us to make the calls."

Right.

"It's good to be the boss," John said, chuckling.

"Isn't it?" Andino grinned. "And what about Michel?"

"It's on my to-do list."

"Oh, you have one of those, too, huh?"

"Apparently."

John found Michel lounging on the back terrace with a glass of whiskey he'd nursed down to the ice in the bottom. "You got a minute?"

Michel peered up at John. "For you, always."

"Hmm."

He took a seat beside his cousin and for a long while, said nothing. Instead, he stared out over the back property where the darkness clung to every corner.

Overhead, the black sky was painted with a yellow moon and dotted with stars. Funny how he related more to the sky and stars at night than he did anything or anyone else.

He was dark, too.

Dark thoughts.

Dark heart.

Dark soul.

Occasionally colored with bright, pretty things.

Michel broke the silence first. "I always wanted to be something more than just a made man."

"You are."

"I am. I'm a husband and a father. A doctor. Yet, I keep going back to my roots, huh?"

John grinned.

How could he not?

"You are a Marcello," he replied.

Michel sighed. "I liked being on the outside of business the most."

"But do you really?"

"I don't know. Certainly thought I did, though."

"You don't owe me shit, Michel. Don't think you have to keep working in this *famiglia* because of me. I—"

"You and Andi made it easy for me to come back and … well, what is it that I even do?"

That was easy. "You have my back."

Michel threw him a look.

John returned it.

"How's Gabbie feel about all of this?" John asked, referring to the man's wife.

"She told me it was inevitable."

"She's probably not wrong."

"Dad said the same."

John did laugh at that one. "You know they all wanted this even if they never explicitly said it to us."

"You mean, all of us in the family business carrying it on?"

"Yeah, exactly that."

Michel let out a heavy breath. "Yeah, they did. I know."

Well, shit.

It was what they all did best.

EIGHTEEN

Cupcakes were passed around the table—each with a mixture of pink or blue frosting on the top with tiny little baby shoes shaped from vanilla-flavored fondant. Siena had no clue what colored cream would be in the middle of the cupcakes once they bit into them. Her doctor's office had sent over the gender of their child to the bakery in Manhattan that delivered the cupcakes to her earlier in the day.

Now, all their family had gathered.

It was time to find out what their baby would be.

A sweet little boy or a precious tiny girl.

She hadn't thought much about it, really. Like her husband, she didn't have a preference one way or the other. All she really wanted was a healthy baby. And no matter what, she loved her child already.

"Your turn," Siena whispered to John.

He laughed, but she heard the stress in the sound. He smiled for their gathered, waiting family, but she saw the tension in his shoulders.

The further along in her pregnancy she became, the more changes she saw in John. Never toward her, but just him in general. She recognized his lack of sleeping, and his up and down moods. She saw his methodical cleaning, planning, and organizing even when he tried to hide it.

She wished he wouldn't hide it.

It was so much harder to settle him back when he hid it.

Leonard would be at their house when they got back—waiting for John, as the man always did. Twice a week, and sometimes more if John felt it was needed, his therapist came for an in-home session.

They never opened up a discussion about John's mental health to anyone who asked. They didn't talk about his meds, his therapy, or anything.

Their choice. John's choice.

Leonard, however, would be there tonight because Siena had made a call and asked for him to come, not John. Sometimes, she needed to do that. Sometimes, she had to be the voice when John was not letting his come through loud enough.

John took the one cupcake Siena offered to him—the only one left. Everyone else around them already had one, and now they were just waiting on him, too.

"My turn," John echoed.

Siena nodded, and smiled. "I love you, John."

"I know you do."

She always would.

"Everybody at the same time," Siena said, directing her comment at the room, yet never looking away from John. "Okay?"

"You got it, babe."

"Now."

Everybody bit into their cupcake, and blue frosting colored up the middle of the sweet cake. John stared at the sweet in his hand for a long while, and Siena reached over to wipe a bit of blue frosting from his bottom lip while cheers lit up the room.

"It's a boy!"

"A boy!"

John barely blinked as his father crossed the room to clap his son on the shoulders, and congratulate them. Jordyn followed behind Lucian, and did the same. Siena and John took a moment to take the congratulations, and the ones that followed from everyone else.

But soon, the room settled, their family faded as John looked at Siena, and it was just them once more. No one else. He had wanted this gender reveal. For his family. To allow them in. Sometimes, he still found it hard to let them in.

The pregnancy was one thing he continued to try to open up for them, but especially for his mother and father.

"Luciano, then," John said.

Siena smiled wider. "Luciano Johnathan Marcello. And he will be perfect, John." So perfect. Just like his father.

Siena hung back in the entryway of the living room. Just out of view of Leonard and John where they sat on opposite ends of the couch while they talked. Without question, when Siena asked for the man to be at their home when they arrived, Leonard agreed.

"I didn't want to bother you," John said. "I know you're—"

"You're not a bother, John. You've never been."

"Even if all I want is to talk?"

"That's what I do best," Leonard replied, never missing a beat.

Siena smiled at that.

Satisfied that her husband had what he needed, and desperately hoping everything that was weighing on John would release him soon, she stepped out of the room to leave him and Leonard alone to their chat. They didn't need her there, she hadn't been invited into it, and she never felt like it was her place to join anyway. She was fine leaving them to it.

In the kitchen, her in-laws waited with a green tea hot and ready for her. She took it from Jordyn with a smile who offered the same back.

Lucian's gaze drifted over Siena's shoulder to where the darkness of the hallway led to the living room. "Better now?"

Siena nodded. "Much better."

"Good."

They hadn't asked to come. John did. Siena figured … that was progress. Then again, their whole marriage had been that. Every day they spent together was simply one step at a time when at one time, they weren't supposed to be at all. She'd take every single step with John as long as he wanted her to.

The rest? It was all a bonus.

NINETEEN

Five months later …

"Harder."

Smack. Smack. Smack.

"Tuck that elbow in tighter, John, come on."

Smack. Smack. Smack.

"Faster, let's go."

Smack. Smack. Smack. Smack.

Each of John's blows landed one after the other with no hesitation against the heavily padded gloves Cree kept high for him to punch. Nothing worked to blow off steam quite like beating the hell out of something did, but in a *healthy* way. Or that's what they kept telling him. Hey, it kept him from getting arrested, and he also had a place to go to work out all the anger that seemed to constantly bubble far too close to his surface.

While he didn't get to see the man nearly as often as he used to—business in Vegas kept Cree busy—he still came into town once a week to visit with his adopted son who lived in Brooklyn with his spouses, *and* he made sure to call John in for a round.

Yeah, he didn't even call them sessions.

Not even close.

"Ten, nine, eight, seven, six, five," Cree said through John's raining punches, counting down to what would be their third five-minute break for him to get some fluids and take a breath. It was also encouragement for John to start hitting as hard and fast as he could, ignoring technique and posture for the moment because that was always how they worked. "Four, three, two … *one.*"

John dropped his hands first and took two bouncing steps back from Cree, grinning behind his mouthguard at the same time. His words came out a bit garbled, but the other man in the ring seemed to understand him just fine all the same. "Better, yeah?"

"Far better," Cree agreed as he pulled the mitts from his hands. He pulled off his own gloves and threw them to the mat at his feet. Tossing his mitts aside, too, Cree headed for the corner of the ring where the water bottles waited with condensation gathering in droplets and dribbling down the sides. He tossed one to John, saying, "Here—drink."

He did.

A half a bottle in one go.

This was hard work.

But *good* work, too.

It focused John's brain in a way nothing—except for maybe fucking his wife—did. He was grateful for this. As a younger man, fighting had simply been a means to an end for John. Something to do with all that anger and rage that constantly festered at the slightest of provocations. His temper was legendary.

This helped that. A great deal.

Cree turned back on John but his gaze drifted to somewhere behind him. "Ah, that's your man, isn't it?"

Spinning around to find who he was referring to, John watched as Michel—smart and entirely out of place in his three-piece suit inside the gym—approached the ring. For the most part, neither his cousin nor Pink stepped in when they knew John was having a session with Cree or Leonard. They didn't take away from his time, and he appreciated that.

"The news you wanted on the upcoming deal with the ..." Michel passed a look to Cree, and then went back to John as though he was waiting for the okay. "We good?"

"Cree is fine," John replied.

Not that Michel knew, but Cree had his own hand in organized crime by way of training assassins. It wasn't really the time for that conversation, though.

"Well, good," Michel said, sighing. "Anyway, the deal is a go so long as you have a personal meeting with the distributor first."

Of course.

Everybody wanted a seat with the boss.

"Thanks," John told his cousin. Then, he pointed at the entrance to the gym saying, "Door's that way unless you plan to change out of that suit and get in this ring."

Michel grinned. "Probably not. Later, man."

"Later."

"That one—he's got an Irish wife, yeah?" Cree asked.

"He does. Gabbie."

Cree hummed under his breath. "Makes a lot of sense."

Turning on the man, John asked, "What makes sense?"

"Things."

The asshole was always doing that shit.

"So, business is good?" Cree asked, picking up John's gloves to ready him for a second round.

"Great."

"And *you?*"

"Waiting on my boy to greet the world."

Cree smiled widely.

A rare sight.

"Well, that is a good thing to be waiting for," Cree said. "Now, let me get a pair of gloves on, and we'll see if I can bruise that face of yours this week."

John laughed. "Fuck you."

"Sorry, my husband doesn't share."

Jesus.

That was Cree for you.

John didn't even get the chance to finish the session that day with Cree before a phone call came in from his mother. Who just conveniently happened to be out with his wife shopping and running other errands.

Siena's water broke on a Manhattan street.

She labored for hours.

John was right there for every single second of it.

Then, his boy made his way into the world. All eight pounds, five ounces of him. Dark-haired, and hazy-eyed. Squalling and *perfect*.

Luciano "Lucky" Johnathan Marcello. He wasn't the first of his name. Not even the second or third, but John bet he would be the best all the same.

In those first few seconds when he met his son and fell in love instantly, John knew everything would be just fine because look at all he had. Sometimes, he still felt like he was waiting for the other shoe to drop. In that moment, he stopped waiting for it to happen.

As for his life?

John would change nothing.

Not a single thing.

ABOUT THE AUTHOR

Bethany-Kris is a Canadian author, lover of much, and mother to four young sons, two cats, and four dogs. A small town in Eastern Canada where she was born and raised is where she has always called home. With her boys under her feet, a snuggling cat, barking dogs, and a spouse calling over his shoulder, she is nearly always writing something ... when she can find the time.

Find Bethany-Kris at www.bethanykris.com

OTHER BOOKS

The Guzzi Legacy

Corrado
Alessio
Chris
Beni
Bene
Marcus

Renzo + Lucia

Privilege
Harbor
Contempt
Forever

Andino + Haven

Duty
Vow

John + Siena

Loyalty
Disgrace
John + Siena: The Complete Duet
John + Siena: Extended

Cross + Catherine

Always
Revere
Unruly
The Companion
Naz & Roz

Guzzi Duet

Unraveled, Book One
Entangled, Book Two
Cara & Gian: The Complete Duet

DeLuca Duet

Waste of Worth: Part One
Worth of Waste: Part Two

Standalone Titles

Effortless
Inflict
Cozen
Captivated
Dishonored

Donati Bloodlines

Thin Lies
Thin Lines
Thin Lives
Behind the Bloodlines
The Complete Trilogy

Filthy Marcellos

Antony
Lucian
Giovanni
Dante
Legacy
A Very Marcello Christmas
The Complete Collection

Seasons of Betrayal

Where the Sun Hides
Where the Snow Falls
Where the Wind Whispers
Seasons: The Complete Seasons of Betrayal Series

Gun Moll Trilogy

Gun Moll
Gangster Moll
Madame Moll

The Chicago War

Deathless & Divided
Reckless & Ruined
Scarless & Sacred
Breathless & Bloodstained
The Complete Series
Maldives & Mistletoe

The Russian Guns

The Arrangement
The Life
The Score
Demyan & Ana
Shattered
The Jersey Vignettes

FANTASY ROMANCE

The Hunted: A 9INE REALMS Novel

Find more on Bethany-Kris's website at www.bethanykris.com.